THE FLETCH CHRONICLE

GREGORY
MCDONALD
THE FLETCH
CHRONICLE

FLETCH
CARIOCA FLETCH
CONFESS, FLETCH

Rediscovery Books
HILL & COMPANY, PUBLISHERS · BOSTON

Library of Congress Cataloging-in-Publication Data

Mcdonald, Gregory, 1937–
  The Fletch chronicle.

  (Rediscovery books)
  Contents: [1] The Fletch chronicle—Fletch—Car-
ioca Fletch—Confess, Fletch.
  1. Fletch (Fictitious character)—Fiction.
2. Detective and mystery stories, American. I. Title.
II. Series.
PS3563.A278A6   1987   813'.54   87-8742
ISBN 0-940595-10-9 (v. 1)

Designed by Milton Glaser, Inc.
Printed in the United States of America

INTRODUCTION

"What's your name?"
"Fletch."
"What's your full name?"
"Fletcher."
"What's your first name?"
"Irwin."
"What?"
"Irwin. Irwin Fletcher. People call me Fletch."

Not long ago, browsing in a bookstore, I heard a young voice unknown to me reading the above aloud from somewhere among the stacks. Little had I known when I wrote those words on a scratch pad in the spring of 1973 the length, the pain, the pleasure of the route I was about to follow.

I thought I might be writing a novel called *The Murder Mystery*, by Christopher Douglas, the first names of my two sons, then very young. I quit after writing a hundred pages. I thought it too unconventional technically, in style, tone, and character ever to be considered for publication. I knew I was using more of a punch-up newspaper lead, more of a jazz/rock structure than a conventional literary form. I had not been much of a mystery reader. (Subsequently, when accused of originality, and of expanding the mystery form, I admitted ignorance.) I thought I was wasting my time. Besides the need to support my family and win the financial freedom to write more, I had been motivated in trying this novel by the desire to let the world know that Bobbi, Creasey and Gummy, rather new to the social scene, existed. A friend, Charles Leo Martin, Junior, dropped by a few days after I had quit this novel and politely inquired how I was spending my time since leaving the newspaper. So he wouldn't think me lazy, however wasteful, I let him read the one hundred pages. His shouts, laughter, banging the desk with his fists and stamping on the floor with his boots (I was downstairs, seriously trying to read something, hearing this demonstration) I took he meant as encouragement to me to continue writing the story, which I did the following morning.

The Fletch chronicle was finished nine novels, thirteen years and many, many problems later.

Incidentally, although Fletch was originally published as a hardback book in December, 1974, by the Bobbs-Merrill Company, Barbara Norville, editor, it was Robert Wyatt, I believe, Hearst's editor at Avon Books, who originally designed the distinctive Fletch cover typography, and put the first page of the novel, the above dialogue, on the cover, which had never been done before, I think, and which since has been imitated universally.

I enjoy problems because I believe in solutions.

The thought never entered my head in writing *Fletch* that there would be a sequel. If it had, I never would have left him in Rio de Janiero, Brazil, with three million dollars. The novel won the 1975 Edgar Allan Poe Award from The Mystery Writers of America. Having been the author of the novel *Running Scared*, published ten years earlier, I worried that the Edgar would forbid my being able to publish anything ever again that wasn't a mystery. (This worry proved justified. *Running Scared* has since been sold to the public as a mystery; it took me thirteen years to get published, on a ten dollar advance, the non-mystery novel, *Safekeeping*, which then won stunning reviews.) Letters arrived asking to read more about Fletch. I spent my spare time that summer sitting under a tree consulting my dog on this issue and wondering if I were to continue how I would solve the problems I inadvertently had set myself. Resolved was that if Fletch hadn't cared about money when he hadn't any, neither would he care about money when he had some. Resolved (and thus commenced the great sequel-followed-by-a-prequel-followed-by-a-sequel sequencing, the cause of critic's errors, botheration to some readers, delight to others, confusion typical of Fletch himself) was that if I could not write the logical sequel to *Fletch* immediately (Fletch in Rio; I hadn't the time or the money to go to Rio at that point; I would have to set the next novel in Boston, Massachusetts, twenty-five miles away, which I could afford to visit, briefly) I would write *Carioca Fletch* someday; resolved also that when time and money permitted I would attempt the novel most necessary to the integrity of any such series, the Fletch father-search novel (*Fletch, Too*), ultimately reporting something of his parentage and moral commitment. Resolved most firmly was that if I were going to attempt a series of novels, for my own pride and from an abhorrence of boring myself, as well as the reader, I was not going to write to formula; that each novel would be different topically, thematically, and that the maturation of the progenitor ultimately would be visible, in whatever order. For all this resolve I was especially pleased when *Confess, Fletch* won the 1977 Edgar, the first time a novel and its sequel each won the award.

Problems continued, of course; that's life. Each novel I would enjoy taking the risk, then curse myself when some people responded obviously. Some people complained because each book was not like the last; because one murder mystery is without a murder; in another the progenitor does not want to solve the murder; because I was cluttering the mystery form with elements extraneous to it, sex, humor, themes, social criticism, the odd foreign phrase; the characters responded to various situations variously, *ad nauseum*, literally. I would console myself each time with the thought that if I were doing anything immediately transparent, understandable, acceptable, I would not be attempting much. A novel to be a novel must be novel, I would recite. Never learning my lesson, I would go set new problems for myself, risk again, curse myself again. Extreme pleasure, extreme pain: such is the author's life.

Profound is my appreciation especially to Ned Leavitt, of William Morris, to Bernard Shir-Cliff, of Warner Books, to Livia Gollancz, of Victor Gollancz, Ltd., for often holding the wheel while I trimmed sails, even unsure, as they sometimes were, as to my course.

Even more profound is my appreciation to people all over the world who let me know that they didn't know where I was going in my Fletch and other novels and they didn't care but that I was providing them with some fun.

In this volume are the novels *Fletch*, which observes that sometimes police control crime; *Carioca Fletch*, which acknowledges man is not bred alone; *Confess, Fletch*, which describes an artful dodge.

—*Gregory Mcdonald*
Camaldon Farm

FLETCH

To Susie, Judy and Lew Clapp

"What's your name?"
"Fletch."
"What's your full name?"
"Fletcher."
"What's your first name?"
"Irwin."
"What?"
"Irwin. Irwin Fletcher. People call me Fletch."
"Irwin Fletcher, I have a proposition to make to you. I will give you a thousand dollars for just listening to it. If you decide to reject the proposition, you take the thousand dollars, go away, and never tell anyone we talked. Fair enough?"
"Is it criminal? I mean, what you want me to do?"
"Of course."
"Fair enough. For a thousand bucks I can listen. What do you want me to do?"
"I want you to murder me."
The black shoes tainted with sand came across the oriental rug. The man took an envelope from an inside pocket of his suit jacket and dropped it into Fletch's lap. Inside were ten one-hundred-dollar bills.

The man had returned the second day to the sea wall to watch Fletch. Only thirty yards away, he used binoculars.
The third day, he met Fletch at the beer stand.
"I want you to come with me."
"Why?"
"I want to make you an offer."

"I'm not that way."

"Neither am I. There's a job I might like to have you do for me."

"Why can't we talk here?"

"This is a very special job."

"Where are we going?"

"To my house. I'll want you to know where it is. Do you have any clothes on the beach?"

"Just a shirt."

"Get it. My car is a gray Jaguar XKE, parked at the curb. I will be waiting in it for you."

"I want to drink my beer first."

"Bring it with you. You can drink it in the car."

Walking away through the beach crowd, the man looked as out of place in his dark business suit as an insurance adjuster at a jalopy jamboree. No one appeared to notice him.

Keeping his shirt over it, Fletch picked up the plastic bag off the sand.

He sat a few feet away from his group, his shirt over the plastic bag beside him. Looking at the ocean, he drank some of the beer he held in his left hand. With his right hand he dug a hole in the sand under his shirt.

"What's happening?" Bobbi asked.

She was belly-down on a towel.

"Thinkin'."

He put the plastic bag into the hole and covered it over with sand.

"I guess I'm splittin'," he said. "For a while."

"Will you be back tonight?"

"I dunno."

Slinging his shirt over his shoulder, he started away.

"Gimme a swallow before you go."

Bobbi jacked herself on her elbow and took some of the beer.

"That's good," she said.

"Hey, man," Creasey said.

Fletch said, "Splittin'. Too much sun."

The license plate of the car was 440-001.

In the car, Fletch sat with the can of cold beer between his knees. The man drove smoothly and silently. Below sunglasses, the man's face was expressionless. On his left hand was a college ring. He used a gold cigarette lighter from his jacket pocket rather than the dashboard lighter.

In the shorefront traffic, the air conditioner was making the car cold. Fletch opened the window. The man turned the air conditioner off.

He took the main road going north from town and accelerated. The car cornered beautifully on the curves going up into The Hills. He slowed, turned left on Hawthorne, then right on Berman Street.

The house was what made Berman Street a dead end. If it weren't for signs on the iron-grilled gate saying PRIVATE PROPERTY — NO TRESPASSING — STANWYK, the road would appear to continue straight onto the driveway. There were two acres of lawn on each side of the driveway in front of the house.

Fletch threw his beer can through the window onto the lawn. The man did not appear to notice.

The house was built like a Southern mansion, with white pillars before a deep verandah.

The man closed the door to the library behind them.

"Why do you want to die?"

The envelope weighed little in the palm of Fletch's right hand.

"I am facing a long, ugly, painful and certain death."

"How so?"

"A while ago I was told I have cancer. I've had it checked and had it rechecked. It's terminal. Nonoperable, nontreatable cancer."

"You don't look it."

"I don't feel it. A kind of general rottenness. It's in its early stages. The docs say it will be a while before it's noticeable to others. Then it will move very swiftly."

"How long will it take?"

"They say three months, maybe four. Not six months, anyway. From what they say, I would guess in a month from now I won't be able to conceal that I have it."

"So? A month's a month."

"When you make a decision like this . . . that you're going . . . to be dead . . . you uh . . . decide to do it as quickly, as soon as possible. You try to cut the dying time."

Hands behind his back, the man was facing the French windows. Fletch guessed he was in his early thirties.

"Why don't you kill yourself? Why do you need me?"

"My company has me insured for three million dollars. I have a wife and child. There is no point in losing the money, which I would, or rather my heirs would, if I committed suicide. On the other hand, for three million dollars it's not worth going through that much pain

5

and unpleasantness. I believe I have made an entirely rational decision."

The paintings in the room were not particularly good, in Fletch's opinion, but they were real.

"Why me?"

"You're a drifter. You suddenly showed up in town. You just as suddenly leave. No one will think about it in particular, or connect you with the murder. There will be no way of connecting you and me. You see, I have planned your escape. It is very important to me that you escape. If you were caught, and talked, as you would, the insurance would be voided."

"Supposing I'm not a drifter. Supposing I'm just on vacation."

"Is that what you're telling me? That you're on vacation?"

"No."

"I've been watching you off and on the last few days. You're on the beach with the dregs of society. You associate exclusively with drug addicts. I must assume you are one yourself."

"Maybe I'm a cop."

"Are you?"

"No."

"You have a deep body tan, Irwin Fletcher. You're as skinny as an alley cat. The soles of your feet are callused. You've been on the road a long time."

"Why did you pick me over the other kids on the beach?"

"You're no kid. You look younger, but you're almost thirty."

"I'm twenty-nine."

"You're not as far gone as the others. You're addicted, I suppose. Otherwise you couldn't stand to live with those freaks. But you still seem able to operate."

"I'm a fairly reliable-looking drifter."

"Don't feel complimented."

Fletch said, "What makes you think I want to commit murder?"

"Twenty thousand dollars. And a guarantee you won't get caught."

After staring out the window, it took the man's eyes a moment to adjust to the room. He was unable to look at Fletch without an expression of mild disgust.

"You can't tell me you don't need money. Addicts always need money. Even beginners. Maybe your taking this opportunity will prevent your committing more genuine crimes."

"Why isn't this a genuine crime?"

"It's a mercy killing. Are you married?"

"I have been," Fletch said. "Twice."

"And now you're on the road. From where are you originally?"

"Seattle."

"So you commit an act of mercy, make some money, and split. What's wrong with that?"

"I don't know. I'm not sure."

"Are you ready for more?"

"More what?"

"More of the plan. Or are you ready to quit?"

"I'm ready. Go ahead."

"I want to die next Thursday, a week from tonight, at about eight-thirty. It should look like the usual murder-robbery scene. The servants will be out, as they are now, and my wife will be at a committee meeting at the Racquets Club.

"These French windows will be unlocked. The damned servants always forget to lock them anyway." He swung the door open and closed it with his hand. "I used to complain about it until I realized their stupidity could be useful. At the moment, we do not have a dog.

"I'll be in this room alone, waiting for you. I will already have opened the safe, and in it will be twenty thousand dollars, in tens and twenties, which will be yours after you have murdered me. I don't imagine opening a safe is one of your skills?"

"No."

"Too bad. It would look better if it were authentically burglarized. At least be sure to wear gloves. I don't want you to get caught.

"In the drawer here," he said, reaching inside the top right-hand desk drawer, "is a gun which is always loaded." It was a .38 caliber Smith & Wesson. The man showed him that it was loaded. "I figure you should use my gun, so no one can trace it to you. Before you come, I will mess up the house a bit to indicate robbery.

"The trick will be to make it look as if I have caught you at burglary, you have already been in my desk, you have my gun, you shoot me. Can you shoot?"

"Yes."

"Were you in the service?"

"Yes. Marines."

"Either the head or the heart. Just make it quick and painless, and, for Christ's sake, make sure you're thorough. Do you have a passport?"

"No," Fletch lied.

"Of course not. Get one. That should be the first order of business, as that will take time. It's not tourist season, so it shouldn't take more than three or four days. But get started tomorrow.

"After you murder me, you will drive the Jaguar, which will be parked out front, to the airport. Leave the car in the Trans World Airlines parking lot. You will be taking the eleven o'clock flight to Buenos Aires. I will make the reservation, and pay for it, in your name, tomorrow. I figure twenty thousand dollars should buy you some fun in Buenos Aires. For a year or two."

"Fifty thousand dollars would buy me even more fun."

"You want fifty thousand dollars? Murder doesn't cost that much."

"You forget you're to be the victim. You want it done humanely."

The man's eyes narrowed contemptuously.

"You're right. Of course. I guess fifty thousand dollars can be arranged without causing suspicion."

The man returned to stare through the French windows. Clearly he did not like looking at Fletch.

"I'm doing everything I can to guarantee that you don't get caught. All you have to remember are gloves and a passport. The gun will be provided, and a seat on the plane will be reserved and prepaid."

The man asked, "Will you murder me?"

Fletch said, "Sure."

TWO

"Clara?"

"Where are you, Fletcher?"

"I'm in a phone booth."

"Are you all right?"

"Sure."

"I was afraid of that."

"I love you, too, bitch."

"Endearments will get you nowhere."

"There's nowhere I want to get with you. Listen: I'm driving up tonight."

"To the office?"

"Yes."

"Why?"

"I think I'm onto something interesting."

"Does it have to do with the drugs-on-the-beach story?"

"As a matter of fact, no."

"Then I don't want to hear about it."

"I'm not going to tell you about it anyway."

"Frank was asking for the drug-beach story again this afternoon."

"Fuck Frank."

"He wants it, Fletcher. That's scheduled as a major magazine story, and you were supposed to be in with it three issues ago."

"I'm doing fine with it."

"He wants it now, Fletcher. With pictures. Frank was pretty boiled this afternoon, and you know how much I love you."

"You'd stick up for me, wouldn't you, Clara?"

"In a pig's ass."

"You can't take me off the story now, and Frank knows it. I've got too much time in on it. Besides, no one else in the office has my tan."

"What we can do is fire you for failure to complete an assignment."

"Why don't you stop talking, Clara? I said I'm driving up tonight."

"There are some people who are just too goddamned obnoxious to have around."

"Meaning me?"

"Which reminds me, Fletcher. Another sleazy lawyer was around the office again this afternoon looking for you. Something about nonpayment of alimony."

"Which wife this time?"

"How the hell do I know? Don't you pay either of them?"

"They both wanted to be free of me. They're both free."

"But the court says you're not free of them."

"When I want legal advice, Clara, I'll ask."

"Keep those bums out of the office. Your alimony problems are not our problems."

"Right, Clara."

"And don't come back here until you have that goddamned story done."

"I can miss a day with the little darlings. I sort of told the kids I was splitting anyway. For a while. I can get back here by tomorrow night. And have another wonderful weekend on the beach."

"I said no, Fletcher. If you've accomplished anything at all down there, you must have caused some curiosity. Going for your car now and driving up to the office would just expose everything. You shouldn't even be in a phone booth talking to me."

"I want to come up to make some phone calls and do some digging."

"On this story? The beach one?"

"No. The other one."

"We don't give a damn about any other story until you finish this one."

"Clara? I'm cold. I'm still in swimming trunks."

"I care. Get off the phone and get doin' what you're supposed to be doin'. It's seven-thirty, and I've had a long day."

"Bye, Clara. Nice talking with you. Don't get any crumbs in Frank's bed."

"Prick."

Running on the beach warmed him. The setting sun made his shadow gigantic, his strides seem enormous. There were people still on the beach, as there always were these days. Taking off his shirt as he ran made his shadow on the sand look as if he were Big Bird trying to take off.

Near Fat Sam's lean-to, he threw his shirt on the sand and sat beside it. His aim had been perfect. Under the shirt he dug up the plastic bag. His fingers told him that the camera was still inside.

With the bag wrapped in his shirt, Fletch ambled back along the beach to the residential section. The houses became more spacious and the distances between them greater.

A checkbook was on the sand. Fletch picked it up. *Merchants Bank.* No depositor's name was printed on the checks, but there was an account number, and a balance of seven hundred eighty-five dollars and thirty-four cents.

Fletch stuck the checkbook into a back pocket of his sawed-off blue jeans.

A man stoking a barbecue pit yelled at him as he cut through a back yard. Fletch gestured at him in Italian.

He picked up his keys in the office and padded over the grease-packed garage floor to where his MG was parked. In the trunk were long jeans and a sweater.

"Hey, jerk!" The guy in the office was fat and bald. "You can't change your pants in here. You can't strip in a public place."

"I did."

"Wise ass. What if some ladies were around?"

"There are no ladies in California."

He flicked on the tape recorder before he left the garage. The safety belt strapped the big tape recorder to the passenger seat. He had put the camera in the glove compartment.

The wire was draped around his neck. The microphone dangled beneath his chin.

"Alan Stanwyk," he said, waving as he passed the man still shouting at him from the office, "after keeping me under surveillance a few days while I have been investigating the source of drugs in The Beach area for the *News-Tribune,* has just commissioned me to murder him in exactly one week — next Thursday night at eight-thirty. His surveillance convinced him that I am in fact a drifter and a drug addict.

"At least I *think* it is Alan Stanwyk who has commissioned me to murder him. I had never seen Alan Stanwyk before, but the man who commissioned me to murder him brought me to the Stanwyk residence on Berman Street, The Hills. I know there is such a person as Alan Stanwyk — as Amelia Shurcliffe of the *News-Tribune* doubtlessly has referred to him a thousand times: Alan Stanwyk, the wealthy young socialite.

"A quick check of the picture files at the office will establish whether or not the man who commissioned me to murder him is in fact Alan Stanwyk.

"I must follow the journalistic instinct of being skeptical of everything until I personally have proved it true.

"Stanwyk's justification for this unique request, that I murder him, is that he is dying of cancer. I am without any diagnostic training, but I must say that to a layman's eye he looks a well and fit man.

"On the other hand, his manner is totally convincing.

"Further justification for the request is that his life is insured for three million dollars. Direct and obvious suicide on his part would nullify the insurance.

"The man who says he is Stanwyk says he has a wife and child.

"The plan he has worked out for his murder is detailed.

"Having a passport, I am to enter the Stanwyk house through the French windows in the library next Thursday evening at eight-thirty. His wife will be at a committee meeting at the Racquets Club. The servants will be gone.

"Stanwyk will have arranged the house to make it appear a robbery has been committed. He will have opened the safe.

"I am to take a .38 caliber Smith & Wesson from the top right-hand drawer of the desk in the library and shoot Stanwyk to kill him, as painlessly as possible. He has shown me that the gun is loaded.

"I am then to drive his car, a gray Jaguar XKE, license number 440-001, to the airport and board the TWA eleven o'clock flight to Buenos Aires. A reservation in my name for that flight will be made tomorrow.

"For this service to Stanwyk, he has agreed to pay me fifty thousand dollars. He will have the cash in the house, in the opened safe, in tens and twenties when I arrive next week.

"Originally, he offered twenty thousand dollars. I pressed the price to fifty thousand dollars, in an effort to gauge his seriousness.

"He appeared serious.

"His investigation of me he believes to have been adequate. He watched me a few days and saw precisely that image I had been assigned to project: that of a drifter and a drug addict.

"He did not know my name or anything else about me.

"What Stanwyk doesn't realize is that I am the great hotshot young reporter, I.M. Fletcher of the *News-Tribune*, who so dislikes his first names, Irwin Maurice, that he never signs them. I am I.M. Fletcher. Down at The Beach trying to break a drug story.

"The questions at this point appear obvious enough.

"Is the man who commissioned me to murder him Alan Stanwyk?

"Does he have terminal cancer?

"Is he insured for three million dollars?

"Does he really mean for me to murder him?

"In the answer to any one of these questions, there is probably a helluva story.

"And although I admit to having been in the killing business for a while, in Indochina, I am now back in the helluva story business.

"Any story concerning Alan Stanwyk is worth getting.

"Therefore, I have agreed to murder Alan Stanwyk.

"My agreeing to murder him gives me exactly a week, in which I can be fairly sure he will not commission anyone else to murder him.

"Dishonest of me, I know.

"But as Pappy used to say about violating virgins, 'Son, if you're not the first, someone else will be.' "

THREE

"Carradine."

"This is I.M. Fletcher."

"Yes, Mr. Fletcher."

"I write for the *News-Tribune*."

"Oh."

"You are the financial editor, aren't you?"

"Are you that shit who wrote that piece saying we are headed for a moneyless state?"

"I did write something of the sort, yes."

"You're a shit."

"Thanks for buying the Sunday paper."

"I didn't. I read it Monday in the office."

"You see?"

"What can I do for you, Fletcher?"

A head peered through the door of Fletch's cubicle and smiled victoriously. The head was about forty years old, male, with bleached blond hair. Seeing Fletch on the telephone, it withdrew.

"I need some information about a man named Stanwyk. W-Y-K."

"*Alan* Stanwyk?"

"Yes."

The picture file on Fletch's desk was clearly of the man he had met yesterday. Alan Stanwyk in business suit, Alan Stanwyk in black tie, Alan Stanwyk in flight gear: Alan Stanwyk who wished to end his life — a murder mystery.

"He married Collins Aviation."

"All of it?"

"He married the only daughter of the president and chairman of the board."

"Job security."

"You should be so lucky."

"Frank, our supreme boss, doesn't have any daughters. Just sons of bitches."

"I believe Stanwyk is executive vice president of Collins Aviation."

"Will wonders never cease."

"I believe he's due to be president, once he gets a little more age on him."

"His future was made with the bed."

"No, I understand he's a competent fellow in his own right. Graduated from Harvard or Wharton — one of those places. A bright fellow who, as far as I know, is a perfectly nice man."

"How is Collins Aviation doing?"

"Very well, as far as I know. He runs the place. His father-in-law is virtually retired. Spends all his time running tournaments at the Racquets Club down at The Beach. And paying for them. The stock is solid. I don't know. I'd really have to look into it more. It's not a very active stock. It is publicly traded, but mostly it's held by Collins and a few of his cronies who are directors."

"So anything could be true, eh?"

"Almost anything. Do you want me to look further into this?"

"Yes."

"What do you need to know?"

"Everything. I want to know everything about Stanwyk, his wife, Collins, Collins Aviation, personal and professional."

"Why the Christ should I do your work for you?"

"You're the financial editor of the *News-Tribune*, aren't you?"

"Yes."

"I'd hate to make a mistake and have it reflect on you."

"Me? How could it reflect on me?"

"I've talked with you already."

"Clara Snow said you're a shit."

"My extension is 705. Many thanks."

"Christ."

"No. I.M. Fletcher."

The telephone book was stuffed into the bookcase behind his desk. While he was pulling it out, ignoring the papers that spilled on the floor from above and below the telephone book, the man who was not blond came in and sat down in Fletch's side chair.

"Mr. Fletcher?"

The man wore an open shirt and love beads.

"Yes."

"I'm Gillett, of Gillett, Worsham and O'Brien."

"No foolin'."

"Your wife's attorneys."

"Which wife?"

"Mrs. Linda Fletcher, as she is now known."

"Oh, really? Linda. How is she doin'?"

"Not well, Mr. Fletcher. Not well at all."

"I'm sorry to hear that. She's a nice kid."

"She is very distressed that since the divorce you have not paid her one cent in alimony."

"I took her to lunch once."

"She has told me about the King-size Relish Burger several times now. Your generosity has been marked. The alimony you owe her is three thousand, four hundred and twenty-nine dollars. Because of your generosity regarding the King-size Relish Burger, the few odd cents can be forgotten."

"Thanks."

COLLINS AVIATION: 553-0477.

"Tell me something, Mr. Worsham — "

"Gillett."

"As an attorney, I mean."

"I would not be allowed to have you as a client. I might add that I would not want you as a client."

"Nevertheless, there you are, sitting in a chair in my office, determined not to be thrown out, while I'm trying to get some work done. I know you come from a very distinguished law firm. Only partners of the most distinguished law firms come out personally to collect bills for three thousand dollars. You've been hanging around all week. It must be that your own office rent isn't paid. Or are you nicking Linda for more than three hundred of the three thousand?"

"What is your question, Mr. Fletcher?"

"As an attorney, Mr. Gillett, do you think it makes any difference that I never agreed to any alimony settlement? I have never even agreed to the divorce."

"I have nothing to do with that now. The court decided that you shall pay, and you shall."

"I mean, doesn't it strike you as peculiar that I came home one night and Linda wasn't there and the next thing I know I'm divorced for abandoning her?"

"This is not the first time this has happened to you, Mr. Fletcher. For a boy in your early or mid-twenties, two divorces on your record seem more than adequate."

"I'm sentimental. I keep believing in the old institutions."

"As long as you keep getting married . . ."

"I promise. I won't get married anymore. Being abandoned is too expensive."

15

"Mr. Fletcher. Mrs. Fletcher has told me a great deal about you."

"Did you ever buy her a King-size Relish Burger?"

"We've talked in my office."

"I thought so."

"She has told me that you are a vicious, violent man, a liar and a cheat, and that she left your bed and board because she absolutely couldn't stand you anymore. She did not abandon you. She escaped with her life."

"Vicious and violent. Bullshit. One night I stepped on the cat's tail."

"You pitched the cat through the window of your seventh-floor apartment."

"The whole place smelled of cat."

"Mrs. Fletcher, thinking reasonably that she might be the next one to go through the window, packed and left the very next time you left the apartment to go to work."

"Nonsense. She didn't smell. She was always in the shower. She washed her hair every half hour."

"Mr. Fletcher, as you have pointed out, I have been looking for you all week. For some reason, your office would not let me know where you were. I have the choice of bringing you back to court, and this time, I assure you, you will appear. Now, do you wish to arrange to make this payment here and now, or do you force me to go back to court?"

"Easier done than said." From his desk drawer Fletch took the checkbook he had found on the beach. The Merchants Bank. "It just so happens, Mr. Gillett, that I've been playing poker all week. I won seven thousand dollars. That's why my office didn't know where I was, of course. I deposited the money last night. If you would just take this check and hold it for ten days . . ."

"Certainly."

"That would leave me enough for taxes and to get the car washed, don't you think?"

"I should think so."

"Now, what was the amount again?"

"Three thousand, four hundred twenty-nine dollars and forty-seven cents."

"I thought we were forgetting about the forty-seven cents. The Relish Burger."

"Yes. All right."

"Every penny counts, you know."

Fletch wrote the check for three thousand, four hundred twenty-nine dollars payable to Linda Fletcher and signed it I. M. Fletcher in an illegible handwriting.

"There you are, Mr. Gillett. Thanks for stopping by. I'm sorry we're not on the seventh floor."

"It's been nice doing business with you, Mr. Fletcher."

Standing at the door, Gillett still held the check between his thumb and index finger. Fletch noticed that his clothes were weirdly cut — the man had no pockets. No pockets at all. How did he get around without pockets?

"By the way, Mr. Fletcher, I read your piece in the magazine regarding what you termed the unfairness of divorce settlements, alimony in particular."

"Thank you."

"I feel obliged to tell you what a stupid and wrong piece that was."

"Wrong?"

"Dead wrong."

"I understand your thinking so. You're a divorce lawyer. Why don't you take an advance in career and become a pimp?"

"I suspect that any divorce attorney, such as myself, could sue you for that piece and win."

"I quoted divorce attorneys."

"None I know."

"I'm only allowed to quote legitimate sources."

Before leaving, Gillett tried to look haughty, but only succeeded in looking as if he were in the early stages of a sneeze.

"Collins Aviation. Good morning."

"Good morning. I wish to talk with Mr. Stanwyk's secretary, please."

"One moment, please."

Beneath his desk, Fletch pried off his sneakers. The linoleum was cool on his bare feet.

"Mr. Stanwyk's office."

"Good morning. This is Bob Ohlson of the *Chronicle-Gazette*," Fletch said. "We're doing a little women's page feature over here, and wonder if you could help us out."

"Yes, certainly."

"This is just a silly little story, of no importance."

"I understand."

"What we're doing is a piece on who the private doctors are of prominent people around town. We thought it would amuse people."

"I see."

"I wonder if you could tell us who Mr. Stanwyk's private physician is?"

"Oh, I don't think Mr. Stanwyk would like to give out that information."

"Is he there?"

"Yes. He came in just a little while ago."

"You might tell him what we want. If we print the name of his doctor, Mr. Stanwyk probably will never get another doctor's bill. Remind Mr. Stanwyk that doctors themselves can't advertise."

"Yes, I see." The secretary's laugh indicated a finishing school with office skills. She had a finished laugh. "Hang on a moment, I'll see."

While he was waiting, Fletch took the envelope with ten one-hundred-dollar bills off his desk and threw it into a drawer.

"Mr. Ohlson? Mr. Stanwyk laughed and said it was all right to tell you that his private physician is Dr. Joseph Devlin of the Medical Center."

"That's great."

The man arranges for his own murder on Thursday night, and on Friday morning laughs at someone's wanting to know who his private physician is. At least Stanwyk had good blood pressure.

"When will the piece appear in the newspaper, Mr. Ohlson?"

"Well, we'll have to get a photograph of Dr. Devlin . . ."

"Can't you guess when? We'd love to see it."

"Friday of next week," Fletch said. "I think."

"Oh, that's fine. I'll tell Mr. Stanwyk so he'll be sure to buy the *Chronicle-Gazette* that day."

"Right. Be sure to buy the *Chronicle-Gazette*. Friday of next week."

Fletch hung up the phone of the *News-Tribune*.

Medical Center, Medical Center . . . Alan Stanwyk expects to be murdered next Thursday night. Failing that, he expects to pick up the *Chronicle-Gazette* Friday morning to read a reference to his private physician. Ah, life: neither was true . . . 553-9696.

"Medical Center. Good morning."

"Dr. Joseph Devlin's office, please."

"One moment."

"Dr. Devlin's office. Good morning."

"Good morning. Dr. Devlin, please."

"Dr. Devlin is seeing a patient. May I be of any assistance?"

"I need to speak with Dr. Devlin himself, I'm afraid."

"Oh, dear."

"We are the carriers of the life and health policies of Mr. Alan Stanwyk . . ."

"Oh yes."

"A little problem has come up regarding these insurance policies . . ."

"One moment, sir. I'll see if Dr. Devlin is free."

Fletch could hear the nurse-receptionist-secretary-whatever saying, "It's Mr. Stanwyk's insurance company. They have some question . . ."

Another phone was picked up instantly. "Yes?"

"Good morning, Dr. Devlin. As you know, we are the holders of the policies on the life of Mr. Alan Stanwyk . . ."

"Yes."

"Who is a patient of yours?"

"In a manner of speaking."

"What does that mean?"

"Well, I'm the Collins' family doctor. John Collins and I were roommates in college. Stanwyk married his daughter, Joan Collins. So I guess I'm his physician. I usually only see him socially."

"How long has Mr. Stanwyk been your patient, doctor?"

"Since he moved out here. Really, since before he married Joan. I'm not being very specific, am I? About six years. I could look it up, if you like."

"No, that's all right, doctor. We're just reviewing some of these cases here. As you know, Mr. Stanwyk is insured for an enormous amount of money."

"Yes, I do know."

"Why is that, by the way? Why is he insured for so much?"

"Oh, that's John's doing. The kid, Alan, loves to fly these experimental planes. You know, he was in the Air Force before he went to business school. He kept up his flying and jumps at the chance to fly any ridiculous-looking thing somebody thinks will go up in the air. I guess his continuing to do so means something to the company. Collins Aviation."

"Would there be a three-million-dollar loss to the family if Mr. Stanwyk were killed?"

"I don't know. I suppose so. The stock would drop, and the family owns most of it. He's the fair-haired boy of the company, and there isn't any other. They would have management difficulties, personnel difficulties. . . . Yes, I suppose the family could lose that much if Alan were killed."

"I see."

"But, frankly, I don't think that's the reason for the policy."

"Oh?"

"John put that policy on him to try to get him to stop flying these gimcracked planes after Julia was born. He thought the premiums would convince Alan he should give up flying. I believe John mentioned that to me over a drink one day at the Racquets Club. I had said that much insurance on somebody would make anybody a target for murder. John didn't think my impugning his daughter was funny."

"Who is Julia?"

"The granddaughter. I mean, Joan's daughter. Joan and Alan. A cute little tyke."

"Mr. Stanwyk is still flying?"

"Oh, yes. Every once in a while we hear of a near scrape. Keep the insurance on."

"When was the last time you examined Mr. Stanwyk, doctor?"

"Not since before you guys took him over. You're giving him a complete physical every six months. How many times a year can a man be examined?"

"You haven't seen him at all?"

"As I say, just socially. At John's for drinks, or dinner at the club."

"What sort of shape would you say he is in?"

"I couldn't say without examining. From seeing him at the pool and in the locker room, I can say he is a slim, well-built young man, muscular and apparently perfectly healthy. He drinks and smokes moderately. He's built like a twenty-year-old boxer. Except for his wind, he could go fifteen rounds with anybody."

"Is it possible he could be seeing any doctor other than you?"

"Anything's possible."

"A specialist?"

"I don't know who would refer him to a specialist, if your insurance doctor didn't. And if he became aware of a problem, he would most likely refer him back to me, and I would refer him to a specialist, if he needed one. If the question is, have I referred him to a specialist lately, or ever, the answer is no."

"Thank you, doctor. Sorry to take your time."

"May I ask the reason for this inquiry?"

"We have to do a summary investigation of these large carriers periodically."

"Three million dollars is a hefty amount of insurance. That much insurance on a man would change his whole way of life, I would think."

"Or his way of death, doctor."

FOUR

"Library."

"I asked for the clips on Alan Stanwyk at a quarter past eight this morning. It is now a quarter to eleven. What the hell's the matter with you people?"

"Is this Mr. Fletcher?"

"It is."

"The chief librarian wants to speak with you."

Fletch had been pleased to get the photo file on Stanwyk before the chief librarian had arrived for work at nine.

"Fletcher?"

"Yes."

"We have the clips on Alan Stanwyk down here for you anytime you want to pick them up."

"Terrific. Such cooperation. I've been waiting two hours while you guys have been playing games."

"Running a morgue is no game, Fletcher. We are not running a delivery service. You have to come down and get the file yourself."

"I said thank you."

"And you have to sign out the file yourself. I've had enough of your denials that you never took something that simply disappeared after it was delivered to you."

"I'll be right down. Try not to have the out-to-lunch sign up when I get there."

Fletch was halfway down the corridor to the library before he realized he had forgotten to put his sneakers back on.

"I would have brought the file to you myself, Mr. Fletcher, but Mr. Osborne said not to." The great round frames to her eyeglasses made the girl look almost attractive.

"Fuck Mr. Osborne."

"He has the file."

Osborne had a large red nose and always looked hung over. He had been a good reporter once.

"Here's where you sign, Fletch; thank you very much. And here's your file. Shitty piece you did last week on the bookie joints."

"Sorry."

"My joint was closed all week. Couldn't make a bet anywhere in town."

"Good for what's left of your character."

"I kept track of the races. I figure you lost me about five hundred dollars."

"I'll send you a check, I get paid so much."

"I'm just saying: thanks very much. Anytime I can do you a favor . . ."

"You can. Fuck off."

"Return this file before you go home, sweetheart, or I'll report you."

"I.M. Fletcher. Reporter."

"For now."

The girl with the nice glasses looked at his bare feet and smiled.

"Fletcher!"

Clara Snow was in the corridor.

"For Christ's sake, Fletcher!"

Beige suit, alligator accessories, all trim and proper for a trim and proper day.

"You just getting in, Clara?"

"For Christ's sake, Fletcher, jeans and a T-shirt are bad enough, can't you wear shoes in the office?"

"I've been here since seven-thirty."

"You're not supposed to be here at all. You're supposed to be at The Beach."

"I told you last night I was coming up."

"And I told you not to come."

"I had to do some research."

"I don't gave a damn. I told you not to leave The Beach until you had that story. Do you have the story?"

"No."

"Fletcher." In the dark of the corridor her face was clearly purple. "I'll talk to you later. I'm late for firing someone. Someone else."

"What? Did you and Frank oversleep?"

"That's not funny. It's not even amusing."

"That's your problem."

Fletch spread the file over his desk. The clips on Alan Stanwyk were from various sections of the newspaper, mainly society and financial, but also sports and run-of-paper. On each clip, Stanwyk's name was circled in red the first time it appeared.

Fletch snapped on the tape recorder he had brought from the passenger seat of his MG. His bare feet on the desk, he leaned back in his swivel chair.

"Eleven A.M. Friday. Re: The Murder Mystery.

"So far we have established only a few things.

"First, from the picture files at the *News-Tribune*, I have established that the man I met last night, who brought me to the Stanwyk house, was Alan Stanwyk.

"Second, he is executive vice president of Collins Aviation, married to Joan Collins and has one child, Julia, age hopefully somewhat less than six.

"His private physician and family friend, Dr. Joseph Devlin, of the Medical Center, confirms that Stanwyk is insured for three million dollars. The reason Devlin offers for the heavy insurance is that Stanwyk's father-in-law and company president, chairman of the board, wishes to discourage Stanwyk from continuing to fly experimental planes. So far, the discouragement induced by heavy premiums hasn't worked. Stanwyk is still flying.

"So far, we have not had a reliable check on Stanwyk's health. Nor do I think we're going to get one.

"Devlin pleaded ignorance regarding Stanwyk's physical condition, which is a queer thing for a family physician to do, unless he were covering himself.

"And, most significantly, the doctor indicated that Collins Aviation stock would fall if word got around that Alan Stanwyk is terminally ill. It's a safe bet the dear old family doctor and friend has a large slice of his savings in Collins Aviation.

"It would be to his benefit to lie and to give Stanwyk all the time possible to put his house in order.

"Therefore, it is unconfirmed and probably unconfirmable whether or not Alan Stanwyk has terminal cancer.

"To me he looked a healthy man, but I'm not better at medical diagnosis than I am at safecracking, to everyone's disappointment."

Leaning over the clips spread out on his desk, Fletch worked the on-off button on the tape recorder microphone.

23

"Let's see. From the *News-Tribune* clips, the Alan Stanwyk file, we have the following:

"Engagement is announced, Joan Collins to Alan Stanwyk, November, six years ago at a big bash at the Racquets Club.

"She is the daughter of John and Marion Collins. The only child. Graduated from The Hills High School, Godard Junior College, and took a year at the Sorbonne. Won Tennis Juniors when she was fifteen and sixteen. Since her year in France, worked in the International Department of Collins Aviation.

"The lady sounds dull.

"Alan Stanwyk, son of Marvin and Helen Stanwyk, Nonheagan, Pennsylvania. Colgate College, Bachelor of Arts degree. Captain, United States Air Force, flew twenty-four missions in Indochina. Purple Heart. Graduated from Wharton Business School.

"At the time of the engagement he was assistant vice president of sales for Collins Aviation.

"January first, it is announced on the financial page that Alan Stanwyk is named executive vice president of Collins Aviation. The old man wanted to see how the boy worked out as a big man in the office before finding out how he worked out as a son-in-law.

"In April, Alan Stanwyk announced a multimillion-dollar government contract for Collins Aviation.

"Big wedding in June at the Collins family home in The Hills. Biographies are the same, but there is no reference to Stanwyk's family attending the wedding. Best man is Burt Eberhart, Colgate graduate, same year as Stanwyk.

"The Stanwyks, the Stanwyks . . . it is announced . . . Joan Stanwyk, Junior League, Symphony Friend . . . a dinner-dance benefit the Symphony at the Racquets Club, in fact, once a year: each October. Julia Collins Stanwyk born in March the year after the wedding. All very proper.

"But interesting: she's here, she's there, she's everywhere at first after becoming Mrs. Alan Stanwyk — teas, lunches, dinners, openings, cocktails. Yet either her activity declined steadily, or the society writers didn't find her very good copy. Which would be unusual, as she is née Collins and the average American blonde who takes a good picture.

"Apparently she has done very little the last six months.

"Oh, Mrs. Stanwyk . . . why have you withdrawn . . . at thirty?

"Alan Stanwyk. Sails as navigator on his father-in-law's yacht, the *Colette*, in the Triangle Race every year. Never won. Never placed.

Skippered by John Collins. A sailing as well as a tennis-playing family. A very rich family.

"Alan Stanwyk becomes member of Racquets Club executive committee. Three years. Treasurer, Racquets Club, the last three years. Makes it to finals tournaments in both tennis and squash. Never wins. Never places.

"Becomes a member of the Urban Club. Reads a paper urging city police to return to foot patrols. Key phrase is: 'Get the cops out of their cars and back into the community.' Yeah, Stanwyk. The police chief answers. The mayor answers. People listen to Alan Stanwyk.

"The next year the paper he delivers to the Urban Club is in defense of jet noise around Collins Aviation. In answer to an earlier paper read to the Urban Club by my boss: *News-Tribune* editor-in-chief Frank Jaffe. Wonder who wrote it for him. Probably Clara Snow, over a cup of Ovaltine. No one answered Stanwyk that time.

"Stanwyk Speaks on F-111. He's in favor of them. Stanwyk Flies F-111 Simulator. Stanwyk Flies this and Stanwyk Flies that. Stanwyk tests Collins cold-weather private-plane equipment in Alaska.

"Stanwyk honored by U.S. aviation writers.

"Stanwyk, Stanwyk, Stanwyk . . . more of the same. I see why his father-in-law married him. There are no flies on Stanwyk. If there were, short of murder, somehow I doubt our sterling journal would print them . . ."

The telephone rang.

Fletch said into it, "So glad you called."

"Fletch, can't you do anything right? Like grow up?"

"Clara, darling! You sound relaxed and subdued, like just after sex. You just fired someone."

"As a matter of fact, I just did."

"Who?"

"A kid in the city room. He had been calling people up and asking them stupid questions, saying he was someone from the Associated Press."

"Really? How awful! I always tell people I'm from the *Chronicle-Gazette*, myself."

"I wouldn't be surprised."

"How did you catch the jerk?"

"He called the French embassy in Washington and asked how to spell *élan*. We got the bill."

"What awful snoops you are."

"He admitted it."

"And you fired him after he admitted it?"

"We can't have people doing that. AP complained."

"Jesus. I'll never confess to anything again."

"Fletcher, we have to talk."

"Are you up to it?"

"That's why I thought we should have lunch. In the cafeteria. Put your shoes on."

"You're not taking me out?"

"I wouldn't be seen in public with you. Even a drugstore lunch counter wouldn't let us in, the way you dress."

"If I had Frank's income . . ."

"Upstairs in the cafeteria, at least people will understand I'm eating with you because I have to."

"You don't have to. I have work to do."

"I have several things to talk to you about, Fletcher. Might as well get it over with. Including your Bronze Star."

"My Bronze Star?"

"See you upstairs. Put your shoes on."

FIVE

Clara Snow had ordered an uncut bacon-lettuce-tomato sandwich on toast. When she bit into it the two edges of toast nearer Fletch gaped as if about to bite him.

"Tell me what I've always wanted to know, Clara, and somehow never expected to find out: how is our editor-in-chief, Frank Jaffe, in bed?"

"Fletch, why don't you like me?"

"Because you don't know what you're doing. You don't know anything about this business."

"I've been employed in this business a lot longer than you have."

"As a cooking writer. You know nothing about hard news. You know nothing about features. You know nothing about the mechanics of this business."

Speaking like a schoolmarm trying to coax a boy full of puberty toward the periodic tables, she said, "Are you sure you don't resent me just because I'm a woman?"

"I don't resent women. I rather like women."

"You haven't had much luck with them."

"My only mistake is that I keep marrying them."

"And they keep divorcing you."

"I don't even mind your going to bed with the editor-in-chief. What I do mind is your being made an editor — my editor — solely because you are going to bed with the editor-in-chief, when you are totally unqualified and, I might add, totally incompetent. Go to bed with Frank if you like. Anything to keep the bastard reasonably sober and relaxed. But your accepting an editorship in bed when you are unqualified is thoroughly dishonest of you."

Even in the cafeteria light, the skin over Clara's cheekbones as she stared at him was purple.

She bit into the sandwich, and the toast yawned at Fletch.

He chewed his calves' liver open-mouthed.

"Such principle," she said, sucking Coke from a straw. "You can't tell me you haven't made every strung-out little girl on the beach."

"That's different. That's for a story. I will do anything for a story. That's why I put penicillin on my expense account."

"You do?"

"Under 'Telephones.' "

"What Frank and I do together, and what our personal relationship is, is none of your damned business, Fletcher."

"Fine. I'll buy that. Just leave me alone, and leave my goddamned copy alone. You chopped hell out of my divorce equity story and made me look like a raving idiot."

"I had to make changes in it, and you were away on a story. I couldn't get in touch with you."

"It came out totally imbalanced, thanks to you, bitch editor. If I were a divorce lawyer in our circulation area, I would have sued the hell out of me by now. You opened me and the newspaper wide for suit, besides making me look like an incompetent."

"I tried to get in touch with you."

"Leave my copy alone. You don't know what you're doing."

"Want coffee?"

"I never take stimulants."

"For now, Fletch, we have to work together."

"Until you build enough of a case against me to get me fired, right?"

"Maybe. Now please tell me how you are doing on the drugs-on-the-beach story."

27

"There are drugs on the beach."

"Lots?"

"On that particular stretch of beach, lots."

"Hard drugs?"

"Very."

"Who are the people there?"

"The so-called kids on the beach are divided into two groups. The first group are drifters, kids on the road, alienated, homeless wanderers, usually incapable of permanent relationships. Some of them are just sun-worshippers, but if they are, they case this particular stretch of beach and move on. The kids who stay are there for the drugs. Because there is a source there, somewhere, of good, clean junk. Some of these so-called kids are forty years old. Although others aren't, like Bobbi."

"Tell me about Bobbi."

"Jesus, she's been listening. Bobbi is as cute as a button, only sexier. She is fifteen, blond, with a beautiful, compact little body."

"Have you been making it with her?"

"She needed someplace to crash."

"A fifteen-year-old. And you talk about me."

"She came out with a guy older than I am. Originally from Illinois. Daddy's a dentist. She fell in love with this guy passing through the local coffee shop, packed a knapsack and came with him. Once she was on the beach and thoroughly hooked, he wandered off. She was hooking when I met her."

"How are you paying for her?"

"Expense account. Under 'Breakfast' and 'Lunch.' "

"Aren't you afraid of the law, Fletcher? A fifteen-year-old?"

"If there is no one to complain for a kid, the law don't give a shit."

"Fletcher's Rule."

"The second group of kids on the beach are the local teenagers. They show up after school in their stripped Volkswagens, with surfboards, and make deals with daddy's hard-earned bread. The fuzz care a lot more about the local kids, as might be expected. In fact, one kid in particular, a kid named Montgomery, they pick up every week, yank him down for questioning. His dad is important in the town or something. Regular as clockwork. But he shows up again, almost immediately, beat up and smiling."

"Why do the kids go to that beach?"

"Because there is a source there."

"Who is the source?"

"An older drifter called Vatsyayana. I'd say he's in his mid-thirties. Balding and bearded. Oddly enough, he's got kindly eyes. Desperately skinny. The local kids call him Fat Sam."

"So why haven't you a story, if you know this much?"

"Because I don't know what Fat Sam's source is. I can't figure it out. He never seems to leave the beach. I spent ten days tailing him. All he seems to do is sell, sell, sell. I know where his stash is. It's in a chink of the sea wall. When word passed that Fat Sam was getting low, I kept my eyes on the stash for thirty-six hours. One: Fat Sam didn't leave the beach. Two: no one else went near his stash. After thirty-six hours, the supply was up again. Rationing was over. I can't figure it out."

"You missed the contact."

"Thanks."

"You've been on the story three weeks."

"That's not so much."

"Why don't we just run with what we've got? Put Fat Sam out of business?"

"Who cares about Fat Sam? The thing would start up again within a month. If you were any kind of a journalist, Clara, you would know we do not have a story until we have Fat Sam's source."

"You've got to stop somewhere. I mean, his source must have a source. Do you plan to follow the sources back to Thailand or some such place?"

"Maybe."

"You've got pictures of Fat Sam dealing, right?"

"Right."

"Let's run with it."

"Negative. You'll get the story when there is one. Putting one little pusher behind bars for twelve hours is not my idea of journalism."

"Frank is anxious."

"You're in charge of relieving Frank's anxieties."

"I wish I could have dessert," she said.

Fletch was eating a strawberry shortcake with whipped cream.

Clara said quickly, "There's a matter of insubordination. Disobedience."

Fletch put a perfect balance of strawberry shortcake and whipped cream on his fork.

"I told you not to leave The Beach today. One: we want you to stay there until that story is done. Two: we don't want you to blow your cover. Whoever Fat Sam's source is could be wise to you by

29

this time, or suspicious. He could be watching you. All you needed to do was jump into your Alfa Romeo or whatever it is you drive, and speed up to the *News-Tribune*, which you have done, and you are dead."

"Good shortcake. It's an MG."

"What?"

"MG."

"I don't understand you."

"My car. It's an MG."

"Oh. You may be dead."

"I'll get the story in first."

"Do you think you should go back to The Beach?"

"Sure."

"Will you be safe?"

"Come with me and find out."

"No, thanks. But I do wonder, Fletch, if we hadn't ought to tell the local police that you're down there. Who you are and what you're doing."

Fletch put down his fork and sat back in his chair. His look was meant to terrify.

"If you do that, Clara, you'll be dead before me. I will kill you. Make no mistake."

"We're responsible for you, Fletcher."

"Then be responsible, goddamn it, and shut the fuck up! You never blow a story! To anyone, at any time, ever! Christ, I wish I didn't have to talk to you, you're such an idiot."

"All right, Fletcher, calm down. People are watching."

"I don't give a shit."

"I won't talk to the police — yet."

"Don't talk to the police or anyone else — ever. If I need help, I'll ask for it."

"All right, Fletcher. All right, all right, all right."

"Stupid bitch."

"Which brings up the last matter — your Bronze Star."

"What about it?"

"While you've been gone, not only have thousands of sleazy lawyers hired by your dozens of ex-wives been prowling the corridors ready to leap at you, but the marine commandant's office has been calling as well."

"So what."

"You won a Bronze Star."

"Years ago."

"You never picked it up."

"Right."

"May I ask why not?"

"Such a thing doesn't belong in a pawnshop."

"What do you mean?"

"That's where they all end up, isn't it?"

"I don't see why."

"You don't have so many ex-wives."

"You are going to pick up the Bronze Star."

"I am not."

"It's all arranged. There is to be a ceremony next Friday, a week from today, in the commandant's office at the marine base, and you are going to be there in a suit and tie *and* shoes."

"What the hell is this to you? This is private business."

"It is not private business. You are I.M. Fletcher, star writer of the *News-Tribune,* and we are going to run you smiling modestly in all editions Saturday."

"You are like hell."

"We are. What's more, the marine commandant is going to have his full public relations staff, including photographers, there."

"No."

"And we're going to try to make a wire story out of it and tell the whole world both about your exploits and the modesty that has kept you from picking up such a high honor all these years. We won't tell them you really haven't picked it up just because basically you are a slob."

"I won't be done with The Beach story by then."

"You will turn in your beach story, whatever it looks like, with pictures, by four o'clock Thursday afternoon. We will run it in the Sunday paper, with a little sidebar saying, *News-Tribune* reporter I.M. Fletcher received the Bronze Star Friday, etc."

"You will do nothing of the sort."

"Frank has decided. The publisher has agreed."

"I don't care. I haven't."

"There is the matter of insubordination. You left an assignment when you were told clearly not to."

"I won't do it."

"I'll put it more simply, Fletcher: you have The Beach story in,

complete, Thursday afternoon at four and be in the marine commandant's office next Friday morning at ten, or you're fired. And I, for
one, will cheer."

"I bet you will."

"You're an obnoxious prick."

"I sell newspapers."

"You heard me, Fletcher. Thanks for wearing your shoes to lunch."

"I didn't."

S I X

"Fletcher, this is Jack Carradine. I tried to call you earlier, but
apparently you were out to lunch."

"I just ran upstairs to get bitten."

"What?"

"I was in the cafeteria getting chewed out."

"I have some information for you regarding Alan Stanwyk, but before I give it to you I'd like to know what you want it for. The
financial department of this newspaper can't be totally irresponsible."

"Of course. I understand." Fletch switched the telephone to his left
ear and picked up a pen. "The truth is," he lied, "we're thinking we
might do a feature story on who the most highly, I should say heavily, insured people are in this area and why they are so heavily insured."

"Is Alan Stanwyk heavily insured?"

"Yes. Very heavily."

"It stands to reason. He has a lot riding on his nose. Who is the
beneficiary?"

"Wife and daughter, I believe."

"I shouldn't think they'd need the money. But since they hold a
lot of stock in Collins Aviation, which he runs almost single-hand-
edly, I suppose they would suffer at least a temporary loss upon his
passing."

"Right," Fletcher drawled. "What have you got?"

"Well, as I just told you, he runs Collins Aviation. He's the executive vice president — has been since he married his wife. His father-in-law is president and chairman of the board, but he really

leaves the running of the company to Stanwyk. It is expected that within two or three years, once he gets a little age on him, he will be made president of Collins. His father-in-law is only in his late fifties but would rather sail his yacht and run tennis tournaments. He seems to trust Stanwyk completely."

"How is the company doing?"

"Beautifully. The stock, what there is of it available, is high and solid. Never been higher, in fact. They declared a stock dividend last year. They're considered a little weak in management, but that doesn't matter so much when you have a man as young and as competent as Stanwyk running the show. And he does, absolutely. He's a hard-working fellow. It is presumed that as his father-in-law's executive team begins to retire in the next few years, Stanwyk will bring in his own fresh young team. It won't be hard for him to do so, because he has made a point of knowing almost everybody in the industry."

"Mind a stupid question?"

"I'm used to them."

"What does Collins Aviation do?"

"They design and manufacture subsidiary parts for airplanes. In other words, they don't make airplanes, but they might make the seats, or engine parts, or control panels, what have you. Without meaning to make a pun, they also have a satellite division that does the same thing for spacecraft. This latter division has grown terrifically under Stanwyk. Apparently he is an attractive, amiable, personable man who always seems to be able to get the right contract for his company at the right time. Someone said, 'He's firm, but he never presses.' "

"How much is a company like that worth?"

"To whom?"

"I mean, what is its net worth?"

"Well, Fletch, you don't really know what you mean. Companies aren't houses that have an approximate aggregate value. Companies are worth precisely what their stock is worth on the market at that moment. It has a considerable gross income, a nifty net return to the stockholders, a big payroll . . ."

"Gimme a figure."

"If it were a house? If it were a house, Collins Aviation might be worth a half a billion."

"Half a billion dollars?"

"Can you count that high?"

"Not even with my shoes off. Who owns it?"

"The Collins family — John, his wife and daughter — continue to own fifty-one per cent of the company."

"Wow."

"They are very rich. Of course, the stock is actually held in foundations and trusts and what-have-you, but it's all John Collins when it comes time to vote. I must add that the Collins family, so you won't think they're complete dopes, have an amount equal to or greater than their investment in Collins Aviation invested through investment houses in Boston."

"Phew. Why Boston?"

"You don't know much, do you, Fletcher?"

"Not about money. I've seen so little of it."

"Boston is the Switzerland of this hemisphere. It is chock-a-block full of quiet, conservative investment bankers."

"I thought it was full of beans."

"It is. Other people's."

"How do people get as rich as Collins?"

"If I knew, do you think I'd be sitting here? Collins is a Harvard graduate who started designing and making airplane equipment with his own hands in a rented garage on Fairbanks Avenue in the early 1930s. Patents led to capital. It's easy. Go do it. Everybody says he's a nice man, quiet, humble. He's good to his friends. Most of the rest of Collins Aviation stock is held by friends of the family. They're all as rich as lords. He's made heavy contributions to Harvard College, the Cancer Fund, muscular dystrophy . . ."

"The Cancer Fund?"

"He's given them something like a total of ten million dollars."

"Recently?"

"Yes. Continuously."

"I see."

"Stanwyk is the perfect man to be Collins's son-in-law, considering Collins doesn't have a son of his own. Stanwyk is from a modest family in Pennsylvania. His father is in the hardware business."

"Still alive?"

"I believe so. Why do you ask?"

"His parents didn't come out to his wedding."

"Probably couldn't afford it. That would have been an expensive trip for them."

"Stanwyk could have paid."

"There could have been lots of reasons why his parents didn't come to his wedding — ill health, business, cost — how do I know?"

"Go on."

"A brilliant student all the way through, and apparently a nice kid. True blue. A Boy Scout; a Golden Gloves champion for the state of Pennsylvania who did not go on to the nationals for some reason; summa cum laude at Colgate, where he did not box but began to play racquet sports; an Air Force flier who flew lots of missions, currently a major in the Air Force Reserves; graduated third in his class from Wharton Business School, which, because you probably don't know, is one of the best; came out here; worked in the sales department of Collins Aviation, where sales immediately jumped; became a vice president at twenty-six or twenty-seven; and married the boss's daughter. Apparently just a magnificent young man in all ways."

"He sounds machine-made."

"Too good to be true, huh? There are people like that. Unquestionably the guy is ambitious, but there is nothing immoral in that. He's done well and he's well liked."

"By the way, Jack, who is your source for all this?"

"I thought you'd never ask. The Collins family has a local stockbroker, an investment man out here who does just little things for them, you know, regarding Collins Aviation stock — little things that run into the millions — name of Bill Carmichael. We play golf together. Needless to say, Carmichael is the son of an old buddy of John Collins. His father died, and Carmichael fell heir to the account. He and Stanwyk have become close friends. Stanwyk has taken him flying. They play squash and tennis together. He genuinely likes Stanwyk. And, incidentally, he says Stanwyk genuinely likes his wife, Joan Collins, which ain't always the case."

"There is no hanky-panky going on?"

"Not as far as Carmichael knows. Between you and me, Stanwyk would have to be out of his mind to be playing around on the side under these circumstances. God knows what Papa would say if Stanwyk got thrown out of bed."

"Does Stanwyk have any money of his own?"

"No, not to speak of. He has savings from his salary invested with Carmichael, but it doesn't amount to much over a hundred thousand dollars."

"Poor fellow."

"He did not buy the house on Berman Street. She did, but it's in both their names. Carmichael says it's worth maybe a million dollars. However, Stanwyk maintains the house and staff, and supposedly all other family expenses, out of salary. Male chauvinist pride, I guess.

Which is why he probably doesn't have more savings out of salary. That's an expensive family to keep up with. Incidentally, the house on Berman Street backs onto the Collins estate on, would you believe it, Collins Avenue?"

"Old John Collins has spyglasses."

"I gather there is a lot of back and forth."

"Doesn't he own a second house anywhere?"

"No. His father-in-law has a house in Palm Springs, one in Aspen, and one in Antibes. The kids use these houses whenever they like."

"Does he own his own airplane?"

"No. Collins Aviation has three Lear jets, with pilots, but Stanwyk flies them when he likes. He also has to do some flying to keep up his Air Force Reserve rank. And he flies experimental planes all over the country, supposedly to test Collins equipment. Carmichael suspects he just gets a kick out of it.

"Stanwyk is also the holder of some stock options in Collins Aviation. So I guess if you put everything together, he is probably a millionaire in his own right at this point, but it's on paper. He couldn't raise a million in cash without upsetting an awful lot of people.

"Oh, I forgot to tell you, Fletcher. Stanwyk and his wife have just converted about three million dollars of her personal stock."

"Converted?"

"Into cash. Carmichael says they intend to buy a cattle ranch in Nevada. He thinks it's an effort to get out from under the heel of Daddy Collins — go do their own thing."

"Is this Stanwyk's idea?"

"Carmichael has the impression it's her idea. At least, she's the one who likes horses. One can have enough of tennis and yachting, you know."

"I didn't know. Why cash?"

"The ranch costs something like fifteen million dollars."

"I can't get used to these figures."

"Inflation, my boy."

"How can a farm be worth fifteen million dollars?"

"Farms can be worth a lot more than that."

"Has Carmichael said anything to you about Stanwyk's health?"

"No. Except that he's a hell of a squash player. You have to be in pretty good shape to play that game. I tried it once. Twelve minutes and I was wiped out. Golf for me. Is there anything wrong with Stanwyk's health?"

"Would it matter if there were?"

"It would matter a lot. I have already mentioned to you that there is a kind of middle-management crisis at Collins Aviation. The whole thing now rests on the shoulders of one Alan Stanwyk. Old John Collins could go back to work, I suppose, but he never was as good a businessman as Stanwyk. He was an inventor who had some luck. Collins now has to be run by a real pro — which Daddy John ain't."

"Would the stock market fall if word got around that Stanwyk was terminally ill?"

"Collins stock sure would. That sort of thing would be very upsetting to that company. Executive personnel would start jockeying for position. Some would leave outright. Things would have to be in a state of confusion for about as long as Stanwyk has been running the place."

"I see. So if he were ill, I mean terminally ill, it would have to be kept a deep, dark secret."

"Absolutely. Is he ill?"

"How would I know?"

"Oh, I forgot. You're working on the insurance angle. Well, young Fletcher, I've told you everything I know about Alan Stanwyk. You see, we are not very close yet to the moneyless state you write about. There is still plenty of it around."

"I guess so."

"Stanwyk seems to be a competent, decent man who happened to marry the boss's daughter. Okay? Mind if I go back and do my own work now?"

"I appreciate your help very much."

"I'm just trying to prevent your writing one of your usual shitty pieces. Anything I could do would be worth that."

SEVEN

Fletch sat on the desk of The Beauty in the Broad-Brimmed Hat, Mrs. Amelia Shurcliffe, Society Editor. He had never heard that there was a Mr. Shurcliffe. Working at her typewriter, her forearms quivered with Who was at the most recent party and Are they getting married.

She finally deigned to notice the one-hundred-sixty-pound object on her desk.

"Why, Fletch! Aren't you beautiful! You always look just right. Faded jeans and T-shirt. Even no shoes. The Shoe Institute wouldn't like my saying this, and of course I'd never write it, but that's exactly what Style should be. Well, darling. Is."

"You're kidding, of course."

"Darling, I'm not."

"You should tell Clara Snow."

"Clara Snow. What does she know? She used to write cooking, you know. And between us, darling, she was terrible at that. Did you ever try to put together one of her 'Recommended Meals'?"

"Somehow, no."

"Desperate, just desperate. The colors all clashed. We tried it once, just for fun, some friends and I at the cottage. We ended up with a Hollandaise sauce, and you know what kind of a yellow that is, and carrots and beets, purple beets, all on the same plate. It was so garish, darling, we had to look away. We ate with our eyes averted. The tastes of things didn't go together either. I believe her cooking column was successful only with blind polar bears."

"You know, she's my editor now."

"Yes, I do know, you poor darling. If she weren't going to bed with Frank we would have upchucked her years ago. Of course Frank has very poor taste, too. Pink shirts and strawberry suspenders. Have you ever seen his wife?"

"Yes."

"A dowdy old thing. She always reminds me of an Eskimo full of baked beans. I mean, she looks as if, if she ever got unfrozen, she would evaporate in one enormous fart."

"Have you ever told her so?"

"Oh, no, darling, I wouldn't. I can't go to bed with her husband, being both overage and overweight, but that doesn't mean I can insult his wife. Somehow it all doesn't matter to me. Frankly, darling, I find Frank as attractive as a hangover. You're much more my type: lean, healthy, stylish."

"I'm horrified at the thought that you think I'm stylish."

"But I do, darling, sincerely. Your style is exactly what Beau Brummel did in his time. All Brummel did, you know, was to bring the lean, simple country style into the city."

"No, I didn't know."

"You should talk with Amelia Shurcliffe more. You see how simple your clothes are; how clean the lines: jeans and T-shirt. Blue and white. The lines couldn't be cleaner. You're not wearing shoes in the newspaper office, which is about as downtown as one can get. Here you can feel the whole city throbbing around you. And you're dressed as if in the middle of a hayloft. Delightful style. Just right."

"I'm amazed."

"Who does your hair?"

"No one."

"What do you mean, 'no one'?"

"When it sticks out someplace, I chop it off."

"Delightful. You're darling."

Amelia Shurcliffe was dressed in a tailored blue suit and white blouse. It was obvious she was liberated enough not to wear a corset. Her belly bulged from too many lunches and cocktail parties a week. The henna of her hair matched her face.

"Well, Fletch, I'm sure you didn't come along simply to have me admire you. You could go anywhere for that. What can I do for you?"

"Alan Stanwyk."

"Joan and Alan Stanwyk. This area's most exciting couple. No, I shouldn't say that. They're beautiful, bright, healthy and rich. But come to think of it, they don't really do anything. In fact, thinking of how exciting they could be, the Stanwyks may be this area's dullest couple."

"Which are they? Exciting or dull?"

"Rather dull, I think. He married her for Collins Aviation, of course."

"You say that straight out?"

"Well, I suppose someone had to marry her, of course. And she's attractive enough, if you like the usual American leggy blonde."

"I do, actually."

"I'm sure you do. I was one, once. Not all that leggy, of course. I was more petite. But Joan Collins Stanwyk is sort of boring, I think. I mean, she's Symphony, of course; gives that bash once a year at the Racquets Club to raise money for the violinists' rosin supply or something, and he always shows up and they stand in the receiving line and all that. Californian Gothic, if you know what I mean. They never seem to be enjoying themselves. They show up at dinners and cocktails, that sort of thing. They never seem to speak unless spoken to. They always seem to be just going through the motions."

"They must do something for fun. I mean, for themselves."

"No, I honestly think they are too busy being ideal. Perhaps they're too aware of their position. I understand he sincerely likes flying. But all the rest of it, the racquet sports, the sailing, what-have-you, seems forced somehow for them. Of course all that money must be oppressive."

"It must be."

"Jack Collins, her father, is a nifty man. Attractive, bright. I've always been slightly in love with him. Of course he's my generation. But one has always had the idea from him, even when he's being formal, that somehow, maybe somewhere else in his mind, he's having fun. Of course his wife, Marion, is a bit tipsy. Never could hold her liquor. Each year they keep her more restrained. That's why I've always thought Joan must mean so much to her father. You see them together at parties, Joan and her father — you know, benefits for cancer, or muscular dystrophy, or some of his other charities — and you always understand that Alan Stanwyk is off being busy with Collins Aviation. Sometimes he makes an appearance just at the end of an evening.

"Joan is in a difficult position, between her father and her husband." Amelia Shurcliffe took a hairpin from her desk drawer and applied it arbitrarily. "Perhaps that's why I think she's never having much fun."

"She has to be hostess for both of them."

"Yes. Instead of being herself, she has to have one hand working for Jack, the other for Alan."

"Reading through your clips, Amelia, on the Stanwyks, it appears Joan Stanwyk has been doing less and less in recent months, making fewer and fewer appearances."

"I suppose you're right."

"At least her name appears in your column less and less frequently."

"Now that you mention it, I'm sure you're right. She has been fading from the scene."

"Why?"

"It could mean many things. She has a child, a little daughter. She could be spending time with her. Joan could be pregnant. She could be worried about her husband. Seeing I have this idea that she doesn't enjoy herself, she could just be bored with the whole round. It has no novelty for her. She's been doing it since she came out, you know, with her father — unofficially acting as his hostess."

"You said she could be worried about her husband. What did you mean?"

"Oh, gracious. What did I mean? Well, her husband, Alan Stanwyk, is running an enormous company, and at an early age. That's an enormous responsibility, you know. He must work very hard and very long. And you know some of these fellows who always show a cool, pleasant face to the world are only able to do so because they fuss and fume at their wives in the privacy of their homes. If anything is wrong with him, she would know it."

"You mean if he were sick?"

"Physically sick?"

"Yes."

"I hardly think so. He looks the picture of health. Always."

"A possible explanation of her withdrawing from society in recent months is that she knows he is very sick."

"I suppose so. Is he?"

"How would I know?"

"Of course. You could speculate endlessly. Maybe she loves him and hates his risking his life in those airplanes all the time. His flying must be a worry to her."

"Amelia, do you think the Stanwyks love each other?"

"I always think so unless I know differently. Why shouldn't they?"

"Well, she seems to be half-married to her father, the wonderfully attractive Jack Collins. It looks to me as if Jack Collins picked Alan Stanwyk to be his daughter's husband. Alan Stanwyk married Collins Aviation instead of a girl named Joan Collins."

Amelia's eyes were the sort one told the truth to; simultaneously they appeared concerned and skeptical.

"Fletch, let me tell you something remarkable. In fact, the most remarkable thing I know. Are you ready for it?"

"All ears."

"I've been a society writer and professional busybody almost all my adult years, and the most remarkable thing I have learned is that people love each other when they have the least reason to, and when you least expect them to. Love-matches, marriages made in heaven, work no better than marriages made in board rooms. Obviously, the Stanwyks' marriage was made by Alan Stanwyk and Jack Collins. Joan just sort of got dragged along. Yet it is entirely possible that she is very much in love with Alan Stanwyk. Do you believe that?"

"If you say so."

"I'm not saying it's true, Fletch. I'm just saying it's possible. Joan and Alan might be terrifically in love with each other."

"Could Alan have a mistress?"

"Of course."

"Would John Collins understand?"

"Of course. I expect neither one of them feels confined to the marital bed. Not in this day and age."

"And you say John Collins would understand."

"Darling: the things I could tell you about John Collins. He didn't spend all his time in that garage twisting propellers."

"Sometimes men feel differently where their daughters are concerned. I had a father-in-law once."

"He wasn't Jack Collins."

"One more question, Amelia: why didn't Stanwyk's parents come for Alan's wedding?"

"My gracious, darling, you young folks do do your research, don't you? I have no idea. I suppose they felt they would have gotten eaten alive."

"Eaten alive?"

"Socially, darling. I suppose they're nobodies from Middle America and would have felt dreadfully out of place."

"Do people still feel that way?"

"Older people do, darling. You'll see."

"I wouldn't miss the wedding of my only child."

"Perhaps our young protagonist. Alan Stanwyk, kept them away for fear they would embarrass him. Maybe their grammar ain't no good. I don't have answers, Fletcher, to all of your questions. I remember at the wedding, whenever it was, six or seven years ago, there was a vague interest in meeting the Stanwyks, but it was explained, if you can call it an explanation, that the Stanwyks couldn't make it. End of vague interest. Maybe they had dentists' appointments that day."

"Amelia, you're a peach. Thank you very much."

"I do have a bone to pick with you, young Fletcher, despite my otherwise unrestrained approval of you."

"Oh oh."

"Has to do with that piece you wrote a couple of months ago, a little ditty called something fresh and original like 'Society Is Dead.' "

"I'm not any more responsible for headlines than you are, Amelia."

"You are partly responsible, however, for the unadulterated rubbish that dribbles down from your byline."

"Yes. Partly."

"That piece was rubbish, Fletcher."

"Oh?"

"Society, as you see, is not dead. There is plenty of it about. Just because you found a few grandnieces and nephews of prominent people hanging about the street corners sniffing pot, or whatever you do with it, saying too loudly and too frequently that they don't care anymore proves nothing. You haven't been reading me."

"Amelia, I've read every word of yours."

"Society changes, Fletcher, but not much. It does not die. It moves. It oozes. It changes its shape, its structure, its leaders and its entertainments. There is always a Society. As long as the instinct for power beats in the breasts of men and women, there will be a restricted clawing called Society."

"And there will always be a society columnist called Amelia Shurcliffe."

"Go off to bed with someone nice, darling, and be sure to tell her how I envy her."

EIGHT

"Trans World Airlines."

"Good afternoon. This is Irwin Fletcher. I asked my office to make a reservation for me today for your flight to Buenos Aires next Thursday night at eleven o'clock. My secretary has left for the weekend, and I just wanted to check and make sure it had been done."

"The name again, please, sir?"

"Fletcher. Irwin Fletcher."

"Flight 629 to Buenos Aires. Departure time eleven P.M. Thursday. Prepaid."

"Do you have a reservation on that flight for Irwin Fletcher?"

"Yes, sir. The reservation was made this morning. It will not be necessary to confirm the reservation again."

"Information. What city, please?"

"In Nonheagan, Pennsylvania, the number for Marvin Stanwyk, please."

"All our numbers are Pennsylvania numbers, sir."

"In Nonheagan."

"In which county is Nonheagan, sir?"

"I don't know. I'm not in Pennsylvania."

"How do you spell it, sir?"

"P-e-n-n-s-y-l — "

"I mean the name of the town, sir."

"Oh. N-o-n — "

"I found it, sir. It's in Bucks County."

"Thank you."

"When people call long-distance information, they are usually calling for Bucks County."

"That's damned interesting."

"Now, what is the name you wanted?"

"Stanwyk. Marvin Stanwyk. S-t-a-n-w-y-k."

"That's the wrong way to spell Stanwyk, sir."

"I'll tell him."

"We have a Stanwyk Marvin on Beecher Road."

"Do you have any other Stanwyk Marvin?"

"We have a Stanwyk Hardware on Ferncroft Road, also misspelled."

"Let me have both numbers, will you?"

"Yes, sir. They're both listed in Nonheagan."

"Mr. Stanwyk? This is Casewell Insurers of California, subinsurers of the subsidiary carriers of a partial policy listed by Alan Stanwyk, who is your son?"

"Yes."

"Glad to catch you in, sir."

"I'm always in."

"Just a few questions, sir. Are you and your wife currently alive?"

"Last time I looked, you damn fool."

"And you're both in good health?"

"Except for a pain in the ass from answering damn fools on the telephone."

"Thank you, sir. And you are the parents of Alan Stanwyk, executive vice president of Collins Aviation?"

"Unless my wife knows somethin' she never told me."

"I see, sir."

"I don't think they should let people like you dial long-distance."

"Very amusing, sir."

"I mean, you must be costing someone a passel of money."

"It's all paid for by the premiums, sir."

"That's what I was afraid of. Some other damn fool, like my son, is paying those premiums just so you can be a jackass coast-to-coast."

"Quite right, sir."

"It's damn fools like you who make me invest in telephone stock."

"Very wise of you, sir, I'm sure."

"The telephone company's the only outfit in the whole country making any money. It's because of fools like you some other fool lets near a telephone. Notice the way I'm keeping you talking?"

"I do, sir. You must own telephone stock."

"I do. Plenty of it. You didn't reverse the charges, did you?"

"No, sir. I didn't."

"Well, you'll be glad to know that both my wife and I are alive. Thanks to telephone stock and damn fools like you."

"When was the last time you saw your son, sir?"

"A few weeks ago."

"A few weeks ago?"

"He drops by every six weeks or so."

"Alan?"

"That's his name. My wife thought it was an improvement on Marvin, although I've never been sure."

"Your son, Alan, visits you in Pennsylvania every six weeks?"

"About that. Give or take a week. He has his own Collins Aviation planes. Jets. A nice young copilot comes with him who just loves Helen's buckwheat cakes. He puts away three plates of them a morning and wants them again for lunch."

"Your son, Alan Stanwyk, flies across country every six weeks in a private jet to visit you?"

"He never was much of a letter-writer. Sometimes he's on his way in or out of New York or Washington."

"Not always?"

"No. Not always. Sometimes he just comes by."

"Then why weren't you at his wedding?"

"How do you know we weren't?"

"Insurance men know some funny things, Mr. Stanwyk."

"They must."

"Why weren't you at the wedding?"

"It's none of your business, even if you are an insurance man, but the answer is that the time got mixed up. We were supposed to go to Antigua for a vacation. Alan was paying. He was doing all right at Collins Aviation. A vice president of sales while he was twenty-something. That didn't surprise me any. I've always been strong in sales myself. So we said all right. We'd never had a real get-on-an-airplane vacation before. The wedding was supposed to be a week after we returned. Smack dab in the middle of our vacation, we get this telegram saying the wedding had been moved forward because of some big business shift in her Daddy's schedule. I think his name is John. We checked the airport, and no connection could be made until the next morning. The wedding was over. We missed it. I sorely would have loved to be there, though. The wife cried a little, but I figure she would have spilled a few tears even if she were there."

"You've never met the Collinses?"

"Never had the pleasure. I'm sure they're nice folks. I've never even met my daughter-in-law. Alan says she hates to fly. Isn't that the damnedest? Her Daddy owns an airplane company and her husband's a pilot and she won't get on an airplane."

"You've never been to California?"

"Nope. But we see a lot of it on television. Especially San Francisco. That place must be an awful pain in the ass to walk up and down. Hills and hills. Everybody in San Francisco must be either slope-shouldered or pigeon-breasted. Now, son, what did you call for?"

"That's all, sir."

"What's all?"

"Just inquiring about you and your wife."

"Seems to me we haven't had a conversation at all."

"If I think of anything more, I'll call back."

"Look here, son, if you think of anything at all, call back. I'd be relieved to hear you're thinking."

"I do have one other question, sir."

"I'm breathless waitin'."

"As far as you know, is your son in good health?"

"When he was fifteen years old, he fought the state Golden Gloves. He's been in better shape every year."

"You think he could win the Golden Gloves championship now?"

"That's not even funny, son."

"Mr. Stanwyk?"

"I'm still listening."

"I won the Bronze Star."

Fletch listened to the silence.

"I take back everything I said, son. Good for you."

"Thank you, sir."

"It's a pleasure being called by you. Is there any chance of your coming east with Alan?"

"He doesn't know me."

"He should. He won a Purple Heart. That doesn't mean as much. He just got in the way of something."

"So did I."

"I bet. I bet you did."

"Where was he wounded?"

"He crashed. A helicopter picked him up. The helicopter crashed. Busy snipers, that part of the woods. In the second crash a piece of metal went into his stomach. He told me it looked like an Amish door hinge. No one ever knew where it came from. Maybe the helicopter. I think it's possible it came from the first crash. A man can carry a door hinge for a while without knowing about it. It's okay. Recovering from it has kept him slim."

"Mr. Stanwyk?"

"Yes, son."

"If you were my dad, I'd pick up the Bronze Star next week."

"You never picked it up?"

"No, sir."

"You must have won it a while ago."

"I did. A long while ago."

"You ought to pick it up. Give the country a boost."

"I don't think so."

"What's your name, son, anyway?"

"James," Fletch said. "Sidney James."

NINE

RESERVED CAPTAIN PRECINCT THREE
Fletch parked there.
He went straight to the bull room.
"Lupo's in back," the sergeant at the typewriter said. "Beating the shit out of a customer."

"I'd hate to interrupt him. Someone might read the customer his rights."

"Oh, they've been read to him already. Lupo's interpretation of the Supreme Court ruling has been read to him."

"How does Lupo's interpretation go?"

"You've never heard it? It's really funny. I can't remember all of it.

He rattles it off. Something like: 'You have the right to scream, to bleed, to go unconscious and call an attorney when we get done with you; visible injuries, including missing teeth, will be reported, when questioned, as having occurred before we picked you up, et cetera, et cetera.' It scares the shit out of people."

"I bet."

The sergeant picked up a phone.

"Lupo? Mr. I.M. Fletcher of the *News-Tribune* is here." The sergeant slid the heavy I.B.M. carriage to three-quarters across the page, punched one key, returned and tabbed once. "Okay."

He hung up and smiled happily at Fletch.

"Lupo said he made a bust Wednesday especially for you. Three dimes' worth for twenty dollars."

"Twenty dollars?"

"He says it's Acapulco Gold. You should be so lucky. It was a bust on advertising executives."

"I pity the poor bastards."

"You don't need three bags full to convict. It's in the second left-hand drawer of his desk."

Fletch took the plastic bag from the second left-hand drawer of the first desk in the third row from the windows.

"Thanks very much."

"The money, Lupo said."

"Do you accept credit cards?"

"Cash. It's for the Police Athletic Fund. Believe me, with his new chick, he needs an athletic fund."

"I believe you. Beating up people all day in the questioning room is a tough way to make a living."

"It's hard work."

"Sweaty."

Fletch dropped two tens on the sergeant's desk.

"We're going to try it on you, one day, I.M. Fletcher. Find out what the hell the initials I.M. stand for."

"Oh, no," Fletch said. "That's a secret that will go with me to my grave."

"We'll find out."

"Never. Only my mother knew, and I murdered her to keep her quiet."

Fletch sat in the sergeant's side chair.

"Seeing Lupo isn't here at the moment, and can't be disturbed,"

Fletch said slowly, "I wonder if you would give me a quick reading on a name."

"What name?" The sergeant put his hand on the phone.

"Stanwyk. W-Y-K. Alan. One 'l.' "

"You looking for anything in particular?"

"Just a computer inquiry. A read-out."

"Okay." The sergeant dialed a short number on his phone and spelled the name slowly. He waited absently a moment and then listened, making notes on his pad. He hung up within three minutes.

"Stanwyk, Alan," he said, "has a six-month-old unpaid parking ticket in Los Angeles. Eleven years ago, Air Force Lieutenant Alan Stanwyk, while flying a training craft, buzzed a house in San Antonio, Texas. Complaint was transferred to Air Force, which reprimanded said Stanwyk, Alan."

"That's all?"

"That's all. I'm surprised, too. I seem to recognize the name from somewhere. He must be a criminal. The only names I ever see are the names of baddies."

"You might have seen it in the sports pages," Fletch said, getting up.

"Oh, yeah?"

"Yeah. He tried out for Oakland once."

Fletch went home.

His apartment was on the seventh floor of a building that had everything but design.

His apartment — a living room, a bedroom, bath and kitchenette — was impeccably neat. On the wall over the divan was a blow-up of a multiple *cartes-de-visite* by André-Adolphe-Eugène Disdéri.

In the bathroom, he dropped his clothes in the laundry hamper and showered. The night before, after being away from his apartment for weeks, he had spent forty-five minutes in the shower.

Naked, he added the day's mail to the stack that had been waiting for him the night before on the coffee table. Sitting on the divan, he rolled himself a joint from the bag supplied by Police Detective Herbert Lupo.

A half hour later he picked up the stack of mail, unopened, and dropped it into the wastebasket beside the desk in his bedroom. They were all bills.

The phone rang.

Fletch shoulder-rolled onto the bed and answered it.

"Fletch?"

"My God. If it isn't my own dear, sweet wifey, Linda Haines Fletcher."

"How are you, Fletch?"

"Slightly stoned."

"That's good."

"I've already paid you today."

"I know. Mr. Gillett called and told me you had given him a great big check."

"Mr. Gillett? Of that distinguished law firm, Jackass, Asshole and Gillett?"

"Thank you, Fletch. I mean, for the money."

"Why do you call Gillett 'Mr.'? His pants don't even have pockets."

"I know. Isn't he awful?"

"I never thought you'd leave me for a homosexual divorce lawyer."

"We're just friends."

"I'm sure you are. So why are you calling me?"

Linda paused. "I miss you, Fletch."

"Jesus."

"It's been weeks since we've been together. Thirteen weeks."

"The cat must have decomposed by now."

"You shouldn't have thrown the cat through the window."

"Anyhow, I bought you lunch more recently than that. You think I'm made of money?"

"Together. I mean together."

"Oh."

"I love you, Fletch. You don't get over that in a minute."

"No. You don't."

"I mean, we had some beautiful times together. Real beautiful times."

"You know, around here now you can't even smell the cat."

"Remember the time we just headed off in your old Volvo and we lived in it a whole week? We didn't bring clothes, money, anything?"

"Credit cards. We brought credit cards."

"Do you still have the old Volvo?"

"No. An MG."

"Oh? What color is it?"

"It's called 'enviable green'."

"I've been trying to get you on the phone."

"Even before you got your check?"

"Yes. Have you been away?"

"Yes. I've been working on a story."

"You've been gone a long time."

"It's a long story."

"What's it about?"

"Migrant workers' labor dispute."

"That doesn't sound very interesting."

"It isn't."

"You must be losing your tan."

"No. I've been staying at a motel with a swimming pool. Are you working, Linda? Last time we talked, you were looking for a job."

"I worked for a while in a boutique."

"What happened?"

"What happened to the job?"

"Yeah."

"I quit."

"Why?"

"I don't know. The owner wanted to make love to somebody else for a while."

"Oh."

"Fletch?"

"I'm still here. Where you left me."

"I mean. I wonder. I mean, the divorce has gone through and all. We couldn't spoil anything by being together."

"Couldn't spoil anything?"

"You know, spoil the divorce. If we had been together while the divorce was going through, you know, it might not have gone through."

"Oh. Too bad."

"Now our getting together wouldn't spoil anything."

"You want to get together?"

"I mean, it's Friday night, and I miss you, Fletch. Fletch?"

"Sure."

"Can we spend the night together?"

"Sure."

"I can be there in about an hour."

"Great. You still have a key?"

"Yes."

"I have to go out for a few minutes. There's no food in the house. I have to get some beer and some sandwich stuff."

"Okay."

"So if I'm not here when you get here, just come in and wait. I'll be back."

"All right."

"I won't be long," he said.

"You'd better be."

"Very funny. Don't bring your cat."

"I don't have a cat. See you soon, Fletch. Right after I shower."

"Yeah. Be sure and take a shower first."

"I'll see you in an hour."

After hanging up, Fletch went to the bureau, put on a fresh pair of jeans, a fresh T-shirt, grabbed his pot from the coffee table, his wallet and keys from the bookcase, turned out the lights, checked to make sure the door was locked, went down in the elevator to the garage, got into his car, and drove the hour and a half back to The Beach.

TEN

When he arrived, the chain light hanging from the ceiling was on. Bobbi was lying naked on the groundmat, on her back, asleep.

The room Fletch had rented at The Beach for the duration of this assignment was over a fish store. It stank.

He had furnished it with a knapsack, a bedroll, and his only luxury in that room, a groundmat.

In an ell of the room, in grossly unsanitary juxtaposition, were a two-burner stove, a tiny refrigerator which did not work well, a sink, a shower stall and a toilet.

For this room he paid a weekly rate that amounted to more per month than his city apartment. It had been rented to him by a fisherman who had the character in his face of an Andrew Wyeth subject. It was impossible to lock the door.

The noise of the pan on the stove woke Bobbi.

"Want some soup?"

She had been up, but now she was down.

"Hi."

"Hi. Want some soup?"

"Yeah. Great."

She remained inert. Her "great" had sounded a proper response to the news that pollution had killed all the rabbits on earth.

Bobbi was fifteen years old and blond. She had lost weight even in the few weeks Fletch had known her. Her knees had begun to appear too big for her legs. The skin of her small breasts had begun to wrinkle. Even with her deep tan, the skin under her eyes, almost to the base of her nose, was purple. Her cheekbones appeared to be pulling inside her head. Each eye looked as if it had been hit with a ball-peen hammer.

On her arms and legs were needle tracks.

He sat cross-legged on the mat with the pan of soup and one spoon.

"Sit up."

When she did, drawing her knees up to make room for him, her shoulders looked narrower than her ribcage.

"Been trickin'?"

"Earlier," she said.

"Make much?"

"Forty dollars. Two tricks. Nothing extra."

"Have some soup."

He tipped the spoon into her mouth.

"One guy had a great watch I tried to hook, but he didn't take his eyes off it once. The bastard."

"Did you spend the forty?"

"Yes. And used it. Now it's gone. All gone."

A childlike, ladylike tear built on the lower lid of her left eye and rolled down her cheek without her appearing to notice it.

"Cheer up. There are always more tricks tomorrow. Where did you get the stuff?"

"Fat Sam."

"Any good?"

"Sure. But he doesn't have much."

"He doesn't?"

"He said he hopes he can deal the weekend."

"Where does he get it, anyway?"

"Why?"

"I was just thinking: his source might be cheaper."

"I don't know. Somewhere on the beach, I guess."

"Did you find him on the beach?"

"Yeah. He's always there."

"He sure is."

"Where did you go, Fletch? You've been gone all day. You smell different."

"I smell different?"

"You smell more like air than like a person."

"Like air?"

"I don't know what I mean."

He said, "I was in an air-conditioned building for a while today."

"Ripping off?"

"Yeah. I was doing some lifting from a couple of stores on the Main. It takes time."

"Get much?"

"A couple of cameras. Tape recorder. Trouble is there's this store dick in one store always hassling me. Minute I show up, he eye-bugs me. I had to wait for him to go to lunch."

"It's lousy the way they always hassle you."

"Shits."

"Rip off much?"

"Twenty-three dollars' worth. Big deal."

"Not so much."

"Not so much."

"I mean, for all day. You were gone this morning, too."

"All fuckin' day."

"Why do they have to hassle?"

"Because they're shits. They just see you coming and they're against you. Fuck 'em."

"Fuck 'em," she said.

"Fuck 'em all. The shits."

"You know, Fletch, you could possibly turn tricks."

"No."

"There are plenty of boys out."

"Kids."

"You got a better body than they have."

"Too old."

"You're only twenty-three."

"Twenty-six," he said.

"So. You could turn tricks. You'd be surprised at the men cruising."

"I've seen them."

"Sometimes they don't know which they want. A guy settled with me once, and a boy cruised by, and he said, 'Forget it,' and went off after the boy. I don't know who was more surprised — the boy, or me."

"I don't know. I don't care."

"It doesn't hurt, Fletch. Honest it doesn't."

"I suppose not."

"You might make more money, is all."

"I guess. Finish the soup."

Between her knees, she stirred the soup in the pan with the spoon, concentrating on how the soup moved.

"I mean, I was just thinking you could make more money."

"I like girls."

"So what. If someone's willing to pay, and it doesn't hurt . . ."

"Maybe I'll try it."

"Sure, you try it. You could get more. I mean, I've only seen you shoot up once or twice, Fletch."

"I can't rip off enough."

"You have this room."

"I haven't paid for it yet."

"How are you staying here?"

"The guy who owns the place fences for me. That's why I get screwed all the time."

"You give him the stuff you rip off from the stores?"

"Yeah."

"That doesn't leave much left over."

"No. Not much."

"The bastard."

"He's always hassling me for more," Fletch said.

"Not a very good arrangement," she said.

"You're from the Midwest."

"Why?"

"You sound it. You sound like you're from the Midwest. Very practical."

Bobbi said, "You don't get to have much junk."

"I pop. You know that."

"I know. But still. Pills aren't good for you. They're not natural."

"They're not biodegradable?"

"Natural substances are better. Like heroin."

"The guy I'd like to rip off," Fletch said, "is Fat Sam."

"Why?"

"All the junk he's got."

"He hasn't got much now."

"Maybe next time it comes. Next delivery. Rip off both the cash and the junk same time. That would be beautiful."

"He's a good man."

"What do you mean?"

"I mean, he's not a department store or something. He's Fat Sam. A person. He takes care of us."

"Think how much you could get if I ripped him off."

"You'll never be able to. You'll never even find his stash."

"He never seems to leave the beach. He never leaves the area of the lean-to."

"He must. To get food," Bobbi said.

"The chicks bring it to him. Wendy and Karen."

"I've brought him food."

"You have?"

"When he's asked. He gives me money and tells me what."

"Where do you get the food?"

"At the supermarket."

"You just go in and take it off the shelves?"

"Yes. How else?"

"I don't know. I'd like to rip him off. Just once. If only I could figure out where the stuff comes from."

"I don't care. It's good stuff."

"You said he's going to be having a delivery in the next few days?"

"He's got to have. He said he was short tonight, but he gave me all I could pay for. He's always been good to me."

"Did he ball you, too?"

"No. Wendy was there and Karen. I think they had just made it together."

"It would be beautiful to rip him off."

With apparent absent-mindedness, Fletch began to play with his wallet. He tossed it up in the air to catch it and a picture fell out.

Bobbi said, "Who's that?"

"Nobody."

She put the soup pan down and picked up the picture. She looked at it a long time.

"It must be somebody."

"His name's Alan Stanwyk. You've never seen him."

"Who's Alan Stanwyk?"

"Somebody I used to know. Back when I was straight. He saved my life once."

"Oh. That's why you carry his picture?"

"I've never thrown it away."

"On the back it says, 'Return to *News-Tribune* library.' "

"I ripped it off from there."

"Were you ever in the newspaper business?"

"Who, me? You must be kidding. I was in with a friend once and happened to see the picture. On a desk. I grabbed it. He saved my life once."

"How?"

"I smashed up a car. It was on fire. I was unconscious. He just happened to be passing by. He stopped and dragged me out. I understand he lives somewhere here on The Beach. Are you certain you've never seen him anywhere?"

"Absolutely certain."

"I never had a chance to say thank you."

Bobbi handed him back the picture. "I want to go to sleep now, Fletch."

"Okay."

Still sitting, he lifted off his T-shirt. When he stood up to take off his pants and turn off the light, she got into the bedroll.

He joined her.

She said, "Are you really twenty-six?"

"Yes," he lied.

"I'll never be twenty-six, will I?"

"I guess not."

"How do I feel about that?" she asked.

"I don't know."

She said, "Neither do I."

ELEVEN

There *are no weekends in this job*, Fletch said to himself.

So on Saturday morning he got up, pulled on a pair of shorts, and went to the beach.

Creasey was there, lying on his back, elbows akimbo behind his head. At first Fletch thought he was catatonic. He may have just awakened.

The beach still had morning dew on it. Up the beach, Fat Sam's lean-to cast a long shadow.

Fletch flopped on his stomach.

"What's happening, man?"

Creasey spoke without looking at Fletch.

"Nothing much."

"Everything's cool with me," Creasey said. "Hungry. Haven't any bread for feed, have you?"

"Twelve cents." Fletch took a dime and two pennies from his pocket and tossed them on the sand near Creasey.

Creasey snorted. He was not impressed by the dime and two cents.

"You must be one of the world's greatest rip-off artists," Creasey said.

"The shitty store dicks know me now."

"You gotta go farther afield, man. Hitch rides to neighboring towns."

"How do I get stuff back to fence?"

"Motorists are very obliging. They'll pick up a man with three portable television sets any day."

Creasey laughed by rolling down his lower lip and puffing air from his diaphragm through rotten teeth.

"I used to be a pretty good house burglar myself," Creasey said. "I even had equipment."

"What happened?"

"I got ripped off. Some bastard stole my burglary equipment. The bastard."

"That's funny."

"A fuckin' riot."

"You should have had business insurance."

"I haven't got the energy now anyway." Creasey imitated a stretch and put the back of his head on the sand. "I'm gettin' old, man."

"You must be takin' the wrong stuff."

"Good stuff. Last night was glory road all the way."

Originally, Creasey had been a drummer in a rock band. They made it big. A big New York record company invested one hundred thousand dollars in them and profited three and a half million dollars from them in one year. They made a record, went on a national promotion tour, made another record, went on a national concert tour, made a third record and followed an international concert tour with another national tour. Creasey kept up, with the drumming, the traveling, the hassling with drugs, liquor and groupies. After the year he had six thousand dollars of his own and less energy than a turnip. The record company replaced him in the band with a kid from Arkansas. Creasey was grateful; he never wanted to work again.

"I used to rip off houses all over The Beach. Even up into The Hills. Beautiful, man. I hit the house of one poor son of a bitch seven times. Every time I ripped him off, he'd go out and buy the same shit. Even the same brands. RCA stereo, a Sony TV, a Nikon camera. And leave them in the same places. It was almost a game we had. He'd buy them and leave them around his house for me, and I'd rip them off. Beautiful. The eighth time I went, the house was bare-ass empty. He had stolen himself and his possessions away. An extreme man."

"No more energy for that, uh?"

"Nah, man; that was work. I might as well be beatin' my brains out on a set."

"Where's the bread goin' to come from now?"

"I don't know, man. I don't care."

"Fat Sam must be paid."

"He must," Creasey said. "Son of a bitch."

Fletch said, "I wonder where he gets the stuff."

Creasey answered, "I wouldn't know about that."

"I'm not asking," Fletch said.

"I know you're not. I'd rip him off in a minute. That way, I'd have my own supply. And he could always get more. But the son of a bitch never leaves the beach. At least not while I'm aware. Can't figure the son of a bitch out."

The last time there had been a panic, when there had been an extraordinary number of junkies around and Fat Sam had declared himself absolutely clean, out of everything, at night, Fletch had sat up the beach in the moonlight and watched the lean-to all night. No one came or went from Fat Sam's lean-to. Fletch spoke with anyone who came near. They were all frantic, desperate people. None of them had a supply.

By eleven-thirty the next morning, word went out that Fat Sam — without leaving his lean-to — was fully supplied again. And he was. The panic was over.

"He's a magician," Creasey said. "A fuckin' magician."

"He must be. Bobbi says he's short now."

"Yeah. Rationing's on this day. Ah, me. Not to worry. He'll get the stuff. I mean, I'm sure he'll get the stuff. Don't you think he'll get the stuff? I mean, plenty of it? Like, he always has. I mean, you know, he always gets the stuff. In time. Sometimes he's short for a day or two, and there's rationing, you know, but he always gets the stuff. He'll get it this time, too."

"I'm sure he'll get it," Fletch said.

"He'll get it."

"I'm sure of it," Fletch said.

"Hey, Fletch. You ever notice the way the same kid is always busted?"

"Yeah."

"Man, that's funny. Always the same kid."

"He's a local kid. Montgomery?"

"Gummy Montgomery."

"His dad's a big cheese in the town."

"Every ten days, two weeks, they pick him up. Question him. Beat the shit out of him all night. Let him go in the morning. In the morning, he's back at Fat Sam's for more."

"I guess he never talks."

"He couldn't. We'd all be cooled if he ever did. Oh, man, the fuzz are stupid."

"They only care about the locals. Montgomery's father is superintendent of schools or something."

"Questioning begins at home. They know none of us would ever talk. So they always pick him up, the same kid, and beat the shit out of him. Funny, funny."

"You have a great sense of humor this morning, Creasey."

"I had a beautiful night. The stars came down and talked to me."

"What did they say?"

"They said, 'Creasey, you are the chosen of God. You are chosen to lead the people into the sea.' "

"A wet dream."

"Yeah. A wet dream."

"I've got to go see the man about some horse," Fletch said.

"I gotta go steal some bread."

Creasey did not move. He remained staring into the sea where he would lead the people on his next high.

Fletch sat cross-legged in the shade of Vatsyayana's lean-to. Vatsyayana was sitting cross-legged inside the lean-to.

"Peace," Vatsyayana said.

"Fuck," said Fletch.

"That, too."

"Some reds," Fletch said.

"I'm fresh out."

"I've got twenty dollars."

"Expecting a shipment any day. Hang in there."

"Need it now."

"I understand." Vatsyayana had the world's kindliest eyes. "No got. I've got what's left of the horse."

"Horseshit."

"Each to his own taste. How's Bobbi?"

"Asleep."

"She really grooves on you, Fletch. She was here last night."

"I know. You didn't ball her."

"Who could? By the time she shows up here, she's had it. Did you ball her last night?"

"No."

"She looks terrible, Fletch."

"Thank you."

"I mean it, Fletch."

"I know. I think she has fetuses going on all the time."

"That's not possible."

"No. She's not strong enough to carry anything."

"Why don't you get her away from here?"

"You think Gummy will talk?"

From the back of the lean-to, Vatsyayana's eyes momentarily brightened. "I don't think so."

"Why not? They keep beatin' on him."

"He hasn't talked yet."

"Why do they keep pickin' on the same kid?"

"He's local. They can put more pressure on him. I guess they figure if they keep hammerin' on the same kid, instead of hammerin' on you one day and me the next, over time they can break him down and get him to turn state's evidence. I've seen it before."

"Will it work? I mean, will they break him down?"

"I doubt it. He's in very deep now. He feels nothing."

"How will we know if he talks?"

"The men in blue with big sticks will come swooping down out of the skies, Society's avenging angels, sunlight glistening from their riot helmets."

"How will we know it's going to happen?"

"It won't happen. Believe me, Fletch. You're all right. It won't happen."

"Fat Sam, I heard someone say he wanted to rip you off."

"Who?"

"I won't say."

"Creasey? These days, Creasey can hardly walk so far."

"Not Creasey. Someone else."

"Who'd want to rip off Vatsyayana?"

"He says he even knows your source."

"No one knows Vatsyayana's source."

"He says he does. He says you get your delivery here on the beach. That someone brings it to you. Is that true?"

"Son, there is no truth."

"He says the next time you get delivery he's gonna be there. He's got some scheme where he picks up both the cash and the junk."

"Not possible. It doesn't work that way."

"What way?"

"It doesn't work any way."

"How do you get it?"

"I pray for it and it comes. You're a good boy, Fletch, but you're not too bright. Has anyone ever told you that before?"

"Yes."

"I bet they have. No one's gonna rip off Vatsyayana."

"Is it possible? I mean, you could be ripped off."

"No way. Not possible. Just relax. By tomorrow noon I should have some reds. Can you make it?"

"Gimme the H."

"Gimme the twenty."

"No one would want you ripped off, Sam."

"If it ever happened, it would be bye-bye highs."

"No one would want that to happen."

"Of course not."

"The Stanwyk residence."

Fletch had turned on the fan in the roof of the telephone booth to dampen the sound of traffic.

"Mrs. Stanwyk, please."

"I'm sorry, Mrs. Stanwyk isn't in. May I take a message?"

"We're calling from the Racquets Club. Do you have any idea where Mrs. Stanwyk is?"

"Why, she should be there, sir, at the club. She was playing this morning, and she said she would be staying for lunch. I think she's meeting her father there."

"Ah, then she's here now?"

"Yes, sir. She planned to spend most of the day at the club."

"We'll have a look for her. Sorry to bother you."

Saturday morning traffic at The Beach was heavy. Down the street was a department store.

Fletch bought a new T-shirt, a pair of white socks, and a pair of tennis shorts.

TWELVE

"Y ou're Joan Stanwyk, aren't you?"
She was sitting alone at a table for two overlooking the tennis courts. A half-empty martini on the rocks was in front of her.

"Why, yes."

"I haven't seen you since your wedding."

"Are you a friend of Alan's?"

"We were in the Air Force together," Fletch said. "In San Antonio. I haven't seen Alan in years."

"You're very clever to have recognized me."

"How could I forget? May I sit down?"

Fletch had left his car in the club parking lot and had gone around the building past the kitchen door to the service entrance to the locker rooms. The freshest sign on a locker door said Underwood. A new member. They and their guests could not yet be well known to the club staff.

When he had come onto the tennis pavilion, the headwaiter had said, "Pardon me, sir. Are you a guest of the club?"

Fletch had answered, "I'm a guest of the Underwoods."

"They're not here, sir. I haven't seen them."

"They're coming later."

"Very good, sir. Perhaps you'd like a drink while you're waiting?"

Fletch had spotted Joan Stanwyk.

"We'll put it on the Underwood bill."

"A screwdriver, please."

He sat at Joan Stanwyk's table.

"I'm afraid my memory isn't so good, although it should be," Joan Stanwyk said. "I can't remember your name."

"No one can," Fletch said. "The world's most forgettable name. Utrelamensky. John Utrelamensky."

"John I can remember."

On the table was a Polaroid camera.

"Are you from this area, John?"

"No. Butte, Montana. I'm here on business. In fact, I'm leaving on a midafternoon plane."

"And what business would that be?"

"Furniture. We sell to hotels, that sort of thing."

"I see. Too bad you won't be able to see Alan. He's at a flying convention in Idaho."

"Alan still flying?"

"Relentlessly."

"Unlike some of the rest of us, he really enjoyed it. I'll never forget the time he buzzed a house in San Antonio with a training jet."

"He buzzed a house?"

"He never told you? Shattered glass. The police were out after him. He was severely reprimanded for it."

"Funny the things husbands don't tell you."

"I expect he's not too proud of it."

"How nice to meet an old friend of Alan's. I mean, meet again. Tell me more."

"Only wrong thing I ever knew of him doing. We weren't that close, anyway. I just happened to be out here the week of the wedding, bumped into him and he said, 'Come along.' "

"But surely you're a good deal younger than my husband?"

"Not much," Fletch said. "I'm thirty."

"You look young for your age."

"The furniture business has been good to me."

"Well, I'm sure Alan will be sorry to have missed you."

"I'm not so sure."

"Oh?"

"We had a political difference at your reception."

"About what?"

"I made some crack about big business. Alan didn't like it a bit."

"How could you?" There was mockery in her eyes.

"I was younger then. I had not yet received a corporate paycheck."

"Did you say anything about his marrying the boss's daughter?"

"No. Is that what he did?"

"He married the boss's daughter — me. He's a bit sensitive about that. That's probably why he got so angry."

"I see. I hadn't realized that. I guess I really goofed."

"Never mind. He's been accused of it enough times. Poor Alan spends all his available time proving he married me for myself and not for Poppa's business."

"He works for your father?"

"I'm not sure at the moment who works for whom. Alan runs the place. Dad runs tennis tournaments. In fact, these days Dad does pretty much what Alan tells him."

"Alan always was very competent."

"Remarkably."

"What sort of a business is this, anyway?"

"Collins Aviation."

"I never heard of it. Sorry."

"You wouldn't have, unless you were in the aviation business. It makes parts for airplanes the actual airplane manufacturers put together."

"Not exactly a dry-cleaning shop."

"Not exactly."

"You see how bad I am at business. I don't even follow the stock market."

"Very little of Collins Aviation stock is available. It belongs mostly to us."

"The whole thing?"

"To us and a few family friends. You know, like the family doctor, Dad's old Harvard roommate, Joe Devlin . . . people like that. All as rich as Croesus."

"How nice."

"It is nice to have everyone you know rich. Problems never come up about who pays the drink bill."

"Would you like another?"

"Why, John. How nice." He signaled a waiter.

"By the way, John, how did you gain entrée to the Racquets Club?"

"I'm a guest of the Underwoods. He and I are doing a little business together. He knew my plane was not leaving until midafternoon, so he suggested I come over, hit a ball and have a swim."

"The Underwoods? I don't know them. They must be new members."

"I'm sure I wouldn't know."

"But where's your tennis racquet?"

"I borrowed one. I just returned it to the pro shop."

"I see."

"A martini on the rocks, please, and a screwdriver," he said.

The waiter said, "Yes, Mrs. Stanwyk."

"The Racquets Club is Daddy's pet. He darn near built the place himself. In fact, he's endowed it so well, the Racquets Club is a major stockholder in Collins Aviation. That very chair you're sitting on was probably designed for an airport lounge in Albany. Does Albany have an airport?"

"Albany, New York?"

"Yes."

"Who cares?"

"Good point. Who cares about Albany, New York?"

"Except the Albanians."

"Except the Albanians. Woo. I usually don't drink martinis after playing tennis in the morning."

"What do you usually do after playing tennis in the morning?"

"I wouldn't mind doing that either," she said. "Alan's away a lot. Mondays and Wednesdays he never gets home before eleven o'clock at night. The ends of the weeks he's apt to get in his airplane and go somewhere on business. Business, business, business. Ah, here's another drink."

The waiter said, "Here you are, Mrs. Stanwyk."

"To business," she said.

"He never comes home until eleven on Mondays and Wednesdays?" Fletch repeated.

"Very late. On Thursdays I have a committee meeting here at the club. Just as well; the servants at home are out. Julie and I have supper here at the Club. Julie's my daughter. You haven't met her yet. I don't know what happens to Alan on Thursdays. That leaves us exactly Tuesdays together. He's always very attentive on Tuesdays."

"I remember Alan got a piece of metal stuck in him overseas."

"He got a scar in his belly and a Purple Heart."

"Is he all right now?"

"Perfect. He's in perfect physical condition."

"He is?"

"Why are you so incredulous?"

"He always worried about having cancer. Every time he lit a cigarette he'd mention it. He called them cancer sticks."

"I have noted no such justifiable neuroticism on his part."

"He's never had cancer?"

"God. Don't even say it."

"Remarkable."

"What is?"

"That he's never had cancer."

"He doesn't smoke all that much. But for you, John whatever-your-last-name-is, there seems nothing wrong with you."

"I never went overseas," Fletch said.

"You seem quite perfect."

"Overflight."

"What?"

"Overflight. I'm trying to think of the name of Alan's best man. Over-something."

"Eberhart. Burt Eberhart."

"That's it. He struck me as a nice guy. Is he still around?"

"You have some memory. He's still around. Fat and balding. He lives here on The Beach, on Vizzard Road. Married to a social climber. Three ugly kids. He's in the insurance business."

"The insurance business?"

"Yes. He handles Alan's insurance, and now the company's insurance, and the club's. He has been well set up. By Alan. They were friends at Colgate."

"Sounds like a good business. Seeing Alan's still flying, he's probably got a lot of insurance on him."

"A foolish amount. My father wanted to teach Alan, via the route of monthly premiums paid by Alan himself, the value of Alan's precious life. An effort to get him to stop flying after Julie was born. It worked not at all. Alan remains perfectly willing to cast his wife and child to the insurance adjuster just to climb through the clouds to sudden sunlight once again."

"Alan pays the premiums? Not the company?"

"When we say 'the company' in my family, we mean my father. Dad obliges Alan to have such insurance coverage as a condition of his employment, but Alan must pay the bill himself. Daddy's very cute at making such arrangements. Pity they never work."

"I should think, from what you say, Alan would need to get away and have some fun by himself once in a while."

"There's the club."

"He relaxes when he flies," he said.

"And everyone else has heart failure. I hate to think what he's flying this weekend. For fun. You wouldn't even recognize those experimental craft he flies as airplanes. They look like the mean, nasty sort of weapons aborigines throw through the air. Horrifying."

"It must be tough on you."

"I wish he'd stop flying."

"One thing I've always wondered about."

"Dad is late for lunch."

"Is he coming?"

"He was supposed to meet me here twenty minutes ago."

"Perhaps I should leave."

"No, no. He'd be happy to meet you. Any friend of Alan's and all that. What were you wondering about?"

"Why Alan's parents didn't come to the wedding."

"Alan's parents?"

"Yes."

"They're estranged. He never sees them."

"He never sees them?"

"Does that surprise you?"

"Yes, it does. I had the idea they were rather close."

"No way. He hates them. Alan always has. I've never even met them."

"How can that be so?"

"You must be thinking of someone else."

"I'm sure Alan used to fly home to see his parents whenever he could. Every six weeks or so."

"Not Alan. His parents were very pushy toward him. The crisis came, I think, at the Golden Gloves."

"The Golden Gloves? I remember Alan had boxed."

"Alan boxed because his father made him. Pushed him right up the ladder or whatever into the state Golden Gloves. When he was fifteen. Every day after school he had to spend in the basement at home, boxing until suppertime. He hated it. He refused to go into the nationals. He and his father have never spoken since then."

"I must be confused."

"You must be. And he's always said his mother is a sickly, neurotic thing. Spends most of her time in bed."

"Aren't you interested in these people? Alan's parents? Aren't you curious to meet them yourself?"

"Not if what Alan says is true about them. And I'm sure it is. Why wouldn't it be? Believe me, honey, I have enough difficult people around me to not want to add in-laws."

"I see."

There was a stir in the pavilion as a handsome, distinguished-looking man in his fifties entered, dressed in white tennis slacks and blue blazer. People reacted like children in a sandbox catching sight of someone coming with a box of popsicles. They waved from their tables. Men nearest the entrance stood up to shake hands. Women beamed. The headwaiter welcomed with happy bows of his head.

"There," Joan said, "is Dad."

Fletch said, "Yes, I remember him."

"Don't be disappointed if he doesn't remember you."

"Why should he remember me?" Fletch said.

"Because you're beautiful," she said. "You really turn me on. Are you sure you have to leave town today?"

"I've got to be back tonight."

"But tomorrow's Sunday."

"Listen," Fletch said, "you and Alan ought to have a place you can go and be by yourselves once in a while. I mean, a place of your own."

"The ranch."

"What?"

"Alan is buying a ranch. In Nevada. For us."

"Great."

"No, it isn't great. It's awful. Who wants a ranch in Nevada?"

"Most people."

"I spent a summer on a ranch when I was a kid. Hot, dusty, dirty. Boring. Incredibly boring. All the men look like pretzels. And when they talk they sound like a Dick-and-Jane book. It comes out slow and it ends up obvious. And you don't talk about anything that hasn't got four legs. I mean, sitting around looking at a cow is not my idea of pleasure."

"Then why are you doing it?"

"Alan wants to. He thinks the ranch is a great idea as an investment. I haven't even been out to look at it. He insists he's taking me next weekend."

"Next weekend?"

"I can't tell you how I'm looking forward to it."

"It's a place you could be alone together."

"Like hell. There's an airstrip in the back yard. I know that already. As long as there's an airplane in the back yard, Alan will be off on an important business deal somewhere and I'll be left staring at cows with a bunch of pretzels in blue jeans."

"So stop it. Stop Alan from buying it."

"Supposedly, he's taking the down payment, the cash, out himself next weekend."

"The cash? As cash?"

"Yes. Isn't that crazy? Cash. He said cash, visible cash is the only way to do business with these people. If he shows up with cash in a brown paper bag or something, flashes the real stuff, he might save percentages from the purchase price."

"They must be more sophisticated than that."

"This is deep in Nevada, honey. How do you know what appeals to a pretzel in blue jeans with a cow on its mind? Oh, Dad."

Fletch stood up.

"This is an old friend of Alan's. They were in the Air Force together. John — "

Shaking hands, Fletch said, "Yahmenaraleski."

"Glad to meet you, Mr. Yahmenaraleski," John Collins said. "Stay and have lunch with us."

THIRTEEN

Fletch brought a chair from a neighboring table and sat in it. John Collins sat facing his daughter. At one o'clock, the sunlit tennis courts were empty. The pavilion was full.

Joan had moved the Polaroid camera.

"John's in the furniture business, Dad. From Grand Rapids, Michigan."

"From Butte, Montana," Fletch said.

"Oh?"

Fletch was correct. Besides no one's being able to remember for long the name he gave, no one cared to inquire too deeply into either the furniture business or Butte, Montana. He believed himself absolutely unmemorable.

"Martinis before lunch?" John Collins said.

"I mean to take a nap this afternoon." Joan stared at Fletch.

"I'm glad to see at least John is drinking orange juice."

"It's a screwdriver."

"Ah. Well. If you drink enough of those, they'll make your head hammer." John Collins beamed at them both. His daughter groaned softly. "You play tennis, John?"

"Just hack about, sir. I enjoy the game, but I have so little time for it . . ."

"You must make time in life to enjoy yourself and be healthy. It's the best way to get a lot done."

"Yes, sir."

"Of course it also helps if you have a very able son-in-law to take over your business and run it for you. Sometimes I feel guilty that I'm playing and Alan is working. How do you know Alan?"

"We were in the Air Force together. In Texas."

"John said that Alan buzzed a house once, in San Antonio. Did he ever mention that to you, Dad?"

"He certainly didn't."

"We were lieutenants then," Fletch said. "He was severely repri-manded. I guess I talked out of school."

"Delighted you did," John Collins said. "Time we had a bit of dirt on Alan. I'll put his nose in it. Got any more dirt?"

"No, sir."

"He's off flying someone's idea of an airplane in Idaho this week-end," John said. "Do you still fly?"

"Only with a ticket in my hand."

"Good for you. I wish Alan would give it up. He's too important to too many people to be taking such risks. Were you overseas with him?"

"No, sir. I was sent to the Aleutians."

"Oh."

Fletch smiled. No one cared about the Aleutians, either.

Without having ordered, John Collins was brought a grilled cheese sandwich and a bottle of ale.

"Aren't you two going to order?" he asked.

"Sliced chicken sandwich," Joan said. "Mayonnaise."

"A grilled cheese," Fletch added. "Bottle of Coors beer."

"How very ingratiating of you," John Collins said.

He was used to young men complimenting him over his choice of lunch.

Fletch laughed. "I'm very happy in the furniture business, thank you."

"Actually, Alan needs more young men around him. Friends. Peo-ple he can trust. He's stuck with all my old office cronies. I keep telling him he should retire them all off, but he's too smart for that. He says he would rather have attrition than contrition."

"Dad. He never said anything of the sort."

"Well, he would have, if he had a sense of humor."

"He has a lovely sense of humor," Joan said.

"Tell me something he ever said that made you laugh," John said. "Anything."

"Well. He said something to Julie the other day. But I can't remember it. Something about going to bed."

"A riot," John said. "My son-in-law is a riot. Did he have a sense of humor when you knew him in Texas?"

"A pretty serious fellow," Fletch said.

"I worry about people who don't have a sense of humor. Here's your lunch. Take everything seriously. They're apt to kill themselves."

"If the cigarettes don't get them first," Fletch said.

"What?" John Collins leaned on him.

"The cigarettes. Alan was always dreadfully afraid of cancer."

"He should be. No one should smoke."

Joan said, "Alan's never mentioned his fear of cancer to me."

"He must be used to it," Fletch said. "Or over it."

"Everybody should be afraid of cancer. Does it run in his family? Of course, how do we know? Never met his family. Ought to look them up and see if they're still alive."

"Alan never speaks of them," Joan said. "I doubt he ever hears from them."

"I don't blame him. Any man who makes his son box is a jackass. A stupid sport. Alan would have been a great tennis player if he had started young and not been forced to waste all his time getting bopped on the nose. Rather, I should say, any man who forces his son to box wants to see him in a coffin."

"You're in top form today, Dad. One right after the other."

"Why not? Pleasant company. His father just never realized what an intelligent lad Alan was and is. Wonder he didn't get his brains knocked out of him."

"Before you came, Dad, we were talking about the damn-fool ranch Alan is buying, in Nevada."

"Yes. Good idea."

"It's a terrible idea."

"This family doesn't have anywhere near enough invested in real estate. And what there is is downtown space. Or the place in Aspen, whatnot. We should be much more heavily invested in land. No one's ever wanted to manage it. I'm glad Alan does."

Joan said, "I hate the whole idea."

"You don't have to go there."

"The way Alan talks, a million acres in Nevada is going to be our spiritual home."

"You'll have to go there once in a while, of course, while Alan goes over things. Do you both good to get away. With Julie. You must be sick to death of your mother and me living on top of you."

"She's not well."

John said, "I remember the first day I saw your mother taking martinis before lunch. Gin is a depressant, my girl."

"My golly. You do live on top of us. I never noticed before."

"Was Jim Swarthout helpful?" John asked.

"Who?"

"Jim Swarthout of Swarthout Nevada Realty. Biggest firm in Nevada. I sent Alan to him when he began talking about the ranch. I understood he's been dealing with him."

"Oh, yes. Very helpful. He's the man who found the ranch for Alan. He's mentioned him several times. He is the real estate broker. We're going down next weekend, cash in hand."

"Cheer up, old girl. Alan's dead right about our investing in a ranch. He couldn't be more right." John Collins drained his ale. "Now the job is to see if we can get young John here a tennis match."

"No, sir. Thank you anyway. I haven't the time, at this point. My plane leaves midafternoon."

"Oh." The man seemed genuinely disappointed. "I'm sorry to hear that."

"This is a beautiful club, though. Joan mentioned the extent of your contribution to it."

"Well, she shouldn't have. But I consider it very important. Young people have to have a place to go, and healthy things to do. You know, I understand young people can't even go to the beach here anymore."

"Oh?"

"Drugs. Goddamn it. Drugs everywhere. On the beach, of all places. Hard drugs. Heroin. Opium. Let alone these pills and amphetamines. Sending a youngster to the beach these days is equal to sending him to hell."

"People literally selling drugs to children. Pushing drugs on them. Can you imagine anything worse than that?" Joan said. "What sort of an insane, evil person would actually urge children to take drugs for just a few bucks?"

"I've had several conversations with the chief of police, Chief Cummings," John Collins said, "urging him to crack down more actively on this business. I've even offered to pay to have special investigators come in, to clean the whole thing up. That's a bill I wouldn't mind paying at all. He tells me he's doing everything he can. He has an informer on the beach, he says, but it's very difficult, as young people drift in and out, live on the beach, go by phony names. Apparently it's much too fluid a situation to control. There are no constants. He said special investigators wouldn't do a darn bit of good."

"I didn't know you made that offer, Dad. How sweet."

"It's not sweet. It's necessary. With the rate of burglaries we're having here at The Beach, muggings and robberies, something has to be done. There's going to be a murder soon, and then people will sit up. But what really bothers me is all these young people staggering around, destroying their brains, destroying their bodies, killing themselves. How very awful for them. They don't know better. Their lives must be just hell."

Fletch said, "I quite agree with you, sir."

"However, the esteemed chief of police is retiring soon, and a man close to retirement isn't apt to be at his most energetic. That's what I keep telling Alan: retire the old farts; give them their money and let them go. They're not doing anything for the company anyway. Chief Cummings is busy setting up some retirement home. He's not paying attention to police business here in town. Might as well get rid of him. Perhaps after he retires, we'll have a better chance to wipe out this nest of vipers and sickies."

Fletch said, "You never can tell. The thing might break by itself, somehow."

"I'd like to see it," John Collins said. "And I'd like to know who is going to do it."

"Well," Fletch said. "The club is just great."

"There are no drugs here," John Collins said, "except for martinis imbibed before lunch by certain dopes."

FOURTEEN

Using his telephone credit card, Fletch spent an hour in an overstuffed chair in the playroom of the Racquets Club. The room was dark and cool, and no one was at the billiard tables or the ping-pong tables or watching the television.

First, he called the home number of Marvin Stanwyk in Nonheagan, Pennsylvania.

"Mr. Stanwyk?"

"Yes."

"This is Sidney James of Casewell Insurers of California."

"How are you, boy? What did you decide about picking up that Bronze Star?"

"I haven't decided yet, sir."

"Doubt you'll ever be offered another one."

"I didn't expect to be offered this one."

"I say you should pick it up. Never know. You might have a son, someday, who'd have some interest in it, or a grandson."

"I don't know, sir. Women don't seem to be having children these days."

"You know, you're right about that. I wouldn't mind Alan and his wife producing a child."

"What?"

"Don't you think it's time they had a child? Been married how long? Six, seven years?"

"They don't have a child?"

"Indeed not. That would get us to come out to California. Boy, girl, anything. We wouldn't miss seeing our grandchild."

"I see."

"Well, Mr. James, I imagine you called to ask how we are again. Mrs. Stanwyk and I are both well. Just beginning to think about lunch."

"Glad to hear it, sir."

"You must be a pretty ambitious fellow, working on a Saturday. I have to go back to the hardware store myself after lunch, but I thought I was the only man left alive who still works on a Saturday. Of course, in your case, you may have to work on Saturday because you spend so much time the rest of the week calling up people."

"We're trying to pin down just how much flying your son does."

"Too much."

"You say he comes to see you every six weeks or so."

"About that."

"How long does he stay with you?"

"A night or two."

"Does he stay in your house?"

"No. He and the copilot or whatever he is stay at the Nonheagan Inn. They have a suite there. Alan's like you. If he's not on the phone forty-five minutes an hour, he thinks the world's going to end. He needs the hotel switchboard."

"How much do you actually see him on a visit?"

"I'm not sure I'll ever get used to your questions, but a man who won the Bronze Star must know what he's doin'. Mostly they come for breakfast."

"They?"

"He and the copilot. Name is Bucky. That's why my wife always makes him buckwheat cakes. He loves them. He can put away more buckwheat cakes than you need to shingle your roof."

"Is it always the same pilot?"

"No. Twice it's been other fellows, but I don't remember their names. Usually it's Bucky. Then, sometimes Alan might come over by himself later, for supper. Not always. We don't see that much of him when he's here, but we guess he just finds his old hometown restful."

"Yes, of course. How long has he been doing this?"

"Visiting us regularly? Since he became the big cheese out at that airplane company. I guess business brings him east more now."

"The last six or seven years?"

"I'd say the last four years. We saw him hardly at all when he was first married. Which is apt to be the way."

"Why do you say he flies too much?"

"Flying's dangerous, son. Especially in a private jet. Anything could go wrong."

"You mean he could get hurt."

"He could get killed. I haven't heard they're making airplanes out of rubber yet. He's already been in one air crash, you know. Two, in fact. Overseas."

"I know. You didn't mind his boxing, though, when he was a kid."

"Who says we didn't?"

"You did mind?"

"We did about everything we could think of to make him stop. Every afternoon down there in the cellar beating the beeswax out of the punching bags. Whump, whump, whump. Till supper time. There was a period when he was out fighting two nights a week. No one's brain can stand that. I was sure his brain was going to run out his ears. Enough ran out his nose."

"Why didn't you stop him from boxing, then?"

"If you ever have a son, you'll find that when he gets to be fourteen or fifteen there are some things you can't tell him not to do. The more you tell them not to smash their heads against the wall, the more they insist upon doing it. They never believe they're going to need things like brains later on in life."

"Then why didn't he go on to the nationals?"

"You can't figure the answer to that question?"

"No, sir."

"Girls, son; girls. No matter how much time fifteen-year-old boys spend thrashing around in the basement, sooner or later they notice girls. And that's the end of their thrashing around in the basement. The boxing gloves were hung up and out came the pocket comb. I admit, though, it took us a while to figure it out. He had sure wanted to go to the nationals, and he was very, very good at out-boxing people. Suddenly, before the nationals, the house stopped shaking, the whumping ceased. We thought he was sick. The night he told us he was not going to the nationals was about the happiest night of our lives. The punching bags are still hanging in our basement. Never touched them since. They need a rest after the beating they took. Then, of course, Alan took to flying airplanes. Sons just don't know how to keep their parents relaxed. I'm sure you weren't a bit kinder to your parents, Mr. James."

"I guess not. Maybe it's just as well your son and daughter-in-law don't have a child."

"Aw, no. Bringing up kids is not the same as eating creamed chicken, but you shouldn't miss it."

"Well, I guess that's all for now, Mr. Stanwyk. Thanks again."

"Say, son?"

"Yes?"

"I'm glad you called back, because I didn't know where to reach you. I've been thinking about your Bronze Star. I want to make a deal with you."

"Oh?"

"Well, you ought to pick it up. What I'm thinking is this. You pick the Bronze Star up and send it out to us. We'll admire it and hold it for you, and someday when you want it, when you have a kid or something, we'll send it back to you."

"That's very nice of you."

"What do you say? If anything happens to us, we'll make sure you get it somehow. We'll leave it with the bank along with my wife's best shoes."

"I don't know what to say."

"It's a long life, son, and your feelings change about things. You send the Bronze Star on to us, and we'll take care of it for you."

"You're a sweet man, Mr. Stanwyk."

"I don't understand that California kind of talk."

"May I think about it?"

"Sure. I'm just thinking it might make the whole thing easier for you."

"Thank you. Thank you very much."

"Call anytime. I bought some more telephone stock last night."

"The Nonheagan Inn. Good afternoon."

"Good afternoon. This is Mr. Alan Stanwyk."

"Hello, Mr. Stanwyk. Nice to hear your voice, sir."

Teenage girls looked into the Racquets Club playroom. Apparently Fletch was not what they were looking for.

"I'm calling myself because it's Saturday and I just decided I might come out next weekend."

"Oh?"

"Why does that surprise you?"

"Sorry, sir. I didn't mean to sound surprised. It's just that we look forward to seeing you every six weeks or so, and you were here just two weeks ago."

"I may change my mind about coming."

"It will be perfectly all right if you do, sir. We'll keep the suite for you until we're sure you're not coming."

"Thank you very much."

"Good-bye, Mr. Stanwyk."

"Swarthout Nevada Realty Company."
"Jim Swarthout, please."
"I'm sorry, sir, Mr. Swarthout is out with a client."
"When do you expect him?"
"Well, sir, it is Saturday afternoon . . ."
"I see."
"May I have him call you after he calls in?"
"No, thanks. He'll be in the office Monday?"
"Yes, sir."
"I'll get him then."

FIFTEEN

Still in tennis whites, Fletch cruised slowly down Vizzard Road. The telephone directory had said the number was 12355.

It was a pleasant Spanish-styled stucco house set back on a cool lawn. In the driveway was a blue Cadillac Coupe de Ville.

Fletch parked in the street.

Going toward the house, he smelled and saw smoke, so he went around to the back.

Inside the pool enclosure was a fat, balding man in Bermuda shorts contemplating a lighted hibachi. Beside him on a flagstone was a large gin and tonic.

"Burt?"

The man looked up, ready to be pleased, ready to greet someone, to be glad; instead, he looked slightly hesitant at someone he had never seen before.

"John Zalumarinero," Fletch said.

"Oh, yes."

Burt Eberhart put out his hand.

"I'm only in town for the day. Just had lunch with Joan Collins and her father at the Racquets Club."

"Oh, yes."

"I asked for you. Joan said you lived here at The Beach and I should pop in to say hello on the way back to the hotel."

"Oh, yes."

79

"I haven't seen you since Joan's wedding. You were best man."

"John!" Burt Eberhart said with a burst of synthetic recognition. He shook hands again. "By God, it's good to see you again. How have you been keeping yourself?"

"Furniture business. Montana."

"That's terrific. You look so young. You say you just had lunch with Joan and her dad?"

"The grilled cheese special."

"Jesus. John Collins and his grilled cheese sandwich. A billionaire practically, and he gives you a grilled cheese sandwich. I'd hate to see what he'd eat if he were poor. I know what you mean, fella. I've had plenty of his grilled cheese sandwiches. At least he could buy you a steak. With his money. He's afraid of putting on a pound. As if anybody cares. Everybody's too busy weighing John's wallet to care what he looks like."

"You look prosperous enough yourself."

"Now no cracks, boy. What can I get you to drink? A gin and tonic?"

"That would be fine."

"It's right here, right here." A bar was in the shade, against the house. "Never be more than ten feet away from your next drink, I always say."

And he looked it.

"We had great fun at the wedding together, you and I," Fletch said. "I guess you don't remember."

"God, I was bombed out of my mind. I don't remember anything. For all I know, I was the one who got married that day. What did you say your last name is again?"

"Zalumarinero."

"That's right, that's right. An Irish boy."

"Welsh, actually."

"I remember now. We did have fun. Wasn't that a beautiful wedding? Oh, God, did we have fun. I remember you: you went right into the pool with your hat on."

"I did?"

"You did. You certainly did. You walked right up to the pool with your hat on and kept right on walking. Splash! Any man who can do a thing like that can't be all bad."

"I don't remember."

"I wasn't the only one putting them down that day, my boy. Here's to your health. Oh, God, it's hot. Why people live in this climate

I'll never know. We all rush to California because of the beautiful climate, and then spend the rest of our lives indoors hugging an air conditioner. Come sit by the hibachi. We're having a few people over later."

Fletch sat in the shade of an umbrella and watched Burt fiddle with the hibachi between gulps of his drink.

"The trick to a good charcoaled steak is to start the fire plenty early. Two or three hours ahead of time. Our ancestors, you know, used to have the fire going all the time. Of course they weren't paying what we are for charcoal. Then, when they wanted to use the fire, it would be right there, ready, and they could control it. You can't control a new fire as well. Golly, I'm awful glad you stopped by, John. You should stay for supper."

"No thanks, I really can't."

"I mean, you should. Anybody who has lunch with John Collins needs a steak supper. And a battle ribbon."

"My plane leaves in a couple of hours."

"Then you should have another drink. I always believe in being at least as high as the plane. That way, if it falls down, you still have a chance."

"How's Alan?"

"Oh, he's terrific. Beautiful. He looks like you. Not an inch of fat on his body. Great shape, great shape. Just watching him makes me tired."

"I think you said at the wedding you and he were great friends at school."

"Colgate, ta-ra! I've been living off him ever since."

"What do you mean?"

"Almost ever since. I had a few lean years before he got married. I had to work for a living. Want another drink? I've got all his insurance accounts. His life insurance, house, cars, inland marine, the Collins Company. That's why I never disagree with John Collins, despite the grilled cheese sandwiches. After all, I've got my future drinking to consider."

"Joan said Alan's life is insured for three million dollars."

"You'd better believe it."

"It's true?"

"Absolutely true. That guy's worth a lot more dead than alive. Except to me. I get the premiums commission. Every night I pray for him. If he dies, I die. I'd even have to go back to work. Jesus. Think of it. Some damn-ass mechanic forgets to tighten a screw on some damn-ass airplane in Idaho this weekend and my life is over. I hate airplanes. I won't even look at any. Put Raquel Welch on one wing stark naked and Ursula Andress on the other wing and put the airplane right in front of me, and I wouldn't even look in its direction. I'm like Al's mother — he flies and I worry. Probably I'll die of worrying and he'll fly a loop-de-loop over my grave."

"How did you know each other in school?"

"Oh, he was beautiful. We were roommates as freshmen. He had boxed Golden Gloves. He was very serious. Work, work, work all the time. You'd think he had a little clock wound up inside him, and if he didn't keep time to it, he'd choke or something. I wanted to get into the fraternity and he didn't. I mean, he didn't care. He went home most weekends. To the ribald town, Nonheagan, Pennsylvania. Jesus, what a boring town. I went home with him one weekend. On Saturday night for excitement we went downtown and watched the bus stop. I said, 'Jesus, Al, you're always so serious. College has more to it than just work, work, work.' I wanted to get him to apply to the fraternity with me. I thought I'd have a better chance. They turned me down and made an offer to him. He hadn't even applied. The most crushing blow of my life. I thought I'd never get over it. I mean, how the hell can kids, seventeen, eighteen years old, make decisions like that about someone else after knowing him only a few months? I mean, turning me down? In a few months this bunch of jerks decided Al was all beautiful and good and I was a shit. And Al didn't even spend the weekends on campus. I rushed the fraternity, and the fraternity rushed Al. Jesus, I wept. Al accepted, on condition they accept me too. His roommate. Jesus, I'll never forget that. The sweetest thing anybody ever did for me. But how did he have the balls to do it? It meant so much, and he stood back cool as a cucumber at eighteen and bargained with this bunch of brass monkeys. I thought he'd never carry it off. He did. They accepted us both, they wanted him so bad. Then he never did a damn thing for the fraternity except honor it by living there. He still went home on the weekends. I stayed at the fraternity weekends. Jesus, we had some beautiful times. I'll never forget that."

"I don't understand. What was so great about Alan Stanwyk?"

"What's so great about Alan Stanwyk? He's thirty-three now, and he's running one of the biggest corporations in the world."

"Yeah?"

"Yeah. I know what you're going to say. You're going to say he married Collins Aviation. He's also brilliant, and he's worked like a son of a bitch. I'm proud to live off him."

"Sorry."

"Believe me, the Collins family wanted him, needed him more than he needed them. I think if it were a toss-up as to whether he saved Alan or Joan, old John Collins would rescue Alan and send his own daughter to the wolves. Alan would be running Collins Aviation today whether he married Joan Collins or not."

"You really think so?"

"I really do. No question about it. You don't know how able this guy is. Corporations should trip over themselves to get Alan, just like the fraternities did. That guy's got everything."

"You're a hero-worshipper."

"Yes, and Alan Stanwyk is my hero."

"Do you actually see much of him?"

"No, not really. We're interested in different things. He's flying, playing tennis, squash, sailing. I'm interested in drinking. He works hard at his business. But he's still very serious about everything. He's incapable of sitting down and having a casual drink as you and I are doing right now. I mean, we're just talking. You're not trying to learn something; I'm not trying to learn something; we're just shooting the breeze. He has to use every moment for some purpose or other. Also, I don't think Joan is too fond of my wife. I'm not either, of course, the little darling. Jesus. You haven't met my wife. With a little luck, you won't. What can I give you to run away with her?"

"So, Burt, you don't really know an awful lot about what Al's doing or thinking these days."

"I never have. No one ever has. That guy plays awfully close to the chest. He could be dying of cancer and he wouldn't tell you."

"Funny you should say that."

"He wouldn't tell his best friend his pants were on fire."

"I thought Joan was very subdued at lunch."

"Well, let me put it this way: you're a friend of Joan's, and I'm a friend of Al's — right?"

Fletch said, "Right."

"So you see things from her side. I see things from his side."

"Right."

"He didn't just marry the girl of his dreams. He married a corporation. He married a business, an omnipresent father-in-law, a board of directors, a staff of servants, a Racquets Club, Christ knows what else. If the average wife is an anchor, that guy is tied to a whole continent."

"Joan said something about their buying a ranch in Nevada."

"Yes. Al's told me about it. I'm to take over the insurance for it when the deal goes through. Sometime in a couple of weeks. Fifteen million dollars' worth of cows."

"Lucky you."

"All these years I've been worrying about Al's dying. Now I have to worry about cows dying. At least cows don't fly airplanes. Maybe now I should worry about Al's dying of hoof and mouth disease."

"Insuring a Nevada ranch seems a little out of your line."

"Al's been very good to me. I'm supposed to be in touch with the real estate broker out there in a couple of weeks. I forget his name. I've got it written down somewhere inside."

"Jim Swarthout?"

"Yeah. That's the name. You know him?"

"Sure. Nice man."

"Hope he knows more about insuring cows than I do. I need all the help I can get."

"I guess the ranch will give them a chance to get away together. I mean Joan and Alan."

"No. It's just more corporation. It's her idea, you know — the ranch."

"It is?"

"Yeah. Al couldn't care less about it. He knows less about cows than I do, and all I know is that a cow is square with legs sticking out at the corners. He doesn't want the damn place. Rancho Costo Mucho."

"I thought it was his idea."

"Negative."

"Then why is Joan so subdued?"

"What do you mean?"

"Maybe I'm wrong, but I thought she acted sort of sad. Over lunch."

"She's worse than he is. Serious, serious, serious. Haven't you ever noticed it before? You'd think with all that money, they'd smile once in a while. It's almost as if they think smiling costs money."

"Sorry I didn't get to meet their daughter, Julie."

"Little brat."

"Little brat?"

"Jesus, I wish she had a sister so I could beat one of them to death with the other one. Have another drink?"

"Burt, no thanks. I've got to go get on that airplane."

"Going back tonight, huh?"

"Just have time to get to the hotel, change, and get to the airport."

"Pity you can't stay and meet my wife. Maybe you'd want to take her with you."

"Nice talking with you, Burt."

"God, she's awful. Don't make it such a long time again, John. Anytime you're in town, drop by."

"I will, Burt. I will."

SIXTEEN

"The fuzz. The fuzz. The fuzz."

Two screwdrivers. A grilled cheese sandwich. Three gin and tonics taken in fast succession. Lying on the beach felt good to Fletch. The sand cooling down in the setting sun had enough warmth to it to permeate his skin, his muscles, his bones. The nearly horizontal rays of the sun were crossed laterally over his body by a twilight breeze.

Unabashedly, he slept.

It was Sando who shook him, saying, "The fuzz. Stash anything you've got. A bust."

Darkness. The bubble lights of the police cars rotated over the sea wall. Silence. Forms carrying riot sticks were ambling down the beach. The people on the beach who were able to move were moving as fast as they could without losing a sense of smoothness, trying not to appear as if they were hurrying away. Some were walking into the ocean. A few went to the edge of the water and strolled one way or the other along it, their profiles on the moonlit surface of the water. The foxes had come into the chicken yard. Fat Sam came to the front of his lean-to and sat cross-legged on the sand. Gummy Montgomery remained propped on his elbows. Fletch did not get up. Nowhere could he see Bobbi's little form.

The police passed to Fletch's right and left. There were seven of them. They wore riot helmets, with the visors pulled down. Chief Cummings, a tall man with heavy shoulders, was with them.

They stood in an imperfect circle around Montgomery. The chief stuck his riot stick into Gummy's stomach and leaned on it, gently.

"Jesus Christ. Why me? Why always me?"

"Your Poppa's worried about you."

"Tell him to go fuck off."

"Let's go, Gummy."

The chief leaned harder on his riot stick stuck in Gummy's stomach.

"I don't have anything. Jesus Christ, I'm clean."

The stick was pressed almost to his backbone.

"Harassment!"

Gummy tried to hit the stick away with the side of his forearm but only succeeded in hurting both his forearm and his stomach.

"Harassment. Big word for an eighteen-year-old."

"I'm seventeen. Leave me alone!"

Another policeman, a short, stocky man, suddenly pounced on Gummy, banging his ear with the back of his hand, his fist closed. He began to swing at his head again from the other side.

Gummy scrambled to his feet to escape more blows.

Fletch, having given the matter some thought, went behind the stooping, off-balance policeman and pushed him over. The policeman's head plowed into the sand where Gummy had been lying.

A third policeman, in surprise, turned to swing his riot stick at Fletch.

With full force, Fletch belted the policeman in the stomach.

A fourth policeman, a big man, in a gesture of bravado, ripped off his helmet and charged at Fletch bare-fisted. Fletch punched him twice in the face, once in the eye, once on the nose.

Fletch heard a crack. Saw a flash of light. Felt his knees pointing toward the sand. He said, "Shit."

His head was in Bobbi's lap. There were true stars in the sky.

"Jesus," he said.

The beach was quiet.

"Does it hurt?"

He said, "Jesus."

"Sando came and got me. I thought they'd killed you."

"Oh, my God, it hurts."

"He said you belted a policeman."

"Two of them," Fletch said. "Three of them. I'm still on the beach."

"What can I do to help you?" Bobbi asked.

"Shoot me."

"I haven't got any stuff."

Fletch hadn't meant that. He decided to remain misunderstood.
"Why am I still at the beach?"
"You thought you'd be in outer space?"
"I thought I'd be in jail."
"You're all right. They're gone."
"Why didn't they arrest me?"
"I'm glad they didn't."
"I expected them to arrest me. I belted three policemen."
"They would have thrown away the key."
Sando stood over them, his shoulders looking bony in the moon-light. He was eating a hot dog.
"Hey, man. How're ya doin'?"
"What happened?" Fletch asked.
"They arrested Gummy again."
"Did they arrest anyone else?"
"No."
"Why didn't they arrest me?"
"They started to," Sando said. "A couple of the apes began to drag you by your ankles."
"What happened?"
"The chief said to leave you there. I guess dragging you over the sea wall would have been too much work for his precious bastards."
"Christ. They didn't arrest me. How long have they been gone?"
"I don't know. A half hour?"
Bobbi said, "What can I do for you? Should we go back to the pad?"
"You go. I can't move."
"I'll help you," Sando said.
"No. I want to stay here."
"It's Saturday night," Bobbi said. "I should be busy."
She was wearing white shorts, a halter and sandals.
"You go get busy," Fletch said. "I'll be all right."
"Are you sure? I mean, it is Saturday night."
"I'll be all right."
"It's going to be a long night," Sando said. "Fat Sam is fresh out."
Pain, anxiety twinged Bobbi's face. She had built a big need.
"Are you sure?" Fletch said.
"Not even aspirin."
Fletch said, "Christ."
"I'll go work up a couple of tricks anyway." Bobbi's voice shook.
"It's Saturday night, and there's always tomorrow."

"Yeah," Sando said. "Sunday."

After Bobbi left, Sando sat silently for a while beside Fletch, saying nothing. Then Sando left.

Fletch built himself a back and head rest in the sand. He was higher on the beach than Fat Sam's lean-to and could see all sides of it. There was a half moon. No one could enter or leave the lean-to without Fletch's seeing him.

The inside of his head felt separated from the outside. Each time he moved or thought of moving his head, the mobile parts hit the stable parts and caused pain.

There was some blood in his hair. Grains of sand had stuck to the blood. During the long night the blood, hair and sand stiffened into a fairly usable abrasive.

After two and a half hours, Fletch gently lifted himself up, walked thirty paces, lowered himself to his knees, and threw up.

Then he walked back to his sand bed.

There was no light in Fat Sam's lean-to.

Someone was walking from the sea wall.

Fletch said, "Creasey."

"Hi." Creasey changed direction slightly and stood over Fletch. "Christ, man. I'm hanging."

Creasey was dressed in blue jean shorts, shirtless, shoeless. He was carrying nothing. Clearly he was carrying nothing.

His hands jerked spasmodically. His eyes moved restlessly. It was true what he had said: he was hanging hellfire.

"Is it true? Fat Sam clean?"

"Yeah."

Creasey said: "I met Bobbi. Jesus Christ."

"You can always try," Fletch said. "Wake the bastard up."

Creasey exhaled deeply. "I've got to. No other way. I've got to see the doctor."

Fletch watched him walk down to the lean-to, bend in the moonlight, walk into the shadow. He heard the voices, one desperate, sharp-edged; the other understanding, conciliatory, cool.

Creasey walked back up to Fletch.

"Jesus," he said. "Nothing. Nothing at all."

"I know."

"Jesus."

Creasey's shoulders were shaking visibly. Shivering.

"Fat Sam said you got fucked by the fuzz. Bobbi said so, too."

"I was cooled."

"Can't you move?"

"Don't want to."

"Fuckin' fuzz."

"They arrested Gummy again."

"Fuckin' fuzz."

Creasey began to take deep breaths. Maybe there was a high to be had in hyperventilation. A relaxation. His stomach went in and his chest filled like a balloon, then collapsed. Again and again. In the moonlight, his eyes were bright.

Fletch said, "Sorry, man."

"You got any?"

"All used."

"Bobbi?"

"You know she has nothing."

"I know she has nothin'. She doesn't store. She uses. Always. Uses."

"What did Fat Sam say?"

"He said he had nothing. Nothing. Nothing."

"When will the candy man come?"

"He said he'd be back in business tomorrow."

"What time tomorrow?"

"Tomorrow morning. Ten. Eleven."

Fletch said, "You'll live."

Creasey said, "Yeah."

He went back up the beach and over the sea wall.

Fletch had had concussions before, and he had suffered shock before, and he had spent nights on the beach before. He dreaded the hours before sunrise. They came. He remained on the beach, overviewing Vatsyayana's lean-to. He forced himself to remain awake. The dew came. His jeans, his shirt became heavily wet. Even the inside of his nose became wet. He was horribly cold. He shivered violently, continuously. Staying awake was then no problem.

He thought of Alan Stanwyk's wanting to die in a few days. His wife, his daughter, his mansion. It was possible, but Fletch had not yet proved it. He had not yet checked everything. Not all the way. He had a good sense of the man, but not yet a complete sense of the man. He tried not to speculate. He went over in his mind, again and again, what he would say into his tape recorder next time. What he knew. What he had checked absolutely. He reviewed all the things he did not know yet, all the facts he had not checked absolutely.

There were many such facts. He reviewed his sources. There we
not many fresh sources left. He counted the days — four, reall
only four — he had left.

Sometime, he would have to sleep. He promised himself slee
Sometime.

Light came into the sky.

Throughout the night with the exception of Creasey, who wa
clearly carrying nothing, no one approached Vatsyayana's lean-to
Fat Sam did not leave the lean-to.

By eight forty-five, Fletch was sweating in the sun.

People drifted onto the beach. Bodies that had remained on th
beach all night moved. Some wandered down to the dunes to reliev
themselves. Some did not bother to go to the dunes. No one spoke
They looked into each other's eyes and got the message that Fat Sa
had not yet received delivery. For a while, Fat Sam sat cross-legge
in the opening of his lean-to, taking the morning sun. No one ap
proached him. To a stranger, it would all look like young peopl
sitting silently, half asleep, on the beach on a Sunday morning. Fletc
saw the fear, the anxiety, the desperation in the darting eyes; th
extraordinary number of cigarettes being smoked; the suppresse
shaking of the hands. He heard the shattering silence. Some of thes
people had been hanging fire two or three days.

At ten-thirty Gummy returned to the beach. He sat alone. Ove
his long jeans he was wearing a Hawaiian shirt like a tent. His shou
ders seemed no wider than the back of his neck. His face in profil
was hawkish. He sat absolutely still, staring straight in front of him

Bobbi came to the beach, and Creasey, and Sando, and July
They sat close to Fletch. No one said a word.

Fat Sam had moved back into the shadows of his lean-to. He ha
withdrawn.

"Jesus," Sando said.

People began to move toward the lean-to. People in shorts, jeans
shirtless. Bikinis. People carrying nothing but money. The store wa
open. Fletch had not perceived a signal of any sort. First Creasey
Then Bobbi. They stood around outside the lean-to, not speaking
looking at their feet, their hands, not at each other, ashamed of thei
desperation. July, Bing Crosby, Gummy, Florida, Filter-tip, Jagger
Fletch stood with them. Milling. In and out of the lean-to. Some
body must have dropped something. There was a supply. Every
thing. Fat Sam was dealing. People who had been served began t
hustle off the beach. Squirrels with nuts to store. They were goin

to stash. They were going to relieve their tensions. They were going to shoot up.

Fletch backed away, imitating the face of someone who had bought. Who was all right. Bobbi had scurried.

Down the beach, Fletch jumped into the ocean. The morning-cold salt water helped glue the separated parts of his head together. The blood was too congealed to wash out of his hair.

Walking back to his pad, past the Sunday-morning-closed stores of ordinary commerce, he heard the church bells ring. It was Sunday noon and everyone was shooting up.

Fletch slept past midnight.

SEVENTEEN

When Fletch woke at a quarter to three Monday morning, he found Bobbi lying in the sleeping bag beside him. He had not heard or felt her come in. It took him a moment to realize she was dead.

The back of his scalp tingling, he scrambled out of the sleeping bag.

As he knelt in the moonlight beside her, his scream choked with horror.

Her eyes appeared to have receded entirely into her head. Her left arm was puffy at the elbow and shoulder. She showed no vital signs.

He guessed she had overdosed.

He spent until dawn ridding the room of every sign of her.

Until eleven o'clock, then, he sat cross-legged on the floor in the center of the room. Rock still. Thinking.

EIGHTEEN

Early Monday afternoon, Fletch spent forty minutes under a warm shower in his own apartment. He had driven up from The Beach at about the pace of a hearse. Bobbi was dead and sort of buried. He washed his hair five times. Finally, the blood, the sand, the congealed mess was gone. A crooked, narrow abrasion under his hair was sore to the touch of his fingertips.

Sitting on the divan under the Disdéri, he ate two delicatessen sandwiches and drank a bottle of milk. On the coffee table in front of him was the big tape recorder. On the wall across from him was a copy of William James's *Cherry Beach*.

After he had finished his sandwiches and milk, he went into the bedroom and lay on the bed. Facing him was a copy of Fredric Weiss's 1968 photograph of a boy apparently walking in midair beneath two roofs, *Boy Jumping*.

Fletch said, "Bobbi," and picked up the phone and dialed the Nevada number.

"Swarthout Nevada Realty Company."

It was the same voice that had answered Saturday.

"Jim Swarthout, please."

"I'm not sure Mr. Swarthout . . . oh, here he is, sir. One moment, please."

Fletch sat up on the bed. He had to put Bobbi out of mind, now. Lighten his voice. Be convincing.

"Jim Swarthout speaking."

"Hi, Jim. This is Bill Carmichael."

"Bill Carmichael?"

"I'm a stockbroker for a bunch of thieves out here on the Coast known as John Collins and all. The John Collins family."

"Oh, yeah. How are you, Bill?"

"I think we've met," Fletch said.

"Well, if you've ever in your life seen an overweight, bald-headed man who was probably drunk at the time, we've met."

"Alan tells me you're doin' a deal with him."

"Alan who?"

"Alan Stanwyk."

"Who's Alan Stanwyk?"

"The guy who married Joan Collins."

"Oh. John's son-in-law."

"Yeah. Anyway, Alan told me about his buying the ranch, and as I might be interested in buying a little piece of real estate out your way myself, I thought I'd give you a ring. The stock market, you know, Jim, isn't all it might be."

"I've never heard from him."

"From whom?"

"Alan what's-his-name. John Collins's son-in-law."

"You've never heard from him?"

"Never. You said he's buying a ranch through me?"

"A big spread. Fifteen million dollars' worth."

"Nope. It's not happening."

"Golly. I thought he said it was quite definite."

"Maybe he's just thinking about it. What's his phone number?"

"Could he be dealing with someone else?"

"No. If there's a fifteen-million-dollar ranch for sale anywhere in Nevada, I'd know about it. There isn't one."

"Amazing."

"I'd know if such a property were available anywhere in the state. And right now there just isn't one. Let me say that over. I can almost perfectly guarantee you that nowhere in the state of Nevada at the present time is there a piece of real estate of such value being sold or bought. Of course there is always the chance of a private deal, between friends or family, where a broker isn't being used or consulted. But even then, I would be very much surprised if I hadn't heard about it."

"In any case, Alan Stanwyk is definitely not using you or your office to buy any real estate in Nevada?"

"Definitely not. As I say, we've never heard from him. I'm sure we could find something for him, though."

"Do me a favor, Jim?"

"Sure."

"Don't call him. You'd just be embarrassing me, and him, too. He mentioned it by the pool last night. He'd had a drink."

"Talking big, huh?"

"I suspect so."

"That's the way it is with these professional in-laws. Always talking about what they're going to do with somebody else's money."

"I guess so. He'd had a drink."

"Well, if he ever gets serious, and if he ever gets his hands on any of his father-in-law's money, send him out to me."

"I will, Jim."

"Now, Bill, you said you were interested in a piece of property yourself."

"I don't know what to say, Jim."

"You were just checking on the old boy."

"Something like that, Jim."

"What are you, the family financial nursemaid?"

"Let's just say I asked a question."

"And you got an answer. I understand. My own daughter is taking art lessons in Dallas, Texas, for Christ's sake."

"Families, Jim. Families."

"I wouldn't trade jobs with you, Bill. But call anytime you want. If old John's hired you to nursemaid Alan what's-his-name, it's all right with me. Just wish I could hire you myself."

"You're a sharp man, Jim. I owe you a drink."

"John Collins does. And from him, I'll accept."

Fletch returned to the living room and sat heavily on the divan. He continued to have a mild headache.

Snapping on the microphone in his hand, he leaned back and closed his eyes. He spoke slowly.

"Although it is my instinct at this point to ramble on regarding the nature of truth, particularly the illusory nature of truth, I shall do my best to confine the following remarks concerning the Alan Stanwyk Murder Mystery to facts as I now know them.

"One comment only for file, which may concern the nature of truth in general, or may, more significantly, concern the nature of facts specifically concerning Alan Stanwyk, to wit: almost every fact adequately confirmed about Alan Stanwyk has also been adequately denied.

"In the case of almost each fact, it would have been easy to accept simple confirmation from an authoritative source. Further checking, however, frequently has resulted in an equally authoritative denial of that fact.

"By now, in my investigation of Alan Stanwyk, I have talked, either in person or by telephone, with his secretary, his personal physician, his father, his wife, his father-in-law, his insurance man who is also his old college roommate. Indirectly, through a third party, I have had testimony from the man's stockbroker. I have had corporate and personal financial views of Stanwyk, and a social view of himself and his wife. I have had a police report on him.

"To the best of my ability, I have run this investigation-in-depth on him without there being any way of his knowing he's being investigated. I have used different names, different identities, and never have I pressed the questioning far enough for the person being questioned to be suspicious, with the exception of Jim Swarthout in Nevada, and I believe I completely cooled his suspicions. He will not report the inquiry to either Stanwyk or his family.

"The portrait of Alan Stanwyk that has emerged so far is that of a bright, healthy, energetic, ambitious man. A man solid in his community, family and business. I would even say a decent man. In fact, perhaps going a bit further than I should, a man of deep loyalties and principles.

"First, he has a clean police record, with the exceptions of a six-month-old unpaid parking ticket from the City of Los Angeles and the complaint that as a lieutenant in the Air Force he buzzed a house with a training jet in San Antonio, Texas.

"From his stockbroker, William Carmichael, we know that Alan Stanwyk is in pretty good financial condition. On paper, he may presently be worth as much as a million dollars. Eventually, because of both the nature of his employment and the nature of his marriage, he will both achieve personal wealth and share in, probably control, one of the world's great fortunes. Even with this ultimate circumstance inevitable, and despite maintaining the highest standard of living available for his immediate family, Stanwyk has salted away over one hundred thousand dollars from salary over a very few years. The last few years, he must have been putting away twenty or twenty-five thousand dollars a year, simply because he hasn't needed it.

"This indicates, at least to me, that such a vice as compulsive gambling can be ruled out. The crime of embezzlement does not seem necessary. Apparently, Stanwyk is not being blackmailed.

"We have from his family physician, and others, good evidence that Stanwyk does not have a drinking problem or a drug problem. Not only is he under consistent close scrutiny by professionals and others who depend upon Stanwyk's physical and mental performance; his way of life, his known, witnessed habits preclude his harboring such addictions. No one can play squash and tennis, sail, and especially fly experimental aircraft with reflexes and nerves shot by depressants.

"I think I can state as a fact that Alan Stanwyk drinks and smokes moderately. Period.

"For what it is worth, from what must be called a streetwalker in the town in which he is currently living, The Hills, a young girl named Roberta 'Bobbi' Sanders had never seen Alan Stanwyk. It might therefore be said that he is not known to have frequented, or cruised, the sexual meat market most convenient to his residence.

"This does not mean that Alan Stanwyk's sexual activity is confined to the marital bed. There is good reason to suspect otherwise.

"However, it does indicate that Alan Stanwyk's sexual activities are controlled in acceptable social patterns.

"His stockbroker and presumed confidant, William Carmichael, doubts strongly that Alan Stanwyk maintains an extramarital sex life. Carmichael believes such an extramarital sex life would place in jeopardy Stanwyk's relations with his wife and thus with his father-in-law employer.

"However, without meaning to visit the sins of the wife upon the husband, I had the distinct impression that his wife, Joan Stanwyk, was perfectly willing to enjoy a sexual dalliance with this investigator. Her ardor may have been the result of tennis followed by martinis. This should be more thoroughly checked later. One expects that if a wife is playing around, a husband is, although the reverse is not always true. If the wife is playing around as openly as it seems, at least she would have little to complain about the husband's extramarital affairs.

"We also have testimony from a contemporary of Stanwyk's father-in-law, *News-Tribune* society writer Amelia Shurcliffe, that extramarital affairs on the part of either Alan or Joan Stanwyk would not greatly disturb John Collins. Apparently the old boy has every reason of his own to be most understanding regarding such matters. According to Mrs. Shurcliffe, his own sexual activities have not been entirely confined to the marital bed.

"Other matters concerning Alan Stanwyk's health are more confusing.

"So far, the only evidence that Alan Stanwyk has terminal cancer is from Alan Stanwyk's own mouth.

"His personal physician denies it. I take that back: his personal physician, Dr. Joseph Devlin of the Medical Center, states that as far as he knows, Alan Stanwyk is in perfect health. He states he has not referred him to any specialist—ever. He also states he has not given him a complete physical examination recently enough to be viable.

"His insurance company examines him every six months.

"Stanwyk's insurance agent and old college chum, Burt Eberhart, also states that Alan Stanwyk is in perfect physical condition. Although he did make an interesting slip, Freudian or otherwise. He said, 'Al plays so close to the chest, he wouldn't tell you if he were dying of cancer . . .'

"I have since confirmed that Dr. Joseph Devlin is heavily invested in Collins Aviation. My source is Joan Collins Stanwyk. I have confirmed from several sources that if it were known that Stanwyk is terminally ill, at least until Stanwyk has a chance to prepare the company for his absence, Collins Aviation would be in financial trouble.

"Burt Eberhart, besides being Stanwyk's personal insurance man, is the broker for all Collins Aviation insurance. One can presume Eberhart is also heavily invested in Collins Aviation.

"Mentioning cancer casually to Stanwyk's wife, father, and father-in-law caused no discernible reaction. Unless everyone is a very good actor, and superbly in control of his emotions, or in complete ignorance, the people closest to Alan Stanwyk are not thinking of cancer in relation to him.

"Therefore, this investigation is drawing a complete blank.

"No aberrations or abnormalities are apparent thus far in Alan Stanwyk's financial, sexual or health areas.

"Alan Stanwyk's social relations seem splendid. According to society writer Amelia Shurcliffe, the Stanwyks present a rather nice, solid, possibly dull image. She even believes they may be in love with each other. Alan Stanwyk could not have fitted into this society of extreme wealth and responsibility without undergoing intensive envious scrutiny. He must have a good glovemaker. Clearly, he has not committed the faux pas of ostentation, silliness, aloofness, what-have-you. He is generally admired and respected.

"The same is true among his intimates. I would say he is intensely admired among family and close friends. Not that he is without criticism. His wife wishes he had more time for her. His father-in-law wishes he had a better sense of humor. His father wishes he wouldn't spend so much time on the telephone. His old friend Burt Eberhart wishes Alan weren't always so serious. Everyone wishes he would stop flying experimental aircraft.

"More publicly, the fact that he married the boss's daughter does not go unnoticed. But as someone pointed out: someone had to. And, after listening to Burt Eberhart, Carradine, Carmichael and John Collins himself, I would guess Alan Stanwyk is the best thing that has ever happened to Collins Aviation. The score seems balanced.

"Alan Stanwyk is not taking a free ride, as one such as Jim Swarthout of Swarthout Nevada Realty is quick to assume.

"Now for a few of the contradictions in facts this investigation thus far has revealed.

"Alan Stanwyk says he is dying of terminal cancer. No one else says so. If he is, no one else knows it.

"Stanwyk's wife and father-in-law say that Stanwyk is estranged from his parents. Yet he visits them all the way across the country every six weeks.

"The reason given for the estrangement is that his father forced him to box. Yet his father insists he urged Alan not to box.

"Despite the fact, confirmed by a call to the Nonheagan Inn, that Alan visits his parents every six weeks, he has never told them that he has a child and that they have a grandchild.

"Everyone says that Alan Stanwyk is buying a ranch in Nevada— his wife, his father-in-law, his stockbroker, his insurance man. Everyone, that is, except the person whom both Stanwyk's wife and insurance man identify as the real estate broker: Jim Swarthout. It was quite clear from his attitude, as well as from his explicit statements, that Swarthout has never done business with, or even met, Alan Stanwyk.

"To some extent, these contradictions can be explained, now that we have some knowledge of the man.

"I take the clue from Burt Eberhart's statement: 'Al plays so close to his chest he wouldn't tell you he was dying of cancer.'

"Although no one knows it, Alan Stanwyk could have terminal cancer.

"There can be an answer to his strange relations with his parents. He could love them very much. Being an only son, he could have a profound sense of loyalty and duty toward them. Apparently he has for his old college roommate, Burt Eberhart. As Marvin Stanwyk says, he could find stopping off in his old hometown frequently a restful experience.

"At the same time, he could realize that the world of Joan and John Collins is no place for Marvin and what's-her-name Mother Stanwyk. He might feel they would be very out-of-place and very embarrassed. Therefore, he might have fudged the date of his wedding, not told them they were grandparents, and told everyone else he was estranged from his parents—solely to save their feelings.

"There is even an answer to the mysterious ranch in Nevada. He could have started to buy the ranch in Nevada for the best reason in the world: a good real estate investment. Neither he nor Joan needed to like the idea of living on a ranch. Thus the confusion in everybody's mind about whose idea the ranch is—Alan's or Joan's. Neither of them really wants to do it. Buying the ranch is simply a good business idea.

"It is possible he took the first steps toward buying the ranch, which first steps for him would have been seeking the advice of his stockbroker, insurance man, wife and father-in-law. After he did this much, he discovered he was dying of cancer. He had to devote his time and energies to cleaning shop at Collins Aviation, subtly, so that no one knew what he was doing. That would take some effort. He knew he would not be able to see the land purchase through, but he could not tell people so without also telling them why, that he has terminal cancer. Therefore, he kept talking about it as if it were a real, developing thing. John Collins referred him to Jim Swarthout. It is very likely that subsequently, when John Collins or whoever asked about Swarthout and the ranch, Stanwyk answered, 'Yes, yes, everything's fine.' Doubtless he even found himself agreeing to take his wife to the ranch next weekend when there isn't any ranch, because Stanwyk knows that for him there isn't any next weekend.

"Even the contradictions can be made to go together.

"Yet there remains one overwhelming question in my mind.

"If Alan Stanwyk wishes to commit suicide, why doesn't he die the way everybody half-expects him to die?

"Why doesn't he crash an airplane?"

Still moving slowly, Fletch disposed of his sandwich wrappings and carton of milk.

In the bedroom, he carefully packed a large suitcase. Into it went tennis whites. Three pairs of blue jeans. Blue jean shorts. T-shirts. Several dress shirts. Neckties. Underwear. His shaving kit. Two suits. Two sports jackets. Two pairs of slacks. His address book. Black shoes. Three pairs of black socks. Three pairs of brown socks. His passport.

He put typing paper and carbon paper into his typewriter case and closed it.

Then he dressed in brown loafers, brown socks, a dress shirt, necktie, trousers and a sports jacket. And sunglasses.

Taking his big tape recorder, typewriter case and suitcase, he went to the apartment garage. He lashed the tape recorder to the passenger seat of the MG. He put the typewriter case behind the front seats and the suitcase in the trunk.

Then he drove to the main gate of Collins Aviation and waited.

NINETEEN

It was four o'clock when Fletch pulled up and parked across from the main gate of Collins Aviation.

At four forty-five, through sunglasses, he saw the gray-uniformed guard at the gate step briskly out of his guardhouse, whistle and wave people aside, clear the road and the sidewalk, and casually salute a car coming through. It was the gray Jaguar XKE, license number 440-001. It turned left into traffic.

Alan Stanwyk was driving.

Fletch followed him.

Joan Stanwyk had said Alan worked late Mondays and Wednesdays. On those two days of the week he seldom arrived home before midnight. He remained at the office.

It was Monday. Stanwyk had left the office before five.

He continued down Stevenson to Main and turned right on Main. Following him, Fletch thought Stanwyk might be heading for the expressway toward the city. But after twelve blocks, Stanwyk turned left on Seabury. At the corner of Seabury and Bouvard he pulled into the parking lot of a liquor store. Fletch waited across the street.

Watching Stanwyk amble into the liquor store and out again, Fletch could only think him a well man. An unconcerned man. A relaxed man. As he went in, Stanwyk's hands were in the pockets of his slacks. His gait was slow and even. His face expressionless. When he came out, his face had the half smile of someone who had just passed pleasantries. In the bag he was carrying were at least three bottles of liquor. It took him a moment to find the right key on his keychain for the ignition.

Continuing the way he had been going, Stanwyk went another

three blocks on Seabury and then turned left on Putnam. A half mile along Putnam, he turned into the tree-shaded parking lot of a garden apartment development. He parked the Jaguar in the shade of the trees at the far side of the parking lot. Fletch parked in the middle row of the parking lot, in the sunlight. Stanwyk locked his car.

Carrying the bag of liquor, he strolled across the parking lot, cutting through the middle row of cars within three cars of Fletch, walked fifteen yards down the sidewalk, turned left on a walk and into a doorway.

Fletch waited ten minutes by his dashboard clock.

Then he went into the doorway himself.

The doorway served two apartments. On the left, the name on the letterbox was Charles Rice. The box was full of mail.

The mailbox on the right was empty. The name on that box was Sandra Faulkner.

A sign in the recessed doorway warned trespassers and solicitors as well as loiterers and burglars. It was signed GREENE BROS. MANAGEMENT.

"Where's Gummy?"

Someone had gotten up enough energy to make a campfire on the beach. It was a reasonably cool night. Farther up the beach there were other campfires.

Vatsyayana said, "Fletch."

In a corner of the parking garage, Fletch had changed into jeans. Having had a sport coat on, he had not realized it had gotten cooler. He wished he had at least put on a T-shirt.

"Where's Gummy?" he asked again.

July said, "I saw him earlier."

"Where did he go? Did he say?"

July said, "No."

"Anyone else seen Gummy?"

No one answered.

Vatsyayana asked, "Where's Bobbi?"

Fletch said, "She's split."

"For where?"

Vatsyayana's look was one of kindly concern.

"That great candy store in the sky."

Vatsyayana said nothing.

Rolled against the base of the sea wall in a blanket, not far from where Fletch had placed the rock the night before, was Creasey.

Fletch stood over him a moment in the dark, not sure whether Creasey was traveling or asleep.

Creasey said, "What's happening, man?"

"I'm looking for Gummy," Fletch said.

"Oh, man, he's gone."

"What do you mean, gone?"

"That kid's had it. I mean, how often can you be a beatin' bag for the fuzz?"

"You don't know he's gone."

Creasey said, "He should have gone. Man, there has to be enough of everything. I mean, the kid's been beatin' and been beatin'. Then he gets home and his daddy whumps him. Everybody's beatin' up on that kid all the time."

Fletch said, "I'm lookin' for Gummy."

"Like my old skins. Man, I feel guilty for beatin' on them. Every night with sticks. Drumsticks. I beat on those skins. I mean, how do we know those skins don't have feeling? Suppose when I hit them they hurt? Really hurt?"

"I don't know about that, Creasey."

"I've got a lot of painin' to do. To make up for what I did."

"Don't you think the drums will forgive you?"

"The Christly drums. That's the idea. Beat up on anybody, anything, as much as you want, even drums, and they must forgive you, because that's what The Man said. Christ."

"I'm looking for Gummy. Have you seen him?"

"No. Where's Bobbi?"

Fletch said, "She's all right."

"She split? I haven't seen her in weeks."

"You saw her yesterday morning."

"Yeah. She was all strung out. She'd had it. Fletch? You know, she'd had it. Last time I saw her."

"I didn't realize it."

"She'd had it. Is she gone?"

"Jesus."

Fletch stood a moment in the dark near Creasey, not looking at the rock, and then moved on.

At another campfire he sat down and waited a moment before speaking. No one was speaking.

"Anyone seen Gummy?"

No one answered.

The kid with the jug ears they called Bing Crosby was looking expectantly at Fletch, as if waiting to hear what Fletch had just said.

"I'm looking for Gummy."

A forty-year-old man with a telephone receiver stenciled on his sweater, with the words under it DIAL ME, said, "He's not here."

Fletch waited a moment before moving on.

At another campfire, Filter-tip said he thought Gummy had gone home. To his parents' house. Jagger said he thought Gummy had been picked up by the police again.

When Fletch stood up from the campfire, he found Vatsyayana standing behind. Vatsyayana walked a few paces with him toward the sea wall.

"Why are you looking for Gummy?"

"Bobbi gave me a message for him."

"Where's Bobbi?"

"She's split."

"Where's Bobbi?"

"Gonzo. Bye-bye."

"Where?"

"With a knapsack I gave her. Full of protein tablets and Ritz crackers I ripped off from a Seventh Day Adventist supermarket."

Vatsyayana stopped. "I said, where's Bobbi?"

"Look. She got her supply up yesterday, didn't she?"

"Yeah."

"So she split."

Vatsyayana was giving him the hard stare through the moonlight. His eyes remained kind.

"Why are you looking for Gummy?"

"I told you. Bobbi gave me a message for him."

"What's the message?"

"It's for Gummy."

"Tell me."

Fletch said, "Hang loose, Fat Sam."

He followed his moon shadow up the beach.

On that cool night, trying to sleep on his groundmat, Fletch missed his sleeping bag. He missed Bobbi. Together they would have been warm in the sleeping bag.

TWENTY

Fletch heard the heavy footsteps on the stairs. They were in no hurry. They came along the short landing to his door and stopped.

The door swung open slowly.

Two policemen looked through the door.

Fletch sat up.

"Good morning," the first policeman said. They both looked showered, shaved and full of coffee.

"What day is it?" Fletch asked.

"Tuesday."

The second policeman was looking for a place to sit down. In his eyes going over the room was comparable pride in his own home, his own furniture.

"Get ready to come with us."

"Why?"

"The chief wants to see you. Questioning."

Fletch was looking at his bare feet on their sides on the ground-mat.

"I guess I'm ready."

"You don't even want to take a leak?"

Fletch said, "Why should I take a leak when I'm going to the police station anyway?"

It was about a quarter to seven in the morning.

One of the policemen held open the back door of the patrol car for Fletch and closed it after he had gotten in.

A heavy wire grill ran between the front seat and the back seat.

The back seat was broken down. It smelled of vomit. Dried blood was on the seat and the floor.

Fletch said, "This is a very poor environment back here. I want you to know that."

"It's nice up here," said the policeman in the passenger seat.

The driver said, "How's your head?"

Fletch had forgotten.

"This is the first time it hasn't hurt. You two aren't the two I belted on the beach the other night, are you?"

"No," said the driver. "I'm the one who belted you."

Fletch said, "You do nice work."

"It's a pleasure."

"How come you guys didn't arrest me the other night?"

"The chief said not to," said the driver. "He was feeling mellow."

"He feels mellow every time he comes back from his retirement home in Mexico. He counts the grapefruit or something. Makes him feel mellow."

"He's retiring soon?"

"Next year sometime."

Fletch said, "I was hoping he'd retire before I got to the station."

They turned onto Main. It was difficult talking through a grill to the backs of heads. Fletch wanted to open the window, but the window jack handles had been removed. The police were probably afraid someone would try to commit suicide by bopping himself on the nose with one.

The smell was beginning to make Fletch feel sick.

He repeated, "This is a very poor environment back here."

From his appearance, Chief of Police Graham Cummings could not have been anything else. Short-cropped iron-gray hair. A jawline like a shovel scoop. Broad, massive shoulders. Steady, brown eyes. A man of his appearance in any town would almost automatically be given the job of police chief.

"What's your name?"

"Fletch."

"What's your full name?"

"Fletch Fletch Fletch."

Alone in the chief's bare, utilitarian office, they sat on either side of a gray aluminum desk.

"By any chance, could Fletch be short for Fletcher?"

"It could be."

"Is Fletcher your first name or your last?"

"My first name."

"What's your last name?"

"Smith."

"Fletcher Smith," the Chief said. "Seems I've heard that name somewhere before."

"Fletcher Smith?"

"No. Just Smith. Where do you live, Smith?"

"I forget the address. Where your goons picked me up this morning."

"You live there?"

"Weekends I spend in Hawaii."

"Do you live alone?"

"Expect for a pet roach."

"And what do you do for a living, Mr. Smith?"

"I'm a shoeshine boy."

"There was no shoeshine equipment in your room."

"I must have been ripped off during the night. I'll file a complaint before I leave."

The chief said, "There seems to be a certain lack of coordination between yourself and your office, Mr. Fletcher."

"I beg your pardon?"

"Your superiors at the *News-Tribune* called here yesterday. Your editor. A Mrs. Snow. Do I have that right? A Clara Snow."

"Shit."

"She informed me you are doing an investigation, for your newspaper, of drugs on the beach. And she asked that we keep an eye out for you. She said she thought you might be getting close to something. If you asked for police protection we were to understand who you are, and to give it."

"Shit."

"You are I.M. Fletcher of the *News-Tribune*."

"You've got the wrong I.M. Fletcher."

"Are you getting close to something, Mr. Fletcher?"

"No."

"Well, Mr. Fletcher."

"Fuck."

The chief did not relax. He remained, forearms on the desk, looking directly at Fletch.

"Mr. Fletcher, it seems you have forgotten certain things. There is a certain little rule, shall we call it, which says that you are supposed to identify yourself as a journalist immediately to any officer of the law with whom you find yourself in conversation—even casual conversation. Had you forgotten that rule?"

"It slipped my mind."

"We have you on a violation of that rule, Mr. Smith."

"Entrapment."

"Second, we know that you have been living here at The Beach
with a young girl named Bobbi."

"I have?"

"Where is Bobbi?"

"She split."

"Where did Bobbi go?"

"I don't know. Home, maybe."

"I sincerely doubt that. Addicts seldom stray far from their source."

"She got a bit ahead. Enough to trip on."

"When did she leave?"

"Sunday night."

"By what method of transportation?"

"She flew."

"Then there is the fact that we found stashed in your room quantities of both marijuana and heroin."

"Did you have a search warrant?"

"We weren't searching. We just happened to find the stuff concealed in the stove."

"I was hiding it from Bobbi."

"You are guilty of possession of hard drugs."

"I made the purchases as evidence."

"From whom did you buy it?"

"Fat Sam."

"Then why was the marijuana in City Police Laboratory bags?"

"Who knows Fat Sam's source?"

"Why would you need to make a purchase of marijuana anyway?
One purchase of heroin would be sufficient evidence."

"I like to write a balanced story."

"That story you wrote last fall about the Police Association wasn't
very balanced."

"What?"

"I remember the story. And the by-line. I.M. Fletcher. You said
the Police Association was nothing but a drinking club."

"Oh."

"You made very little of the fact that we have seminars, when we
meet, on police techniques. That we raise money for the Police
Academy. That last year we donated an ambulance to Ornego, California."

"Thanks for reading me."

"Do you get my point, Mr. Fletcher?"

"I'm getting it."

"I want you out of town. Immediately."

"Some police protection."

"You may have some excuses for the matters I have already mentioned, including the possession of heroin, but I have on my staff three police officers who can attest to having been struck by you while in the course of their duty last Sunday night."

"You didn't arrest me then."

"We were trying to subdue another prisoner."

"It took seven of you to subdue a seventeen-year-old junkie?"

"Due to your intercession, three of the seven were wounded."

"Why didn't you arrest me the other night?"

"Did you want to be arrested, Mr. Fletcher?"

"Golly, gee, no, chief."

"Mr. Fletcher, I am going to give you two orders, and you are going to obey both. The first is that any evidence you have regarding drugs on the beach you turn over to us. Do you have any evidence at all?"

"No."

"None?"

"Just Fat Sam."

"You really aren't very good at your work, are you?"

"I get a lot of help from the office."

"The second order is that you get out of town before noon. And not come back. Ever. Is that clear?"

"What are you afraid of?"

"We're not afraid of you."

"Seems like it."

"We are conducting our own investigation of the drugs on the beach, Mr. Fletcher. This is police work. These investigations have been ongoing for some time."

"Two or three years."

"We're looking for a break sometime in the next few months. This is a difficult, complicated business. A private investigation, even by your newspaper, could ruin all our work to date. I think I've made myself clear: get out of town, or we'll run you through a course that will begin immediately with jail, and will end with your suffering a very long and very expensive legal battle. Possession of heroin and assault upon three separate officers while in performance of their duties should be enough to convince you."

"I'm convinced."

"You will leave town immediately?"

"Never to darken your dungeon again."

TWENTY-ONE

I t was a quarter to nine, and the sidewalks were as full as they ever got in the business district of The Beach. Traffic on Main Street was bumper to bumper.

A block and a half from the police station, an approaching gray Jaguar XKE slid against the curb. License number 440-001. The car Fletch was to steal after murdering Alan Stanwyk in sixty hours. The horn honked.

Fletch got into the front seat.

Stanwyk moved the car back into the line of traffic.

"What were you doing at the police station?"

"Being questioned."

"About what?"

"A kid I know disappeared. A girl named Bobbi."

"Are you involved in her disappearance?"

"No, but I sure want to get out of town soon. How did you know I was at the police station?"

"I asked at the beer stand. Which was open at eight o'clock in the morning. Some life you lead. A kid with jug ears said he saw you this morning in the back of a patrol car."

"French fries are good for breakfast."

Again Stanwyk lit a cigarette without using the dashboard lighter. He used a gold lighter from his pocket. He was wearing sunglasses.

Fletch said, "What do you want?"

"To see how everything's going. Do you have your passport?"

"I should have it tomorrow."

"And the gloves?"

"I'll get a pair."

"You *have* applied for the passport?"

"Oh, yes, I even had my picture taken."

"Fine. Are you clear in your mind about what you are going to do?"

"Perfectly. You still want it done?"

Stanwyk blew out a stream of smoke. "Yes."

"Are you sure you're dying of cancer?"

"Yes. Why do you ask?"

"You look fine."

"It takes a while for it to show. I want to be gone by then."

They were sitting at a red light.

"I remember reading that you fly airplanes," Fletch said. "Test air planes. Whatever you call them."

"What about it?"

The car crossed the intersection.

"So why don't you kill yourself in an airplane?"

The shoulders of Stanwyk's suit jacket moved more than anothe man's would when he shrugged. He had powerful shoulders.

"Call it pride, if you like. If you spend your life trying to keep airplanes in the air, it's sort of difficult to aim one for the ground."

"An expensive pride."

"People have spent more than fifty thousand dollars on pride be fore."

"I guess so."

"You remember where the house is?"

"At the end of Berman Street."

"That's right. And how are you going to get there?"

"I'm going to take a taxi to the corner of Hawthorne and Main and walk from there. It's a different district, but only about two mile away."

"Good for you. And you remember the flight number?"

"No. You never gave it to me."

Stanwyk was looking at him through the sunglasses. "It's the eleven o'clock TWA flight to Buenos Aires."

"I know that," Fletch said. "But I don't know the number."

Stanwyk said, "Neither do I."

He glided the car against the curb.

"I don't believe you and I should know each other too well," he said. "I'm trying not to know you. What I mean is, I think you should forget what you read about me in the newspapers."

Fletch said, "I just happened to remember that."

"Forget it. I'll let you off here."

"We're on the other side of town. I was going in the other direc tion."

"You can hitchhike back."

"Thanks a lot."

Stanwyk said, "See you Thursday night."

TWENTY-TWO

Fletch rang the bell of 15641B Putnam Street and looked back the few feet to where his MG was parked at the curb. Through sunglasses, the green of the car seemed the same as the green of the lawn.

An elfin voice said, "Yes? Who is it?"

Fletch bent and shouted into the mouthpiece: "Greene Brothers Management, Miss Faulkner."

"Just a minute."

Fletch smoothed his tie beneath his buttoned suit jacket.

Sandra Faulkner's face was not particularly friendly when she opened the door. She was wearing black slacks and a loose blouse. Her hair was bleached blond and touseled.

Fletch was astonished. Sandra Faulkner was nowhere near as attractive as Joan Collins Stanwyk. She must be better in bed.

"I'm from Greene Brothers Management," he said sternly.

She said nothing. She was looking at him as if he were a piece of month-old fish.

"The people who manage these apartments."

"So what do you want?"

"We want to talk with you."

"Do you have some identification?"

"If I were you, miss, I would not take this opportunity to be insolent."

"What?"

"We've had complaints from the neighbors about you, and we're here to discuss the possibility of evicting you on morals charges."

"You must be kidding."

"We are not kidding at all. Now, if you wish to continue standing here on the doorstep talking about it, it's all right with me. If you prefer to go inside, out of earshot of your neighbors, we can."

She drew back, leaving the door open.

He entered and closed the door.

"What in God's name are you talking about?"

"You know perfectly well what I'm talking about," he said. "Are you alone now?"

"Jesus Christ!"

He stalked into the living room, which was furnished in what once had been termed Danish modern.

"The use of foul and abusive language will do nothing to further your defense."

"Defense? What defense?"

He pushed open the door of the bathroom, which struck him as peculiarly empty. In the bedroom was a king-size bed, with a mirror suspended from the ceiling over it. The bed was made, at ten-thirty, with a red silk coverlet smoothed over it. On a sideboard in the kitchen was a used bottle of vermouth, a half-empty bottle of vodka, and an empty bottle of California chablis.

"What in Christ's name are you talking about?" Sandra Faulkner asked.

"What's that suspended from the ceiling of the bedroom?"

"It's a mirror. What-the-hell business is it of yours what it is?"

"Miss Faulkner, your lease precisely prohibits hanging anything from the ceiling of this apartment."

"Jesus."

Nowhere in the apartment were there signs of anyone packing.

Fletch sat on a living room chair. He took a notebook and pen out of his pocket.

"Is your real name Sandra Faulkner?"

"Yes. Of course. What's all this about, anyway?"

"Miss Faulkner, you live in a residential community. There are young families who live in these apartments around you. Families with young children."

"I know. So what?"

"It has become clear to some of the mothers, and, I might add, some of the fathers, that you have no visible means of support."

"Jesus."

"You haven't worked in some time."

"Why is that anybody's business?"

"There is a question of whether your hanging around all the time is good for the moral fiber of the community's young."

"Wow. Who'd believe this?"

"Second, it is quite clear what your means of support are. You keep this apartment solely by your means to sexually entertain."

"My God! You're something from the last century."

"Greene Brothers Management is responsible for these apartments, Miss Faulkner, and responsible to some extent for what goes on inside them. At least we must be responsive to complaints."

"You can just get the hell out of here."

Fletch said, "How long have you known Alan Stanwyk?"

Her face changed from fury to suppressed horror mingled with sickness.

"Sit down, Miss Faulkner."

She did. On the edge of the divan.

"How do you know about Alan?"

"Neighbors recognized him. His picture is frequently in the newspapers, after all."

"Jesus. Leave Alan out of this."

"He is paying for this apartment and your support, isn't he?"

"Yes."

"All right, then. You're keeping this apartment through illicit means. You had better tell us everything."

"Why?"

"Miss Faulkner, would you like to see Alan Stanwyk named in an eviction action? An eviction action taken on moral grounds?"

"Oh, my God. I can't believe this is happening. Who complained?"

"It is our policy not to report that sort of thing?"

"Make the world safe for informers, huh?"

"We're very grateful to people who tell us when things are amiss among our apartments. How else would we know? Now, I suggest that you take our attempt to grant you a fair hearing sincerely, and tell us all."

Sandra Faulkner was looking at Fletch as a lady-in-waiting caught rolling in the hay with a court violinist might have looked at Queen Victoria.

"Do you always wear your sunglasses in the house?" she asked.

"I have a failing in the eyes," Fletch said, "which is not a subject for general conversation."

"I see. Wow. Okay. What do you want to know? I used to work as a receptionist at Collins Aviation. Alan Stanwyk is sort of important at Collins Aviation."

"We know, Miss Faulkner."

"I'm not Miss Faulkner. I'm Mrs. Faulkner. My husband was a test pilot. For the navy. One day, trying to land on an aircraft carrier, he missed and crashed. I couldn't work for a long time thereafter.

Jack and I had put off having children, thinking there would be plenty of time . . ."

"This person you refer to as Jack was your husband?"

"My husband. The insurance ran out. Unemployment ran out. I was drinking heavily. Very heavily. At first, Alan Stanwyk's office would make a call to see how I was doing. It was just professional courtesy, I think. One morning, very early, I was drunk out of my mind, and I told the secretary to go fuck herself. The next day, Alan Stanwyk showed up at the door with his secretary and some flowers. This was more than a year after Jack had died. They put me in a hospital for a while. And paid for it. Alan is a flier himself. He was overseas. He has a scar on his belly from where he was wounded. The day I was released, Alan picked me up in his car and brought me home. It's been that way ever since."

"You see him twice a week?"

"Yes, about that. He's given me something to live for. Himself. I hope someday to have his child."

"He comes here on Mondays and Wednesdays?"

"The neighbors don't miss much, do they? The sons of bitches."

"Mrs. Faulkner, do you have any intention of ever marrying Mr. Stanwyk?"

"Why, no. He's married. Joan Collins. He couldn't divorce her. She's the daughter of the chairman of the board, or something. John Collins."

"You've never thought of marrying him?"

"No. We've never discussed it."

"Yet you hope to have his child?"

"Yes. There's nothing wrong with that."

"Are you currently pregnant?"

"No."

"In other words, Mrs. Faulkner, you intend to maintain this affair, unchanged, in this apartment, for the foreseeable future?"

"Yes. I do."

"And Mr. Stanwyk has not indicated to you any desire for change?"

"What do you mean?"

"Well, it hardly needs pointing out, Mrs. Faulkner, you have no rights here. Alan Stanwyk could disappear next week, and you wouldn't have a leg to stand on."

"Fine. If that's what he wants to do. He owes me nothing. I could get a job now. I'm fine."

"Is Mr. Stanwyk in good health?"

"Yes. Terrific. I wish I hadn't let myself go so long."

"And has he indicated any change in your relationship in the foreseeable future?"

"What do you mean?"

"Has he indicated to you that you might be taking a trip together?"

"No. I think I'm kept pretty much in the background. And I've never asked for any such thing."

Fletch closed his notebook. He had written nothing in it.

"Very well, Mrs. Faulkner. I'll make my report to Greene Brothers. I will ask them not to take any action on this matter, as it seems to be a discreet, adult affair."

"Thank you."

"There aren't any other men who use this facility, are there?"

"By 'this facility,' do you mean this apartment, or me? The answer is no to both."

"I see." Fletch stood up. "Thank you very much, Mrs. Faulkner."

She said, "You have a lousy management company."

"What did you say?"

"I said you have a lousy management company. Not only are you nosy parkers, but these apartments are not adequately protected against burglary."

"Why do you say that?"

"I was robbed last night."

"You were?"

"Yes. All my cosmetics."

"Your cosmetics?"

"All of them."

"What on earth are you talking about?"

"Come. I'll show you."

In the bathroom, she opened the medicine chest.

"This morning, that window was open, and all my cosmetics were missing."

The medicine chest was bare, as were other shelves in the bathroom.

"Only your cosmetics were missing?"

"Some aspirin. My toothpaste."

"Your towels are here."

"No. One towel is missing."

"One towel is missing. They must have used it to carry off the cosmetics."

"That's what I figure."

"Surely, Mrs. Faulkner, that window is not large enough for an adult."

"I wouldn't think so."

"Some child in the neighborhood must have broken in and stolen your cosmetics."

"I would say so."

"Probably afraid to venture farther into the apartment."

"I'm glad you're so busy protecting the morals of the children in this neighborhood, Mr. Whatever-your-name-is, Greene Brothers Management. I'd hate to have them thinking dirty thoughts while they're in jail for burglary."

TWENTY-THREE

I t was lunchtime. The corridors of the *News-Tribune* were cool and empty.

Fletch dropped two wrapped sandwiches and a carton of milk on his desk and took off his suit jacket.

He picked up the phone and dialed the number of the managing editor.

"This is Fletcher. I want to talk to Frank."

"Are you in the office, Fletch?"

"Yes."

"He's at lunch. He'll be back at two o'clock. Can you wait till then?"

"I'll twiddle my thumbs. Please make sure I see him at two."

Fletch loosened his tie and sat down.

While eating the sandwiches, he found the subpoena. Ordered to appear in court Friday morning at ten o'clock. Failure to pay alimony to Barbara Ralton Fletcher. Contempt of court. Failure to appear will cause instant arrest.

"Jesus Christ."

Friday morning he had the choice of receiving a Bronze Star and thus being arrested, or facing contempt charges in court and thus being fired.

"Jesus Christ."

The phone rang.

"Hello, for Christ's sake."

"Is this Mr. Fletcher?"

"If you insist."

"What?"

"Who is this?"

"This is Mr. Gillett, of Gillett, Worsham and O'Brien."

"Jesus Christ."

"Mr. Fletcher, I regret to tell you that the check you gave me the other day as payment of back and present alimony to Mrs. Linda Fletcher, in the amount of three thousand, four hundred and twenty-nine dollars, is no good."

"You bastard. I asked you not to cash it for ten days."

"I didn't try to cash it, Mr. Fletcher. However, I did take the precaution of making an inquiry at the bank. You don't even have an account in that bank, Mr. Fletcher."

"What?"

"You do not now, you never have had an account in the Merchants Bank. Not a checking account, not a savings account. Nothing."

"Nice of you to tell me."

"Where did you get that check, Mr. Fletcher?"

"I'm sorry, I didn't hear you. I was clearing my throat."

"It doesn't matter. What does matter is that I warned you when we met in your office last Friday that if you didn't play straight with us from now on, I would lower the boom on you. I would bring you back to court. You have provided me with ample opportunity for doing precisely that."

"Mr. Gillett —"

"You listen to me. This morning I have gone into court and seen to it that contempt charges are filed against you. A subpoena ordering you to appear in court Friday morning at ten o'clock will arrive within minutes."

"No."

"What do you mean, 'No'?"

"I can't be there Friday morning."

"Why not?"

"I've already been subpoenaed to appear in court Friday morning at ten o'clock to answer contempt charges for not paying alimony to my first wife, Barbara."

"Mr. Fletcher, I can't care about that."

"Well, I can't be in two places at the same time."

"At least we know Friday morning you will not be before a justice of the peace getting married again."

"Anyway, Friday morning at ten o'clock I'm also supposed to be in the marine commandant's office receiving a Bronze Star."

"Really, Mr. Fletcher. I've had enough of your stories."

"It's true. If I don't pick up the damned Bronze Star, I'll get fired. Then where will all my wives be?"

"They'll still be in court, Mr. Fletcher, hopefully represented by able attorneys."

"Jesus."

"What's more, Mr. Fletcher, in further implementation of my threat to lower the boom on you, this morning I also filed criminal charges against you for fraud."

"Fraud?"

"Fraud, Mr. Fletcher. It is against the law, Mr. Fletcher, to present checks against bank accounts that don't exist."

"How can you do this to me?"

"I'm obliged to. As an attorney practicing law in the state of California, I am an officer of the court, and I would be derelict in my duty to know that a crime has been committed without reporting it to the authorities."

"You reported me. Criminal charges."

"I was obliged to, Mr. Fletcher."

"You just bit the hand that feeds you. How can I support my ex-wives if I'm in jail?"

"I have bitten the hand which has refused to feed us. You haven't yet supported your ex-wives."

"Mr. Gillett."

"Yes, Mr. Fletcher?"

"I wonder if you and I might not meet in some quiet, out-of-the-way place, a bar, or take a ride in the country, spend a night or two . . ."

"Are you serious?"

"Of course I'm serious."

"I think that's a delightful idea. I don't know how you guessed, but I am rather attracted to you, Mr. Fletcher. But I really think we had better put these legal matters behind us first, don't you?"

"I was thinking this might be a very good way of putting our legal matters behind us."

"Your legal problems, Mr. Fletcher, are between you and your wives. And now, of course, a criminal court. Any relationship you and I might have should have nothing to do with your legal matters."

"Are you sure?"

"Mr. Fletcher. Are you pulling my leg?"

"That's what I'm pulling. Yes."

Gillett breathed three times before speaking again.

"Mr. Fletcher, I don't know whether you are a very, very cruel boy, or just thoroughly confused. I would prefer to think the latter. I am a member of the Anglican faith. If you are confused, I would be extremely pleased to continue our relationship more affectionately at some future time. For the moment, however, I advise you that a subpoena to face contempt of court charges Friday morning is immediately forthcoming. And I also advise you that criminal charges for fraud have been filed against you, and, although I am not your attorney, I would suggest to you that you present yourself at the main police station this afternoon, identify yourself, and allow yourself to be arrested. This should permit you to be out on bail in time for your other court appearances Friday morning."

"Thank you very much, Mr. Gillett. See you in church."

Fletch was chewing the second half of his first sandwich, feeling guilty about what he had done to Sandra Faulkner, when the phone rang again.

"Hello?"

"Fletch? This is Barbara."

"Barbara, my first wife?"

"I've been calling you every half hour for days. I was hoping to talk to you before the subpoena arrived."

"I'm having it for lunch."

"I'm sorry about that, Fletcher."

"Tut, tut, my dear. Think nothing of it. What's a little contempt of court charge between old friends?"

"It's the lawyers who are doing it, Fletch. They insist. They're real worried about the eight thousand dollars you owe me."

"Is it that much?"

"Eight thousand four hundred twelve dollars."

"Golly. I should have taken care of that. How careless of me."

"It really isn't my fault, Fletch. I meant the contempt of court thing. I didn't do it."

"Not to worry, Barbara. A little enough matter. Easy to straighten out. I'll pop down to court Friday morning and straighten things out in a switch of a lamb's tail."

"You're wonderful, Fletcher."

"Tut tut."

"I mean, it's not the money I care about, or anything. I know how much you earn from the newspaper. You can't afford it."

"I understand precisely."

"You do?"

"Certainly, Barbara."

"Fletcher, I'm still in love with you."

"I know. Isn't it awful?"

"It's been two years."

"That long?"

"I never even see you around town anymore. I've put on weight."

"You have?"

"I've been eating too much. I heard you got married again and divorced again."

"Just a temporary defection from my one true love."

"Really? Why did you get married again?"

"It came over me one day. With chills and prickly heat."

"Why did you get divorced?"

"Well, Barbara, it came down to a question between the cat and me. One of us had to go. The cat went first."

"I didn't call you all the time you were married."

"Thank you."

"I just heard you got divorced last week. I bumped into Charlie."

"How's Charlie?"

"Fletcher, do you think you and I could make it together again?"

"How much weight did you say you've gained?"

"A lot. I'm really gross."

"I'm sorry to hear that."

"I don't like the place I'm living. Are you still in the apartment on Clearwater Street?"

"I still live on the Street of Magnificent Plumbing."

"I'm sorry I divorced you, Fletch. I really regret it."

"Ah, well. Easy come. Easy go."

"That's not funny."

"I'm trying to eat a sandwich."

"What I'm trying to say is, I'm trying to apologize to you. For divorcing you."

"Don't give it a thought."

"I've grown up a lot."

"It comes with gaining weight, I think."

"The girls really bothered me, you know."

"Girls? What girls?"

"Oh, Fletch. You were just making love to everybody in town. All the time. You'd be gone for days on end. Sometimes I think you were making love to five or six different girls a week. I mean, you never hesitated."

"I get seduced easily."

"I thought it was awful. Every girl I looked at on the street, complete strangers, their eyes would say: I've made love to your husband, too. It was spooky. I mean, you never hesitated to make love to anybody."

"It's good exercise."

"Anyway, I think I've grown up. To accept that."

"You have?"

"Yes, Fletch. I understand. You're a male nymphomaniac."

"I am not."

"You are, Fletch. You just run around the city fucking people."

"Well . . ."

"You can't deny it."

"Well . . ."

"I think it's cute. I can accept it, now. You do understand that at first it bothered me."

"I don't know why it should."

"It did. But it won't anymore. I'm all grown up now, and you can play with anybody you like."

Fletch drank from the carton of milk.

"Fletch?"

"Yes, Barbara?"

"What I mean is: can we live together again?"

"What a wonderful idea."

"Are you serious?"

"Sure, Barbara."

"My lease runs out the end of this week —"

"Move in Friday."

"Really?"

"Friday morning. Sorry I won't be able to help you, but as you know, I have to run down to court for a few minutes."

"I know. How awful."

"But it would make everything all right, if you're there at the apartment when I get back."

"I've got a lot of junk now. I'll need a whole moving van."

"That's all right. You just back the moving van up to the service elevator and get yourself moved in. Arrange things as you like. And then when I get back from court, we'll have a nice lunch together."

"Terrific. Fletcher, you're beautiful."

"Just like the old days, Barbara."

"I'd better get packing."

"See you Friday. Maybe I'll take the weekend off."

"Fletcher, I love you."

As Fletch was reaching for the second half of the second sandwich, the phone rang again. It was almost two o'clock.

"I.M. Fletcher's line."

"Fletcher, that's you."

"Linda — my second wife."

"What happened to you the other night?"

"What other night?"

"Friday night. You told me to rush right over. To the apartment. You weren't there."

"I got held up."

"It wasn't funny, Fletcher. I mean, if that's your idea of a joke."

"Are you sore?"

"Of course not. At your apartment, I got all ready. I washed my hair and everything. It took me a while to find the dryer. The hair dryer."

"You washed your hair?"

"And I waited and waited. I slept on the couch."

"Poor Linda."

"It wasn't very funny."

"I told you I was stoned."

"What happened to you?"

"I ended up at The Beach."

"Couldn't you have waited for me?"

"I didn't know I was going."

"Did you spend the night with a girl?"

"Yes."

"You're something else."

"Linda, I've been thinking . . ."

"Doesn't sound it."

"I mean, since the other night. I had to go think."

"I understand. You always had to go think."

"I've been thinking about you since the other night. What I mean is, you know, I don't earn much here on the newspaper."

"I know. By the way, Mr. Gillett says there was something funny about your check."

"I know. He has me in court Friday morning."

"Poor Fletch."

"I agree. We must do something, Linda."

"Like what?"

"Well, I mean, I'm not earning much, and you've lost your job at the boutique, and it just doesn't make sense for us to be running two apartments."

"We're divorced."

"Who cares about that? You wanted to move back in last Friday night."

"I still do."

"So why don't you? Give up your apartment, and move in?"

"I want to."

"So okay. Do it."

"When?"

"Friday morning. That way we can spend the weekend together."

"You mean, move in permanently?"

"I mean, give up your apartment, get a moving van, and move your junk back into our apartment Friday morning, put everything away, arrange things as you like, and be there when I get back from court."

"Really?"

"Really. Will you do it?"

"Sure. That's a wonderful idea."

"I think it makes great sense, don't you?"

"I hate this place I'm living in, anyway."

"Maybe you'll even have lunch ready when I get back. Maybe we'll go to The Beach for the weekend."

"Wonderful idea. I really do love you, Fletch."

"Me, too. I mean, I love you, too. See you Friday."

TWENTY-FOUR

"Clara Snow is an incompetent idiot. She knows nothing about this business. She is too stupid to learn."

Frank Jaffe, editor-in-chief of the *News-Tribune*, was sober only a few moments a day. Two o'clock in the afternoon was not one of those moments. At nine in the morning he was bleary-eyed and hung over. At eleven he was reasonable, but also reasonably nervous: he saw everyone as being in the way between him and his first luncheon martini. At eleven-thirty he would dash through the city room to commence drinking his lunch. From two to four-thirty he was coherently drunk. At five he was impatient, irascible. Evening drinking began at six. By nine he was incoherently drunk. In the evening he would phone the office frequently shouting orders no one could ever understand. He would spend much of the next day countermanding the orders he could remember which nobody had understood anyway. From the editor-in-chief's office would flow daily a sheaf of oblique "clarifications" which disturbed everyone and made no sense to anyone.

Fletch wondered how he had the energy for Clara Snow.

From across his oak desk, Frank's eyes behind glasses appeared to be trying to focus on him from the bottom of a jar of clam juice.

"What?"

"Clara Snow is an incompetent idiot. She knows nothing about newspapering. She is so stupid she can't learn."

"She's your boss."

"She is an incompetent idiot. She almost got me killed. She might yet."

"What did she do?"

"I've been working on this drugs-on-the-beach story —"

"For too goddamn long a time, too."

"Clara Snow reported to the chief of police at The Beach that I was there on an investigation and getting close to something."

"What's wrong with that? You might need police protection."

"What's wrong with it is that I believe the chief of police is the source of the drugs on the beach."

"You're kidding."

"I'm not kidding."

"Chief Graham Cummings? I've known him for ten years. Fifteen years. He's a wonderful man."

"He's the drug source."

"The hell he is."

"The hell he isn't."

Frank found it difficult to focus on people. "Fletcher, I think I'm taking you off this assignment."

"The hell you are."

"You've spent too goddamn long at it, and you've come up with nothing. You've just been horsing around at The Beach."

"If you take me off it, Frank, I will write it for the *Chronicle-Gazette* and publish it with the statement that you refused to publish it."

"We've been knockin' the police too hard lately."

"Graham Cummings is a drug source."

"What evidence do you have?"

"I'll write it."

"You have no evidence."

"Besides that, he's thrown me out of town. If I had been honest with him this morning and told him I have evidence, I think he would have killed me. If he gets one whiff of the evidence, he will kill me. I asked Clara Snow not to call the police."

"And Clara asked me and I said 'Go ahead.' "

"It was a damn-fool thing to do, Frank. When a man's on a story, he knows what he's doing. If I had wanted police protection, I would have sought it. It is not for you guys, you or Clara, to sit back here, setting me up as a clay pigeon."

"Did you tell Clara you suspected Cummings?"

"No. Because when I was talking to her last Friday I didn't suspect Cummings."

"So what are you saying?"

Frank looked like an unhappy frog sitting on a pad. As what Fletch was saying went through his mind, his chest expanded, his cheeks expanded and his eyes widened. His face became red.

He turned his swivel chair sideways to his desk. That way he didn't have to look at Fletch at all.

"Look, Fletcher, you and I have quite a bit to talk about. Clara says you've been pretty obnoxious. She says you dress like a slob, never wear shoes in the office, never answer your telephone, that she never knows where you are, that you're not working very hard, not working at all, that you don't accept editing, that you're sort of rude. . . . She says you're insubordinate and disobedient."

"Gee, boss, no wonder she set me up to be murdered."

"You're being rude now. Clara didn't know she was setting you up to be murdered, and I don't believe it yet. Graham Cummings is a decent guy."

"You have me saying Clara's an idiot, and Clara saying I'm an idiot. Doesn't that lead you to some conclusion?"

"What conclusion?"

"Separate us. If you insist on her being an editor, let her go make someone else's life miserable."

"I won't do that. You'll live with her."

"No. You live with her."

Frank's full face snapped to Fletcher. He tried to glare. Instead, his face just turned redder.

Frank said, "You're hanging on here by a thread now, boy."

"I sell newspapers."

"If it weren't that you're scheduled to pick up a Bronze Star Friday, I'd fire you in a minute."

"What I'm really saying, Frank, is that I am on a story, an investigation of the source of the drugs at The Beach. I'm not being dramatic, but I might be killed. If I am killed, some superior ought to know why. I believe the chief of police at The Beach, Graham Cummings, is the source. Clara Snow has tipped him off that I am on his heels. This morning he called me in to ask me what I know. This was after I tried to get arrested Sunday night. I tried very hard to get arrested. I belted three cops, in the chief's presence. I got a crack on the head, but I did not get arrested. This morning I played dumb. Very, very dumb. I told him I know nothing but the obvious. He told me to get out of town. It's reasonable to expect that if he begins to believe I've got hard evidence on him, he might want to kill me. You and your incompetent idiotic Clara Snow will have killed me."

"You're dramatizing yourself."

"Maybe."

"So what are you saying? You don't want to finish the story?"

"I'll finish it."

"When will you have it finished?"

"Pretty soon."

"I want to see it."

"You'll see it."

"You'd better pick up the Bronze Star Friday morning."

"By all means, Frank. Have reporters and photographers there. I look forward to having my face splashed all over the newspaper Saturday morning. That would surely get me killed."

"You collect that medal."

"Definitely, Frank. Friday morning, ten o'clock, the marine commandant's office."

"You pick up that medal, Fletcher, or Friday's will be your last paycheck."

"I wouldn't think of disappointing you, Frank."

"By the way, Clara also says you've got sleazy divorce lawyers all over this office. Keep them out of here."

"Right, Frank."

Fletch stood up and changed his tone of voice entirely. "What do you think of Alan Stanwyk?"

"He's a shit."

"Why?"

Frank said, "Stanwyk has fought every sensible piece of noise pollution legislation brought up in the last five years."

"And he's won?"

"Yes, he's won."

"What else do you know about him?"

"Nothing. He's a shit. Go get killed. Then maybe we'd have a story."

"Thanks, Frank."

"Anytime."

TWENTY-FIVE

"Good afternoon, sir." The headwaiter recognized him, even dressed in a full suit. The man was wasted on a tennis pavilion. "Are you looking for the Underwoods?"

"Actually, I'm looking for Joan Stanwyk," Fletch said.

"Mrs. Stanwyk is playing tennis, sir. Court three. There's an empty table at the rail. Shall I have a screwdriver brought to you?"

"Thank you."

Fletch sat at the round table for two. Along the rail were flower boxes. In the third court away from Fletch, Joan Stanwyk was playing singles with another woman.

"Your screwdriver, sir. Shall I charge this to the Underwoods?"

"Please."

Half of court three was in the shade of the clubhouse. This made serving difficult half the time for both players. One would think Joan Collins Stanwyk could get a better court at the Racquets Club.

Half the people on the tennis pavilion were still dressed in tennis whites. The other half were dressed for the evening. It was five-twenty.

Joan Collins Stanwyk played tennis like a pro, but utterly without the flash of passion that made a champion. She was smooth, even, polished; a well-educated, well-experienced tennis player. It was difficult to get anything by her, or to outthink her, yet she didn't seem to be deeply involved — paying attention. She was also without the sense of fun and of joy that a beginning tennis player has. She was competent, terrifically competent, and bored.

She won the set, walked to the net, shook hands with her opponent and smiled precisely as she would have if she had lost. They both collected sweaters and ambled up to the pavilion.

Fletch turned his chair to face the entrance.

She had to greet many people, using the same shake of the hand and smile as she used at the net. It was a moment before her eyes wandered along the rail and found Fletch.

He stood up.

She excused herself and came over immediately.

"Why, John. I thought you were in Milwaukee."

"Montana," Fletch said.

"Yes, of course. Montana." She sat at the table.

"Just before leaving for the airport Saturday, my boss called and asked me to stay a few more days. Some customers to see."

"Why didn't you call me?"

"I was busy seeing customers." He was sitting at the table, finishing his drink. "Besides, I thought I would come by on Tuesday."

"Why Tuesday?"

"Because you said Tuesday was the day your husband came home from the office at a reasonable hour."

Beneath her tan, her cheeks turned red.

"I see."

"Didn't you say your husband has Tuesdays reserved for you?"

"You're rather putting it to me, aren't you, John?"

"I hope to."

Joan Collins Stanwyk, keeping her eyes in his, laughed. She had a lovely throat.

She said, "Well, now. . ."

He said, "I'm sorry I can't offer you a drink."

"You ask a great many more questions than you appear to ask, John. And what's more, you listen to the answers. You must be very good at what you do."

"What do I do?"

"Why, sell furniture, of course. Isn't that what you said?"

"I'm really quite expert on beds."

She said, "Would you believe that I have one?"

She had one, at the Racquets Club, a three-quarter-sized bed in a bright room overlooking the pool area. She said it was her "changing room." It had a full bathroom and a closet full of tennis dresses, evening gowns, skirts, sneakers and shoes.

She had given him directions to the door on the corridor above the dining room.

By the time he arrived, she was out of the shower and wrapped in an oversized towel.

Joan Collins Stanwyk was more interested in making love than in playing tennis. But again, she was educated and experienced without the flash that makes champions. And she was without the playful joy of the beginner.

"It's really remarkable, John."

"Isn't it?"

"That's not what I mean."

"What's remarkable?"

"Your bone structure."

"I have one."

"One what?"

"One bone structure. I'm very attached to it."

"I should think you would be."

"Yes, yes."

"But you never noticed."

"Never noticed what?"

"Never in the showers in Texas, or whatever."

"It's been a long time since I took a shower in Texas."

"Al's bone structure."

"Al's bone structure? What about it?"

"It's identical to yours."

"My what?"

"Your bone structure."

"What do you mean?"

"I mean the width of your shoulders, the length of your back, your arms, your hips, your legs are identical to Alan's."

"Your husband's?"

"Yes. Didn't you ever notice? You must have been in shower rooms with him in Texas, or something. The shape of your head — everything."

"Really?"

"You two don't look a bit alike. You're blond and he's dark. But actually you're just alike."

"Something only a wife would notice."

"He weighs ten or twelve pounds more than you do, I'd say. But your bone structures are the same."

"That's very interesting."

She rolled onto her elbows and forearms, looking closely at his mouth.

"Your teeth are perfect, too. Just like Alan's."

"They are?"

"I'll bet you haven't a cavity."

"I haven't."

"Neither has he."

"How very interesting."

She said, "Now I bet you're insulted."

"Not a bit."

"I don't suppose it's polite to compare you to my husband just after we've made love and made love."

"I find it interesting."

"You're saying to yourself. 'The only reason this broad was attracted to me is because I have the same bone structure as her husband.' Is that right?"

"Yeah. Actually, I'm terribly hurt."

"I didn't mean to hurt you."

"I'm going to cry."

"Please don't cry."

"I'm dying of a broken heart."

"Oh, don't die. Not here."

"Why 'not here'?"

"Because if I had to have your body taken away, I'd be absolutely stuck trying to pronounce your last name. I'd be so embarrassed."

"Is it embarrassing being in bed with a man whose last name you can't pronounce?"

"It would be if he died and had to be taken away. I'd have to say at the door, 'His name is John, an old friend of the family, don't ask me his last name.' What is your last name again, John?"

"Zamanawinkeraleski."

"God, what a moniker. Zamanawink — say it again?"

"— eraleski. Zamanawinkeraleski."

"You mean someone actually married you with a name like that?"

"Yup. And now there are three little Zamanawinkeraleskis."

"What was her maiden name? I mean, your wife's?"

"Fletcher."

"That's a nice name. Why would she give up a nice name like that to become a Zamabangi or whatever it is?"

"Zamanawinkeraleski. It's more distinguished than Fletcher."

"It's so distinguished no one can say it. What is it, Polish?"

"Rumanian."

"I didn't know there was a difference."

"Only Poles and Rumanians care about the difference."

"What is the difference?"

"Between Poles and Rumanians? They make love differently."

"Oh?"

"Twice I've made love Polish style. Now I'll show you how a Rumanian would do it."

"Polish style was all right."

"But you haven't seen the Rumanian style yet."

"Why didn't you make love Rumanian style in the first place?"

"I didn't think you were ready for it."

"I'm ready for it."

It was eight-thirty.

In forty-eight hours Fletch was scheduled to murder her husband.

TWENTY-SIX

Wednesday morning, Fletch had a great interest in not being seen by the police at The Beach. Doubtless, Chief Cummings had told his officers to pick up Fletch on sight. The man could not bear investigation. And he had enough ammunition to use against Fletch to make life very difficult for him. Possession of marijuana. Possession of heroin. Physical assault upon three separate police officers. And when Chief Cummings ran out of charges at The Beach, he could turn Fletch over to the city police to face a charge of fraud. Fletch was careful in his stepping.

In jeans, shoeless and shirtless, he started shortly after sunrise looking for Gummy.

It was a quarter to nine when July said he had just seen Gummy parking a Volkswagen minibus on Main Street.

Fletch found the flower-decorated bus and waited in the shadow of a doorway.

At twenty to ten Gummy appeared. While he had been waiting, Fletch had counted five police cars passing on Main Street.

Gummy was unlocking the driver's door to the bus.

Fletch stepped beside him and said, "Take me around to my pad, will you, Gummy? I need to talk to you."

Gummy's face pimples twitched.

"Come on, Gummy. I've got to talk to you. About Bobbi."

In the room, Fletch said, "Bobbi's dead, Gummy."

Gummy said, "Oh."

Fletch smashed him in the face with his fist.

Gummy's head snapped back and turned, his long hair twirling. His feet moved slowly. He did not fall. He turned back, his head low, looking at Fletch through watering eyes. The look was resentful. The kid had never been hit before.

"I said Bobbi is dead, Gummy, and 'Oh' is not a proper response. You killed her. And you know it."

Gummy stepped toward the door.

Fletch said, "I've got bad news for you, Gummy. Bobbi's death means the heat's on. Fat Sam is turning state's evidence."

"Bullshit."

"He has written me a nice little deposition naming Chief Graham Cummings as the source. Everything is in the deposition, including your Hawaiian shirt. He's pinning the actual sale of drugs on you. He insists he was just a receiver."

The kid had stopped moving toward the door. His eyes were wide and innocent.

"I never pushed. I was just carrying."

"You were transferring, baby."

Gummy had blood at the corner of his lip.

"I never sold any of the stuff."

"Fat Sam is laying it on you."

"The bastard."

"And he has signed the deposition in big, flowing handwriting with his real name — which I forget for the moment."

"Charles Witherspoon."

"What?"

"Charles Witherspoon."

"That's right."

"Where is this what-do-you-call-it?"

"Deposition. I left it in the city. Do you think I'd be crazy enough to bring it down here? He signed it Charles Witherspoon."

"Shit."

"Let me help you, Gummy." Fletch opened the case of his portable typewriter. He placed an original and two carbon sheets in the carriage. "You need help."

Gummy stood in the dark room with his hands in his back pockets.

"By the way, Gummy, I'm I.M. Fletcher of the *News-Tribune*."

"You're a reporter?"

"Yeah."

"I knew there was something funny about you. I saw you riding in a gray Jaguar last week — I think Thursday night."

"Did you tell anybody you saw me?"

"No."

Gummy sat on the floor. He leaned his back against the wall.

"Does this mean I go to jail?"

"Maybe not, if you turn state's evidence."

"What does that mean? I fink?"

"It means you write a deposition and sign it. You say what role you played in supplying the beach people with drugs."

"I carried the drugs from the chief of police to Fat Sam."

Fletch was sitting on the floor cross-legged before his typewriter.

"You've got to tell us more than that. Tell me everything. I'll write it down. And you sign it."

"You know everything."

"I need to hear it from you."

"What are you going to do with the deposition?"

"I'm going to turn it over to a friend of mine who works in the district attorney's office. We were in the marines together. He'll know what to do."

"I'll get killed. Cummings is a mean son of a bitch."

"I'm going to ask for police protection for you."

" 'Police protection'? That's funny."

"Not the local police, Gummy. I agree Cummings is a dangerous man."

"Who then? The state police?"

"Probably federal narcotics agents. Or the district attorney's office. I don't know. You'll be taken care of. I want you to nail Cummings."

"All right." The light from the dirty windows was white on Gummy's long face. "Cummings was the source of drugs."

"All the drugs?"

"Yes. All."

"What is his source?"

"I don't know. He goes back and forth to Mexico every few weeks. He tells people he's building a house down there, or something. For when he retires. He brings the drugs back with him. No one questions the chief of police going through customs."

"How does customs know he's a police chief?"

"Aw, hell, have you ever seen his car? I mean, his own car? Plates front and back say 'chief of police.' He has a bubble machine on top. A police radio. He even has a Winchester rifle hanging from brackets under his dashboard."

"I've seen it. He uses that car to get through customs?"

"Yes."

"Does he wear his uniform going through customs?"

"I don't know. I've never been with him. With that car, he doesn't need a uniform."

"Does he take his wife to Mexico with him?"

"I know he has. And his teenage daughter."

"How do you know he has?"

"I've seen them leaving town. When I've known where they were going."

"Okay, Gummy. Now tell me how you get the drugs."

"Every week or ten days, they arrest me. They pull me down to the station house for questioning."

"Who picks you up?"

"Town police. Two of them, if I'm alone on the street. If I'm with you guys, I mean the guys on the beach, they send more. Like Sunday. There were seven of them. All dressed for a riot. They always expect somebody to jump on them. Like you did Sunday. By the way, Fletch, why did you do that Sunday?"

"I wanted to get arrested. I wanted to go to the station house with you and see precisely what happened."

"They really cracked your head. It sounded like a gunshot."

"It did to me, too. Is Chief Cummings always with the cops who pick you up?"

"No. But they always say the chief wants me for questioning. They're a stupid bunch of cops."

"What happens when you get to the station house?"

"I wait in the chief's office. He comes in and closes the door. He pretends to question me. I give him the money, he gives me the drugs. As simple as that. Sometimes they keep me in a jail cell over night. It looks better."

"How does the chief know that it's time to pick you up — that you're carrying money for him?"

"I park the minibus so he can see it from his office window."

"How much money do you turn over to him, on the average?"

"It averages about twenty thousand bucks."

"Every two or three weeks?"

"Every ten days or so."

"How do you transfer the money?"

"You said Fat Sam's already told you."

"I want to hear it from you."

"In a money belt. Under my Hawaiian shirt."

"And that's how you bring the drugs to Fat Sam?"

"Yeah. I carry the drugs in the money belt under the Hawaiian shirt."

"How do you actually give it to Fat Sam?"

"I don't. I just walk to the back of the lean-to and drop it. He knows where to pick it up. Then I line up like everyone else and make a phony cash buy."

"I've seen that. You really fooled me. So what do you get out of this?"

"Free drugs. Like the man said, all I can eat."

"No cash?"

"No cash. Never."

"How did you pay for the minibus?"

"That belongs to Fat Sam. You should know that. Didn't he tell you that?"

"No, he didn't. I've never seen him use it."

"He never leaves the beach."

"Why does he never leave the beach?"

"He's afraid someone would try to rip him off. Everyone thinks he's carrying. Either drugs or money. He's not, of course. I am."

"How does he give you the money?"

"In the money belt. I pretend to buy drugs every few days. When I see the money belt rolled up at the back of the lean-to, I sit down and put it on under my shirt."

"Okay, Gummy. You're doin' fine."

"Yeah."

"When Chief Cummings takes the money and gives you the drugs, are you always in the room alone with him?"

"Yes. With the door shut."

"Has there ever been another police officer or anyone else with you at the transfer of the drugs and money?"

"No. Never."

"Do you think any of the other police officers know that the chief is the source of the drugs at The Beach?"

"They're dumb bunnies. None of them know. None of them have ever figured it out."

"Aren't they suspicious that you, and only you, are brought in for questioning every week or ten days?"

"My Dad's superintendent of schools. They think Cummings has a particular concern for me. I also think they think I'm informing. I suspect some of them even think I'm working for the chief, as a spy."

"How long has this routine been going on?"

"How many years?"

"Yeah. How many years?"

"About four years."

"How old are you, Gummy?"

"Seventeen."

"So you couldn't have been using the minibus as a signal to the chief originally. What were you using?"

"My bicycle. I'd chain it to a parking meter. He'd be able to see it through his office window. My bike had a purple banana seat and a high rear-view mirror."

"How did you get started being the go-between?"

"I got hooked my first year in high school. The runner was a senior named Jeff. He blew his brains out with a shotgun. I didn't know he had been the runner until next time I went to Fat Sam."

"Was it Fat Sam who got you going?"

"No. The day after I was turned off I was pretty uptight, you know, pretty nervous. It was all beginning to hang out. In fact, I don't think I had really known I was hooked until that day. Until Jeff killed himself and the supply turned off. A couple of cops met me at the bicycle rack, at the school. They picked me up and brought me to the station. I was scared shitless. The chief closed the door to his office, and we had our first talk. We made our first deal."

"It was the chief who first got you going?"

"Yes."

"Was it Fat Sam who gave you your first drugs?"

"No. It was Jeff. At the high school. He got his free. He had extra. He gave it to me. I guess, seeing I was the son of the superintendent, they figured getting me hooked would give them some extra protection. At least regarding the drugs in the school. After a few months, Jeff stopped giving it to me free and sent me to Fat Sam. He said I wanted too much. For a while, until Jeff blew his brains out, I had to pay for it."

"How did you pay for it?"

"I burglarized my parents' house three times."

"Your own house?"

"Yeah. I was afraid to burglarize anyone else's. I was just a little kid. I really hated stealing the color television."

"Did your parents ever suspect you?"

"No. They would just report the burglary to Chief Cummings. Buy new stuff with the insurance money."

"Do your parents know you are a drug addict?"

"Yes. I guess so."

"Have they never talked to you about it?"

"No. Dad doesn't want to make an issue out of it. After all, he's superintendent of schools."

"Okay, Gummy. Just sit there and let me type a minute."

Fletch typed almost a whole page, single-spaced. He had Gummy sign the three copies. Lewis Montgomery. He had the handwriting of a nine-year-old boy. Fletch witnessed the signature on each copy.

"Is Bobbi really dead?"

Fletch said: "Yes."

"She OD'd?"

"Yes."

"Shit, I'm sorry."

"So am I."

"It's time this whole scene broke up. You know what I mean?"

"Yeah."

"I mean, I've been wondering how it would stop. Jeff blew his brains out."

"I know."

"I do feel badly about Bobbi."

"I know."

Fletch put the third copy of the deposition folded into his back pocket. He put the typewriter back into its case.

Gummy said, "What will happen to me now?"

"Tomorrow morning at eleven o'clock, I want you to be waiting at the beer stand. Fat Sam will be waiting there with you. You'll be picked up. Probably by plainclothesmen. Until tomorrow at eleven o'clock, I want you to shut up."

"Okay. Then what will happen? What will the fuzz do to me?"

"They'll probably bring you to a hospital and check you in under another name."

"I've got to come down, huh?"

"You want to, don't you?"

"Yes. I think so."

Fletch did not understand why Gummy did not leave. The boy remained sitting on the floor, his back against the wall, his face toward the window.

It was a moment before Fletch realized Gummy was crying.

Fletch walked into the lean-to carrying the typewriter.

Fat Sam was lying on his back on a bedroll on the sand, reading Marcuse's *Eros and Civilization*. The bedroll stank. Fat Sam stank.

"Hello, Vatsyayana."

In a back corner of the lean-to was a pile of empty soup cans. They stank.

Fletch handed Vatsyayana Gummy's deposition.

"I.M. Fletcher, of the *News-Tribune*."

Fat Sam put the book face-down on the sand.

While Fat Sam read the deposition, Fletch sat cross-legged on the sand and opened the portable typewriter case. Again he put an original and two carbons in the carriage.

Fat Sam read the deposition twice.

Then he sat up. His look remained kind.

"So."

"Your turn."

"You even have the name spelled right. Charles Witherspoon. It's been a long time since I've heard it."

"I guess Gummy got it from the registration of the Volkswagen."

"Oh, yes," Vatsyayana looked out at the sunlit beach. "You expect a deposition from me."

"I want to get Cummings."

"I don't blame you. A most unsavory man."

"Either you hang him, or you'll hang with him."

"Oh, I'll hang him all right. With pleasure."

Fat Sam reached for a book: Jonathan Eisen's *The Age of Rock*. In the back of the book was a folded piece of paper. Fat Sam blew the sand off it and handed it to Fletch. It read:

Sam — Jeff killed himself tonight. The boys investigating report of a gunshot found him on the football field. We need a new runner. Maybe the Montgomery kid. He may show up in the next day or two with the money belt. We need someone local. — Cummings.

"Is that hard evidence, or not?"

"That's hard evidence."

"Note, if you will, my dear Fletch, the gentleman wrote and signed it in his own hand."

"I do so note. How did you get it?"

"Would you believe it was delivered to me in a sealed envelope by an officer of the law? I've never known what to do with it. When there isn't the police, who is there? I forgot about the power of the press."

"You have wanted to turn Cummings in?"

"Always. I have been his prisoner, you see. Just as surely as if I were sitting in the town lock-up."

"I don't see."

"When I first came here from Colorado, I had a supply of drugs, thanks to my dear old mother's insurance. To support myself here, on this magnificent beach, I sold some of it off. The eminent chief of police had me arrested. He had the evidence. I either went to jail for a very long time, or worked for him. I chose not to go to jail."

"You mean you have never made a profit from this business?"

"No. Never. I have been a prisoner."

"Fat Sam, you're smarter than that. You're an intelligent man. You've known you could go over the head of the local police and turn Cummings in."

"You do realize, Fletch, that I am an addict, too?"

"Yes."

"I became addicted while teaching music in the Denver public school system. I was really at the end of my rope when my mother died, fortuitously leaving me fifteen thousand dollars in life insurance."

"You could have stopped the whole thing here anytime. Especially once you had this note."

"I realize that. The chief has continuously had evidence against me. Current evidence. Two, I am an addict. My profit from my partnership with the eminent chief of police has been free drugs all these years. Just like Gummy. The chief pays off only in merchandise. Three, I have always hoped for a guarantee of some sort, if I am to turn state's evidence. Do you have such a guarantee, Fletch?"

"Yes. I'll have you picked up at the beer stand tomorrow morning at eleven o'clock. You and Gummy."

"How very considerate of you. And then, I presume, you will splash this sordid affair all over your newspaper?"

"The whole story will be in tomorrow afternoon's *News-Tribune*. The first afternoon edition appears at eleven-twenty in the morning. If you are not at the beer stand at eleven, you will probably be dead by three o'clock in the afternoon."

"Oh, I'll be there. In fact, I would say you are pulling it rather close."

"I don't want to tip my hand until the morning."

"I see. And will you need photographs?"

"I have them already. Several fine shots of you, dealing. In fact, I had them developed and made yesterday at the office. They are awaiting captions."

"How very efficient. I remember once saying you weren't very bright. I think you are a very good actor."

"I'm a liar with a fantastic memory."

"That's what an actor is. How did you catch on?"

"I watched the drop three times before I realized it was Gummy. It was his Hawaiian shirt. It was his being picked up by the police regularly. He was the only one ever picked up by the police. And he was picked up only when your supply was running low. Actually, I think it was Creasey who mentioned the repetitious coincidence of timing. He didn't realize what he was saying. Then, Sunday night, when I tried to get arrested with Gummy and I belted three cops and they didn't arrest me, I knew Cummings did not want anyone with Gummy at the station. They wanted him alone."

"Of course."

"Then someone else mentioned the chief's frequent trips to Mexico. I heard that the first time last Saturday noon, from a very unlikely source."

"Who?"

"A man named John Collins."

"I don't know him."

"You don't play tennis."

"I used to. Back when I was alive. And how did you get the deposition out of Gummy?"

"I told him you had already signed one, naming him as pusher."

"That was dirty pool. And why would Gummy believe that I had signed a deposition?"

"Because Bobbi is dead, Fat Sam. She really is dead."

"I see. I'm sorry. She was a pretty child. Where is her body?"

"It's about to be found."

"And her body being found will trigger a whole chain of events. Supercops will flood The Beach."

"You wouldn't have a chance."

Fat Sam lit a joint and inhaled deeply. He handed it to Fletch.

"Peace."

"Fuck."

"That too."

Fletch inhaled twice.

"It's time," Fat Sam said. "It's time."

"Gummy said the same thing."

"I wonder if I have any life left. I am thirty-eight and feel one hundred."

"You'll get help."

"Now I wish they would put me in jail for a long time." Fat Sam inhaled again. "I suppose I don't really. I'm smoking a joint. I shot up two hours ago. Oh, Buddha."

"It's time to do the deposition."

"No, son. Move away from the typewriter. I'll do it myself."

Fletch lay down on the sand with the rest of the joint.

Fat Sam sat at the typewriter.

"Now let's see if Vatsyayana remembers how to type. Let's see if Fat Sam remembers how to type. Let's see if Charles Witherspoon remembers how to type."

To Fletch, stoned on the sand, the typing seemed very slow.

TWENTY-SEVEN

"It is Wednesday afternoon at three o'clock. Although I have what can be termed fresh intuitive evidence, I cannot pretend that I have much fresh factual evidence.

"My best guess at the moment, based on no factual evidence, is that Alan Stanwyk is absolutely straight — that what he says is the truth: he is dying of cancer; he wishes me to murder him tomorrow night at eight-thirty."

Fletch had returned to his apartment, taken a shower, eaten a sandwich and poured a quart of milk down his throat.

On the coffee table before him were the two depositions and their copies, and the original of Cummings's incriminating note to Fat Sam.

There was also the big tape recorder.

"Yesterday morning, Alan Stanwyk picked me up in his car again and confirmed my intention to murder him. We reviewed the murder plan.

"Conversationally, he asked me the flight number of the Trans World Airlines plane for Buenos Aires. I denied knowing the flight number, as he himself had not mentioned it to me. In fact, I did know the flight number, as I had confirmed the reservation with the airline.

"My apparent failure to know the flight number should have meant two things to him: first, he should continue seeing me in character, as a drifter — that is, I'm apparently as stupid and trusting as he thinks I am; second, he should be satisfied that if he is being investigated, I am not the source of the investigation.

"Conversationally, without appearing out of character, I was able to ask him one of my major questions: why, if he wishes to commit suicide, doesn't he crash in an airplane, as everybody half-expects?

"His answer was one of pride: that after years of keeping airplanes in the air, he couldn't aim one for the ground.

"This is an acceptable answer. As he pointed out, people do spend more than fifty thousand dollars in support of pride. Any man who lives in a house worth more than a million dollars can be expected to spend fifty grand on a matter such as this, which would so profoundly affect his most personal pride.

"Alan Stanwyk has a mistress, a Mrs. Sandra Faulkner, of 15641B Putnam Street. He spends Monday and Wednesday evenings with her.

"Mrs. Faulkner is a widow who used to work at Collins Aviation. Stanwyk and Mrs. Faulkner did not particularly know each other while Mrs. Faulkner worked at Collins Aviation.

"Sandra Faulkner's husband was a test pilot who was killed while attempting to land on an aircraft carrier, leaving her childless.

"At the time of the death, Sandra Faulkner left her employment at Collins Aviation, ran through her insurance money and whatever other sums she had available, and in the process became a drunk.

"It was approximately a year after the death that Alan Stanwyk discovered the straits she was in and came to her with what can only be described as a genuine instinct of mercy. Being a test pilot himself, it can be properly assumed his sympathy for the widow of a test pilot was entirely sincere.

"He paid for her hospitalization and has been supporting her ever since. I would estimate this affair has been going on about two years.

"Sandra Faulkner does not deny that she and Stanwyk have a sexual relationship.

"Joan Collins Stanwyk is unaware of the fact of this relationship, as she is quick to refer to her husband's working late at the office on Mondays and Wednesdays.

"However, I have subjective knowledge that Joan Collins Stanwyk herself is unfaithful to her husband.

"Returning to Sandra Faulkner: Stanwyk's mistress is unaware that Stanwyk is terminally ill, if he is. She is unaware of any change in the relationship in the foreseeable future, such as the possibility of sudden death.

"Her apartment and other belongings show no sign of being packed up.

"She is of the opinion that Stanwyk's health is excellent, and that their relationship will continue unchanged for the foreseeable future.

"Otherwise, I would characterize the relationship of Stanwyk and his mistress as generous on his part, even noble. Here is a woman of no great attraction, a heavy drinking and emotional problem, who desperately needs a friend. Stanwyk, really from a great distance, perceives that problem and becomes the friend she needs. He has no real reason to exercise such a sensitivity toward the widow of a man he never knew, or toward an unknown and unimportant ex-employee of Collins Aviation.

"Yet he does.

"This is the most consistently surprising element in Alan Stanwyk's character. The man has a peculiar principle and a unique sense of profound loyalty.

"Evidence of this rare personality trait can be found in his extraordinary, frequent, and reasonably secret trips to his hometown, Nonheagan, Pennsylvania, where his mother and father still live; in his refusing to join a fraternity at Colgate until the fraternity had made his roommate, Burt Eberhart, equally welcome; his subsequent loyalty to this same ex-roommate, Eberhart, in virtually setting him up in a business, supporting him royally as his personal and corporate insurance man, when the two men really have nothing in common at this point, if they ever did have; in his relationship with a mistress from which the mistress has benefited far more than he, and not just in worldly goods, but in mental, emotional and physical health.

"Despite Stanwyk's obvious personal ambition, which may be evidenced by his marrying the boss's daughter, which remains possible as a result of genuine love, as Amelia Shurcliffe pointed out, one really must conclude that Alan Stanwyk is a remarkably decent and honest man. What he says is true.

"Nevertheless, I am professionally obliged to retain my skepticism to the ultimate moment.

"It is entirely possible I have not assembled the right facts, or noticed them, or put them in the right order. It is possible I have not asked the right questions.

"I must continue to believe that Stanwyk's basic statement, that he is dying of cancer, is not true until I have proved it true.

"So far I have not proved this basic statement true."

Fletch turned off the tape recorder and stood for a moment in front of the divan, studying the Disdéri — four photographs of a dreadfully unattractive woman in nineteenth-century bathing costume. In it were so many truths; the truth of momentary fashion, the truth of what the woman thought of herself, thought of the experience of being photographed, the hard truth of the camera.

Fletch put down the microphone and rewound the Alan Stanwyk tape.

Wandering around the room, he listened to the tape, his own voice droning on, at first against a background of traffic noise, then in the silence of this same room, remembering that at first, less than a week ago, he wasn't sure who Alan Stanwyk was. The voice continued, not always succeeding in separating fact from speculation, observation from intuition, but nevertheless cutting through to a reasonable sketch of a man, his life and affairs: Alan Stanwyk.

Fletch played the tape again, going over the six days in his mind, trying to remember the smaller observations and impressions he had failed to record on the tape — clearly irrelevant matters. Joan Stanwyk was visibly lonely and drinking martinis before lunch on the Saturday her husband was flying an experimental airplane in Idaho. Dr. Joseph Devlin had answered the phone too fast when he heard the call concerned Alan Stanwyk — and he did not appear to question that the call had come from the insurance company. Sandra Faulkner's apartment had been burglarized, apparently by a child. But Eberhart thought Alan's daughter, Julie Stanwyk, a brat. Alan Stanwyk did not use the cigarette lighter on the dashboard of his car. He, Fletch, had not yet bought a pair of gloves. Fletch sat on the divan again and picked up the microphone.

"Alan Stanwyk is a decent man. A man of principle and profound loyalty. A strong man. An ambitious man.

"Everything in his life is intelligible and consistent — with one exception.

"I do not understand his relationship with his parents.

"He didn't invite his parents to his wedding. He hasn't told them they have a five- or six-year-old granddaughter.

"Yet he visits them across country every six weeks.

"The answer has to be that his relationship is not with his parents, but with Nonheagan, Pennsylvania."

Fletch turned off the tape recorder and went into the bedroom to use the phone.

It was four-thirty, Wednesday.

TWENTY-EIGHT

"**M**r. Stanwyk? Believe it or not, this is Sidney James of Casewell Insurers again."

"I thought you'd call again. Once you long-distance dialers learn a telephone number, you're apt to ring it a lot."

"I expect this will be the last time I bother you, sir."

"That's all right, son. I hope it isn't. I bought some more telephone stock yesterday."

"The hardware store must be doing pretty well."

"It's doing all right. Ever since the price of labor went sky-high, people have been rushing to the hardware store to buy the wrong equipment for jobs around the house they never intend to do anyway. You've heard of selling used equipment? I bet half the stuff I sell never gets used in the first place."

"I thought you said the telephone company is the only business making money these days."

"The hardware business is doing pretty good, too. Although I'd only admit it long-distance to California."

"You seem to have things pretty well figured out, sir."

"How are you figuring these days? You picking up that Bronze Star?"

"Yes, sir, I am."

"That's good, son. That's fine. Can we keep it for you?"

"I noticed a space in the back of my sock drawer where I think it would fit."

"I thought you'd make the right decision. There never was a country that didn't need to decorate people."

"Thanks for the offer, anyway. How's Mrs. Stanwyk?"

"Oh, I forgot: you're a pulse-taker. When I was home for lunch,

Mrs. Stanwyk was still ticking over nicely. The older models are the best, you know. Better built, and they use less fuel."

"Say, Mr. Stanwyk, the last time we talked you said your son, Alan, gave up boxing, refused to go to the nationals after winning the state's Golden Gloves, because of girls."

"Yes, I did say that."

"Is that what you meant?"

"Well, son, I believe a man of my age has sufficient motor memory to mean approximately the same thing when he says 'girls' as a young buck of your age. If I remember rightly, girls have a couple of legs under them, a hank o' hair up top, and a couple of protuberances about grab height. That about right?"

"That's about right, sir."

"I thought so."

"What I mean is, did you mean *girls*, or *girl*?"

"I'm in the hardware business, son. I'm apt to speak in gross lots."

"Did you mean any girl in particular? Was there any one particular girl who was the cause of Alan's giving up boxing?"

"There certainly was."

"Who was she?"

"You insurance men ask some funny questions."

"We'll be through with this case very soon, sir. We'll stop bothering you."

"Mr. James, you sound more like a private investigator or somethin' than an insurance man."

"Going over this policy, Mr. Stanwyk, we noticed a small bequest we don't understand. We have to check out whether the person is a relative or not, whether or not she is still alive, the current address, etc."

"I should think all that would be up to Alan, the insured."

"Your son's a very busy man, Mr. Stanwyk. You'd be surprised how people fail to maintain the proper information on policies of this sort."

"I suppose I would."

"They experience the death of a friend, or get a postcard saying a friend's address has changed, and it never occurs to them to update such a thing in an insurance file."

"I guess I understand. But if you hadn't won a Bronze Star, Mr. James, I think I'd be inclined to tell you to go leap into the Pacific Ocean. Are you near the Pacific Ocean out there?"

"I can see it through my window, Mr. Stanwyk. Who is the girl?"

"Sally Ann Cushing. Or, as she is now known, Sally Ann Cushing Cavanaugh."

"Alan and she were in love?"

"They were thicker than Elmer's Glue. Sticky. For years there, you hardly saw one without seeing the other one attached. If they weren't kissin', they were holdin' hands. Here in town we had to widen the sidewalks for them. You couldn't pry 'em apart."

"Alan gave up boxing because of Sally Ann Cushing?"

"As the old song says, 'Love walked in.' She set him on his ass like no long-armed middleweight ever did. He gave up boxing. He almost gave up everything, including breathing normally, for that girl. We had a hard time gettin' him to go to school."

"What happened?"

"Well, he went to Colgate and she went to Skidmore."

"They're reasonably close together, aren't they? I mean, as colleges?"

"Scandalously close. That's why the kids picked 'em. And every weekend they came home and continued being a sexual inspiration to us all. You never saw two kids so in love."

"So why didn't they get married?"

"They did, but not to each other. Spring of their senior year in college, Sally Ann was visibly pregnant. I do believe my wife noticed it before Alan. Naturally, we thought it was Alan. We thought it was Alan's kid. It wasn't. I guess their relationship had been as pure as the driven snow. Alan was shaken to his foundation. The kid was caused by a man named Bill Cavanaugh, a town boy. Sally Ann said that she had had too much to drink at a party here in town one night, while Alan was at school, and Cavanaugh had driven her home. She said he had taken advantage of her. She insisted it happened only once, but as Mother Goose said, once is enough. At least it was that time. Or, more likely, she wasn't telling the truth. I've always suspected she was a little impatient with my son. You know, Alan always played everything remarkably straight. There comes a time when a girl wants to get laid, and I suspect Alan was keeping the girl he intended to marry as untried as next year's car."

"So Sally Ann Cushing married Cavanaugh?"

"Yup. And Alan took up flying those damn-fool aircraft. Between the boxing and the flying, there was a hot and heavy romance with Sally Ann Cushing. Frankly, I think my son has always had a bit of a death urge. Although I suppose I shouldn't tell you that. Your bein' his insurance man. A bit of the daredevil, except when it came to young love. He treated that very carefully. A bit too carefully, I'd say."

"This explains a lot."

"Does this explain that small bequest on the insurance policy?"

"Yes. The name is Sally Ann Cushing Cavanaugh."

"That's good. She's a nice girl. I've always been a bit in love with her myself. Cavanaugh is a skunk, I've always thought. Never have liked him. The boy, young Bill, is about twelve years old now. One or the other frequently comes in the store, Sally Ann or young Bill. I feel toward them almost like family. Despite the pregnancy, Alan and Sally Ann still thought of getting married. But Cavanaugh had his rights, and he exerted them. Sally Ann was quite a catch for him. He's in the insurance business, like you, only he's no good at it."

"The Cavanaughs still live in Nonheagan?"

"Well, yes and no. That's what I was going to tell you. I can't be too sure of Sally Ann's address at this point."

"Why not?"

"Sally Ann and Bill Cavanaugh got divorced a while back. I'm not sure exactly when. There was a separation. I know they were getting divorced, and she must have gotten it, because she sold her house and left town, taking the boy with her."

"When? When did she leave town?"

"Yesterday."

"Yesterday?"

"Yup. They sold everything. Furniture, washer, dryer, beds and kitchenware. There was no moving van at all. She and the boy packed suitcases and took a taxi to the airport. It's a bit of a mystery around here. According to my wife, they were very vague about where they were going. The kid said he was going to go live on the West Coast — out somewhere near you. In California. I expect that after almost thirteen years of marriage to that bum Cavanaugh, she just wanted to burn her bridges behind her. Find a new life somewhere. Anyway, be shut of this town. Cavanaugh gave her a pretty rough time."

"Mr. Stanwyk, thank you very much."

"Well, if there's any question about that little bequest to Sally Ann, you be a good fella and see that she gets what Alan wants to give her. Sally Ann is a wonderful person, and she's had a rotten time."

"One other question: when your son would visit you in Nonheagan, did he ever see Sally Ann?"

"Why, no. He was at the Inn on the telephone all the time, as far as I know. She was married. I suppose he could have seen her. He never mentioned it."

"Again, many thanks, Mr. Stanwyk. You've been a great help. We won't bother you again."

"Any time, Mr. James. I'm very happy to have the opportunity to help out Alan."

Fletch went through the routine with five local hotels before finding the right one.

"Desk, please."

"Desk."

"Has Mrs. Sally Ann Cavanaugh checked in yet?"

The sixth hotel desk answered, "Yes, sir. Mrs. Cavanaugh and her son checked in yesterday. Do you want their room number?"

"No. Thanks. We want to surprise her with some flowers. Can you tell me when she intends to check out?"

"She's keeping the room through Thursday night, sir, but she told us she would actually be leaving Thursday evening after supper. Tomorrow night about nine o'clock."

"That should give us plenty of time to send her flowers. Thanks very much."

"Trans World Airlines. Reservations."

"On your flight 629 to Buenos Aires tomorrow night," Fletch said, "do you have a reservation for a Mrs. Sally Ann Cushing Cavanaugh and son?"

"What's the name, sir?"

"Mrs. Cavanaugh and son, William."

"No, sir. We do not have reservations under that name. Should we make these reservations, sir?"

"No, no. That's all right. Do you have a reservation under the name of Irwin Fletcher for the same flight?"

"Irwin Fletcher. Yes, sir. Flight 629 to Buenos Aires. Departure time eleven P.M. Thursday. That reservation has been confirmed."

"And you do not have a Sally Ann Cushing Cavanaugh registered aboard that flight?"

"No, sir. We do not have either a Cushing or a Cavanaugh listed as passengers aboard flight 629."

Fletch said, "Thank you very much."

Before making the next telephone call, Fletch spent a few moments wandering around the apartment. In the kitchen he drank a glass of milk. In the bathroom he brushed his teeth. Back in the bedroom he spent a few minutes looking into the telephone directory.

Then he picked up the phone.

"Command Air Charter Service?"

"Yes. Hello. Command Air Charter Service."

"This is Irwin Fletcher. I'm calling regarding my reservation for tomorrow night . . ."

"Yes. Mr. Fletcher. We're glad you called. Your cashier's check arrived this morning, as we arranged. The flight is prepaid. An executive jet will be standing by tomorrow night from ten-thirty P.M. to twelve midnight for your flight to Rio de Janeiro. You don't expect to be arriving later than twelve midnight, do you, sir?"

"No. I don't. At the airport, aren't you right next to Trans World Airlines?"

"Yes, sir. We use the same parking facilities."

"I see."

"We haven't known where to call you, Mr. Fletcher, as you left no telephone number when we talked Friday of last week. You didn't indicate whether or not you'd be traveling alone, sir."

"No. Does it matter?"

"No, sir. Our only question is whether or not you wish a steward flying aboard."

"Is one usual?"

"Well, sir, if you're flying alone, the copilot usually can take care of such things as drinks and food . . ."

"I see."

"Will you wish a steward, sir? It makes no difference in cost to you. It just means one of our able stewards will be flying to Rio and back."

"Yes. I will want a steward."

"Yes, sir. That's fine. We'll have a steward on board."

"Thank you."

"Thank you, Mr. Fletcher. And thank you for calling in. This flight will not need to be confirmed again."

After replacing the telephone receiver, Fletch remained sitting on the bed. It was ten minutes past seven.

There were twenty-five hours and twenty minutes before he was next scheduled to meet Alan Stanwyk.

Fletch went over in his mind precisely what he had to do in that twenty-five hours and twenty minutes, and ordered the doing of these things in a time sequence. After making the plan, he adjusted it and then reviewed it.

There was plenty of time for what he had to do.

At seven-thirty Fletch fell asleep with his alarm set for one-thirty Thursday morning.

At three-twenty Thursday morning, Fletch parked his car on Berman Street, The Hills, three hundred yards from the Stanwyk driveway.

In sneakers and jeans and a dark turtleneck sweater, Fletch entered the Stanwyk property by the driveway. Leaving the driveway immediately, he approached the side of the house by walking in an arc across the left lawn.

He entered the library of the Stanwyk house by the French window. He reflected that it had even been true that the servants perpetually forgot to lock that door.

Using only moonlight, he slid open the top right drawer of the desk.

As he suspected, the .38 caliber Smith & Wesson revolver was still in the drawer.

And, as he had suspected, the bullet clip had been removed.

He returned the empty gun to the drawer.

At five-fifteen Thursday morning, Fletch was in his office at the *News-Tribune*, writing a story for Thursday afternoon's newspaper.

TWENTY-NINE

or 1st Thurs. p.m. BODY FOUND w/cuts: R. Sanders Fletcher

The nude body of a 15-year-old girl was discovered buried in the sand off Shoreside Blvd., The Beach, by police this morning.

The body was found encased in a sleeping bag in a shallow grave in the shade of the sea wall as the result of a tip from an anonymous caller.

The body has been identified as that of Roberta "Bobbi" Sanders, believed to be originally from Illinois.

It is expected that, in his report, coroner Alfred Wilson will estimate the time of death sometime late Sunday night or early Monday morning and the cause of death as an overdose of drugs.

According to a police spokesman, the sleeping bag is a popular brand and there is little expectation it can be traced to its owner.

The girl, abandoned at The Beach by a 30-year-old male traveling companion some months ago, had no known local address.

Her friends are not known to police.

She had no known means of support.

The anonymous caller this morning was described by police as "probably male." It is reported by the receiving officer that an obvious attempt was made by the caller to muffle or disguise the voice.

The Beach police are making every effort to locate the girl's family in Illinois.

It is believed her father is a dentist.

for 1st Thurs. p.m. (fp) POLICE CHIEF IMPLICATED Fletcher w/exhibits: 1) Montgomery affidavit; 2) Witherspoon affidavit; 3) Cummings's handwritten note — enclosed, captioned w/cuts: Cummings, Witherspoon, Montgomery — u have in rack.

The *News-Tribune* delivered to the district attorney's office this morning evidence implicating Chief of Police Graham Cummings in illegal drug trafficking in The Beach area.

The evidence includes: an affidavit signed by Charles Witherspoon, alias Vatsyayana, alias Fat Sam, who identifies himself in the affidavit as "the disseminator of [illegal] drugs in The Beach area," an affidavit signed by Lewis Montgomery, who identifies himself in the affidavit as "the drug runner to Fat Sam," and a handwritten note to "Sam" regarding the drug-running problems signed "Cummings."

These affidavits identify Chief Cummings as the source of illegal drugs in The Beach area.

The affidavits are dated with yesterday's date.

This morning, The Beach police discovered the body of a 15-year-old girl, Roberta "Bobbi" Sanders, buried in a shallow grave near the main sea wall at The Beach, dead of a drug overdose. (See related story.)

The evidence implicating Cummings is the result of a special investigation by the *News-Tribune* beginning a month ago.

Both Witherspoon and Montgomery were placed in protective custody before noon today.

The arrest of Chief Cummings by federal narcotics agents is expected later today.

According to the affidavits, Cummings, 59, under the guise of establishing a home in Mexico preparatory to his retirement a year hence, has been smuggling drugs in from Mexico on a monthly basis for more than four years.

Street prices for these drugs have totaled as much as $75,000 a month.

Cummings's personal car, which he used on his frequent trips to Mexico, is a late-model dark blue Chevrolet sedan, with plates front and back reading "Chief of Police." The car is equipped with a police radio. A rotating, flashing light similar to those used on official police cars is on the roof of Cummings's privately owned car. A high-powered Winchester rifle is slung beneath the dashboard.

It is unknown whether Cummings also wore his police uniform while going through customs.

It is known that his wife and teenage daughter frequently have made the trip with him.

Cummings has been a member of The Beach police force 19 years. Prior to his police career, he was a career non-commissioned officer in the U.S. Army.

Montgomery is the son of James Montgomery, superintendent of schools at The Beach.

According to the affidavits, town police regularly would pick up young Montgomery for "questioning."

Once alone in the office of the chief of police, the transfer of drugs for cash would take place between Montgomery and Cummings.

Montgomery states the belief these transactions were completely unknown to other police officers.

Montgomery would transfer both drugs and money in a money belt concealed beneath a loose Hawaiian shirt.

Pretending to make a purchase of drugs from Witherspoon, Montgomery would in fact drop the drug-laden money belt in a place prearranged for Witherspoon to find it.

Although the widespread presence of illegal drugs in The Beach area was visible, the method of how the drugs came to be in the area was invisible.

An earlier drug-runner, a 19-year-old simply identified in the affidavits as "Jeff," reportedly committed suicide four years ago.

The handwritten note allegedly from Cummings was written at the time of "Jeff's" suicide. It refers to the problem of replacing "Jeff" as a drug-runner by Montgomery.

According to his own affidavit, Montgomery has been running drugs since the age of fourteen.

Originally, when it was time for another transfer, Montgomery would signal Cummings by leaving his bicycle chained to a parking meter visible through the window of the office of the chief of police. The bicycle had a distinct, purple "banana" seat and a high rear-view mirror.

Later, the signal that Montgomery wanted to be "picked up for questioning" so a transfer of money for drugs could take place would be his parking a flower-decorated Volkswagen minibus within sight of the police chief's office window. The vehicle is registered to Witherspoon.

Witherspoon, 38, has been living apparently undisturbed by police in a lean-to on the beach for years.

He identifies himself as a former music teacher with the Denver, Colo., public school system.

In his affidavit, Witherspoon states that he and only he has been selling the drugs supplied by Cummings in The Beach area.

Both Witherspoon and Montgomery state they had no share in the profits from the illegal drug trade. Self-attested addicts, they profited only by having their own drug needs supplied free of charge by Cummings.

They both attest that they were forced to continue in this traffic by Chief Cummings, who threatened them with evidence in his possession that they had been involved in drug-dealing.

Witherspoon had sold drugs illegally in The Beach area before becoming an agent of the police chief.

Witherspoon stated, "I was as much a prisoner of the chief of police, both by my need for drugs and by evidence he had on me, as I would have been if I were sitting in the town jail."

As chief of police, Cummings had refused offers of assistance from private sources to have the town's drug problems investigated by outside experts. Such a repeated offer by John Collins, chairman of the board of Collins Aviation, was repeatedly refused.

According to Collins, Cummings always insisted he was "within a few months" of breaking the case.

He made a similar insistence to the *News-Tribune* Tuesday of this week.

After handing in the originals and duplicates of both stories to the copy desk of the afternoon newspaper, Fletch spent time identifying the photographs he had ordered processed two days before and drafting captions for them. The photographs were of Roberta Sanders, Police Chief Graham Cummings (which had been in the *News-Tribune* picture files), Charles Witherspoon outside the lean-to handing a small cellophane-wrapped package of heroin to Creasey, who was not identifiable in the photograph, and of Lewis Montgomery dressed in a Hawaiian shirt standing beside the Volkswagen minibus.

He Xeroxed two copies each of the affidavits and Cummings's handwritten note and turned both copies over to the copy desk. One clear copy of each would be photographed, engraved and printed in the *News-Tribune* with his second story.

The originals of the affidavits and the handwritten note he brought back to his office and placed in an addressed envelope. He telephoned for a city messenger. Then he sealed the envelope.

It was only then that Fletch made the telephone contacts he had already reported in news stories already being printed.

"Beach Police. Please state your name and the number from which you are calling."

With his handkerchief between his mouth and the telephone receiver, Fletch said, "I want to report a body."

"Please state your name and the number from which you are calling."

"There's a body buried on the beach, of a girl — the girl Bobbi. She is buried in a sleeping bag. She's dead."

"Who is this?"

"This is not a hoax. Bobbi is buried on the beach near the sea wall. The only place along the sea wall where the sand is perpetually in the shade. Where it curves and the sidewalk overhangs. Up the beach from Fat Sam's lean-to. There is a rock from the sea wall placed over the exact spot where she is buried. Have you got that?"

"Please repeat."

"The body of Bobbi is buried on the beach, next to the sea wall not far from Fat Sam's lean-to. There is a rock placed precisely on the sand where she is buried."

"Please identify yourself. Who is this calling?"

Fletch said, "Please find Bobbi."

At seven forty-five Thursday morning, the city messenger appeared in Fletch's office. He was about twenty-five years old, wearing a black leather jacket and carrying a motorcycle helmet.

Without saying anything, Fletch handed him the envelope containing the original affidavits and the original of Cummings's handwritten note.

The messenger read the address and, without saying anything, left.

At seven-fifty, Fletch dialed a suburban number.

"Hello?"

"Good morning, Audrey. You sound as fresh as a morning glory."

"Fletcher? Is that you?"

"Sharp as a tack, too."

"Why are you calling at this hour? I'm trying to get the kids off to school."

"I just wanted to make sure you're awake and have the coffee on for Alston."

"He's had his coffee. He's just leaving for the office."

"Call him back, will you, Audrey? I need to speak to him."

"He's right here. Trying to kiss me good-bye."

"How could he, ever?"

"Fletcher, you're sweet. Here's Alston."

"Is this Alston Chambers, our distinguished district attorney?"

"Hiya, buddy. I'm not district attorney. I'm what is known as the district attorney's office. That means I just do all the work."

"I know. Audrey sounds pretty fresh for eight o'clock in the morning."

"She makes up for the coffee with morning sprightliness. I can't stand either. That's why I leave for the office so early. What's up, buddy?"

"Alston, I'm sending over to your office by messenger a couple of depositions or affidavits or whatever you legal types call them, and a signed, handwritten note. They should be in your office by the time you get there."

"Okay. What do they say?"

"They should be self-explanatory. Briefly what they say is that Graham Cummings, the chief of police at The Beach, is and has been

157

for at least four years the source of illegal drugs in The Beach area."

"Wow. Graham Cummings? He's as clean as a hound dog's tooth."

"We thought he was as clean as a hound dog's tooth."

"I'm sorry to hear this."

"Actually, so am I."

"Has anybody arrested him yet?"

"No. That's a bit of a problem, as you can see. You'll have to arrange that."

"Right, Irwin. It will take time."

"Time?"

"A few hours. First, I have to get your depositions and copy them. Then I'll have to get in touch with federal narcotics agents, show them the depositions, and so forth. Then they'll have to send someone down there, after having gotten an arrest warrant."

"Don't be too long about it. If you miss him, he'll probably head for the Mexican border in his own car, which looks like a police car, bubble machine and all. He has a police radio in the car and a high-powered rifle. Apparently he's used it to fool customs a lot. Anyway, it's a dark blue Chevrolet sedan, license number 706-552."

"Give me the number again."

"706-552."

"Okay. Sure you're right about this?"

"Yup."

"Boy. Graham Cummings. I can't believe it."

"Look, Alston, even before you pick up Cummings, there's something else I want you to do for me."

"You've already given me a morning's work."

"I know, but I want the two people who signed these affidavits to be picked up and put in protective custody."

"Right. Where are they?"

"At eleven o'clock this morning, they'll be waiting to be picked up at the beer stand at the main section of The Beach. You know, the beer stand that you can see from Shoreside Boulevard."

"I know the place."

"They'll be there waiting."

"What are their names?"

"Witherspoon and Montgomery. A couple of terrible-lookin' fellas. Witherspoon's thirty-eight; Montgomery's seventeen. Their names will be on the depositions."

"Of course."

"And Alston, be quick about this, will you? I've already got the story splashed all over the afternoon paper, and you know that comes off the presses at eleven-twenty-two."

"Ah, yes: Fletcher, the terrific journalist."

"And there is a death involved here —"

"Murder?"

"No. A fifteen-year-old girl found overdosed this morning at The Beach. Cummings could turn into a dangerous man very easily."

"Fletcher, did I ever tell you you're a great journalist?"

"No."

"Irwin Fletcher, you are. You really are. I hope the *News-Tribune* appreciates you."

"They're about to fire me."

"Nonsense."

"Something about my not wearing shoes in the office."

"Hey, old buddy Irwin, I get to see you honored tomorrow."

"What do you mean?"

"Thanks for inviting me to witness your receiving the Bronze Star."

"I didn't invite you."

"I got an invitation from the promotion department of the *News-Tribune*."

"I didn't send it."

"You must have made up the invitation list."

"I made up no invitation list."

"I'm coming anyway. All of us old comrades-in-arms are very proud of you, you know. All I ever won in the marines was a disease coffee doesn't cure."

"Do you still have it?"

"No. I lost it on a toilet seat."

"At City Hall, I hope."

"Probably. I thought you picked up the Bronze Star years ago."

"I never picked it up."

"Will you pick it up tomorrow?"

"Sure," Fletch said. "Sure, sure, sure."

"I'll be there."

"You be there. Better look pretty — there will be photographers."

"I'll wear a smile. See you then, Fletch."

"See you then."

"Fletcher!"

It was nine-thirty in the morning, and Fletch was going home for the day. He had waited to see the front-page proof at nine-fifteen.

It was beautiful. Both stories began above the fold, with pictures of Bobbi and Cummings. The jumps, with more pictures, would be on page three, with full reproductions of the affidavits and hand-written note and more pictures. A blockbuster. Copy editors had changed very little of his copy. A veritable one-two helluva block-buster.

He had the key in the ignition of the MG.

"Oh, hello, Clara."

She had parked her gray Vega station wagon down the line of cars waiting to take their owners home again.

"How are you, sweetheart?"

"Fletcher, this is Thursday."

"I know."

She was leaning over his car door like a traffic officer.

"Where are you going?"

"Home."

"I haven't seen the beach-drug story yet."

"I know."

"I told you you're to have that story in by four o'clock this after-noon."

"When would you run it?"

"I don't know. I'll have to do some work on it first."

"Would you run it tomorrow?"

"I don't know. It depends on how much work we have to do on it."

"Would you run it in the Sunday paper?"

"I don't know. Frank said something about holding it for a week or two. He said you had some crazy idea Graham Cummings is im-plicated."

"Did I say that?"

"They're friends."

"Oh."

"Is Cummings implicated?"

"His name is mentioned in the story."

"It's up to Frank and me when the story runs in the paper. It's your job to get the story on my desk by four o'clock this afternoon."

"Have I ever disappointed you yet, Clara?"

"I'm serious, Fletcher."

"Have no fear. You'll see the story this afternoon."

"You're sure?"

"Clara: I'm absolutely sure. This afternoon you'll see the drug-beach story."

"I'd better."

"You will."

"And you'd better plan on being in the marine commandant's office at ten o'clock tomorrow morning."

"Don't worry about that, either."

"Okay. Your job is on the line."

"I'd hate to lose it," Fletch said. "You know how I love working with you."

Fletch turned the ignition key.

"Fletch, I'll see you by four o'clock at the latest."

"You'll see the story by four o'clock," Fletch said. "Maybe even a little earlier."

THIRTY

Fletch spent most of Thursday alone in his apartment.

He ate.

He slept.

He destroyed the Stanwyk tape.

He typed a letter to John Collins. He typed an original and a single carbon copy of the letter. And threw the original of the letter away. The copy he placed folded in the inside pocket of his suit jacket.

He emptied the wastebaskets.

At eleven-thirty, the phone began ringing persistently. He knew it was Clara Snow and/or Frank Jaffe or any one of several other *News-Tribune* executives who characteristically became excited, one way or the other, in pleasure if they were real professionals, in anger if they were not, when a staff member had snuck a genuine, unadulterated piece of journalism over on them. In all newspapers Fletch had seen there was always a hard core of genuinely professional working staff which made it possible to commit genuine journalism occasionally, regardless of the incompetence among the executive staff. The afternoon newspaper was on the streets. The excited callers apparently went out to lunch at one o'clock. The phone did not begin ringing relentlessly again until two-thirty.

At three o'clock the lobby doorbell rang.

Fletch pressed the buzzer to unlock the downstairs lobby door and waited.

In a moment his own apartment doorbell rang.

He opened the door to Joan Collins Stanwyk.

"Good afternoon, Mr. Fletcher."

"Good afternoon, Mrs. Stanwyk."

"Fletcher, as I said, is a name I can remember."

"You know who I am?"

"Thank you, I do."

"Won't you come in?"

She entered and sat on the divan.

"May I offer you a drink?"

"No, thank you, Mr. Fletcher. But you may offer me an explanation."

"Ah?"

Fletch remained standing, taking a step this way, a step that. In the eleventh hour, his cover had been blown.

"Mr. Fletcher, why are you investigating my husband? Or is it I you are investigating?"

"Neither of you," Fletch said.

Also, he found this Mr. and Mrs. business a bit cumbersome between two people who had made love both Polish and Rumanian style only two days before.

"What makes you think I am investigating you?"

"Mr. Fletcher, I have been born, bred and educated to do a job, as I gather you have, because clearly you are very good at your job. My job is to support and protect my father and my husband. And I'm rather good at it."

"In fact, protect Collins Aviation."

"And its investors, and the people it employs, et cetera."

"I see."

"One can't have this subtle job for as many years as I've had it without developing certain subtle instincts. At lunch at the Racquets Club Saturday, when you and I first met, after a while my intuition told me I was being questioned. For the life of me, I could not figure what I was being questioned about. So I took your picture."

Without looking at it, she transferred it from her purse to the coffee table. It was a three-quarter Polaroid shot of Fletch in a tennis shirt in the Racquets Club pavilion.

"While you were getting another chair for the table, after my father joined us. I turned your picture over to Collins plant security Monday morning. It was just this morning I received their report. You are I.M. Fletcher of the *News-Tribune*. Your identity was confirmed by a city policy detective named Lupo, and has since been confirmed by the newspaper itself."

Fletch said, "Wow."

Prowling the room, watching her, Fletch had the sudden, irrational desire to marry Joan Collins Stanwyk.

"Now, Mr. Fletcher, when a newspaper reporter ingratiates himself into one's acquaintanceship — in this case, I might even say into one's intimacy — under a false name, an entirely false identity, one can safely assume one is being investigated."

"Right."

"But you say you're not investigating us."

"Right. Your father. John Collins. I wanted some information from him."

"Your phone is ringing."

"I know."

"Seeing you apparently don't answer your phone, may I ask what information you wanted from my father?"

"Whether or not he had ever offered to subsidize a private investigation of the source of drugs at The Beach, and whether or not the chief of police, Graham Cummings, had ever refused his help."

"Of what conceivable use could that piece of information be to you?"

"I've already printed it. Have you seen this afternoon's *News-Tribune*?"

"No, I haven't."

"I busted your local drug story wide open. Cummings is the source of the drugs. In one paragraph, I believe paragraph thirty-four, I report your father's offers. If I had asked your father officially or directly, he would never have told me, for fear it would reflect upon the chief of police, never dreaming it is the chief himself who is guilty."

"How very interesting. You go to that much effort for one paragraph?"

"You should see the efforts I go to sometimes for paragraphs I don't even write."

"But I have the distinct impression it was my father who first brought up the topic of drugs, not you."

"You can't be sure, can you?"

"No, I can't. Have you ever known my husband?"

"No."

"How were you so able to convince us that you had known him and known him well? That you had even attended the wedding?"

"Newspaper research. Plain old homework."

"But you even knew that he had buzzed a house in San Antonio, Texas, years ago. We didn't know that."

"How do you know it's true?"

"I asked him."

"You asked him?"

"Yes. He was embarrassed, but he didn't deny it."

"That's funny."

"How did you know it?"

"It's on his police record. That and a six-month-old unpaid parking ticket in Los Angeles."

"And why would you look up his police record if you are not investigating him?"

"I wanted to have some detail of information to convince you that I knew him."

"I'm having greater difficulty believing you would go to such lengths for one, unimportant paragraph in a news story which really doesn't concern us."

"Believe me. I'm absolutely honest."

"Your phone is ringing."

"I know."

Joan Collins Stanwyk said, "In trying to focus upon what your line of questioning was, if there was one, I believed it had to do with your curiosity concerning my husband's health."

"How is he, by the way?"

"Fine, as far as I know. But your questions concerned his health. You even pinned down the name and address of his insurance agent. And I think — I'm not sure — you even mentioned the name of the family doctor."

Standing in the room, looking at Joan Collins Stanwyk sitting with dignity on the divan, Fletch was full of joy. She was wonderful. A woman who penetrated his sense of play, could reconstruct it, come close to understanding his moves, he should love forever.

And in a few hours he was scheduled to murder her husband — at the request of the man himself.

He said, "I have no idea what you're talking about. All that was idle chatter."

"Secondly, you directed a great many questions to me, and virtually none to my father. With him, again the question of Alan's health came up."

"What else is there to talk about? The weather. When one has nothing to talk about, one talks about either the weather or someone's health."

"Do you know anything about my husband's health that I don't know?"

"Honestly, I don't."

"How did you get into the Racquets Club, Mr. Fletcher?"

"I bought a pair of tennis shorts and said I was a guest of the Underwoods."

"Do you know the Underwoods?"

"No. I read the name from a locker."

"I will have to reimburse them for any expenses you incurred."

"It shouldn't be much. Two screwdrivers."

"Nevertheless, I will reimburse them for two screwdrivers. You don't even play tennis?"

"I play with people. Somehow I don't like the word 'court.' Not even 'tennis court.' Once playing with people gets close to a court, things are apt to get boring."

"Is that because in a court there are rules?"

"It may be."

"Your phone is ringing."

"I know."

"Was our going to bed together Tuesday night a part of your investigation?"

"No. That was on my own time."

"I sincerely hope so."

"Do you intend to tell your husband about I.M. Fletcher of the News-Tribune?"

"Mr. Fletcher, how can I?"

Fletch finally sat on the divan.

"People call me Fletch."

"I have a committee meeting at the Racquets Club. It's Thursday evening. I have to pick up Julie. The servants are away."

"There's always time."
"Fletch. Your phone is ringing."
"I know."

At six o'clock the apartment doorbell rang again. Fletch was alone. He had showered and put on a suit. The downstairs lobby bell had not rung.

At the door were two very young, very scrubbed men who were very obviously police detectives.

"Mr. I.M. Fletcher?"

Fletch said, "I'm sorry, Mr. Fletcher isn't in. I'm his attorney, Mr. Gillett of Gillett, Worsham and O'Brien. Is there anything I can do for you?"

"You're his attorney?"

"That's right."

"We have a warrant for the arrest of I.M. Fletcher of this address to face charges of criminal fraud."

"Yes, I know. I've advised Mr. Fletcher on this matter."

"Where is he?"

"Well, gentlemen, I'll tell you. The man is as guilty as sin. He's spending this afternoon and evening trying to wind up personal business. You do understand."

"This isn't the first time we've come here trying to locate him."

"Never fear. I promise you I will bring Mr. Fletcher to the main police station tomorrow at ten o'clock, where he will surrender himself. He just needs tonight to iron things out for himself."

"What's tomorrow, Friday?"

"He will surrender himself Friday morning at ten o'clock."

"In your recognizance?"

Fletch smiled patronizingly, as attorneys always do when police officers use large legal terms.

"In my recognizance."

"What's your name again?"

"Mr. Gillett, of Gillett, Worsham and O'Brien. My firm is here in the city."

Fletch watched one of the policemen write in a notebook: "Gillett — Gillett, Worsham and O'Brien."

The other policeman said, "You do realize, sir, that if you do not surrender I.M. Fletcher tomorrow morning, you too will be liable for criminal arrest?"

"Of course I realize it," Fletch said. "After all, I am a member of the California bar and an officer of the court."

"Okay."

Fletch said, "Wait a minute, officers, I'll walk out with you. Which way is the elevator?"

"This way, sir."

"Oh, thank you."

Fletch then drove to the Stanwyk residence on Berman Street.

THIRTY-ONE

It was eight-thirty Thursday night.

Dressed in a full business suit, shirt and tie, Fletch opened the French windows to the library of the Stanwyk house and entered.

Alan Stanwyk, smoking a cigarette, was waiting in a leather chair the other side of the desk. He had bleached his hair blond.

"Good evening, Mr. Stanwyk. I.M. Fletcher, of the *News-Tribune*. May I use your phone?"

Stanwyk's left knee jerked.

Fletch picked up the phone and dialed.

"This won't take a minute."

He took the folded copy of the letter from his inside suit jacket and handed it across to Stanwyk while listening for the phone to be answered.

"Here, you can read this while you're waiting. Copies go to those people indicated at midnight, unless I make a coded phone call saying not to send them. Hello, Audrey? Fletcher. Is Alston there?"

Stanwyk had leaned forward across the desk and taken the letter.

Mr. John Collins,
Chairman of the Board,
Collins Aviation
#1 Collins Plaza
Greenway, California

Dear Sir:
Alan Stanwyk murdered me tonight.

The charred remains are mine, regardless of the evidence of the Colgate ring and the gold cigarette lighter identified as belonging to Stanwyk.

Stanwyk boarded a plane chartered from Command Air Charter Service in my name for Rio de Janeiro, where he intends to establish residence under my name with the aid of my passport.

For the purpose, he has bleached his hair blond. He stole the bleach from the apartment of his mistress, Sandra Faulkner, 15641B Putnam Street, Monday night.

With Stanwyk in Rio de Janeiro are a Mrs. Sally Ann Cushing Cavanaugh, and son, William, of Nonheagan, Pennsylvania. Stanwyk has been visiting Mrs. Cavanaugh in Nonheagan on the average of every six weeks for at least four years. This can be confirmed by a pilot called "Bucky" in your employ. Mrs. Cavanaugh was recently divorced from her husband.

Also with Stanwyk in Rio are three million dollars in cash. This money is the result of sales of stock by broker William Carmichael, who believed the cash was required as down payment for a ranch in Nevada being bought through Swarthout Nevada Realty.

Sincerely,
I.M. Fletcher

cc: Joan Collins Stanwyk
    William Carmichael
    Burt Eberhart
    Alston Chambers

"Hello, Alston? Fletch."

"The world's greatest journalist?"

"The very same. How did everything go?"

"Terrific. The affidavits are fine. That handwritten note from Cummings is beyond belief. We picked up your little birds, Witherspoon and Montgomery, and they've been singing all afternoon."

"Are they all right?"

"We have them in protective custody under assumed names in a hospital far, far away from here."

"That's great." Stanwyk was reading the letter a second or a third time. "You do nice work, Alston."

"You made quite a splash in the afternoon paper, Irwin. This case is the biggest local sensation of the year."

"Would you believe I never saw it?"

"You ought to read your own newspaper."

"I can't afford to buy it on a reporter's salary."

Beside the desk were neatly placed two matching attaché cases.

"There is one thing more, Alston."

"What's that, old buddy?"

"You haven't arrested the chief of police yet. It's only a small matter, I know, a minor detail, but the son of a bitch just followed me in his car."

"Where are you?"

"He followed me from The Beach to The Hills."

"Is he still with you?"

"I guess so. It was his car all right. The private car that looks like a police car."

"Fletch, there are federal narcotics agents waiting for him both at the police station and at his home. They've been there for hours."

"Couldn't they get up off their tails and go out into the streets and find the bastard?"

"They don't know the area. You can't outfox a police chief in his own town. If worse comes to worst, we'll catch him at the border."

"Terrific. What about me?"

"Just shout out the window at him. Tell him to go home."

"Thanks."

"Don't worry about a thing, Fletch. They'll get him. And I'll see you in the marine commandant's office at ten in the morning. Be sure to shine your shoes."

"Pick the son of a bitch up."

"We will, we will. Good night, Fletch."

Stanwyk was sitting in the red leather chair with the copy of the letter in his hand. On the table beside him were his Colgate ring and the gold cigarette lighter.

He was staring calmly at Fletch.

"I guess you don't get to do what you want to do," Fletch said.

"I guess not."

"The thing that tipped me off was something your wife said the other night when we were in bed together."

Fletch sat at the desk.

"She said you and I have identical bone structures. We look nothing alike. You're dark, I'm blond. You weigh ten or twelve pounds more than I do. But our bone structures are alike. That's why you picked me from all the drifters on the beach.

"Your plan was to murder me somehow — probably, as you've boxed, with your hands — knock me unconscious, strangle me. Then fake a car accident. Only as a burned corpse could I pass for you. I would be wearing your clothes, your shoes and your ring and carrying your cigarette lighter, burned to death in your car. No one would question it."

"Quite right."

"Are there three million dollars in those attaché cases?"

"Yes."

"You needed a chartered plane to avoid an airlines baggage check. Carrying three million dollars in cash on a commercial airliner would be noticed."

Stanwyk said, "Remarkable. At no point during this last week have I had the slightest sensation of being investigated."

"You thoroughly expected to murder me tonight."

"Yes."

"After investigating you off and on all week, I must say that puzzles me. Generally speaking, you're a decent man. How did you intend to justify murder to yourself?"

"You mean, morally justify it?"

"Yes."

"I have the right to kill anyone who has agreed to murder me, under any circumstances. Don't you agree?"

"I see."

"Putting it most simply, Mr. Fletcher, I wanted out."

"Many people do."

"And now, Mr. Fletcher, what do we do?"

"Do?"

Stanwyk was standing, hands behind his back, facing the French windows. He could not see through the transparent curtain from the lighted room into the dark outdoors. The man was thinking furiously.

He said, "I see I've put myself into a rather difficult position."

"Oh?"

"I can see you are probably going to do precisely as I asked: you are going to murder me."

Fletch said nothing.

"I have arranged the perfect crime against myself. We are alone. No wife, no servants. There is nothing to connect you and me. And

I imagine that in your investigating me this week, you were very careful not to connect you and me."

"I was."

"I have guaranteed your escape. Only you take the charter flight rather than the TWA flight."

"Right."

"The difference is that there are three million dollars at your feet, rather than fifty thousand. Surely that's enough to make any man commit murder."

In the air-conditioned room, Stanwyk's face was gleaming with perspiration.

"The only thing you don't know is that the gun in the desk drawer is empty."

"I do know that. I checked it early this morning. You're right. The servants always do leave the French windows unlocked."

"Therefore, I would guess you have brought your own implement of death, your own gun, and you do mean to kill me. Am I right?"

Fletch opened the top right-hand drawer of the desk.

"No. I just brought a full clip for this gun."

While Stanwyk watched from the windows, Fletch picked up the gun in one hand; with the other hand he took a full .38 caliber clip from his pocket.

"You pointed out to me the benefit of using your gun."

He removed the blank clip from the gun and inserted the full clip.

Stanwyk said, "You're not wearing gloves."

"Nothing a quick dust with a handkerchief can't fix."

"Christ."

"You've not only arranged your own murder perfectly, you've even given me a moral justification for it. You say you have the right to kill anyone who has planned to murder you. Isn't that what you said?"

"Yes."

"So why shouldn't I murder you, Stanwyk?"

"I don't know."

"For three million dollars rather than fifty grand. Alone with you in your house, as you nicely arranged. Using your gun. Nothing to connect us to each other. With a prearranged, guaranteed escape. And a moral justification, provided by yourself. I'm sure I can make it look exactly like the usual burglary-murder you originally described."

"You're playing with me, Fletcher."

"Yes, I am."

"I repeat my original request: if you're going to murder me, do it quickly and painlessly."

"Either the head or the heart. Is that what you said?"

"Have some decency."

"I'm not going to murder you."

Fletch put the gun in his pocket.

"I'm not going to murder you, rob you, blackmail you or expose you. I can't think of a single reason why I should do any of those things. You'll just have to find another way to establish life with Sally Ann Cushing Cavanaugh.

"Good night, Mr. Stanwyk."

"Fletcher."

Fletch turned at the door to the front hall.

"If you're not going to do any of those things, why did you go to all this effort?"

Fletch said, "Beats tennis."

The room shattered.

The light curtains over the French windows billowed forward as if caught by a sudden puff of wind. There were two explosive cracks. Glass tinkled.

The front of Stanwyk's chest blew open. His arms and chin jerked up. Without his having stepped, his body raised so that the toes of his black shoes pointed downward.

From that position, he fell to the floor, his knees thudding against the rug. Stanwyk rolled to his right shoulder and landed on his back.

"Christ."

Fletch knelt beside him.

"You've been shot."

"Who? Who shot me?"

"Would you believe the chief of police?"

"Why?"

"He thought you were me. We have the same bone structure, and you bleached your hair blond."

"He was trying to kill you?"

"Stanwyk, you've killed yourself."

"Am I dying?"

"I don't know how you're breathing now."

"Fletcher. Nail the bastard. Use the money. Nail the bastard."

"I already have."

"Nail the bastard."
"Okay."

With his handkerchief, Fletch removed his fingerprints from the gun and the gun clip. He exchanged clips and returned the gun to the drawer. He dusted the handle to the desk drawer, the telephone, the desk itself, and the outside handle to the French window.

Stanwyk was dead on the rug.

The copy of the letter he had addressed to John Collins was on the table beside the leather chair. Fletch folded it and put it back in his pocket.

Then, taking the two attaché cases, Fletch carefully let himself out of the house.

His MG was parked in front.

THIRTY-TWO

"Ah, Mr. Fletcher."

"I just have to make a phone call. It will take me about twenty minutes."

"Then we'll take your luggage aboard, sir. Just the suitcases and these two attaché cases?"

"Yes. Is there a phone?"

"Use the phone in the office, sir. Just dial nine and then your number. We'll be ready for departure when you are."

Fletch dialed nine and then the recorder number of the *News-Tribune*. He sat at the wooden desk. The door with the opaque glass to the Command Air Charter Service lobby was closed.

"This is Fletcher. Who's catching?"

"It's me, Mr. Fletcher. Bobby Evans."

"How are ya doin', Bobby?"

"Helluva story this morning, Mr. Fletcher."

"Thanks for reading the *News-Tribune*. Look, Bobby, no one's expecting this one. Will you square with the desk for me? I'm in sort of a hurry."

"More of the same?"

"Sort of. I want to get out of here. Another thing, Bobby. I haven't written this story yet. I'm just dictating off the top of my head."

"Okay, Mr. Fletcher."

"So if you hear anything wrong, grab it right away. I can't go back over it."

"Okay."

"Another thing. When I get done with the story I'd like you to take a little note to Clara Snow."

"That isn't usually done."

"I know, but I won't be in the office in the morning. I'm going to have to miss an appointment."

"Okay."

"Is the blower on?"

"Go ahead, Mr. Fletcher."

"Friday A.M. parenthesis fp unparenthesis Stanwyk Murder Fletcher.

"Alan Stanwyk, *one l, a, w-y-k,* thirty-three-year-old executive vice president of Collins Aviation, was shot and killed in the library of his home on Berman Street, The Hills, last night."

"Wow."

"Chief of Police of The Beach, Graham Cummings, is being questioned about the murder."

"Wow, wow. Mr. Fletcher, there hasn't been anything on the police radios about this yet."

"I know. Paragraph three. Police estimate the time of the murder at nine-thirty.

"Paragraph. The body was discovered by the victim's wife, Joan Collins Stanwyk, upon her return from a committee meeting at the Racquets Club at eleven o'clock."

"Mr. Fletcher?"

"What?"

"You said the body was discovered at eleven o'clock."

"I know."

"It's only ten-fifteen now, Mr. Fletcher."

"I know."

"Paragraph. According to a police spokesman, Stanwyk was shot twice in the back through a window by a high-powered rifle. Death was instantaneous.

"Paragraph. Ballistic tests are being made this morning to determine if the murder weapon is the same as the high-powered Winchester rifle Cummings kept slung from the dashboard of his private car.

"Paragraph. Cummings, fifty-nine, was named in a *News-Tribune* report yesterday afternoon concerning the source of illegal drugs in The Beach area.

"Paragraph. Evidence presented to the district attorney's office yesterday morning by the *News-Tribune* included affidavits signed by a self-admitted drug peddler, Charles Witherspoon, thirty-eight, alias Vatsyayana, alias Fat Sam, and a self-admitted drug runner, Lewis Montgomery, seventeen, alias Gummy two *m's, y*. Other evidence was a note written in Cummings's hand to Witherspoon concerning the drug traffic.

"Paragraph. Both affidavits named Cummings as the principal source of illegal drugs at The Beach.

"Paragraph. Beach police yesterday discovered the body of a fifteen-year-old girl, Roberta quote Bobbi unquote Sanders no *u*, buried in a sleeping bag in the sand near Witherspoon's lean-to. She died of a drug overdose.

"Paragraph. Warrants for the arrest of Cummings were issued yesterday afternoon.

"Paragraph. Cummings had not been taken into police custody at the time of the murder at the Stanwyk residence.

"Paragraph. This reporter saw Cummings alone in his private car in the area of the Stanwyk residence at eight-thirty last night, and reported seeing him by telephone to assistant district attorney Alston Chambers one *l*.

"Paragraph. There is no evidence that Stanwyk and Cummings knew each other, although Stanwyk's father-in-law, John Collins, president and chairman of the board of Collins Aviation, several times had pressured Cummings as chief of police to discover and destroy the source of illegal drugs in The Beach area.

"Paragraph. Collins lives within walking distance of the Stanwyk house.

"Paragraph. Reportedly, Joan Stanwyk expressed surprise at finding the victim's hair bleached blond. Her husband had dark hair and had not been known previously to bleach it.

"Paragraph. This morning the victim's widow is under heavy sedation in the care of the family physician, Dr. Joseph Devlin of the Medical Center.

"Paragraph. Insurance agent Burt Eberhart has confirmed that Stanwyk's life was insured for three million dollars. The extraordinary amount of insurance coverage is explained by Eberhart as being related to Stanwyk's frequent piloting of experimental aircraft.

"Paragraph. Stanwyk, a native of Nonheagan, Pennsylvania, N-o-n-h-e-a-g-a-n, was a graduate of Colgate College and the Wharton School of Business. As a captain in the Air Force, he flew twenty-four missions over Indochina. Shot down twice, Stanwyk was a recipient of a Purple Heart.

"Paragraph. He served as treasurer of the Racquets, plural, Club. He was a member of the Urban Club.

"Paragraph. Besides his wife, Stanwyk leaves a daughter, Julia, five, and his parents, Marvin and Helen Stanwyk, of Nonheagan, Pennsylvania. Thirty. You got that?"

"Mr. Fletcher?"

"Yes?"

"You mean this all happened last night?"

"No. Tonight."

"But how can you report a murder and even name the murderer when the body hasn't even been found yet?"

"Just make sure everything is spelled right, will you, Bobby?"

"But you say the body is discovered at eleven o'clock and it's only ten-thirty."

"Yeah. I want to make first edition."

"But, Mr. Fletcher, it hasn't happened yet."

"You're right, Bobby. Advise the desk that photographers should be sent out to the Stanwyk residence, but ask them please to wait until the widow gets home and discovers the body. It's only decent. For first edition they can use pictures from the library."

"Okay, Mr. Fletcher."

"One other thing, Bobby. I think I forgot to put in Mrs. Stanwyk's age. She's twenty-nine."

"Right."

"Please insert it."

"What about the note you want me to take to Clara Snow?"

"Oh, yeah. Dear Clara. Leaving; area too hot tonight. Frank says you're lousy in bed, too. Love, Fletch."

"Really?"

"Really."

"You want me to write that?"

"I sure do. Just don't indicate you were the one who typed it. Good night, Bobby."

"Anytime you're ready, Mr. Fletcher."

"I'm ready."

"A woman and child are waiting in the lobby. For some reason she won't say for whom they are waiting. Are they waiting for you? We haven't put their baggage aboard . . ."

"No, they're not waiting for me."

"The boy has mentioned an 'Uncle Alan.' We have no other flights tonight."

Sally Ann Cushing Cavanaugh and son William were standing in the lobby with five pieces of baggage at their feet. The boy was looking through the opened office door at Fletch.

She looked like a wonderful person. A real person. The sort Marvin Stanwyk would like, as would his son. The sort Alan Stanwyk would never have forgotten and always would have needed. The sort of girl who could make a boy give up boxing and a man give up flying. She looked like home.

The boy's stare was level and curious.

"No," Fletch said. "They're not waiting for me."

On the chartered jet was a heavy leather swivel lounge chair into which Fletch buckled himself.

His suitcase and the two attaché cases he had seen stored behind a drop-curtain in the stern.

With a minimum of fuss, and a maximum of silence, the Lear jet lifted into the sky.

It was eleven o'clock Thursday night.

"Would you like a drink and something to eat, Mr. Fletcher?"

"Yes."

The steward wore a white coat and black bowtie.

"Perhaps a drink first?"

"Yes. What's aboard?"

"Beefeater gin. Wild Turkey bourbon. Chivas Regal scotch —"

"What is there to eat?"

"We've stocked both a capon dinner for you, and club steak."

At ten o'clock in the morning, he would not have to be standing in court facing contempt charges for failing to pay his first wife, Barbara, eight thousand four hundred and twelve dollars in alimony.

"That sounds very nice."

"Yes, sir."

"Vermouth?"

"Yes, sir."

"Lemon?"

"Yes, sir."

At ten o'clock the next morning, he would not be standing in court facing contempt charges for failing to pay his second wife, Linda, three thousand four hundred twenty-nine dollars and forty-seven cents in alimony.

"Would you like a martini, sir?"

"I would like two martinis."

"Yes, sir."

"Each made fresh."

At ten o'clock the next morning, he would not be standing in the marine commandant's office, with photographers' flashbulbs popping, having the old tale told again, receiving the Bronze Star.

"Of course, sir."

"Then I would like the capon. Do we have an appropriate wine?"

"Yes, sir. A selection of three."

"All for the capon?"

"Yes, sir."

At ten o'clock the next morning, he would not be standing before the booking desk at the main police station being charged with criminal fraud.

"After the capon, I would like two scotches."

"Yes, sir."

"Cracked ice."

"Of course, sir."

At ten o'clock the next morning, his two ex-wives, Barbara and Linda, each having given up her own apartment, would be moving into his apartment, to live with each other.

"Then I would like the club steak. Fairly rare."

"As another supper, sir?"

"Yes."

"I see, sir."

And shortly after ten o'clock in the morning, a warrant for the arrest of Gillett, of Gillett, Worsham and O'Brien, would be issued, for aiding a fugitive escape justice.

"With the steak I would like an ale. Do we have ale on board?"

"Yes, sir."

"That's fine. It should be very cold."

"Yes, sir."

Fletch was flying over Mexico with three million dollars in tens and twenties in two attaché cases.

"Would you like your first martini now, sir?"

"We'd better start sometime. We're only going as far as Rio."

CARIOCA FLETCH

ONE

aturally the samba drums were beating, rhythms beside rhythms on top of rhythms beneath rhythms. Especially just before Carnival did this modern city of nine million people on the South Atlantic reverberate with the ever-quickening rhythms of the drums. From all sides, every minute, day and night, came the beating of the drums.

"You cannot understand the future of the world without first understanding Brazil." That was the way the trim, forty-year-old Brazilian novelist Marilia Diniz spoke. Informative. Instinctual. Indicative. The umbrella over the cafe table on Avenida Atlantica shaded her eyes, leaving her mouth in the afternoon sunlight. She shrugged her thin shoulders. "Unfortunately, Brazil is beyond anyone's understanding."

Marilia sat across from Fletch in a light dress with only straps over her pale shoulders. Marilia Diniz was the rare *carioca* who never went to the beach.

Laura Soares, more appropriately dressed in shorts, sandals, a halter, more appropriately tanned golden brown, sat to Fletch's right. Laura would always go to the beach.

Fletch was dressed in the uniform he had learned to be innocent, egalitarian: shorts and sneakers.

In front of Marilia and Laura were glasses of beer, *chope*. Fletch had the drink he liked best in all the world: *guaraná*.

"Now that Fletch sees the *Praia de Copacabana* he will never go anywhere else," Laura said. "Maybe I will never even be able to get him to come back to Bahia."

"I'll go back to Bahia anytime," Fletch said. "If your father lets me."

"He'll embrace you. You know that."

"I don't know."

"The first truth about Brazil," Marilia said, "is its absolute toler-
ance."

"Does Brazil tolerate intolerance?"

"I suppose so." Marilia wrinkled her nose. "You see, you cannot
understand."

Across the *avenida* stretched the huge, dazzling Copacabana Beach,
from the Morro do Leme to his left, to the peninsula separating Copacabana from the beaches of Arpoador, Ipanema and Leblon to his
right.

On the beach, among the brightly colored umbrellas and blankets,
were thousands of golden brown bodies, all ages, sexes, their swim-
suits so small on them only their skin, really, was visible, exercising,
taking turns at the provided chin-up bars, reclining on sit-up boards,
running. Within sight of the beach, Fletch counted fourteen soccer
games in progress. Small children played at the water's edge, but
most of the people in the water were doing disciplined swimming.
Proportionately few on the beach were resting. The temperature was
thirty-three degrees centigrade, about ninety degrees Fahrenheit;
it was four o'clock in the afternoon, and the people's energy shim-
mered up from the sand more positively than reflected the strong
sunlight.

At street corners to the right and left of where they sat drummed
samba bands. Boys, men, from fourteen years of age to whenever,
beat on drums of various sizes, various tones as if this were their last
chance to do so, ever. The band to the right wore canary yellow
shorts; to the left, cardinal red shorts. Immediately around each band,
pedestrians stayed to give in totally to the samba awhile, dancing on
the sidewalk, up and down the curb, among the cars parked pride-
fully anywhere. One or two drummers might stop a moment to wipe
the sweat from their chests, bellies, forearms, drink a *chope* to make
more sweat, but a samba band itself never stops, when it moves,
when it stays in one place. A samba band's stopping is as fatal a
thought as your own heart's stopping.

And the people passing on the sidewalk in front of the cafe, the
pedestrians, going from corner to corner, band to band, businessmen
dressed only in shorts and sandals, sometimes shirts, carrying brief-
cases, women in bikinis lugging bags of groceries, barefoot children
running with a soccer ball, walked, lugged, ran, keeping the beat of
the drums in their feet, their legs, their hips, their shoulders. This
moving to the samba instead of just moving gives Brazilians the most
beautiful legs in the world, having a true balance, an ideal proportion

between muscular calves and slim thighs. The groups of gap-mouthed begging children, the cloth of their shorts worn so it almost did not exist, kept their bare feet moving to the rhythm of the drums, making the stillness, the steadiness of their huge dark eyes the more shocking, imploring. To provide a deception of class difference for the tourists, the cafe waiters wore black long trousers and white open shirts and real shoes, but even in their brushing crumbs from the tables, begging children away from someone they had implored too long, they somberly kept the samba beat.

"*Cidade maravilhosa!*" In his chair, Fletch stretched his arms over his head.

"Mysterious city," said Marilia. "Mysterious country."

Fletch said: "The guidebook says something like, 'At first sight of Rio de Janeiro instantly you forgive God for what's visible of New Jersey.' "

"I like New Jersey," said Laura. "Isn't that where Pennsylvania is? I thought so."

"If you cannot understand the future of the world without first understanding Brazil," Fletch said, "I would like to understand more of Brazil's past. Granted, I came to Brazil rather quickly, without really expecting to, without being prepared, but once here I can find out very little of Brazil's history. Even Laura's father —"

Laura giggled and put her hand on his thigh. "Brazil has no past. That's what makes us so mysterious."

Marilia shot a glance at Laura. "You have not heard of *queima de arquivo?*"

A begging child came by and placed one peanut in front of each of them.

Laura laughed. "A while ago a Brazilian airliner crashed on a runway. As anyone's airliner might. Within minutes a crew showed up to paint over the Brazilian how-do-you-call-them? insignias on the airplane. It is our way of preventing what has already happened."

"It means 'burn the record,' " Marilia said.

"It means 'cover up,' " Laura said. "It is the Brazilian way of life. That is why we are so free."

"It has happened more than once," Marilia said. "A government takes power. In disapproval of all that has gone before, it burns the records of previous governments. Like confession, the idea has been to give us a fresh beginning."

"So we are a nation of anarchists," laughed Laura. "We are all anarchists."

"All histories are shame-filled," Marilia said. "Brazil's shames we have expunged by setting fire to them, sending them away on the wind."

At a little distance from them, the pixie, a boy about six years old, watched them with disappointment. They were not eating their peanuts.

Marilia put her sunglasses on her nose and sat back in her chair. "And you, Fletcher?"

Slowly, Fletch ate his peanut.

Instantly the small boy stepped forward and offered to sell Fletch a bag of peanuts.

Fletch took *cruzeiros* out of his sneaker and gave too many to the boy.

He opened the peanut bag and held it out to Marilia.

She shook her head. "Do you practice *queima de arquivo?* Are you in Brazil to burn your record?"

"Many are."

"It would make him Brazilian," Laura said. "Honorary Brazilian."

"Is that why Laura's father does not like you?"

"My father likes him," said Laura. "Loves him. It's only that —"

"Her father," Fletch said, "is a scholar. A professor at the university. A poet."

Now a dozen begging children were around his chair, whispering at him.

"Of course. Otavio Cavalcanti. I know him well. Laura is almost my niece. She should be staying with me, here in Rio."

"He is intolerant of North Americans. I am a North American."

Standing on the sidewalk near the curb, standing uncommonly still, was an old woman, a hag. A long, shapeless white dress hung from her neck. Dark pouches high in her cheekbones made it seem as if she had four dark eyes. All four eyes were staring at Fletch.

"That's not it, precisely," Laura said. "Fletcher can come here to Brazil, to sit in this cafe, drink *guaraná* and watch the women walk. My father is not permitted into the United States of the North anymore, to read his poetry at Columbia University. My father is intolerant of that."

"I have read your father," said Fletch. "He speaks on behalf of the people."

Across the sidewalk the woman in white was staring at Fletch as if he had dropped from the moon.

"And there is something else." Laura shifted in her chair. "You must admit it, Fletch."

"What is it?" Marilia asked.

"My father feels Fletch does not see the difference in the Brazilian people."

"There is no equality like Brazilian equality," Fletch said. "I love that."

"It is not the equality. . . ." Uncomfortably, Laura was looking at Marilia.

"Oh, yes," Marilia said.

"My father says Fletch keeps trying to understand the Brazilian people through other people he has known. He cannot see the other side of us."

"There is much I don't understand," Fletch said.

"There is much you do not accept."

Fletch grinned at his own joke: "There is much I cannot see."

"My father —"

"Your father is a member of a *Candomble*," Fletch said. "An intelligent man like that."

Marilia twisted the cloth braided around her left wrist.

"But he loves Fletch. He says Fletch is surprisingly open, as a person," Laura said.

"As a North American."

"You cannot understand Brazil," Marilia said from behind her sunglasses. "Brazil accepts thieves. The United States of North America will not accept scholars and poets who speak on behalf of the people."

"Am I a thief?" Fletch asked. Clearly the hag staring at him from across the sidewalk thought he was something extraordinary.

"You said you came here rather quickly."

"True."

"You said you did not expect to come here. You were not prepared."

"True."

"You do business with Teo da Costa."

"True."

"Teodomiro da Costa is my good friend. In fact, I understand I will see you both at dinner at his house tonight."

"Good."

"Teodomiro da Costa makes a good business changing hard currencies, like dollars, into *cruzeiros*, into hard commodities, like emeralds, gold. He has become very rich doing so."

At the word *cruzeiros*, the pixies around Fletch stepped even closer and raised the pitch of their imploring whispers.

Fletch said, "I thought he drove a taxi."

"Teodomiro da Costa does not drive a taxi."

Fletch took more money from his sneaker and gave it to Laura to pay the waiter. When Laura paid, speaking Brazilian Portuguese, the bill was sometimes as much as ninety percent less. He gave some *cruzeiros* to the smallest begging child.

"Marilia," Laura said. "In Brazil, a man's past is burned."

"You may burn Fletcher's past," Marilia said. "That is all right. Laura, I do not want to see you burn your future."

"There is no future, either," said Laura. "There is the piano."

"The Brazilians wish for a future," Marilia said.

"Past . . . future," Fletch muttered.

"I said something wrong," Laura said.

"You are staying at The Yellow Parrot?" Marilia asked.

The Hotel Yellow Parrot was on Avenida Atlantica and known to be among the most expensive.

"Yellow Parrot," said Fletch. "You must admit some things in Brazil do not make sense."

"Fletch is okay," Laura said. Then she said something rapidly in Portuguese. "My father loves him."

Down the sidewalk to the right, stepping warily around the samba band sweating in canary yellow shorts, through the dancers, came a North American woman, clearly from the United States, clearly newly arrived, in a light green silk dress moving on her body as she moved, green high-heeled shoes, wearing sunglasses and stupidly carrying her purse like a symbol of rank dangling from her forearm: the California empress.

Laura put her hand on Fletch's forearm. "You okay, Fletch?"

"My God! I mean, why not?"

"Suddenly you turned white."

"Let go of me." Fletch flung off her hand.

He ducked beneath the table and began retying his sneakers.

Instantly there were the seven or eight heads of the pixies under the table with him, to see what he was doing.

Laura's head joined him under the table, too.

"Fletch! What's the matter?"

"*Estou com dor de estomago!*"

The pixies groaned in sympathy for him: "Oooooooohh!"
"You are not sick from the stomach!" Laura said.
"*Estou com dor de cabeca!*"
"Oooooooohh!"
"You are not sick from the head!"
"*Febre . . . nausea . . . uma insolacao. . . .*"
"Oooooooohh!"
Seen relaxed in the shade under the table, Laura's legs were great to look at. Marilia's, although pale, were not so bad either. The sight made him feel better.
"Fletcher! What is the matter with you? Why are you so suddenly under the table?"
"That woman. That woman in green passing by. Don't look now."
The heads of the pixies looked back and forth from Fletch to Laura intelligently, as if they understood.
"So? What about her?"
"She probably thinks I murdered her husband."

T W O

"*Janio!*" With a frightening rush of long white dress through heavy green leaves, the old hag emerged from the bushes in front of them in the small forecourt of The Hotel Yellow Parrot. She was pointing her arm, her arthritically bent index finger at Fletch's face. "*Janio Barreto!*"
Fletch took a step back. His hand gripped Laura's arm.
The hag took a step forward, her finger in Fletch's face. "*Janio Barreto!*"
He thought they had done quite well. They had left Marilia at the cafe, walked half a block to their right, through the samba band on that corner, ignoring the gestures to stay and dance for awhile, turned right, right again on Avenida Copacabana, along that a few blocks, turning right again at the street just beyond The Hotel Yellow Parrot, carefully, looking first, hurried around the corner and the short way along the sidewalk and into the forecourt of the hotel. They were to use the beach entrance to the hotel, as Fletch was not wearing a shirt.

He had forgotten about the hag.

Now she was blocking their way into the hotel entrance.

"Janio Barreto!" she accused, wagging her bent finger in his face. "Janio Barreto!"

Laura stepped forward. She put her hand on the old woman's sleeve and spoke in a soothing voice. Fletch recognized the Portuguese word for *mother* in what Laura said.

"Janio Barreto!" the hag insisted, pointing at him.

Laura spoke quietly to the woman some more.

The uniformed doorman appeared through the main door of the hotel and came through the forecourt to Fletch. "Is there a problem, sir?"

"No. I don't think so. I don't know."

The two women were talking quietly.

"Give her some money," the doorman said. "For charity."

The hag was speaking rapidly now, to Laura.

The old woman kept glancing at Fletch. She was fairly tall and fairly slim, and clearly she could move fast to have gotten to the hotel before them, to have caught them. The leanness of her hands made her fingers seem all the more misshapen. Her brown eyes were huge, clear and intense; her face more wrinkled than drying, caked earth. Thin, iron-gray hair fell from her head like photographed lightning. Her high, cracked voice came through a few blackened teeth.

Now Fletch was hearing the Portuguese words for *wife, husband, father, sons, daughter, boat.*

Listening to the old woman, Laura began taking long, surmising looks at Fletch. Her looks seemed unsure — not of what the old woman was saying, but somehow of Fletch. She was looking at him as if she had never seen him before, or seen him in quite this way.

His face politely averted, the doorman was listening too.

"What is she saying?" Fletch asked.

Laura waited until the old woman finished her sentence.

"She says you are Janio Barreto."

"Who? What?"

"Janio Barreto."

"Well, I'm not . . . whatever. Whoever. Let's go."

Laura's chin came forward a few centimeters. "She says you are."

The hag spoke some more, clearly repeating what she had said before, something about a boat.

Looking into Fletch's eyes, not smiling, Laura said, "She says you are her husband."

"Her husband. Ayuh."

Laura repeated with firmness: "She says you are Janio Barreto, her husband."

Now Laura had the old woman's hands cupped in her own, gently, protectively.

"Of course," said Fletch. "Naturally. Certainly. She's not the first to say that, you know. Or the second. Tell me, does she have a settlement lawyer in California?" The doorman, having heard all, having understood all, turned his head and looked at Fletch. "Tell her she'll have to get in line with her settlement lawyer."

He smiled at the doorman.

The doorman was not smiling at him.

Laura said, "You are her husband, Janio Barreto."

"Hope she sues for settlement under that name. What is this? What's going on? Laura!"

Laura said, "You died forty-seven years ago, when you were a young man, about as you are now. When you were this lady's young husband."

"Good grief."

"You are, how do I say it? Janio Barreto's aura. His other person. His same person." Laura smiled. "She is glad to see you."

"I can tell." Standing in the little forecourt of the hotel, surrounded by thick, deep green bushes, hearing the cars going by in the *avenida*, the voices of the children playing, hearing, of course, the beatings of the samba drums, Fletch felt coldness breaking over him, prickling his skin. "Laura . . ."

Still gently holding the woman's hands, Laura said, "With this woman you have two sons and a daughter. Grown now, of course. They have children of their own. She wants you to meet them."

"Laura, she wants money. I'm not taking on an extended Brazilian family."

The doorman was still studying Fletch.

"You were a sailor," Laura said. "You earned your living from the sea."

The old woman had turned, was facing Fletch, presenting herself to him.

Quietly, Laura said, "She wants to embrace you."

"Laura! My God . . ." Fletch could not help himself from moving somewhat backward, somewhat sideways. There were tears on the old woman's cheeks. Laura had let go of the old woman's hands. He felt a branch of one of the bushes against his bare back. "Laura, what is this? What are you doing?"

"The important thing is . . . ."

The old woman came to Fletch. She raised her arms, put them around his neck. Approaching him, her eyes were soft, loving.

"Laura!"

The doorman held up his hand as if to stop traffic. "Wait, sir. There is more."

The hag's cheek, wet with tears, was against Fletch's. She smelled terribly, of cooking oils, of fish, and of a million other things. Her body pressed against his.

He did not want to breathe. He wanted to gag. The branches from the bushes were stabbing into the skin of his back.

"The important thing is . . . ." Laura's head was lowered. She spoke respectfully. "Is that forty-seven years ago, when you were a young man, in another life, you were murdered."

From the back of his throat, Fletch coughed over the old woman's shoulder.

Then Laura looked up at Fletch, her brown eyes moving rapidly from his left eye to his right to his left. "Now you must tell your family who murdered you!"

Also with his eyes on Fletch's, the doorman nodded solemnly.

Her eyes settled in Fletch's, Laura said, "Clearly you cannot rest until you do."

THREE

"Of course," Fletch said, coming out of the bathroom, a towel wrapped around his waist, "I really don't know how reasonable I want you to be."

"I am very reasonable."

Naked, long, lean, she lay across the rumpled white sheets of the bed reading *Newsweek*. Her wavy black hair fell over her face. The late afternoon sun through the shaded balcony window made consistent the gold in her skin.

"Laura Soares," he said. "From São Salvador da Bahia de Todos os Santos. Studied piano at the university in Bahia, then two years at the London Conservatory."

"I did not like London Conservatory. There is little understanding of Brazilian music there. In a conservatory they conserve music, you know? They don't like to let it expand."

"Sometimes gives concerts. Daughter of Otavio Cavalcanti, scholar and poet. And your mother cultivates orchids and takes photographs."

"My mother grows flowers and takes pictures of them. She is trying to beat time."

Fletch opened the shade more. Their room was at the back of the hotel, overlooking utility areas. Through tall windows in the building across the area, Fletch watched a man painting a room. The man, in undershirt and shorts, had been painting the room during the day and well into the evening since they had arrived at The Yellow Parrot. It looked an ordinary, albeit big, room. The man was either a meticulous painter or had no other work waiting for him.

Fletch said nothing for a moment.

He had gone directly into the shower. The odor of the old woman had clung to him. His face was sticky from her tears, the back of his neck pasty from her caresses.

He had gotten himself thoroughly soaped when the shower curtain drew back and Laura stepped in. She helped him wash, even putting him on his knees in the bathtub, doubling him over, to scrub the back of his neck. She was kneeling before him in the bathtub, the shower water cascading off her head, shoulders, breasts. He began to clean her thighs with his tongue.

After they messed up the bed and each other to the sound of the samba drums coming through the windows, and lying quietly awhile until the sweat dried and made him feel cool, he went back into the shower.

Standing at the window he said, "Questions . . ."

Reading from the magazine, the lean, naked Laura said, "Half your diet should be carbohydrates."

"You're reading about diets? You don't need to improve yourself."

"My mother will be glad to hear about the carbohydrates. Am I saying 'carbohydrates' right?"

"No. But I understand."

"I don't think they talk about carbohydrates in London. I never heard the word. Pasta!"

"Don't you have any questions?" he asked.

"About pasta?" Still she did not look up from the magazine.

"About the woman in the green silk dress. I told you she probably thinks I killed her husband. She's come here to find me."

"So?"

"You haven't asked me about that."

"That has to do with your past. Anyone can make up a story and say it is the past."

"You're not curious?"

"About the future. What time is it?"

He looked at his watch on the bureau. "Nearly seven."

"We cannot be too much on time at da Costa's for dinner. It is not polite to the servants. It gives them too much to do at once. Makes them nervous."

"I have questions."

"Probably. You are a Northamerican."

"Your father is Otavio Cavalcanti. You are Laura Soares."

"That is the past, Fletcher old top."

"I don't get it."

"It has to do with who had the name in the past. Then you forget it. This article says you should eat much more chicken and fish than red meat. It says nothing of rice and beans. *Feijoada.*"

"Are you going to talk to me about that old woman?"

"Forget it, for now. She is not *Yemanjá.*"

"I am not Janio Barreto. Whoever."

"She says you are. She recognized you. She says she studied you carefully while we were at the cafe. Did you notice her?"

"Yes."

"She said you have the identical legs of her husband, the same stomach muscles from pulling the fish nets, the same proportion between your shoulders and your hips. She said the slight slash of your navel is identical."

"Laura . . . ."

"Well, she should know."

"I have never pulled fish nets."

"You have the muscles from Janio Barreto."

"Laura, not many Brazilians have my basic light coloring."

"Some do. Janio Barreto did. Your heads are identical, she says, your eyes."

"I had a similarity to the husband of the woman in the green dress, too."

"Similarity has nothing to do with it. She says you are Janio Barreto, her husband."

"Who was murdered forty-seven years ago."

"Yes."

"I'm a ghost? Is that what she's saying?"

"Partly that. No, you are yourself. You are Janio Barreto. You see, you came to Brazil. You see why, don't you?"

Fletch exhaled deeply. "What is the old woman's name?"

"Idalina. Idalina Barreto."

"What bothers me is that you listened to her. The doorman —"

"Why not?" Laura turned the page of the magazine. "She was talking."

"Laura, you seem to have no regard for the real past. Yet you listen to these impossibilities."

She was studying some health chart in the magazine. "What's real?"

"Which is more real to you?"

"Bananas are good for potassium," she said. "I think I knew that."

"You won't let me explain. You won't explain to me."

"Forget Idalina Barreto, as much as you can, for now."

She flung the magazine aside and looked at him standing between the window and the bureau.

"How are we to know each other?" he asked.

She rolled more onto her back and held one leg, one arm in the air. "By sharing your banana with me."

He laughed.

"I need more potassium."

"Potassium gluconate, I hope."

"Come, come, Janio. I want some more of your potassium."

"I'm not Janio."

"Janio's potassium. Your potassium. Harvest your banana and feed me your potassium."

"You're crazy."

"Come, come, my Janio. It is ripe. I see that it is ripe. I will peel it with my teeth. Let me taste your banana."

"Where's my shoe?" He regretted kneeling on the floor in his long white trousers to look under the bed for his shoe.

She came into the room and stopped. In the bathroom she had bathed and done her hair and also dressed in white slacks and an open white shirt.

"Why is this stone under our bed?"

Sitting back on his haunches, he showed her the small carved stone he found under the bed. "It's a toad. It looks like a toad."

"That," she said.

"Why is there a stone toad under our bed?"

"The maid must have left it there."

"The maid left a stone toad under our bed?"

"Put it back," Laura said. "It may be important to her."

FOUR

"My father's here!" Laura dumped three teaspoonsful of sugar into her *cachaça*. "I hear his voice."

Courteously, Fletch took his glass of *cachaça* from the silver tray held out to him by a houseman. *Cachaça* is a brandy made of sugar cane juice. In Brazil it is courteous to offer guests *cachaça*. It is courteous of guests to accept *cachaça*. Fletch had tried it with some added sugar, much added sugar, no added sugar. *Cachaça* was a taste he had not acquired.

With his glass of *cachaça* in hand, he followed Laura out onto the terrace.

Teodomiro da Costa's house was built somewhat upside down. Entering at street level, one went downstairs to the bedrooms and a small family sitting room, upstairs to the grand living room filled with splendid paintings and other *objets d'art*, upstairs again to a huge reception room complete with full bar. Off the reception room, high above Avenida Epitacio Passoa, overlooking the truly beautiful lagoon Rodrigo de Freitas, was a handsome terrace decorated with green, red, yellow flowering jungle plants.

Now in the reception room a long table had been set with crystal and silver for twelve.

Teodomiro da Costa did well exchanging currencies and commodities. Fletch had invested his money with him.

On the terrace Laura and Otavio were greeting each other with hugs and kisses and rapid talk in Brazilian Portuguese.

Wordlessly, Otavio then shook Fletch's hand.

"Boa noite," Fletch said.

"Otavio has come here to meet with his publisher," Laura said. "He is staying nearby, with Alfredo and Gloria. Have you met them? Alfredo is a marvelous man, true Brazilian, so full of life, generous to a fault. Gloria is a marvelous woman, truly bright, so charming, with a large feminine soul."

"Are they here?"

Laura looked around at the other people on the terrace. "I don't see them."

"They are preparing for the Canecao Ball tomorrow night," Otavio said. "I do not need to prepare. Poets are born in disguise."

"And your mother?" Fletch asked Laura. "She did not come from Bahia?"

"My mother," said Laura. "Orchids you can never leave."

"They are worse than children," agreed Otavio.

"Worse than I was, anyway," Laura said.

Teodomiro da Costa came across the terrace to them. He was a tall man of sixty with the head of a bald eagle. "Fletcher, it is good to have you back. Did you enjoy Bahia?"

"Of course."

"Good. For dinner we are having *vatapa*, a typical dish from Bahia."

Fletch smiled and took Laura's free hand. "I made friends there."

"But Cavalcanti is my friend." Teo kissed Laura on the cheek. "And Laura too."

Otavio said, "We are all friends."

Teo took Fletch's *cachaça* and placed it on the tray of a passing houseman. He said something to the houseman. "I have ordered you a screwdriver," he said to Fletch.

"Is it called a screwdriver in Portuguese?"

Teo laughed. "I called it orange juice, vodka, and ice."

"I must figure out the words for it."

"Not hard."

"To say it rapidly. With firmness."

"Come. I want you to meet da Silva." Slowly Teo guided Fletch by the elbow across the terrace. "Is Laura with you, or with her father?"

"With me."

"Ah! You are so lucky." Teo then introduced Fletch to another sixty-year-old businessman, Aloisio da Silva.

Immediately, da Silva said, "You must come to my office. I have a new computer system. The very latest. Digital. From your country."

"I would be very interested in it."

"Yes. You must come tell me what you think."

The houseman brought Fletch his screwdriver.

"Also, perhaps you have noticed my new building going up. How long have you been in Rio?"

"I was here for three weeks, then I was in Bahia for two weeks. I am back three days."

"Then perhaps you have not noticed my building?"

"Rio is so vibrant."

"Of course. It is in the Centro. Near Avenida Rio Branco."

"I did notice a new building going up there. Very big."

"Very big. You must come and see it with me. You'd be very interested."

"I'd like that."

"It is amazing what a difference computers make when it comes to building a building."

Marilia Diniz appeared with her glass of *cachaça*. She kissed Aloisio and Fletch on their cheeks.

"Are you well, Aloisio?"

"Of course."

"Rich?"

"Of course."

Marilia forever remained a surprise to Fletch. She had to be the only person in Rio with no sun-color in her face. She saw people from a different perspective.

"Marilia," Fletch said. "Something happened to us after we left you."

"Something always happens in Rio." She sipped her *cachaça*. "Listen. Teo has some new paintings. He has promised to show us them after dinner."

"Otavio, perhaps you would help me to understand something."

"Yes?"

Fletch and Otavio Cavalcanti stood alone at the edge of the terrace, looking at the moonlight on the lagoon. Otavio was drinking Scotch and water.

In Brazil, even distinguished scholars and poets are to be called by their first names.

"Does the name 'Idalina Barreto' mean anything to you?"

"No."

"She is not a famous eccentric?"

"Not that I know."

Laura was across the terrace talking with the Vianas.

"I wonder if it is a scam."

"A what?"

"A swindle. Some sort of confidence trick."

"Ah, yes. Trick."

"This afternoon Laura and I were accosted by an old woman, a *macumbeira* of some sort, maybe, dressed in a long white gown, an old woman. She said her name is Idalina Barreto."

From the terrace the samba drums could be heard only faintly.

"Yes?"

"She said I was her husband."

Otavio turned his head to look at Fletch.

"Her dead husband. Janio Barreto. A sailor. Father of her children."

"Yes . . ."

"That Janio was murdered when he was young, at my age, forty-seven years ago."

"Yes."

"Are you hearing me?"

"Naturally."

"She demands that I tell her who murdered me."

Otavio was looking at Fletch as had Laura, as had the doorman at The Hotel Yellow Parrot. Then his eyes shifted in a circle around Fletch's head.

"Will you help me to understand this?"

Then Otavio took a drink. "What's there to understand?"

At the long table at dinner they talked of the magic in much Brazilian food which provides so much energy, the masses of sugar usually placed in the coffee, in the *cachaça*, the sweetness of *cachaça* anyway, the *dende* oil in the *vatapa* they were having for dinner. The drink, *guaraná*, is without alcohol and also gives energy. It was said by the Indians that it cleared the blood channels going to and coming from the heart. Fletch had discovered that it relieved tiredness.

Down the table, Laura said, "Bananas are good for you, too. There is potassium in bananas."

Then Marilia asked about the paintings Teo had bought.

"I'll show them to you after dinner. Perhaps, first, Laura will play for us."

"Please," said the Viana woman.

"Certainly."

"Then I will show them to you," Teo said.

Aloisio da Silva asked Fletch, "Have you visited the Museu de Arte Moderna?"

"Yes."

"I should think you'd be very interested in that building."

"I am very interested in the building. It is a wonderful building. And I had a splendid lunch there." The people at table became silent. "There were few paintings in the museum when I was there."

"Ah, yes," Marilia said.

"I was thinking of the building," Aloisio said.

"There was a fire . . ." Teo said.

"All the paintings were burned up," the Viana woman said. "Very sad."

"Not all. A few were left," Viana said.

Aloisio blinked at his plate. "I was thinking the building would interest you."

Fletch said, "The paintings in the museum got burned. Is this another case of *queima de arquivo?*"

The silence at the table was complete.

From the head of the table, Teodomiro da Costa looked down at Fletch. A virus a few years before had given da Costa's left eye a permanent hooded effect, which became worse when he was tired, or wished to use it on someone. He was now using it on Fletch.

"It is a good thing, I think," Fletch said into the silence, "for the artists of each generation to destroy the past, to begin again. I think perhaps it is necessary for them."

It was many moments, then, before conversation flowed smoothly again.

"You have Laura, I see. I am glad." Viana sat next to Fletch on the divan in the living room. They were waiting for Laura Soares to play the piano. "You must be very careful of women in Rio."

"You must be very careful of women everywhere."

"That is true. But women in Rio." He sipped his coffee. "Even I. Late at night. Have found myself dancing with one of them. A man, you know. An operated-on man. It is more easy than you think to be tricked."

"Not anything is as it seems in Brazil," Fletch said.

"It is easy to be tricked."

Laura played first some Villa Lobos, of course, then some of her own arrangements of the compositions of Milton Nascimento, somehow keeping in balance his romantic sweetness, his folkloric virility, his always progressing, complicated, mysterious melodic lines. At the side of the room, in a deep armchair, Otavio Cavalcanti dozed over his coffee cup. Then she played arrangements of other deeply folkloric Brazilian music Fletch did not recognize.

Laura Soares must have used piano technique she learned at the London Conservatory, but she played none of the music she had learned there.

After everyone except Otavio, her father, had applauded, Laura said, "Not so good." She smiled at Fletch. "I have practiced little the last two weeks."

"We have come to see your new paintings, Teo!" So the young man first into the reception room announced. With his white open shirt and slacks he wore a forest green cape, a green buccaneer hat, green shoes. Immediately, his eyes found Fletch across the room.

"I've been waiting for you," Teo said from the bar.

Just suddenly they were there, four young men dressed expensively, tailored perfectly, each in his own style, moving slowly, expectantly into the big reception room at the top of the house like a theatrical troupe taking over a stage. All but one had lithe bodies, the graceful ways of moving one would expect from fencers, acrobats, or gymnasts. The fourth was heavier, duller in the eye, maybe a little drunk, and moved unevenly.

"Toninho!" the women cried.

The Viana woman smothered him with kisses.

"Tito! Orlando!" No one seemed to greet the fourth young man immediately. Someone finally said, "Norival! How do you find yourself?"

Tito was dressed entirely in black. His shirt and slacks had to have been fitted to him while they were wet. No seams showed in his clothes.

Orlando wore blue stripes down the sides of his white slacks, blue epaulettes on his shoulders.

And Norival was dressed as expensively, but somehow the earthbrown pockets in his light green slacks and shirts did not seem so amusing.

The people had surrounded the four young men, three of whom were uncommonly handsome, and were talking in Portuguese and laughing. Laura had gone to give each of them a hug and kisses.

Fletch ordered a *guaraná* from the barman.

Not only had the dinner been cleared from the long table in the reception room during Laura's recital, the long table itself had disappeared.

Their backs to the room, some paintings had been placed on the floor along one wall.

One easel had been set up in the best light of that room.

Now Toninho stood in that light, in front of the easel, making gestures with his arms which made his green cape ripple in that light. Whatever he was saying was making the people around him laugh. He seemed to be charming even his companions, Tito, Orlando, and Norival.

Laura's eyes were shining happily when she came back to Fletch.

"Who are they?" he asked.

"The Tap Dancers. They are called the Tap Dancers. Just friends of each other. It's just a name."

"Do they dance?"

"You mean, professionally?"

"Yes."

"No."

"Sing?"

"No."

"Do tricks?"

"They are just friends."

"Fashionable, I think."

"Aren't they sleek?"

Hand emerging from his cape, Toninho came forward to shake hands with Fletch.

"Toninho," Laura said happily. "This is I.M. Fletcher."

"Ah, yes." Toninho's eyes were as brilliant as gems and as active as boiling water. "Janio Barreto. I am Toninho Braga."

"You know about that?" Fletch shook hands.

Toninho flung his arms up, sending his cape back over his shoulders. Clearly, in his eyes, he was enjoying his own act; possibly, confident in his virility, he was satirizing fashion, fashionable behavior. "The whole world knows about that!"

Teo da Costa came into the group.

Laura said something to Toninho in Portuguese. Toninho answered, briefly, and she laughed.

"Fletcher," Teo da Costa said quietly, "within the next day or so, I would like to talk with you. Privately."

"Of course."

"Your father is not here. Not looking into your life . . ."

With great dignity, Teo's face was averted.

"Of course, Teo. I'd appreciate it."

"Come, Teo!" Toninho exclaimed. "The paintings! We came to see your new paintings!"

One by one, Teo placed the paintings on the easel and let his guests study, enjoy them. They were by Marcier, Bianco, Portinari, Teruz, di Cavalcanti, Virgulino. For the most part they were clear, even bold, in the bright, solid earth colors. Especially did Fletch like one of a mother and child, another of a child with a cage. All the rhythms and colors and feelings and mysteries of Brazil were in the paintings, to Fletch.

Later, Fletch sat on the divan next to the sleepy Otavio Cavalcanti.

"You like the paintings?" Otavio asked.

"Very much."

"Better than the museum building?" Otavio smiled. "You are a Northamerican. Everyone expects your passion to be for buildings and computers and other machines."

"Yes."

"Teo perhaps has the best collection, now that the museum is just a wonderful building again."

"He must be careful of fire."

To that, Otavio did not respond.

"Perhaps you can tell me this," Fletch said to Otavio. "Getting dressed tonight, looking for a shoe, I discovered a small carved stone under my bed."

Otavio raised one eyebrow.

"A small stone. It was carved into a toad. A frog."

Otavio sighed.

"Why would the maid put a stone toad under my bed?"

Slowly, heavily, Otavio Cavalcanti lifted himself off the divan. He went to the bar and got himself a Scotch and water.

"Come on." Laura samba-walked across the room, holding her hands out to Fletch. He sat alone on the divan, thinking of *Ilha dos Caicaras*. He was thinking of himself as *Ilha dos Caicaras*, a small island in the lagoon. "I worked enough. I played a little concert. Let's go with the Tap Dancers."

"Where are they going?"

Otavio was drinking alone at the bar.

"Seven-oh-six. Toninho wants us to go with them. To hear the music. To dance."

"Everyone?"

"Just you and me. And the Tap Dancers."

Fletch got up from the divan. "Why do I keep asking your father questions? Great scholar. I have never gotten an answer yet."

Laura glanced at her father at the bar. "Come on. If you have foolish questions, the Tap Dancers will have foolish answers for you. You'll get along fine together."

FIVE

"Toninho must always make an entrance," Laura said in the dark nightclub. "I think he does so on purpose."

"Do you really think so?" Fletch mocked.

Fletch and Laura had driven in his yellow two-seater MP convertible directly from the sidewalk in front of da Costa's house to the sidewalk in front of 706.

The Tap Dancers had disappeared in their own black four-door Galaxie.

At the door, Laura spoke to a young waiter, and instantly three tables for two were pushed together for them. Of course the band in the club was playing. The music would be nonstop. As soon as Laura and Fletch sat at the table, a waiter brought a bottle of whiskey with a marked strip of tape down its side, a pitcher of water, a bucket of ice and many glasses.

"What did you tell the waiter?" Fletch asked through the sound of the drums.

"That the Tap Dancers are coming."

"They are that famous?"

"Everyone loves the Tap Dancers."

"They're sleek."

"Yes. They're sleek."

In a moment, they appeared in the door. Each wore the mask of a cat over his face. There were four girls with them.

Even without making noise, they soon had everyone's attention. They began to sniff up and down the walls, along the tables, through a foreign lady's bouffant, curious about everything, until they found their own table.

Even the man who was singing at the moment laughed. The sound of his laughter through the amplifier in the middle of a song was delightful.

As the catlike Tap Dancers found their table and sat down, even those who were dancing applauded them.

One squeezed in beside Fletch and took off his mask. Toninho. Fletch expressed the appreciation of having been tricked that he had learned was appropriate in Brazil.

Fletch said, "Laura suspects you make big entrances on purpose."

Smiling, face flashing even in the near-dark, Toninho took off his buccaneer's hat. "What's fun?"

Fletch said, "What's fun?"

"Moving." Toninho looked at his hand on the table, directing Fletch's attention to it. He raised and lowered his ring finger. "That's fun," he said. He raised his ring finger, little finger and thumb, and lowered them. "That's more fun." Then his hand on the table became terrifically animated, the fingers fluttering, doing their own crazy dance, the hand itself becoming some sort of a crazed rabbit trying to keep up its own wild beat. Watching it, Toninho laughed. "That's most fun."

"Have you ever had experience with paralysis?" Fletch asked. "Have you ever been paralyzed?"

Toninho's big brown eyes swelled. "I have the wisdom to know that one day I will be."

Introductions to the girls were made. Fletch got none of their names right, over the sound of the music. They clearly were glad and impressed to be there, to hear such good music, have access to the Scotch. Fletch calculated it had taken the Tap Dancers less than ten minutes to find these girls.

"Toninho," Fletch said. "Why would the hotel maid place a small carved stone toad under my bed?"

"A toad?"

"A frog."

"Was there a frog under your bed?"

"Yes. There still is."

"How do you know?"

"I found it while I was looking for my shoe."

Toninho's eyes twinkled. "What did you do with it?"

"I put it back."

"That's good." Toninho shed his cape then, and took a girl dancing to the dance floor.

For a while they all danced. The music was marvelous. Rather, Fletch danced. The Brazilians, including Laura, simply continued their being Brazilian, keeping the rhythm of the constant music anyway, their constant rhythmical movements anyway, onto the dance floor where they simply glided into full reaction to the music.

A young girl in leather jeans and a jersey which did not make it to the top of her jeans began to sing. She was extraordinarily good. They all sat at the table to listen to her.

The tape which ran down the side of the whiskey bottle was marked off in ounces. To calculate the bill, the waiter counted the ounces of whiskey missing from the bottle and charged them for that. The Tap Dancers' girls moved the whiskey level down the tape with happy alacrity.

The band did not stop when the girl put the microphone back on its stand. Everyone stood to cheer her and she danced into the dark at the back of the nightclub.

One of the Tap Dancers' girls, who had been staring at Laura, finally asked, in Portuguese, "Are you Laura Soares, the pianist?"

"I play piano."

Tito was sitting across from Fletch.

"How did you people know about Janio Barreto?" Fletch asked him.

"About your being Janio Barreto?" Tito seemed to be correcting him.

"About that incident this afternoon."

"Is it not something to know?" Tito's face was handsome and happy, too, but his eyes could not have Toninho's sparkle.

"How did you hear of it?"

Tito leaned forward across the table. "We're all very eager to hear what you will have to say."

"About what?"

"About how you came to die. Who murdered you."

"Tito, Tito. Am I never to get sensible answers?"

"Tell me one thing, Janio."

"Don't call me Janio."

"Fletch. How do you think you came to be in Brazil?"

"I am a newspaperman from California. I had an airplane ticket."

"How did you come to have the airplane ticket?"

"Sort of by accident."

"You see?"

"No. I don't see."

"Look around this room." Without moving his head, Tito shot his eyes all the way to the left and moved them slowly in a straight line all the way to the right. There was something spooky in this controlled use of his eye muscles. "Do you see others here like you?"

"What do you mean?" Mostly the room was full of young Brazilians, a few older Argentinians, the foreign lady with her large bouffant and small escort.

"Other newspapermen from California who 'had an airplane ticket' and came here 'sort of by accident'?"

"Tito . . ."

"No. You are here."

"Why was I born?"

"Maybe that too." Tito sat back. "Now that you know what you must do, you will never rest until you do it."

"What must I do?"

"Tell us who murdered you. Murder is the most serious crime."

"Tito . . ."

A conspiracy of girls yanked Tito dancing.

Fletch finally poured himself a Scotch and water and sat back.

Then he and Laura danced awhile.

When it was very late in the night he found himself sitting at the end of the table with Norival, who was having difficulty keeping his eyes open and his tongue straight, being told, even being asked, about various kinds of fish available in the South Atlantic.

Slowly it occurred to Fletch that Norival was talking to him as Janio Barreto, who had fished these waters fifty years ago.

Fletch decided it was time to leave.

As he stood up, he said to Norival, "Much has changed in these waters in fifty years."

He went to the dance floor and cut in on Orlando and asked Laura if they could leave.

Outside the nightclub, on the sidewalk, Toninho called after him.

Fletch turned around.

Again, Toninho said, "Fletch," but he did not approach. He stayed near the door of 706.

Laura sat in the MP.

Fletch went back to Toninho.

It would be dawn soon.

"Fletch." Toninho cupped his hands around Fletch's left ear and put his lips in his cupped hands. "A woman puts a frog under their bed to keep her lover from leaving her."

Fletch stood back. "It wasn't the maid?"

"Are you the maid's lover?" Toninho laughed. He slapped his thigh with his hand. "Oh, Fletch!" He put his hand on Fletch's shoulder and shook him. "Be glad." Then he laughed again. "Also because traditionally it is a live frog!"

S I X

"Restless."

"Of course," she said.

This was the third time he had gotten out of bed in a half hour.

The first time, he went to the bathroom and drank from the bottle of mineral water. Then he tried snuggling up next to Laura so that all of his front touched all of her back. She breathed deeply, asleep. The second time he put his head through the drapes and saw the daylight of another morning. No electric lights were on. In bed again, he tried lying straight on his back, his hands folded across his chest as if he were in a coffin, and breathing deeply. Even at that hour, from somewhere in the city he could hear the samba drums.

Now he put on his light running shorts.

Laura raised her head from the pillows and looked at him.

"I'm going for a run on the beach," he said. "Before the sand gets too hot."

"Okay."

"I can't get to sleep."

"I know," she said. "Poor Fletch."

She put her head back down on the pillows.

SEVEN

" **C**an you buy me a cup of coffee?"
Joan Collins Stanwyk.
She was waiting for him, smoking a cigarette, at a little
table in the forecourt of The Hotel Yellow Parrot when
he came back from his run. There were three crushed cigarette butts
in the ashtray on the table.

Her eyes ran over the sweat gleaming on his shoulders, chest,
stomach, even on his legs.

Having finished his run with a sprint, he was breathing heavily.

"That's the least I can do for you," he said.

Two miles up the beach there had been a crew of men dressed in
orange jackets fanned out like a search party cleaning the beach, and
Fletch had run to them, and back. As he ran barefoot, he avoided
several *macumba* fires smoldering from the night before. And he passed
many dead wallets, purloined, stripped and dropped. Even at that
hour, many other people were running on the beach. And a group
of Brazilian men easily in their sixties were playing a full game of
soccer barefooted in the sand.

Coming back across Avenida Atlantica, the roadway was almost
unbearably hot on his bare feet, and it was not yet seven o'clock in
the morning.

The bar, which was the middle door at the front of The Hotel
Yellow Parrot, of course was closed. Fletch pressed the service bell
beside the door.

"Let's see if that brings someone." He sat across from Joan at the
little table.

He folded his slippery arms across his slippery chest.

The forecourt, with thick green bushes headhigh on three sides,
had brilliant streaks of morning sunlight in it.

This morning Joan Collins Stanwyk looked less the California empress. She was dressed in a light, tan slack suit, white silk shirt, and
sandals. Her hair was not in its usual impeccable order. Her face

looked haggard, her eyes sleepless. She might still have been suffering jet lag; she might also have been suffering from her martinis and her cigarettes and, of course, from her recent widowhood.

"How are you?" he asked.

"I've been better."

"Did you come here to find me? I mean, to Rio?"

"Of course."

"How did you work it out? Where I went?"

"Did you forget Collins Aviation has its own security personnel? Mostly retired detectives who are very good at finding out things? Although, I admit, sometimes not fast enough." There was no humor in the irony of her statement. "And did you forget that I was born, bred, and educated to do a job? And that I'm rather good at it?"

She was the daughter of John Collins, who had built a mammoth airplane company out of his own garage in California. Wife, now widow, of Alan Stanwyk, the late chief executive officer of that company. A famous socialite, executive hostess for both her father and her husband, famous blonde, long-legged, tennis-playing Californian beauty who had known her function in that world of fast cars and slow parties and had once, shortly before, surprised Fletch at how well she had performed, or tried to perform.

"I haven't forgotten."

A waiter appeared.

Fletch ordered coffee for Joan and *guaraná* for himself.

She said, "You're absolutely gorgeous, wet with sweat. You have the same build as Alan had, but there is so much more light in your skin."

He tried to shave the sweat off his chest and stomach with the side of his index finger. "I don't have a towel. I've been running. I —"

A slight jerk of her head stopped him. There was something smoky about her eyes. He was looking at a woman whose life, whose whole world, had been deeply violated by circumstances, probably for the first time in her life.

"If you came here for a full explanation —"

She stopped him. "I need your help." Her hand shook before she put her fingers against her cheek and stroked the area in front of her ear. "Let's forget for now why I came here. Ironically enough, you're the only person I know in Rio, and I have to ask you to help me." Her voice was very soft.

She collected herself while the waiter set coffee in front of her, the can of *guaraná* and a glass in front of Fletch.

"I knew you were here," Fletch said. "I saw you yesterday on the *avenida*. You were wearing a green silk dress. And carrying a handbag."

"Oh, yes," she said bitterly.

"I hid from you." He poured his *guaraná*. "I was just so surprised to see you. How did you find out where I was staying?"

"I just called all the best hotels, and asked for Mister Irwin Maurice Fletcher. I knew, of course, you could afford the very best accommodations." Again, naturally, there was no humor in her irony. "Just went down the list of first-class hotels. When I asked for you here, at The Yellow Parrot, they rang your room. No answer. So I knew where you were staying."

"Why are you sitting in the forecourt waiting for me at six-thirty in the morning?"

"I had no choice. It was the next thing to do, the only thing to do. After the most horrible night . . . I walked down from the hotel. While I was still up the block I saw you starting out for your run, going across the street. I wasn't about to run after you up the beach."

"No."

"I was robbed," she said.

"Oh."

"You say that with such aplomb. As if you knew it."

"I guessed it."

"How?"

"You don't know about Rio?"

"I guess not enough."

"It's a marvelous place."

"Terrific," she said.

"You going to give me all the details?"

"You sound like you've already heard them."

"I think I have."

"Robbed twice."

"Not a record."

"Robbed of everything." A tear appeared in the corner of her eye.

"Baptized," he said.

"Last night, after I found out which hotel you were in, I considered coming and camping out in the lobby until you showed up, but from what I've heard of Rio nightlife, that didn't make much sense."

"No."

"At least not for such a healthy, wealthy, attractive young man."

At first Fletch thought he would let this irony pass over him. Then he said, "I wasn't in."

"So I went out myself. I went for a walk. Right along here." She indicated the *avenida* beyond the hedge. "Sat in a cafe, had a drink, watched the people, listened to the drums. Walked further, to another cafe, had a drink. Couldn't pay the bill. My purse was gone."

"Yes." In his saying "yes," Fletch heard an echo of Otavio Cavalcanti. *Yes. Of course. What is there to understand?*

"My wallet was gone. All my cash. My credit cards." Tears now were in both her eyes. "My passport."

"It happens to everyone I have heard of," he said.

"My necklace was gone!" She seemed astounded. "A diamond pin I was wearing on my dress!"

"Yes."

"What bothers me most is that pictures of Alan in my wallet are gone. Of Alan and Julia." Julia was her young daughter. "No matter what you may think, I wanted those pictures of Alan. They're irreplaceable."

Tears rolled down her cheeks.

Fletch said: "Yes."

She reached for a purse that wasn't there. "Damn! I don't even have a handkerchief."

Fletch shrugged his bare shoulders. "I don't even have a sleeve."

She sniffed.

"I explained to the waiter as best I could that I couldn't pay him. I'd been robbed. That I would come back and pay him today." Joan Collins Stanwyk sniffed again. "I swear, Fletch, all during my walk, nobody even touched me. No one bumped into me. How did they get my necklace? The pin off my dress? There wasn't even a tear in my dress. I felt nothing!"

"The future of Brazil," said Fletch, "is in surgery."

"I went back to my hotel."

"And your room had been burglarized."

"How did you know?"

"You said you'd been robbed twice."

"Everything!" she said. "Everything except my clothes. My jewel case, my traveler's checks."

"Everything."

"Everything. I haven't a thing. This morning I don't have a dollar, a *cruzeiro*, a credit card, a piece of jewelry."

Fletch said: "Yes."

"I went downstairs to the hotel manager immediately. The assistant manager, that time of night. He came to the room with me, clucked and hissed and t'ched like a barnyard, figured the thieves must have come in over the balcony, scolded me for leaving the balcony door unlocked — Good heavens, I'm on the ninth floor. It was a warm night."

"Took no responsibility."

"I spent hours with him in his office. He said I should have left all my valuables in the hotel safe. Apparently they handed me a slip of paper when I checked in with that written on it. He took me back to my room and showed me the sign on the inside of the door advising me to lock the balcony doors, to put my valuables in the hotel safe. We went back to his office. I filled out lists of things that are missing. I kept asking him to call the police. For some reason, he never called the police."

"No reason for disturbing them."

"What do you mean?"

"They've heard the story, too."

"Fletch, I was robbed. Of thousands and thousands of dollars worth of things. Money, jewelry, my credit cards."

Again Joan Collins Stanwyk sniffed.

"The police would know all that."

"Will you help me?"

"Of course."

She clutched her hands in her lap. "I feel so violated."

"Disoriented?"

"Yes."

"Stripped naked?"

"Yes!"

"Totally lost without all your possessions?"

"Yes, yes!"

Fletch sat back in his chair. His sweat had dried in the air. "I think that's part of the idea."

"What are you talking about?"

"Who are you?"

"I am Joan Collins Stanwyk."

"Can you prove it?"

Her eyes searched the stone floor of the forecourt. "As a matter of fact, I can't. No credit cards. No checkbooks. No passport."

"How does it feel?"

"How does what feel?"

"To be whatever you are right now."

Her eyes narrowed. "I did not come to you for psychological therapy, Mister I.M. Fletcher."

"Thought I'd throw it in. No extra charge."

"I need money."

"Why?"

"I want to get out of that damned hotel. I want to pay my bill and get out of that damned hotel. I don't even have taxi fare."

"Okay. But why don't you call home? To California? Your father?"

"He's on his yacht. The *Colette*. Trying to recuperate from Alan's —"

"And you came here, to look for me."

She shrugged. "Recuperation."

"Doing your job. As you see it."

"Yes."

"Striving. Being Joan Collins Stanwyk, come hell or high water."

"Are you going to help me? I want to go —"

"Tell me. Your family has offices stuffed with people looking out for you. Security personnel. Lawyers. Accountants. Why haven't you called them?"

Her head lowered. After a moment, she said, softly, "It's Saturday. In California, it's before dawn Saturday morning."

He laughed. "And you can't wait? You'd rather come to me, whom you pursued to Rio de Janeiro, than wait until your daddy's offices open?"

"I want to get out of that hotel. That man made me so angry."

"It is essential to you, under the circumstances, that you talk to someone who knows who you are."

She blinked at him. "What?"

He put his forearms on the table. "I was robbed. Wallet, cash, driver's license. Not my passport. My watch. My Timex watch."

"Within the first twenty-four hours you were here?"

"Within the first six hours. People warn you, but you cannot believe it. You have to go through it yourself. It's a baptism."

"What do you mean, *baptism?*"

"You learn to use the hotel safe, carry what money you need immediately in your shoe. And to not wear jewelry. Not even a watch."

"Fletcher, I lost thousands of dollars, everything I have with me."

"You lost your identity."

"Yes. I did."

"You lost your past."

"Yes." Joan Collins Stanwyk was frowning at the bushes.

"Do you feel more free?"

Now she was frowning at him. "What?"

"Now you are equal, you see."

"The people who stole my possessions aren't equal."

"Oh, sure. That's widely dispersed. Come here a moment, will you?"

He got up from the table and stood in the opening of the hedge.

After a moment, she got up and came to him.

Together they looked across the city sidewalk where people were beginning to go about their daily business, across the wide city avenue filling up with taxis and commuters, to the beach, beginning to fill up with people of all ages walking, running, jumping, doing pull-ups, swimming.

Drums could be heard from down the road.

"There's not a pair of long trousers in sight, is there?" he asked.

"Very few shirts," she said.

"No wallets. No identities. No class paraphernalia: no jewelry." He looked at her tan slack suit, silk blouse, high-heeled open-toed sandals. "They have their bodies. Their eyes, their arms, their legs, their backs."

"Their fingers, damn them."

"I think we're being told something."

"Have you gone Brazilian? In just a month?"

"Naw. I won't be *carioca* until I can walk across that *avenida* in bare feet at high noon."

She turned to go back to the table. "Sounds to me like you're giving some fantastic intellectual, political rationale for their out-and-out thievery." She sat down at the table. "But I guess you have every reason to."

"To what?"

"To understand."

"This lady I know . . . ." Fletch too sat down at the table. "She writes novels. I doubt I've got it straight, but she told me there is some ancient ritual here, a religious ritual, for which the food, in order to be acceptable by the ritual-masters, must be stolen."

Joan Collins Stanwyk sighed. "Enough of this. I've been robbed. I need help. If I weren't desperate, I wouldn't have come to you."

"I guess so."

"Will you please come to the police station with me?"

"If that's what you want."

"I must report this."

"It won't do any good."

"Fletcher, I've been robbed, of thousands of dollars —"

"You have to pay a fee."

"What?"

"To report a robbery to the police, you have to pay a fee."

"You have to pay the police money to tell them you were robbed?"

"It's a lot of paperwork for them."

She swallowed. "Is that all it is? Paperwork?"

"Yes. I think so. In most cases." He scraped his chairlegs on the stone pavement. "You are warned, you see. Robbery here is not uncommon. No one can deny that. It is also common in New York, Mexico City, and Paris."

She was beginning to have to squint into the sunlight to see him. A beam of sunlight was coming through a break in the hedge. "But here, you say, they're doing you a favor to rob you."

"You might as well think that."

"They rob you with philosophy."

"It's not considered such a bad thing to relieve you of your possessions, your identity, your past. What is yours is theirs is mine is ours . . ."

Her white face was stonelike. Her jaw was tight.

He said, "I'm just trying to make you feel better."

"Fletcher, are you going to let me have some money? Right away?" Her fingers gripped her temples. Her whole head shivered. "At the moment, we won't go into the source of that money."

"Of course. I'll bring some to your hotel. I have to get out of these wet shorts and shower and get them to open the hotel safe."

"Very well."

When she stood, she looked very pale and she seemed to sway on her feet. She closed her eyes a moment.

"You all right?"

"I'll be all right."

"What hotel are you in?"

"The Jangada."

"Very posh."

"Bring lots of money."

"We'll have breakfast together. At your hotel."

"Yes," she said. "Come straight to my room with the money. Room nine-twelve."

"Right." He had been in a bedroom of hers before.

He walked with her to the break in the hedge.

"I'd send you back in a taxi," he chuckled, "but I'm not wearing shoes."

Distantly, she said, "I'd rather walk."

EIGHT

There was no answer when he tapped at the door of Room 912.

He knocked louder.

Still the door did not open.

He knocked again and then placed his ear against the door. He could hear nothing.

As quietly as possible, in his own room at The Hotel Yellow Parrot, Fletch had showered and changed into fresh shorts, a shirt, sweat socks and sneakers. Laura was still sleeping. He left a note for her, *I have gone to the Hotel Jangada to have breakfast with someone I know.*

He had driven the short distance between the hotels in his MP.

After knocking on Joan Collins Stanwyk's door at The Hotel Jangada, he went back down to the lobby and called the room on the house phone.

No answer.

At the hotel desk, he asked the clerk, "Please, what is the number of Joan Collins Stanwyk's room? Mrs. Alan Stanwyk?"

The clerk consulted his plastic-tabbed file. "Nine-twelve."

"She hasn't checked out, has she?"

The clerk squinted at his file. "No, sir."

"*Obrigado.* Where is your breakfast room, please?"

Joan Collins Stanwyk was not in the breakfast room. She was not in the bar, which was open.

On the terrace of The Hotel Jangada were two swimming pools, one which was in the morning sun, the other which would be in the sun in the afternoon. Already a few were sunning themselves around one pool. Around the pool in the shade a few were having breakfast. Two fat white men had their heads together over Bloody Marys.

Joan Collins Stanwyk was not in the pools area.

On the ninth floor, Fletch knocked at her door again.

From the lobby he called her room again.

At the desk, he left her a note: *Came to have breakfast with you as arranged. Can't find you anywhere. You fell asleep? Please call me at Yellow Parrot. If I'm not there, leave message. Enclosed is taxi money.* — *Fletch.*

"Will you please leave this for Mrs. Stanwyk? Room nine-twelve."

"Certainly, sir."

Fletch watched the desk clerk put the sealed envelope in the slot for Room 912.

"Teo? *Bom dia.*" Fletch phoned from The Jangada.

"*Bom dia*, Fletch. How are you?"

"Very pleased by your new paintings. Thinking of them has made me happy."

"Me, too."

"When do you want to see me?" Three Northamerican oil-rig workers in heavy blue jeans got off the elevator, staggered across the lobby of The Hotel Jangada, and went straight into the bar.

"Any time. Now is fine."

"Shall I come now?"

"We'll have coffee."

NINE

"Y ou do want coffee, don't you?"

"I guess I need it."

A houseman had led Fletch downstairs in Teo da Costa's house to the small family sitting room. Dressed in pajamas, a light robe and slippers, Teo sat behind his glasses in a comfortable chair reading *O Globo.*

"Have a busy night?" Teo folded the newspaper.

"We went to Seven-oh-six. With the Tap Dancers."

"It's a wonder you've had any sleep."

"I've had no sleep."

Standing, Teo nodded to the houseman, who withdrew.

"You look fresh enough. You look like you've been out jogging."

"I have been."

A look of concern flickered across Teo's haughty face.

Fletch said, "I don't feel like sleeping."

"Sit down," Teo said. "Is there anything bothering you?"

Sitting, Fletch said, "Well, I arranged to have breakfast with this person I know, from California. When I went to the hotel, she wasn't there."

"She went out on the beach, perhaps."

"I had arranged to meet her less than an hour before I went to the hotel. She could have fallen asleep."

"Yes, of course. In Rio, night and day get mixed up. Especially as Carnival approaches."

The houseman brought two cups of coffee.

Teo sipped his standing up. "People don't realize it, but Brazil's second-largest export is tea."

After the houseman left, Fletch asked, "You wanted to talk to me, Teo. Privately, you said."

"About what you're doing."

"What am I doing?"

"What are you going to do?"

"I don't understand you."

"Brazil is not your home."

"I feel very comfortable here."

"What would you most like to do in this world?"

"Sit on Avenida Atlantica in Copacabana, eat *churrasco*, drink *guaraná*, and watch Brazilian women of all ages walk. Listen to Laura play the piano. Go to Bahia, occasionally. Run, swim. Jump up and down to the drums. Love the people. I am learning a little Portuguese, a few words."

"Do you mean to stay in Brazil?"

"I haven't thought."

"How long have you been here now? Six weeks?"

"Something like that."

"You've bought a car. You've met Laura." Teo sipped his coffee. "Don't you have any plans?"

"Not really."

Teo put his cup and saucer on a table. "A young man should have plans. You're a young man. From everything I can see, a very healthy young man. You are attractive. You have a brain. Because of the business we have done together, I know how much money you have. I do not know the source of that money, but I know you are not a criminal."

"Thanks."

"I am only speaking to you, Fletch, because I am sixty, and you are only in your twenties. Your father is not here. . . ."

"I appreciate it."

"It is not good for a young man to live without a plan."

"Are you saying I should leave Brazil, Teo?"

"Brazil is a difficult place, even for Brazilians." Teo scratched the back of his head and laughed. "Especially for Brazilians."

"Is this about Laura, Teo?" Fletch fixed Teo in the eye. "Did Otavio Cavalcanti ask you to speak to me?"

Teo used his hooded eye on Fletch. "Brazil is not that way. Not intolerant."

"Otavio is."

Teo laughed. "Otavio Cavalcanti is one of the most liberal men we have. So liberal he cannot go to New York and read his poetry at a university."

"About some things he is liberal. About his daughter . . . ?"

"And what do you think of Otavio?"

"He is a great scholar and poet who does not answer my questions."

"Brazil is difficult to understand."

"Did Otavio speak to you last night, Teo?"

"Yes," Teo admitted. "He did. That is not what concerns me."

"Laura put a frog under our bed."

"Yes," Teo said. "So Otavio told me. You know what that means?"

"I do now."

"You see, you do not know Brazil. Perhaps cannot know Brazil. There is so much here that came from the Nago and the Bantu, particularly the Yoruba. You can have no feeling for it."

"*Saravá Umbanda!*"

"What did you do before you came here? You were a journalist?"

"I worked for a newspaper."

"Then you must make a plan to work for a newspaper again. Buy your own small newspaper, somewhere you want to be. Understand the new technology of communications. Grow along the course you were on."

Fletch sat silently a moment.

Then he finished his coffee.

"Teo, have you heard about this Janio Barreto . . . situation? That I am someone who was murdered here forty-seven years ago — ?"

"Yes. I was told about it last night. It worries me."

"Why?"

"It worries me that you might not understand."

"Of course I don't understand. Perhaps you could help me to understand."

"I'm sure the woman — What's her name?"

"Idalina. Idalina Barreto."

"I'm sure the woman is entirely sincere in what she believes. There is no scam, swindle. There is no trick involved, as you asked last night."

Upstairs, a vacuum cleaner was being run.

"Teo, do you personally give any credence to such a thing?"

"Do I think you are a peri-spirit?" Teo smiled. "No."

Fletch said, "Phew!"

"I worry that you won't know what to do about it."

"What do I do about it?"

Teo hesitated a long moment. "I don't know either. Brazil is one of the most modern nations on earth . . ." His voice dwindled off.

"I think I understand what you are saying, Teo." Fletch stood up. "I promise I will think."

"It's just that your father is not here."

"I will think of a plan."

In shaking, Teo held Fletch's hand a long moment. "The Tap Dancers," he said. "Your father would not want you to become a tap dancer on life."

TEN

"Laura?"

The window drapes were open. The room had been made up. Fletch pushed the ajar door to the bathroom all the way open.

"Laura?"

There was a note for him on the bureau.

Fletch —

Otavio called. He is feeling too tired to stay for Carnival in Rio. He wants to be home in Bahia. He said this morning he feels too tired to travel alone, through all the Carnival crowds. So I am helping him travel to Bahia.

Surely I will be back Sunday. Enjoy the Canecao Ball tonight even without me. If you get too lonely without me, I have left you Jorge Amado's *Dona Flor and Her Two Husbands* — a great Brazilian classic. And I will bring you a present from Bahia — something I want for you.

Ciao,
Laura

Across the utility area, the man was still painting the room.

The phone rang.

"Janio?"

"Not here, at present."

"Is Fletcher there?"

"Yes, he's here. I think."

"Toninho Braga, Fletch."

"How are you? Have you slept?"

"We thought you might like to spend the day with us. Drive up to a place we know in the mountains. Laura can go shopping."

"Laura's gone to Bahia with her father."

"That's well. Then will you come? A place we know, very amusing, very relaxing. It is important to get away during Carnival."

"Toninho, I haven't slept. I went running."

"This place is very relaxing. You can have a sleep there, after lunch."

"Teo da Costa is expecting me for the Canecao Ball tonight."

"Oh, we'll be back in plenty of time for that. We are going to the ball, too."

"Who's 'we'?"

"Just Tito, Norival, Orlando, and myself. Get away from the women a few hours."

"I think I should try to sleep."

"You don't understand."

"I don't understand anything."

"We are downstairs in the lobby, expecting you."

"Toninho."

"You will come?"

Fletch looked at the freshly made bed. "*É preciso terno?*"

Such was a tourist joke. In Brazil a suit was never necessary.

"You will need no clothes. Do you have money?"

Fletch felt the wad of *cruzeiros* in his pocket he had taken out of the hotel safe for Joan Collins Stanwyk. "Yes."

"Good. Bring your money. We will gamble. We will gamble and take your money away from you."

"Okay."

"You coming right down?"

"Yes."

"You didn't say that."

"I'll be right down."

Before leaving the telephone, Fletch called The Hotel Jangada and asked for Room 912.

There was no answer.

He took a full liter of mineral water from the bathroom.

Before leaving the hotel room, Fletch checked under the bed.

The frog was still there.

ELEVEN

"*Bum, Bum,*" Toninho said.

The black four-door Galaxie was on the sidewalk close to the hedge in front of The Hotel Yellow Parrot. Around it, dressed only in shorts and sunglasses, were the Tap Dancers. Norival, the only one with his belly hanging over his belt, held a can of beer in his hand.

"*Bom dia,* Fletch," Tito said.

"*Tem dinheiro?*"

Tito grinned. "*É para uso pessoal.*"

In front of the hotel, half in the road, half on the sidewalk, a samba band was beating its drums at full strength in the strong Saturday morning sunlight. At their center was an old pickup truck casually decorated with palm fronds, some of which had been dyed purple and red. Seated in the back of the pickup trick, facing backward, was a huge black *papier-mâché* monster. Its arms were out, to embrace; its eyes were big and shiny; its smile was friendly. A girl dressed only in a G-string and pasties sat on the monster's head, her legs dropping over its face. Of course she had gorgeous legs and a flat belly and full breasts. Her long black hair fell over her face. On the ground near the truck, a tall man in a long black evening gown and cherry-red face rouge danced wildly to the drums. A nine-year-old girl also danced in a black evening gown, while puffing a cigarette. A bare-legged middle-aged man danced while holding his briefcase. Perhaps there were fifty or sixty people dancing around the band.

"*Bum, bum, paticum bum,*" Toninho said.

Fletch tossed his plastic liter bottle of water onto the backseat of the Galaxie.

"*Senhor Barreto,*" the doorman said quietly.

In one swift motion, Tito pulled Fletch's tennis shirt over his head and off him.

Orlando put his forefinger against Fletch's chest. "Look! Skin!"

"He has skin?" Norival asked, looking.

Tito ground a couple of knuckles into Fletch's back. "Muscle!"

"He is there?" Norival asked. "Really there?"

"*Senhor Barreto,*" the doorman said. "Mister Fletcher."

"*Bum, bum,*" Toninho said.

Behind the doorman, tall, stately in her white gown, big-eyed Idalina Barreto came through the crowd. On each side of her she had a child by the hand. Three older children were in her wake. The children were clean enough, but the jerseys on the girls were too big or too small. Below his shorts, from above his knee, the ten-year-old boy had a wooden leg.

"*Janio Barreto!*" the hag shrieked over the sound of the samba band.

"Ah," Toninho said solemnly. "Your wife."

The doorman stood back.

Tito handed Fletch his shirt rolled up into a ball. Fletch threw it into the car.

The old woman cackled rapidly. She was presenting the children to him.

"She says they are your great-grandchildren, Janio," Tito said. "Are you catching their names? The boy is called Janio."

Fletch put his hand on the head of one of the small girls.

At first, Idalina Barreto smiled.

As Fletch ducked into the backseat of the black Galaxie, her voice became shrill. She pressed forward.

Toninho got into the driver's seat. "Aren't you going to ask your wife if you may go gambling?"

Orlando got into the front passenger seat. Entering from the other side, Tito sat in the middle, beside Fletch. Norival sat near the left window of the backseat.

Fletch handed two of the children money through his back window.

Toninho started the car. *"Bum bum,"* he said.

As the car rolled forward, the hag's face continued to fill Fletch's window. Her shrieking voice filled the car.

"Ah, wives," Tito said.

Soon the car bumped off the sidewalk and got into traffic on the *avenida.*

Through the rearview mirror, Toninho was staring at Fletch.

There were many cans of beer on the floor of the backseat of the car.

"Bum, bum, paticula bum," Toninho said, driving through traffic.

"Carnival." In the front seat, Orlando stretched. "How nice."

Toninho shook his head sadly. "Think of driving off and leaving your wife and great-grandchildren that way! To go gambling! What is the younger generation coming to!"

"Um chopinho?" Norival held out a can of beer to Fletch.

"Not yet."

Stuck in traffic, Norival handed the beer through the window to a child no more than twelve. Then he opened one for himself.

In the traffic near them was a big, modern bus. All that could be seen through the windows of the bus were bare, brown upper torsos, moving like fish in a net, the arms flailing the insides of the bus, the feet apparently stomping the floor with the rhythm, the faces raised in some song. The bus was being used as a drum, being played from the inside by more than one hundred fists, more than one hundred feet. The bus' being used as a drum from the inside did not seem to impair its modern beauty or impede its rollicking progress through the traffic.

Finally the Galaxie turned into a side street and picked up speed for a short way until they came to another samba band almost clogging the street. A small seventy-year-old lady, all by herself, dressed in a red dress and red shoes, a red plastic handbag hanging from one forearm, danced to that band, taking perfect small steps with perfect dignity.

Creeping the car past the samba band, Toninho shouted through the window at them, *"Bum, bum, paticum bum, prugurundum!"*

Some of the people who heard him waved.

"Bum, bum, paticum, prugurundum," Fletch tried to say. "What's that?"

"An old carnival song," Tito said, picking a beer off the floor.

Norival was swallowing his third beer since getting into the car.

"What does it mean?"

"Nothing."

After a while they were free of the city, and the car began climbing the narrow, twisting mountain roads. Behind walls and hedges were suburban homes. The higher they climbed, the more expensive were the houses.

Shortly Norival had to be let out to water some of the bushes. Then he started another beer.

Occasionally through the heavy green growth, the hedges, Fletch caught glimpses of Christ the Redeemer, thirty meters tall, over a thousand tons heavy, a half mile in the sky above Rio on Corcovado, arms stretched wide to welcome and embrace the whole world. Enough times, Fletch had heard the story of the Argentine fisherman who spent days outside *Baia de Guanabara* waiting for the statue to wave him in. Finally, he sailed his catch of fish home to Argentina.

At one point, Toninho said in English, "You are not here long before you discover Brazilian music is not only the *bossa nova* of Vinicius de Moraes and Tom Jobim."

"That is for export." Norival licked the lid of his beer can.

"Perhaps Brazilian music is too complicated for others to understand," Tito said.

"The melody, too, comes from the drums," Fletch said. "People are not used to listening to the drums for melody."

For the most part, the Tap Dancers discussed which samba school would win the Carnival Parade. This matter is discussed in Brazil as fervently, as passionately, as who will win the World Football Cup or the presidential election is discussed in other parts of the world.

Each of the big *favelas*, slums in Rio de Janeiro, presents a finished samba school for the Carnival parade, complete with a newly written song and huge, ornate, intricate floats; hundreds of trained, practiced drummers; brilliant, matching costumes for thousands of people. The Carnival Parade is the total competition of sound, melody, lyrics, rhythm; sights, the stately floats, dazzling costumes, the physical beauty of the people dancing from that *favela*, the magical quickness of the kick-dancers; originality and vitality; minds and hearts of the people of each of the slums.

All the people in each *favela* work all the year on their *favela's* presentation, being careful that their song for that year is well written, then spending many nights and every weekend practicing it, playing it, singing it, dancing it, promoting it in the streets; designing and making each of the costumes, for men and women, each more complicated than a wedding garment, by hand, designing and building their samba school float, usually as big as a mansion. Every spare moment and every spare *cruzeiro* goes into making each *favela's* presentation as beautiful, as stunning to the ear and the eye, the mind and the heart, as exciting as possible.

And the competition is most strictly judged, and therefore, of course, always the subject of much controversy.

As Fletch heard the Tap Dancers discuss these matters, which school had the best song for this year, possibly the best costumes and floats, as they knew of them, the best drummers and dancers, which did win and might have won last year, the year before, he heard the names and snatches of the songs that were now being heard everywhere, on the streets, from the radio and television. Months before Carnival, the new song of each samba school is offered the people like a campaign pledge and promoted like a political platform or an advertising slogan. The Tap Dancers discussed the various samba schools one by one, from the oldest, *Mangueira*, to one of the newest, *Imperio da Tijuca;* from one of the more traditional, *Salgueiro*, to the overpowering drum section of *Mocidade Independent de Padre Miguel.* Toninho seemed to think this year's winner would be *Portela*, judging the song that school was offering and what he knew of the costumes. Orlando thought *Imperatriz Leopodinense* had the better song. Tito agreed with Toninho about *Portela*. Norival drank his beer, belched, and just said, *"Beija-Flor."*

Fletch wiped the sweat off his skin with his rolled-up shirt.

Breaking into English, Toninho said, looking through the rearview mirror, "Fletch, you should hope for Santos Lima to win."

"Then I do." Leaning forward, Norival gave Fletch a lopsided look. "But why should I?"

"You used to live there. That was your place. That is where Janio Barreto lived. And was murdered."

For a moment, there was silence in the car.

Then Orlando began humming the song offered this year by *Imperio da Tijuca*.

"Orlando! Toninho!"

In the mountains, they had driven down a deeply shaded drive and pulled into the sunlight-filled parking area in front of an old run-down plantation house.

Immediately there appeared on the front porch of the house an

225

enormous woman, a good three hundred pounds, her arms out in either greeting or sufferance, in the identical posture of Christ the Redeemer.

"Good Lord," Fletch said when he saw her through the car window.

Orlando and Toninho had gotten out of the front seat and opened the back doors.

On the other side of the car, clearly Norival did not care whether he moved.

Fletch got out his side of the car. The mountain air was cooler on his skin; but, still, the sun was biting.

Around the corner of the house appeared a skinny young teenage-girl dressed only in shorts. Her eyes seemed as sunken as in a skeleton's skull.

"Tito?" the woman shouted.

Tito got out of the car, grinning.

The other side of the car, Norival lumbered out, went quickly to the bushes not far away, and relieved himself.

Then behind the enormous woman imitating a statue there appeared a real statue, a *mulata*, a girl six-foot-four easily, perfectly proportioned, an amazing example of humanity. Her shoulders were broad, her waist narrow, her legs long. Each of her breasts was as large and as full as an interior Brazilian mountain seen from the air. Each of her eyes was bigger than a fist and darker than a moonless night. Her black hair was long and flowing. Her skin was the color and texture of flowing copper. Dressed only in slit shorts and high-heeled shoes, she moved like a goddess in no great hurry to go out and sow the seeds of humanity upon a field. This amazing creature, this animate statue, smiled at them.

Fletch gulped.

"You brought me someone new!" the fat older woman yelled in English. "Is he Northamerican? He is so beautiful!"

"He has special problems, Dona Jurema," Toninho laughed. "He has special needs!"

"My God," Fletch said. "Where am I?"

Tito punched Fletch's bicep. "At a different height in heaven."

TWELVE

"Tricked," Fletch said. " 'A little place we know in the mountains.' You guys have brought me to a brothel."

Towels wrapped around their waists, he and Toninho were sitting in long chairs in the shade near the swimming pool. The back of the plantation house was even more dilapidated than the front. Paint was thin and chipped. The back door was lopsided on its hinges. The flower borders had gone years untended. Lilies grew in the swimming pool.

"Very relaxing," Toninho said. "I did say it was very relaxing."

"So why do the well-loved Tap Dancers need a brothel?"

"Everyone needs a few uncomplicated relationships, no? To relax."

They had entered the plantation house, each being fondled by the massive Dona Jurema as he passed her, her laugh volcanic, her fat layered like lava. The younger woman, Eva, smiling happily, stood aside, looking even more Amazonian inside the house. They had crossed the scarred foyer, gone through a large, vomit-smelling dark ballroom turned into a tavern, and out the back door.

Coming again into the sunlight, each of the Tap Dancers dropped his shorts and plunged into the swimming pool. With the encouragement of Dona Jurema and the smiles of Eva, Fletch had followed suit.

There were five white towels waiting for them when they came out of the pool. Their shorts had been piled neatly on a table near the back door.

The skinny young teenage girl brought them a tray with five glasses of *cachaça* and a sugar bowl.

Norival downed his *cachaça* in a gulp, asked for another, and collapsed on a long chair on the long side of the pool.

Tito was doing disciplined laps in the pool, stroking through the lily pads.

Orlando went into the house.

"What is that new Northamerican verb?" Toninho asked. "Interact. It is tiresome having always to interact, especially with women. The women here do not expect anything so profound as interaction."

Dona Jurema came through the back door and let herself down the steps like a big bag of glass.

"So good of you to come, Toninho," she said. "Not many of the girls are up. Ah, it's a hot day. We had a busy night. We will have lunch for you in a while."

"This man." Toninho put his hands on Fletch's forearm. "This man has special needs."

Jurema beamed at Fletch. "It would be a sin if he is having difficulties."

"He is not having difficulties, I think," Toninho said. "Are you, Fletch?"

"Only with the *cachaça*." He put his glass down on the burned-out grass.

"A special need I'm sure you can satisfy, Jurema."

Arms akimbo, the woman shrugged her shoulders. It was a seismic upheaval. "We can satisfy any need. Why, an Air Force General we had here — "

"Toninho," Fletch said. "I have no special needs."

"But you do," Toninho said. "A very special need. I am your friend. It is important to me that your special need be fulfilled."

"I need sleep," Fletch said, leaning back in his chair, closing his eyes.

"I know what you need." Solemnly, Toninho said, "My friend needs a corpse."

Fletch's eyes popped open. His head snapped up. "What?"

"I said you need a corpse. For the purpose of copulation." To Jurema, he said, "My friend has the great need to make love to a corpse."

Jurema was not laughing. She was answering Toninho in rapid Portuguese. Her eyes, her face, her voice bespoke someone doing business.

"Because," Toninho said, "my friend is a corpse. Partly a corpse. Part of him has not had a woman in forty-seven years. Clearly, if we are to get the truth from him, his peri-spirit must be awakened."

"Toninho!" Fletch said.

"It is true," Toninho said to Jurema.

Behind Fletch's long chair, Jurema bent over. She put her hands on his breasts and put at least part of her weight on them. Pressing hard, she ran her hands all the way down his stomach, under his towel to his pelvis, then raised her hands.

She erupted in laughter. "He seems alive. If the other part of him is as healthy . . ."

A cool breeze blew over Fletch. He resettled his towel.

"You see the problem," Toninho said with dignity. "Now. How can you help my friend?"

"Toninho. Stop it. You're gross."

"A corpse for my friend? Someone young, dead, and pretty."

"Toninho, this isn't funny."

"Probably by Tuesday," Jurema said. "There are always such corpses available during Carnival."

"Find a good one," Toninho said.

Jurema waddled a short distance. Speaking to Toninho in Portuguese, incredibly enough she stooped over and picked a weed out of the burned grass. Her face flushed. She then lifted herself up the back stairs and into the house.

"Tuesday," Toninho said. "She'll have one for you Tuesday."

"Toninho, I hope this is another of your jokes."

Abruptly, in the same tone of voice, Toninho said, "Your friend, Teodomiro da Costa, is to be respected."

"I met with him this morning." Fletch watched the sunlight flashing on Tito's shoulders as he swam. "He had advice for me, which I respect. Especially at the moment."

"In this country, seventy percent of the business is run by the government, you see. To do well on your own, as Teo has, is to do very well indeed. Now tell me. In North America, there is a car which has what is called a slant-six engine. Can you describe it to me, please?"

Fletch told Toninho what he understood of the slant-six engine, and that it had an especially long life. Sitting on Saturday morning in the mountains above Rio de Janeiro looking out into the sunlight, he felt his eyes crossing. He had not had that much of the *cachaça*. One moment Toninho was talking seriously of necrophilia and the next just as seriously about a slant-six car engine.

The young girl brought Norival his third *cachaça*.

"Ah," Toninho said. "Norival is an *arigó*. A simpleton, a boor, but a good fellow. If he were not from a rich, important family, he would be an *arigó*. His brother, Adroaldo Passarinho, is the same, exactly like him in every way. Look the same, act the same. His father has sent Adroaldo to school in Switzerland, in hopes there will be someone in the family this generation less than simple. *Arigó*."

Tito climbed out of the pool and, not drying himself, dropped naked belly down on the grass.

In high seriousness and in great detail, Toninho then wanted to know about this new robot he had read about in *Time* magazine supposedly capable of understanding and obeying one hundred thousand different orders. Designed in Milan, manufactured in Phoenix with Japanese parts. What was the nature of the computer which ran it? How were the joints designed, and how many were there? What would the robot say when given conflicting orders? Would the robot know, better than a person, when it is breaking down?

In his towel, holding a fresh glass of *cachaça*, Orlando stood on the back steps of the plantation house. He sang. Of the four Tap Dancers, Orlando's muscles were the heaviest. His voice was deep, and he sang well.

O canto de minha gente
Assediando meu coração
Semente que a arte germinou
E o tempo temperou
Amor, o amor
Como é gostoso amar.

Norival raised his head from his long chair and hissed. Even from a distance, it could be seen Norival was not focusing. His head dropped back.

"Ah, the *arigó* never sobered from last night," Toninho said.

"What's the song?" Fletch asked.

"An old Carnival song. Let's see." Toninho closed his eyes to translate. Fletch had been slow to see how long Toninho's lashes were. They rested on his cheeks. " 'My people's song makes my heart leap. The seed is sown by art and tempered by time. Love, love, how good it is to love.' "

"That's a good song."

"Oh, yes."

With his glass of *cachaça*, Orlando wandered down to where they were sitting.

"Orlando," Toninho said. "Give Fletch a demonstration of *capoeira*, of kick-dancing. You and Tito. Make it good. Kill each other."

Raising his head beside the pool, Tito said, "You, Toninho."

"Perform for the gods," Toninho said.

Orlando looked into his glass. "I've had a drink."

"You won't hurt each other," Toninho said.

"You and Orlando," Tito said from the grass.

"It is important Janio sees *capoeira* from close up," Toninho said. "So he will remember."

Glass still in hand, Orlando went to Tito and with his bare feet stood on Tito's ass. Standing thus, he drained his glass, leaned over, and put it on the grass. Then he began to walk slowly up Tito's back.

"I can't breathe!" Tito said.

"And you can't talk?" Toninho asked.

"I can't talk, either."

Then he wriggled free, spilling Orlando to the side, and jumped to his feet.

In a wide arc, he swung his right foot, aiming for Orlando's head.

Orlando ducked successfully, turned sideways and slammed his instep into Tito's side, against his rib cage. Orlando's towel dropped.

"Wake up," Orlando said.

In a short moment, Tito and Orlando had the rhythm of it, had each other's rhythm. Gracefully, viciously, rhythmically, as if to the beating of drums, with fantastic speed they were aiming kicks at each other's heads, shoulders, stomachs, crotches, knees, each kick coming within a hair's breadth of connecting, narrowly ducking, sidestepping each other, turning and swirling, their legs straight and their legs bent, their muscles tight and their muscles loose, their fronts and their backs flashing in the sunlight, the hair on their heads seeming to have to hurry to keep up with this frantic movement. With this fast, graceful dance, easily they could have killed each other.

Eva had come onto the porch to watch. Her eyes flashed. A few faces of other women appeared in the upper windows of the plantation house. *Everyone loves the Tap Dancers. . . . They're sleek.*

"Remember . . ." Toninho was saying. "A skill developed by the young male slaves, in defense against their masters. They would practice at night, to drums, so if their masters came down from the big house, to look for a woman, they could pretend to be dancing. Thanks to — what is the word in English? — miscegenation, such skills ultimately were not needed. . . ."

There was a loud *Thwack!* and Tito began to fall sideways. He had taken a hard blow to the head from the instep of Orlando's foot. The blow could have been much, much harder. Tito did not fall completely.

"I told you to wake up," Orlando said regretfully.

Recovering, Tito charged Orlando like a bull, right into his midriff. Orlando fell backward, Tito on top of him. Laughing, sweating, panting, they wrestled on the grass. At one point their bodies, their arms and legs, were in such a tight ball perhaps even they could not tell which was whose.

Eva, moving like Time, went down to them.

Finally, Orlando was sitting on Tito and giving him pink-belly, pounding Tito's belly hard repeatedly with his fists. Tito was laughing so hard his stomach muscles were fully flexed and no harm was being done.

Standing over them, behind Orlando, Eva laced her fingers across Orlando's forehead and pulled him backward, and down.

Kneeling over Tito as he was, sitting on him, bent backward now so that his own back was on the ground, or on Tito's legs, Orlando looked up Eva's thighs. He rolled his eyes.

He jumped up and grabbed Eva by the hand.

Together Orlando and Eva ran down the grassy slope from the swimming pool and disappeared.

"You see?" Toninho said. "Uncomplicated."

After resting a moment on the ground, breathing hard, Tito rolled over and over and on into the pool of water.

"Your *Moby Dick*," Toninho said abruptly. "By Herman Melville?"

Fletch looked at Toninho, wondering what new surprise was coming. "Yes," Fletch said. "I read it while waiting for a bus."

" 'Call me Ishmael,' " Toninho quoted.

"Not a bad beginning," Fletch said. "Simple."

"Is it?" Toninho finished his *cachaça*. At the long side of the pool, Norival was finishing his fourth. "Is that Ishmael meant to be some spirit of the United States? Some guardian?"

"Almost anything can be said," Fletch said. "And has been."

"In a way, *Ismael* is the guiding spirit of Brazil."

Fletch said nothing. Necrophilia, slant-six car engines, the nature of *arigó*, robotics, *capoeira*, now a discussion regarding American literature.

"I'm quite certain Melville stopped in Brazil on his voyages. Have you ever thought of that interpretation of *Moby Dick*?"

"Melville meant Brazil is the guiding spirit of the United States?"

"Maybe of the hemisphere."

"Toninho . . ." Tito's forearms were flat on the edge of the swimming pool, holding his head up. Water streamed down his face from his hair. His right ear was red from Orlando's kick. "I think we should do Norival a favor."

Toninho looked over at Norival stretched out in the sunlight. Norival bubble-belched. "Yes."

Toninho stood up.

Together Toninho and Tito tipped the slow-reacting Norival out of the long chair.

Fletch went to watch what new trick they would play.

Each taking an arm, they dragged Norival, belly down, to the bushes. The towel dragged off him in the dirt. Then, methodically, standing behind him, Toninho and Tito each picked up one of Norival's feet. They raised him so that his shins were on their shoulders.

Not all that gently, somewhat from the sides, they kicked Norival's soft, upside-down belly with the insteps of their feet, once, twice, some more.

"*Arigó*," Toninho said, kicking Norival's upside-down stomach.

"Empty out the sack," Tito said. "Very practical."

It didn't take too many kicks for Norival to begin vomiting his four *cachaças*, his numerous *chopinhos*, whatever was still in him from the night before.

Once he began vomiting, they dropped his legs on the ground.

Tito grinned at Fletch. "Very efficient, yes?"

"It seems to be working."

The other side of the swimming pool, Orlando and Eva were climbing back up the slope.

"Ah," Toninho said, watching them. "Five minutes is a long time in the life of such a *mulata*."

Norival now was on his hands and knees, emptying himself into the bushes.

Bleary, drooling vomit, he looked up at them.

"*Obrigado*." In Portuguese, he said to them, "Thanks, guys."

THIRTEEN

After lunch, it rained.

The five young men sat in their muddy towels at a round table on the back porch of the old plantation house playing poker.

The humidity was complete, and even in the rain Fletch and Orlando and Tito had been in and out of the pool between hands. They would be either wet with sweat or wet with water, and the rain water, the pool water, seemed cooler. The only reason they sat under the roof to play was to keep the cards reasonably dry. Near them, their shorts were still piled on a small table, but the pile was messed up, as Norival had gone to his shorts and swallowed two pills from its pockets. They drank beer. There were many crushed cans near Norival's feet.

From under the porch roof, as he played, Fletch watched the rain fall on the pool and make mud puddles in the dead garden. He watched the flower-kissing birds sustain themselves with wings which beat so fast they were almost invisible, like auras on either side of their bodies, as they sucked sugar water from small vessels in the rafters.

Kick-dancing and flower-kissing birds.

After two or three hours of poker playing, it was clear who the winner was. Norival was careless, concerned more with his next *chope* than the cards. He seemed keyed-up anyway — for someone who had had so much to drink, even though properly evacuated before lunch. Fletch yawned. Tito, Orlando, and Toninho played cards in a way odd to Fletch. They did not seem to see the cards as they were, but as something else, something more. Always they believed in the next card too much. They believed in what the cards might be instead of what they were.

Fletch was collecting all the chips.

At one point, Toninho said, "Of course you cannot understand Brazil, Fletch. Three of us — all but Norival — have been to school in the United States. We cannot say we understand the United States, either. Everyone there is so anxious."

"Very nervous," Orlando said.

"Worried," Tito said. "Do I drink too much, smoke too much, make love too much, too little? Is my hair all right? Might someone see that my ankles are fat?"

"Does everyone *like* me?" Orlando guffawed.

"I'm so pretty!" Toninho said in falsetto. "Don't touch me!"

Fletch strummed the table with his fingers. *"Bum, bum, paticum bum, prugurundum."*

The noise of the rain pounding on the tin roof increased.

Eva came through the back door and stood, watching them.

She stood behind Norival and watched his last chips disappear in careless play.

She took his feverish head in her hands and turned it sideways, and leaned his cheek against her bare stomach. "Ah, Norival," she said in Portuguese. "You are getting drunk again."

"*Arigó,*" Toninho said, clearly hoping for a picture card and playing as if he had one.

Eva rotated Norival's head so that he was slipping off the chair. The front of his face was against her stomach. He breathed deeply a few times through his nose.

In a moment, Eva led Norival indoors.

Tito, Orlando, Fletch, and Toninho played silently.

Occasionally, concentrating, Toninho's lips would move as if he were talking, but no sound came out.

When Orlando won anything, no matter how much he had lost, his face would break into a marvelous grin. He would be ready to lose more.

At one point, when Fletch was raking in chips again, Tito murmured, "Your peri-spirit is with you."

"Is he telling you what cards we have?" Toninho asked.

"Doesn't need to," Fletch said. "I play with what I see I have against what I see you have."

From inside there was a short scream.

Toninho chuckled. "I guess Norival has a few surprises in him yet."

"We know he cannot hurt Eva," Tito said. "He is only a stick in her fire."

Then there was another, horrible, long drawn-out scream. It pierced the sound of the rain.

"They are playing," Orlando said.

"Norival!" Toninho called in Portuguese. "Mind your manners!"

Naked, Eva fell through the back door. "Norival!"

Her hair was messed up. Her eyes were wild.

She sucked in breath and spoke in a rush.

Toninho said, "She says Norival has stopped moving. That he has stopped breathing."

Eva was shouting Portuguese over the sound of the rain.

"He has passed out," Tito said.

"No." Alarmed, Toninho stood up. "She says he has stopped breathing!"

They all rushed inside.

More slowly, Fletch went with them, suspecting some new trick.

In the little room on the first floor, Norival lay on the rumpled, dirty sheets of an extra long bed. He was partly on his side, as if

235

rolled into that position. He was naked and his stomach was slack. There was still a streak of mud on his leg.

Norival was grinning.

There was a happy, wicked gleam in his eye.

From the door, Fletch watched Norival's grin remain idiotic.

Norival's eyes did not blink.

Fletch joined the Tap Dancers at the side of the bed. With his fingertips he felt for a pulse in Norival's neck. There was none. Norival's pleased eyes did not blink.

As Fletch watched, slowly the grin disappeared from Norival's face. The lips became straight.

The happy gleam remained in his eyes.

A few inches in front of Norival's penis, the bed sheet was wet and stained.

"He is dead!" Orlando said in Portuguese.

Under his breath, Tito whistled.

Standing, his back straight, Toninho said, "Norival. You died *arigó*."

"What do we do?" Orlando asked. "Norival is dead!"

"How did he die?" Tito asked. "Surely he has done this before. It hasn't been fatal."

Orlando said, "He can't be dead. Wake up, Norival! You'll miss Carnival!"

"He is dead," Toninho said. "Norival is dead!"

Eva filled the door of the small, dark room. Talking rapidly but more quietly now, she kept gasping, imitating a belch, grabbing her huge left breast with both hands.

"Died of a heart attack while copulating, I guess," Fletch said.

Orlando said, *"Way to go, Norival!"*

"No wonder he was smiling!" Tito said.

"You saw him smiling?" Toninho asked.

"Definitely he was smiling," Tito said.

Orlando nodded. "When we came into the room, he was smiling!"

"He is not smiling now," Tito said.

"But look at his eyes," Toninho said.

"His eyes are still happy," Tito said.

"And why not?" Orlando asked. "Why not happy?"

At the door, Eva was beginning to look pleased with herself.

"But he's dead!" Tito said.

"But how he died!" Orlando said. He looked ready to shake Norival's hand. "Well done, Norival!"

"A death in ten million," Toninho said. *"Arigó!"*

FOURTEEN

The tall, slim, naked young man stood in the dead garden, the rain pouring down his body, his feet wide apart in the mud, his face up to the rain, his arms held high as if to catch the sky.

From the back porch, Fletch heard what Toninho said to the sky:

With God he lays down, with God he rises,
With the grace of God and the Holy Spirit.
May Thine eyes watch over him as he sleeps.
Dead, will You light his way
Into the mansions of eternity
With the tapers of Thy Trinity?

Fletch went down to Toninho in the garden.

"A prayer." Toninho's face and arms lowered. His shoulders sagged.

Then Toninho looked over the hedges, out into mountain space in the rain. "Not a worry." Fletch could not make sure if there were tears mixed in with the rain on Toninho's cheeks. "When you die copulating, you are certain to come back to life, soon."

FIFTEEN

"Toninho! What do we do?" Tito asked in a hushed voice.

Toninho shook his head as if to clear it.

"Still, Norival is dead," he muttered thickly.

While Fletch and the Tap Dancers were out of the room, Dona Jurema, the young teenaged girl, and one other woman from the house had washed Norival, put a fresher sheet under him, and laid him out straight.

Now in the small, dark room, Norival lay on his back, clean, naked. His eyes were closed. In his hands folded over his stomach were a few flowers which had seen better hours. A candle flickered at the head of the bed; another candle at the foot of the bed.

Leaving a full bottle of whiskey in the room, Dona Jurema left the young men sitting around the bed in straight wooden chairs.

So they had sat for two or three hours. The thick candles had burned down only a few centimeters.

There was no measurement tape on that whiskey bottle. Their next drink from it would probably be their last. Fletch had had three or four good swallows from the bottle.

Even on the straight wooden chair across the bed, Orlando sat with his legs out straight before him, his chin on his chest, his thumbs hitched into the tops of his shorts.

"We must do something," Tito said.

Toninho blinked.

"We cannot leave Norival here," Tito said.

To Fletch, Toninho said, "Norival comes from a rich, important family. His uncle is an admiral!"

"To die in a whorehouse," Tito said. "Full of booze . . ."

"And pills, I think," Fletch said.

"His mother would be disappointed," Tito concluded.

"But what a way to go!" Orlando muttered without opening his eyes or raising his chin from his chest.

"We must do something," Tito said.

"We must move him." Toninho drank from the bottle, saw that it was nearly the last of the whiskey, and handed the bottle to Tito.

"We must arrange some other death for Norival," Tito said.

"Burn the record," Fletch agreed. "I see the point."

"For the sake of his mother," Tito said.

"He must not have died here," Toninho said carefully. "Not in the arms of Eva."

"No," said Tito. "It would make her too famous."

"Still." Toninho winked. "People will know."

"Yes," Tito said. He passed the bottle over Norival to Fletch. "People will know how Norival died."

"What a way to go!" Orlando muttered.

"But not his mother," said Toninho.

"Not his mother," agreed Tito. "Not his sisters."

For a moment, while Fletch held the bottle, they were silent.

The candles flickered and Norival did not breathe.

Through the open window came the sound of the rain on the tin roof.

"We must do something," Tito said.

"The important thing is," Toninho said, trying very hard to keep his tongue straight and to see things clearly, "is to prevent an autopsy."

"Yes!" Tito said forcefully at this great wisdom.

"Because Norival was full of booze and pills."

"Despite our having emptied him out once," Tito put in.

"And that would disappoint his mother," said Toninho, losing his tongue in his mouth.

"Worth it," Orlando muttered from his chest. "A death in ten million. Good old Norival."

"Wake up, Orlando," Tito said. "We must think."

"No."

Toninho kicked Orlando's legs and Orlando nearly fell off his chair.

Blinking, he looked at Norival laid out on the bed, holding the wilted flowers.

It was not yet dark, but the rain made the candles bright in the small room.

"Orlando, we must think of something."

"Queima de arquivo," Fletch said. "I am learning Portuguese."

"Truly," Orlando said. "We must do something. We must move him."

"His boat," Toninho said.

"Yes." Orlando shook his head solemnly. "His boat. Who now will want his boat?"

"Exactly," Toninho said.

"Exactly what?" Tito asked.

Fletch took his drink from the bottle and handed it back across Norival to Orlando.

"Clearly." Toninho spoke slowly, carefully. "Norival died on his boat."

"Clearly." Tito looked at Norival as if for agreement. "Norival would have liked that."

Orlando said, "I think Norival was satisfied enough with the way he died."

"But we can say he died on his boat, Orlando," Tito said.

"Off his boat," Toninho corrected him. "He died off his boat. He drowned. That should prevent an autopsy."

"Yes," Tito said. "Poor Norival drowned. That should make his mother happy."

"You're all crazy," Fletch said.

"But Toninho," Tito asked, "how do we get Norival to his boat? It is way down in the harbor. There is a gate to the docks. Guards. There are always guards at the gate."

Again there was silence, as they considered the gate and guards leading to the dock where Norival's boat was.

Toninho took the bottle of whiskey from Orlando and finished it. "We walk him."

He placed the empty whiskey bottle on the bed, within Norival's reach.

Tito said something in Portuguese.

"We walk him right by the guards."

Orlando said, "This is a night the dead walk."

"Broomsticks." Toninho's eyes were now fully open. He was speaking perfectly clearly. "Jurema must have brooms."

Tito looked at the floor. "I sincerely doubt that, Toninho."

"Everyone has brooms. Tito, you get rope and rig a harness around Norival's chest. Under his arms. Orlando, you get brooms from Dona Jurema and saw them down to size. You know? So they will fit from the harness under his arms to his waist, so we can hold him up. We need some thick thread for his legs." Orlando and Tito were studying Toninho carefully with their eyes, putting all this together. Toninho jumped up. "There is a book of tide tables in the glove compartment of the car. I shall figure out exactly where Norival must drown to come ashore and be found in the morning."

"His wallet is in the car, too, Toninho," Tito said. "In the glove compartment. Norival must wear his wallet when he drowns, so when they find him in the morning, they will know who he is."

"Otherwise they will not report the body," Orlando said.

"They will report the body fast enough, if it's a Passarinho," Tito said. "Norival Passarinho."

"You help too, Fletch. You get Norival's clothes, including his shirt."

"You're all crazy," Fletch said. "What if we get caught with a corpse?"

Standing over Norival, Tito rubbed his own hands together. "Not a worry, Norival," he said. "We'll see that you died decently."

SIXTEEN

"**D**rive carefully, Toninho," Tito said. "We don't want an accident."

Although he was not going fast, Toninho was not being all that successful at keeping the black four-door Galaxie to the right. They were swerving down the wet, twisting mountain-side road. It was now fully dark. A Volkswagen, climbing the road, had just blared its horn at them.

"We don't want to be stopped by the police," Orlando said.

"Drive as if you are driving a hearse," Tito advised.

"I am driving a hearse," Toninho said, swinging the wheel too much.

At Dona Jurema's, Orlando had sawed two broomsticks down to size. Tito bound Norival's chest with a rope harness. Toninho stud-ied the tide tables and decided exactly where Norival was to drown in the South Atlantic Ocean. Together they fit the broomsticks into the harness and then dressed Norival.

While watching them carry Norival out of the old plantation house, Dona Jurema said to Fletch, "Come Tuesday. I'll have a corpse for you."

"Cancel the order," Fletch said. "We have a corpse."

Toninho sniffed. "Norival is not that sort of corpse."

As they swerved down the mountainside, Norival sat propped up in the backseat between Tito and Orlando. The broomsticks were not visible beneath his shirt.

When they came to the first flat, wide road on the outskirts of Rio de Janeiro, Tito reminded Toninho again to drive slowly, to stay to the right. Toninho drove very slowly. Even two children on roller skates passed them.

Toninho looked through the rearview mirror. "Norival never looked better. He holds his head up nicely."

The car swerved a little.

"Careful, Toninho," Tito clucked.

"The way he died, he should," Orlando said. "Not everybody —"

From behind them came the sound of a police siren.

"Oh, oh," Toninho said.

"Go fast, Toninho!" Tito said. "We have a corpse in the car!"

"No, no," Orlando said. "Stop."

The result of following these conflicting orders was that the car shot forward a few meters and then bucked to a stop.

On the backseat, Norival rolled forward. His head struck against the back of the front seat.

"Oh, Norival!" Tito said in exasperation.

"It's all right," Orlando said, pulling Norival back into a sitting position. "He won't bleed."

"Quick!" Toninho said. "Open his eyes! He looks more real that way!"

Orlando reached over with his fingers and opened Norival's eyes.

The police car drew alongside.

Apparently staring straight ahead through the windshield, Norival's eyes gleamed with a wicked joy.

"What did I do wrong?" Toninho asked. "These people have no respect for the dead!"

The conversation with the policeman of course was in Portuguese.

While it was going on, Fletch sat perfectly still in the front seat, trying not to look interested or concerned.

After they drove away from the policeman, Toninho, Orlando and Tito, choking with laughter, repeated the conversation in English for Fletch.

Policeman: Why are you driving so slowly?

Toninho: It's Carnival, sir. I don't want to hit any revelers.

Policeman: No one else is driving so slowly.

Toninho: Perhaps no one else is as good a citizen as I, sir.

Policeman: Back there, you swerved. You almost hit a parked car.

Toninho: I sneezed.

Policeman: God bless you, my son.

Toninho: Thank you, sir.

Policeman, shining his flashlight around the inside of the car, finally leaving it for a moment on Norival's joyfully beaming, unblinking face: Why does that guy look so happy?

Toninho: He always looks that way during Carnival, sir.

Policeman: Is he stoned?

Toninho, whispering: He's not all there, sir.

Policeman: Oh. Well, drive faster.
Toninho: Yes, sir.

"Tito, you stay with the car. Drive to where I showed you on the map. The beach. We'll be there in a few hours."

Correct. They had driven by the gates to the dock where Norival's boat was. The gates were closed and locked. Not one but three guards stood at the gate chatting, two outside and one inside.

They drove up the street and parked the car against the curb.

It had stopped raining. The moon was threatening to come out.

They lifted Norival out of the backseat and stood him in the road between Toninho and Orlando.

"Here, Fletch." Toninho handed Fletch a ball of heavy thread he had taken from Dona Jurema. "Tie Norival's left ankle to Orlando's right, his right ankle to my left. See? It will work out. That way, Norival will appear to walk."

Fletch tied Norival's left ankle to Orlando's right.

They lifted Norival a little off the ground on his broomsticks and Orlando walked in a circle around Toninho. Norival's movement was too slow.

"No, Fletch," Toninho said, "the line must be tighter. Norival must appear to be taking the same size steps as Orlando."

Kneeling on the wet road, Fletch retied the thread tighter, and then tied Norival's right ankle to Toninho's left.

Somewhere in the harbor, a ship's whistle blew.

Toninho and Orlando walked Norival up the road a little way. "How do we look, Tito?"

"Lift your side higher, Toninho," Tito said. "His foot is dragging a little, your side."

Toninho hitched Norival higher. "That better?"

"Perfect," Tito said. "You'd never know he's dead."

"Fine. Then we should go. See you at the beach in a few hours, Tito. Here, Fletch, you walk a little in front of us, in case things do not look exactly right."

Slowly, in bare feet, Fletch walked down the rain-slicked road and up onto the sidewalk toward the gate to the boat dock. Each pocket of his shorts was bulging with a wad of *cruzeiros* he had won at poker.

He could not help looking around.

Eyes beaming in complete joy, arms stiff at his sides, although his shoulders propped up by broomsticks did look a little high, Norival walked almost in step between Toninho and Orlando. Three close friends going down the street together. The harness kept Norival's head high.

Norival did trip going up the curb.

Down the road, Tito was driving the car away.

The three guards watched the four young men approach.

"*Boa noite*," Fletch said to them.

"*Boa noite*," they answered lowly, suspiciously.

Fletch stood aside.

"Ah, Doctor Passarinho!" One guard threw away his cigarette.

Again the conversation was in Portuguese.

Fletch kept looking up at the heavy, scudding clouds, hoping the moon would not take that moment to appear.

Guard: "You are not going out on your boat tonight, are you?"

Toninho answered in his normal voice, not even trying to conceal the movement of his lips. "Yes. Rio is so crowded. From Carnival. I need some peace and quiet."

Orlando took a few steps in his circle so that the faces of Norival and Toninho were turned a bit away from the guards.

Guard: "But there has been a heavy rain! It might rain again!"

Toninho/Norival: "That will help keep the sea calm."

Guard: "They say the wind will come up."

Toninho/Norival: "Yes, well, I feel like a vigorous sail."

Second guard: "You look uncommonly happy, Doctor Passarinho."

Toninho/Norival: "I think I have met the love of my life."

Guard: "That will do it."

Toninho/Norival: "Yes. I doubt I will ever love anyone else."

Third guard (inside gate): "Ah, to be in love! To be young and in love! You look so happy, Doctor Passarinho!"

Guard: "But if you go sailing now, you will be missing the parties! The grand balls! How can there be Carnival parties without the Tap Dancers?"

Orlando: "No. Only Norival is going sailing. Because he is so stuck in love, you see. We came just to see him off. We will swim ashore. Off Copacabana."

Second guard: "I understand everything perfectly. He is in love. . . . From the stiff way he walks, I should say he should not be with the young lady just now. . . ."

Guard: "Is that it? Ah! I see! So Doctor Passarinho, even though it is the middle of the night during Carnival, goes sailing!"

Third guard: "What a man!"

Guard: "What a gentleman!"

Toninho/Norival: "Something like that."

Guard: "Norival Passarinho must do what is best, for himself and his young lady!" He signaled the guard inside to open the gate. "What consideration!"

Orlando and Toninho marched Norival through the gate. True, Norival did walk as if he suffered one of the more virulent social diseases.

Fletch fell in behind them.

Toninho/Norival: *"Obrigado! Boa noite!"*

Aboard, Orlando removed the sail covers and had the mainsail up in almost no time at all.

Toninho released the bow line and gathered it in.

As soon as the mainsail caught wind, Fletch, at the tiller, released the stern line and, letting it trail in the water, took in the main sheet.

Facing aft in the cockpit, Norival beamed delightedly at his friends taking him sailing.

While Orlando was running up the jib, Toninho came aft and took the tiller. "I know the harbor," he said. "We do not want to run into someone's boat in the dark while one of us is dead."

Fletch gathered in the stern line. "Not in the *S.S. Coitus Interruptus.*"

The moon came out.

In the moonlight, Norival's whole face beamed. But when the boat heeled, he fell over sideways.

"Can't have him rolling around," Toninho said. "He might go overboard before we mean him to."

Fletch relieved Norival of his rope harness and the broomsticks and sat him up in the leeward corner of the cockpit. He tied a light line around his shoulders to a stanchion behind him.

"The things we do for our friends," Toninho muttered, coming about.

Now Norival was sitting to windward, leaning unnaturally forward as if being seasick. But he was still beaming.

Orlando joined them in the cockpit.

Laughing, then, they translated the conversation with the guards for Fletch. *"What a gentleman!"* Orlando kept repeating.

Then Orlando said, "Norival loved this little boat."

At the tiller, Toninho said, "Who'd think Norival would be one to go down with his ship?"

Orlando laughed. *"What a gentleman!"*

"We're just about there," Toninho said.

Ashore, as they came around a point, a car's headlights went on and off three times.

"Yes!" Toninho said. "There's Tito. He must see us."

At first, sailing south in *Baia de Guanabara*, Fletch had tried to sleep. He lay on the deck, a cushion under his head. He regretted leaving the rest of his mineral water in the car. Despite the drinks he had had, sleep was impossible.

The sky was clear now. The breeze was from the northeast and steady. The little sloop moved nicely through the water.

To starboard, *Cidade Maravilhosa*, Rio de Janeiro, passed slowly, laid out under the moonlight. There were a few fires on the beach. The street lights, the lights in the tall apartment buildings and hotels along the shore dimmed the stars above. From offshore, the samba drums were heard from all parts of the city in a soft jumble. Like no other city Fletch had seen from such a perspective, Rio has peculiar black holes in its middle, the sides of its cliffs, *Morros da Babilonia, de São João, des Cabritos, Pedra dos dois Irmãos*, its surprising, irrepressible jungle growth within the city. Above all in the moonlight, arms out in forgiveness, stood the statue of Christ the Redeemer.

At some point, sitting in the cockpit opposite Norival, Orlando had said, "We will have to go to Canecão Ball."

"Yes," Toninho said. "However late."

"We will have to find the Passarinhos," Orlando said, "and say that Norival went sailing."

"Janio, you must stay with us so we will be believed."

"I should return to The Yellow Parrot."

"No, no. There will not be time. You come to my apartment. You can wear my costume from last year. We are the same size."

"I seem to be the same size as everybody," Fletch said. "Alan Stanwyk, Janio Barreto, Toninho Braga . . ."

"Tito will drive fast and we will dress and go in a hurry."

"The tickets Teo gave me for the ball are at The Yellow Parrot."

"You can use Norival's. He won't be needing it."

They sailed another few kilometers. Ashore, again Tito flashed his headlights three times.

"All right." Toninho punched Fletch's leg. "Take the tiller, Senhor Barreto. It is no surprise to us you know how to run a boat. Orlando, assist Norival. Make sure he has his wallet in his pocket."

"He has his wallet."

"His death would never be reported, unless they know who he is. Whoever finds a Passarinho body will expect money for reporting it."

Fletch sat, tiller in hand, keeping the course along the shore.

Toninho went below.

Soon from the small cabin came a heavy pounding. The a splintering sound. Then gurgling.

The boat veered to port. Instantly, it became unmanageable. The sails luffed.

Fletch released the tiller.

Toninho came up the companionway and tossed a hammer overboard.

"We are near enough the rock for people to believe he hit it," Toninho said. "And now for Norival."

Together, Toninho and Orlando lifted Norival, his eyes still beaming happily in the moonlight, brought him to the gunwale. Gently, they dropped him overboard.

For a moment, the two young men stood on the deck, staring down into the water. Toninho's lips moved. Orlando crossed himself.

"He'll be on the beach by dawn," Toninho said.

The little boat first had come about, put its nose up into the wind, both sails luffing. Then the bow began to sink. As it did so, it fell off the wind, the sails filled again, and, twisting, it began to capsize.

"Come, Janio!" Toninho shouted. "You don't want to keep dying at your age!"

Orlando dove overboard.

Only after Fletch dove did Toninho scramble off the sinking boat.

The water was exactly body temperature, as was the air. In irrepressible, sensuous delight, Fletch stroked through the buoyant water toward *Cidade Maravilhosa.*

The wads of money in the pockets of his shorts came to feel like stones in the water.

After a hundred meters, he stopped swimming. He looked around to see if anything of the boat was still visible. He could not be sure. There was something white on the water, possibly the side of the hull, possibly the sails.

Then, from near the boat came a loud yell. *"Aaaaaaaaaarrrrrgh!"* Water was thrashed.

"Toninho!" Fletch called. "What's the matter?"

Silence.

"Toninho! What happened?"

Fletch was just starting to swim back when Toninho's steady voice came calmly across the water surface: "I swam into Norival. . . ."

SEVENTEEN

"We must be very casual," said Tito, now a movie Indian.

They were entering the Canecão Night Club.

"What is the number of the Passarinho box?" Orland asked.

"They're always in box three," Toninho answered.

"Da Costa is in box nine," Fletch answered.

Relieved of the corpse, Tito drove the black four-door Galaxie back to Copacabana fast enough to satisfy any police.

In the car, Fletch gulped down the rest of his liter of water.

At Toninho's apartment on rua Figueiredo Magalhaes, Toninho, Tito, Orlando, and Fletch shaved and showered in assembly-line fashion.

The Tap Dancers were to dress as movie Indians in breechclouts, soft thigh-high boots, and war paint. Norival's breechclout did not fit Fletch, unless he wanted to spend the rest of the night holding it up with his hand.

Toninho dug his last year's costume out of a closet and tossed it to Fletch: a one-piece shiny satin movie cowboy suit, complete with mask, frayed leggings, and spangles. Fletch wriggled into it.

"Toninho. This is a scuba suit?"

"It fits you perfectly. Here are the boots, the hat, the mask."

"It fits like a scuba suit."

Toninho, Tito, and Orlando then sat in a circle decorating each other's faces, chests, backs with movie war paint, with great speed. Finished, they looked as if they had already sweated through a war.

While they were doing that, Fletch decorated Toninho's apartment by draping wet *cruzeiros* every conceivable place, to dry.

"Remember," Tito said. "Very casual."

At Canecão Night Club, Orlando opened the door to the Passarinho box.

"Orlando!" people exclaimed. "Tito! Toninho!"

The people in the box just stared at the masked movie cowboy.

Below them, the huge floor of the Canecão Night Club was jammed with people in bright costumes at little tables, on the dance floor, wandering around. Across the hall on the large stage was an enormous band, mostly of samba drums, but of horns and electric guitars as well.

Everyone in the Passarinho box made much of the Tap Dancers' costumes. As there wasn't much to the costumes, in fact they were making much of the Tap Dancers.

In turn, Toninho, Orlando, Tito exercised the courtesy of not knowing who people were and expressing great surprise when, for example, Harlequin revealed himself to be Admiral Passarinho.

"You're very late!"

"Oh," Toninho equivocated. "We just found the box."

"Who's this?" a woman asked.

"Janio Barreto," Toninho muttered.

"I.M. Fletcher."

Senhor Passarinho was dressed as *Papai Noel*.

"Where's Norival?"

"He went sailing," Tito said.

"Sailing? It is storming out!"

"The storm is over," Orlando said.

"Sailing? On the night of the Canecão Ball?"

"We saw him off," Toninho said. "Fletch did too."

"Sailing? Why would he go sailing the night of the Canecão Ball?"

With apparent concern, Toninho said, "Norival has been acting very serious lately."

"He has been talking of taking up a career," Orlando said.

"That would be nice," said *Papai Noel*.

"It is a question of what he does best," Tito said.

"Norival has his talents," Orlando said.

Toninho said, "Perhaps he wanted to think."

"Norival becoming serious?" asked Harlequin. "Then it is time for me to retire!"

"No, no," Toninho said. "You don't know Norival as we do. When Norival sets his mind to something, he is apt to die trying."

"Norival can be very sincere," Orlando said. "About some things."

"Yes." Accented by war paint, Toninho's eyes crossed. "Norival is one to die trying."

"Norival is not coming to the ball at all?" Harlequin asked.

"He went sailing," Toninho said lamely. "To come to some conclusion . . ."

"Ah, what a son!" *Papai Noel* said. "Probably drunk somewhere! These tickets cost three hundred Northamerican dollars each! Norival Adroaldo. . . . Why does a man have sons? As soon as they grow as big as he is, they ignore him! They take, but do not give!"

Fletch was introduced to Senhora Passarinho, who sat aside, watching the dancers on the floor. A lady with mild, vague eyes, she was dressed as a circus clown.

"Ah!" she said. "Norival went sailing! Of course, he never was one for parties! A quiet, sensitive boy, always. He wrote poetry, you know, when he was younger. I remember one poem of his, where the cockatoo bird was meant to represent his school principal . . ."

"You see," Tito said aside to Fletch. "We could not disappoint that lady with the truth."

"Clearly."

"It would kill her."

"Have a drink!" ordered Harlequin. *"Cachaça?"*

Toninho grinned broadly. The worst was over. *"Nao, Senhor.* We must go find girls."

"Of course you must!" boomed *Papai Noel.* "The night is as young as you!"

"Just make sure they're not men disguised surgically!" Harlequin warned.

"If I find someone special, I shall bring her to you," Toninho said, "to check out."

Harlequin roared in laughter.

Outside the box, Fletch said, "Toninho, are you going back to the beach in the morning to make sure Norival came ashore?"

"Oh, no." Toninho adjusted the top of his boot against the bare calf of his leg. "Today is Sunday. We must go to Mass."

Teodomiro da Costa was standing at the little bar at the back of his box.

"Who is this?" he exclaimed. "I don't recognize you!"

Fletch stared at him the appropriate time through his mask.

Everyone else in the box was facing forward, listening intently to the singer of the moment.

What was left of the Tap Dancers had gone looking for girls.

"You scare me, Senhor Gunslinger! What do you want?"

"It's me, Teo."

"Who?" Teo leaned forward, staring through the eyeholes of Fletch's mask.

"Fletch!"

"Ah!" Teo feigned a look of great relief. "Then come have a drink."

The barman Teo had brought from his house began to make Fletch a screwdriver.

"It's so late," Teo said. "It is nearly three o'clock in the morning. Did you fall asleep?"

"No."

"I thought not."

"Without Laura, I went for a tour of the suburbs. Got back late."

"In a bus?"

"Something like that. A big car."

The singer stopped singing.

"Oh, Fletch! Beautiful costume!" the Viana woman said. "Where did you get it?"

"I mugged someone on my television set."

"It fits you. . ." She looked below his waist. ". . .handsomely."

"Frankly, I feel like I'm walking behind myself."

"You are, darling. You are."

Teo introduced Fletch to his other guests. Besides the Vianas and the da Silvas, there was a famous Brazilian soccer player who could not stop dancing around the box by himself; his wife, who was taller than he, and probably heavier; a broker and his wife from London, who put on their Wegman — Man Ray masks for Fletch; Adrian Fawcett, who wrote about music for *The New York Times*; an Italian racing car driver and his girl friend, who was very young indeed; and the young French film star Jetta.

Everyone marveled at Fletch's costume, and he at everyone's. Teo was dressed somewhat as a tiger, with a short tail. His tiger head rested on the bar table. Staring unblinkingly through glass eyes, the tiger head reminded Fletch somewhat of Norival in his last moment. But Norival's eyes were much happier.

Jetta was dressed in a nurse's cap and costume, white shoes. Her nurse's skirt was not even as long as the Tap Dancers' breech-clouts.

In films, he had seen more of Jetta.

Fletch took off his mask and movie cowboy hat and stood at the rail and watched the swirl of color and flesh below him.

A few of the drummers were going off the stage; others were coming on. The music would never stop.

At three places on the huge floor, between the dancing area and the tables, were tall, raised gilded cages. Inside, three or four magnificent women dressed only in G-strings and tall headgear writhed to the music. Outside, crawling around the cages, trying to attain sufficient footholds in their high-heeled shoes to writhe to the music, nine or ten women dressed in G-strings and tall headgear crawled around like big cats on their hind legs. Each of the gilded cages was a locus of writhing brown bare asses and huge, shaking brown bare breasts.

Beside him, Teo said, "The floors of the cages are elevators; they go up and down so the women can get in and out without being accosted by the crowd."

"They must be seven feet tall," Fletch said.

"They are all over six feet."

"What about the women outside the cages?"

"They were not women." Teo sipped his drink.

"They are."

Teo said, "They are exhibiting the superb work of their Brazilian surgeons."

From a distance, Fletch could see no difference between the women inside the cages and the women outside the cages.

Once before, in New York, he had been fooled.

"No one hardly ever accosts them," Teo said. "Very sad, for them."

The music picked up, and all the people, those dancing, those at the tables, those in the boxes, began singing/chanting the song presented by *Imperio Serrano* that Carnival. Fletch stumbled over the lyrics. He could never make his Portuguese sibilant enough.

All the tanned people, the brown people, the black people were moving to the rhythm and singing the lyrics of the song presented by a single samba school together, something about how indebted Brazilian people are to the coffee bean, and how they should respect the coffee bean like an uncle.

Adrian Fawcett, drink in hand, stood at the rail to Fletch's left. "Brazil is what the United States would like to think it is."

"I used to work for a newspaper," Fletch said. "A reporter."

"What do you do now?"

"Do? Why must I do? I am."

Jetta stood the other side of Fletch. After Eva, after watching the women in the gilded cages, Jetta-off-the-screen seemed small.

"Really what do you do?" Adrian asked.

Fletch said, "I don't know."

Jetta said, "Teo said there would be someone young for me to dance with."

"I feel one hundred years old at the moment."

"I have heard that story," she said. "You are someone who died, years ago, murdered, and has come back to life to reveal your murderer."

"Did you ever hear anything so crazy?"

"Yes," she said. "Will you dance?"

Fletch wanted to crawl into a corner of the box, to sleep. He was sure he could do so, despite the drums, the horns, the guitars, the singing. "Of course."

Excusing themselves from the box, they went to the dance floor.

The people swirling around them were dressed as rabbits and rodents, harlequins and harlots, grande dames and playschool children, villains and viscounts, convicts and cooks, pirates and priests.

Surprising to Fletch, Jetta seemed a wooden dancer. She clung to Fletch as she might to a log in the middle of the sea. He suspected she resisted such music.

A few meters away, Orlando, breechclout flapping, was dancing wildly with a woman in a blond wig. The concentration in his eyes as he danced put him in another world. The woman's dress exposed only one breast totally.

At the edge of the dance floor, a dozen men stood absolutely still, staring up, their mouths agape. Above them was a woman sitting on the rail of a box, her bare buttocks hanging over the rail. The woman herself was not visible: just her bare buttocks hanging over the rail.

Jetta followed Fletch's gaze. "Brazilians are so relaxed about their bodies," said the young French film star. "So practical."

Feeling almost intoxicated with sleeplessness, Fletch envisioned Tito and Toninho turning Norival upside down in the bushes, kicking the vomit out of his stomach; Tito and Orlando, naked, kick-dancing, then wrestling, laughing, on the burned-out grass; the magnificent Eva standing in the door of the small, dark room where Norival lay dead, clutching her left breast with both hands, looking mildly pleased with herself; harness and broomsticks and calculating where a corpse dropped into the tide would be by dawn. . . .

Jetta ran her hands up the smooth sleeves of Fletch's shirt to his shoulders and said, "You were so late in coming."

Even though dancing, sleep passed through Fletch's brain like a curtain dragging across a stage. "I had to sit up a sick friend."

EIGHTEEN

Alone in his room at The Hotel Yellow Parrot, Fletch first dialed The Hotel Jangada and asked for Room 912.

There was no answer in Room 912.

Not even taking off his movie cowboy suit, he fell on his bed. He thought he would sleep immediately. It was nearly seven o'clock in the morning. He was not used to going to sleep at seven o'clock in the morning.

Getting up, he dropped his clothes on the floor. Then he crawled beneath the sheet.

Even at that hour of the bright morning, the sound of a samba combo could be heard from somewhere in the street. He rolled onto his side and pulled the pillow over his ear. Eyes closed, flesh wavered everywhere in his mind: big, soft, pliant breasts with huge nipples swinging to the beat; long, smooth backs danced away from him; brown buttocks dimpled as they moved; gorgeous long legs bent and straightened as feet pressed gently against the earth, the dance floor in the rhythm of the melodic samba drums.

Fletch got out of bed and called Room Service for breakfast.

While he waited, he took a long, hot shower.

Alone, a towel around his waist, he ate breakfast sitting in a corner of his room. Sunday morning. For once, the man across the utility area was not painting the room.

He called The Hotel Jangada again, again asked for Mrs. Joan Stanwyk in Room 912.

Again there was no answer.

He closed the drapes against the bright morning and got into bed.

He tried lying like a statue on a crypt, like Norival dead on the bed at the old plantation house, flat on his back, his hands crossed on his stomach. He tried counting the members of a woman's pole-vaulting team leaping over the barrier. At the nineteenth redhead taking her turn with the brunettes and blondes going over the barrier, he knew sleep was unattainable.

He called The Hotel Jangada again.

Heavily slogging around the room, he opened the window drapes.

He pulled on clean shorts, a clean tennis shirt, socks, and sneakers.

Outside the hotel, in the brilliant sunlight, the small boy, Idalina's great-grandson Janio Barreto, was waiting for him.

The boy grabbed Fletch's arm. He hobbled along with Fletch, speaking rapidly, softly, insistently.

Fletch shook the boy off and got into his MP.

On his wooden leg, the ten-year-old Janio Barreto ran after Fletch's car, calling to him.

NINETEEN

"*Bom dia*," Fletch said to the formally dressed desk clerk at The Hotel Jangada. "There is a problem."

Instantly, the man was solicitous. He put his forearms on the reception counter and folded his hands. "Are you a guest of this hotel?"

"I am staying at The Hotel Yellow Parrot."

The desk clerk was only a little less solicitous. The Hotel Yellow Parrot was a good hotel, too, more traditional, not so flashy. All the good hotels in Rio de Janerio exactly doubled their rates during Carnival.

Fletch had already telephoned Room 912 on the house phone, gone to the door, checked out the breakfast and pool areas. No sign of Joan Collins Stanwyk. The note he had left for her was still in the Room 912 box behind the reception desk.

He spoke slowly and distinctly: "Someone who is staying at your hotel, a Northamerican woman named Mrs. Joan Stanwyk, talked to me yesterday morning at about this time, at my hotel. We arranged to meet almost immediately here, for breakfast. She was to walk from there to here. All I had to do was to get something from the safe of The Hotel Yellow Parrot, shower, change clothes (I had been jogging), and follow her in my car. I left The Hotel Yellow Parrot about a half hour after her, and drove straight here. She did not answer the house phone. She did not answer when I knocked on her door. She was not in the breakfast room, the terraces, the swimming pool areas, the bar. She still doesn't answer. I'm afraid something must have happened to her."

The desk clerk smiled faintly at this story of a jilted lover. "There is nothing we can do, Senhor. We must respect the privacy of our guests. If the lady does not wish to see you, or hear from you . . ." Raising his hands from the counter, he shrugged.

"But, you see, she needs something from me. Money. She had been robbed of everything."

Again the man shrugged.

"I left her a note." Fletch pointed to the note still in its slot behind the man. "The note is still there."

"People change their plans rapidly in Rio during Carnival." The man smiled. "Sometimes they change their whole characters."

"Will you let me into her room, please?" Fletch had already tried to jimmy the lock to Room 912. It was an advanced lock, designed for only the most advanced burglars. "I worry that something must have happened to her. She may need help."

"No, sir. We cannot do that."

"Will you go yourself?"

"No, sir. I cannot do that."

"Will you send a maid in?"

"It's Carnival." The desk clerk looked at the lobby clock. "It is early. People sleep odd hours. They do not want disturbance."

"She's been missing twenty-four hours," Fletch said. "It is now a police matter."

The man shrugged.

Fletch said, *"Onde é a delegacia?"*

"Is there a police officer who speaks English?"

"Spik Onglish," the police officer behind the tall desk said. "Quack, quack."

Fletch turned his head so a younger police officer down the counter could hear him. "Anyone here who can speak English?"

Down the counter, the younger officer picked up a phone, dialed a short number, and spoke into it.

After he hung up, he held the palm of his hand up to Fletch, either ordering him to stop or suggesting he wait.

Fletch waited.

The lobby of the police station was filled with regretful revelers. On the floor and along the bench sat and lay men and women of all shapes, sizes, colors, in nearly every state of dress and undress, sleeping, trying to sleep, blinking slowly, holding their heads. Some of the revelers were in Carnival costumes, now in tatters: a queen, a mouse; ironically, a magistrate. One hairy man, asleep with his mouth open, was dressed only in bra, panties, and garter belts. A fat woman, eating cookies from a bag, was dressed as the Queen of Sheba. Five or six of the men had cuts and bruises on their heads; one had a nasty long cut down the calf of his leg. Even with no glass in the windows, the room smelled putrid.

While Fletch waited, a man dressed only in tank trunks entered. A long-handled knife stuck into the area between his chest and his shoulder. He walked perfectly well. With dignity, he said to the police officer at the high counter, *"Perdi minha máquina fotográfica."*

From the bottom of a flight of stone stairs, a heavy police officer beckoned Fletch to come to him.

"My name is Fletcher."

The man shook hands with him. "Barbosa," the man said, "Sergeant Paulo Barbosa. Are you Northamerican?"

"Yes, sir."

The sergeant heavily led Fletch up the stairs. "I have been to the United States. To New Bedford, Massachusetts." He led Fletch into a little room with a desk and two chairs. The sergeant sat in the chair behind the desk. "I have cousins there, in New Bedford, Massachusetts." He lit a cigarette. "Have you been to New Bedford, Massachusetts?"

"No." Fletch sat down

"It is very nice in New Bedford, Massachusetts. Very sealike. It is on the sea. Everyone there fishes. Everyone's wife runs a gift shop. My cousin's wife runs a gift shop. My cousin fishes." The sergeant brushed cigarette ashes from his shirt when there were no cigarette ashes on his shirt. "I truly believe the Portuguese bread is better in New Bedford, Massachusetts than the Portuguese bread in Rio de Janeiro. Some of it. Ah, yes. New Bedford, Massachusetts. I was there almost a year. I helped my cousin fish. Too cold there. I could not stand the cold."

The man sat sideways to the desk, not looking at Fletch. "Are you enjoying Carnival?"

"Very much."

"Ah, to be young, handsome, healthy in Rio during Carnival! Can you come closer to heaven? I remember." Then he brushed cigarette ashes off his shirt which were truly there. "And rich, too, I suppose."

In a corner of the room behind the desk was a gray steel filing cabinet, with three drawers.

"It must be a busy time for the police."

"It is," the sergeant agreed. "We get to enjoy Carnival very little. Everything goes topsy-turvy, you see." He smiled at Fletch, slyly proud of this idiom. "Topsy-turvy. Men become women; women become men; grown-ups become children; children become grown-ups; rich people pretend they're poor; poor people, rich; sober people become drunkards; thieves become generous. Very topsy-turvy."

Fletch's eyes examined the typewriter on the desk. It was a Remington, perhaps seventy-five years old.

"You were robbed. . . ." the sergeant guessed.

"No," Fletch said.

"You were not robbed?"

"Of course I was robbed," Fletch said. "When I first came here." The sergeant seemed to be relieved. "But I am not bothering you with such a small, personal matter."

The man smiled happily, in increased respect for Fletch. He turned and faced Fletch, now ready to listen.

Again, slowly, carefully, Fletch told Sergeant Paulo Barbosa the facts of his meeting Joan Collins Stanwyk at The Hotel Yellow Parrot, arranging to bring money to The Hotel Jangada, as of course she had been robbed, to have breakfast with her . . . her not being at the hotel yesterday or today . . . not picking up the note he had left for her . . .

Another cigarette was dropping ashes on the sergeant's shirt. He was quick to brush them away.

"Ah," he said, "Carnival! It explains everything."

"This is not a crazy lady." Fletch said. "She is a woman of many responsibilities. She is a healthy, attractive blond woman in her early thirties, expensively dressed — "

"Topsy-turvy," the sergeant said. "If you say she is not a crazy lady, then during Carnival, she becomes a crazy lady! I know! I have been on this police force twenty-seven years. Twenty-seven Carnivals!"

"She has been missing for over twenty-four hours."

"Some people go missing all their lives! They come to Brazil because they go missing from some place else. Don't you know that?"

"Not this lady. She has a magnificent home in California, a daughter. She is a wealthy woman."

"Ah, people during Carnival!" The sergeant puffed on his cigarette philosophically. "They are apt to do anything!"

"She could be kidnapped, mugged, hurt, run over by a taxi."

"That is true," the sergeant said. "She could be."

"It is very important that we find her."

"Find her?" The sergeant seemed truly surprised at the suggestion. "Find her? This is a huge country! A city of nine million people! Tall buildings, short buildings, mountains, tunnels, parks, jungles! Are we supposed to look on top of every tall building and under every short building?" He sat forward in his chair. "At this time of year, everyone becomes someone else. Everyone wears a mask! There are people dressed as goats out there! As porpoises! Tell me, are we to look for a goat, or a porpoise?"

"For a blond, trim Northamerican woman in her early thirties. . . ."

"Topsy-turvy!" the sergeant exclaimed. "Be reasonable! What can we do?"

"I am reporting the disappearance of a female Northamerican visitor to Brazil —"

"You've reported it! If she walks into the police station, I'll tell her you're looking for her!"

"I don't see you taking notes," Fletch said firmly. "I don't see you making up a report."

The sergeant's eyes grew round in amazement. "You want me to type up a report?"

"I would expect that, yes."

"I should type up a report because some Northamerican woman changed her plans?"

"A report should be filed," Fletch insisted. "Any police force in the world — "

"All right!" The sergeant opened his desk drawer. "I'll type up a report! Just as you say!" He took a key from his desk. "You want me to type up a report, I'll type up a report!" Standing, he went to the filing cabinet and inserted the key into its lock. First he looked in the top drawer, then the middle drawer. "Anything to keep the tourists happy!"

From the bottom drawer, he took out a typewriter ribbon. It appeared to be just about as old as the typewriter.

The sergeant blew dust off the typewriter ribbon.

"Never mind." Fletch stood up. "I get the point."

From a telephone kiosk on the sidewalk outside the police station, Fletch called Teodomiro da Costa.

Teo answered the phone himself.

"Teo? Fletch. I knew if you were asleep, your houseman would tell me."

"I have to wait for some Telexes from Japan. I am preparing to sell some yen."

"Teo, that woman I mentioned to you yesterday morning, the Northamerican, is still missing. The note I left for her at The Hotel Jangada has not been picked up. She has no money, no identification. I have been to the police. They tell me there is nothing they can do. The people at The Hotel Jangada will not let me into her room. She may be very sick, Teo, or — "

"Of course. I understand. I think the first thing is to inspect her room. She was a healthy woman, you say?"

"Very healthy. Very sensible."

"Where are you now?"

"Outside the police station."

"I'll meet you at The Hotel Jangada."

"Teo, you've been awake all night."

"That's all right. This could be a very serious matter, Fletch. Just let these Telexes arrive, and I will be right there."

"Thanks, Teo. I'll wait in the bar."

TWENTY

"What is the woman's name?"

"Joan Collins Stanwyk," Fletch answered. "Room nine-twelve."

Fletch was on his second *guaraná* when Teo appeared in the door of the bar of The Hotel Jangada. Even in shorts and a tennis shirt, the dignity of Teodomiro da Costa was absolute.

At the reception counter, Teo spoke with the same clerk with whom Fletch had spoken.

Fletch stood aside and listened.

Clearly, in Portuguese, Teodomiro da Costa introduced himself, explained the situation as he knew it and stated his request: that they be permitted to inspect Room 912.

Again, with all apparent courtesy, the desk clerk refused.

The conversation became more rapid. Teo said something; the desk clerk said something; Teo said something, smiling politely; the desk clerk said something.

Finally, drawing himself up, giving the desk clerk his hooded eye, Teodomiro da Costa asked the rhetorical question which is magic in Brazil, which opens all doors, closes all doors, causes things to happen — or not happen, according to the speaker's wish — which puts people in their places: *"Sabe com quem está falando?*: Do you realize to whom you are speaking?"

The desk clerk withered.

He got the desk key to Room 912 and led the way to the elevator.

"Do you see anything amiss?" Teo asked.

While the desk clerk stood at the door of Suite 912, jangling the key in his hand, Teo and Fletch had searched through the living room, bedroom, bathroom, terrace as well as they could.

"Not a damned thing," Fletch answered. "Except that Joan Collins Stanwyk isn't here."

The rooms were freshly made up, the bathroom undisturbed, the bed not slept in. Going through the drawers, closets, even going through the medicine chest and suitcases, and other immediately conceivable hiding places, Fletch had found no money, no jewelry.

"One thing is significant, Teo," Fletch said. "Yesterday morning, Joan was wearing a tan slack suit and a silk shirt. I cannot find the slack suit and the shirt here in the suite."

"She could have sent them to the hotel cleaners. You don't know what other clothes she had."

"Not likely. She wanted to move out of this hotel as soon as I brought money."

"Then it is likely she disappeared somewhere between The Hotel Yellow Parrot and here."

"Yes."

Standing back on his heels at the door, the desk clerk rattled the key against its chain.

"What do we do now?" Teo asked. "You're the investigative reporter, newly retired."

"Check the hospitals, I guess."

Teo thought a short moment. "There is really only one hospital where they would have brought anyone sick or injured between The Yellow Parrot and here. We can check that one out."

Fletch said, "Let's do so."

"What do we do now?" Teo asked again.

They stood in the hospital lobby.

Teo had explained to the hospital administrator the disappearance of a blond Northamerican woman, in good health, more than twenty-four hours before, who had already been robbed of her money and identification.

The administrator clucked about Carnival, was most understanding although not alarmed, and permitted Teo and Fletch to walk through the seven floors of the hospital, checking the beds of every reasonable unit.

The administrator had said there were many people without identification in the hospital during Carnival. She would be grateful to have any of them identified.

"I don't know." Fletch's eyes wanted to close in sleep, in discouragement, perhaps to think.

"I don't see what else we can do," Teo said.

"Neither do I."

"Once in a while you have to let time pass. . . ." Teo said.

"I guess so."

"Let things right themselves."

"She could be anywhere," Fletch said. "Anything could have happened to her. Should I check all the hospitals in Rio?"

"That would be impossible! Then check all the hotels and hospitals and jails in Brazil, one by one? You can't live so old!"

"I guess not."

"Let time pass, Fletch."

"Thank you, Teo. Sorry to keep you up."

"You have done your best, for now."

"Yes . . . ." Fletch said, uncertainly. "I guess so."

TWENTY-ONE

Before again pulling the drapes closed in his room at The Hotel Yellow Parrot, Fletch noticed that across the utility area the man was back painting the room. "If he doesn't finish soon," Fletch said to himself, "I'll go across and help him."

In bed again, hearing the samba drums from two or three combos in the street, Fletch tried his best to sleep. He breathed deeply, evenly, a long time, to convince his body he was asleep.

His body was not fooled. He was awake.

His mind was crowded with wriggling flesh, with people dressed as rabbits and rodents, harlequins and harlots, grande dames and playschool children, villains and viscounts, convicts and crooks, pirates and priests. *Clearly, you cannot sleep,* Laura had said. *Did you fall asleep?* Teo had asked. *I thought not.* With a fat Queen of Sheba eating cookies from a bag. With the sight of a man walking well with a long knife sticking out of his chest, reporting to police that he had lost his camera.

Idalina Barreto had been on the sidewalk in front of The Hotel Yellow Parrot when he returned. The wooden-legged great-grandson was with her. She had some sort of rag doll in her hand.

As he hurried into the hotel, she yelled and shook the rag doll at him.

Again he put the pillow over his head. Again he insisted he go to sleep. He thought how tired his legs were, from dancing with Jetta, from . . .

It was no good.

"Bum, bum paticum bum."

Heavily, he got out of bed. He opened the drapes again.

He looked up the number of Marilia Diniz in the telephone book.

"Prugurundum."

He dialed her number. It rang five times.

"Marilia? Good morning. This is Fletcher."

"Good morning, Fletcher. Are you enjoying Carnival?"

"Marilia, I know it is Sunday morning, during Carnival; it is wrong of me to call; but I need to talk to you. I have not slept since Thursday."

"You must be enjoying Carnival."

"It is not exactly that. Are you too busy? Can we meet somewhere?"

"Right now?"

"If I don't get sleep soon . . . I don't know what will happen."

"Where's Laura?"

"She went to Bahia with her father. She'll be back later today."

"You need to see me, before you can sleep?"

"I think so. I need to understand something, do something. I need advice."

"You are disturbed?"

"I lack in understanding."

"Come over. Do you know how to get to Leblon?"

"Yes. I have your address from the telephone book. Are you sure it's all right if I come now?"

"I ignore Carnival. I am here."

"Trouble between you and Laura?" Marilia asked.

In her little house in Leblon, behind a high wooden fence, Marilia Diniz led Fletch into a small study.

"I saw you in a car with the Tap Dancers yesterday."

Fletch did not dare ask her what time of day, or night, she saw them; whether all the Tap Dancers were blinking. "I relieved them of some money, playing poker."

At the side of the study, Marilia was adjusting a disk in a word processor. "The Brazilian male," she said, "is known for his energy."

"There's magic, high energy in the food."

"The Brazilian male is slow to give up his . . . what? . . his immaturity." She started the word processor and watched it operate a moment. "At seventy, eighty, the Brazilian male is still a boy."

The word processor was whizzing away, typing manuscript. "Forgive me," Marilia said. "This is my routine for Sunday mornings, making manuscript of my week's work." She sat in a comfortable chair near her desk and indicated Fletch should sit on a two-person sofa. "I used to have a typist, but now? Another job lost. Teodomiro arranged this word processor for me."

Fletch sat.

"You look healthy enough," pale Marilia said. "Glowing."

"I have already been to the police station this morning. A woman I know, from California, showed up at my hotel yesterday morning, early. She had been robbed. I told her I would bring her money, immediately. Walking between my hotel and hers, she disappeared."

"Ah, Carnival . . ."

"Really disappeared, Marilia. With Teo's help, I checked her suite at The Jangada. Her clothes are still there. She has no money, no passport, no credit cards, identification."

"You are right to be concerned," Marilia said. "Anything can happen during Carnival. And does. Is there any way I can help you?"

"I don't think so. We went through the hospital for that district. Teo says I just must wait."

"Waiting is hard."

"That's not why I came to see you. As I said on the phone, I have not slept since Thursday."

"No one sleeps during Carnival." Then Marilia said, "So I guess you don't want any coffee."

"No, thanks. Do you know about this old woman who says I am her murdered husband come-back-to-life?"

"Someone mentioned something about it, the other night at Teo's." Marilia glanced at her word processor. "You tell me about it."

"Okay." On the divan, Fletch put his hands under his thighs. "When you, Laura, and I were having that drink at the cafe on Avenida Atlantica, Friday afternoon, an old woman in a long white dress came along the sidewalk and apparently saw me. She stopped near the curb. She stared at me until we left. Did you happen to notice her?"

"I'm ashamed to say I didn't."

"She was behind you."

"Is the old woman the reason you disappeared under the table?"

"No. That was because of this other woman, from California, who walked down the street just then. I was surprised to see her."

"The woman who has since disappeared?"

"Yes."

Marilia got up and checked her word processor, scanned the processed manuscript.

"When Laura and I entered the forecourt of The Yellow Parrot, this old hag jumped out of the bushes at us. She was screaming and pointing her finger at me. Laura talked to her calmly." Marilia sat down again and listened to Fletch expressionlessly. "The old woman said that she recognized me. In an earlier life, I had been her husband. Janio Barreto. That forty-seven years ago, at about my present age, I had been murdered. And now I must tell her who it was who had murdered me."

Marilia said nothing.

Fletch said, "Laura said, 'Clearly you will not rest until you do.' "

"And you have not rested."

"I have not slept."

"You think the woman has put a curse on you?"

"Marilia, she hangs around outside my hotel, accosts me every time I go in or go out. She brought her great-grandchildren to the hotel to meet me. This morning she was there on the sidewalk, yelling at me and shaking some kind of a voodoo doll at me."

"A *calunga* doll."

"Whatever."

The word processor finished its work and turned itself off.

Marilia said, "An interesting story."

"No one will help me to understand," Fletch said. "Otavio Caval-canti will answer none of my questions, about anything. He just nods and says Yes. Teo says he doesn't understand, doesn't know what to do. I can't understand whether Toninho Braga is making a joke out of it or whether there is some part of him that is serious. Worst of all, I can't understand Laura at all. She's an intelligent woman, a concert pianist. She seems to have no curiosity about my background, but she seems to give this Janio Barreto matter some credence."

Marilia sighed. "Ah, Brazil."

"I can't tell if everyone here is playing some kind of an elaborate joke, a trick on me."

"What do you think?"

"I don't know. Laura says I won't rest until I reveal this murderer, and I haven't. Teo seems to say he is not surprised I am not sleeping. The Tap Dancers just don't expect me to sleep. How can I figure out what happened in Rio de Janeiro a generation before I was born? Am I to die of sleeplessness?"

"Did the old woman say you wouldn't sleep until you answered her?"

"I don't know. Laura talked to her. In Portuguese that was way above my head. I believe the old woman did say so. Why else would Laura have said so?"

"And you believe all this?"

"Of course not. But I'm nearly going crazy with sleeplessness."

Marilia's eyes traveled around the stacks of books in her study. "What's the question?"

"First, could this all be an immense practical joke Laura and the Tap Dancers are playing on me? The Tap Dancers seemed to know all about it before they ever met me."

"Could be," Marilia said.

"They're all friends. I'm the foreigner. Surely it is easy enough to hire an old woman, some children, a ten-year-old boy on a wooden leg?"

Marilia frowned. "A small boy on a wooden leg?"

"Yes. Supposedly the great-grandson. Named Janio Barreto, of course."

Marilia said, softly: "Or it could be that you are Janio Barreto, and you were murdered decades ago, and you have come back to Rio to reveal who murdered you."

Fletch stared at her. "Are you in on this, too?"

"Fletcher, my new friend from Northamerica, you must understand that most of the people in this world believe in reincarnation, in one form or another." Marilia stood up and went to her word processor.

She began to tear and stack the pages of her manuscript.

"Marilia, may I point out to you that while you and I have been sitting in this room talking about ghosts and curses and *calunga* dolls, a magnificent, modern piece of technology quietly has been typing your manuscript in the corner?"

"This will not be read in your country." She placed the stack of new pages under a manuscript on her desk. "I am not translated and published in the United States of the North. The publishers, the people there have a different idea of reality, of what's important, what affects people, what happens, of life and death." She sat in her soft chair. "Have you at least had breakfast?"

"Yes."

"Then what shall we do?"

"Tell me straight out if I should take this matter seriously."

"It is serious, if you're not sleeping. You can become quite ill from not sleeping. You can drive your car into a lamp post."

"Marilia, nothing in my background prepares me for this. I was employed as an investigative reporter for a newspaper, dealing with real issues, police corruption — "

"This is not real?"

"Can it be real that I was murdered forty-seven years ago? That I have come back from the grave?"

Marilia chuckled. "It's real that you've come back to Rio de Janeiro. It's real that some old woman thinks so. It's real that you're not sleeping. Ah, Carnival!" Marilia said. "People go crazy during Carnival!"

"I don't intend to be one of them."

"Reconciling differing realities," Marilia apparently quoted from somewhere. "What does your education and training, as an investigative journalist, tell you to do in a situation which perplexes you?"

Fletch thought a short moment. "Find out the story."

"My training says that, too. So let's go find out the story. Where do the Barreto family live?"

"Someone mentioned . . . Toninho mentioned . . . Santos Lima. Toninho said I had lived in the *favela* Santos Lima."

"Let's go there, then." Marilia stood up and took a bunch of keys from her desk. "Let's go find out the story."

TWENTY-TWO

"Have you ever been in a *favela* before?" Marilia asked.
"I have been in slums before. In Los Angeles, New York, Chicago."
They had driven slowly past The Hotel Yellow Parrot. None of the Barreto family was at that time waiting in front of the hotel.

Fletch had parked the MP where Marilia told him to, on a city street a few blocks from the base of the *favela*.

"Last week, our industrial city of São Paulo produced ten thousand Volkswagen cars," Marilia said. "And twelve thousand, eight hundred and fifty babies. That is the reality of Brazil."

The *favela* of Santos Lima rose straight up a mountainside not all that far from the center of Rio de Janeiro. For the most part it was made of hovels stuck together by various materials, bits of lumber from here and there, packing crates, tar paper. A single roof might be made of over a hundred pieces of wood, tin, aluminum. A favorite patch is a flattened tin can nailed over a hole. A few were old, solid houses, all very small, and most of these had been painted at one time or another, purple, green, chartreuse. Some of the little stores, which mostly sold rice and beans and *chope*, looked somewhat permanent. As with most residential districts, the houses looked more solid, slightly more prosperous, the higher they were in the *favela*. The sewage from the higher houses flowed down muddy streets to settle under the lower houses.

As they entered the *favela* and began to climb, radios blared music from every direction. In a nearby shack, a packing crate really, a samba drum was being tuned. At a distance a large *bateria* of drums could be heard practicing.

Marilia Diniz and Fletch attracted much attention. Almost instantly they were surrounded by thirty, forty, fifty small children barefoot in the mud and sewage. The teeth of a few of the older children had rotted to stumps. Only a few of the very young had the distended bellies and skinny legs of malnutrition. Generally the bodies of the children old enough to fend and rummage for themselves, those over the age of six, although skinny, were well formed, as quick as darting fish. Their fingers tugged lightly at Marilia and Fletch; their imploring voices were low. For the most part, their eyes were bright.

"Well over half the population of Brazil is under nineteen years old," Marilia said. "And half of them are pregnant."

Marilia then asked the children for directions to the home of Idalina Barreto. In response, they fought for her hand to guide her there.

Fletch followed along with his own gaggle of children. Perhaps a dozen times he felt their hands slip into and out of the empty pockets of his shorts.

The women looked at him through their doorless doors and glassless windows with blank expressions on their worn faces, neither friendly nor unfriendly, not particularly curious. Their expressions indicated more that they were thinking about him, the life he led that they had glimpsed here and there; the big, clean buildings he had lived in, the airplanes he had flown in, the restaurants he had dined in, the accoutrements of his life, cars, telephones, air conditioners. There was little resentment in their look, as there was little resentment in their not being familiar with snow. His was a different life, vastly different, as different as if he had lived on Venus or Mars: too different to generate emotion.

A man called to Fletch in Portuguese from a bar counter under a tin roof. "Come! I'll buy you a little beer!"

"Thanks," Fletch answered in Portuguese. "Maybe later!"

And of course Fletch wondered about their lives as he walked through their world. To do without everything he knew, even a little money, privacy, machinery, in most cases, work. To do without everything but each other. He wondered if he could adapt to such a life, but only as he wondered if he could adapt to life on Jupiter or Saturn.

As they passed a small home, a toothless, bald old woman in a rocking chair in the shade looked at Fletch through rheumy eyes. *"Janio!"* she shrieked. *"Janio Barreto!"*

She tried to get out of her chair, but fell back.

Fletch just kept moving.

As they turned the corner around a sizable pink building, Fletch spotted young Janio Barreto down the dirt track. The boy hurried away on his wooden leg — doubtless, to broadcast the news that Fletch was coming.

The Barreto home was not very high in the *favela*.

Idalina Barreto stood tall in the door to her home, hands on her hips. Janio and other small children were in front of the house. Her eyes narrowed as Marilia and Fletch approached.

"*Bom dia,*" Marilia said. She introduced herself. She explained that they had come to hear all about Janio Barreto and what had happened to him forty-seven years before.

The hag pointed to Fletch and, in her crackly voice, asked some question about Fletch.

Marilia said, "She wants to know if you will tell her what happened. Why you were murdered, and who murdered you."

There was no humor, no irony, in Marilia's face.

Sleepless, slightly dizzy in the bright sunlight, surrounded by a swarm of whispering children, Fletch shook his head. "I don't know."

As Idalina Barreto led Marilia and Fletch into her home, she dispatched children to find various relatives and bring them here.

The inside of the house was a space protected from some of the elements by walls of many boards of different shapes and sizes, nailed together at different angles under a patched tin roof.

The interior was impeccable. The dirt floor was reasonably dry and freshly swept. Plates, pans, cups, and glasses near the basin sparkled. A round table in the center of the room was polished. On it was a pretty embroidered cloth, and on the cloth was a bowl of fresh flowers. The *calunga* doll was also on the table. Chairs of various styles and sizes were around the walls of the room.

On the wall, either side of a battery radio, were magazine pictures of Jesus and the Pope.

A vast crowd was collecting outside the house.

Marilia said, "Idalina would like to know if you'd like coffee."

"Yes. Thank her."

Idalina flicked her wrist, and more children darted out.

Then she sat in a tall-backed wooden chair with wide arms. She gathered the hems of her long white dress around her ankles.

She indicated with a sweep of her hand that Marilia and Fletch should be seated in chairs of their choosing.

Fletch took a humble seat in a kitchen-styled chair.

As they waited silently, children brought them cups of very strong, very sweet coffee.

A few adults came into the room, four women, two men. They were introduced to Fletch as Idalina's children and grandchildren. Fletch stood to greet each of them and didn't really get their names.

Each stared at him, round-eyed. They didn't seem willing or able to breathe normally. They backed into chairs along the walls.

Finally, the one for whom everyone apparently had been waiting arrived: a man in his fifties, shirtless, in proper black shorts and sandals. His hair was neatly combed.

"I speak English," he said, shaking Fletch's hand. "I am Janio Barreto Filho. I have worked many years as a waiter, in Copacabana." He stared into Fletch's eyes a long, breathless moment. Then, old enough to be Fletch's father, he said, "I am your son." In one movement, he hugged Fletch to him and embraced him hard. There was a choked sob in Fletch's ear. "We are so glad you have come back."

TWENTY-THREE

"I will speak English so good as I can," the middle-aged Janio Barreto Filho said. "Mother says to me you want me to bring to life for you the facts of what happened."

"Yes," Fletch said. "Please."

"If this will help you tell us who murdered you . . ."

Barreto Filho sat in a cushioned chair along the back wall of the house. Stately as a duchess, Idalina Barreto sat in her tall chair along the side wall. Fletch and Marilia sat along the other side wall.

Adult relatives sat in the other chairs. Four stood near the door. Children sat on the dirt floor. The windows were filled with people listening.

The area in front of the house was crowded with people.

From somewhere in the neighborhood the distinct sound of a television ceased.

But, of course, practicing drums could still be heard.

As Janio Barreto Filho spoke, he was interrupted, questioned, reminded, and corrected by his mother and other adults inside and outside the house. Marilia helped translate the difficult parts.

Listening intently, as the room under the tin roof in the sun became hotter, the air thicker, Fletch put together a continuous narrative to take away with him, to dissect and analyze later.

This may be a story, Janio Barreto Filho said, of a father who may have been right.

After all these years, my mother would like to know.

My father, Janio Barreto, was a handsome man, fair of hair and skin, well built, very lively, believed to be the best dancer in all the *favela*, maybe all of Rio de Janeiro. At least people say they enjoyed watching him the most. Sometimes, serving young people from Northamerica, one or two from Chile or Argentina, in the hotels of Copacabana, I have thought of him, as this was always as he was described to me, light in color and as unconcerned with the sad little things in life as a rich person.

It is said he came from near São Paulo, perhaps the descendant of one of the Northamericans from the South of the United States who came to that area at the end of your Civil War, to try to continue their plantation, slave-owing lives there. Many such came, and, of course, such is the beauty and seductiveness of our women, it was not long before they too became a part of the Brazilian population, their children having black and Indian blood and therefore unable to keep their brothers and sisters in bondage.

But you were truly fair, and came to the *favela* Santos Lima like a welcome thunderstorm in midwinter heat, casting your bolts of lightning everywhere. Why you came here, perhaps you could tell us now.

You were fourteen or fifteen when you arrived, full of your juices, full of laughs and smiles, being here, there, everywhere at once. As soon as you came to the *favela*, everyone could not have enough news of you: *Where is Janio? What has Janio done now? Did you hear what Janio did last night?* When the pantaloons of the corrupt policeman were pasted on the statue of Saint Francis, when the new bicycle of the storekeeper was found in a bedroom of the brothel, when the shit-dam suddenly appeared around the big house a few of the faithful had built for the strict Northamerican missionary, everyone knew you did it, and laughed with you, and stroked your fair hair.

The prestige of any girl you lay with rose in the *favela*. I suppose some of the girls lied about this, as it seems impossible to me — a man who enjoys life as much as any other — that one boy could have granted such prestige to so very many girls. In my own youth, being your acknowledged son, too much was expected of me. Going down the street I had to protect myself, not only from girls, but from their mothers, as well. It is true that the *favela* Santos Lima is known to have many more fair people than any other *favela* in Rio de Janeiro.

Of course you took on friends, a gang of three or four boys, two of whom were Idalina's brothers. Together you spent the days on the beaches, wrestling, swimming, playing soccer, the nights drinking and dancing and gambling, increasing the prestige of girls individually and raising mischief.

Now, Idalina's father was a man of great dignity. Although he worked as a conductor on a trolley car, he spent his life studying to be a bookkeeper. He never succeeded in finding work as a bookkeeper, but he prepared himself. It was his fervent wish at least to hand on to his sons the idea of being a bookkeeper.

He did not share in the *favela's* general idolatry of Janio Barreto. He felt you were leading his sons astray, giving them a liveliness that was not natural to them or in keeping with the idea of keeping books.

Through people he knew at the samba school, finally he succeeded in getting his sons jobs on a fishing boat. But the old men who owned the fishing boat made the condition highly irksome to old Fernando that they would only hire his sons to work on the fishing boat if they could hire Janio Barreto as well. Whether the idea was that they believed my uncles needed your leadership and brains, even though at first you knew nothing about the sea, being from the interior of Brazil, or whether it was the idea of the elders to get you to sea and therefore away from the *favela* some hours of the week and therefore cut down on the mischief and population growth, or whether they wanted, by being your employers, to be the first to know and tell of your pranks is unknown to me. To get his sons employed, Fernando had no choice but to agree.

So you went on the fishing boat with the Gomes brothers, and soon there were stories of a dead cold fish five feet long being put in the bed of the most precise bachelor in the *favela* while he slept (it was said he never slept in his bed or ate fish again), of a fishing-boat race which caused an older captain, whom you had taunted unmercifully, to become so determined to win at any cost that he rammed his own dock under full sail at such high speed he smashed his boat to slivers.

Fernando put up with all this with resignation. At least his sons had jobs, and there was hope that after a while working hard at sea, they would come to the idea of bookkeeping.

But when you began to call upon his daughter Idalina, coo to her through the window, spread flowers you stole from the cemetery all over the roof of the house, Fernando went into a rage.

Nor did he consider it funny when, on the night of his Saint's Day and perhaps he had had a bit too much to drink and lay in a stupor, you came along and shaved off only half of his mustache.

Then, at the age of eighteen, when most young men consider it wise and appropriate to be humble, apparently goaded by Fernando's open disapproval of you, you announced to the whole *favela* your intention of making Idalina your wife.

The *favela* was delighted. They knew marriage would do you no harm, not slow you down or make you less entertaining.

Idalina was delighted. It did not disturb her to be marrying the liveliest boy in the *favela*, or that her bond to you in marriage would have to be made of elastic.

Fernando fell into a mood so black for weeks he could not think of bookkeeping. He spent his time keeping his eye on Idalina. He argued with the air.

"Am I the only sane man in the world to see that Janio Barreto is a bad boy and no match for my Idalina? He has done enough to me, in keeping my sons from thinking in assets and debits! Why does he want a wife when he has every girl in the *favela* spitting at each other over him? He will never stop! Does he want to marry my daughter and continue his wild life just to torment me? It is as natural for him to be a husband as it is for a tomcat to pull a wagon!

"Idalina, he is no good! At the first difficulties of life, he will wander away! Already he has wandered from his home once! I want to know why! Once a man has wandered from his home, he is never to be trusted! He will wander again!

"Believe me, he will end up beaten in a gutter! That will not be a husband to be proud of!

"Probably dead! Some day someone will put a knife to him, and that will be the end of your husband, Janio Barreto, and of your marriage!"

The weight of the *favela* was on the side of the young lovers, of course, as people who are not directly involved in a situation always prefer romance to reason, and while Fernando stewed in his deep gloom, you and Idalina were married.

Now, as you must remember, not only were you known to be able to dance better and for a longer time than anyone, with more admiring eyes upon you, also you brought to the *favela* many new things about kick-dancing, *capoeira*, it being a skill which really developed in the interior. You taught the young men in Santos Lima more about *capoeira* than people knew in all the other *favelas* in Rio.

At that time, the Carnival Parade was beginning to become more organized from just a street competition among the *favelas* to the more formal presentation and attraction it is today.

Immediately, the samba school of Santos Lima became most famous for its troupe of *capoeiristas* you had trained. Santos Lima still has the reputation as having the best *capoeira* group in Rio de Janeiro.

But the first prophecy of Fernando came true.

You did not return immediately from Carnival that year. For days afterwards you were missing.

Finally you returned to Santos Lima from somewhere in the city. It was clear you had been physically beaten, and very badly. Your body was black with bruises. There were knife cuts on your upper arms and shoulders. Your face was as lumpy and welted as the bed or a couple married fifty years. You dragged yourself home like a beaten dog. Obviously, you had ended up beaten in a gutter.

People remarked, in hushed voices, the change in you. Silently you sat in your little house, licking your wounds. You never said what happened. You spoke to no one. Your laughter was not heard anywhere in the *favela*. You never went out and embarrassed Idalina by being with other women, to such an extent Idalina was beginning to lose her pride in you.

This is as I have the story from my mother and my uncles. Is your life beginning to come alive for you?

Then the second prophecy of Fernando came true.

After sitting quietly at home, not working, not playing, for almost all of Lent, you rose up and, carrying nothing, taking nothing with you except the working shorts you wore roped around your waist, you walked down the *favela* without a salutation to anyone, and disappeared. You wandered away.

Everyone was sure you were gone for good. Fun had gone from the *favela*.

Everyone commiserated with Fernando for having an abandoned daughter and two small grandchildren living out of his pocket, and congratulated him on the accuracy of his prophecies.

But the next winter, nine months later, you came back. You sailed into Guanabara Bay in a fishing boat you said was your own, a big boat ten meters long. You said you won it playing cards in Uruguay. The name painted on her side was in Spanish, *La Muñeca*. Surely you had sailed a long way. You were as thin as a street dog and very badly sunburned across your nose and shoulders. Some people said you went to Uruguay and stole the boat. Did you?

So now you had your own fishing boat.

In the inactivity caused by your absence, one of the Gomes brothers had become too fat to fish, the other too drunken. They both said they wanted to stay ashore now and think about bookkeeping.

You took on another young man, younger than you, named Tobias Novaes, to help you fish.

You worked hard. Shortly, you had a house near the top of the *favela*, higher even than Fernando's house. And for every married year, you had a child from your wife, Idalina. And every one of those children had children to play with their own ages who were also partly fair and looked as much like them as cousins.

At about your present age, it happened that a girl younger than you, who was as fair of hair and skin as yourself, came to the *favela*. Immediately, the *favela* said, "Oh, poor Idalina! This one will be serious! If they love themselves, how can they not love each other?"

And it was noticed that you became more serious then, worked longer hours, seldom looked up from your work. It was as if you were trying to ignore the inevitable: Ana Tavares, her name was.

But the inevitable is the inevitable, and as if your seed were transmitted by the wind, it was soon seen that Ana Tavares was glowing in her pregnancy.

This was especially noted as Ana Tavares was only waiting

out the year to be old enough to join the convent of The Sacred Heart of Jesus. People marveled that a girl who spent so many hours of the day and the night kneeling before the statue of the blessed Virgin could become pregnant. They attributed it to the wind.

Spending just as much time in prayer as always, Ana did not explain or complain.

Her father, however, whose life had not been as saintly as is recommended, was outraged. It had been his fondest wish to have a daughter a nun to pray for his soul before and after it departed.

You, having no father or brothers to attack, and being too young and strong, too expert a *capoeirista*, to attack, laughed for days after old Tavares attacked your father-in-law, Fernando, for his trouble-making son-in-law. Your father-in-law did not defend you. He too carried such rage at you that he yelled back at Tavares, and the two fathers of women became so enraged thinking about you that soon they were beating each other with their fists, then rolling on the ground, apparently fighting about which had the greater rage against you.

In truth, the son of Ana Tavares was entirely fair. She became the wife of a carpenter, and the boy — most likely another of your sons — became a *Puxador de Samba*, a singer of great repute in the samba school.

Yes, Oswaldinho there, in the window, is a son of that son of yours. You see how fair he is? Clearly, he has your blood, as have I.

Then the third prophecy of old Fernando came true — really came true.

One night you did not come home. You did not come home most nights. You were still young and perhaps by now considered it your obligation to entertain the *favela* with your tricks and to continue increasing your ever-growing audience by copulation.

But after this night in particular, after a heavy sea storm, you were found on the beach, facedown, with your throat slit ear to ear. Your blood had drained from your neck into the sand. Your shorts and hair and skin were caked with salt water, as if you had swum a long way to shore.

People say that in that particular spot on the beach, it has been impossible to light a fire or even light a match, ever since.

Your boat, *La Muñeca*, was missing, and never seen again.

Never seen again also was the boy who had helped you on the boat, Tobias Novaes.

For many years it was believed you had been murdered by young Tobias, although that surprised people, as it was generally believed he was a good boy. People thought he had slit your throat and stolen your boat.

But years later, his father got a letter from him, saying he had become a monk in Recife. Instantly, they had a letter written to him, asking if he had murdered you and stolen your boat.

The answer came back, eventually, that he hadn't known you were dead and that he felt himself greatly indebted to you as it was your example, and the example of your life, which had made the unworldly, serene, contemplative life of a monk seem so ideal to him.

For all these years your murder has been a mystery. There were so many people who could have killed you. Someone in the *favela* who did not like a trick you played on him? Did Tobias murder you for the boat? Did Uruguayans come and murder you and take back their boat? Or had the boat wrecked in the storm? How about old Tavares? He believed your preventing his daughter, Ana, from becoming a nun, surely condemned him to hell . . .?

My grandfather Fernando made three predictions about you. That you would end up beaten in the gutter. You were beat up, but you survived it, became your old self again. That, sooner or later, you would wander away. You did, but came back. That some day, someone would take a knife to you and kill you. That happened.

My mother, Idalina, who is very old now, as you see, wants to know the truth of these things. Who murdered you, and why?

How is it that her father was so right about you?

TWENTY-FOUR

"What Laura says is true," Fletch said to Marilia Diniz across the lunch table. "Anyone can tell you any story, and say it is the past."

Leaving *favela* Santos Lima totally unsatisfied, Fletch and Marilia led a parade of plucking pixies and curious adults down the hill and along the city street to his car. He had made his courtesies, thanked Janio Barreto Filho for the story, shaken hands with all the adults, thanked Idalina for her coffee and hospitality, generally wished the *favela* well in the parade of the samba schools that night, but left the airless little house as soon as he could. The heat in the room had become almost unbearable. But the eyes of everyone told him how unsatisfied they were. They had expected the story of Janio Barreto to so bring his memories alive he could tell them before leaving who had been his murderer.

Solemnly, Fletch promised he would think over the whole story.

He and Marilia drove to Colombo, a sparkling clean tearoom noted for its great pastry.

Marilia asked, "Do you still think it is a joke being played on you by Laura and the Tap Dancers?"

"I don't see how it can be. All those people in the door and windows, all those people in the street had heard the story before, knew parts of it well enough to correct Janio, add elements to it — and all with high seriousness. If it is a trick, it's the most elaborate trick conceivable."

Their waffles were warm and tender.

"You have heard the story now," Marilia said.

"What is the answer?"

"How would I know?"

Marilia's eyes flickered at him. "All right. But use what you do know, use your training. You were trained as an investigative reporter. . . ."

"Yeah: investigating how come the city's water pipes run an extra five kilometers to avoid the property owned by the water commissioner. Big deal. This is not quite the same sort of situation."

"Nevertheless . . ."

"Investigative reporters do not make guesses just to satisfy people with a conclusion to a story."

"But investigative reporters do think, don't they?"

"Think about documented facts. How can I think about something that happened on a beach in Rio de Janeiro forty-seven years ago? However long I am in Brazil, I will never be that prescient. Or post-scient."

"What will you tell them?"

Fletch made sure there was syrup on each part of his waffle. "I suppose I'll tell them the kindest thing I can think of: Uruguayans came and slit his throat and took their boat back. It would be kinder than blaming someone in the *favela* dead or alive."

"Janio said he won the boat playing cards." Marilia chewed thoughtfully. "There is some evidence he did."

"What evidence?"

"If you stole a boat, even from a different country, wouldn't you change its name?"

"Of course. I suppose so."

"The name of the boat was in Spanish. *La Muñeca.* He never changed its name. They said after Janio was found dead, *La Muñeca* was missing. Never seen again."

Fletch sighed.

Marilia said, "And if Uruguayans killed Janio Barreto, why didn't they kill Tobias Novaes as well? He would have been on the boat with Janio."

"Perhaps the Uruguayans appeared after they docked."

"Could be," Marilia said.

"After Tobias wandered off to become a monk. Marilia, that's too big a coincidence in timing. How could Tobias wander off to become a monk without telling anyone what he was doing, just before Janio got his throat slit?"

"There had been a storm at sea. I have heard of people becoming very religious, very suddenly, during storms at sea. They make deals. Spare my life, oh Lord, and I will devote the rest of my life to singing Thy praises."

"Maybe."

"I think the boat sank. And both Janio and Tobias swam ashore. Tobias to join a monastery; Janio to get his throat slit."

"That's fine. It's great to guess. But how can we know?"

Again, Marilia's eyes flickered.

Fletch said, "Tobias himself is a good bet as the murderer. Surely he wouldn't be the first to commit a heinous crime and then, after a while, so weighted with guilt, he hies off to a monastery to spend the rest of his life atoning."

"True. Tobias could have killed Janio. He could have stolen the boat. But after years of being a monk, could he have lied about it?"

Somewhat in imitation of Tito Granja, Fletch crossed his eyes.

"After years of atonement," Marilia said, "Tobias would know he would be risking his soul to lie."

"Risking his soul," Fletch repeated. "That brings up the father of the girl who was going to be a nun. What was his name? Tavares. Apparently he thought he was going to end up in hell anyway. Why wouldn't he have killed Janio?"

"He might have. Still, murder is the greatest crime. And there is always the possibility of personal salvation."

Fletch looked at Marilia's bracelet. It was made of rotting braided cloth. He had seen many such bracelets in Brazil. He had difficulty understanding the significance of them.

"Fernando," Fletch said. "Idalina's father. Certainly he hated Janio. Over a long period of time. He got into a fistfight over him."

"Kill his son-in-law? Leave his daughter a widow, his grandchildren fatherless?" Slowly, Marilia said, "I suppose so. Fernando apparently thought Janio not a very good husband or father."

"And he had reason to be envious of him. Fernando could never find work as a bookkeeper. Then Janio shows up with his own boat. Becomes a prosperous man. Even gets to live in a house higher up in the *favela* than Fernando."

Marilia, a slim, trim woman, surprised Fletch by ordering one of the bigger, more sugary pastries.

Fletch said, "You know, once you make prophecies about someone, there is the instinct to help them become fulfilled."

"Fernando said someone would take a knife to Janio and kill him, and it wasn't happening fast enough to satisfy Fernando, so he did the job himself?"

"I suppose prophets have to work at their reputations, as much as anyone else."

"Mmmmm. So what will you do, Fletcher? What will you tell these people?"

"I don't know. I'm not about to point the finger at a monk. Or at the grandfather of the family. Or at the memory of some other deceased citizen whose daughter was deflowered by the victim. Any one of hundreds of people could have done in Janio."

"Now that you've heard the story, will you be able to sleep?"

"Will I?"

They finished their pastries in silence.

Fletch said, "Marilia, tell me about that bracelet you're wearing."

Self-consciously she touched it with the fingers of her other hand. "Oh, that."

"I see many people, men and women, wearing these cloth, braided bracelets."

"Just a superstition, I guess." Her face flushed. "You make a wish, you know, for something you hope will come true. As you make the wish, you put on this braided bracelet. You wear it until what you wished for comes true."

"Supposing what you wish for doesn't come true?"

Slightly red-faced, she laughed. "Then you wear it until it falls off."

"You believe in such a thing?"

"No," she said quickly.

"But you're wearing such a bracelet."

"Why not?" she asked, resetting it on her wrist. "It does no harm to act as if you believe in such a thing, just in case it is true."

Outside the restaurant they stopped at a kiosk. Marilia bought *Jornal do Brasil* and Fletch bought *Brazil Herald* and the *Latin America Daily Post*.

A healthy-seeming curly-haired man of about thirty was leaning against Fletch's MP. It appeared he was waiting for them.

He spoke rapidly, happily to Fletch.

Then, seeing he wasn't being understood, he spoke to Marilia.

She answered him, happily enough. While talking with him, she opened the small purse tied to her wrist, took out some money, and gave it to him.

The man stuffed the money into his shoe.

Then he leaned against the next car, a Volkswagen bug.

In the car, Fletch asked, "What did he want?"

"Ohhhh. He said he had been taking care of the car for us while we were away. It is for him to take care of the cars along this section of curb, he said."

"Is it?"

"He says so."

"Who gave him charge of this section of curb?"

"No one. It is just something he says."

Fletch started the car. "If it is just something he says, then why did you give him money? Why didn't you just tell him to get lost?"

Flustered, Marilia was looking into her handbag, perhaps rearranging the interior, "I suppose I owe it to him because I just had such a nice lunch."

TWENTY-FIVE

"Fletch?"

"Yes?"

"Toninho Braga, Fletch. Look what time it is."

"Shortly after noon."

"That's right. And so far no one has reported finding Norival's body."

Over the phone, Toninho's voice sounded more hushed than alarmed.

Fletch had driven Marilia Diniz to her home in Leblon, thanked her for accompanying him to the *favela*, repeated he still had no way of solving a forty-seven-year-old murder mystery, but he would return to the hotel to try to sleep.

His room at The Hotel Yellow Parrot had been cleaned. The unslept-in bed had been freshly made up.

He telephoned The Hotel Jangada and asked for Joan Collins Stanwyk in Room 912.

No answer.

Across the utility area, the man was still painting the room.

He was about to strip, to shower, to darken the room, to get into bed again, to try to sleep, when the phone rang.

"Toninho," he said. "It's Sunday. A big day of Carnival. Communication is slow."

"That's exactly it, Fletch. There would have been hundreds, thousands of people on that beach, shortly after dawn."

"Finding a body —"

"Norival is not just a body. He is a Passarinho. That would be news."

"First the police have to be summoned —"

"Yes, the police would be summoned. But we left plenty of identification on Norival's body. The people who found the body would be quick to tell the Passarinho family, the radio stations. The police would be even quicker. They would compete for the attention of the Passarinho family."

"I don't see what you're saying. You put Norival's body in the water. He was dead. He has to come ashore somewhere, sometime, if you were right about the tides."

"I was right about the tides. Where's Norival?"

"How would I know?"

Fletch looked down at the soft, smooth countenance of the bed.

"Fletch, we must go make sure someone finds the body of Norival."

"Toninho, I'm not sure I can take many more disappearances today, of persons dead and alive."

"You must come help us look, Fletch. That will make four of us. We can comb the beach."

"You want to go beachcombing for a corpse?"

"What else can we do? We put Norival's body there to be found, not to be lost. What if he were lost forever? There would be no Funeral Mass. He would not be properly buried. His family might think he ran away."

"His boat would be missing."

"Sailed away. To Argentina! Think of his poor mother!"

"His poor mother."

"Such a thing would kill her. Not to know what happened to her son."

"Toninho . . . . I still have not slept."

"That's all right."

" 'All right'?"

"You must help us. Four searching is better than three searching. It is a long beach."

"Toninho . . ."

"We'll pick you up in ten minutes."

The phone line died.

TWENTY-SIX

"Perhaps we should check with Eva," Tito said. "Norival might have gone back to her."

"Norival was happy with Eva," Orlando said.

Of the four young men walking along the beach, only Fletch wore sandals. He knew himself not sufficiently *carioca* to walk along a beach in the midday sun in bare feet.

Toninho, Tito, and Orlando had picked Fletch up in the black four-door Galaxie.

On the sidewalk in front of the hotel, the youngest Janio Barreto on a wooden leg silently watched Fletch get into the car and be driven away.

The drive to the beach where Norival was scheduled to appear had been as fast as possible through the Carnival crowds.

At one place on Avenida Atlantica perhaps as many as a thousand people in tattery costumes jumped up and down around a big samba band moving forward only a few meters an hour on the back of a flatbed truck. Never had he seen so much human energy spent in so little forward motion.

On the way to the beach they listened silently to the loud car radio.

The discovery of Norival Passarinho's body was not yet news.

The beach was filled with bright umbrellas, mats. Families and other groups picnicked and played.

Orlando said to Fletch: "It is said if a person dies copulating, he is guaranteed to return to life soon."

"For Norival, the process might have been very quick," said Tito.

Spread apart only somewhat, they walked along the water's edge, looking for Norival perhaps washed up dead but thought asleep, some crowd of gossips with news of something unusual having happened, the corpse of the Passarinho boy being found, police barriers, markers, something, anything.

"Do people say the same thing in the United States of Northamerica?" Orlando asked.

"I don't think so," Fletch said. "I never heard it."

"People in the United States of Northamerica don't die while copulating," Toninho said. "They die while talking about it."

"They die while talking to their psychiatrists about it." Orlando laughed.

"Yes, yes," said Toninho. "They die worrying about copulating."

"People of the United States of Northamerica," Tito scoffed. "This is how they walk."

Tito began to move hurriedly over the sand, his head and shoulders forward of his body, legs straight, not pivoting his hips at all, his hands dangling loosely beside him like a couple of cow udders, his eyes staring straight ahead, an expectant grin on his face, each foot landing flat on the sand. The impression was of a body being pushed at the shoulders, falling forward, each foot coming out and landing at the last second to keep the body from falling flat on its face.

Fletch stopped walking and laughed.

For a while, then, he walked slightly behind his friends.

"Yes," Tito said. "Norival may have revived."

Fletch asked, "Is it true everyone goes slightly crazy during Carnival?"

Toninho said, "Slightly."

"If the way to life eternal," Fletch asked, "is to die copulating, then why don't people just copulate constantly?"

Orlando sniffed. "I do my best."

A man carrying two metal cylinders containing iced *mate* passed them. Each container easily weighed one hundred pounds. He would sell the *mate* in little cups to people on the beach. The man was in his sixties and he was walking rapidly enough to pass the four young men. His legs looked like the roots of trees hardened by time.

"This is crazy," Fletch said. Perhaps lying in the sun on the beach would make him drowsy enough to sleep.

Dead wallets, stolen and emptied, were on the beach like birds shot from the sky.

Toninho scanned the surface of the ocean. "There is not even a sign of his boat. That, too, should have come ashore."

"The boat sank," Tito said.

"Maybe Norival sank," Orlando said.

"Maybe Norival is alive and we are dead," Fletch said.

Orlando looked at him as if he had just offered a possibility worth consideration.

They were coming to the end of the beach.

Nearby was a group of very young teenage girls in bikinis. Five of the eight were pregnant.

Toninho said, "Absolutely, Norival was to come ashore somewhere along here."

"Let's ask," Fletch said. "Let's ask the people on the beach if they've noticed a Passarinho floating by without a boat."

"It leaves only one thing to do," Toninho said.

"Go home to bed," Fletch said.

"Swim along the beach," Toninho said.

"Oh, no," Fletch said.

Toninho was looking into the water. "It is possible Norival is lurking somewhere just below the surface."

"That would be just like Norival," Orlando said. "Playing some trick."

"*Arigó*," Toninho said.

"I need sleep," Fletch said. "Not a swim."

"Yes," Tito said, "Norival was apt to be a bit slow, sometimes, to show up."

"Last night, when I swam into Norival," Toninho said, "he was more under the surface than I would have expected."

"Right," said Tito. "We shall swim along the shore and see if we bump into Norival."

"Oh, no," said Fletch.

"Leave your sandals here," said Orlando. "Not even a Northamerican can swim well wearing sandals."

On the way back in the car they listened to a long news broadcast. Mostly, it was about Carnival Parade that night, and certain controversies which had arisen concerning it. One samba school was insisting the theme they had chosen to present had been usurped a little bit by another samba school. At least, the themes of the two schools were believed by one school to be dangerously similiar.

In all that long broadcast, the discovery of the corpse of Norival Passarinho was not reported.

TWENTY-SEVEN

"You're not becoming a Brazilian," Laura Soares said over the dinner table. "You're becoming a Carnival Brazilian."

When Fletch dragged himself back to his room at The Hotel Yellow Parrot, sunburned, caked with salt, the bottoms of his feet fried from just the walk up the beach from the ocean to the car, Laura was waiting for him, curled up in a chair studying sheet music, full of questions about where they would dine, full of enthusiasm for spending the night watching the Carnival Parade from Teodomiro da Costa's box.

Tiredly, he greeted her. She helped him shower. On the bed he wanted to sleep. She teased him into giving her a warmer greeting than he thought possible in his sleepless condition. They showered again.

She was dressing when he came out of the bathroom.

On the white trousers and white shirt he had laid out to wear that night, she had placed a wide, bright red sash.

"Is this for me?" he asked.

"From Bahia."

"Am I to wear it?"

"To the Carnival Parade. You will look very Brazilian."

"I am to wear a red sash without a coat?"

"Why would anyone wear a coat over such a beautiful red sash?"

"Wow." After he dressed, she helped him adjust it. "I feel like a Christmas present."

"You are a Christmas present. A jolly Christmas present wrapped in a red ribbon for Laura."

They decided to dine in the dining room which was on the second floor of The Hotel Yellow Parrot.

Through the floor-to-ceiling open windows they could see the *macumba* fires on *Praia de Copacabana*. Believers spend the night on the beach tending a fire, having written a wish, or the name of their illness, on a piece of paper which they launch in the first moments of the outgoing tide. On the first night of the year especially there are thousands of fires on the beach.

The hotel restaurant was said to be one of the best in the world. It was rare in that the restaurant's kitchen was exactly twice as big as the seating area.

They ordered *moqueca,* another Bahian speciality.

"You did not even read Amado's *Dona Flor and Her Two Husbands* while I was gone."

"Tell me about it."

"You said you could not sleep, of course, but you did not even read."

"Somehow I kept busy."

"Gambling with the Tap Dancers."

"I relieved them of some of their inheritances."

"I dare not even ask you about this country inn they took you to."

"It had a swimming pool."

"Riding around all day. So late to the Canecão Ball. Cristina said you were dressed as a movie cowboy."

"An outfit I borrowed from Toninho."

"I saw it in the closet."

"I looked real sleek."

"That you danced hours with that French film star, Jetta."

"There was no one else to dance with her."

"I'm sure." Laura mixed her *pirao* with her *farofa com dendê.* "Brazilians are not like this all the time. Only during Carnival. Brazilians are a very serious people."

"I'm sure."

"Look at our big buildings. Our factories. Our biggest-in-the-world hydroelectric plant. Everything here runs by computer now. At the airport, all the public announcements, in each language, are done by computer voices. And you can understand what they are saying perfectly."

Through the window Fletch started to count the *macumba* fires on the beach.

"Marilia Diniz and I went this morning to the *favela* Santos Lima to see the Barreto family, to hear the story of Janio Barreto's life and death."

Laura did not seem interested in that. "You should read the novels of Nelida Piñon. Then you would know something of Brazilian life. Not just Carnival foolishness. Things are very different here in Brazil."

"I know," he said. "The water goes down the drain counterclockwise."

"Anyway . . ." She removed a bone from her fish. "Last night, in Bahia, I agreed finally to do this concert tour."

"Concert tour? You're going on a concert tour?"

"Pianists who stop playing the piano stop being pianists," she said.

"Where are you going? When?"

"In about a month. Bahia first, then São Paulo, Rio de Janeiro, Recife. Friends of my father have been urging me to do this, setting it up for some time."

"I guess they want you to get serious."

"I am an educated pianist. I've had good reviews. I like the idea of bringing so much Brazilian music to the piano."

"You will have to work very hard to go on such a tour."

"Very hard."

"Practice a lot."

"A very lot."

"Do you want dessert?"

"Of course."

They ordered cherry tarts.

"Fletcher," she asked, "what are you serious about?"

"Sleeping."

"Serious."

"I'm serious about sleeping."

"Sleeping is necessary, I guess."

"I am seriously worried. You remember that woman I was to have breakfast with yesterday morning at The Hotel Jangada?"

"Who is she?"

"The woman in the green dress we saw on the *avenida*."

"You didn't want to see her."

"I do now. Her name is Joan Collins Stanwyk. She's from California."

"That was clear, from looking at her. Her eyes looked as if she were watching a movie."

"She's disappeared."

"People disappear in Brazil, Fletch." Laura didn't seem to want to hear about that, either. "What time are we to arrive at Carnival Parade?"

"Teo suggested about ten o'clock. I doubt he'll be there much earlier than that."

"I've never watched Carnival Parade from a box before."

"I think he suspects this is the only year I'll be here for it."

Laura said nothing.

For a moment, Fletch watched her finish her cherry tart.

Then Fletch gazed through the window at the *macumba* fires on the moonless beach. A cheer was sent up from a samba crowd on the *avenida*.

He said, "Carnival . . ."

"The point of it is to remember that things are not always as they appear."

TWENTY-EIGHT

"Welcome to the Samba School Parade!" Teodomiro da Costa said in the tone of a ringmaster. He stood just inside the door of his box overlooking the parade route. He wore jeans and a T-shirt. On front of the T-shirt were printed a black bow tie and ruffles. In a more personal tone, he asked, "Have you eaten?"

"At the hotel."

He looked into Fletch's eyes and spoke just loudly enough for Fletch to hear him over the fantastic noise. "You have not slept."

"Not yet."

"Have a drink."

"*Guaraná*, please."

Teo repeated the order to the barman.

"Laura!" Teo hugged her to his chest. "Did Otavio get home all right?"

"Of course. He just pretended to need help."

"I think that's what you do with daughters. You pretend to need their help when, actually, you do."

The box was bigger than Fletch had expected, big enough for twenty people to move around in comfortably, to see, even dance, plus room for the sandwiches and drinks table, the barman.

Adrian Fawcett, the writer for *The Times*, was there, the Vianas, the da Silvas, the London broker and his wife, the Italian racing car driver and his girl friend. Jetta looked at Fletch with the resentment of someone who had been danced with but not loved. She did not look at Laura at all.

Everyone marveled at everyone else's costumes, of course. Laura was dressed as an eighteenth-century musician, in breeches and knee socks, ruffled shirt front, gray wig. The Viana woman asked Laura if she had brought her piano to accompany her costume.

As Fletch moved forward in the box, glass of *guaraná* in hand, he had the sensation that Rio's volume knob was being turned up. Thousands of drums were being played in the area. Hundreds of thousands of people were singing and chattering and cheering.

Across the parade route, the stands were a sea of faces inclined toward the sky. Above the bright lights aimed on the route, thick, hot, smoky air visibly rolled up the stands and formed a thin gray cloud overhead.

"Rio de Janeiro's Carnival Parade Class One-A is the biggest, most amazing human spectacle in the world," Teodomiro da Costa had said, inviting Fletch. "Except war."

The parade starts at six o'clock Sunday afternoon and continues until past noon Monday. About twelve samba schools, of more than three thousand costumed people each, compete in the parade.

"I'm not sure I can stand three more days of Carnival." Even speaking over the noise, Adrian Fawcett's voice was a deep rumbling chuckle. "Days of elation or depression have the same effect on people, you know. I'm drained already."

"It's a mark of character to be able to survive Carnival intact," Laura answered. "It's a matter of having the right attitudes."

She beamed at Fletch.

Fletch said: "It's all beyond belief."

"Next is *Escola Guarnieri.*" Teo peered over the rail at the *bateria* in the bull pen. "Yes, that's Guarnieri." Then he said to Fletch, "After that comes *Escola Santos Lima.*"

The parade route, on Avenida Marques de Sapucai, is only a mile long.

To the left along the parade route are the stands, built as high as most buildings, crammed with tens of thousands of people. They arrive in the stands, take and protect their seats, bake in the sun, eat their sandwiches, hold their bladders, chatter and sing beginning at noon, a full six hours before the parade starts. Almost all stay in their seats for the full twenty-four hours.

To the right along the parade route are the boxes, vastly expensive vantage points, some done up in bunting. In the boxes are government dignitaries, Brazilian and foreign celebrities, and people who are simply rich.

The parade route between its two sides is as wide as a three-lane road.

It is as wide as the line between shade and sun, sickness and health, tin and gold.

Also along the right-hand side of the route, ten meters high in the air, are the watchtowers where sit the various parade judges, one for costumes, one for floats, one for music, one for dancing, etc. They sit immobile, expressionless, alone, many behind dark sunglasses so that not even a flicker of an eye may be a subject of comment and controversy. Their names are not released to the public until the day of the parade. And so complicated and controversial is their task that the results of their judging are not announced until four days later, on Thursday.

Diagonally across the parade route from da Costa's box, to the left, is the bull pen filled with hundreds of costumed *ritmistas*, the *bateria* of drummers of *Escola Guarnieri*. Their drums are of all sizes and tones. It takes the drummers up to an hour to put themselves into their proper places in regard to each other, to get their rhythms up, their sound up. Now their rhythm and their sound are full, and fill everyone at the parade, fill their ears, their brains, their entire nervous systems, control the beatings of their hearts, make their eyes flush with blood, their hands and feet move involuntarily, their bones to vibrate. This is total sound, amplified only by human will, as primitive a sound as Man ever made, the sound of drums, calling from every human, direct, immediate response, equalizing them in their numbness before the sound.

Everyone in da Costa's box is standing at the rail. Laura has taken off her wig and opened the collar of her eighteenth-century-styled shirt. The faces of everyone at the rail shine with sweat. Their eyes, their lips protrude slightly, as if the sound of the drums reverberating within them were seeking a way to burst out of them. The veins at their temples throb visibly to the beat of the drums. Being host, Teo stands back behind the people at the rail. Being tall, he can still see everything.

Down the parade route from the left, passing the *bateria* in the bull pen like the top of a T comes the *Abre-Alas*, the opening wing of Guarnieri's presentation. This group of *sambistas*, moving of course to the sound of the drums, wear bright, ornate, slightly exaggerated costumes presenting a hint of the time and place of the samba school's theme, in this case nineteenth-century Amazon plantation ball gowns, their hoop skirts a little too wide, the bodices a little too grand, the bouffants a little too high; for the men, spats a little too long, frock coats a little too wide in the shoulders, top hats a little too high. This is the slave's view of plantation life. The exaggeration is a making fun. The exaggeration also expresses victory over such a life.

Immediately behind the *Abre-Alas* comes a huge float stating the literary theme of Guarnieri's presentation. On the slowly moving truck invisible beneath the float is a mammoth book open for all to see the letters G. R. E. S. GUARNIERI (*Gremio Recreativo Escola de Samba Guarnieri*). It is desired that the spectator know that it is of history that the school portrays, a kind of written, authoritative history, which may be a kind of joke, too, or an exaggeration, as there is very little authoritative, written history.

Then comes the *Comissão de Frente*, a line of formally dressed men doing a strolling samba. It is desired that the spectators accept these aging *sambistas*, honored for their contributions to past Carnival Parades, chosen for their grace and dignity, as the samba school's board of directors. Few, if any, actually are directors. The real directors are working hard in the school's parade, all sides of it at once. The presentation — dancers, drummers, floats on trucks and flatbeds, floats that are pushed by hand — must move at exactly one mile an hour, without gaps or holes, keeping the balances of colors and movements perfect.

Behind this line of dignitaries comes the first and most distinguished dancing couple, the *Porta Bandeira* and the *Mestre Sala*, the Flag Bearer and the Room, or Dancing Master. These are mature people, in their prime, dressed in lavish eighteenth-century costumes regardless of the theme, those decided by everyone in the *favela* to be absolutely the best dancers, those dancers everyone else most enjoys watching. Their dance step is incredibly complicated, to most people an incomprehensible wonder, with patterns within patterns, movements within movements. They too must move forward in their dancing at exactly one mile per hour. And while she dances, the lady of the couple must carry a flag, the samba school's emblem on one side, the symbol of that year's theme on the other side, waving it so that both sides are visible to everyone.

It is obligatory that every person in the parade, every dancer, dignitary, drummer, director working or parading must constantly be singing the *samba enredo*, the song presented by that school that year, as loudly and as well, as continuously, as he or she can.

As the *alas* come by, the theme of the school's presentation becomes more and more clear, however broad the theme may be. An *ala* is a group of hundreds of vigorously dancing people identically dressed depicting some aspect of the theme. Here one *ala* is costumed as Indians from the Amazon Basin, dancing steps suggestive of that cultural area. Another *ala* is again of plantation life, the costumes modified, of course, so that the beauty of the people of that *favela*, their flesh and movement, the joy of the dancers' bodies may be revealed and enjoyed by all.

In among the *alas* come the *Figuras de Destaque*, the prominent figures which relate to the theme, in this case mythically huge figures of Amazonian plumed birds and monkeys.

All these groups cross in front of the *bateria* of drummers filling the air with sound in the bull pen.

In da Costa's box, Jetta in particular wilts. Her greatly abbreviated costume of a Foreign Legionnaire looks hot and heavy over her breasts and hips. Her back leans against a stanchion. Her chin is on her chest. Her eyes are open, watching, but glazed.

The most important obligatory *ala* of any presentation is that which honors the earliest history of the samba parade in Rio de Janeiro. After the drought of 1877, women who had emigrated from Bahia danced slowly down the main street of Rio in their long white gowns on the Sunday before Lent, inviting the men to join them, as they had done in Salvador. So here comes the *Ala das Baianas*, scores of older women, usually the blackest in the *favela*, dressed, dancing in the flowing white robes of Bahia.

The *passistas* cause the greatest excitement and appreciation. Young people from the *favela*, the youngest fully formed, girls and boys, the most beautiful and most handsome, clearly the most athletic, as near naked as possible without being cumbersomely nude, dance down the parade route together acrobatically, tumbling, doing cartwheels, climbing each other, leaping off, being caught by others a centimeter before disaster, all the while singing, of course, doing all this in a choreography so intricate, so closely timed it has taken them the full year to study it, learn it, practice it. Some of the young men may have developed a *capoeira* routine which is so graceful while so vicious, so rife with genuine danger, that the sight of it might stop the spectator's heart if the drums weren't controlling the heart, keeping it going.

Adrian Fawcett says something to Fletch.

Fletch yells, "What?" but cannot hear even his own voice.

Adrian cups his hands over Fletch's ear and yells with his full voice, virtually taking a full breath to blow out each word: "Think if all this energy, planning, work, skill the year 'round went into revolution instead!"

Fletch nods that he heard him.

Interspersed among the *alas*, a few *alegorias* have passed, huge floats depicting scenes from the Amazon, one a section of jungle bejeweled by women in G-strings suggesting plumed birds in their tall, bright, feathered headpieces; slim boys-men with the heads of snakes slithering over the rocks; children with the heads of monkeys dancing in the trees. Another *alegoria* depicts an Indian village, live fire centering thatched huts, costumed Indians dancing with mythical fish-headed and monster-headed figures.

In the middle of the presentation comes a small float, a disguised pickup truck, really a sound truck with amplifiers aiming every direction. On the back of the truck-float, dressed formally like a nightclub singer, stands the *Puxador de Samba*, microphone close to mouth, singing over and over at fullest personal volume, belting out the lyrics of the samba school's song for that year:

Like the Amazon flows our history,
Deep, mysterious and wide,
Of many brooks and streams,
Magically providing us with life.

After a few more *alas* does the *bateria* begin to pull out of the bull pen and join the parade. An entire army of drummers, perhaps a thousand or more powerful men from the ages of fifteen to whenever, uniformly dressed in dazzling costume, all beating their drums in patterns practiced all year, all singing, all dancing despite the size of their drums, pass by. The sound is overpowering. It is perhaps the maximum sound the earth and sky can accept without cracking, without breaking into fragments to move with it before dissipating into dust.

Near the end of the parade comes the samba school's principal *alegoria*. In this case, for *Escola Guarnieri* that year, a nineteenth-century riverboat slowly comes down the parade route, if not full-sized at least impressively huge — as white, as delicate, as ornate as a wedding cake. Its prow moves majestically down the street high above the heads of the *bateria*. The bridge is proud in its height. Steam comes from its funnels. The cap of its whistle funnel rises and lowers, and doubtlessly the sound of a steamboat whistle comes out, but so high is the level of sound generally that even a steamboat whistle cannot be heard fifteen meters away. The white, gleaming hull moves by slowly. The mere sight of the upper decks and into the interior cabins and ballroom of the ship instantly creates the feeling of a grander day, grander people, a grander way to travel, to move, to be. Sedately move the side wheels of this riverboat, exactly as if they were thrusting water behind them. And as the riverboat passes, its stern turned up to be high above the final dancing *ala* behind it, the last to disappear down the stream of swirling costumed dancers and drummers, instant yearning for it fills the heart, the instant and full desire to experience again the passing of this ghost, this *alegoria* of the past.

"I think you're going to have to tell me that there is life after Carnival," Fletch said.

At the bar table at the back of the box, Teo laughed and handed him a sandwich.

Other people were coming to the back of the box for drinks and sandwiches.

"Does everything become real again?" Fletch asked.

Adrian Fawcett said, "Reality has hunkered down somewhere in my gut, assumed the fetal position, and promises only in whispers to return."

The sound level had lowered to the merely very loud. Across the parade route, the *bateria* of *Escola Santos Lima* was organizing itself in the bull pen.

Jetta put her hand on Fletch's shoulder. "Are you supposed to be some kind of a present?"

She looked thoroughly sound-struck, sight-struck, mind-blown, and jaded.

He smoothed his bright red sash.

"I'm a present," Fletch said. "Maybe I'm a past. Maybe I'm a future."

"And did you come *par avion?*"

Chewing, Teo said, "Did you and Laura come by subway?"

"Yes, Teo," Fletch said honestly. "Never have I seen an underground transportation system so modern, so quiet, so clean."

Dressed like a Christmas package and as an eighteenth-century musician, Fletch and Laura had ridden Rio's subway to Carnival Parade at Teo's suggestion. Everyone had told them they could not get a car or a taxi within kilometers of Avenida Marques de Sapucai.

The ten-year-old Janio Barreto had followed Fletch and Laura from The Hotel Yellow Parrot to Avenida Marques de Sapucai.

In the subway station he ducked under the turnstile onto the platform. Fletch thought the underground official saw him, but the man took no notice. Who would keep a wooden-legged boy off public transportation because he had no money? On the train, Janio stood away from them, not looking at them, not speaking to them.

Fletch pointed him out to Laura, briefly told her about him.

She seemed particularly disturbed by being followed by a small boy on a wooden leg.

Janio hobbled after them through the dark back streets to the Carnival Parade. At the entrance to the boxes he was stopped. Security was very heavy there, very official. Even with tickets, Fletch and Laura physically had to force, squeeze themselves through the bodies of the guards. They would not let anyone, even or especially a ten-year-old boy on a wooden leg, through the entrance to the boxes without a ticket.

"Yes." Fletch was aware Teo was watching his face. "A magnificent subway."

The Italian racing-car driver came to the bar table. "There are some Indians out there calling for you."

"Me?" Fletch asked.

The racing-car drive jerked his thumb over his shoulder, indicating the area beyond the box rail.

Laura was dancing in the center of the box with Aloisio da Silva. The heat had caused her leggings to drop over her patent leather shoes.

On the packed earth between the box and the pavement of the parade route stood Toninho Braga, Orlando Velho, and Tito Granja. Again they were dressed as movie Indians. In that light, their shoulders and stomach ridges shone with sweat.

"Jump down!" Toninho shouted.

Fletch put perplexity on his face.

Cupping his hand over his mouth, Orlando shouted, "We need to talk to you!"

"Later!" yelled Fletch.

"About Norival!" shouted Toninho.

Tito waved his arm to encourage Fletch to jump down to them.

Fletch turned around.

Dancing with Aloisio, Laura's eyes were on Fletch's face.

Her own face was so expressionless it was unfathomable.
From behind him, Fletch heard the name *Janio* shouted.
He jumped the three meters from the box down to the Tap Dancers.

TWENTY-NINE

Toninho clapped Fletch on the shoulder. "You look Brazilian with that red sash. Probably just the way you did fifty years ago."

"Laura brought it to me from Bahia."

The four young men walked along the area between the boxes and the parade route.

Fletch said, "I was in a *favela* this morning. I don't see how the people in a *favela* can afford to put on such a presentation, all these drums and costumes and floats."

"It takes every *cruzeiro*, and then some," Toninho said. "By the way, I have lots of your money, your poker winnings, at my apartment. It's safe there. And dry."

"Thousands of beautiful costumes," Fletch mused. "Each must be individually made."

Tito said, "Everyone in a *favela* pays dues to the samba school every week. Also, the samba school gets some subsidy from the government for Carnival Parade. It's good for tourism."

"The *jogo do bicho*," Orlando said. "The *jogo do bicho* pays a lot."

"The illegal numbers game," Toninho said. "The people who run the illegal numbers games give a lot of money to the samba schools for Carnival Parade. It's their way of giving some of the money back, paying taxes —"

"Because they've been stealing from the people all year," Tito said. "Stealing their false hopes."

"It's good public relations for *jogo do bicho*," Tito said. "A business expense."

They had passed two or three of the judges' viewing towers.

Tito turned around and walked backwards. "Here comes *Escola Santos Lima*, Janio. Some of your descendants are parading."

"*Escola Santos Lima* has the best *capoeiristas* in all Rio de Janeiro,"

299

Orlando said. "Maybe all Brazil. A huge what-would-you-say squad-
ron of them."

Toninho held Fletch's elbow. "Listen. Norival has not appeared."

"You miscalculated, Toninho. Miscalculated the currents. His body
must have been carried out to sea."

"Not possible. Remember last night when I was swimming ashore?
I swam into Norival. That proves that already he was floating toward
the beach."

Against the noise of Carnival Parade the four young men held their
heads close together as they walked.

"It would be terrible if Norival were eaten by a shark," Tito said.

"You don't see Norival as fish food?" Fletch asked.

"If it looks like he has just disappeared," Orlando asked practica-
bly, "how do we tell his family he is dead?"

"His poor mother," said Tito.

"His father will be awfully angry," said Toninho. "And Admiral
Passarinho . . ."

"They will never forgive us for burying Norival at sea without them,"
Tito said.

"How would they ever believe us?" asked Toninho.

"You have a problem," Fletch admitted.

"The tide has been in and out and soon comes in again." Toninho
looked sick. He looked as if the tide, with all its wiggly life, were
passing through his own stomach and head.

"What do we do?" Orlando asked.

Fletch said, "Got me."

"What does that mean?"

"I haven't any idea."

"You are our friend, Fletch." Toninho still walked with Fletch's
elbow in hand. "You helped us with Norival."

"Now you must help us think," said Tito.

"I don't think I can," said Fletch. "Someone I know who is alive
has disappeared. Other people tell me I died forty-seven years ago
and must name my murderer. I haven't slept. I am drunk with the
sound of the drums. Norival has died and disappeared. Everything is
becoming less real. How can I answer if I don't understand?"

They had walked half the length of the parade route.

Fletch stopped. "I must go back."

"Yes," said Tito. "He must see Santos Lima parade."

"You will tell us if you think of anything?" Toninho asked.

"Sure."

"Now we cannot fish the whole ocean hoping to catch the corpse of Norival," Orlando said.

"We'll telephone you," Toninho said. "Tomorrow, after the parade is over."

If it were not for his wounds, Fletch would have been willing to believe that finally he fell asleep and dreamed the most horrible dream.

As it was, later he was unsure of when he had been conscious and when he had been unconscious.

Dizzy with sleeplessness, having somewhat the sensation of intoxication from the constant sound of Carnival drums, perhaps staggering a little, alone he began to walk back along the parade route to Teodomiro da Costa's box. His eyelids were heavy, his vision diminished in that glaring light. The *Abra-Alas* of *Escola Santos Lima* passed by, the first *alegoria* reminding the spectators to expect a literary theme. The walk back to da Costa's box seemed as big a chore as crossing all Brazil on foot. He was aware of the passing of the *Commisão de Frente*. He stopped, swaying, trying to focus in the glare on the dancing of the *Porta Bandeira* and the *Mestre Sala*. Their dance steps were too quick, too intricate for him to follow with his eyes. At the first *ala*, he staggered forward again, only dimly aware of the passing of the thousands of dancing, singing people, the swirling costumes and flesh to his right.

Once back in Teo's box he would curl into a corner and sleep. For only an hour. People might be amazed or insulted at his sleeping during Carnival Parade, but he could not help it. He would arrange with Laura to wake him after an hour so people would not be too insulted. Even in that noise, he could, he had to sleep.

Just as he was comforting himself with this decision, using it to strengthen him to make it all the way back to Teo's box, strong hands pushed suddenly and hard against his left shoulder.

Instead of looking at who had pushed him, Fletch tried to save himself from falling. The edge of the parade route's pavement shot out from under him.

Someone pushed him again.

He fell to his right, into the parade.

A foot came up from the pavement and kicked him in the face.

Staggering from the blow, arms raised to protect his head, he looked around him. He was just inside the edge of perhaps a hundred young men doing their murderous, practiced kick-dancing. A foot landed flat against his stomach. Immediately, the air was gone from Fletch's lungs. Gasping, he tried to duck sideways, back to the edge of the parade.

Again he was pushed, hard.

Spinning, he fell more deeply into the group of *capoeiristas*. He was surrounded by fast-moving, swinging legs striking at crotch height, stomach height, shoulder height, head height. A blow landed against the back of his right knee. He fell against someone. All around him flashed intense eyes. *Aw, shit*, was in Fletch's head, *I'm messing up their presentation. A damned Northamerican, a tourist.* He was being kicked from all sides. The eyes of the *capoeiristas* were seeing him, popping in amazement at his being there, but usually only after they had pirouetted, when it was too late for them to stop their momentum, avoid kicking him.

I don't belong here.

Someone had pushed him into the *capoeira* troupe, not just once but three times. Whoever pushed him doubtlessly was still between him and the edge of the parade. Arms over his head, Fletch ducked. Keeping as low as possible, he began to scurry across the parade route to the far side, toward the stands.

A hard kick in the stomach lifted him off his feet. He came down hard on his left foot. He kept moving forward, through the muscular bare backs shining with sweat, the wildly flailing legs, balancing arms. Without air or the ability to breathe, he felt he was drowning in an ocean of churning arms and legs. The sound of the drums, the sound of the men singing in short, practiced phrases, rushed in his ears. He was being kicked and kicked. Even the gray pavement of the parade route was heaving beneath his feet.

He didn't see the foot that came up from the pavement and kicked him in his face. A cracking noise blasted his ears as his head snapped up and back.

A firm hand against his waist ejected him from the parade.

There was hard-packed earth beneath his feet. The *capoeiristas* were now a meter behind him.

Blood was on his hands. From his nose and ears and mouth blood was pouring down inside and outside his white shirt. It disappeared into his red sash.

He turned, half-conscious, to see if he could spot whoever had pushed him into the *capoeira* troupe.

The *Ala das Baianas* was passing by. A few of the tall black women in long white robes saw him, grimaced at his bloody appearance as they sambaed to the edge of the pavement and turned back.

His eyes wanted to close. He knew he had to go to ground somewhere.

Clutching his ribs, he turned toward the stands. A few people were pointing to him. Most were moving their heads, their shoulders to look beyond him, at the parade.

He staggered, fell toward the stands.

People he approached on the bottom tiers of seats stood up in horror at his appearance, to get away from him. Maybe one or two women were screaming. A few men were shouting at him, angrily, pointing at him. He could not hear the women screaming or the men shouting. He could only see their mouths move.

He knelt down and put his head and shoulders between the second and third tiers of seats. Whoever had pushed him into the *capoeiristas* had intended murder. Perhaps he had succeeded. Chances were good he would follow his quarry until he was sure he had killed him. His head under the seats, Fletch reached out, grabbed a couple of metal uprights and pulled himself through.

Fletch crawled beneath the stands.

He lay on his back on the dirt, the bottoms of the seats, the bottoms of the spectators just above him. He had been kicked in the stomach so many times he could not breathe.

Vomiting turned him over, got him up on his knees, got him gagging, breathing again. Blood from his nose and lips joined the more forceful stream of vomit.

On his knees, he backed away from his mess.

Stomach muscles quivering from the blows, arms and legs shaking, he remained on hands and knees coughing, trying to clear his throat of vomit and blood.

A meter ahead of him, the people who had risen from their seats, allowing him to crawl under the stands, were sitting in their seats again, pounding their feet like pistons again in rhythm to the drums, cheering on the biggest and most amazing human spectacle in the world except war. Fletch knew they could not hear him retching and choking. He could not hear himself. He was sure his appearance to them was as unreal as the rest of the spectacle they were watching.

After a while he crawled backward farther to give himself more headroom, more air.

Sitting cross-legged then, he put his head back to try to stop the bleeding from his nose. He remembered the crack he had heard when he got that final kick in the face. He did not think his neck was broken, nor his back, nor his head.

Above him rose, as far as he could see, the undersides of the stands. Pieces of skirts, the undersides of thighs, a few dangling feet. A sandwich wrapper floated down and landed near him in the dirt.

The light under the stands was weird. It was midnight. There was no illumination under the stands. The powerful light from the parade route filtered under the stands through the densely packed bodies above. Nodes of light, apparently sourceless, quivered in midair.

Streams of light wavered at odd angles to each other.

His crotch hurt, his stomach hurt, his ribs. His head had been hit from every direction.

Fighting the temptation, his body's demand to stretch out, to go to sleep, become unconscious, he lifted himself to his feet. It took him three tries to become upright.

He fell forward, and caught himself. A *chope* can fell from the stands and landed near his foot. He put one foot forward and fell on it. Maintaining upright balance seemed important to him. One hand rubbed an ear; the other tightly held his ribs. He gasped.

Later, he supposed he had moments of unconsciousness as he stood there.

He saw a man walking along under the stands. About to wave to him, make some gesture he needed help, Fletch noticed how oddly the man walked. Fletch looked more closely. The man's steps were short, high, fast. He landed first on his toes and then his feet rolled forward to his heels.

The man's feet were backward. His toes were behind his legs.

The hand pressing against his ribs Fletch lowered to press against his stomach.

He blinked blood from his eyes.

A headless mule cantered out of the dark under the stands, slowly turned, and cantered away.

Fletch fell forward on his feet several steps. Now truly he was the walking Northamerican, falling forward. Each step, his feet barely prevented his falling on his face.

Out of the dark at Fletch's left appeared another man, walking, bouncing slowly. He was to cross in front of Fletch.

As he passed Fletch, the man's head, backward on his shoulders, turned and smiled. His eyes and teeth shone even in that light.

In an impossible angle from his head, one of his arms raised. He pointed to Fletch's right.

Standing very close to Fletch was an old man in an oversized coat. The man's hair was thin and gray. His eyes were sad.

He raised his arms toward Fletch.

Fletch backed away.

Only hair came out of the old man's sleeves, not hands or wrists.

Again, Fletch's head snapped.

Someone kicked him hard, on the muscle of the upper left side of his back.

Brushing away the old man with hair for hands, Fletch spun slowly on the hard-packed earth.

He saw the second blow coming at his chest. He did not know how to avoid such a blow from the foot. He could not duck it. Moving sideways, slowly, stupidly, he still caught the full force of the blow.

His feet caught him as he fell backward.

A man, a wiry old man, was kick-dancing in front of him. Groggy, Fletch admired the perfectly executed pirouette.

And as the man's face turned to him, a beam of light through the stands shone fully on the face of a goat. Through the mask's eye-holes gleamed steady brown eyes.

The man's instep hit Fletch hard on the side of the head.

Fletch's head felt it was traveling through space by itself.

Reeling, Fletch saw the small boy standing not too far away on his wooden leg.

"Janio!" Fletch yelled. Blood bubbled from his throat to his lips.

In all that noise, he could not even hear his own voice.

His shoulders pumping unnaturally, the small boy ran away.

The *capoeirista* was real. He was in front of Fletch, behind him, all around him. The blows from his feet were real.

The man behind the goat mask was kicking Fletch to death.

Fletch tried to keep his legs together, yet not fall over. He tried to keep his back to the man, which was impossible. Hunkered down, he tried to keep his hands over his head, his elbows protecting his ribs. Falling this way, that, he tried to get away. The *capoeirista* was on all sides of him at once. Each blow from his feet opened Fletch's body for another blow.

Fletch received a hard kick in his throat, perhaps a killing kick.

Then one more kick in the back of his head.

He was face down in the dirt.

Consciousness was coming and going like an old song on a high wind. Blood was pouring from his face, particularly his nose again, but he could not get a hand to it.

His legs would not get him up. They would not obey orders, they were well beyond the necessary impulse to get up and run.

The man in the goat's mask grabbed Fletch's hair and twisted his head sideways and up. Fletch's whole body rolled sideways. He was lying on one hip.

A knee either side of him, the man knelt over Fletch.

For a second the man's hand was flattened on the ground in front of Fletch's nose. In one of the odd flashes of light, Fletch glimpsed a ring on the man's finger. A ring with a black center. Intertwined snakes rose from that center.

Farther along the ground, Fletch saw a piece of wood sticking into the ground again and again as it came closer. Paired with the stick of wood was a boy's leg.

Pulling Fletch's hair, the man in the goat mask twisted Fletch's head forward and back.

With his other hand, the man was doing something under Fletch's chin.

Fletch felt a nice warmth on the side of his neck.

The nice warmth of blood.

The man was slitting Fletch's throat.

Then, as if hit by a great wind, the man was blown sideways. He sprawled into the dirt beside Fletch.

Above them were many legs, strong men's legs.

In one incredibly smooth, lithe movement the man was up, on his feet, on one foot. The other foot on a straight leg was whirling through the air. From the ground, Fletch saw all the other legs, the legs of his rescuers, back away.

The toes of the man in the goat mask then dug into the ground with the grip of a sprinter. They were gone in a blur.

Heavily, the other feet went after him.

The wooden leg still stuck in the ground nearby, next to the boy's bare leg.

"Janio, I need help." On the ground, Fletch managed to get a hand to his throat. He stuck his finger in the knife hole. *"Janio! Socorro!"*

Fletch knew he was not being heard. He could not even hear himself.

It was not sleep then, into which Fletch fell.

THIRTY

He was conscious when the phone began ringing, but it rang five or six times before he could get rolled over, stretch his arm out to it, and pick up the receiver from the bedside table.

"*Bom dia*," Fletch said into the phone, not believing a word of it.

"Fletch! Are you better?"

By now, Fletch knew Toninho's voice over the telephone.

"Better than what?"

"Better than you were when we found you."

Fletch's memory was far from perfect. His brain had begun to clear only shortly before noon. He still tasted blood.

Lying on the ground under the stands at Carnival Parade, he remembered seeing from close up the creases of Toninho's or Tito's belly.

He remembered being carried, it seemed for kilometers, under the stands. The sky was full of human feet and legs pounding in rhythm. The noise was no longer of singing, pounding samba drums. It was all just roar.

Then they were out from under the stands, and still he was carried a long, long way. The sounds abated. The air became clearer. The sky was high and dark.

"We're getting good at lifting bodies around," Tito said. Why was he speaking English?

"Bury me at sea," Fletch instructed them. "The fish will appreciate dessert."

As they carefully fitted him into the backseat of the four-door black Galaxie, Fletch saw the ten-year-old boy standing next to the car. His eyes were round.

"Hey, Janio," Fletch said. "*Obrigado.*"

During the ride in the car, he lost consciousness again. He remembered none of it.

He remembered being walked into the lobby of The Hotel Yellow Parrot. Orlando was holding him up.

The doorman and the desk clerk hurried around, each questioning Toninho and Tito in Portuguese. Toninho and Tito were placating.

The ride in the elevator took forever.

Finally, Fletch was on his own bed. Being on his bed was so unexpected, so wonderful, he sucked in great gobs of breath. And passed out again.

He remembered Toninho working up and down his naked body, squeezing, testing, looking for breaks in Fletch's bones.

"My neck," Fletch said. "Is my head on straight?"

Orlando came in from the bathroom with wet towels. He and Toninho washed Fletch down, even turning him over, gently, to do so.

As the towels passed in and out of Fletch's sight, they became pink, and then red.

The formally dressed desk clerk arrived with bandages and bottles of antiseptic.

He took away the wet, bloody towels and Fletch's blood-soaked clothes.

"Not my sash," Fletch complained. "Not my beautiful red sash."

"Your bloody red sash," Toninho said.

"Laura gave me that bloody red sash," Fletch said. "She brought it from Bahia."

"He says he'll burn your clothes," Tito said. "A sacrifice to the gods. They get only a little of your blood. You live."

"Ow."

Toninho was applying antiseptic to a hundred places over Fletch's body. He stuck the antiseptic-soaked face cloth into the small slit in Fletch's throat.

Consciousness was lost again.

They rolled Fletch this way and that, to put a fresh, dry sheet under him. The desk clerk was back in the room. He was trying to fold a wet, bloody sheet while not letting it touch his clothes.

With his fingers, Fletch discovered plaster stuck to various parts of his body: his shins, ribs, face, neck. He did not remember their being put on.

"Should I stay with him?" Tito asked.

"He'll be all right," Toninho said. "He needs a few hours of meditation. There's nothing really wrong with him."

"Except that someone tried to kill him," Orlando said.

"Yes," Toninho said. "It looks that way."

"He did not succeed," Fletch announced from the bed.

"No," Toninho said. "He did not succeed."

Softly, Tito said, "He almost succeeded."

The room was black. Fletch did not remember their leaving.

Through the dark night he listened to the samba drums. The sound was not coming from the street. It was coming from various televisions throughout the hotel, around the neighborhood. An announcer's voice came and went over the sound of the drumming and singing. Rio de Janeiro's Samba School Parade was continuing.

He did not sleep. Some unconsciousness other than sleep came and went like a presence in the dark room. It came closer and went away.

He did not move. No part of his body wanted to move. Every muscle in his body had been kicked at least once. The skin and tissue against his bones throbbed. For a while, the thighs of his legs would hurt; he would think about them, then his shoulders; and he would think about them, his back, the area high in his stomach just below his ribs. Even his fingers and toes hurt. Anything was better than thinking how his head hurt. His head felt as if the inside had been kicked loose from the outside and rattled.

Laura would return. Sometime during the morning. Or perhaps within an hour after the parade was over, by two or three in the afternoon. How could she know, at the parade, he had been kicked almost to death? All she knew was that he had left the box to take a walk with the Tap Dancers. She would return.

Daylight came through the balcony drapes. Then direct sunlight entered the room. The television coverage of Carnival Parade continued. The room grew hot.

In his bed he experimented moving an arm. Then the other. One leg. He dug his fingers into his left leg to cause it to move. Slowly, he rolled his head back and forth on the pillow.

His head was clearing. He had not been unconscious for a long time now.

It was nearly noon when he could resist no longer.

Slowly he rolled himself to the edge of the bed. Heavily he lifted himself up. The semi-dark room went out of focus for a minute. He took a step forward. There was no part of his body which did not hurt.

After using the toilet, he turned on the bathroom light and looked at himself in the mirror. To his regret, his head was on frontwards and stared back at him. Swollen eyes, bruised cheekbones, jaws. One ear was inflamed. There was still blood in his hair. A shower would cause his bandages to fall off. Backing up, he saw the blue bruises on his upper arms, his chest. The top of his stomach was purple.

Brushing his teeth gingerly, he spat blood into the basin.

Then he returned to bed and waited.

Laura would come and they would have food. He would tell her what had happened to him. Would she listen? What had happened to him? Would she be interested, or would this be a level of reality which didn't interest her much? While he talked, would she be hearing something else? As he was leaving the box to join the Tap Dancers, her face had been inscrutable. What did the fact of the wooden-legged boy following them through the subway mean to her it did not mean to him?

Laura had not returned by the time Toninho called.

"You must be better," Toninho said. "You've had almost twelve hours to meditate."

"I need twelve years."

"Who tried to kill you?"

"I'm thinking about that."

"Ah, Carnival," Toninho said.

"He was wearing a goat mask," Fletch said. "A man in his sixties, I'd say. He tried to kick me to death."

"He must have slipped into the personality of the goat. Carnival does that."

"No goat has such training in *capoeira*." Fletch wanted to switch the phone to his other ear. Then he remembered his other ear had slipped into the personality of a tomato.

"The news is that Norival has showed up."

"Great! In one piece?"

"Yes. He came ashore way down the coast, a hundred kilometers south of where we thought."

"I always thought that boy would go a long way."

"Apparently he got caught in a current, which took him south, then ashore. He was on the beach this morning. A jogger found him. They are bringing his body up now."

"Good. Great. All your worries are over."

"The report so far is that he drowned. His boat broke up and he drowned."

"That's good. So Norival did die at sea. His mother will be so glad. Admiral Passarinho will be ecstatic."

"So we'll see you at the funeral home in about a half an hour."

"What? No way. Toninho, I can't move."

"Of course you can move."

"Why should I go to the funeral home?"

"To help us distract the officials." Toninho's voice fell to the con-spiratorial. "To distract them from any idea of an autopsy. We need to stand around in a circle and say, yes, he drowned. We saw him go sailing and indeed he certainly did drown. They're more apt to believe you, you see. They don't know you as well as they know us."

"I don't think I can move."

"You must move. If you don't make yourself move now, you'll stiffen up, like Norival, and not be able to move for days."

Fletch hesitated. He remembered past injuries. "You're probably right."

Still, he had had no real sleep.

"Of course I'm right. The funeral home of Job Pereira. On rua Jardim Botanico. The business part of the road."

"I'll find it."

"I'll bring all your gambling winnings to you."

"You needn't bribe me." Fletch tried sitting up in bed. "On the other hand, maybe you do."

THIRTY-ONE

At the funeral home of Job Pereira, Fletch tried to find a doorbell to ring, a door on which to knock. There was neither.

It was a large stucco and stone house sitting in the deep shade of its own trees.

"Hello?" he called. "Anyone?"

The quiet from inside the building was tomblike.

He stepped into the coolness of the foyer. There was no reception desk, still no bell to ring. There were short, dark potted palms in each corner.

"Hello?" Fletch called.

The only response was a faint echo of his own voice.

It had taken him longer than the promised half hour to get from The Hotel Yellow Parrot to the funeral home of Job Pereira.

Sitting on the edge of his bed, he had ordered food from Room Service.

While still at the telephone, he called The Hotel Jangada and asked for Room 912.

No answer.

No, Mrs. Joan Collins Stanwyk had not yet picked up the envelope Mr. Fletcher had left in her box.

Every step, every movement, however small, caused him pain. He opened the drapes to the balcony. Across the utility area, the man was painting the room. Perhaps the man's permanent job in life was to paint that room. Fletch opened the door to the balcony. The air was warm and dry and felt good. The televisions were still blaring the news of Carnival Parade.

Life goes on.

Shaving was like walking barefoot through a field of glass. Finished, he had to affix one more bandage to his face.

Alone, with stinging lips and sore jaws, he ate breakfast.

Every minute, he thought Laura might return.

Finally dressed in a pair of clean shorts and a T-shirt, sneakers and socks, he went down in the elevator. The desk clerk and the few other people in the lobby glanced at him and immediately looked away. Despite the glue stuck to various parts of his face and body, he gathered he no longer looked like a Christmas package.

The *avenida* in front of the hotel was emptier than he had ever seen it. Citizens either were still watching Carnival Parade or were worn out by it and sleeping.

Finally a taxi picked him up. All the streets were empty. All the way to the funeral home, the taxi radio kept up an excited description of the late *escola* to parade.

"Hello? Anyone here?"

The funeral home was lifeless. There was not even the sound of a radio or television reporting the parade.

Fletch limped into a big room to the left of the foyer. Heavy, waisted velvet drapes on the windows cut down the light in the room.

Several open coffins were on display in the room. Each was on its own fancy trestle. He looked in one. It was empty. A coffin sales room. He moved from coffin to coffin, looking in each. The coffins ranged from polished pine to brass-studded mahogany.

He heard a sound behind him.

A seemingly tired, lazy voice said, "Hello?"

Fletch turned around.

In the door to the room, white as sea foam, the brighter light from the foyer behind him softening his outline, clearly stood Norival.

Norival Passarinho.

Dressed in white shoes, white slacks, white shirt. His belly hung over his belt. Damp hair fell onto his forehead. His face was puffy.

Norival Passarinho!

Fletch blinked.

Norival blinked.

Fletch sucked in cool air from the coffin display room.

"Ah, Janio Barreto." Norival shambled toward Fletch. Norival even put out his arm to take Fletch's hand. "At last I get to meet you properly!"

The room rose.

Fletch fell.

THIRTY-TWO

Fletch knew he was in a small, dark place.

Becoming conscious, he could hear no natural sounds except the sound of his own breathing. The air was stale.

He was lying on his back. His head was on some kind of pillow.

Only when he moved his right hand and immediately came to the edge of the space, a soft wall, did he realize how small the space was. The same was true when he moved his left hand.

The space he was in clearly was no wider than a long, narrow bed. He ran his hands up the satiny walls. The ceiling of the space was immediately on top of him, only a few centimeters above his chest, his chin, his nose.

A very small space indeed.

His fingers brushed against something else. Paper, fairly stiff paper. Both hands felt over the object lying beside him in the small space. His fingers told him it was a paper bag, with papers in it.

Fletch tried to think where he had last been, what had happened to him, at what he had been looking when . . . Coffins!

"Aaaaaaaaarrrgh!" Fletch's roar surprised and deafened himself. "I'm not dead?"

In that terrible enclosure, he tried to get his hands up, to press up, raise the lid of the coffin. His heart was pounding in a lively manner. His face poured sweat.

"Hey, out there!"

Horrified, he realized he might be trying to yell through six feet of sod.

"Hey, up there! I'm not dead yet! I swear to it!"

He could not get his arms, hands at the right angle to lift. The coffin lid was heavy. His beaten muscles quivered and ached but accomplished little.

"Aaaaaaaaarrrgh! Somebody! Anybody! Listen! I'm not dead yet!" The air in the coffin had become exceedingly warm. *"Socorro!* damnit!"

By itself, it seemed, the coffin lid rose.

Instantly, the air became fresh and sweet.

He blinked stupidly at the light of day.

Laura's head was over the coffin, looking in. "Ah, there you are," she said.

Lying flat, sucking in the good air, Fletch said nothing.

"What are you doing in a coffin?"

Fletch panted.

"You do look like you belong in a coffin."

"I saw Norival," he said. "Norival Passarinho."

"Norival's dead," she said.

"I know!"

"Apparently he went sailing alone at night. His boat hit a rock or something. He drowned."

"I know!"

"His body washed up this morning. Very sad. Poor Norival."

"I know all that, Laura. But, listen! I came here to the funeral home. Toninho asked me to. I was alone, in this room." Fletch peered over the edge of his coffin and established that he was still in the coffin display room. "And I turned around, and there, in the door, stood Norival! Norival Passarinho! Blinking!"

"Norival?"

"He spoke to me! He said, 'Janio Barreto.' He came forward. He walked across the room at me. He tried to shake my hand!"

Laura wrinkled up her nose. "Norival Passarinho?"

"Yes! Definitely!"

"After he was dead?"

"Yes! I know he was dead!"

"It couldn't have been Norival Passarinho."

"It was Norival Passarinho. Dressed in white. All in white."

"You saw Norival Passarinho walking around after he was dead?"

"He said, Norival said, 'Ah, Janio Barreto.' " Fletch lowered his voice to the sepulchral. " 'At last I get to meet you properly.' "

"You saw Adroaldo Passarinho."

"What? Who?"

"Adroaldo. Norival's brother. They're just alike."

Fletch thought a moment. "Adroaldo?"

"Yes. Adroaldo was very surprised when he put out his arm to shake hands with you, and you fainted."

"I fainted?"

"Well, you fell on the floor without apparent what-do-you-call-it? premeditation."

"Adroaldo Passarinho?"

"You didn't know Norival had a brother?"

"Yes. Of course. But he was so white!"

"He's been in school in Switzerland all winter."

"Laura . . ."

"Fletch, I think you're not surviving Carnival. It's beginning to affect your mind."

"What am I doing in a coffin?"

Laura shrugged. "I suspect the Tap Dancers put you in there. After you fainted."

"Why?"

"One of their little tricks." She giggled.

"Very funny!" Stiffly, he began to pull himself up, to sit up in his coffin. "God! I thought . . ."

"It is funny."

He picked up the paper bag and looked into it.

"What's that?" she asked. "Your lunch? Enough to tide you over to the other world?"

"My poker winnings."

"Ah, they buried you with all your worldly wealth. All your ill-gotten gains. So you can tip Charon after he rows you across the River Styx."

His time in the coffin had stiffened his muscles again. "How come you're here?"

"Toninho called me at the hotel. Said you had fainted. I should come in the car and pick you up. Adroaldo and the others had to go with Norival in his coffin to the Passarinho home."

Fletch's heart had slowed, but he was still sweating. "What if you hadn't come? I could have run out of air —"

"Why wouldn't I have come?"

"Supposing the car had broken down, or —"

"You could have gotten yourself out of there."

"I could have died of cardiac arrest."

"Were you that frightened?"

"Waking up in a closed coffin is not something one expects to do — under any circumstances."

She was studying his face. "You're a mess."

"I got nearly kicked to death."

"They told me. Your whole body like that?"

"At the moment, I am not very sleek."

"Was there any reason for it you know of? I mean, getting attacked?"

"I think so, yes. Help me out of this damned coffin, if you don't mind."

"Also, there was another message for you at the hotel." She balanced him by holding onto his hand. "A Sergeant Paulo Barbosa of Rio de Janeiro police would like you to call him."

"What did he say?"

"Just left a message. How much trouble are you in?"

"Oh, my God." A body wounded in every part is painful to lift out of a raised coffin and set on two feet on the floor.

"You really are a mess," Laura said. "The car is just outside."

"You'd better drive."

"Seeing the last vehicle you tried to drive is a coffin . . ."

"Not by choice, thank you."

"We'll go back to the hotel. The Parade is over. It was really wonderful. You missed most of it."

"I'm sorry about that."

"Fletch, you always seem to be someplace you're not supposed to be, doing something you're not supposed to be doing."

"Got any other news for me?"

"Yes." They were crossing the wide, cool foyer of the funeral home of Job Pereira, heading for the dazzling sunlight beyond the front door. "Paul Bocuse is the chef at Le Saint Honoré. I've made reservations for tonight, in your name. Have you forgotten the ball at Régine's? That's tonight. Tomorrow, I thought we'd drive up and have a quiet lunch at *Floresta*."

"You mean Carnival still isn't over?"

"Tomorrow night it's over. I'm not at all sure you'll make it. I'll have to start preparing for my concert tour soon enough. Not a worry. We'll go back to the hotel and rest now."

"No."

"No? You want to go play soccer now?"

"I want to go to *favela* Santos Lima now." Over the top of the small yellow convertible, she gave him a long look. "I'll never rest until I do. You said so yourself."

"I don't think I know the way."

"I do." He lowered himself gently onto the hot passenger seat. "Just follow my directions."

THIRTY-THREE

Sore with wounds, dazed with sleeplessness, Fletch walked into *favela* Santos Lima like a *Figura de Destaque*. The sun was searingly, blindingly hot.

Laura traipsed along a few steps behind him.

The children of the *favela* followed him too, of course, but they walked at a distance from him, quietly. As they climbed the hill, adults from the little houses and the little shops followed them.

By the time they were in front of Idalina Barreto's house, they were a large crowd.

The tall old woman recognized Laura immediately. Hands on her hips in the doorway of her little house, she began talking to Laura even before Laura got to the front of the house. The old woman asked, repeated some question of Laura.

The crowd outside the house was quiet. They wanted to hear Fletch's answer.

Laura said, "She wants to know if you've come to identify your murderer."

Fletch said, "I think so. Tell her I think so."

Laura frowned. "Are you serious?"

"Is anything serious?"

"How do you mean to do that?"

"I mean to walk slowly through the *favela*, look into everyone's eyes. I shall identify my murderer."

"Just like that?"

"Just like that."

"I don't believe . . . " She looked around at all the people quietly awaiting Fletch's response.

"What don't you believe?" he asked. "What do you believe?"

Fletch waited a long time for her to answer. He asked, "Would you like to believe I'm about to perform magic? That I'm about to do a trick?"

Still Laura did not answer.

"Would you like to believe, as some of these people do, that I am Janio Barreto returned from the dead after forty-seven years to point out my murderer?"

"I believe . . . " In the heat of the sunlight, Laura took a deep breath. "I don't believe you should play with these people."

"Am I playing?"

"At least some of these people believe this story. Because the old lady wants them to believe. The others are just curious. They love any story."

"Anybody can make up a story and say it is the past. Right?"

"Identifying someone as your murderer, as the murderer of Janio Barreto, would be a very serious thing for these people."

"I hope so."

"You have no idea what they might do to such a person."

"I can guess."

"Fletch, you must tell me what you know."

"You want a fact?"

"I want something."

"Okay, Laura, here's a fact: The person who murdered Janio Barreto forty-seven years ago truly believes I am Janio Barreto returned."

"How do you know that?"

"Look at me."

"I don't think you should play with the, what's-the-word? credibility of people."

"I am taking advantage of the credulity of only one of these people."

"Someone believes —"

"Someone either believes I am Janio Barreto returned. Or he has decided to act as if he believes I am Janio Barreto returned, just in case it is true."

In the sunlight, Laura sighed.

Now there were even more people standing around outside Idalina Barreto's house awaiting his answer.

The child Janio Barreto had appeared. Of all the people in the *favela*, he stood closest to Fletch.

"Please tell the old woman I am here to identify my murderer."

Laura started to speak to Idalina, but then stopped.

Instead, she said to Fletch: "You're putting it to me too, aren't you?"

"Hell, Laura, we haven't even gotten to know each other."

"All this will be on your head," she said.

"Fine. My head is so sore now, it doesn't matter."

Speaking loudly, as if making an announcement, Laura answered the old woman.

The crowd cheered. Many gave the thumbs-up sign.

The old woman asked another question.

Laura said, "Do you really mean to just walk through the *favela*, up and down the streets, until you point someone out?"

"I want to see, to look into the eyes of everyone in the *favela*. Tell her, if the murderer is here, I will find him."

Laura translated, in a less robust voice.

Idalina Barreto came out of the shade of her doorway.

In the sunlight, she took Fletch's arm.

Together, Laura walking behind them, the people from the *favela* all around them, Fletch and Idalina Barreto began to walk through *favela* Santos Lima.

"I know your trick," Laura finally said to Fletch in a low voice. They had been walking a long time. Her hair had collapsed with perspiration. "You're going to walk through the whole *favela* and point no one out."

"Maybe," Fletch answered. "Would that permit me to sleep?"

Favela Santos Lima was far more extensive than he thought. It was a senseless warren of streets and alleys and footpaths. The banged-together, stuck-together hovels seemed placed by the whimsy of the moment, or some invisible convenience. On some of the paths only he and Idalina could walk abreast. The stream of their followers flowed a kilometer behind them in some places.

"We're having our own Carnival Parade," Fletch said to Laura.

"Not bloody likely."

Sweating, the middle-aged Janio Barreto Filho appeared and asked what was happening. His mother told him *Janio Barreto* wished to look into the eyes of everyone in the *favela*. He would identify his murderer.

Janio Barreto Filho organized boys and men to walk ahead of Fletch and Idalina and get all the people out of their homes so Fletch could look into their eyes as he passed.

It was the afternoon after the Samba School Parade, and most of the people in the *favela* were sleeping. Barreto's squad called through the windows of their homes, entered, awakened people, and politely asked them to come outside. *No, no, it is not the police. It is an important matter. To solve an ancient matter having to do with the* favela. *We are about to find out who murdered Janio Barreto, a long time ago.* Shy of most clothes, faces puffy with tiredness, the people stood at their doors rubbing their eyes in the sunlight.

Perhaps they understood a feat of legerdemain was about to happen: a voice from beyond the grave was about to speak. Perhaps they understood nothing but that someone had asked them to wake up and stand outside a moment. Something interesting was passing by. Sleepy or curious, they cooperated.

Fletch asked Laura, "Are you deciding what you believe now?"

"All these people." Laura looked back at the river of people following them. "Many of them are laughing at you."

"I would hope so," he said.

"Turning this into a joke. Is that what you're doing?"

"Isn't it a joke?"

"You're going to lead them around in a circle and then say there is no such person as your murderer here."

"Perhaps."

As he walked, Fletch was becoming less stiff. He was thirsty. The sun was stinging his various wounds on his face and arms. His head throbbed like a samba combo. A few times, the bright sunlight dimmed on him unnaturally. He stumbled. Idalina Barreto's grip on his arm was strong.

Of course he did not know if he was going up and down every path in Santos Lima. He had to leave that to his guides. It certainly felt as though he was going up and down every path, looking into the eyes of every person in Santos Lima.

"I'm going back," Laura said. "Here are the car keys. I'll take a taxi."

"No," said Fletch. "Stay with me."

"I don't care to see out the end of this act of yours."

"It's not an act."

Fletch was seeing the people of *favela* Santos Lima. He was seeing males and females, the old, the young, the tall, the short, the beautiful, the ugly, the misshapen, the healthy, the insane, the doddering, the dignified, the ashamed. . . .

Ahead of him on a narrow path, he saw a lean, gray-haired man dressed only in shorts leave a house. He crossed the path and entered another house.

Walking more quickly, Fletch approached that house.

In excitement, Idalina Barreto gripped his arm even tighter. She kept up with him.

Young Janio Barreto looked up into Fletch's eyes. Then, calling others, he ran ahead and into the house.

Fletch entered the house. It was empty. There was a doorless back door.

From behind the house came the sound of young Janio Barreto calling loudly.

As Fletch went through the house, the mob following gathered speed. They went through the house and round the house.

Now they had the idea they were pursuing someone.

"What are you doing?" Laura said. "Madman!"

Fletch looked back. A wall of the little house they had just gone through fell flat in the dust. The other three walls fell forward but did not collapse. The twisted tin roof kept three of the walls up.

"You're out of your mind!" Laura said. "There is no understanding this!"

Above the little house he came to a wider path. To his left down the path, young Janio Barreto held onto the black shorts of the gray-haired man he knew Fletch was pursuing. Other boys, men, surrounded the man.

More slowly now, Fletch walked toward the group in the middle of the path.

As he approached, one of the young men said to the gray-haired man, "Just let him look into your eyes, Gabriel."

"Gabriel Campos!" Idalina Barreto shrieked in her highest crone's voice. "Gabriel Campos!"

Clearly the man wanted to bolt. He was surrounded now by twenty strong young men, by more than thirty children. He was being approached by more than one hundred fellow citizens of his *favela*.

With dignity, he stood his ground. His body was mostly light, sinewy muscle. The top of his stomach was pumping hard. The man had not moved that far, not moved that fast, to be so out of breath. Not for a man in his condition. A disingenuous smile played on his lips.

"*Gabriel Campos!*" Idalina shrieked. Then she shouted something about Janio Barreto.

Standing close to him, Fletch looked into the eyes of Gabriel Campos. He had seen those eyes before.

Gabriel Campos' eyes flickered. He looked at the crowd and back at Fletch.

His smile came and went like a flashing light.

Slowly, Fletch raised his hand.

He pointed his index finger at Gabriel Campos' nose.

Fletch already had checked the ring the man was wearing. It had a black center. Intertwined snakes rose from that center.

Instantly, Gabriel Campos ducked. Throwing back his elbows, he darted backward through the circle of young men, children, knocking over a child.

Idalina Barreto shrieked.

Others began to yell, move forward.

Two of the young men grabbed for Gabriel Campos.

Campos kicked one in the stomach; the other in the face.

It seemed everyone was trying to lay a hand on Campos. With tremendous skill, ducking and dancing, he kicked free of the crowd.

He turned and ran up the path.

Shouting, young men ran after him. Tripping over each other, almost all the men and children who had been following Fletch joined the pursuit. Yelling, some lifting their skirts up, many of the women pursued Gabriel Campos as well.

Shrieking *Gabriel Campos! Gabriel Campos!* tall old Idalina Barreto went after him in her rapid, sturdy pace, losing ground in the midst of this marathon.

Fletch sat on a nearby rock.

Dor de estomago . . . de cabeca . . . febre . . . nausea.

A few meters away, Laura Soares was in a group of women from the *favela*. They were all talking at once. Most of them were pregnant and therefore could not join in the pursuit of Gabriel Campos.

Laura was asking questions. She kept looking across at Fletch.

Higher up in the *favela*, the chase was still going on. On a road along a ridge, Fletch saw Gabriel Campos running between the houses. Easily one hundred people were streaming after him. He had a good lead on them.

Idalina Barreto's high, shrill shriek dominated all other sounds. "*Gabriel Campos! Gabriel Campos!*"

From somewhere down in the depths of the *favela* came the sound of a samba drum.

After a while, Laura came over to Fletch. She stood over him a moment without speaking.

Fletch said, "I'm awfully tired. And I still have to call Sergeant Barbosa of the Rio police."

Laura said, "His name is Gabriel Campos."

"I heard." He looked up to where Idalina Barreto was. The old lady had climbed far fast. "I hear."

"The women say he was your friend when you were boys. He, one other boy, and the Gomes brothers. Who are the Gomes brothers?"

"Idalina's brothers."

"See?" she said. "You do know."

"I was told, Laura. Yesterday. I was told."

"You taught them all the skill of *capoeira*. Of everyone, Gabriel learned the best. After you were killed, he was master of the *capoeira* school of *Escola* Santos Lima. For years, he was famous for it. One year, he was even *Mestre Sala.*"

"I see. He wanted Janio — his teacher — out of the way."

"He was placed on the board of directors of the samba school."

"He would never have had such honors if Janio were alive."

Laura made some sign in the dust with the tip of her sandal.

"I must get sleep." High in the *favela*, the pursuit, the shouting continued. Fletch said, "I wonder what they will do with him."

"I don't want to know. How, why did you pick out Gabriel Campos? You must tell me."

"You mean, did Gabriel Campos murder Janio Barreto forty-seven years ago?"

"Did he?"

"I don't know." Beyond exhaustion, Fletch stood up from the rock. "But I do know that, disguised as a goat, last night he tried to slit my throat."

THIRTY-FOUR

"I forget if you said if you have ever been to New Bedford, Massachusetts," Sergeant Paulo Barbosa asked.

"No," Fletch said into the phone. He sat heavily on his bed in The Hotel Yellow Parrot. "I have never been to New Bedford, Massachusetts."

Laura had gotten Sergeant Barbosa on the line. Placing the call had seemed too complicated to Fletch in his sleepless condition.

"It is very nice in New Bedford, Massachusetts," Sergeant Barbosa told him again. "Much too cold, of course, for me. When you go back to your country, you must visit New Bedford, Massachusetts." Fletch noticed the presumption that sooner or later everyone does go back to his country. It was the same presumption Idalina's father made of Janio Barreto. "You must visit my cousin's gift shop in New Bedford, Massachusetts. She has everything in her gift shop that every other gift shop has."

"All right." Fletch's head was nodding. "I promise."

"That would be very nice. Now, about that Northamerican woman you lost . . ."

Fletch's eyes popped open. "Yes?"

"I don't think we have found her."

"Oh."

"What we have is a telephone call from the mayor of a very small town on the coast, south of here three hundred kilometers. The town of Botelho. It is very nice there. Very sealike. It is on the ocean. You should visit there anyway."

"Yes," Fletch said drowsily. "I'll visit there, too. I promise I will."

Laura was pulling the drapes closed against the sunlight. She had already stripped for bed.

"The mayor of Botelho said that on the weekend, Saturday, I think it was, a Northamerican woman showed up there in Botelho."

"Perhaps somebody told her she should visit."

"Very likely. It is a nice place. I have taken my wife and children there."

"Did you have a nice time?"

"A very nice time."

"Good."

"The mayor said this woman just wandered around for the afternoon by herself, on the beach and so forth, you know?"

"An American tourist —"

"After dark, she went into the very excellent seafood restaurant they have there. I brought my wife and children to eat there."

Kneeling before him, Laura was taking off Fletch's sneakers and socks.

"Was it good?"

"Excellent. This woman ate her dinner."

"A Northamerican woman tourist went to a small resort town —"

"Botelho."

"Botelho, yes. Spent the afternoon on the beach and then had dinner in a seafood restaurant."

"Yes, that's right. After dinner, she said nothing. Instead of paying she went straight into the kitchen and began washing dishes."

Laura pushed Fletch onto his back and began taking off his shorts.

"That's not Joan Collins Stanwyk."

"She's been there ever since. Two days. Washing dishes. Eating. The man who owns the restaurant has given her a little bed to use."

"Joan Collins Stanwyk never washed a dish in her life. She wouldn't know how."

"She is a blond Northamerican or English lady. She speaks no Portuguese."

"How old is she?"

Kneeling over him on the bed, Laura was taking off his shirt. The telephone wire went through the sleeve.

"Quite young, the mayor says. Slim. In her twenties. Maybe her mid-twenties."

"Sounds to me like some female derelict from the Florida Keys washed up on a Brazilian beach."

"Botelho. The beach is very nice there."

"I'm sure." Laura was sliding Fletch's legs under the sheet. "Why did the mayor of Botelho call the Rio police about this lady?"

"Saturdays a tour bus from Copacabana hotels stops in Botelho. The mayor thought she might have gotten off the bus. So he called this police station. He asked if we were looking for a murderess of her description."

"A murderess?"

"Truth, he doesn't know where she came from. Or why. Botelho is a small town. He is a small mayor."

Finally in his bed, to sleep, Fletch thought a moment. Then he said, "I don't think so, Sergeant. Joan Collins Stanwyk didn't have any cash on her, but she is a wealthy, responsible lady, a lady of great dignity. She has many options open to her. All the options in the world. I can't see her ever going to a resort and getting a job washing dishes in a fish-and-chips joint."

"Fish-and-chips? Ah, you are speaking London English."

"Anyway, Joan Collins Stanwyk is in her thirties."

"I didn't think this would be the lady."

"I'm sure it's not."

"Topsy-turvy. Do you remember what I said about topsy-turvy?"

"In fact, I do."

"This is a very topsy-turvy world. Twenty-seven years I have served with the Rio police. Believe me, I have seen topsy-turvy."

"I'm sure you have. Thanks for being in touch with me, Sergeant."

Laura was in the bed beside Fletch.

"So," she said, "they have not found the woman you are looking for."

"No. Just some English-speaking woman has showed up washing dishes in some fish restaurant down the coast."

Into the dark, Laura said, "The police just want you to think they are doing something about the disappeared lady."

"Probably." He turned on the bedside light.

"What are you doing?"

"Just calling The Hotel Jangada," Fletch said. "See if she has returned."

"Want me to help you?"

"This one I can do myself," he said. "I've been practicing."

At The Hotel Jangada, Room 912 did not answer.

The desk clerk said Mrs. Joan Collins Stanwyk had not checked out.

Nor had she picked up the note Fletch had left for her.

THIRTY-FIVE

Fletch —
I could not wake you up.
I tried and tried. A few times I thought you were awake,
because you were talking. What you said made no sense.
Did you know you talk in your sleep?

You said you were on a big white riverboat, and the sky was
full of buttocks.

You said you had your goat, or someone was trying to get your
goat. You seemed afraid of a kicking goat. Then, remarkably, you
babbled on about an ancient Brazilian mythical figure, the dancing
nanny goat.

How do you know about such things? Sometimes, when you
were talking in your sleep, your eyes were open, which is why I
thought I was succeeding in waking you. You said something about
a man with his feet turned backward, another mythical figure, and
when I asked, "Fletch, do you mean the *capoeira?*" you just stared
off like some sort of a *alma penada*, a soul in torment. You also
mentioned other Brazilian hobgoblins, the man with his head on
backward, the headless mule, and the goblin with-hair-for-hands.
You talked about being pursued by a one-legged boy, and when I
asked, "Fletch, do you mean the *saci-perêrê?*" you stared a long time
before saying, "Janio Barreto . . . Janio Barreto . . ."

Amazing thing is, you didn't know the names of any of these
Brazilian scary figures. You seemed to be seeing them in some sort
of a nightmare. You were sweating profusely. Do you think you
had a fever? I am amazed you have such bad dreams of such
hobgoblins, like a Brazilian child, when you have never heard of
them or read of them, as far as I know.

Later, when I tried again to wake you, you said, "Leave the dead
alone!"

Maybe you frightened me. A little.

I canceled our reservation for dinner at Le Saint Honoré. I gave
our tickets to the ball at Régine's to Marilia, who gave them to
some people she knows from Porto Alegre.

Your body is a real mess.

I decided what you need is rest.

I have gone back to Bahia. Carnival is almost over, for this year. I must start organizing my music for the concert tour.

Perhaps you would come to Bahia and advise me of what music you think should be included in the programme.

Now maybe my father will be interested in talking to you — now that he knows you have studied up on such things as the *boi-tatá* and the *tutu-marambá!*

Ciao,

Laura

Fletch had awakened into bright sunlight. He was very hungry. He was very stiff. His body was sticky with sweat.

For a long moment, he thought it was still Monday afternoon and the sun had not yet set.

"Laura?" The hotel room was totally quiet. There was no noise from the bathroom. "Laura?"

From the bed, he noticed that her cosmetics, all those bottles which issued smells if not beauty, were gone from the bureau. None of her clothes were around the room. Her suitcase was gone from the rack.

His watch was on the bedside table. It read five minutes past eleven. Even in a topsy-turvy world, the sun did not shine brightly at five minutes past eleven on Monday nights.

Slowly it dawned on him it must be five minutes past eleven Tuesday morning.

He had slept seventeen hours.

Having to ask individually each part of his body to move, he got up from his bed and walked across the room.

Instead of Laura's cosmetics on the bureau was Laura's letter.

He read it twice.

Had he really talked so much in his sleep, said all those things to Laura? What's a *boi-tatá* and a *tutu-marambá?* Indeed, he must have frightened her.

Vaguely, he remembered having bad dreams. The boy, Janio Barreto, was following them down that crowded, dark slum street to Carnival Parade. In bright floodlights, Fletch was hunkered down in a swirling mass of bodies, brown eyes popping in surprise at seeing him there, being kicked from every direction. Again he was under the stands at Carnival, where he did not belong, looking through his own blood at a man walking by slowly, his head on backward, turning to smile at him. . . .

In the bathroom, he tore the bandages off himself. Scabs had formed nicely. Red marks had turned purple, and purple marks had turned black.

Hadn't Laura seen the big white riverboat floating sedately down the stream of swirling costumes? Hadn't that been real?

Gingerly, adding no more cuts to his face, Fletch shaved.

Janio Barreto following them through the subway to Carnival Parade had meant something to Laura it had not meant to him. What had her letter said? *Saci-perêrê*. What's a *saci-perêrê*?

The warm water of the shower felt good on his body. The soap did not feel so good on some of his wounds.

In fact, Laura had not really asked him what happened to him under the stands at Carnival Parade. She thought anyone can tell a story and say it is the past. Even after his pointing out Gabriel Campos at Santos Lima, she did not really ask. She only asked how, why he pointed out Gabriel Campos.

He did not dry himself after the shower. Instead, he just wrapped the towel around his waist. The air felt too good on his wet body.

His mind a jumble, he went out into the balcony. A small samba combo was playing, probably outside a nearby cafe. Across the utility area, the man was still painting the room.

Laura thought it was funny the Tap Dancers had left him in a closed coffin with his bag of money. He had seen Norival Passarinho walk after he was dead. On broomsticks, his ankles tied to the ankles of Toninho and Orlando. Then Fletch had seen Norival Passarinho really walk after he was dead, really talk. Adroaldo Passarinho. Well, it *was* funny.

Fletch was dead. He had died forty-seven years ago. At Dona Jurema's mountain resort the Tap Dancers had tried, maybe as a joke, to arrange a corpse for him. People believed he could answer a question older than himself. Who had murdered Janio Barreto? And he had answered it. Apparently, Fletch had seen mythological figures which were not a part of his own culture. Of course, they must have been just costumed revelers under the stands. Were they? He had helped the dead Norival Passarinho walk, in a crazy, drunken scheme. Then he had believed he saw Norival Passarinho walk, heard him talk. Fletch had come back to life. He was in a closed coffin.

For Fletch, the line between life and death had become narrower. It was so narrow, it really could be funny.

Across the utility area, the man painting the room looked at Fletch.
Fletch had not realized he was staring at the man.
Fletch waved.
Grinning, the man waved back at him. He waved his paintbrush.
Fletch blinked. *He has damned little paint on that paintbrush, if he does not hesitate to wave it at someone, in a room he has been painting for days!*
Fletch laughed.
The man waved his paintbrush again.
Across the utility area the two men laughed together.
Fletch gave the man the thumbs-up sign, then went back into his room.

He telephoned The Hotel Jangada.
Room 912 did not answer.
Mrs. Joan Collins Stanwyk had not checked out.
Yes, there was a message awaiting her in her mail slot.
Drinking mineral water from a plastic liter bottle, Fletch read Laura's note a third time.
Then he called Teodomiro da Costa and arranged to meet with him that night. He would be late, Fletch said, as he intended to drive to the village of Botelho and back.
Teo recommended the seafood restaurant there.
Reluctantly, Fletch knelt. His cuts and bruises protesting, he leaned over until his head was only a few centimeters from the floor.
He peered under the bed.
The small, carved stone frog was gone.

THIRTY-SIX

"What are you doing here?"
Joan Collins Stanwyk, dressed in shorts which were too big and a T-shirt which had some slogan on it in Portuguese, stood across the rough restaurant table from Fletch.
"Eating."
"But how do you come to be here?"

"I was hungry." He continued eating.

"Really," she said. "How did you find me?"

Her eyes were round in amazement.

"Brazilian police apparently are not always as casual as they like to appear."

The restaurant was a patio with a roof over it on the beach.

"Can you join me?" Fletch asked. "Or aren't the help allowed to sit with the customers."

"I can buy you a cup of coffee," she said.

In sandals, she went across the restaurant to the serving tables.

He had enjoyed the drive through Rio's suburbs, through the Brazilian countryside down the coast. He enjoyed sucking in good air and seeing the real things of the countryside, real rocks and trees, real cows and goats. Good roads had been laid out against the day Brazil's past would catch up with her future. As he drove farther, most of the traffic he passed was on foot.

It had not taken him long to tour the village of Botelho. A short dock poked into a long ocean. The fish warehouse was no more than a shed. In the tiny church was a powerful, crude crucifixion. Less than a dozen fisherfolk bungalows facing the sea dozed in the shade of their own groves.

At the entrance to the open-air seafood restaurant he spotted Joan. Standing with her back to him in the kitchen area, Joan Collins Stanwyk, Mrs. Alan Stanwyk, was placing plates and glasses in a vat of steaming water. He watched her dry her hands and begin shelving clean plates.

It was early for dinner. The only other customers in the restaurant were five fishermen at one table chatting over *chopinhos*. A young waiter gave Fletch a menu and understood as Fletch pointed to a soup and a fish entree.

Brown paper sack on the bench beside him, Fletch gazed out over the beach to the ocean. Sooner or later, Joan Collins Stanwyk would turn, look through the serving apparatus, see him. He left her the option of ignoring his presence. He would go away again without speaking, if that was what she wanted.

The fish chowder was the best he'd ever had.

He was halfway through his fish entree when Joan crossed the restaurant and spoke to him.

Now she sat across from him at the long, rough table. She had placed a cup of coffee before each of them.

"I'm glad you're all right," he said, still eating.

"Have an accident?"

"No, thanks. Just had one."

They both laughed nervously.

"You look like someone really beat on you." Especially did her eyes fasten on the small scar on his throat.

"I ran into an enraged nanny goat." Her face put on patience. "That is the story I have decided to tell, to say is the past."

Joan's face looked better than when he saw her Saturday morning. There was good color in her skin and her eyes were clear. So far, she had not lit a cigarette, which was unusual for her. She was wearing no makeup at all. It was also obvious her hair had received little attention in the previous four days.

"It really was good of you to seek me out," Joan said. "Have I been much trouble?"

"I was worried about you. I've been stood up for dinner before, often, but seldom for breakfast."

"Not very nice of me."

"It's okay. I had breakfast anyway."

"Well." She looked into her coffee cup.

"The food here is very good."

"Isn't it? I love it."

"Very good indeed. You wash dishes in this establishment?"

"Yes."

"Didn't think you knew how."

"It's not one of the more artful skills." She showed him her hands. "Aren't they beautiful?" They were red and wrinkled.

"They look honest."

She fluttered her hands and put them in her lap. "I feel like a schoolgirl who's been caught playing hookey."

"It's just nice to know you're alive."

"Any questions I might have had about you and Alan's death . . ." She looked into Fletch's face, then at the scar on his neck, then into her own lap. ". . . I don't have now. The money —"

"I'm willing to do my best to try to explain."

In truth, Fletch wondered if Joan, in her extreme competence, was making some sort of a bargain with him.

"Not necessary," she said. "I know as much as I want to know. I pursued you to Brazil out of some sense of duty." Numbly, she repeated, "Some sense of duty."

He pushed his empty plate away. He realized Joan Collins Stanwyk was expected to wash it.

He sat silently, gazing out to sea. He waited until she understood that he was not questioning her.

She was sitting on her bench, her back straight, leaning on nothing. "I walked away from you that morning, Saturday morning, away from your hotel, to walk to my own hotel. You had said some things I had never heard before. I became angry in a way I had never been angry before.

"Suddenly I realized that here I was, a grown woman, stumbling along in the morning sunlight in tears because someone had stolen my little pins. My pinky rings! Little plastic cards with my name on them!"

Fletch said, "Also irreplaceable photographs of your husband, Alan, and your daughter, Julie."

"Yes. That profoundly bothers me. But I realized what a spoiled brat I was. I am. Skinny little beggar children were dancing all around me as I walked along, their hands out, whispering at me. I waved my arm at them, and through tight jaws shouted, *Oh, go away!* Couldn't they understand that I had lost a few of my diamonds, my credit cards, to me a negligible amount of cash? How dare they bother me at seven o'clock in the morning for money for food?

"I became truly angry at myself. What a superficial, supercilious bitch. What a hollow person. I had spent the night whining at the poor assistant manager at the hotel. I rushed to you at first light, to whine to you. And here I was virtually swinging at hungry kids."

She said, "Joanie Collins had lost a few pins."

Fletch sipped his coffee.

"Then I had a second thought, based on what you had said." Her index finger was feeling along a short crack in the table. "In a most peculiar way, I was free. I had been relieved of my identity. My credit cards had been stolen, my passport. It almost meant nothing that I was Joan Collins Stanwyk. At least, I couldn't prove it immediately to anybody. I couldn't go up to anybody, in a store or something, and say, 'I'm Joan Collins Stanwyk,' and make it mean anything. As you said, I was just arms and legs: one more person walking naked in the world.

"I liked that thought. Suddenly I liked the idea of being without all that baggage."

From behind the serving apparatus, a tall, slim man was peering out at them. He was looking from Joan to Fletch to Joan again with apparent concern.

Fletch said, "You're still Joan Collins Stanwyk."

"Oh, I know. But, for the first time in my life, it didn't seem to mean much. I saw that it didn't have to mean much."

Again Fletch permitted his question to remain tacit.

"When I got to The Hotel Jangada, a tour bus was waiting. I didn't know where it was going. I joined the people, the women in their short silk dresses, the men in their plaid shorts, and got on it. No one asked me for a ticket, or money. Obviously I belonged to a group from The Hotel Jangada. I belonged with these people. I stole a bus ride here."

Fletch smiled. "Thievery is infectious."

"The bus stopped here for lunch. I didn't have lunch. I couldn't pay for it. What a new fact! What a new feeling! I wandered around the beach. I let the bus leave without me.

"I wondered who I was. Really was. Really am. I wondered if I could survive a full day without cash, without credit cards, without my identity. I wondered what life would be like, for just a few moments, if I couldn't pull something out of my purse and say, 'Here I am, now do as I ask, please; give me . . .'" She smiled at herself. "It was getting dark. So I came here and had dinner. I sat over there." She indicated a bench near the door. "I felt as guilty as hell." She put her elbows on the table in a most unrefined way, her chin on her hands. "Then I went and washed dishes for them."

"Is it fun for you?"

"It's harder than tennis. I daydream about having a proper massage. God, last night I wanted a martini so badly." She shrugged. "I can't understand a word of the language. It's so soft, so sibilant."

The tall man, wiping his hands on an apron, finally was approaching them.

Joan's face was happy. She said, "This noon, a well-dressed couple arrived for lunch. German, I think. In a Mercedes, behind a uniformed driver. I found myself looking at her over my pile of dirty dishes. Somehow it made me angry that she only picked at her lunch. Of course I understood. She has to keep her figure. . . ."

The man stood behind Joan, looking at Fletch. He put his hand on her shoulder.

She put her hand on his.

"Fletch, this is Claudio."

"Bom dia, Claudio."

Fletch half rose, and they shook hands.

"Claudio owns this place, I think," Joan said. "At least he acts as if he owns the place. He acts as if he owns the world. It may just be Brazilian masculinity."

Assured she was all right, and apparently without conversation in English, Claudio left the back of his hand against Joan's cheek for a moment, then went back to the kitchen.

"Are you here forever?" Fletch asked. "Have you decided upon dishwashing as a career?"

"Oh, no. Of course not. I love Julie. I love my father. I must get back. I have responsibilities. To Collins Aviation. I'm the best fundraiser Symphony has."

Fletch put the brown paper sack on the table.

"Just leave me here for a while," Joan said quietly. "Let me play truant from life for a short while, from being mother, daughter, from being Joan Collins Stanwyk. Leave me be."

"Sure." He pushed the paper bag across the table at her.

"What's that?" she asked.

"The money I was bringing you Saturday — enhanced by poker earnings. For when you decide to get back." She looked into the bag. "Surely enough to get you back to Rio, pay a hotel bill for a few nights, pay for Telexes."

"How very nice."

"Poverty is easier to slip into," Fletch said, "than to climb out of."

She reached across the table and took his hand. "How do you know so much?"

"Just the wisdom of the masses. Also," he said, "you must still have the key to your suite at The Hotel Jangada."

"I must have. It must be in a pocket of that pants suit I was wearing."

"Get it for me. I'll check you out of the hotel. I'll leave your luggage with the concierge, for when you want it."

"I will want it," she said. "I'm sure I will."

While Fletch paid the waiter, Joan told him about bathing in the warm ocean, how hot the sun was at midday, how much she liked the smell of fish, it was so real, the sounds of something she thought might be tree-frogs at night.

"You sound like you're at summer camp," he said.

"No. At summer camp someone else washed the dishes. And," she smiled, "there were only girls."

Fletch waited by his car while she got the key to her suite at The

Hotel Jangada. It was still daylight. Customers were beginning to arrive for dinner.

As Joan crossed the small parking lot to him, some of the customers stared after her, perplexed.

"Do me one other favor, will you?" she asked.

"Sure." Fletch had known there would be a second part to the bargain. There are always two parts to a bargain.

"When you go back to the States, to California, back to your own reality, don't ever tell anyone that this crazy thing happened to me, that I did this crazy thing. That you found me washing dishes in a fish joint in some nameless little town in Southern Brazil."

"The town has a name."

She laughed. "You know, I don't know what it is?"

"Botelho."

"Will you promise me that?"

"Sure."

"I mean, everyone needs a vacation from life. Don't you agree?"

"A vacation from reality."

She handed him the key. "I'm paying for a suite at The Hotel Jangada, and sleeping more or less on the beach in Botelho."

Fletch said: "Topsy-turvy."

THIRTY-SEVEN

"Did you enjoy your dinner in Botelho?" Teodomiro da Costa asked.

"It was excellent," Fletch answered.

"Yes, that's a good restaurant. I'm not sure it's worth the ride. . . ."

It was late when Fletch got back to Rio, by the time he arrived at Teo da Costa's home on Avenida Epitacio Passoa.

When the houseman had shown Fletch into the downstairs family sitting room, Teo was looking sleepy in a dressing gown in a comfortable chair. He was reading the book 1887 — *The Year Slavery In Brazil Ended.* From under the reading light, Teo's eyes traveled over Fletch's various visible wounds, but he did not comment on them.

"Want a nightcap?"

"No, thanks. I won't be here that long."

Stiff from Carnival, from his wounds, from the long ride, Fletch sank comfortably into the two-seater divan.

In the little sitting room was a handsome big new painting by Misabel Pedrosa.

"And did Laura enjoy Botelho?"

"Laura has gone back to Bahia. Yesterday, I finally fell asleep. She couldn't wake me up. She had to go back to begin preparing for her concert tour."

"Yes," Teo said slowly, "I gathered you might have cleaned up that mystery of who murdered Janio Barreto forty-seven years ago. There was a most peculiar report in O Globo this morning. A small item, saying Gabriel Campos, past capoeira master of Escola Santos Lima, was found on the beach, his throat slit. A woman from the favela, Idalina Barreto, is helping the police in its inquiries."

"I pity the police."

"Apparently she was found on the beach lighting matches trying to set fire to the corpse of Gabriel Campos."

"Did she succeed?"

"That's what's peculiar about O Globo's report. It says that legend has it that no one has ever succeeded in lighting a fire in that exact spot on the beach in almost fifty years."

"Teo, I'd like some of the money you've invested for me to be available for the education of the current young generation of the descendants of Janio Barreto."

"Easily done."

"Especially young Janio. He has a wooden leg. It will be harder for him to make a living without an education."

"Yes."

Fletch fingered the scar on his throat. "I believe he saved my life." Then he chuckled. "He might even think of becoming a book-keeper."

Teo placed his history book on the table beside his chair. "And did you find your lady friend from California? What's her name, Stanwyk?"

"Yes. She's all right."

"What happened to her?"

"She fell out of her cradle. She's enjoying a few moments crawling around the floor."

Obviously tired, Teo cast his hooded eye across the darkened room at Fletch.

"Brazil is the future," Fletch said. "Who can see the future?"

"And you," Teo asked, shifting comfortably in his chair. "Did you enjoy Carnival?"

"I learned some things."

"I'd love to know what."

"Oh, that the past asserts itself. That the dead can walk." Fletch thought of the small carved stone frog that had been under his bed. "That the absence of symbols can mean as much as their presence."

As if digesting all this, Teo blinked his hooded eye. He did not ask questions.

"Teo, driving so far today by myself, through the incredible Brazilian countryside, I think I settled on a plan."

"No need to tell me what it is," Teo said. "Any more than there is to tell your father what it is. As long as you have a plan."

"I've decided to try writing a biography of the Northamerican western artist Edgar Arthur Tharp, Junior. It seems an opportunity to get some things said about the Northamerican's view of the artist, the intellectual, of the Northamerican spirit."

Teo repeated, "As long as you have a plan."

"It is the spirit of things which is important, isn't it?"

Teo said, "Norival Passarinho's funeral is tomorrow. Will you attend?"

Fletch hesitated. "Yes." He stood up. "Why not?"

Teo stood up as well. "And will you visit Bahia before you leave?"

At the door, Fletch said: "To say good-bye."

For a moment, Fletch sat quietly in the dark in the small yellow convertible outside Teodomiro da Costa's home.

A few doors from Teo's, a last Carnival party was in progress. It was Shrove Tuesday night.

A couple dressed as the King of Hearts and the Queen of Diamonds scurried across the sidewalk from a taxi into the house.

There was the sound of laughter coming from the house. Singing. Above all, the sound of a samba combo. Of samba drums *beating, rhythms beside rhythms on top of rhythms beneath rhythms. From all sides, every minute, day and night, came the beating of the drums.*

"*Bum, bum, paticum bum.*" Fletch started the car. "*Prugurundum.*"

Most people in the world Fletch had known had stopped hearing the melodies from the drums.

CONFESS, FLETCH

TO *Judy and Lew, Susie and Chuck, Stuart,*
    Karen and Rupert, Jennette and Alan,
    HoRo, HoHo, Susi, Chris and Doug

ONE

Fletch snapped on the light and looked into the den.
Except for the long windows and the area over the desk,
the walls were lined with books. There were two red leather
wing chairs in the room, a small divan, and a coffee table.
On the little desk was a black telephone.

Fletch dialed "O."

"Get me the police, please."

"Is this an emergency?"

"Not at the moment."

The painting over the desk was a Ford Madox Brown — a country
couple wrapped against the wind.

"Then please dial '555-7523.' "

"Thank you."

He did so.

"Sergeant McAuliffe speaking."

"Sergeant, this is Mister Fletcher, 152 Beacon Street, apartment
6B."

"Yes, sir."

"There's a murdered girl in my living room."

"A what girl?"

"Murdered."

Naked, her breasts and hips full, her stomach lean, she lay on her
back between the coffee table and the divan. Her head was on the
hardwood floor in the space between the carpet and the fireplace.
Her face, whiter than the areas kept from the sun by her bikini, eyes
staring, looked as if she were about to complain of some minor discomfort, such as, "Move your arm, will you?" or "Your watchband is
scratching me."

"Murdered," Fletch repeated.

There was a raw spot behind the girl's left ear. It had had time neither to swell nor bleed. There was just a gully with slim blood streaks running along it. Her hair streamed away from it as if to escape.

"This is the Police Business phone."

"Isn't murder police business?"

"You're supposed to call Emergency with a murder."

"I think the emergency is over."

"I mean, I don't even have a tape recorder on this phone."

"So talk to your boss. Make a recommendation."

"Is this some kinda joke?"

"No. It isn't."

"No one's ever called Police Business phone to report a murder. Who is this?"

"Look, would you take a message? 152 Beacon Street, apartment 6B, murder, the name is Fletcher. Would you write that down?"

"156 Beacon Street?"

"152 Beacon Street, 6B." Through the den door, Fletch's eyes passed over his empty suitcases standing in the hall. "Apartment is in the name of Connors."

"Your name is Fletcher?"

"With an 'F.' Let Homicide know, will you? They'll be interested."

T W O

Fletch looked at his watch. It was twenty-one minutes to ten. Instinctively he timed the swiftness of the police.

He returned to the living room and mixed himself a Scotch and water at the sideboard. He would not bother with ice. He concentrated on opening the Scotch bottle, making more of a job of it than was necessary. He did not look in the direction of the girl.

She was beautiful, she was dead, and he had seen enough of her.

Sloshing the drink in his glass as he walked, he went back into the den and turned on all the lights.

He stood at the desk, looking closely at the Brown. The cottage behind the country couple was just slightly tilted in its landscape, as if it, too, were being affected by the wind. Fletch had seen similar Browns, but never even a reproduction of this painting.

The phone made him jump. Some of his drink splashed onto the desk blotter.

He placed his glass on the blotter, and his handkerchief over the stains before answering.

"Mister Fletcher?"

"Yes."

"Ah, good, you did arrive. Welcome to Boston."

"Thank you. Who is this?"

"Ronald Horan. Horan Gallery. I tried to get you earlier."

"I went out to dinner."

"Your letter mentioned you'd be staying in Bart Connors's apartment. We did some restoration work for him a year or two ago."

"It's very good of you to call, Mister Horan."

"Well, I'm very excited by this Picasso you mentioned in your letter. You said it's called 'Vino, Viola, Mademoiselle'?"

"It's been called that. God knows how Picasso thought of it."

"Of course, I'm puzzled why you came all the way from Rome to Boston to engage me as your broker. . . ."

"There's some evidence the painting is in this part of the world. Possibly even in Boston."

"I see. Still, I expect we could have handled it by correspondence."

"As I wrote in my letter, there may be one or two other matters I'd like to consult you about."

"Yes, of course. Anything to be of service. Perhaps I should start by warning you that this painting might not exist."

"It exists."

"I've looked it up, and there is no record of it anywhere that I can find."

"I have a photograph of it."

"Very possibly it does exist. There are a great many Picassos in existence which have never been recorded. On the other hand, the body of Picasso's work very often has been victim to fakes. I'm sure you know his work has been counterfeited more than the work of anyone else in history."

"I do know, yes."

"Well, I wouldn't be giving you professional service if I didn't bring these matters up to you. If such a painting exists, and it's authentic, I'll do everything I can to find it for you and arrange for the purchase."

Rotating blue lights from the roofs of police cars stories below began to flash against the long, light window curtains. There had been no sound of sirens.

"Are you free to come by tomorrow morning, Mister Fletcher?"

Fletch said, "I'm not sure."

"I was thinking of ten-thirty."

"Ten-thirty will be fine. If I'm free at all."

"Good. You have my address."

"Yes."

"Let's see, you're on Beacon Street across from the Gardens, right?"

"I think so."

Fletch pushed the curtains aside. There were three police cars in the street. Across the street was an iron railing. The darkness beyond had to be a park.

"Then what you do is this: Leave your apartment and turn right, that is, east, and go to the end of the Gardens. Then turn left on Arlington Street, that is, away from the river. Newbury Street will be the third block on your right. The gallery is about two and a half blocks down the street."

"Thank you. I've got it."

"I'll send someone down to open the door to you at ten-thirty precisely. We're not a walk-in gallery, you know."

"I wouldn't think so. I'm sorry, Mister Horan. I think there's someone at my door."

"Quite all right. I look forward to seeing you in the morning."

Fletch hung up.

The door buzzer sounded.

It was seven minutes to ten.

THREE

"My name's Flynn. Inspector Flynn."

The man in the well-cut, three-piece, brown tweed suit filled the den doorway. His chest and shoulders were enormous, his brown hair full and curly. Between these two masses of overblown brown was a face so small it had the cherubic quality of an eight-year-old boy, or a dwarf. Even with the hair, his head was small in proportion to his body, like a tiny, innocent-looking knob in control of a huge, powerful machine. Nothing indoors had the precise color of his green eyes. It was the bright, sparkling green of sunlight on a wet spring meadow.

Below the break of his right trouser leg were a half-dozen dots of blood.

"Pardon my pants. I'm fresh from an axe murder."

For such a huge chest cavity, for anyone, for that matter, his voice was incredibly soft and gentle.

Fletch said, "You're an Irish cop."

"I am that."

"I'm sorry." Fletch stood up. "I meant nothing derogatory by that."

Flynn said, "Neither did I."

There was no proffer to shake hands.

As Flynn vacated the doorway, a younger and shorter man came in, carrying a notepad and ballpoint pen. He had the grizzled head of someone fried on a Marine Corps drill ground a score of times, like a drill sergeant. The rubbery skin around his eyes and mouth suggested his eagerness to shove his face in yours, tighten his skin, and shout encouraging obscenities up your nose. In repose, the slack skin gave him the appearance of a petulant basset. His suit and shirt were cheap, ill-fitting, but spotless, and his shoes, even this late on a drizzly day, gleamed.

"This is Grover," said Flynn. "The department doesn't trust me to do my own parking."

He settled himself in a red leather chair.

Fletch sat down again.

It was twenty-six minutes past ten.

He remained waiting in the den. A young, uniformed policeman waited with him, standing at parade rest, carefully keeping his eyes averted from Fletch. Beyond the den, other police, plainclothesmen, moved around the apartment. Fletch wondered if any reporters had sneaked in with them. Fletch heard the murmur of their voices, but caught nothing of what they said. Occasionally, a streak of light from a camera flashbulb crossed the hall, from either the left, where the bedrooms were, or the right, where the living room was.

An ambulance crew entered, rolling a folded stretcher across the hall, toward the living room.

"Close the door, will you, Grover? Then make yourself comfortable at the wee desk there. We don't want to miss a word of what this boyo in the exquisite English tailoring has to say."

The uniformed policeman went through the door as Grover closed it.

"Has anyone read you your rights?" Flynn asked.

"The first fuzz through the door."

"Fuzz, is it?"

Fletch said, "Fuzz."

"In more human language," Flynn continued, "I ask you if you don't think you'd be wiser to have your lawyer present while we question you."

"I don't think so."

Flynn said, "What did you hit her with?"

Fletch could not prevent mild surprise, mild humor appearing in his face. He said nothing.

"All right, then." Flynn settled more comfortably in his chair. "Your name is Fletcher?"

"Peter Fletcher," Fletch said.

"And who is Connors?"

"He owns this apartment. I'm borrowing it from him. He's in Italy."

Flynn leaned forward in his chair. "Do I take it you're not going to confess immediately to this crime?"

He used his voice like an instrument — a very soft, woodland instrument.

"I'm not going to confess to this crime at all."

"And why not?"

"Because I didn't do it."

"The man says he didn't do it, Grover. Have you written that down?"

"Sitting here," Fletch said, "I've been rehearsing what I might tell you."

"I'm sure you have." Elbows on chair arms, massive shoulders hunched, Flynn folded his hands in his lap. "All right, Mister Fletcher. Supposing you recite to us your opening prevarication."

The green eyes clamped on Fletch's face as if to absorb with full credulity every word.

"I arrived from Rome this afternoon. Came here to the apartment. Changed my clothes, went out to dinner. Came back and found the body."

"This is a dandy, Grover. Let me see if I've got it in all its pristine wonder. Mister Fletcher, you say you fly into a strange city, go to an apartment you're borrowing, and first night there you find a gorgeous naked girl you've never seen before in your life murdered on the living room rug. Is that your story, in short form?"

"Yes."

"Well, now. If that doesn't beat the belly of a fish. I trust you've got every word, Grover, however few of them there were."

Fletch said, "I thought it might help us all get to bed earlier."

" 'Get to bed,' he says. Now, Grover, here's a man who's had a full day. Would you mind terribly if I led the conversation for a while now?"

"Go ahead," Fletch said.

Looking at his watch, Flynn said, "It's been a near regular custom I've had with my wife since we were married sixteen years ago to get me home by two o'clock feeding. So we have that much time." He glanced at the glass of Scotch and water Grover had moved to the edge of the desk blotter. "First I must ask you how much you've had to drink tonight."

"I've had whatever's gone from that glass, Inspector. An ounce of whiskey? Less?" Fletch asked, "You really have inspectors in Boston, uh?"

"There is one: me."

"Good grief."

"I'd say that's a most precise definition. I'm greatly taken with it, myself, and I'm sure Grover is — an Inspector of Boston Police as being 'good grief.' The man has his humor, Grover. However, we were speaking of the man's drinking. How much did you have to drink at dinner?"

"A split. A half bottle of wine."

"He'll even define 'split' for us, Grover. A remarkably definitive man. You had nothing to drink before dinner?"

"Nothing. I was eating alone."

"And you're going to tell me you had nothing to drink on the airplane all the way across the Mediterranean Sea and then the full girth of the Atlantic Ocean, water, water everywhere. . . ."

"I had coffee after we took off. A soft drink with lunch, or whatever it was they served. Coffee afterwards."

"Were you traveling first class?"

"Yes."

"The drinks are free in first class, I've heard."

"I had nothing to drink on the airplane, or before boarding the airplane. I had nothing to drink at the airport, nothing here, wine at the restaurant, and this half glass while I've been waiting for you."

"Grover, would you make a note that in my opinion Mister Fletcher is entirely sober?"

"Would you like a drink, Inspector?" Fletch asked.

"Ach, no. I never touch the dirty stuff. The once I had it, the night after being a student in Dublin, it gave me a terrible headache. I woke up the next morning dead. The thing is, this crime of passion would be much easier to understand if you had a bottle or two of the old juice within you."

"You may find that is so," Fletch said. "When you find the murderer."

"Are you a married man yourself, Mister Fletcher?"

"I'm engaged."

"To be married?"

"I expect to be married. Yes."

"And what is the name of this young lady whose luck, at the moment, is very much in question?"

"Andy."

"Now why didn't I guess that myself? Write down 'Andrew,' Grover."

"Angela. Angela de Grassi. She's in Italy."

"She's in Italy, too, Grover. Everyone's in Italy except he who has just come from there. Make a social note. She didn't come with you due to her prejudice against the Boston weather?"

"There are some family problems she has to straighten out."

"And what would the nature of such problems be?"

"I attended her father's funeral yesterday, Inspector."

"Ach. Dicey time to leave your true love's side."

"She should be coming over in a few days."

"I see. And what is it you do for a living?"

"I write on art."

"You're an art critic?"

"I don't like the words 'art critic.' I write on the arts."

"You must make a fortune at it, Mister Fletcher. First class air tickets, this lavish, opulent apartment, the clothes you're wearing. . . ."

"I have some money of my own."

"I see. Having money of your own opens up a great many careers which otherwise might be considered marginal. By the way, what is that painting over the desk? You can't see it from where you are."

"It's a Ford Madox Brown."

"It's entirely my style of work."

"Nineteenth-century English."

"Well, that's one thing I'm not, is nineteenth-century English. And who with a touch of humanity in him would be? When did you notice it yourself? The painting, I mean?"

"While I was calling the police."

"You mean to say, while you were calling the police to report a murder, you were looking at a painting?"

"I guess so."

"Then, indeed, you must be a most relentless writer-on-the-arts. I understand you used the Police Business phone to report the heinous deed rather than Police Emergency."

"Yes."

"Why is that?"

"Why not? Nothing could be done at the moment. The girl was clearly dead. I'd rather leave the Emergency line clear for someone who needed the police immediately, to stop a crime in progress, or get someone to a hospital."

"Mister Fletcher, people with stutters and stammers and high breathlessness call the Police Emergency number to report a cat in a tree. Did you look up the Police Business number in a book?"

"The operator gave it to me."

"I see. Were you ever a policeman yourself?"

"No."

"Just wondering. Something about your sophistication regarding bodies in the parlor. The conciseness of your answers. After a murder, usually it's only the policemen who want to get to bed. Where was I?"

"I have no idea," Fletch said. "In the nineteenth century?"

"No. I'm not in the nineteenth century, Mister Fletcher. I'm in Boston, and I'm wondering what you're doing here."

"I'm here to do research. I want to try a biography on the Western artist, Edgar Arthur Tharp, Junior. He was born and brought up here in Boston, you know, Inspector."

"I do know that."

"The Tharp family papers are here. The Boston Museum has a great many of his works."

"Have you ever been in Boston before?"

"No."

"Do you know anyone here?"

"I don't think so."

"Let's go over your arrival in Boston again, Mister Fletcher. It makes such a marvelous story. This time, tell me the approximate times of everything. Again, I remind you that Grover will take it all down, and we're not supposed to correct him later, although I always do. Now: when did you land in Boston?"

"I was in the airport waiting for my luggage at three-forty. I set my watch by the airport clock."

"What airline? What flight number?"

"Trans World. I don't know the flight number. I went through customs. I got a taxi and came here. I got here about five-thirty."

"I understand about going through customs, but the airport is only ten minutes from here."

"You're asking me? I believe Traffic Control is also considered Police Business."

The representative of Boston Police said, "Ach, well, so, of course it was five o'clock. Where in particular did you get stuck?"

"In some crazy tunnel with a dripping roof and chirruping fans."

"Ah, yes, the Callahan. I've sat in there myself. But at five o'clock the traffic in there usually gets stuck going north, not south."

"I shaved and showered and changed my clothes. I unpacked. I left here I would guess a little after six-thirty. I took a taxi to the restaurant."

"Which restaurant?"

"The Café Budapest."

"Now, that's interesting. How did you know enough to go to such a fine restaurant your first night in town?"

"The man sitting next to me on the plane mentioned it."

"Do you remember his name?"

"He never mentioned it. We didn't talk much. Just while we were having lunch. I think he said he was some kind of an engineer. From someplace I think called Wesley Hills."

"Wellesley Hills. In Boston we spell everything the long way, too. Did you have the cherry soup?"

"At the Budapest? Yes."

"I hear it's a great privilege, for those who can afford it."

"I tried to walk home. It had seemed like a short ride in the taxi. I left the restaurant shortly after eight and got here, I would say, just before nine-thirty. In the meantime, I got thoroughly lost."

"Where? I mean, where did you get lost?"

Fletch looked around the room before answering. "If I knew that, would I have been lost?"

"Answer the question, please. Describe to me where you went."

"God. A Citgo sign. A huge, gorgeous Citgo sign. Remarkable piece of art."

"There, now, you see, that wasn't so difficult, was it? You turned left rather than right. That is, you went west rather than east. You went into Kenmore Square. What did you do then?"

"I asked a girl for Beacon Street, and it was right there. I walked along it until I came to 152. It was a long walk."

"Yes. That was a long walk. Especially after a Hungarian dinner. So you came into the apartment, and went into the living room. Why did you go into the living room?"

"To turn off the lights."

"So you must have gone into the living room the first time you were in the apartment and turned on the lights."

"Sure. I looked around the apartment. I don't remember whether I left the lights on in the living room or not."

"Undoubtedly you did. Anyone as likely a murderer as you are is apt to do anything. Now, why were you in Rome?"

"I live there. Actually, I have a villa in Cagna, on the Italian Riviera."

"Then why didn't you fly from Genoa, or Cannes?"

"I was in Rome anyway."

"Why?"

"Andy has an apartment there."

"Andy-the-girl. You've been living with Andy-the-girl?"

"Yes."

"How long?"

"A couple of months."

"And you met with Bartholomew Connors, Esquire, in Rome?"

"Who? Oh, no. I don't know Connors."

"You said this is his apartment."

"It is."

"Then how are you in it, if you don't know Mister Connors?"

"Homeswap. It's an international organization. I think its head-quarters is in London. Connors takes my villa in Cagna for three months; I use his apartment in Boston. Cuts down on the use of money."

"You've never met?"

"We've never even corresponded. Everything, even the exchange of keys, was arranged through London."

"Well, I'm sure I'll catch up again with this world, one day. Don't write that down, Grover. So, Mister Fletcher, you say you don't know Bartholomew Connors at all, and you don't know Ruth Fryer either?"

"Who is she?"

"You answered that question so perfectly I'm beginning to believe I'm talking to myself. Mister Fletcher, Ruth Fryer is the young lady they have just taken out of your living room."

"Oh."

" 'Oh,' he says, Grover."

"Inspector, I believe I have never seen that young lady before in my life."

"Taking your story as the word from John — that's Saint John, Grover — when you discovered the body, didn't you wonder where the young lady's clothes were? Or are you so used to seeing gorgeous girls naked on the Riviera you think they all come that way?"

"No," Fletch said. "I did not wonder where her clothes were."

"You came in here and looked at a painting, instead."

"Inspector, you've got to understand there was a lot to wonder about at that moment. I was in a state of shock. I didn't know where the girl came from. Why should I wonder where her clothes went to?"

"They were in your bedroom, Mister Fletcher. With the bodice torn."

Fletcher ran his eyes along a shelf of books.

"I'm not sure I've ever heard the word 'bodice' spoken before. Of course, I've read it — in nineteenth-century English novels."

"Would you like to hear my version of what happened here tonight?"

"No."

"Let me run through it, anyway. I can still get home in time for two o'clock feeding. You arrived at the airport, having left your true love in Rome, but also after having been confined to her company for two months, living in her apartment, the last few days of which have been sad days, seeing her to her father's funeral."

"Sort-of funeral."

"You escaped the dearly beloved with divine celerity, Mister Fletcher. That's a nice alignment of words, Grover. Have you got them all?"

"Yes, Inspector."

"In their proper order?"

"Yes, Inspector."

"You came here and introduced yourself to this huge, impressive apartment. Your sense of freedom was joined by a sense of loneliness, which is a potently dangerous combination in the loins of any healthy young man. You shave and you shower, spruce yourself up, never thinking ill of yourself for a minute. Are you with my version of the story so far?"

"I can't wait to see how it comes out."

"You take yourself out into the drizzle. Perhaps you do the obvious and stop in at the first singles bar you come to. You put forth your noticeable charm to the most attractive girl there, possibly a little under the drizzle from gin — by the way, Grover, we'll want to know what's in that girl's stomach — entice her back here, to your bedroom, where she resists you, for some reason of her own. She promised Mother, or had forgotten to take her pills, or whatever it is young ladies say these days when they change their minds. You tear her clothes off her in the bedroom. Thoroughly frightened, she runs down the corridor to the living room. You catch up to her. She continues to resist you. Perhaps she is screaming, and you don't know how thick the walls are. You're in a new place. You left your fiancée this morning in Rome. Here's the classic case of adults in a room, and one of them isn't consenting. In frustration, in anger, in fear, in passionate rage, you pick up something or other, and knock her over the head. To subdue her — get her to stop screaming. Probably even you were surprised when she crumpled and sank to your feet."

Flynn rubbed one green eye with the palm of his huge hand.

"Now, Mister Fletcher, why isn't that the obvious truth?"

"Inspector? Do you think it is the truth?"

"No. I don't."

He pressed the palms of both hands against his eyes.

"At least not at the moment," he said. "If you'd been drinking — yes, I'd believe it in a moment. If you were less attractive, I'd believe it. What else do these girls hang around for, if it's not the Peter Fletchers of the world? If you were less self-possessed, I'd believe it. It's my guess it would take less cool to get rid of a resisting girl than go through an initial police questioning for murder. Never can tell, though — we all have our moments. If you hadn't called the Police Business phone, I'd be quicker to believe in your being in an impassioned, uncontrollable state. No. I don't believe it, either."

Grover said, "You mean, we're not arresting him, Inspector?"

"No, Grover." Flynn stood up. "My instinct is against it."

"Sir!"

"I'm sure you're right, Grover, but you must remember I haven't the benefit of your splendid training. I'm sure any experienced policeman would put Mister Fletcher behind bars faster than a babe can fall asleep. It's times like these, Grover, that inexperience counts."

"Inspector Flynn. . . ."

"Tush, tush. If the man's guilty, and he most likely is, there'll be more evidence of it. If I hadn't seen the suitcases in the hall myself, I'd think the whole thing was a pack of lies. I suspect it is, you know. I've never met a writer-on-the-arts before, but I've not considered them such a randy subspecies before, either."

Fletch said, "I expect you're going to tell me not to leave town."

"I'm not even going to say that. In fact, Mister Fletcher, I'd find it very interesting if you did leave town."

"I'll send you a postcard."

Flynn looked at his watch.

"Well, now, if Grover drives me home, I'll be just in time for my cup of camomile with my Elizabeth and my suckling."

"I will, Inspector." Grover opened the door to the empty apartment. "I want to talk to you."

"I'm sure you do, Grover. I'm sure you do."

FOUR

Expecting the normal delays in completing a transatlantic telephone call, as well as the normal difficulty of getting Angela de Grassi on the phone any time of the day or night, Fletch made his effort while remaining in bed in the morning.

He was greatly surprised when the call went through immediately, and Angela answered on what appeared to be the first ring.

"Andy? Good noon."

"Fletch? Are you in America?"

"Arrived safely. Even you can fly to Boston and arrive in one piece."

"Oh, I'd love to."

"Are you eating lunch?"

"Yes."

"What are you having?"

"Cold asparagus with mayonnaise, a few strawberries. Have you had breakfast?"

"No. I'm still in bed."

"That's nice. Is it a nice bed?"

"Sort of big for one person."

"Aren't they all?"

"No. This bed kept me awake all night, calling out 'Andy! Andy! Where are you? We need you. . . .' "

"My bed asked for you, too. Is the weather good there?"

"I don't know. I can't see it through the fog. How goes the battle?"

"Not so good. I spent all day with the lawyers and the commissioner of this and the commissioner of that. We're never going to get this straightened out. All the legal officials tell us he's dead, we must consider him dead, adjust to it and go live our own lives. Which is why we had the funeral service. But the lawyers insist everything must be left up in the air until we know more. Remember Mister Rosselli? He was at Poppa's funeral Monday. Poppa's lawyer. Chief mourner. Very big with his handkerchief. A day later, yesterday, he's putting his hands in the air saying there's nothing they can do until more is known."

"What are you going to do?"

"Keep trying, I guess. Everyone's being very sympathetic."

"But nothing's getting done."

"I've always heard lawyers will fiddle around forever, milking an estate — is that the expression? — like a cow, until they have grabbed everything in fees and nothing is left. Even a little estate like my father's."

"Sometimes it happens."

"And Sylvia, of course, darling stepmother Sylvia, is acting her usual bitch self. She announces about every ten minutes that she is the Countess de Grassi. Every doorman in Rome must know she is the Countess de Grassi by now. I get to tag along like a poor waif."

"Why don't you forget about it all and come over here?"

"That's the point, Fletch. Everyone tells us we must adjust, accept the facts, and go back to living our own lives. But we can't do that without some kind of income from the estate. They've turned everything off."

"I don't see that it matters. You and I get married, and it doesn't matter how many years it takes to settle the estate. I mean, who cares?"

"I care. Listen, Fletch, I don't care how long it takes to settle the estate. I don't care about the rotten old house or the income. All I want is the will read. I want to know to whom the bulk of the estate goes — my father's third wife, or my father's only daughter. That matters to me."

"Why?"

"If it goes to Sylvia, fine. That's my father's prerogative. I would never contest it. So I'd lose my family's home. Okay, I can walk away from that. Never again would I think of the old servants as my responsibility. Remember, Fletch, Ria and Pep brought me up. If most of the estate goes to me, they're my responsibilities. Right now I can do nothing about them. Not even answer the questions in their eyes. They are my responsibility. Sylvia can take her precious countess-ship and walk into the sea with it."

"Andy, Andy, this is an emotional matter. Between two women."

"You bet it's an emotional matter. The whole situation is bizarre enough without everything being left up in the air this way. I don't care if the will is never executed, is that how you say? All I want to know is what the will says."

"I'm sort of surprised you can't get the substance of the will some-how out of Rosselli."

"This man! He dandled me on his knee when I was a baby. Now he will tell me nothing!"

"He's still dandling you on his knee."

"And Sylvia doesn't leave me alone for a moment. When she's not two paces in front of me announcing to the world she is the Countess de Grassi, she is two paces behind me trying to find out what I do. Every minute she asks, 'Where did Fletcher go? Why did he go there? What is he doing in Boston?'"

"What have you told her?"

"I said you went to Boston on personal business. Something about your family."

"Look, Andy. Don't forget why I am in Boston."

"And you'd better find them, Fletch. It's becoming very important. Even if Sylvia inherits most of the estate, she will never take care of the responsibilities. What's happened so far?"

"Horan, the man from the gallery, called last night. Almost the minute I arrived."

"What did he say?"

"He never heard of such a painting. I'm meeting him this morning."

"He says he never heard of the Picasso?"

"That's what he said."

"How did he sound to you?"

"What can I say? He sounded authentic."

"This is crazy, Fletch. At least you don't have Sylvia, the Countess de Grassi, to contend with."

"Listen, Andy, would you do me a favor?"

"Anything, Fletch of my heart."

"Will you go up to Cagna?"

"Now?"

"This guy, Bart Connors, who took the villa. One of us ought to have a look at him."

"Why? Isn't the apartment all right?"

"Yeah, it's fine. It's just that something has come up which makes me sort of curious about him."

"I'm supposed to drive all the way up to Cagna because you're curious about someone?"

"I flew all the way to Boston because you're curious about someone."

"Fletch, if I leave Rome, leave Rosselli and the other old baboons to Sylvia. . . ."

"Nothing will happen. My curiosity about Connors is more than casual, Andy. I need to know what sort of a person he is."

"Really, Fletch."

"Take the Porsche, take the train, fly to Genoa, rent a car, do whatever is easiest for you. You need to get away a day or two, anyway."

"Is that what you're really thinking?"

"No. I really want to know about Bart Connors."

"Your precious villa."

"You'll go?"

"Of course. How can I say no?"

"I thought you were saying no."

"I wouldn't think of it, darling. I'll leave my father's estate to wolf lawyers and vixen Sylvia, and fly to see if your tenant is happy."

"I'll appreciate it."

"Anything else I can do, Big Boss?"

"Yeah. After you look at Connors, come to Boston. Have you ever made love in the fog?"

"Fletcher, I have to straighten things out here."

"Forget it. The whole estate isn't worth a fart in a gale of wind. We can take care of your precious Ria and Pep."

There was a silence on the line.

"Andy?"

"I'll come as soon as I can, Fletch. Until then."

F I V E

A cross the Charles River the Cambridge Electric sign, still lit, looked dull through the fog. Cars going along the highways on both sides of the river used parking lights or headlights.

After he shaved and took a cold shower, he did his hundred pushups on the bedroom carpet, a towel spread under him.

Not dressing, he padded down the corridor.

The girl had run along here the night before. She had found herself in a situation she had had every right to think playful and fun but which suddenly went wrong, desperately wrong, hopelessly out of her control. She fled. Would she have fled the apartment naked?

Or was her running down the corridor, perhaps pretending to be frightened, part of her play?

In the living room, Fletch sat on the stool of the baby grand piano and stared at the spot where she had lain. The dim morning light, the shadows between the divan, beyond the coffee table, did little to alleviate the original shock of her presence, her smooth, sun-touched skin, the youthful fullness, leanness, shape of her body, the queer angle of her head, the discomfort in her face, her being dead.

Ruth Fryer. Ms. Fryer. Fletch knew more about her. She was about twenty-three. She had been brought up in health and self-confidence by loving parents. Boys, men had loved her. She had loved them, loved her freedom. She trusted. She had always been treated gently, considerately. Until last night.

Last night she had been murdered.

He went through the dining room, pushed open the swing door to the kitchen, and snapped on the light.

There was no milk or cream in the refrigerator, but there were five eggs and some butter. He would scramble eggs with water. Instant coffee was in a cupboard.

While he was scrambling the eggs he heard the old iron grill of the elevator door clang shut. Then he heard a key in a lock.

To his surprise, the swing door from the front hall opened.

In the door stood a woman, carrying a plastic shopping bag by its handles. Her eyes were wide-set and huge, her cheekbones high, her lips curiously long and thin. Her raincoat was open, loose. Around her hair was a red, blue, and black bandanna. She was in her mid-fifties.

"Good morning," Fletch said, staring from the stove.

"I'm Mrs. Sawyer. I clean here Wednesdays and Saturdays."

"I'll try to remember."

"That's all right." Her smile was directed more at Fletch's confusion than his nakedness. "I run naked around my place, too."

"You arrive early."

"Don't apologize. I don't buy those magazines, but I'm not so old I don't enjoy seeing a naked man. 'Course, you aren't black, Honey."

Fletch took the fork out of the frying pan.

When he turned, she was standing directly before him, searching his eyes.

"Before I do anything," she said, "you answer me."

Fletch was not about to back against the stove.

"You kill that girl last night?"

Fletch answered her eyes. "No."

"You ever kill anybody, anytime?"

Fletch could not answer her eyes. "Yes."

"When?"

"In a war."

"All right." She put her shopping bag on the table. "Your eggs are burning."

"How do you know about it?"

"It's in this morning's *Star*. Mister Connors said to expect a Mister Fletcher."

"Do you still have the newspaper?"

"No. I left it in the subway." She took off her coat and laid it neatly across the table. "Here, give me that pan."

Fletch looked down at himself.

She said, "So old Anne Sawyer can still do that to young men. My, my. I'll remember that, Saturday night."

"Does Connors like women, too?"

"Oh, yes. Especially after his wife left him for another woman. There's been a parade through here. Everything but the brass bands and the fire trucks."

Fletch said, "I'll get dressed."

"Your eggs are ready. From your tan marks, I'd say you're not too used to wearing all that many clothes anyway, regular."

"I'll get dressed."

"Your eggs will get cold."

Fletch said, "I'm cold."

"All right."

S I X

The eggs were cold. They were also watery.

Mrs. Sawyer had set a place for him at the dining room table.

He presumed the telephone was for Bart Connors.

Mrs. Sawyer pushed open the kitchen door.

"It's for you. A Mister Flynn."

Fletch took his coffee cup with him, across the dining room, through the living room, through the hall, to the den. He also took the hotel room key.

"Good morning, Inspector."

"Now who would this be?"

"Fletcher. You called me."

"Oh, yes. Mister Fletcher. I forgot who I was calling."

"Inspector, you'll be glad to know I passed a lie detector test this morning."

"Did you, indeed?"

"Administered by a Mrs. Sawyer, who comes in to clean twice a week. She arrives very early."

"How did she administer it?"

"She asked me if I killed the girl."

"And I daresay you had the gall to say you didn't?"

"She stayed to do her work."

Flynn said, "I was reasonably startled when a live woman answered your phone this morning. I said to myself, 'What is this boyo we have here?' I thought of giving the woman some warning."

"Which makes me think, Inspector. Did your men find a key to this apartment among the girl's possessions?"

"Only a Florida driver's license. And that was in her left shoe."

"No key? Mrs. Sawyer had a key."

"Cleaning ladies are apt to have keys. Girl friends aren't. But I take your meaning, Mister Fletcher. Other people might have keys to that apartment."

"Mrs. Sawyer found a key this morning. Just off the carpet in the corridor."

"A key to your apartment?"

"No. A hotel key."

"How very interesting."

Fletch looked at it in his hand.

"The tag on it says 'Logan Hilton — 223.' How could your men have missed it?"

"How, indeed? It's possible, of course, they didn't miss it — that it wasn't there at all. The suicide note hasn't been found yet, either."

"What?"

"Isn't that the theory you're working on this morning, Mister Fletcher? That the young lady let herself into your apartment with her own key, undressed in your bedroom, went into the living room, and hit herself over the head?"

"I'm not working on any theory this morning, Inspector."

"I know you're not. You're just trying to be helpful. Even your defensive theories are peculiarly lame. I've never known a man so indifferent to a murder he might have committed."

"What did the driver's license say?"

"That Ruth Fryer lived in Miami, Florida."

"That all? Is that as far as you've gotten this morning?"

"Plodding along, Mister Fletcher, plodding along. Today should turn up some interesting facts."

"I'll keep this key for you."

"We have turned up one curious fact already. I called customs officials this morning. You did arrive from Rome yesterday at about three-thirty. Trans World Airlines flight number 529."

"What's curious about that?"

"Your name isn't Peter Fletcher. The name on your passport is Irwin Maurice Fletcher."

Fletch said nothing.

Flynn said, "Now, why would a man lie about a thing like that?"

"Wouldn't you, Inspector, if your first names were Irwin Maurice?"

"I would not," said Flynn. "My first names are Francis Xavier."

SEVEN

Fletch hesitated at the corner of Arlington Street before turning left.

Walking along the brick sidewalk he turned up the collar of his Burberry. Lights were on in the offices of the brownstones to his right. After months of sun, the cool October mist felt good against his face.

He did not hesitate under the canopy of the Ritz-Carlton Hotel. He had seen the sign from a block and a half away. He went through the revolving door, across the lobby to the newsstand and bought a map of Boston and a *Morning Star*.

Turning away from the counter, he saw there was a side door and went through it. He was on Newbury Street.

He turned the pages of the newspaper as he walked. The story was on page five. It was only three paragraphs. No picture. He was identified in the second paragraph as "Peter Fletcher" and was attributed with calling the police. The third paragraph said, according to police sources, he had been alone in the apartment with the murdered girl.

The bare facts made it seem he was guilty. And the Boston press did not care much about the story.

He knew. The only follow-up expected from such facts would be the indictment of Peter Fletcher. Not much of a story. No mystery.

Classified advertisements were in the back of the paper, just ahead of the comics page. He tore out the strip concerning "Garages For Rent" and stuffed the rest of the newspaper into a small rubbish basket attached to a post at the corner. He put the piece of newspaper and the map in his coat pocket.

In the next block was the Horan Gallery. Of course, there was no sign. A building, an old townhouse, a thick, varnished wood garage door to the left, a recessed door with a doorbell button, two iron grilled windows to the right. The windows on the second, third and fourth floors were similarly grilled. The place was a fortress.

The brass plate under the bell button gave the address only — no name.

The door opened as Fletch pushed the button.

The man, in his sixties, wore a dark blue apron from his chest to his knees. He also wore a black bow tie with his white shirt, black trousers, and shoes. A butler interrupted while polishing silver?

"Fletcher," Fletch said.

To the right of the hall, in what had once been a family living room, was no furniture other than objects of art. Passing the door, Fletch saw a Rossetti on an easel. On the far wall was a Rousseau, over a standing glass case. On a pedestal was a bronze Degas dancer.

Going up the stairs, Fletch realized the house was entirely atmosphere-controlled. With thermostats every five meters along the walls, the temperature was absolutely even. The air was as odorless as if man had never existed. Few of the world's major museums afforded such systems.

The man, remaining wordless, showed Fletch into a room on the second floor and closed the door behind him.

Facing the door was a Corot, on an easel.

Horan rose from behind a Louis Seize desk, made a slight nod of his head which would have passed in Europe for an American bowing, and strode across the soft Persian carpet with his hand extended.

"I understand now," he said. "You're younger than I expected."

Horan hung Fletch's damp coat in a tight closet.

A Revere coffee service awaited them on a butler's table between two small, comfortable, upholstered divans.

"Cream or sugar, Mister Fletcher?"

"Just the coffee will be fine."

"I spent a pleasant half-hour reading you this morning — your monograph on Edgar Arthur Tharp, Junior. I should have read it before this, of course, but it was unknown at the Athenaeum until I requested it."

"You do your homework."

"Tell me, was it originally done as a doctoral thesis? It had no university imprimatur on it."

"I did it originally about that time in life, yes."

"But you've only printed it recently? Of course, you're still not much older than the average graduate student. Or are you one of these people blessed by the eternal appearance of youth, Mister Fletcher?"

Horan was a far more attractive man than Fletch had expected. In his early fifties, he was slim but heavily shouldered. His features were perfectly even. Without wrinkles, his complexion had to have been cosmetically kept. Over his ears, his hair, brushed back, was silver, not gray. Hollywood could have sold tickets to films of him dancing with Audrey Hepburn.

"Of course," he continued after Fletch's silence, "I haven't yet gotten my enthusiasm up for the bulk of American artists. Cassatt, Sargent, all right, but your Winslow Homers and Remingtons and Tharp all seem so indecently robust."

"Michelangelo and Rubens you would not call robust?"

"The action in the work is what I mean. The action, the moment, in the bulk of American work seems so existential. It is overwhelmed by its own sense of confinement. It does not aspire." Horan tasted his coffee. "I shall leave my lecturing for my class at Harvard, where I am due at twelve o'clock. About this Picasso?"

Fletch said, "Yes."

Being offered a seat was one thing; being put in his place another.

"What is there to say about the work I haven't already said?" Horan asked the air. "It may not exist. Then again it may. If it exists, where is it? And can it be authenticated? Believe it or not, the job of authentication is easier, now that the old boy is dead. He was prone to claim works he liked, whether he did them or not, and to deny works he probably did do, if he didn't like them. Then, after we find it, there is the question of whether whoever owns the work is willing to sell, and for how much. You may have come a long way for nothing, Mister Fletcher."

Fletch said nothing.

"Or did you really come to Boston to expand upon your work on Tharp?"

"Actually, I did," Fletch said. "I'm thinking of trying his biography."

Horan's forehead creased.

"Well," he said. "If I can be of any help. . . . Introduction to the Tharp Family Foundation. . . ."

"Thank you."

"You want the Picasso purely for your private collection?"

"Yes."

"You represent no one else?"

"No one."

"There is the question of credit, Mister Fletcher. Most of the people I deal with, I've dealt with for years, you understand. Other than your monograph, privately printed. . . ."

"I understand. The Barclough Bank in Nassau will establish what-ever credit for me you require."

"The Bahamas? That might be very useful."

"It is."

"Very well, sir. You mentioned you have a photograph of the Pi-casso?"

Fletch removed the envelope from his inside jacket pocket. He placed the photograph on the table.

"The photograph was made from a slide," he said.

"As I thought," Horan said, picking it up. "Cubist. And Braque did not do it." He tapped the photograph against his thumbnail. "But we don't know if Picasso did."

Fletch stood up.

"You'll make enquiries for me?"

"By all means."

"How long do you think it will be before you know something?"

Horan was following him.

"I'll get on the phone this afternoon. It may take twenty minutes, or it may take twenty days."

On a little table next to the closet door was a copy of the *New York Times*. Fletch's notoriety had not penetrated the Horan Gallery. He looked at the front page.

"I never bother with the Boston newspapers," Horan said.

"Not even the society pages?"

Horan held his coat for him.

"I believe anything of sufficient importance to warrant my atten-tion will appear in the *New York Times*."

Horan opened the door. The houseman, still in his apron, waited on the landing to show Fletch out.

Fletch said, "I'm sure you're right."

EIGHT

Apparently doing nothing but consulting his map, Fletch stopped across the street and looked at the Horan building. On each side of the roof, along the lines where the building joined with roofs of buildings to its left and right, ran a high, spiked iron fence. Its forward ends curved over the edge of the roof, fanning halfway down the fifth story. The windows on the third, fourth, and fifth storeys were barred, too.

Ronald Horan liked his security.

Using his map, Fletch crossed to Boylston Street and walked into Copley Square.

There, at the State Street Bank and Trust Company — after long, albeit courteous, delays, interviews with everyone except the most junior teller, proving his identity over and over again, including showing his passport, listening five times to the apologetic explanation that "all this is for your own protection, sir" — he picked up the twenty-five thousand dollars in cash he had had sent ahead. He took the money in fifty and one hundred dollar denominations.

He observed how much easier it always is to put money into a bank than it is to take it out. Even one's own money.

"That's what banks are for, sir."

"Of course."

Then he lunched on a tuna fish sandwich and Coke.

He taxied to five used car lots, in Boston, Brookline, Arlington, Somerville, and Cambridge, before he found precisely the van he wanted. It was last year's Chevrolet, light blue, with an eight-cylinder engine, standard shift, heating, and air conditioning. He paid cash for it and had the garageman replace all four tires. The garageman also obliged him by providing the legally necessary insurance for the van, through his sister-in-law, who ran an office across the street. The insurance bill was outrageous in relation to the cost of the vehicle.

Comparing the map with the list of garages for rent he had torn from the newspaper while going back to town in the taxi, he told the driver to go to the Boston underground garage. It was not far from his apartment. Once at the garage, he rejected it immediately — there would be no privacy there, typical of most government-run facilities the world round. He wanted walls.

He walked to a garage advertised on River Street, even closer to his apartment. First he woke up the housekeeper left in charge of the negotiation by its owner. She had to find the key. In broken-down, red house shoes, describing her osteitis in jealous detail, she showed him the garage. The monthly rent was exorbitant. But the place had brick walls and a new, thick wooden door. He paid two months' rent in cash and took the key, as well as a signed receipt (made out to Johann Recklinghausen) shortly after the interminable time it took the woman to find the receipt book.

He advised her to see a doctor.

After standing in line for forty-seven minutes at the Commonwealth of Massachusetts Registry of Motor Vehicles at 100 Nassau Street before being able to present his driver's license, purchase agreement marked "Cash — Paid," and application for insurance, he was given his vehicle registration (for a light blue Chevrolet caravan) and two license plates.

They attached his license plates for him at the used car lot in North Cambridge.

Driving back into Boston, he stopped at a corner variety store and bought twenty-five issues of that evening's *Boston Globe*. The curiosity of the storekeeper and his wife made Fletch wonder if indeed he was mentioned in that evening's newspaper. In the van, he went through one newspaper quickly. He wasn't.

He also stopped at a hardware store and bought a quart of black paint, a cheap brush, and a bottle of turpentine.

It was dark when he returned to River Street. Leaving the garage door open and the van outside with its lights on, he spread the *Globe* all over the cement floor.

Then he drove the van into the garage, onto the paper, and closed the door.

Being careful of his clothes, doing a purposefully messy job by the headlights reflected from the front wall, he climbed on top of the van and wrote, "YOU MUST BE HIGH" on the roof. Climbing down, again over the windshield, he wrote, in huge, dripping letters, on the left panel, "FEED THE PEOPLE." On the right panel, "ADJUST!"

As the truck was wet from the mist before he began, the mess he created was perfect.

After cleaning his hands with the newspapers and turpentine, he locked the garage.

Then he taxied to the Sheraton Boston Hotel and rented a two-door, dark blue Ford Granada Ghia, which he drove to his apartment and parked on the street.

NINE

Lights were on in the apartment.
Taking off his coat, Fletch went directly into the den. He flung the coat over an arm of a chair.
On the desk was a note for him.
It read, "Call Countess de Grassi at Ritz-Carlton — Mrs. Sawyer."
Aloud, Fletch said, "Shit!"
"Would it be more bad news for you, Mister Fletcher?"
Inspector Flynn was looking in at him from the hall.
"I fear we must add to it."
Grover joined Flynn from the living room.
"Your Mrs. Sawyer allowed us to remain after she left," Flynn said, "after we had fully proven ourselves not only Boston Police officers but fully virtuous men as well."
Fletch left the note upside down on the desk.
"If you want to talk to me, let's not sit in here," he said. "I got sort of tired of this room last night."
"Precisely why we were waiting for you in the living room." Flynn stepped back to let Fletch pass. "It's airier."
"Do you gentlemen want a drink?"
"Don't let us spoil your pleasure."
Fletch abstained.
He sat in one of the divans at the fireplace — the one nearer where the corpse had lain, and therefore not in view of the site.
"You've led us a merry chase," Flynn said, letting himself down in the opposite divan. "After you disappeared this morning, you would have found it impossible to leave the City of Boston — at least by public transportation."
"Disappeared?"
"Now you can't tell us you went in one door of the Ritz-Carlton and out the side door in a flash, thereby dropping our tail on you, out of the purest of all innocence!"
"Actually, I did," Fletch said. "I just stopped in to buy a newspaper."
"Such an innocent man, Grover. Have we ever met such a bliss-

fully innocent man? Here, stalwart men of the Boston Police have been staking out all the terminals all the day, the airport, the train stations, the bus stations, armed with the description of our murder suspect here, and our Mister Fletcher pops up at the cocktail hour like a proper clubman with the entirely reasonable explanation that he went in one door of a hotel and out another simply to buy a newspaper!"

"I bought a map of Boston, too."

"We were just about to leave," Flynn said, "having heard you rented a car a half hour ago. A blue Ford Ghia, whatever that is — I suppose it's got wheels — license number what-is-it, Grover?"

"R99420," Grover read from his notebook.

"By the by, Grover. Go call off that all-points-bulletin on that car. Let the troopers on the Massachusetts Turnpike relax tonight. Mister Fletcher is at home."

Grover returned to the den to use the telephone.

Flynn said, "Is that turpentine I smell?"

"It's a new men's cologne," Fletch answered. "Eau Dubuffet. Very big in France at the moment."

"I'd swear it's turpentine."

"I can get you a bottle of it," Fletch said.

"Ach, no, I wouldn't put you to the trouble."

"No trouble," Fletch said. "Honestly."

"Is it expensive stuff?"

"Depends," Fletch said, "on whether you buy it by the ounce or the quart."

"No offense intended," Flynn said, "but I'm not sure I'd want to smell that way. I mean, like a housepainter coming home. Supposed to be manly, is it?"

"Don't you think it is?"

"Well, noses play funny tricks on people. Especially the French."

Grover came back into the living room.

"Inspector, I smell turpentine," he said. "Do you?"

Flynn said, "I do not."

Grover stood in the middle of the room, white at the wrists, wondering how he should settle.

"Do you want me to take the conversation down, Inspector?"

"In truth, I don't want you to take anything down, ever. I have a very peculiar talent, Mister Fletcher. Being a writer-on-art you must have a heightened visual sense. I gather you have a more refined olfactory sense as well, as you pay a fancy price for a French cologne which smells remarkably like turpentine to me. My talent is I never forget a thing I've heard. It's these wonderful Irish ears." The green eyes gleamed impishly as the big man pulled up on his own ears. "Ears of the poets."

Grover was in a side chair, his notebook and pen in his lap at the ready.

In his soft voice, Flynn said, "Grover gave me quite a scolding last night, Mister Fletcher, on the drive home. For not arresting you, you understand. He's convinced we have enough evidence to make a case."

"You're not?" Fletch asked.

"We have evidence," Flynn said, "which is getting thicker by the minute. I explained to Grover I'd rather leave a man his own head and follow him. It's easier to get to know a man when he's free and following his own nature than it is when he's all scrunched up and defensive with his lawyers in a jail cell. A terrible scolding I had. And then this morning you slip our tail, all quite innocently, of course, and fritter away the day doing we know not what."

Fletch did not accept the invitation to report his day.

"In the meantime," he said, "aren't you afraid I might murder someone else?"

"Exactly!" blurted Grover from the side of the room.

Flynn's look told Grover he was a necessary evil.

Softly, Flynn said, "It's my argument that Irwin Maurice Fletcher, even alias Peter Fletcher, would not murder a gorgeous girl in a closed apartment — at least not sober — and then routinely, almost professionally, call the police on himself. He could have wiped things clean, repacked his suitcases, gone back to the airport, and been out of the country in the twitch of a rabbit's nose."

"Thank you," said Fletch.

"Even better," Flynn continued his argument with the side of the room, "he could have dressed the body, taken her down the back stairs in the dark of the night, and left her anywhere in the City of Boston. It wouldn't have disturbed his plans at all."

Fletch had thought about that.

"Instead, what does our boyo do? He calls the police. He doesn't precisely turn himself in, but he does call the police. He deserves some credit, Grover, for his remarkable and demonstrated faith in the institution of the public police."

Grover's ears were red. For a single, impetuous word in argument with his superior he was receiving a considerable chewing out.

"However," said Flynn in a more relaxed manner, "evidence developed today adds considerable weight to Grover's argument. Are you interested in it at all, Mister Fletcher?"

"Of course."

"First of all, what's your understanding as to when Mister Bart Connors went to Italy?"

"I don't know," Fletch answered. "He had occupancy of the villa as of last Sunday."

"And this is Wednesday," Flynn said. "Mrs. Sawyer confirms that Connors was here with her on Saturday, and that he asked her to come in Monday night for a few hours and do a special clean-up because of your arrival Tuesday, yesterday. She did so. Therefore, wouldn't it be natural to assume Connors left for Italy sometime between Saturday night and Monday night?"

Fletch said, "I guess so."

"To this point, we have not been able to establish that he actually did so," Flynn said. "A check of the airlines turned up no transatlantic reservations in the name of Bartholomew Connors."

"He could have flown from New York."

"He didn't," Flynn said. "And as Mister Connors is a partner in an important Boston law firm, I can't believe he would travel under a false passport, unless there is something extraordinary going on here at which we can't even guess."

Fletch said, "I suppose I could call the villa in Italy and see if he's there."

"We may come to that," said Flynn, "but let's not roust the quail until its feathers are wet."

"What?"

"Next we come to Mrs. Sawyer. A widow lady with two grown daughters. One teaches school in Mattapan. She does not live with her mother. The other is in medical school in Oregon. Mrs. Sawyer confirms she has a key to this apartment, but that no one had access to it other than herself. She spent Sunday with a gentleman friend, who is a sixty-year-old divorced accountant, visiting his grandchildren in New Bedford."

Fletch said, "Would you believe I never did suspect Mrs. Sawyer?"

"She had a key," Flynn answered. "Never can tell what bad man might have been taking advantage of her, for reasons of his own. She says that six months ago Connors suffered a particularly — I might even say, peculiarly — painful separation from his wife. There will be a divorce, she says, and I don't doubt it. She says there have been one or more women in this apartment since the separation. She finds their belongings around when she comes to clean. As clothes have never been left, in closets and drawers, she believes she can say no woman has actually lived here since the separation. It substantiates her belief that there has been 'a parade of women through here.' It also substantiates her belief that none of them was ever given, or had, a key."

Grover sneezed.

"As there appear to be paintings in this apartment of great value — is that not right, Mister Fletcher? — we may suppose even further towards certainty that Mister Connors did not dispense keys to this apartment like jelly beans."

"Great value," said Fletch. "Very great value."

He had not toured the paintings to his own satisfaction yet, but he had seen enough to be impressed. Besides the Brown in the den, there was a Matisse in the bedroom, a Klee in the living room (on the wall behind Grover), and a Warhol in the dining room.

"The last thing to say about access to the apartment is that there is a back door, in the kitchen. The rubbish goes out that way. There is no key to it. It is twice bolted from the inside. Mrs. Sawyer tells us she is most faithful about bolting it. In fact, when we arrived last night, both bolts were in place. No one could have gone out that way."

"But someone could have come in that way," said Fletch, "bolted the door behind him and gone out the front way."

"Absolutely right," said Flynn. "But how would they, without having known the back door was unbolted?"

"By chance," said Fletch.

"Aye. By chance." Clearly Flynn did not think much of chance.

"Now we come to you," said Flynn.

Grover sat up and clicked his ballpoint pen.

"Washington was good enough to send us both your photograph and your fingerprints." Flynn smiled kindly at Fletch. "Ach, a man has no privacy, anymore."

The kindly smile increased Fletch's discomfort.

"A man is many things," said Flynn. "A bad check charge. Two contempt of court charges. Non-payment-of-alimony charges longer than most people's family trees. . . . "

"Get off it, Flynn."

". . . All charges dropped. I do not mean to act as your lawyer," said Flynn, "although I seem to be doing a lot of that. May I recommend that as all these charges were mysteriously dropped, you do something to get them off your record? They're not supposed to be there. And you never know when an official, such as myself, might come along and view them with extreme prejudice. On the principle, you know, that where there's a hatrack there's a hat."

"Thanks for your advice."

"I see you also won the Bronze Star. What the notation 'not delivered' means after the item, I can't guess."

Grover looked around at Fletch with a drill sergeant's disdain.

Flynn said, "You're a pretty dodgy fellow, Irwin Maurice Fletcher."

Fletch said, "I bet you wouldn't even want your daughter to marry me."

"I would resist it," Flynn said, "under the prevailing circumstances."

"You guys don't even like my cologne."

"None of the gentlemen who drive the taxis in from the airport have identified you so far."

"Why do you care about that?"

"We'd like to know if you came in from the airport alone, or with a young lady."

"I see."

"Even the driver who delivered someone from the airport to 152 Beacon Street yesterday afternoon can't identify you. Nor is his record clear on whether he was carrying one passenger or two."

"Terrific."

"Those fellows who work the airport are an independent lot. Fearful independent. And four taxis went from this area last night to the Café Budapest. None of the drivers can identify you or say whether you were alone or not."

"I'm greatly indebted to them all."

"Not everyone is as cooperative as you, Mister Fletcher."

"The bastards."

"Nor did the waiters at the Café Budapest recognize you at all. For a man who wears such an expensive cologne, the fact that you can spend an hour or two in a fashionable restaurant and have no one — not even the waiters — recognize you the next day must cut."

"It slashes," said Fletch. "It slashes."

"You'd think waiters would remember a man eating alone, taking up a whole table, even for two, all by himself, wouldn't you? It affects their income."

It was ten minutes to eight.

"That we discovered with your photograph. From your fingerprints we also found out some interesting things."

"I can hardly wait."

"You touched two things in this room — middle-A on the piano keyboard, with your right index finger. I had no idea you are musical."

"I'm not."

"Did I say two things in this room other than the light switches? I meant to. I would guess when you first came into this apartment and were looking around, you turned on the wall switch in the living room, went to the piano, hit middle-A, went into the dining room and then the kitchen, leaving the lights on like a 1970 electric company executive."

"I suppose I did."

"The only other things your fingerprints were on in this room were the whiskey bottle and the water decanter."

"That would be right."

"It was a fresh bottle. You opened it."

"Yes."

"Mister Fletcher. The whiskey bottle was the murder weapon."

The green eyes watched him intensely. Fletch felt them in his stomach. To his side he had the impression of Grover's white face, watching him.

"There were no other fingerprints on the bottle, Mister Fletcher. It had been dusted. Liquor bottles are apt to be dusted while being set out."

"What other fingerprints were in this room?" Fletch asked. "I mean, whose others?"

"Mrs. Sawyer's, the girl's — that is, Ruth Fryer's — and the prints of one other person, a man's, we presume to belong to Bartholomew Connors."

"Were there many of the girl's?"

"A few. Enough to establish she was murdered here. They were the fingerprints of a live person."

Fletch considered his wisdom in saying nothing. At the moment he doubted he could say anything, anyway.

"The disconcerting thing is, Mister Fletcher," continued Flynn with a nerve-shattering gentleness, "that if you remember your laws of physics, the whiskey bottle would be a far more reliable, satisfactory, workable murder weapon when it is full and sealed than after it has been uncapped and a quantity has been poured out."

"Oh, my God."

"By opening the whiskey bottle and pouring a quantity out, you meant to remove the whiskey bottle from suspicion, as the murder weapon."

"It didn't work," said Fletch.

"Ah, that's where my inexperience comes in. A more experienced police officer might have discounted the whiskey bottle completely. I remember having to persuade Grover to send it along. It took a few words, didn't it, Grover? Not having come up through the ranks myself, and never having had the benefits of a proper education, I insisted. The boyos in the police laboratory were very surprised the murder weapon was an unbroken, open bottle."

"How do they know it was?"

"Minute traces of hair, skin, and blood that match the girl's."

Flynn allowed a long silence. He sat quietly, watching Fletch.

Either he was waiting for Fletch to adjust to this new trauma or he was waiting for Fletch to be indiscreet.

Fletch exercised his right to remain silent.

"Now, Mister Fletcher, would you like to call in a lawyer?"

"No."

"If you think by not calling in a lawyer you're convincing us of your innocence, you're quite wrong."

Grover said, "You're convincing us of your stupidity."

"Now, Grover. Mister Fletcher is not stupid. And now he knows we're not stupid. Maybe he wants to skip the formalities of a lawyer altogether and go ahead with his confession, get the dastardly thing off his chest."

Fletch said, "I know you're not stupid. But I don't know why I'm feeling stupid."

"You look angry."

"I am angry."

"At what?"

"I don't know. I suppose I should have been doing something about this the last twenty-four hours. This murder."

"You haven't been?"

"No."

"Your trust in us has been the most perplexing element in this whole affair," Flynn said. "You're not a naive man."

"You read the record."

"I take it you're not confessing to murder at this point?"

"Of course not."

"He's still not confessing, Grover. Take that down. The man's re-sistance to self-incrimination is absolutely metallic. Let's go on, then." Flynn sat forward on the divan, elbows on knees, hands folded be-fore him. "You said last night you had never seen Ruth Fryer before in your life."

"Never to my knowledge," answered Fletch.

"With the key number you provided us we went to her hotel, which, by the way, is at the airport. We went through her belong-ings. We interviewed her room-mate. Then we interviewed her su-pervisor. Never having seen her before, can you guess what she did for a living?"

"You're not going to say airline stewardess, are you?"

"I am."

"Dandy."

"Trans World Airlines, Mister Fletcher. Temporarily assigned to the job of First Class Ground Hostess at Boston's Logan Airport. On duty to receive passengers aboard Flight 529 from Rome, Tuesday."

"I never saw her! I would remember! She was beautiful!"

Flynn moved back on the divan, possibly in alarm, when Fletch jumped up.

Fletch went up the living room to the piano.

Grover had stood up.

Fletch banged the middle-G major chord.

Then he said, "This has something to do with me."

Flynn said, "What?"

Fletch walked back toward Flynn.

"This murder has something to do with me."

"That's your reaction, is it? Sit down, Grover. Clever man, this Mister Fletcher. It's only taken him twenty-four hours to catch on."

"You've done some wonderful work," said Fletch.

Flynn said, "Oh, my god. Now it's innocent flattery."

"What am I going to do?"

"You might try confessing, you blithering idiot!"

"I would, Inspector, I would." Fletch paced the room. "I still don't think it's personal."

"Now what do you mean by that?"

"I don't think the person who killed Ruth Fryer knows me person-ally."

"If you're saying you were framed, Mister Fletcher, you've already told us you know no one in town."

"I didn't say I don't know anybody in the world. Lots of people hate me."

"More every minute," said Flynn. "Take Grover there, for example."

"Everybody in Italy knew my plans. Everyone in Cagna, everyone in Rome, everyone in Livorno. The Homeswap people in London. I began making these plans three weeks ago. I wrote old buddies in California saying I would try to get out there while I was in the country. I wrote people in Seattle, Washington."

"All right, Mister Fletcher, we'll put the rest of the world in prison and leave you free."

"But that's not what I'm saying, Inspector. I don't think this is a personal frame. Some sort of an accident happened. I happened to be the next guy in this room after a murder."

"Oh, boyoboyoboy. Like a French philosopher thirty years after he's born he decides he might be involved with the world."

Fletch said, "You guys want to join me for dinner?"

"Dinner! The man's crazy, Grover. As a matter of fact, Mister Fletcher, we were both thinking of asking you to join us."

"I don't care," Fletch said. "Either way. You know the city."

"Well, the truth is," Flynn said to the air, "to this minute the man hasn't acted involved in this case. He's acted as innocent as a reliable witness. He still does. That's the biggest puzzle of all. What are we going to do with him, Grover?"

"Lock him up."

"A very succinct man, this Grover."

"Charge him."

"You know the man can afford to hire fancy lawyers, detectives, make bail, protest all over the press, get postponements, appeal, and appeal all the way to the Supreme Court."

"Lock him up, Frank."

"No." Flynn stood up. "The man didn't leave town yesterday. He didn't leave town today. One may presume he won't leave town tomorrow."

"He'll leave town tomorrow, Inspector."

"Life is simpler this way. We haven't got this man far enough in a corner yet. Although I thought we did."

"What more evidence do we need?"

"I'm not sure. We have pounds of it. I had a hat when I came in.

Oh, there it is. It's not polite to talk in front of a man as if he were dead, Grover."

In the hall, Flynn settled the hat on his small head.

"I'm going to get another scolding, Mister Fletcher, I'm sure, all the way home. Maybe Grover can convince me you're guilty. So far you haven't. Good night."

TEN

As it was late (and as Fletch had just discovered he was apparently invisible in a restaurant, anyway) he did not go out to dinner. Tiredly, he searched the kitchen cupboards and came up with a can of hash.

The telephone rang three times while he fed himself.

The first, while he was working the can opener, was a cable from Cagna.

"Connors nice hurt man. Nothing new on father. Much love — Andy."

So Connors was in Italy. Nice, hurt at this moment were irrelevant. He was definitely in Italy.

The second call came before Fletch put the frying pan onto the burner.

"Is this really the hot-shot journalistic wizard, cogent writer *non pareil*, the great I.M., the one and only, now-you-see-him, now-you-don't Irwin Maurice Fletcher?"

"Jack!" The voice of his old boss, his city editor when he worked in Chicago, Jack Saunders, was too familiar to Fleth ever to confuse with any other voice in the world. For more than a year he had had to listen to that voice, on and off the telephone, for hours at a time. "Where are you?"

"So you've been passing yourself off as Peter Fletcher, eh? I just found an identity-correction advisory from the Boston Police Department on my desk."

"In Chicago?"

"No, sir. Right here in Beantown. You are talking to the night city editor of the *Boston Star*."

"You left the *Post?*"

"If I had realized that murder story involved the great I.M. Fletcher I never would have put it on page seven."

"Page five."

"I would have run it front page with photos linking you and the murdered girl indelibly in the public mind."

"Thanks a lot. So I do know someone in Boston."

"What?"

"How come you left the *Post?*"

"Boston offered more money. Of course, they didn't tell me it costs a lot more to live here in Boston, Taxachusetts. And after you left the *Post*, Fletch, the old place wasn't the same. All the fun went out of it."

"Yeah, sure."

"You made me look real good. Hey, you want a job?"

"Not at the moment. How are Daphne and the kids?"

"Still Daphne and the kids — face powder and peanut butter. Why do you think I work nights?"

Fletch had never known why Jack had remained married. He didn't even like to look at his wife. He considered his kids a big noise.

"Hey, Fletch, they going to indict you?"

"Probably. Who's this Flynn character?"

"You got Frank Flynn? You're in luck. That's why you're not in the slammer already."

"I know."

"They call him Reluctant Flynn. He's very slow to make an arrest. But he's never made a mistake. If he arrests you, boy, you know you've had it."

"What's some b.g. on him?"

"Don't have much. He showed up here in Boston about a year and a half ago, which is very unusual. Cops hardly ever change cities, as you know. I don't even know where he came from. He was the rank of Inspector. Family man. Musical. He plays the violin or something."

"He's good, uh?"

"Cracked about a dozen major cases since he's been here. He's even reopened cases people never expected solved. If you're guilty, he'll get you. By the way, are you guilty?"

"Thanks for asking."

"Free for lunch?"

"When?"

"I was thinking I better get you tomorrow. Visiting people in prisons depresses the hell out of me."

"Working nights you probably want a late lunch, right?"

"About two o'clock. Can you make it?"

"Sure."

"If you have necktie, we can go to Locke-Ober's."

"Where's that?"

"You'll never find it. It's in an alley. Just ask the taxi driver for Locke-Ober's. Want me to spell it?"

"I've got it."

"There are two dining rooms, Fletch. Upstairs and downstairs. I'll meet you downstairs."

"Okay."

"Stay loose, kid. Please don't knock anyone else off without calling the *Star* first. We've got the best photographers in town."

"Bye, Jack."

The third call came while he was eating the hash.

"Fletcher. Darling."

It was Countess de Grassi. The Brazilian Bombshell. Sylvia, Andy's stepmother.

"Hello, Sylvia."

"You didn't return my call, Fletcher."

"What call? Where are you?"

"In Boston, darling. I called earlier and left a message."

"Oh, that Mrs. Sawyer," Fletch said.

He took the message off the desk, crumpled the paper, and threw it hard against a drape.

"I'm at the Ritz-Carlton."

"You can't afford the Ritz-Carlton, Sylvia."

"I'm the Countess de Grassi. You can't expect the Countess de Grassi to stay in, what do you call it, fleabag."

"However, the Ritz-Carlton will expect the Countess de Grassi to pay her bill."

"You're being very unkind, Fletcher. This is none of your business."

"What are you doing here, anyway, Sylvia?"

"What did Angela tell me? You came to Boston to visit your family in Seattle? Even I have a map, Fletcher. I came to visit your family in Seattle, too."

"Sylvia, what I'm doing here doesn't concern you even a little."

"I think yes, Fletcher. You and Angela are, how do you say, pulling some game on me."

"What?"

"You aim to deprive me of what is rightfully mine."

"What are you talking about?"

"First that terrible thing happens to Menti darling, and then you two conspire about me."

"As the grieving widow, aren't you supposed to be in Rome? Or Livorno?"

"You and Angela plan to rob me. Cheat me. Menti would be so mad."

"Nonsense."

"You come over to the hotel right now, Fletcher. Tell me it's not true."

"I can't, Sylvia. I'm miles from the hotel."

"How far? How many miles?"

"Eighteen, twenty miles, Sylvia. Boston's a big city."

"Come in the morning."

"I can't. I'm tied up."

"What does that mean, you're tied up?"

"I have appointments."

"Lunch, then."

"I have a lunch date."

"Fletcher, I come here to catch you. I'll call the police. They'll listen to the Countess de Grassi at the Ritz-Carlton Hotel."

"I'm sure they would. Sylvia, did Menti ever tell you you're a bitch?"

"You're a son of a bitch, Fletcher."

"That's no way for a Countess to talk."

"I can say worse things in Portuguese and French."

"I've heard them. All right. I'll come to the hotel."

"When?"

"Tomorrow. Late afternoon. Six o'clock."

"Come to my room."

"I will not. I'll meet you in the bar. Six o'clock."

"Six-thirty I call the police if you're not here."

"Don't use their business phone. It upsets them."

"What?"

"Shut up."

The rest of the hash he flushed down the toilet.

E L E V E N

"Look what some son of a bitch did to my truck!"

Fletch, dressed in jeans, sweater, and boots, led the manager of the auto body repair shop through the door.

Now that he knew he was to be followed, Fletch had unbolted the kitchen door and used the back stairs. Actually, the back alley had been a shortcut to the garage on River Street.

He drove the smeared van to the auto body shop feeling as conspicuous as a transvestite at a policemen's ball.

The manager's eyes read "FEED THE PEOPLE." He shook his head slowly.

"Kids."

Hands in his back pockets he walked slowly around to the "AD-JUST!" side.

The sun appeared between clouds.

"There's more on the top, too," Fletch said.

Coming back, the manager stood on tiptoes and stretched his neck to see the top.

"Have to paint the whole thing."

"Shit," Fletch said.

"Little jerks," the manager said. " 'Feed the people,' but screw whoever owns this truck."

"Yeah," Fletch said. "Me."

"You got insurance?"

"Sure."

"Want to check your coverage?"

"Got to have the truck," Fletch said, "whether insurance covers it or not. Can't use it this way."

"What do you do?"

"I'm a plumber," Fletch said.

"Yeah. I guess not too many people would like that truck in their driveways. You might lose a few customers."

"Lose 'em all. Paint it. I'll pay you and knock the insurance company up later myself."

"Same blue?"

"Wouldn't work, would it?"

"Naw. You'd be able to read the black right through it."

"Better paint it black, then."

"Sons of bitches. Even dark red wouldn't work. Even dark green. Ought to have their asses whipped."

"Paint it black."

"You want it black?"

"No, I don't want it black. If I wanted a black truck I would have bought a black truck."

"You'll look like a hearse."

"Friggin' hearse."

"You got the registration?"

"What for?"

"Got to take it into the Registry. Report the change in vehicle color."

"Screw 'em."

"What?"

"Look." Fletch laid on anger. "I'm a victim of a crime. If the fuzz were doin' what they're supposed to be doin', instead of makin' us fill out papers all the time, my truck wouldn't have been vandalized."

"Sounds reasonable."

"Let 'em go screw. I'll notify 'em when I'm good and ready."

"You want it black, uh?"

"No. But it's gonna be black."

"When do you need it?"

"Right now. I'm late for work right now."

"You can't have the truck today. No way. Tomorrow morning."

"Okay, if that's the best you can do."

"You goin' to go into the Registry?"

"I'm goin' to work. I'll go into the Registry when I get damned good and ready."

"Okay. I understand. We'll paint the truck. You go into the Registry."

"Damned kids," Fletch said. "Weirdos."

"If you get picked up, just don't say where you got the truck painted."

Fletch said, "Screw 'em."

TWELVE

Fletch listened to the old elevator creak and clank as it climbed to the sixth floor.

The door to apartment 6A opened. A miniature poodle preceded a woman on a leash. It was immediately obvious the woman was tipsy at one-thirty in the afternoon. While Fletch held the elevator door, she rummaged in her purse for her key. The dog watched Fletch curiously. Apparently satisfied she had her key, the woman slammed the door.

"Watch your step," Fletch said.

The woman tripped anyway.

He pushed the "L" button. They sank slowly.

"You the man taking Bart's apartment?"

"Yes," Fletch said. "Name of Fletcher."

How could the woman not have heard of the murder next door? Some drunk.

Fletch patted the dog.

"When did Bart leave, anyway?"

"Saturday," Fletch said. "Sunday. He's using my house in Italy."

"Oh," the woman said.

Fletch wondered how far she could walk the dog.

"That couldn't be," she said.

"What couldn't be?"

"I saw Bart Tuesday."

"You did?"

"Tuesday night. At the place right up the street. The Bullfinch Pub."

"What time?"

She shrugged. She was tired of the conversation.

"Drink time. Six o'clock."

"Are you sure it was Tuesday?"

"He wore a tweed sports jacket. I knew he hadn't just come from the office. Thought it odd. Pretty girl with him."

"What did she look like?"

"Pretty. Young."

The elevator clunked to a stop.

Fletch opened the door.

"Are you sure of this?" he asked.

Passing him, she said, "I'm in love with Bart."

Thinking, Fletch watched her walk unevenly across the lobby.

He caught up to her at the door. He put his hand on the knob to open it.

"Did you speak to Bart Tuesday night?"

"No," she said. "I hate the son of a bitch."

He trailed her through the door.

"That's a nice dog you have there."

"Oh, that's my love. Mignon. Aren't you, Mignon?"

On the sidewalk she extended a gloved hand to Fletch.

"I'm Joan Winslow," she said. "You must come by sometime. For a drink."

"Thank you," Fletch said. "I will."

THIRTEEN

"The arrogance of the press," Fletch said, standing to shake hands.

It was two-fifteen. Knowing full well Jack Saunders would be late, Fletch had ordered and sipped a vodka martini. Through the window he had watched the plainclothesman standing in the alley. A day of quickly traveling clouds, sunlight switched on and off in the alley as if someone were taking time exposures of the discomfited cop. There had been no place for him to park his car. Through the dark window glass of Locke-Ober's the man he was supposed to be watching was sitting at a white-clothed table, sipping a martini, watching him. Fletch had toyed with the idea of inviting him in for a drink.

Jack Saunders said, "Sorry to be a little late. The wife got her eyelashes stuck in the freezer door."

Sitting down, Fletch said, "A reporter is always late because he knows there is no story until he gets there. Still drink gin?"

Jack ordered a martini.

He had not changed much — only more so: his glasses were a

little thicker, his sandy hair a little thinner. His belly had let out more than his belt.

"Olde times," Jack said in toast. "With an 'e'."

"To the end of the world," said Fletch. "It will make a hell of a story."

They talked about Jack's new job, where he was living now, their time together on the *Chicago Post*. They had a second drink.

"God, that was funny," Jack was saying. "The time you busted the head of the Internal Revenue Service in Chicago. The Infernal Revenue Service. The guy was as guilty as hell. They had him in court. They couldn't get the evidence on him because his wife had all the evidence, and they couldn't call her to testify because she was his wife, even though they were separated."

"The newspaper was being very polite about it," Fletch said, "following the court in its frustration, as the man Flynn might say."

"Journalistic responsibility, Fletch. Journalistic responsibility. Will you never learn?"

"Sloppy legwork," Fletch said. "I didn't do anything any junior-grade F.B.I. man couldn't have done."

"What did you do, anyway?"

"I can't tell you."

"Come on, I'm not your boss anymore."

"You might be again one day, though."

"I hope so. Come on, we're not in Illinois, the guy's in jail. . . ."

"Why the hell should I give you ideas? You were reporting the court record as docilely as the rest of the idiot editors."

"Yeah, but when you got the story, I ran it."

"Yes, you did. Of course, you did. I'm supposed to be grateful? You won a prize and then made a bloody long speech about team efforts."

"I let you hold the prize. Ten or fifteen minutes. I remember handing it to you."

"And I remember your taking it back."

"You're ashamed. You're ashamed of what you did."

"I got the story."

"You're ashamed of how you got it. That's why you won't tell me."

"I'm a little ashamed."

"How did you do it?"

"I poured sugar in the wife's gas tank and followed her home. When her engine died I stopped to help her. Did the whole bit, fiddled under her hood, pretended to adjust things, told her to try it again."

"That's funny."

"Drove her home. It was eight o'clock at night. She offered me a drink."

"You entrapped her."

"Is that the word? The friendship ripened. . . ."

"How was she in bed?"

"Sort of cold."

"Jeez, you'd do anything for a story."

"She had her good points. They weren't far from her chin."

"I'm sure you told her you were a member of the press."

"I think I told her I sold air-conditioning units. I don't know how the idea occurred to me. Something about the cool breezes from her every orifice."

"But you plugged her in." Jack's eyes were wet from laughing. "And plugged her in. And plugged her in. And plugged her in."

"Look, the lady was blackmailing her husband and therefore he was embezzling from the United States government. The courts couldn't get at her because she was still legally his wife. What did she deserve?"

"Yeah, but I still don't know how you did it."

"Well, we took a vacation together. In Nevada. The dear thing was divorced before she knew it."

"I remember the expense account. Oh, boy, do I remember the expense account. The Accounting Department did a dance all over my ass. With hiking boots. You mean the *Chicago Post* paid for somebody's divorce?"

"Actually, yes. Well, it freed her as a witness."

"Oh, that's funny. If they only knew."

"I listed it properly — legal fees incurred while traveling."

"Jeez, we thought you got busted for pot or something. Maybe got caught with your pants down in a casino. . . ."

"Don't ask. I told the lady we had to go back to Chicago to get married. Had to get my birth certificate, that sort of thing, you know."

"You actually told her you were going to marry her?"

"Of course. Why else would she get a divorce? I mean, under those circumstances?"

"You are a bastard."

"So my father said. Anyway, once the lady realized she was divorced and about to land at O'Hare International Airport in Chicago, she panicked. She envisioned all sorts of men in blue suits waiting for her when she got off the plane. So I convinced her the best thing

to do was to give me the evidence, pack her bags, and split immediately."

"Which she did?"

"Which she did. All the evidence, plus a signed deposition, all of
which, you may remember, we published."

"We certainly did."

"I told her I'd meet her in Acapulco as soon as I found my birth
certificate."

"What happened to her?"

"I never heard. As far as I know, she's still waiting in Acapulco."

"Oh, you're a terrible man. You're a son of a bitch. You're a shit,
Fletcher. But you're funny."

"It was a pretty good story," Fletch said. "Shall we eat?"

They dug into their Châteaubriand.

"Did you see the *Star* this morning?" Jack asked.

"No. Sorry."

"We gave more space to your story this morning. Ran a picture of
the girl."

"Thanks."

"Had to. Pretty damning evidence they've got on you, Fletch. Your
fingerprints were on the murder weapon."

"The police gave you that?"

"Yup."

"Trying to build a public case against me. The bastards."

"Poor Fletch. As if you never did such a thing yourself. What's the
next development to expect?"

"My confession. But don't hold your breath."

"I figure if Flynn hasn't arrested you, he's got a reason."

"If you look through the window to your right, you'll see my flat-
footed escort."

"Oh, yeah. Even paranoids have enemies, I've heard."

"Actually, I think I've got the case cracked. It was an impersonal,
coincidental frame."

"So, who did it?"

"One of two people. Rather not go into it now."

"You always did play stories close to the chest. Until you had
them on paper."

"Twists and turns, Jack. Twists and turns. Every story has its twists
and turns. By the way, do you think you'd let me use your library?
There are some people I'd like to look up."

"Sure. Who?"

"This guy, Bart Connors, for one. I'm using his apartment."

"Don't know much about him. Partner in one of those State Street law firms. He's taxation or something."

"Maybe I could come in some afternoon, while you're there."

"You bet. Mondays and Tuesdays I take off. You'll probably want to come sooner than that."

"Yeah. God knows where I'll be next Monday."

"I've been to Norfolk Prison," said Jack. "It's not bad, as prisons go. Clean. Got a good shop. Overcrowded, of course."

"Maybe that's why Flynn hasn't arrested me."

"I don't think you should come into the office using the name Fletcher, though. The publisher might resent a murder suspect going through our files."

"Okay. What name should I use?"

"Smith?"

"That's a good one."

"Jones? I've got it — Brown."

"Has a nice ring to it."

"I'm not as inventive as you are, Fletch."

"How about Jasper dePew Mandeville the Fourth?"

"That's a good one. Very convincing."

"I'll use the name Locke."

"John?"

"Ralph."

"Ralph!"

"Somebody's got to be called Ralph."

They both had their coffee black.

Jack said, "For some reason, I've hesitated to ask you what you're doing these days. I guess I'm afraid what you might tell me."

"I've gone back to writing about art."

"Oh, yeah. You were doing that in Seattle. Not quite as exciting as investigative reporting."

"It has its moments."

"How can you afford it? I mean, you're not writing for anyone, right?"

"An uncle left me some money."

"I see. I.M. Fletcher finally ripped somebody off. Always knew you would."

"Did the de Grassi story come over the wires?"

"De Grassi?"

"From Italy. Count Clementi de Grassi."

"Oh, yeah. That's a weird one. I don't think we used it. What was the story? He was kidnapped, and then when the ransom wasn't paid, he was murdered, right?"

"Right. I expect to marry his daughter, Angela."

"Oh. Why didn't they pay the ransom?"

"They didn't have the money. Nothing like it."

"A great tragedy."

"There's only the young wife, the present Countess de Grassi, about forty, and Angela, who is in her early twenties. They haven't got a dime. Ransom was over four million dollars."

"Then why was he kidnapped?"

"Somebody got the wrong de Grassi family. They have the title, you know, a falling-down palace outside Livorno, and they keep a small apartment at a good address in Rome."

"Pretty horrible story. Maybe we should have run it."

"I don't think so," said Fletch. "It's far away, has nothing to do with Boston. No use in advertising crime."

Jack Saunders paid the bill.

"Nice eating off a newspaper again," Fletch said. "As a kindness, I guess I should go get that cop off his flat feet. For him, I'll take a taxi home. Otherwise, I would walk."

"Congratulations," Jack said. "I mean, about getting married."

Fletch said, "This is the real thing."

FOURTEEN

It would be nine-thirty at night in Cagna, Italy.

Fletch wandered around the apartment, with his coat and tie off. He toured the paintings.

He had evidence, from an unreliable witness, Joan Winslow from apartment 6A, that Bart Connors had been in Boston the night of the murder. Tuesday night. No, he had more than that. Flynn had said there was no evidence from the airlines Connors had flown out of the country anytime between his being seen by Mrs. Sawyer on Saturday night and Tuesday night. Yet yesterday, Wednesday, Andy had seen him in Cagna.

Should he tell Flynn what the woman in 6A had said?

Fletch had worked with the police before. With them, against them, around them. Flynn was pretty good, but it was Fletch's freedom Fletch was fighting for. So far, he had been entirely too trusting.

He'd roust the quail whether its feathers were wet or not.

Fletch checked his watch again, and placed a call to his villa in Cagna.

"Hello?"

"Andy?"

"Fletch!"

"What are you doing in Cagna?"

"You asked me to come up."

"That was yesterday."

"Why did you call here, Fletch?"

"Did you spend the night?"

"Oh, I had car trouble."

"The Porsche?"

"Bart said it was the diaphragm or something."

" 'Bart said!' This is the second night, Andy."

"Yes. The car will be ready in the morning."

"Andy!"

"Wait until I turn the record player down, Fletch. I can't hear too well."

She came back in a few seconds and said, "Hello, Fletch, darling."

"Andy, what are you doing spending the night at my house with Bart Connors?"

"That has no business for you, Fletcher. Just because I marry you has nothing to do with where I spend last night."

"Listen to me, will you? Is Bart Connors there?"

Andy hesitated. "Of course."

"Then get out of that house. Sneak out and run down to the hotel or something."

"But, darling, why?"

"There is some evidence your host has a terrible temper."

"Temper? Nonsense. He's a kitten."

"Will you do as I say?"

"I don't think so. We're just beginning dinner."

"I think you'd better come here, Andy. To Boston."

"I have to go back to Rome. See what the grand Countess is doing."

"The Countess is here."

"Where?"

"In Boston. Sylvia is here."

"The bitch."

"Why don't you fly from Genoa?"

"I can't believe you, Fletch. This is something you're putting on. For jealousy. I'm not jealous of the people you spend time with."

"Andy, you're not listening."

"No, and I'm not going to. I don't know why you called here, anyway. I'm supposed to be in Rome."

"To talk to Bart Connors."

"Then talk to him."

"Andy, after I talk to Connors, please come back on the phone." She said, "I'll get him."

The pause was interminable.

"Hello? Mister Fletcher?"

"Mister Connors? Everything all right at the villa?"

"Your girlfriend dropped in yesterday. She'd lost a necklace here. We put on quite a search for it."

"What's wrong with the car?"

"What car?"

"The Porsche."

"It's quite a long drive to Rome. Isn't it?"

"When did you arrive in Cagna?"

"Yesterday."

"Wednesday?"

"Yes, that's right."

"I thought you were going out on Sunday."

"My plans got mixed up. The person I thought was coming with me couldn't make it."

"You waited for her?"

"My powers of persuasion were not adequate to the task. Good thing I didn't become a trial lawyer."

"You flew through New York?"

"Montreal."

"Why Montreal? Is that better?"

"I had a late business dinner there. It's very nice of you to call, Mister Fletcher, but it's sort of expensive for a chat. I hope you called collect — on your phone."

"And Ruth said she wouldn't go with you?"

"What?"

"Ruth. She said she wouldn't go with you to Cagna?"

"Who's Ruth?"

"The girl you were trying to take to Cagna with you."

"I don't understand you, Mister Fletcher."

"Mister Connors, I think you had better think of coming back to Boston."

"What?"

"A young woman was murdered in your apartment. Tuesday night. I found the body."

"What are you talking about?"

"Her name was Ruth Fryer."

"I don't know anyone named Ruth Prior."

"Fryer. She was hit over the head with a whiskey bottle."

"Am I crazy, or am I just not understanding you?"

"A girl named Ruth Fryer was killed in your apartment Tuesday night."

"Did you do it?"

"Mister Connors, it appears you are a suspect in a murder case."

"I am not. I'm in Italy."

"You were in Boston at the time of the murder."

"I had nothing to do with it, and I'm going to have nothing to do with it. No one could have gotten into that apartment. You're the only one who has a key."

"And Mrs. Sawyer."

"And Mrs. Sawyer. My key is here. Is this some kind of a joke?"

"You were seen in Boston on Tuesday night, Mister Connors."

"I stayed at the Parker House Monday night. I had already moved out of the apartment and didn't want to mess it up. Look, Fletcher, I don't know what the hell you're saying. Was there any damage to the apartment itself?"

"No."

"I have nothing to do with this. I don't know anyone named Ruth Fryer. And who the hell are you to question me, anyway?"

"Another suspect in the same murder case."

"Well, don't lay it off on me, pal. I'm sorry somebody's dead, and I'm sorry somebody's dead in my apartment, but I don't know anything about it."

"You're a kitten."

"What?"

"Will you let me talk to Andy again?"

"If I came running back, then I would be involved. The newspapers would question me. I'm a lawyer in Boston, Fletcher. I can't afford that. Jesus Christ, did you kill somebody in my apartment?"

"No. I didn't."

"Whom have the police questioned so far?"

"Me."

"Whom else?"

"Me."

"Fletcher, why don't you move out of my apartment?"

"No, I'm not going to do that."

"I'll call the law firm. Somebody's got to protect my interest."

"I thought you didn't have an interest."

"I don't. Jesus. You've ruined dinner. Do you have another bottle of gin somewhere?"

"Yeah. In the lower cupboard in the pantry. It's Swiss."

"This is a terrible thing to happen. I'm staying away from it."

"Okay. Let me talk to Andy."

Connors exhaled into the mouthpiece.

Then the line went dead.

He had hung up.

If Fletch had accomplished nothing else, he had ruined their evening together.

"Pan American Airways. Miss Fletcher speaking."

"What?"

"Pan American Airways. Miss Fletcher speaking."

"Your name is Fletcher?"

"Yes, sir."

"This is Ralph Locke."

"Yes, Mister Locke."

"Miss Fletcher, I'd like to fly from Montreal to Genoa, Italy, late Tuesday night. Is that possible?"

"One moment, sir, I'll check." It was scarcely a moment. "TWA's Flight 805 leaves Montreal at eleven P.M. Tuesday evening, with a connection in Paris for Genoa, Italy."

"What's your first name?"

"Linda, sir."

"Linda Fletcher? You weren't ever married to someone named Irwin Maurice Fletcher, were you?"

"No, sir."

"You didn't sound familiar. How long does it take to fly to Montreal from Boston?"

"About forty minutes, actual flying time, sir. Eastern has a flight at eight P.M., which would give you plenty of time."

"Is there a later flight?"

"Delta flies to Montreal at nine-thirty P.M. That would still give you plenty of time."

Talking to her, as obviously she was pushing buttons on a computer console, was like talking to someone in space. A short delay preceded her every answer.

"Should I make these reservations for you, Mister Locke?"

"Perhaps later. I'll call back. Where are you from, Miss Fletcher?"

"Columbus, Ohio, sir."

"Ohio's a nice place," Fletch said. "I've never been there."

Fletch shaved, showered and put on a fresh shirt. It was almost six o'clock.

At six-thirty the Countess was going to call the police on him, if he didn't meet her in the Ritz bar.

Instead, the police called him.

Necktie over his shoulders, he answered the bedroom phone.

"How are you today, Mister Fletcher?"

"Ah, Flynn. I wanted to talk to you."

"Did you want to confess, by any chance?"

"No, that wasn't what I was thinking."

"Sorry if I appear to be ignoring you, but a City Councilwoman was murdered in her bath this morning and since it's a politically sensitive case, I've been assigned to it. I've never held with taking baths in the morning, anyway, but when you're in politics god knows how many baths a day you need."

"What was she killed with?"

"The murder weapon? An ice pick, Mister Fletcher."

"Messy."

"Aye, it was that. She took the first thrust in the throat, which seems peculiarly appropriate. I mean, it makes it seem far more the political crime, doesn't it?"

"I wouldn't like your job, Flynn."

"It has its downs. She was a chubby old thing."

"Inspector, I've discovered a few things which might be of interest to you."

"Have you, indeed?"

"The woman in the next apartment, 6A, name Joan Winslow, says she saw Bart Connors in Boston Tuesday night, at about six o'clock, having a drink up the street at the Bullfinch Pub with an attractive young woman."

"Now, that's interesting. We'll talk with her."

"I suspect she's not too reliable a witness. But I've talked with Bart Connors in Italy."

"Have you? And now that you've talked with him, will he stay in Italy?"

"Apparently. He refuses to come back."

"Small wonder. It's not his coming this direction I worry about. We have an extradition agreement with Italy, whereas we don't with one or two other countries he might find attractive."

"He says he flew to Genoa through Montreal late Tuesday night."

"We know. The nine-thirty Delta Flight 770 to Montreal; the eleven o'clock Trans World Airlines Flight 805 to Paris."

"He had plenty of time to do murder here."

"Yes, he did."

"But the important thing is that he said the reason for his delay in departure, by two or three days, was that he was trying to talk a girl, a specific girl, into going to Italy with him."

"But Ruth Fryer wasn't in Boston until Monday night."

"He may have been waiting for her."

"He may have been."

"Bought her a drink up the street, brought her back here for further persuasion, lost his temper, and bashed her."

"It sounds very reasonable."

"I would guess he's been through a tough time emotionally lately."

"There's no way of knowin' that. Every time I've made guesses as to what goes on between a married couple, I've been wrong. Even when they're divorcing."

"Anyway. . . ."

"At least your theories in defense of yourself are becoming fuller. More cogent, if you know what I mean. I'm pleased to see, for example, you're beginning to accept the idea that someone else hit Ruth Fryer over the head with a bottle — not that she bopped herself and put the bottle back carefully on the tray across the room before expiring."

"You'll talk to the Winslow woman?"

"We will. In the meantime, we have the autopsy report on the Fryer girl. She was killed between eight and nine o'clock Tuesday night."

"The airport is ten minutes away. Connors' flight was at nine-thirty."

"It is ten minutes away. When the Boston police are succeeding at their traffic duty. She had had about three drinks of alcohol in the preceding three or four hours."

"At the Bullfinch Pub."

"That can't be determined. Despite her naked condition, she had not had sexual relations with a male in the preceding twenty-four hours."

"Of course not. She refused him."

"Mister Fletcher, would a man of Mister Connors' age and experience, in this advanced age, murder a girl because she refused his sexual advances?"

"Certainly. As you said, if he'd had enough to drink."

"I would think, even with liquor he'd have to have a deep-seated psychological problem to do in a young lady who said 'No.' "

"How do we know he hasn't?"

"I'll grant you, Mister Fletcher, there is some evidence against your landlord. And, under the circumstances, I don't even perceive your trying to pin it on him as being particularly ignoble."

"I have the advantage, Flynn. I know I'm not the murderer. I'm trying to find out who is."

"However, the evidence against yourself is a great deal stronger. Ruth Fryer was the Ground Hostess for First Class passengers of Trans World Airlines Flight 529 from Rome Tuesday. Your Ground Hostess. Several hours later, after having been dressed for the evening, she's found murdered in your apartment. Your fingerprints were on the murder weapon."

"Okay, Flynn. What can I say?"

"You can confess, Mister Fletcher, and let me get on with the City Councilwoman's murder."

"Person, Inspector."

"What's that?"

"Councilperson. City Councilperson."

"Fat lot of good the distinction will do her now she's been slain in the tub. Will you confess, lad?"

"Of course not."

"Do you still think the murder's an accidental and impersonal co-incidence? Is that still your lame stand?"

"Yes."

"Grover's of the fixed opinion we should arrest you and charge you with murder before you do harm to someone else."

"But you're not going to."

"I'm inclining very much that way."

"Did you ever find that girl who gave me directions in that square Tuesday night? The square with the Citgo sign?"

"Of course not. We haven't even looked. We'd have to interview the entire female population at Boston University, and that still wouldn't cover all the young women who might be in Kenmore Square at that time of night. There are night clubs there."

"Oh."

"It's no good, lad. The evidence is piled up. I doubt we'll ever get more."

"I hope not."

"It's not precisely warm of me to ask you to confess by telephone, but there is this other murder."

"Will you stop giving the evidence you have to the newspapers? You're convicting me."

"Ach, that. Well, that puts as much pressure on me as it does on you."

"Not quite, Inspector. Not quite."

"Well, I'll leave it alone for a while. Give you time to think. Get a lawyer. I have a natural instinct to not do precisely what Grover tells me to do. You might even get a psychiatrist."

"Why a psychiatrist?"

"It's your seeming innocence that puzzles me. I sincerely believe you think you didn't kill Ruth Fryer. The evidence says you did."

"You mean you think I blacked it out."

"It's been known to happen. The human mind plays amazing tricks. Or am I doing the wrong thing in giving you a line of legal defense?"

"I guess anything's possible."

"The thing is, Mister Fletcher, what I'm saying is, you have to keep an open mind to the evidence. Even you. You might start to begin to believe the evidence. You see, we have to believe the evidence."

"There's a lot of evidence."

"I shouldn't be doing this on the phone. But there's this other body."

"I understand."

"I suppose we could work a thing whereby the court appoints a psychiatrist for you. . . ."

"Not yet, Flynn."

"Do you agree this interpretation of the crime and its solution is a possibility?"

"Yes. Of course."

"Good lad."

"But it didn't happen."

"I'm sure you don't think so."

"I know so."

"That, too. Well, that's my best guess at the moment. Got to get back to my chubby City Councilperson."

"Inspector?"

"Yes?"

"I'm about to go to the Ritz-Carlton."

"Yes?"

"Just warning you. You'd better have your men keep a pretty sharp eye on the side door this time."

"They will, Mister Fletcher. They will."

FIFTEEN

Fletch walked the "eighteen, twenty miles" to the Ritz-Carlton, which was around a corner and up a few blocks.

He hung around the lobby, looking at the books on the newsstand, until his watch said six-thirty-five.

Then he went into the bar.

Countess Sylvia de Grassi was receiving considerable attention from the waiters. Her drink was finished, but one was dusting the clean table, another was bringing her a fresh plate of olive hors d'oeuvres, a third was standing by, admiring her with big eyes.

Sylvia, near forty, had brightly tousled bleached hair, magnificent facial features, smooth skin, and apparently the deepest cleavage ever spotted in Boston. Her dress was cut not to cover her breasts but to suggest the considerable structural support needed. Clearly there was nothing holding them down. They preceded her like an offering.

"Ah, Sylvia. Nice trip?"

He kissed her cheek as a socially acceptable alternative.

"Sorry to be a little late." All three waiters held his chair. "Mrs. Sawyer got her eyelashes caught in the freezer door."

"What's this, Mrs. Sawyer — freezer door?"

Sylvia's big brown eyes were puckered with impatient suspicion.

"Just the best excuse I've heard all day."

"Now, Flesh, I am not going to have any of your double-talk in English. I want the truth."

"Absolutely. What are you drinking?"

399

"Campari in soda."

"Still watching your figure, uh? Might as well. Everyone else is."
He said to all the waiters — as he could get the eye of none of them
— "A Campari and soda and a Bath Towel. You don't have a Bath
Towel? Then I'll just have a Chivas and water. Now, Sylvia, you
were saying you were about to tell the truth. Why are you in Bos-
ton?"

"I come to Boston to stop you. You and Angela. I know you conspire against me. You plan to rob my paintings."

"Nonsense, dear lady. What makes you think a thing like that?"

"Because. In Angela's room I found your notes. Your address, 152
Beacon Street, Boston. Your telephone number. Also a list of the
paintings."

"I see. From that you reasonably concluded I came to Boston to
find the paintings."

"I know you did."

"And you followed me."

"I come ahead of you. I fly Rome, New York, then Boston. I wanted
to be waiting when you got off the airplane in Boston. I wanted you
to run right into me."

"What fun. What held you up?"

"I missed the connection in New York."

"You mean, you were here in Boston on Tuesday?"

"I was. Five o'clock I arrived Boston."

"My, my. And all that time I thought I knew no one in Boston.
What did you do then?"

"I came here to the hotel. I call you. No answer."

"I went out to dinner."

"I call you next day, yesterday, leave a message. You never call
back."

"Okay, so you killed Ruth Fryer."

"What you say? I kill no one."

She retracted her supercarriage while the waiter served her drink.
"What's this talk of kill?"

Fletch ignored the drink in front of him.

"Sylvia, I don't have the paintings. I've never seen the paintings. I
don't know where the paintings are. I'm not even sure I've got the
story about the paintings straight."

"Then why are you in Boston with a list of the paintings? Tell me
that."

"I'm in Boston to do research on a book about an American painter named Edgar Arthur Tharp, Junior. I brought a list of the mythical de Grassi paintings with me, just in case I ran across any reference to them. Boston's a center of culture."

"How do the Americans say it? Bullshit, Flesh! You're engaged to marry my daughter, Angela. The day after her father's funeral, you jump on a plane with the list of the missing paintings in your pocket, and come to Boston, U.S. America. What else to think?"

"Stepdaughter. Angela is your stepdaughter."

"I know. She is not mine. She plans to rob me."

"Has Menti's will been read?"

"No. Bullshit lawyers will not read it. They say, too much confusion. Police say, this matter settled, go away, Countess, cry. Bullshit lawyers say this matter not settled. So Countess go away and cry some more. All this time, Angela, you rob, rob, rob me."

"Angela's mentioned the paintings. Menti mentioned the paintings. You talk about the paintings. I've never seen the paintings. I don't even know they ever existed."

"They exist! I've seen them! They are my paintings, now that Menti is dead. Poor Menti. They are what I have in the world. He left them to me."

"You don't know that. The will hasn't been read. They're the de Grassi paintings. He might have left them to his daughter, who is a de Grassi. He might have left them to both of you. Do you know what Italian estate laws are concerning such matters? They might not even be mentioned in the will. They've been gone a long time. He might have left them all to a museum in Livorno, or Rome."

"Nonsense! Menti would never do that to me. Menti loved me. It was his great sadness that we had the paintings no more. He knew how I loved those paintings."

"I'm sure you did. So what makes you think the paintings are in Boston?"

"Because you come here. The day after the funeral. You and Angela have your heads together. Angela wants those paintings. She's going to rob me!"

"Okay, Sylvia. I give up. Tell me about the paintings."

"The de Grassi Collection. Nineteen paintings. Some, Menti had from his parents, others he collected himself. Before World War Two."

"And I suspect during and after World War Two."

"Before, during, after World War Two."

"He was an Italian officer during the war?"

"He did nothing about the war. The de Grassi's turned their palace, Livorno, into a hospital."

"Palace? Big old house."

"They took care of Italian soldiers, citizens, German soldiers, American soldiers, British soldiers — everybody soldiers. Menti told me. He spent his fortune. He hired doctors, nurses."

"And picked up a few paintings."

"He had the paintings. Them he did not sell. Even years after the war. Angela was born. He sold his land, bit by bit, the de Grassi land, but never sold a painting. You know what the paintings are. You have the list."

"Yeah. From what I've been able to find out so far, they've never been recorded. Anywhere. No one knows they exist."

"Because they have always been in a private collection. The de Grassi Collection. See? You are looking for them!"

Fletch said, "I made an inquiry."

"You son of a bitch! You are looking for them. You lie to me!"

"Andy gave me the list. I said I would make an inquiry. I've asked one dealer about one painting. Please don't call me a son of a bitch anymore. I'm sensitive."

"You and Angela are not going to rob me of my paintings!"

"You've made that point pretty well, too. You're accusing me of robbery. Go on with the story. When were the paintings stolen?"

"Two years ago. Stolen overnight. Every one of them."

"From the house in Livorno?"

"Yes."

"Weren't the servants there?"

"Ah, they're no good. Very old, very sleepy. Deaf and blind. Ria and Pep. Menti had great loyalty for them. Last two de Grassi servants. I told him they stupid old fools. Never should he leave such a fortune in paintings to their charge."

"They heard nothing and saw nothing?"

"Flesh, they didn't even realize they were gone until we came back to the house and said, 'Where are the paintings?' They were so used to them. They had seen them all their lives. They didn't even recognize when they were gone. All the time we were away, they never even went into front of the house!"

"And the paintings weren't insured?"

"Never. Stupid old Italian counts do not insure things they've always had, always been used to."

"Menti was a stupid old Italian count, eh?"

"About insurance, he was as bad as the rest of them. As bad as the Catholic Church."

"He probably couldn't afford the premiums."

"He couldn't afford the premiums. Then, whoosh, one day they were gone. The police did not care so much. Just some paintings, they said. There was no big insurance company making them find the paintings and kill the people who stole them."

"You weren't in Livorno when the paintings were stolen?"

"Menti and I were on our honeymoon. In Austria."

"That's not far." Fletch tried one of the olives. "So where are the paintings, Sylvia?"

"What do you mean, 'Where are the paintings, Sylvia?'"

"I think you stole them yourself. Is that what you don't want me to find out? Is that why you're here?"

"Stole them myself!"

"Sure. In your mid-thirties, you marry a sixty-seven-year-old Italian count, with a palace in Livorno and an apartment in Rome. You're his third wife. He's your second husband. Your first husband was Brazilian?"

"French." Her face vacillated between studied amusement and murderous rage.

"You have, let's say, international connections. You marry the old boy. You go on your honeymoon. You discover he's broke. Or, he has very little money. Nothing like the fortune you thought he had. You realize his whole fortune is in these paintings. He's thirty years older than you. You think he might leave the paintings to his daughter, to a museum. After all, you told him you married him for love, right? So you arranged to have the paintings stolen. You stashed them away. Did you even arrange to have Menti kidnapped and murdered? Now you're scared to death I'm going to catch you."

The amusement in her face was agonized.

She said, "I hate you."

"Because I'm right."

"I loved Menti. I would do nothing to harm him. I did not steal the paintings."

"But you, too, left Rome the day after the funeral."

"To catch you."

"It's one thing for the prospective son-in-law of the deceased to leave town the day after the funeral. It's something else for the grieving widow to skip."

"If I killed anyone, I would kill you."

"Which brings up another question, Sylvia. Did you come to my apartment Tuesday night? Was the door opened by a naked young lady who said she was waiting for Bart Connors? Not being able to make sense out of her, did you hit her with a bottle of whiskey?"

"I not make sense out of you."

"Of course not."

"You say your apartment is twenty miles away. That's what you said."

"It's just around the corner, Sylvia. And you know it."

"I don't know what you're talking about. 'Killing a girl.' First you say I kill Menti, and then you say I kill some girl. You're crazy in the head."

"I've already admitted that possibility today."

"Who is this man you talked to about the paintings?"

"I have to have a few secrets of my own."

Fletch stood and neatly put his chair back under the table. "Thanks for the drink, Sylvia."

"You not paying?"

"You invited me. It's a whole new world, babe. You pay."

SIXTEEN

"I guess it's a pretty good job," Fletch said. "I can't read the shit through the paint."

"It's a nice job if you like hearses," the manager said. "What will a black truck do for your plumbing business?"

"I don't know," Fletch said. "Might improve it."

"Neighbors will think you're carrying out a body."

Friday morning was cool and cloudy again.

The manager said, "Did you get down to the Registry?"

Fletch said, "I brought cash for you."

"I'll get the bill."

Fletch paid him off and took the keys to his black panel truck.

"Okay, fella," the manager said. "You get stopped in that truck and the registration don't match, don't say where you got it painted."

"I'll get to the Registry tomorrow," Fletch said. "Saturday."

When he was getting into the truck, the manager said, "Don't suppose you got a spare minute?"

"Why? What's the matter?"

"Leak. In the men's room."

"No, thanks," said Fletch. "Don't need to."

SEVENTEEN

"Will you tell Mister Saunders that Mister Ralph Locke is in the lobby waiting to see him?"

The smile of the woman at the reception desk was a widow's smile. In her fifties, she had learned to smile again, after a funeral, after someone had given her a job, a new but lesser life. Fletch guessed she was a widow of a journalist — perhaps one of those later names inscribed in a long plaque on the lobby wall, starting with 1898 and dribbling through years of war, collisions with fire trucks, and accidents with demon rum.

"A copy boy will be right down to get you," she smiled.

In mid-afternoon, Fletch had gone down to the Ford Ghia parked at the curb.

There were six parking tickets under the windshield wipers.

Knowing the two men in the car across the street were plainclothesmen assigned to watch him, he tore the six parking tickets up and dropped the pieces in the street.

They did not arrest him for destruction of public records, contempt, or littering.

So he led them to the *Boston Daily Star* building.

It was a wet, graystone building in the bowels of the city. The narrow streets around it were clogged with *Star* delivery trucks.

Fletch found two places to park.

He drove the Ghia into one.

And waved the policemen into the other.

A copy boy led him through the huge, smelly old city room.

Jack Saunders was waiting for him near the copy desk.

Fletch said, "I see the publisher has paid off the mortgage."

Shaking hands, Jack looked around the large, yellow room. A hundred years of nicotine had attached themselves to the walls, ceiling, and floor.

"I think he's almost got it paid off. Another few payments."

In the morgue, Jack said to the young help behind the counter, "Randy, this is Ralph Locke, *Chicago Post*, here working on a story."

"I know your by-line, Mister Locke," the kid said.

"Ah, shit," said Fletch.

Jack laughed. "Show him around, will you, Randy?"

Fletch knew the alphabet. He also knew left from right.

Very shortly he got rid of the young hypocrite.

First the regional *Who's Who*.

An item on page 208 read:

Connors, Bartholomew, lawyer; b. Cambridge, Mass. Feb. 7, 1936; s. Ralph and Lilliam (Day) C.; B.A. Dartmouth, 1958; Harvard Law, 1961; m. Lucy Aureal Hyslop, June 6, 1963; Tullin, O'Brien and Corbett, 1962–; partner, 1971. Harvard Club, Boston; Harvard Club, New York. Boylston Club; Trustee, Inst. Modern Art; Director Childes Hospital, Control Systems, Inc., Wardor-Rand, Inc., Medical Implements, Inc. Home: 152 Beacon St., Boston. Office: 32 State St., Boston.

An item on page 506 read:

Horan, Ronald Risom, educator, author, art dealer; b. April 10, 1919, Burlington, Vt.; s. Charles N. and Beatrice (Lamson) H.; B.A. Yale, 1940, U.S. Navy, 1940–45 (Commander); M.A. Cambridge, 1947; Ph.D Harvard, 1949; m. Grace Gulkis, Oct. 12, 1948 (d. 1953). Harvard fac. 1948–; ass't. prof., dept Fine Arts, 1954–. Cont. ed., *Objects*, 1961–65; cont. ed., *Art Standards International*, 1955–. Author, *Themes and Images*, September Press, 1952; *Techniques in Object Authentication*, September Press, 1959. Director, Horan Gallery, 1953–. Lecturer, Cambridge, 1966. Athenaeum, St. Paul's Society, Bosely Club; Advisor, Karkos Museum, 1968–. Home: 60 Newbury St., Boston. Office: Horan Gallery, 60 Newbury St., Boston.

There was no item in *Who's Who* for Inspector Francis Xavier Flynn.

There was little in the newspaper clipping files directly concerning either Connors or Horan.

Connors was represented by a single clipping. Once he had issued to the press and public the recent tax statements of a then-gubernatorial candidate, a client and Harvard Law School classmate, who did not win.

The story referred to Connors as "senior partner of the State Street law firm, Tullin, O'Brien and Corbett and son of former U.S. Ambassador to Australia, Ralph Connors."

Connors' photograph showed a fair-sized, athletic-looking man.

The file on Ambassador Ralph Connors apparently had been cleaned out, except for the obituary. Until becoming Ambassador, he had been Chairman of the Board of Wardor-Rand, Inc. He died in 1951.

There was no photograph of Ronald Risom Horan.

The only news item concerning Horan reported an attempted burglary of the Horan Gallery in 1975. From the way the item was written, Fletch guessed it had been taken straight from a police spokesperson. There was no actual confirmation. There was no follow-up story.

The obituary of Grace Gulkis Horan preceded her husband's folder in the file. A graduate of Wellesley College and heiress to the Gulkis fortune (Gulkis Rubber), she was mostly noted for being owner of the Star of Hunan jade. She was a victim of leukemia.

There were perhaps forty-five clippings under Francis Xavier Flynn's name — all dating within the last eighteen months.

Fletch did not read through all the reports, but he noticed they followed a pattern.

A crime would be reported. A follow-up story would report Flynn had been assigned to it. After a few days of absolutely static news stories, in which there would be no new news, there would be the "public outcry" story: Why has this crime not been solved? Impatient city editors who believed they were getting a runaround from the police were quick to report to the public its indignation. Immediately thereafter a police spokesperson would announce an imminent arrest. Not immediately thereafter, Flynn would be quoted, in response to questioning, as saying, "Nonsense. We're not arresting anybody." At first, this announcement would be followed by another "public outcry" story or one which regretfully questioned the competence of the Boston police.

Not in response, absolutely on his own time schedule, Flynn would announce an arrest. Frequently the arrest report appeared as a small item, on a back page.

Halfway through the file, references began to appear to Inspector Francis "Reluctant" Flynn. The "public outcry" and "police incompetence" stories became less frequent and then stopped altogether. The press had discovered they couldn't push Flynn. They had also discovered he was pretty good.

One of the earliest reports referred to Flynn as "formerly Chicago precinct chief of detectives."

"Do you need anything, Mister Locke?"

The young hypocrite ambled up the row between the file cabinets.

"No, thanks, Randy." Fletch shut the drawer. "I guess I'm done."

"What's the story you're working on, Mister Locke?"

"Nothing very interesting. Feature on the history of New England celebrations of the American Revolution."

"Oh."

The kid appeared to agree it wasn't very interesting. If Ralph Locke was working on such a nothing story, he wasn't very interesting, either.

"I expect you'll read it," Fletch said. "It will be under my by-line."

EIGHTEEN

Fletch found Jack Saunders in the city room.

Someone had handed him a wire photo, which he showed to Fletch.

It was a picture of the President of the United States trying to put on a sweater without first removing his vizored cap and sunglasses.

"That's news, uh?"

"Actually, it is," said Fletch. "I always thought he stepped into his sweaters."

Jack dropped the picture on the copy desk.

"Send it over to the Sunday feature section. Maybe they'll run it under 'Trends.' "

"Jack, I'd like to see your art critic."

"So would I," said Jack. "I'm not sure I ever have. We get a lot of phone calls for him. Mostly angry. His name's Charles Wainwright."

They walked down a long, dark corridor to the back of the building.

Fletch said, "Do you remember Inspector Flynn in Chicago?"

"What Flynn? 'Reluctant' Flynn?"

"Yeah. Your copy said he was a precinct Chief of Detectives in Chicago before coming here."

"The *Star* said that?"

"Your very own newspaper."

"Frank Flynn was never in Chicago. Not two years ago. And not with that rank. I would have had to know him."

"I don't remember him, either."

"That's a mystery," said Jack.

"That's a mystery."

Charles Wainwright was the filthiest man Fletch had ever seen indoors.

His face was only relatively shaved, as if his beard had been pulled out in tufts. In his fifties, particularly his nose and chin gave sustenance to many black-headed pimples. His shirt collars were turning up in decay. And on the shirt front, where the protruding stomach had stopped their fall, were evidences of at least a dozen meals. Tomato sauce had dribbled onto egg yolk.

"This is our great art critic, Charles Wainwright, Ralph," Jack said. "Charles, Ralph Locke is from Chicago, here working on a story."

Fletch braced himself to shake hands, but the slob didn't require it.

"Do what you can for him, eh?"

"Why should I?"

It took Jack a second to realize the question was serious.

"Because I ask you too."

"I don't see why I should do this man's work for him. I have work of my own to do."

Fletch said, "Actually, I'm not working on a story, Mister Wainwright. There's a rumor around Chicago that one of your Boston dealers might donate a painting to the museum there, and the publisher just asked me to stop by and have you fill me in on him."

"What do you mean? You want me to do a story on him?"

"If the guy actually donates the painting, I'd think you'd be the first person we'd call."

"Who is it?"

"Horan."

"Ronnie?"

"Is that what he's called?"

Not concealing his disgust, Jack said to Fletch, "Good luck," and left.

In the small office newspapers and books were piled everywhere, other newspapers and books thrown on top of them. And on top of that was mildew and then dust.

Wainwright sat at his desk. He rather sank among the piles.

"I've known Ronnie for years."

There was no other place in the room to sit. Although apparently permanent, none of the piles looked stable enough to bear weight.

Wainwright said, "We went to Yale together."

"Hygiene Department?"

"I guess he could give a painting to Chicago, if he wanted to. I can't think why he'd want to."

"Ah, the old city still turns a few people on. Rare beef and frequent wind, you know. Gets the blood up."

"Maybe Grace had some connection with Chicago. Maybe that's it. Her family was in the rubber business. Grace Gulkis. Gulkis Rubber."

"Not following you."

"Ronnie married Grace after the war. When he was back taking his doctorate at Harvard."

"And she's rich?"

"Was rich. She died after they had been married a few years. One of those terrible diseases. Cancer, leukemia, something. Ronnie was heartbroken."

"And rich."

"I suppose he inherited. He started the gallery back about that time. And you don't start a gallery like that off the pay of a Harvard instructor."

"He never married again?"

"No. I've seen him with a lot of women over the years, but he never remarried. Ever hear of the Star of Hunan jade?"

"What is it?"

"It's a big rock. A famous jewel. Grace used to own it. I'm just wondering now what became of it. I must ask Ronnie."

"You'll ask him what he did with his wife's jewels?"

"There's no such thing as an improper question — just an improper answer."

"So Horan has plenty of money."

"I don't know. I don't know how much he inherited from Grace, how much went back into her family coffers. These are things you don't know about people, especially in Boston. You know what's happened to money since the 1950s."

"Heard rumors."

"He lives well, in that castle on Newbury street where he has his gallery. The top two floors are his penthouse apartment. He drives a Rolls-Royce. And anyone who drives a Rolls-Royce must be broke."

"Doesn't he have another house somewhere?"

"Maybe. I don't know."

"I mean, he can't just live over the shop."

"I've never heard he has another place."

"Was he in the service?"

"Yes. Navy. Pacific Theater during World War Two. He was an aide to Admiral Kimberly."

"That was before he married La Gulkis?"

"Yes."

"So how did he have enough political muscle to land a cushy Admiral's aide job?"

"Well," Wainwright said, "he went to Yale. A very smooth, attractive guy. Very polished."

"Where's he from, originally?"

"Some place up-country. Maine or Vermont. I forget. There's no money there. He was broke at Yale."

"I see."

"He still teaches at Harvard. Some kind of a freshman art survey course. He's written a couple of turgid books."

"Turgid?"

"Academic. I was never able to get through them. You know the kind of book where the author spends one hundred and fifty thousand words correcting the opinion of someone else who didn't matter anyway."

"Turgid."

"Your name is Ralph Locke?"

"Yeah."

"What paper?"

"*Chicago Post.*"

"You write on art?"

"Oh, no," said Fletch. "I'm a sports writer. Hockey."

"Vulgar."

"Rough."

"Primitive."

"Simple."

"Violent."

"I take it you like writing on the arts." Fletch looked around the room. "You must have a great visual sense."

The filthy man sitting in the filthy room neither confirmed nor denied the assertion.

411

Fletch said, "Tell me more about the Horan Gallery. Is it doing well?"

"Who knows? As an art dealer, Ronnie's the *crème de la crème*. Horan is not a walk-in gallery. He's an international art dealer making deals that are so private even the parties involved aren't sure what they're doing. He has to play very close to the chest. He could have made millions. He could be stone broke, for all I know."

"Which do you think?"

"Well, the art market in recent years has had extraordinary ups and downs. First, the Japanese came along and invested heavily. Then, some of them had to dump on the market. Then Arabs came along, trying to bury petrodollars. Many Japanese weren't deeply schooled in Western art. And Islam has a distinct prejudice against representations of the human or animate figure. So there have been funny, unpredictable distortions in the market. Plus, of course, the art market reflects every distortion in the nature of money itself. Some people have made killings off the market. Others have gotten badly stuck."

"And you don't know which has been Horan's experience."

"No. But I'm interested to hear he might give a painting to Chicago. I might use the item in my column."

"By all means, do," said Fletch. "I'm very grateful to you for all your help."

NINETEEN

Fletch led the plainclothesmen through Friday evening commuter traffic back to his apartment house.

After sharing Charles Wainwright's critical vision, Fletch felt badly in need of a wash.

Taking his complimentary copy of the *Boston Star* with him (a quarter of the front page was devoted to the bathtub murder of the City Councilperson), Fletch walked up the five flights of stairs which squared the lobby elevator shaft and quietly let himself in the front door of his apartment.

Mignon did not bark.

After he washed, he went through the front door again, closing it quietly behind him.

He pushed the button for the elevator. It creaked up to the sixth floor.

He pulled open the iron-grilled doors. They clanged shut on their own weights.

After he waited a moment, he rang the bell to apartment 6A.

It took another moment for Joan Winslow to collect herself and open the door.

"I'm afraid I've locked myself out," Fletch said. "By any chance do you have a key to 6B?"

The smell of gin was not stale, but it was mixed with the odor of an air purifier.

From beside the skirt of Joan's housecoat, Mignon was looking at him with her usual polite courtesy.

"Who are you?" Joan asked.

"Peter Fletcher. I'm using Bart's apartment. We met in the elevator yesterday."

"Oh, yes." She lurched heavily on her left foot as she turned to the small hall table. "You're the man Bart dumped the body on."

"Ma'am?"

The drawer of the hall table held many keys.

"The police were here. An enormous man. Name of Wynn, or something."

"Flynn."

"He spoke so softly I could hardly hear him. Came this morning. He showed me a picture of the murdered girl. I forget her name."

"Ruth Fryer."

"Yes."

She stirred her hand through the key drawer.

Fletch said, "Yes?"

She pulled out a key with a white tag attached. It read, "Bart's — 6B."

"There it is."

She lurched toward the doorway, apparently thinking Fletch was still standing in it.

"Oh," she said, finding him. "Now use this key and give it right back to me so next time one of you lock yourselves out I'll have it."

Key in hand, Fletch asked, "Did you let anyone into the apartment Tuesday night?"

"No. Of course not. I've never let anyone into that apartment. Except Bart. Lucy. And now you. Anyway, I wasn't here Tuesday night. I had drinks and dinner with some friends."

413

"Where did you have drinks?"

"Bullfinch Pub." She knew she was repeating herself. "Just up the street."

"I see."

"That's where I saw Bart. And the girl."

Fletch crossed the small hall and opened the door to 6B with Joan Winslow's key.

Handing it back to her, he asked, "Was the girl you saw with Bart Tuesday night the same girl in the photograph the police showed you?"

"Yes," Joan Winslow said. "Of course."

"Did you tell the police that?"

"Certainly. I'd tell anybody that."

She whisked Mignon behind her with the long skirt of her house-robe.

"Come in," she said. "It's drinks time."

"Thank you."

"Don't you want a drink?"

"I'll be right with you."

Fletch crossed the small elevator landing, closed the door to his apartment, and returned to Joan's. He closed the door behind him.

Swaying over a well-stocked bar in the living room, her face was that of a child at a soda counter.

Her living room was a counterpart of Connors', in its large size and basic solidity, but far more feminine. Instead of polished leathers and dark woods the upholstery was white and blue and pink, the furniture light and spindly. The paintings on the walls were originals, imitative modern junk.

"Seeing it's Friday night, shall we have a martini? Why don't you make it?" She waved her hand airily at the bar. "Men make martinis so much better than women do."

"Oh, yes?"

She placed the ice bucket centrally on the service table.

"I'll make crackers and cheese," she said.

She walked flat-footed, placing most of her weight on the heels of her house slippers, prepared at each step to prevent a fall sideways. Joan Winslow was accustomed to being crocked.

"Well." On the divan, her legs curled up under her houserobe, she bit into a bare cracker. "Isn't this nice?"

Fletch poured.

"Have you known the Connorses long?"

"Years. Ever since they were married. The apartment next door was being prepared for them while they were on their honeymoon and I was in Nevada getting a divorce. We all arrived back within a day or two of each other and just fell into each other's arms."

"You hadn't known each other before?"

"No, indeed. If I had laid eyes on Bart Connors before Lucy, she wouldn't have had a chance. He was a darling. And we'd all be much better off."

She took the tiniest sip of her martini.

"Um, good. Men can make better martinis than women."

"I used a little vermouth."

"You see — what's your name, Peter? That doesn't seem right to me, somehow, but I'll use it — they were just getting used to marriage, and I was just getting used to divorce. My husband, a structural engineer, had accepted a contract in Latin America, in Costa Rica, the year before. The poor, empty-headed boob remarried there. I found out some months later. I mean, I had no choice but to divorce him, did I? Why put a person in jail just because he's a booby? Don't you think it was the best thing to do?"

"Absolutely," Fletch said firmly.

"Only the Connorses never did get used to marriage." She drank half her martini in a single swallow. "And I have never gotten used to divorce."

The woman, at the most, was in her early forties. She had probably been attractive, in a petite, helpless, feminine way. She probably could be again, if she would put down her glass.

"At first," she continued, "it was great fun. They didn't know the building, or the district. I got the janitorial service to work for them — there was always something abrasive about Lucy — and found them a string of apartment cleaners. People were doing things for the Connorses because I asked them to. Lucy quite turned people off."

She finished her drink. Fletch did not pour her another.

"After a year or so, it was pretty obvious she turned Bart off, too. When I had a dinner party, I usually had the Connorses as guests. They invited me, with or without escort, when they were throwing a bash. What could we do, really? There were only two apartments on this floor, and we were friends. We had to be."

She poured herself a fresh drink.

"One night, after they had been here for dinner, Bart came back. All the other guests had gone. We had a nightcap. A big one. We

415

both had too much to drink. Lucy was frigid, he said. Always had been. Or so he thought.

"There was a year of psychiatry for her. During that time, I sort of played psychiatrist for Bart. He'd come over late at night. We'd have a drink, and talk. As you can imagine, Lucy became a little cool with me. I could never make out whether it was because I was intimate with the family secrets, or because I was getting too much attention from Bart. I can tell you one thing. During all that time, and it went on for a long time, Bart was completely faithful to Lucy. He couldn't have been otherwise, without his telling me. I was his good friend. His drinking buddy.

"Lucy dropped psychiatry after a while. Bart found her another shrink, but she refused to go. You see, I think she had discovered what the so-called problem was.

"Then I noticed a young woman coming in and out of the apartment house, and it sort of puzzled me, as I knew no one had moved in. I saw her during the daytime. Then I realized she was going to 6B. I assumed it was some old friend of Lucy's. Then I met her at a cocktail party at the Connorses. Her name is Marsha Hauptmann. It was announced she and Lucy were starting a boutique together. How nice. All very reasonable.

"Until the servant we had in common in those days — that was before Mrs. Sawyer, who now comes to me on Tuesdays and Fridays, she just left, and you on Wednesdays and Saturdays — told me Lucy and Marsha were taking showers together! How else can I say it? They were using the bed together.

"Incidentally, I fired the person who told me that. Servants must not be allowed to gossip in the neighborhood. And, in truth, I had not wanted to know any such thing. Do you believe that?"

"Of course," Fletch said.

"Then I did rather a stupid thing. I thought it was right at the time. I never told Bart. We had always been strictly honest with each other, but I just couldn't tell him that. I thought the news coming from me would destroy his faith in his own manliness, his own perceptions, if you see what I mean. He had to find out by himself. Instead, I encouraged infidelity."

"With you?"

"I was in love with Bart. Please, would you pour me another touch more?"

Fletch poured into her glass.

"I'm ashamed to say I did," she said. "I had never been a seductress before, although I had been seduced enough. I'm afraid I was rather clumsy at it. Bart couldn't understand. He thought of me as a friend of Lucy's. I was his old drinking buddy. Suddenly, I turn all hot and passionate. I should say, I let him see how hot and passionate I always had been towards him.

"He rejected me. There's no other way to say that, either.

"Months went by. No more mutual dinner parties. No more drinking with Bart.

"I guess finally she told him she was leaving him for another woman. The poor jerk still hadn't caught on."

Fletch said, "After Lucy accepted her lesbianism, why did she wait so long before divorcing Bart?"

"Those adjustments take time, I expect. Maybe she thought it was a momentary thing. She had been told she was frigid enough times, by Bart and Bart's psychiatrists. I knew that. Here was a person who turned her on. It happened to be another girl.

"Anyway," Joan continued, "Lucy had nothing and Bart is rich. His father built Wardor-Rand, you know. Bart inherited most of it. Haven't you noticed the paintings in his apartment? You can't buy those with cheesecake. His father ended his days being our ambassador to Australia."

"I see," Fletch said. "But ultimately, she did tell him, and she told him the truth."

"I guess so. Can you realize what that must do to a man? Realize he's been married to a girl who doesn't, who can't have the slightest interest in him, sexually?"

"She could have."

"I'm sure it didn't seem that way to Bart. Every man wants to believe he's married to a red-hot mama, who loves him sexually. My husband did. Twice, apparently. To discover your wife prefers girls — to the point where she is leaving you for a girl — can't do much for your ego, no matter how modern you are."

"I guess not."

"And I'm sure Bart tried to be understanding. He would."

"Were the facts of this affair public?"

"Everyone knew about it. Everyone in our circle. That's how I knew the great moment of revelation had come. By that time, you see, neither one of them was talking to me."

"He must have felt a little foolish."

"Innocent, anyway. Bart, despite his age, was a very innocent man. He went to one of the up-country colleges. Was never in the service.

Worked like hell through law school and during his first years at the firm, having to work with Wardor-Rand simultaneously. His father was dead. When he married Lucy, he was very naive."

"He isn't now."

She offered the plate of bare crackers to Fletch. There was no cheese anywhere in sight.

He refused them.

"So why do you still hate Bart?" he asked.

"Hate him? Did I say I hate him? I suppose I do.

"After the incident, the revelation, he didn't come to me. I waited, politely.

"Then one day I heard him on the landing. I opened my door and put my arms out to him. I guess I was crying. It was morning. I said, 'Oh, Bart, I'm so sorry.' I tried to hug him. He took my arms away from around his neck."

"He rejected you again."

"He even said something rather cutting about my drinking habits. After all the drinks I had poured nursing him. Something unforgiveable."

Fletch said, "I expect the poor guy was feeling a little sour on all womanhood at that moment."

"It's not that." Her tears were as big as drops of gin. "He not only rejected me as a woman. That I could understand, at the moment. What hurts is that he rejected me as a friend."

"I see."

Unabashed, Joan continued talking through her tears, her whole mouth working to get the words out comprehensibly.

"Then there was that endless stream of girls who poured through here. Pony tails. Frizzy hair. Blue jeans. Little skirts. It's been going on for months."

Fletch waited for her breathing to become more regular.

"So you think he finally killed one of them."

"Of course, he did. The bastard."

She flat-heeled over to the serving table and poured herself a slug of straight gin and poured it down her throat.

"It wasn't any girl he was killing. Any Ruthie what's-her-name. It was Lucy. He was killing Lucy."

For a moment, Fletch sat, saying nothing.

Mignon, sitting on the divan, was looking anxiously at her mistress.

Finally, Fletch said, "Is there anything I can do for you?"

"No." She brushed hair back from her forehead. "I think I'll take a bath and go to bed."

"No supper?"

"I'm too tired."

Fletch dropped her key to Bart's apartment on the coffee table. "We can get a sandwich somewhere. It's early yet. What about this pub you've mentioned? Up the street."

"Really," she said. "I'm much too tired. The police were here this morning. About Bart."

"I understand." Standing up, he said, "Someday I'd like to take Mignon for a nice long walk."

"She'd love that."

Joan Winslow showed him to the door. Her face looked dreadful. "Good night."

When he got to his own door he realized that supposedly he didn't have the key.

Her door closed.

He shrugged, took his own key out of his pocket, and let himself in.

TWENTY

Fletch was still wondering about the source of his own supper, trying to remember the name of the pub up the street, when his doorbell rang.

"Oh, my god."

The Countess de Grassi was standing among her luggage on the landing.

A head with a taxi driver's hat on it was descending down the elevator shaft.

"Eighteen, twenty miles you say! It's no eighteen, twenty miles."

"I said it wasn't."

"All the time you lie, Flesh." She tried, but not very hard, to pick up one of her suitcases, the biggest. "A nice man let me in downstairs."

"Sylvia, what do you think you're doing?"

Sylvia could turn an elevator landing into a stage.

"You say Ritz too expensive for me." Helplessness was expressed by widened eyes, arms thrown wide — even her cleavage seemed wider. "You right. They present me bill."

"Did you pay it?"

"Of course I pay it. You think the Countess de Grassi some sort of crook? Everybody rob the Countess de Grassi. The Countess de Grassi rob no one!"

Fletch remained in the center of the doorway.

"But why did you come here?"

"Why do I come here? What you think? Why should Countess de Grassi stay in too-expensive hotel when her son-in-law live around corner in magnificent apartment?"

"I'm not your son-in-law. Ye gods."

"You marry Andy, you become my son-in-law. You become member de Grassi family. I, Countess de Grassi!"

"I've heard." He faltered back a step. "What the hell is this? Son-in-step-law? Step-son-in-law? Son-in-law-step?"

"No! No English double-talk in American, please."

"Me? Wouldn't think of it."

She entered through the small space his body left in the doorway. He closed the door on her luggage.

"Very nice." Her quick glance through the living room door was followed by a quick glance through the den door. "Okay enough. Very nice."

"Sylvia, there are other hotels."

"Not for the Countess de Grassi. Always number one place. What would poor, dead Menti say if Countess de Grassi stay in fleabag?"

"I think he'd probably say, 'Thank God. I left a lousy estate.' "

"He left no lousy estate. He left magnificent estate. My paintings!"

"There are more middle-class hotels, Sylvia."

"Middle-class? You crazy in the head, you bullshitting son of a bitch. The Countess de Grassi is not middle-class."

"I see."

She flounced the white gloves in her hands, substituting the action for removing them. They had never been on. It was doubtful they would fit over her rather impressive diamond ring.

"Now. Where my room?"

"Sylvia, you wouldn't be here just to keep an eye on me, would you?"

"Eye on you? Devil eye on you!"

Her eyes spit into his.

"Because, honestly, I'm not doing anything about your paintings. I know nothing about your paintings." Fletch thought a shout would be worth trying. "I'm here researching a book about an American artist, and you'd be in my way!"

"You bet your cock I'll be in your way!" One should never try to outshout a Brazilian who had been married to both a Frenchman and an Italian. And who was not middle-class. "You no make one move without me! I at the hotel! I might as well be in Rome! In Livorno! I'm not here to buy you a drink and go away again! I'm here to catch my paintings!"

"Sylvia, I know nothing about your paintings."

"Now. Where is my room? Servants can bring in the luggage."

"Sylvia, there are no servants."

"No servants! Always you lie. Who answered your phone the other day? The woman who puts her eyelashes in the refrigerator!"

"Oh, boy."

The Countess de Grassi marched down the corridor to the bedrooms, snapping on lights as she went.

While Fletch was still in the reception hall, the telephone rang.

He answered it in the den.

"Hello, Mister Fletcher?"

"Yeah."

"This is Mister Horan, of the Horan Gallery."

"Oh, yes."

"Sorry to bother you on a Friday night, especially after seven, but I thought you'd be pleased to hear my good news."

"Oh?"

"Yes. I've succeeded in locating the painting you were interested in, Picasso's 'Vino, Viola, Mademoiselle.' "

"That's wonderful."

"I've talked with the present owner. Like the rest of us, I guess, he's suffering somewhat from a shortage of cash, and I think he was rather pleased that someone has come forward at this time with an interest in buying it. I suggested to him that as you had sought the painting out, he might get a slightly higher price than if he were simply to offer it on the market himself now or in the near future."

"I hope you didn't make his mouth water too much."

"No, no. Simply a negotiating device. But of course a seller does do better when a negotiation is initiated by the buyer. You do understand."

"Of course."

"He does slightly better. If, after we see the painting, you are still interested in its purchase, I will do my best to get it for you at the most reasonable price."

"Tell me, Mister Horan, where is the painting?" There was a hesitation on the phone. "Who is its present owner?"

"Well, I don't usually like to answer that question. I'm a private dealer."

Fletch said nothing.

Horan said, "I guess there's no reason why I shouldn't answer you, in this instance. The painting is owned by a man named Cooney. In Dallas, Texas."

"Texas. Texas is still big in the art market, eh?"

"There are some superb private collections in Texas. Mister Cooney has not been an active collector, to my knowledge, but he does have this piece and some others I know of. The Barclough Bank in Nassau has given you a credit reference more than adequate. Therefore, I have asked Mister Cooney to fly the painting up for our inspection. It should be here by morning."

"The painting is coming here?"

"It should already be on its way. I tried to get you by phone this afternoon. Truth is, I had to spend considerable time advising Mister Cooney on the work's proper crating and insurance."

"I'm very surprised the picture is coming here."

"Well, I want to see it myself. If it's authentic I might want to purchase it myself, or find another purchaser for it, should you decide not to purchase it. Once an owner gets over what might be called a psychological hump and makes the basic decision that he might consider selling an object of art, if the price is right — as our Mister Cooney did this afternoon after lunch in Dallas — then a dealer should go forward with him and arrange a sale."

"You did all this by telephone?"

"Oh, yes. I'm not unknown in Texas."

"Well, that's wonderful. What else can you tell me about Mister Cooney?"

"Not much. I was put on to him by a curator, friend of mine, at the Dallas Museum. My source knew Cooney owned a Picasso of your general description, but had never seen it. I called Mister Cooney last night and asked him bluntly if he owned a Picasso entitled 'Vino, Viola, Mademoiselle,' an impossible title. I gather he dropped his bourbon bottle. He answered in the affirmative. I said I might have a purchaser for it. He thought about it overnight. I believe he's in ranching. Has something like eight children."

"That's why he needs some cash, right?"

"In any case, Mister Fletcher, albeit tomorrow is Saturday, I believe if you came here — is nine-thirty too early? — we could look at the painting together and perhaps make Mister Cooney an offer before the bourbon begins to flow again."

"Yes. That would be fine. You say the painting is coming by air tonight?"

"Yes. If all goes well. If it's not here in the morning, I'll give you a ring. But I'm sure it will be here."

Fletch said, "Okay, I'll see you in the morning."

Sylvia stood in the doorway to the den.

"You'll see who in the morning?"

At least she had not been listening on the extension.

"I have to see a man about a horse."

"A Degas horse?"

"No, Sylvia. A pinto."

"What is this, pinto horse. A painted horse, right?"

Now in a more kittenish manner, she sat in one of the leather chairs.

"What about my dinner?" she said.

"What about it?"

"No servants. Don't you expect me to eat, Flesh? I am your guest!"

"Right," Fletch said. "You've never tasted my cooking, have you?"

"You cook?"

"Like a dream." He kissed the tips of his fingers and exploded them before his face. "Um! Better than the Ritz! Let's see." Thoughtfully, he paced the small room. "To begin with, a *potage au cresson*, yes? *Timbales de foies de volaille.* Good! *Homard à l'américaine!* Then, of course, a *fricassée de poulet à l'indienne*, with *pois frais en braisage.* What could be better! Eh? For dessert, *charlotte Chantilly, aux framboises!* Splendid!" He considered her anxiously. "Would that be all right, do you think? Countess?"

"It sounds all right."

"Of course, it will take me some time."

"I'm used to eating late. I want to see these things you cook."

"I'd offer you a drink, but of course, I never would before such a dinner."

423

"Of course not. I'll take nothing to drink."

"You sit right there. I'll get busy in the kitchen."

Briskly, Fletch crossed the reception hall and went through the swing door to the kitchen.

He also went through the kitchen, out its back door, and down the stairs to the alley.

He ran to the garage on River Street.

Not taking time to figure a new route to 60 Newbury Street, he drove down Beacon Street, past his own apartment. The two plain-clothesmen in the parked car across from 152 Beacon Street looked like bags of laundry. But they had their eyes firmly on the front door of the apartment house. Fletch scratched his left temple while passing them.

He turned left on Arlington Street and right on Newbury. Double parking outside a pharmacy, he ran in and ordered two sandwiches and some soft drinks to go. He also ordered two cups of coffee.

There was a place to park diagonally across the street from the Horan Gallery.

He turned off his lights and engine and settled down to wait.

It was then he realized he would need more than his suit jacket. He was cold.

Within twenty minutes the garage doors at 60 Newbury Street opened. Fletch saw the grille of a Rolls-Royce with its headlights on.

The sixty-year-old houseman, or gallery assistant or whatever he was, closed the doors after the Rolls pulled out.

There was only one way the Rolls could go on Newbury Street, it being a one-way west, and the car went west.

In the van Fletch followed Horan in the Rolls.

They went by several cross-streets. They went west to the end of Newbury Street.

After stopping at a red light, they crossed Massachusetts Avenue and dipped down a ramp onto the Massachusetts Turnpike Extension. And kept going west.

The Rolls proceeded at a stately fifty-five miles per hour. It went through a toll booth, making its proper genuflection to the exact change machine, and continued westward.

It curved right before the second toll booth. "WESTON," Fletch read, "128 NORTH/SOUTH."

At the end of the off-ramp, there was another toll booth.

In his own lane, Fletch caught up to Horan. He waited a moment before throwing change out the window, as if he were having trouble finding the exact change.

The Rolls preceded him onto the Weston Road.

After stopping at a light, the two vehicles veered right. The road from there curved and climbed gently, past woods, a golf course, well-spaced antique farmhouses, and more contemporary estate houses.

Fletch dared not let the Rolls' taillights get more than one hundred and fifty meters ahead of him.

Even that was almost too much, on that road.

After a curve the taillights were no longer ahead of him. Slowing imperceptibly, Fletch saw a car going through woods down a driveway to his left. The headlights were high and round, the shape of the car boxy, the taillights huge. It had to be the Rolls.

Fletch drove around the next curve and pulled over. He left his parking lights on.

He ran along the soft shoulder of the road back to the driveway he thought Horan had taken. The mailbox read MILLER.

Lights in a house further down to his left went on.

The mailbox on that driveway read HORAN.

Stepping around in the dark, he explored the area across from the driveway.

There was a break in the stone wall, with a rusty chain across it. The wall was only two meters from the road.

Fletch returned to his truck and turned it around.

Before reversing, to put the back bumper of his truck against the chain, he turned out its headlights.

The chain snapped easily.

Crunching through brush, Fletch backed up, turned the wheel, and then drove forward to the wall.

Through a light screen of brush in front of him, he had a perfect view of the Horan driveway.

In the silent dark, he had one sandwich and a cup of coffee.

He watched the lights go out in the Horan house. At a quarter to twelve all the lights were out in the neighbors' house.

At one-thirty, Fletch walked up the shoulder of Horan's gravel driveway. Moonlight came and went through the clouds.

After a patch of woods, a lawn appeared to the left, in front of the house. It had two levels. The upper level apparently was used as a patio. Under a green striped awning, white, wrought iron furniture remained outdoors in October.

The house was a rather imposing, three-storied structure. Its slate roof reflected moonlight.

Going around the right of the house, Fletch had to cross a patch of gravel. He took off his shoes to do so.

A garage was connected to the house.

Around the garage ran a dirt car track, to an unused, three-sided tractor shed. The extensive gardens at the back of the house had fallen into decay.

He examined the windows at the back of the house. All, including the windows in the kitchen door, were wired with a burglar alarm system.

Woods came up to the far side of the house.

Fletch returned to his van and had his second sandwich and the cold coffee.

By three-thirty he was cold enough to look in the back of the van for something to wrap around himself, although he was sure there was nothing there.

In fact, the painters had left a long piece of tarpaulin. The splattered paint on it was dry to the touch.

Returning to the driver's seat, he wrapped the tarpaulin around him.

He was getting comfortably warm when dawn arrived.

Almost immediately, rain sounded against the truck's roof. It obscured vision through the windshield.

Turning on the ignition, but not the engine, Fletch sent the wipers over the windshield every few minutes.

At a quarter past eight, he saw the grille of the Rolls-Royce in the driveway opposite.

It had been Fletch's plan to pull the truck further back into the woods if he had forewarning of Horan's departure. He had had none.

He hoped the combination of the rain and the screen of brush in front of him protected him somewhat from being seen.

The Rolls did not stop. It turned right, without hesitation, back the way it had come the night before.

After Horan went around the curve, Fletch extricated the truck from the bushes and followed him.

He followed him back to 60 Newbury Street.

Fletch was parked — halfway down the block — before the manservant opened the garage in response to Horan's horn. The Rolls backed across the sidewalk into the garage.

It was ten minutes to nine, Saturday morning.

At nine-fifteen, Fletch drove to the pharmacy. There he bought a razor, a blade, and a can of shaving foam. He also bought a cup of tea to go.

In the truck he loosened his collar, threw out the tea bag, and, using the tarpaulin, as well as the razor, the blade, the shaving foam, and the tea, shaved himself.

At nine-thirty he rang the doorbell of the Horan Gallery.

TWENTY-ONE

The Picasso was on the easel in Horan's office.

"Ah, good morning, Mister Fletcher. Wet morning."

" 'Fraid I came away without my raincoat." The weather would take the blame for his disheveled appearance. "Hard to get a taxi in the rain."

"Always," sympathized the impeccable Ronald Horan. "Well. There it is."

Fletch had stopped in front of the painting.

Damned fool title but what could the painting be called but "Vino, Viola, Mademoiselle"? The basic shape was repeated three times. The first image, or the fourth, was the true shape.

"Magnificent," he said.

"I believe I can guarantee its authenticity."

"I'm speechless," Fletch said.

"I'm curious as to why you want to purchase this piece in particular? I'm always curious about that."

"I saw a slide of it," Fletch said, "at a little showing in Cannes, sometime well after Picasso's death. It just sped by with a lot of other slides. It struck me as possibly the key cubist work, even more refined than others of the same theme."

Horan was looking at the painting as well.

"You may be right," he said.

"But let's not tell Mister Cooney."

Fletch walked around the easel. "It's all right? It arrived without damage?"

"No damage at all." Horan joined him behind the painting. "And, I may add, I believe this is the original stretcher. Although it may not be."

"You picked it up at the airport yourself?"

Horan moved to the front of the painting.

"I rather indicated to Mister Cooney we'd be in touch with him sometime early today. Although we needn't be, of course. It's up to you."

"What's your advice?"

"You might start with six hundred and fifty thousand dollars."

Fletch wandered to a chair from which he could see both Horan and the painting.

"You say Mister Cooney is not an active collector?"

"Well, he's not in the business of collecting," Horan answered. "I've bought one or two other things from him in the last year or two. They've always proven to be right."

"You've bought two other paintings from him within the last two years?"

"As I say, the man doesn't have a professional reputation to uphold, as a dealer would have, or a museum, but his other sales, at least through this gallery, have been entirely successful."

Tall, slim, suave, graying Horan prowled the rug, arms behind his back, in an attitude of respectful waiting.

Quietly, firmly, Fletch said, "I'm interested in the painting's provenance."

"Ah!" Horan responded as if a whole new topic had been introduced — an original question from a slow student. "I'm not sure you'll be entirely satisfied there."

"No?"

"You see, in many private sales provenance is not offered." The man was lecturing again. "Especially in a case of this sort. There is no record of this painting in existence — at least none I've been able to find. Of far more importance, there appears to be no record of this painting's ever having left another country, or ever having entered this country. Governments, with their taxes and other requirements, their increasing interest in preserving national cultural objects, these days, you know, can be a bit sticky."

"I know. Which, of course, makes my having the provenance of this painting all the more important."

"Yes, I can see that. You live in Italy, don't you?"

"I sometimes do."

"Of course, we can ask Mister Cooney the provenance."

"You haven't done so?"

"I know what he'll say."

"Let me guess," said Fletch. "He'll say he bought it from a reputable dealer in Switzerland sometime in the past, and he doesn't remember precisely when."

"Well, yes." Horan was pleased by the slow student's perceptive answer. "I expect that's what he would say."

"There are more reputable art dealers in Switzerland than there are citizens of France. Piled on top of each other, they are that nation's national culture."

"As I guess you know, Swiss dealers seldom confirm sales."

"I think we should ask, Mister Horan."

"By all means, we should."

"I wish to know the source, and the history of this painting."

"Of course, when a provenance isn't offered, Mister Fletcher. . . ."

"I would be derelict in not asking for the provenance."

"You said you represent yourself?"

"I would be derelict in my obligations to myself, my estate, as well as to those parts of the art world which consider their responsibilities. Frankly, I'm fairly shocked you cannot say you have already asked for a complete provenance."

Below Horan's silver-streaked temples appeared a flush of red.

"I don't think you understand, Mister Fletcher, how usual this situation is. Very common, indeed. Art is the international language. It is also an international currency. The art market, by its nature, is international. It cannot recognize arbitrary, national borders. Governments have been poking more and more into matters which are beyond their natural province. People must insist upon privacy in their affairs, especially in esthetic matters."

"Ah, yes."

"You remember, I'm sure, the deluge of art objects flooding out of Britain in late 1975, as a result of incredible legislative mistakes by the Labor government. Were you unsympathetic?"

"I understood the movement."

"Incidentally, it is entirely possible 'Vino, Viola, Mademoiselle' is one of those objects of art which found its way here from Britain."

"It's also possible it's not. In any case, even if it is, I must protect myself, Mister Horan."

"My dear Mister Fletcher! You are protected. Entirely protected. We are not new in this business. After spending a little more time with this painting, I'm sure I will have no hesitation in authenticating it. If you wish a second authentication, or even a third, such can be arranged locally within a matter of days, if not hours."

"Very good of you."

"You will have bought the painting through the Horan Gallery in Boston, with proper authentication. My reputation has never been questioned. If asked, which I doubt I would be, I will state happily the seller is James Cooney, of Dallas, Texas. When asked, he, in turn. . . ."

". . . will say he bought it sometime in the past from a reputable dealer in Switzerland," Fletch said. "And the reputable dealer in Switzerland will refuse to come forward with the record, which is his right, as a Swiss citizen."

"Bless the Swiss," said Horan. "They still have some sense of privacy left — although it is dissipating."

"I understand all this, Mister Horan."

"In the meantime, and forever, your investment is absolutely protected."

"It remains my obligation to ask the question. I want to know where Cooney got the painting, even if it is in the nature of private, undocumented information."

"Yes. Of course, you're right, Mister Fletcher. We should ask the question. In the meantime, would you care to mention a specific price to Mister Cooney?"

Horan stepped behind his Louis Seize desk to answer the telephone. The ring had been muffled.

"Hello? Yes, this is Mister Horan. . . . Who wishes to speak to me? . . . Hello? No, operator, no . . . I will accept no calls from anyone in Chicago today. . . . This is the third call I've had from the *Chicago Tribune* . . . I have already denied that story. . . . What's your name? . . . Mister Potok? . . . Two others of your reporters have already called here this morning, Mister Potok. How many times do I have to deny a story? . . . I am not giving, nor have I ever intended to give a painting to the Chicago museum. . . . What do you mean, what painting am I *not* going to give? My god. . . . I have no idea where the Boston newspaper got the story. I believe it was the *Star*. I haven't read the story. I expect it was their idiot critic, Charles Wainwright, who has never gotten anything right. . . . Listen, Mister Potok, I am not giving a painting to the Chicago museum; I never intended to give a painting to the Chicago museum; I never will give a painting to the Chicago museum. . . . What do you mean? I have nothing against the Chicago museum. . . . Mister Potok, I am running out of patience. The story is entirely fallacious. Please don't call here again."

His footfalls on the rug repeated the quiet firmness with which he had hung up the phone.

"Some damn fool Boston newspaper reported I am going to give a painting to the Chicago museum." Horan shook his head. "Totally untrue. Where do they get things like that?"

"There's no accounting for the press," said Fletch.

"We were discussing price."

Fletch stood. He remembered he didn't have a coat.

"Yes. We were," said Fletch. "I think we might offer Mister Cooney two hundred and seventy-five thousand dollars."

Horan looked slapped.

"That would be totally unacceptable."

"I know. I'll go higher, of course. But tell Mister Cooney I am deeply anxious about the source of this painting."

"I doubt he'll talk in response to such an offer."

"He might talk — a lot."

TWENTY-TWO

"Who's there?"

"The big, bad pomegranate."

It was eleven-thirty Saturday morning.

Fletch had had to go a little out of his way to find a hardware store on his way home from Newbury Street. He had bought a screwdriver, a pair of pliers, and a small can of household oil — all of which he had left in the truck.

After putting the truck in the River Street garage, he had cut through the alley and up the iron, cement-walled back stairs to his apartment.

He had forgotten Mrs. Sawyer would be there. Naturally, she had locked the back door.

"You go away," she shouted through the door. "Nothing gets picked up on Saturdays."

"It's Mister Fletcher, Mrs. Sawyer! Please open up."

"What are you doing out there?"

The two bolts slid free of the door.

"Well, look at you!" she said. "Out caterwauling all night! Where's your coat? You're wet like a puppy."

"Good morning."

"You have a European countess sleeping in your own bed, and you're not even home to enjoy it."

"In my bed?"

"She calls herself the Countess del Gassey."

"She should."

"I've never seen so much luggage. She expect to be buried here?"

"She slept in my bed?"

"Didn't you leave her there?"

"I did not. Where is she?"

"She said something about going shopping. Then she said something about going to the museum and visiting some galleries."

"Great."

"I fed her, and she's gone. Mercy, Lord, was she hungry! You'd think no one had fed her in a month."

"No one has." The bright, white kitchen was a complete contrast to the cold, dark, wet truck. "I'm wet."

"Your hair looks like you spent the night tunneling through a haystack. Maybe that's what you were doing. You want something to eat?"

"Sure would. Where are the countess's things?"

"You'll see. All over the apartment. I never met such a bossy woman. She talked to me like I was a platoon."

"Would you move everything of hers into a guest room, please? And then close the door. Tight."

"I'm not sure it will all fit! You want breakfast, or lunch?"

"Anything warm would be great. By the way, where are the telephone books?"

After standing in a warm shower, he sat on the edge of his bed and checked all the local telephone books.

There was no listing for Lucy Connors.

However, there was a listing, on Fenton Street, in Brookline, for Marsha Hauptmann.

He dialed the number and waited through four rings.

"Hello?"

"Hello. This is Martin Head, of *Très Magazine*. Is Ms. Connors there?"

Fletch guessed it was Ms. Hauptmann who said, "Just a moment, please."

Another voice came on the line. "Hello?"

"Ms. Connors, this is Martin Head, of *Très Magazine.* I've been trying your number all week."

"Yes?"

"Ms. Connors, I'd appreciate your listening very carefully to what I have to say, and see if you can't agree to it."

"I doubt I will."

"Please. You'll see our intention is good and, with your cooperation, the result may be good."

"You've got me mystified. I don't read your magazine."

"We would like to do a sensitive, personal story — without mentioning any names, or using any photographs — on women who have declared themselves lesbian, especially after having gone through a few years of married life."

"Where did you get my name?"

"Your husband."

"Bart's in Italy. I can't believe that."

"We met him Tuesday night, in Montreal. Apparently he's far more understanding, or trying to be far more understanding, than many husbands in similar circumstances we have met."

"Bart? I suppose so."

"I believe you could give our readers some genuinely sensitive insights into what you've been through — some real understanding. You'd be an ideal interview."

"I don't think so. Is it Mister Head?"

"Martin."

"Does this have anything to do with the murder?"

"What murder?"

"There was a murder in my husband's apartment the other night. I wouldn't want to comment on it. It's perfectly irrelevant."

"I didn't know about that." Fletch's eyes wandered around Lucy and Bart Connors' old bedroom. "If it's irrelevant, why should it be mentioned?"

"I don't think so, Martin. This has been bad enough, without publicity."

"Lucy, think how bad it is for other women in the circumstances you were in. I daresay you felt pretty alone, going through it."

"Certainly did."

"It sometimes helps to be able to read that someone else has been through it. You've resolved your problems, fairly successfully, I gather. . . ."

"You're a very convincing fella, Martin."

"Furthermore, I guarantee you, there will be no personal publicity. You'll be referred to as 'Ms. C.,' period. Nice, tasteful drawings, probably abstracts, will be made up as illustrations."

"And what if you don't?"

"You can sue us. We know we're trespassing here on personal, intimate affairs. We're doing a story on your feelings, rather than the facts. We're not out to expose anybody, or anything."

"I see. Would you let me read the story and okay it before it's published?"

"We don't like to do that. The editors sort of feel that's their job."

"I won't talk to you unless I see the story before it's published."

Fletch forced himself to hesitate. "Okay, Lucy. I agree. It will have to be between us, but I'll let you see the story before I hand it in. When can I see you?"

"Marsha and I are going shopping this afternoon if this rain ever lets up. And we're seeing friends tonight."

"May I come tomorrow morning?"

"Okay. About ten?"

"Ten-thirty. 58 Fenton Street?"

"Apartment 42."

"Will Ms. Hauptmann be there?"

"You bet. You goof up one little bit, Babe, and we'll both stomp you."

TWENTY-THREE

After steak and eggs, provided and prepared by Mrs. Sawyer, Fletch got into his freshly made bed with yesterday's edition of the *Boston Star*.

The murder of Ruth Fryer received little space compared to the space devoted to the City Councilperson's murder. Obviously there was no new news concerning Ruth Fryer's murder. The City Councilperson's murder was reported in the greatest detail, together with her full biography, with pictures of her throughout her career, a personal recollection piece by the paper's chief local reporter, a sidebar of quotes from notables, political and nonpolitical, friends and enemies, all conspicuously generous. She was a jowly, mean-eyed woman. Indeed, she must have been an unpleasant sight, bloody in her bath.

After more than an hour, Fletch saw an advertisement for an Alec Guinness matinée double bill, *The Lavender Hill Mob* and *The Man in the White Suit*. It was the right thing to do, on a rainy Saturday afternoon. According to his map, the theater was not far.

While he was dressing in slacks, loafers, open shirt, sweater, and tweed jacket, he heard the door buzzer ring and presumed it was some enterprise of Mrs. Sawyer. She was trying to restock the kitchen shelves.

Coming down the corridor, then, he was surprised to see Inspector Flynn in the hall. His Irish-knit sweater made his chest and shoulders look even more huge, his head even more minute.

"Ah!" Flynn grinned amiably. "I was hoping you'd be at home."

He was carrying a package which was clearly a bottle of something.

"Where's Grover?" Fletch asked, coming into the hall.

He took Flynn's outstretched hand.

"I have some time of my own, you know," Flynn said. "The department lets me off the leash sometimes on the weekend. Had to come nearby — wanted to pick up a Schönberg score the store doesn't have in yet — and happened to consider the City of Boston owes you a bottle of whiskey."

He presented his package with the full joy of giving.

"That's damned nice of you."

It was twelve-year-old Pinch.

"Hope I'm not disturbing anything?"

"Oh, no. I was just going to see a couple of Alec Guinness pictures at the Exeter Street Theater. That's nearby, isn't it?"

"What a darling man! He's Irish, you know. Most English people you think of with talent are." He rubbed his hands together. "I thought it being a rainy Saturday afternoon, you might like to sit with me over a taste . . . ?"

"I thought you never touch the stuff?"

"I never do. But, like work itself, I never mind watching another man partake." He turned to Mrs. Sawyer. "I don't suppose you keep a camomile tea?"

She said, "I think we've got Red Zinger."

"Any herb tea will do. Perhaps you'd bring a glass, some ice and water into the study as well, for Mister Fletcher here."

The thing seemed decided.

Flynn stepped into the den.

Fletch snapped on the lights and began to open the odd-shaped bottle.

Flynn rummaged around inside his sweater, having driven his hand through the neck of it, and pulled two sheets of folded paper from his shirt pocket.

"I was able to secure the complete passenger list for Flight 529 from Rome last Tuesday." He handed it to Fletch, who put down the open bottle. "I wonder if you'd cast your eye along that and see if there are any names you know."

"You think Ruth Fryer's murder might have something to do with something I was doing in Rome, eh?"

"Mister Fletcher, you said yourself, people hate you all over the world. Surely, one might spend an airfare to wreak your undoing."

Most of the names on the list were Italian; most of the rest were Irish — modern-day pilgrims on a flight between Rome and America in search of spiritual consolation or material attainment.

Flynn stood, hands in his pockets, chin back, the amiable grin still on his face.

"Supposing we were friends, Mister Fletcher," he said. "What would I call you? Surely not Irwin Maurice. Are you used to the name Peter, yet? Or are you down to calling yourself 'Pete'?"

"Fletch," Fletch said. "People call me Fletch."

"Fletch, is it? Now that's an impudent enough name. Couldn't an Irish poet dance a Maypole playing with a name like that, though?"

"I recognize no one's name on the list."

Fletch handed it back to him.

"I was afraid you'd say that."

"And I should call you Francis Xavier, right?"

"People call me Frank," said Flynn. "Except my wife, who calls me Frannie. She has a kindlier, softer view of me."

Mrs. Sawyer entered with a tray.

"I had the hot water on, anyway," she said.

On the tray were an ice bucket, an empty glass, a water carafe, a teapot, cream, sugar, a cup, saucer, spoon.

"Ah, that's lovely." Flynn rubbed his hands again. "Tell me, Mrs. Sawyer, when you left here after cleaning up Monday night, was there water in the carafe in the living room next to the whiskey bottle?"

"No, sir. Of course, there wasn't. That had been washed out, dried out, and stoppered."

"I wouldn't think so. Who'd leave water out to go stale, when it's so easily replaceable? Was the whiskey bottle there when you left?"

"What whiskey bottle? Which whiskey bottle?"

"There was more than one?"

"There were a lot of bottles on that table. That was Mister Connors' little bar. There were Scotch bottles, bourbon bottles, gin bottles, sherry and port decanters. Plenty of clean glasses."

"What happened to them?"

"Mister Fletcher put them away. I found them all in a cupboard in the kitchen. I figured he couldn't stand the sight of such things anymore than I can."

Flynn looked his question at Fletch.

"No," Fletch said. "I didn't."

"And," Flynn asked Mrs. Sawyer, "I suppose you've been rummaging around in that cupboard, touching the bottles and thus obliterating any fingerprints which might have been on them?"

"Of course, I've been touching the bottles. I've been shoving them back and forth. They've been in the way of the sugar, salt, and pepper."

" 'The sugar, salt, and pepper.' A most active cupboard. No use," said Flynn. "Thank you, Mrs. Sawyer."

"You want anything else, you just let me know," she said. "I'm so far behind in my own work, I have no hope of finishing, anyway."

"Salt of the earth," said Flynn, pouring out his tea. "Salt of the earth." Across the hall, the kitchen door swung shut. "Of course it's always the salt of the earth that destroys the evidence."

They sat in the red leather chairs, two men in sweaters, one in a jacket as well, one with a cup of tea, the other with a Scotch and water.

Through the light curtains of the long windows was a dark sky. Every few moments a gust of wind from the Boston Gardens splattered a sheet of rain against the windows.

From six storeys below they could hear the hiss of tires going along Beacon Street.

"A dark, gloomy day like this," said Flynn, "reminds me of when I was a boy in Munich, growing up. Dark days, indeed."

"Munich?"

"Let's see. On a day like this, a rainy fall Saturday afternoon, I'd be obliged to be in the gymnasium — the real gymnasium, the sports place — doing push-ups, scrambling up ropes, wrestling until the blood was ready to burst our heads."

437

"You're Irish."

"That I am. Or we'd be out running miles in the wet, around the countryside, looking out for the little red markers, sweat and rain mixed on our faces, the air heavy in our lungs, the ground just turning hard beneath our feet. What a splendid way to bring a boy up. No doubt I owe my current hardy constitution to it."

"To what?"

"I was a member of the Hitler Youth."

"You what?"

"Ah, yes, laddy. A man is many things, in his past."

"The *Jugendfuehrer*?"

"You've got it just right, laddy."

"How is that possible?"

"As you've said yourself: Anything is possible. Is this whiskey all right?"

"Very good," said Fletch.

"Not being a drinking man myself, I'm shy in making choices for others. I'm afraid it was the peculiar shape of the bottle that caught my eye."

"It's fine."

"I don't suppose one should buy the whiskey for the bottle?"

"One might as well."

"For all you drink, you mean. I see you're not a gulper."

"Not in front of you, anyway. How could Francis Xavier Flynn be a member of the *Jugendfuehrer*?"

"Now, haven't I asked myself that same question a thousand times?"

"I've just asked you again."

"The Republic of Ireland, of course, had little to do with the war. Relentlessly neutral, as they say, on the side of the Allies. My Da was the Republic's consul to Munich. Is it getting clearer?"

"No."

"In 1938, when I was about seven years old, it was decided, because of the unusual world circumstances, that I would stay on in Munich with my parents, instead of returning home to school by myself, as would have been normal. I spoke German as well as any boy my age, had had my first years in German schools, looked and dressed German. And, as my Da said, entrusting me with this great responsibility, I had reached the Age of Reason.

"So my Da took up agreein' with the Nazis in public, although he hated their ideas as any decent man would. We remained in Germany throughout the war. I remained in the German school, became a member of the Hitler Youth. The short pants, the neckerchief, the salute, the whole thing. Marched in the rallies. Was the young star at some of the gymnastic shows. People forgot I was Irish altogether."

"Flynn, really. . . ."

"Believe it, if you will. I was a perfect member of *Jugendfuehrer*.

"But, you know, you'd be surprised what a wee boy in short pants and a Hitler Youth shirt and a bicycle and a camera can do. He can roam the countryside, sometimes with his friends. Tours of installations would be set up for us. You'd be amazed how soldiers and officers will show things to a wee boy they wouldn't show their own mothers. Anything I didn't understand, I'd take a picture of; anytime I came across what I suspected was a Nazi dignitary, I'd get his autograph. You'd be surprised at the number of high Nazi officers who'd be moving about in great secrecy but would stop to sign their names on a slip of paper for a small boy. Ah, I was a wonder, I was.

"And I had a couple of friends I corresponded with all during these years, in Dublin. One was Timmy O'Brien, Master Timothy O'Brien, and the other was Master William Cavanaugh. I used to write them excited letters about my life, where I'd been and what I'd seen. I was full of the old Nazi malarkey — a bragging schoolboy, I was, if you read the letters. Sometimes I'd get letters back, doubting my word. I'd send photographs and autographs, and every proof I had.

"Of course, my Da was the ghostwriter of my side of the correspondence. And both Masters O'Brien and Cavanaugh had their actual address in London, at headquarters for British Intelligence."

"My God."

"An unusual way to grow up. My father also was using the consulate to help sneak British and American fliers out of the country, home again. It was all very difficult on my mother."

"Is this true, Flynn?"

"I was fourteen at the end of the war. Munich was rubble. There was no food to be had. I expect you've seen the pictures. It's all true.

"Before the Nazis withdrew, they shot my parents. Each of them. A single bullet between the eyes. In the kitchen of our apartment. I don't think the Nazis had any evidence against them. I think it was one of those arbitrary murders. There were lots of such incidents, those days. I found them after standing an air raid watch."

"What did you do then?"

"Oh, there were weeks and months to go yet. At first, I lived with the family of a friend. They didn't have any food or heat, either. I was on the street, living under things that had already fallen down. Even after the surrender, there were weeks and weeks of wandering around. You see, I was afraid to go up to the British or American soldiers. An odd thing. I was afraid of them. Of course, I was half-crazy.

"One night, sleeping in an alley, I got the toe of a boot in my ribs. Someone spoke to me in the lilt. A soldier was standing over me. You can believe he got an earful of Irish like he'd never had!

"Then it was home for me, back to Dublin. I was put in a Jesuit seminary, if you'd believe it. I guess it was my choice. I'd seen hell, you see.

"I learned another logic, got my health back. By the age of twenty I was tired of truth. Can you understand that?"

"Of course."

"The celibacy had worn thin, too. So I wrote a friend of mine, Master William Cavanaugh, in London. I sent the letter direct this time. Asking for a job. I gather the letter caused a great laugh, among the old boys.

"The rest of my life is a blank."

"I know you didn't work in Chicago."

"I know you know that. You did work in Chicago. What were you doing at the newspaper the other day, if you weren't enquiring about me?"

"You became a spy again."

"Did I say that?"

"But you married, and had kids."

"I did that. An unusual thing for a lad who thought he'd be a priest to do."

"Odd for a spy, too."

"I wouldn't say that, precisely."

"Are you Catholic now?"

"Are the Catholics Catholic now, I'd want to know. My kids enjoy something or other, but what it is, I don't know. They disappear on the Sundays with their guitars and violins and bang around in some church, shaking hands and kissing each other. They tell me it's very exhilarating."

"Your wife is Irish? American? What?"

"She's from Palestine, a Jewish girl. I had a job of work to do out there in that area at one time. Would you believe we had to go to Fada to be married when she was pregnant? Neutral territory."

"Flynn, your being a Boston policeman is a cover. It's your cover."

"Why don't you pour yourself some fresh whiskey, lad?"

"That's why you've said you have no experience as a policeman. You've never actually been a policeman."

"I have to bumble along," said Flynn. "Bumble along."

"You became a Boston policeman just at the time the intelligence agencies were being investigated by Congress and everyone else throughout the world."

"Have I said too much?" Flynn's face was a study in innocence. "It must be the tea talking."

"Can you still speak German?"

"In a way, it's my natural tongue."

"As a member of the Hitler Youth, did you ever actually have to pick up a gun and use it?"

"I did, yes."

"What happened?"

"In my confusion, I almost shot myself. I couldn't shoot at the Allied troops advancing on Munich. I couldn't shoot the lads I had been brought up with."

"What did you do?"

"I cried. I lay down in a ditch of mud and I cried. I wasn't fifteen yet, lad. I doubt I'd do anything different today."

A heavy gust blew a sheet of rain against the windows.

"Now it's your turn, Fletch."

TWENTY-FOUR

Fletch mixed himself a second drink.

He said, "I doubt I have anything to say."

Even through the thick walls of the building they could hear the wind.

"I've done this much on you," said Flynn, from his chair. "Born and raised in Seattle. You have Bachelor's and Master's degrees from Northwestern. You didn't complete your Ph.D."

"The money ran out."

Fletch sat down again in his chair.

"You concentrated in journalism and fine arts. You wrote on the arts for a newspaper in Seattle. Broke a story there regarding the illicit importing of pre-Columbian Canadian objects. You joined the Marine Corps, were sent to the Far East, and won the Bronze Star, which you have never accepted. You then worked as an investigative reporter for the *Chicago Post*. You broke several big stories there, as you did later for a newspaper in California. As an investigative re- porter — not as a critic."

"There's a difference?"

"About eighteen months ago, you disappeared from southern Cal- ifornia."

"It's hard to get full cooperation from a newspaper these days," said Fletch. "One doesn't get to be a newspaper executive without politi- cal savvy — which is utterly destructive to the newspaper."

"You've been married and divorced twice, and there has been a continuous flap in the courts about your refusal to pay alimony. Charges against you, from fraud to contempt — all, I suspect, in- curred in your line of duty — were all dropped. Incidentally, after enquiring about you through several California police agencies, I re- ceived a personal phone call from the district attorney, or assistant district attorney, somewhere out there, a Mister Chambers, I think he said his name was, giving you high marks for past cooperation in one or two criminal cases."

"Alston Chambers. We were in the Marines together."

"Where have you been the last eighteen months?"

"Traveling. I was in Brazil for a while. The British West Indies. London. I've been living in Italy."

"You returned to this country once, to Seattle, for your father's funeral. Did you say you inherited your money from him?"

"No. I didn't say that."

"He was a compulsive gambler," Flynn said.

Fletch said, "I know."

"You didn't answer the question as to where your money came from."

"An old uncle," Fletch lied. "Died while I was in California."

"I see." Flynn accepted the lie as a lie.

"He couldn't leave his money to my father, could he?"

"So there are a good many people in your past who'd like to do you harm," Flynn said. "That's the trouble with crime in a mobile society. People wander all over the face of the earth, dragging their pasts with them. A good investigation these days is almost completely beyond a local police department, no matter how good."

"Your tea must be getting cold," Fletch said.

"Just as good cold as hot." Flynn poured himself some more. "We Europeans aren't as sensitive to temperature as you Americans are."

Fletch said, "You're thinking my past may have caught up with me in some way. Someone has followed me here and purposely put me in this pickle."

"Well, I'd hate to have to fill up the other side of the page that contains the list of your enemies. Isn't it said that a good journalist has no friends?"

"I think you're wrong, Inspector. As Peter Fletcher I was the victim of an accidental frame-up. Someone committed murder in this apartment and arranged things to hang the blame on the next person coming through the front door."

"Take this Rome situation, for example," said Flynn. "Can you explain it to me?"

"What do you mean?"

"Well, now, I not only observe what a man does do, but what he doesn't do, if you take my meaning. You told me the other night that you're here to do research into the life of the painter Edgar Arthur Tharp, Junior, the pinto painter, for a biography."

"That's right."

"Yet, since Wednesday morning, mind you, until last night, you had not been in touch with either the Tharp Family Foundation, or the proper curator at the Boston Museum of Fine Arts."

Fletch said, "I've been busy."

"In fact, you haven't been. Our boyos watching you say you lead the life of a proper Boston old lady. Lunch at Locke-Ober's, then drinks at the Ritz. You spent a couple of hours in the offices of the *Boston Star*. Otherwise, you've been at home here, in someone else's apartment."

"I guess that's true, too."

"Do you sleep a lot, Mister Fletcher?"

"I've been putting together my notes."

"Surely you would have done that in the sunny climate of Italy before you came here."

"Well, I didn't."

"Except for Wednesday, of course. We don't know what you did on Wednesday. That was the day you slipped in one door and out the other at the Ritz-Carlton. Innocent as a honeybee, of course. That was before we knew we were onto a retired investigative reporter who has an innocent instinct for losing his tail. All we know is that you did not go to either the Museum or the Tharp Foundation Wednesday."

"You've got to understand, Inspector. I had been traveling. Jet lag. The shock of the murder. Realizing I was a suspect. I guess I just can't account for myself."

"Indeed?" Before the curtains and the leaden sky, the green eyes could have been cosmic lights. "You're engaged to be married to Angela de Grassi."

"You're good at names."

"I've lived many places. Now who is she?"

"She's a girl. An Italian girl. Daughter of Count de Grassi."

"Count de Grassi?"

"Count Clementi Arbogastes de Grassi."

"Is that the gentleman who died last week?"

"We think so."

" 'We think so!' What sort of an answer is that?"

"He's dead."

"You said you attended a 'sort of funeral.' "

"Did I?"

"You did."

"I guess I did."

"Fletch, why don't you tell me the truth, straight out, instead of making me work like a dentist pulling teeth. It's my day off, you know."

"And you paid for the whiskey yourself?"

"I did. And you might start by telling me why you're really here in Boston."

"Okay. I'm here looking for some paintings."

"Ah! That's the boy. Flynn finally gets to hear the story. Don't stint yourself, now. Be as expansive as you like."

"Andy de Grassi and I are engaged to be married."

"A blissful state. Does the young lady speak English?"

"Perfectly. She went to school in Switzerland and for a while here in this country."

"Very important to have a common language between a husband and wife, when it comes to arguing."

"A collection of paintings was stolen from her father's house, outside Livorno, a couple of years ago. Very valuable paintings."

"How many?"

"Nineteen objects, including one Degas horse."

"A Degas horse, you say? Bless my nose. And what would you say these nineteen objects are worth, taken all in all?"

"Hard to say. Possibly ten million, twelve million."

"Dollars?"

"Yes."

"By god, I knew I shouldn't have taken up the viola. Is it a rich family, the de Grassis?"

"No."

"Of course, you'd say that, being rich yourself."

"Andy was up in the villa with me, at Cagna."

"Enjoying premarital bliss."

"You love a story, don't you, Flynn?"

"Show me an Irishman who doesn't!"

"Your years in the Hitler Youth did you no harm that way."

"Made me hungrier for a good story."

"I get catalogues from around the world," Fletch said. "You know what catalogues are, in the art world? They're published by museums of their collections, or of special shows. Dealers put them out as a means of offering what they have to sell, or, frequently, as it works out, what they have sold."

"I see. I think I knew that."

"One day Andy is going through a particular catalogue issued by a gallery here in Boston, the Horan Gallery."

"I've never heard of it."

"It's on Newbury Street."

"It would be."

"She recognizes one of the de Grassi paintings — a Bellini — sold."

"This is two years after the robbery?"

"About that."

"She shows me, and together we go through earlier Horan catalogues. Two issues back, there's another de Grassi painting — a Perugino — also sold."

"And this is the first you'd heard of the paintings since the robbery?"

"Yes."

"They show up for sale in Boston."

"It might be more accurate to say, they show up sold through Boston."

"I've got you."

"Andy's very excited. We pack our bags, jump into the car, and head for Livorno."

"Where the Count is. Is there a Countess?"

"I'm afraid so. But she's not Andy's mother."

"You're not too keen on her."

"Oh, she's all right, I suppose. Andy's not too high on her."

"Understandable."

"We were going to show the Count the two catalogues from the Horan Gallery."

"You didn't call ahead?"

"We were too excited, I guess. We came off the beach, changed, packed, jumped into the car. I don't think we even showered."

"Must have been an itchy ride."

"It was."

"You said you were 'going to show' the catalogues to the Count?"

"On the way down to Livorno, we hear on the car radio that Count Clementi Arbogastes de Grassi has been kidnapped."

"Kidnapped? My god. That's gotten to be altogether too popular a crime."

"Andy begins screaming. I drive even faster. We stop for cognac. I go like hell again. She stops to phone ahead. It was quite a ride."

"You got there."

"Usual kidnap story. Except that the ransom demand was for something over four million dollars."

"Good heavens."

"And the de Grassis are broke. After the paintings were gone, they had nothing. They had not been insured. The de Grassi *palazzo* outside Livorno is just a weedy, run-down old place. No land. Two old servants who are virtually retired."

"You said she had an apartment in Rome. How did they live?"

"The three of them, the Count, the Countess and Andy, had been living off an annuity which comes to about fifty thousand dollars a year."

"Not precisely broke."

"Not up to paying a four million dollar ransom."

"And you couldn't pay it yourself? I mean, from what your uncle left you."

"No way."

"I mean, this being your prospective father-in-law and all."

"Absolutely not. I couldn't do it. The de Grassi family has been inactive for decades now. They had no credit."

"So?"

"So we published statements, saying such a ransom was impossible. We received more messages, saying, essentially, pay up in full, or we murder him. I talked the ladies into publishing an audited accounting of the family's worth. The annuity, incidentally, is absolutely frozen. There was no way even that capital could be turned to cash. In Italian law, you see, the family is still more important than any individual in the family, including the head of the family."

"The Italians are famous for sticking together," said Flynn, "even at the sacrifice of one of them."

"Just more messages. Pay up or we murder. In five days. A week went by. Silence. Two weeks. Three weeks. We heard nothing more."

"So he was murdered?"

"So the Italian police believe."

"How long ago was this?"

"More than a month now. The authorities advised the de Grassis to put the matter out of their minds. To accept the fact the Count was dead. 'He could be buried anywhere in Italy, or off its shores,' was their exact phrase. We had a memorial service for him last Monday."

"The 'sort of funeral.' "

"The sort of funeral. It seemed real enough."

"So you, an ex-investigative reporter of some repute, decide to take matters into your own hands and come here to Boston to see what you can find out."

"That's about it."

"Have you talked with this man Horan?"

"Yes. Wednesday."

"That's where you were Wednesday."

"Yes."

"Then, of course, you went in one door of the Ritz-Carlton and out the Newbury Street door. The gallery is on Newbury Street!"

"Yes."

"By god, the man is relentlessly innocent. And does the man Horan have the rest of the paintings?"

"A dealer doesn't have paintings, Frank. He deals in them. The trick was to find out the source of the two de Grassi paintings he had already sold. His reputation checks out as clean as a whistle."

"I suppose you went about it in your usual direct manner."

"Difficult being direct with an art dealer, Frank. I asked him to find another painting for me. Another painting on the de Grassi list. A Picasso named 'Vino, Viola, Mademoiselle.' "

"Did he turn it up?"

"After a few days, yesterday, he told me it belongs to a man in Dallas, Texas. He also says he has bought a couple of other paintings from this same man, within the last year or two. I mean, he has sold them for him, through his gallery."

"You have the Texan's name?"

"I have."

"And tell me, Fletch, to whom do these paintings belong, if you do find them?"

"That's the question. Menti's estate can't be settled for years."

" 'Menti'?"

"The Count's. The will can't be read until the body is found. Or enough years to pass for him to be declared dead."

"So, after you find the paintings, you have to find the body."

"No way I can do that. If the Italian police can't."

"No one knows whether the paintings belong to the daughter, or the widow?"

"No. What makes it worse is that until Menti's body is found, they don't even have an income."

"I daresay both ladies have eyes only for you at the moment."

"One would think so."

"Ach! And I thought your biggest problem at the moment was being a murder suspect."

"I suppose that's why I reacted so slowly at first to the idea I was a murder suspect."

"I knew you had a more-than-natural view of the murder, what with your calling the Police Business phone and all. If you had told me you once had been a reporter, I would have understood your professional reaction to a body in the living room a little better." Flynn shook the pot and poured himself a third cup of tea. "It's not every man who bounces blissfully from a kidnapping to a murder to another murder."

"Inured I think is the word."

"A good one, that."

"Do I understand, Inspector Francis Xavier Flynn that you think there might be some connection between what went on in Italy — I mean, Menti's kidnapping and murder — and the murder of Ruth Fryer here?"

"I might."

"You had me check the airline's passenger list."

"There might be a connection, Irwin Maurice Fletcher, but at the moment I don't know what it is."

"There is a connection," said Fletch. "Someone did come from Rome with me."

"And who might that be?"

"The Countess. She flew through New York. She arrived in Boston Tuesday about an hour after I did."

"And did she know you were coming to this apartment?"

"She had my address and telephone number."

"She's hot after the paintings, is she?"

"Boiling after them."

"And how did she know you were looking for them?"

"I guess she read some notes I left Andy — my itinerary, that sort of thing. She knew I had a list of the paintings with me."

"But why would she kill Ruth Fryer?"

"Ruth may have been here in the apartment, naked, waiting to surprise Bart, not knowing he was in Italy. She opened the door to the Countess."

"The irate step-mother-in-law?"

"Well, damned angry and suspicious."

"Naturally, she thinks you're grabbing the paintings for Andy."

"Naturally."

"Are you?"

"Naturally."

"It's no good," said Flynn. "The bodice was torn."

"That could have happened any number of different ways. She could have done it herself, taking it off."

"Ruth Fryer didn't have a key to the apartment."

"But Joan Winslow does."

"The woman next door? She has a key? We forgot to ask that. Terrible thing, being an inspector of police inexperienced at the job. I should have asked. But why would she let Ruth Fryer in?"

"She probably wouldn't — if Joan were sober. She let me in."

"Did she, indeed? How very interesting. And where is the Countess now?"

"She moved in last night."

"Moved in here?"

"Yes. The Ritz-Carlton was too expensive."

"Ah! The Countess is the dish you had drinks with at the Ritz the other night. Ah, yes. The boyos were rather taken with her. And they said you didn't even pay the check!"

"I didn't."

"The Countess is rather cramping your style?"

"She'd like to."

"Well, well, now." Flynn gazed at the bottom of his empty teacup. "Haven't we learned a lot about each other?"

Fletch said nothing. His second drink was gone.

Flynn said, "I guess I should be shovin' home to my family."

The rain was still audible.

In the hall, Fletch asked, "How's the chubby City Councilperson's murder coming?"

"It's not coming at all. Not at all. You'd think with such a murder, someone would step forward and take the credit, wouldn't you?"

"Thanks for the Scotch, Inspector."

Fletch pushed the elevator button.

Then he said, "Get me off the hook soon, will you, Frank?"

"I know. You want to go to Texas, trailing your entourage of women."

He went through the clunky elevator doors.

Descending the shaft, he said, his voice as quiet as always, "You're the best suspect I've got yet, Fletcher, no matter how you dance on the head of a pin. You might save me the bother by confessin'."

TWENTY-FIVE

It was just past five o'clock in the afternoon, and Fletch was sleepy. The drinks with Flynn had unwound him.

He said good night to Mrs. Sawyer, had a bowl of her stew, and, despite the hour, crawled into bed.

It was midnight, Rome time.

"Flesh, darling."

Someone was nibbling his ear.

A long, cool body pressed against his. A nipple grazed his forearm.

It was a fuller body than Angela's. Much.

A leg stroked the back of his own legs. Up and down.

"Sylvia!"

Even in the dark room, there was no mistaking the tousled hair of his step-mother-in-law-to-be against the pillow.

"Jesus Christ, Sylvia!"

"It's too late, darling."

She slipped her right hip under his.

"You read in the Bible, 'They knew each other in his sleep?' "

"This is incest!"

"So was that, darling."

She was fully under him, her hips moving.

Her breasts were back-breaking.

"God!"

It was too late.

There was only one thing he could do to prevent either one part of his body, or another, from breaking.

"It was not incest, darling."

Flat on his back, finally, Fletch read the luminous dial of his wristwatch. It was only eight o'clock at night.

"Did you have something to eat?" he asked.

"Of course," she said. "You expect me to put up with your tricks forever?"

"You've got some pretty good tricks of your own, Countess de Gassey."

"Where did you go last night? One, two hours I wait for my dinner."

"I went out."

"I know that. Son of a bitch." She sat up. "That's what you do! You tell me some crazy story and then you leave me with nothing! You're no grand chef! You're son of a bitch! You'll do the same thing with the paintings — tell me lies, lies! Leave me with nothing!"

He put his hand on her back.

"I left the front door unlocked for you. Did you get a nice man to let you in downstairs?"

"I had to wait, and wait. You didn't answer the buzzer."

"I was asleep."

Sitting up in the bed, in the dark, the Countess de Grassi began to cry.

"Oh, Flesh! You will help me."

"I will?"

"You have to help me!"

"I do?"

"Menti's dead. I'm an early widow. With nothing. Nothing!"

"Yeah."

"I have nothing, Flesh."

"Actually, you have a few things going for you."

"Angela's young, and she's pretty. Clever. She has her whole life ahead of her. Me? I have nothing."

"She's a de Grassi, Sylvia."

"Me? I'm the Countess de Grassi!"

"I've heard."

"I married Menti."

"And his paintings."

"They are my paintings. Menti would want me to have them. I know this. Many times he spoke of 'our paintings.' "

"Sylvia, will you listen? Whose paintings they are is not for me to say. Either Menti mentioned them in his will, or he didn't. If he did mention them, they go to you, Andy, both of you, neither of you — whatever he directed in his will. If he didn't mention them, then it is for the Italian courts to decide — if we ever recover the paintings, that is."

She crawled inside his arm, snuggled next to him.

Fletch remembered seeing, on the beach at Cagna, her toes, with the nails polished.

She said, "If the paintings are in this country, then, how do you say, possession is the first law of nature."

"Self-preservation is the first law of nature, Sylvia — an instinct you have fully developed."

"I mean, possession."

"I know what you mean."

"Flesh, tell me the truth. You know where the paintings are."

"Sylvia, I am in Boston working on a biography of Edgar Arthur Tharp, Junior."

She slapped him lightly on the chest.

"You lie. All the time you lie to me."

"I am."

"You writing on such a big book, then where the typewriter? Where the papers? I looked all over the apartment last night. Nobody's writing a book here."

"I haven't started yet. I've had distractions."

" 'Distractions!' You find the paintings." He could feel breath from each nostril going against his side. "Where are the paintings?"

He was awake. And he was beginning to want it.

He said nothing.

She placed the side of her knee over his crotch and moved it.

She said, "Where are the paintings? Eh, Flesh?"

"You're a hell of a negotiator, Sylvia."

"You will help me, Flesh. Won't you?"

"You help me first."

"America!" Fletch shouted.

It was at the worst possible moment that the telephone rang.

It was a cable. From Andy. Angela de Grassi.

"ARRIVING BOSTON SUNDAY SIX-THIRTY P.M. TWA FLIGHT 540. IS SYLVIA WITH YOU. MUCH LOVE. — ANDY."

Fletch said, "Oh, shit."

She never could keep herself to ten words or less.

He said, "Oh, Christ."

He said, "What, in hell, am I doing?"

Sylvia said, "Come on, Flesh."

He said, "All right."

It was a somewhat better moment the next time the telephone rang.

Fletch said, "Hello?"

"Are you drunk?"

It was Jack Saunders. Fletch could hear the city room clatter behind him.

"No."

"Were you asleep?"

"No."

"What are you doing?"

"None of your fucking business."

"I've got it. Are you about through?"

"Buzz off, will you, Jack?"

"Wait a minute, Fletch. I'm stuck."

"So am I."

"Really stuck. Will you listen a minute?"

"No."

"Fires are breaking out all over Charlestown. A torch is at work. I haven't got the rewrite man I need."

"So?"

"One is drunk and ready for the tank. The other one is pregnant and just left for the hospital to have a baby. Nothing I can do about it. I can't find the day guy. His wife says he's at a ballgame somewhere. I'm three short on the desk, two with vacations and one with the flu. The guy I've got on rewrite now is a kid; he's not good enough for a big story like this."

"Sounds like very poor organization, Jack."

"Jeez, who'd think all hell would break loose on an October Saturday night?"

"I would."

"Can you come in?"

"For rewrite?"

"Yeah."

"You're crazy."

"I can't handle it myself, Fletch. I've got to remake the whole paper."

"What time is it?"

"Ten minutes to nine."

"What time do you go to bed?"

"We'll front-page big cuts for the first edition which goes at ten-twenty."

"Jack, I'm a murder suspect."

"Ralph Locke isn't."

"I don't know the city."

"You know how to put words together."

"I'm rusty."

"Please, Fletch? Old times' sake? I can't talk much longer."

Fletch looked through the dark at Sylvia, now on his side of the bed.

"I'll be right there. Bastard."

T W E N T Y - S I X

"Frank?"

"Who do you want?"

The young voice was sleepy.

It was two-twenty-five Sunday morning.

"Inspector Flynn."

The telephone receiver clattered against wood.

At a distance from the phone, the voice said, "Da'?"

After a long moment, Flynn answered.

"Now who might this be?"

"I.M. Fletcher."

"God bless my nose. Where are you, lad? Would you be seizing upon this odd hour of the night to confess?"

"I'm at the *Star*, Frank."

"Now what would you be doing there? Have you rejoined the enemy?"

"Charlestown is on fire. Someone is torching it."

"I see."

"An old friend from the *Chicago Post* asked me to come in and help out."

"You have an old friend in Boston?"

"I guess so."

"Where was he the Tuesday last? Did you ask?"

"I know he has Monday and Tuesday nights off."

"No matter how much you talk to a man, ply him with drink, there's always more to learn."

"Frank, could I make this call quick?"

"You didn't have to make it at all."

"I'm sorry to wake you up."

"It's all right, lad. I was just filling in my time by sleeping, anyway."

"I can't get your Boston Police spokesman to listen to me."

"And who's speaking for us tonight?"

"A Captain Holman."

"Ach, he's a police spokesman, all right. That's precisely what he is."

455

"He calls every fifteen minutes with new facts, but I can't get him to listen."

"That's what a spokesman is: a person with two mouths and one ear, a freak of nature. What would you like to say to him?"

"I've got some facts, too. We've got more reporters in the field than you have bulls."

" 'We' now, is it? An inveterate journalist, I do believe is Mister I. M. Fletcher."

"Listen, Frank. It's very simple. Eleven fires have been set since seven o'clock. Mostly tenements, a few warehouses, one church. Nothing consistent."

"All empty?"

"Yes."

"Then that's consistent."

"Right. At the third, fifth, seventh, eighth, and ninth fires, empty, two-gallon containers of Astro gasoline have been found. You know, the kind of containers a gas station sells you when you're out of gas on the road somewhere?"

"Yes."

"I've sent a reporter back to the other fires to see if he can spot Astro containers there, too."

"Haven't the Fire Department's arson boys caught on, yet?"

"No. They're doing the usual. Watching the spectators. They won't listen to the reporters who keep finding these containers. They're just taking pictures."

"I know their method. They'll have a meeting in the morning, to compare notes. It gives them something to do, with their coffee."

"The arsonist should be pinned tonight."

"I agree," said Flynn. "All that smoke is air polluting."

"All these fires are taking place around Farber Hill. All sides of it, more or less equally. First a fire starts on the north side, then one on the south side, then one on the northwest side."

"That could cause a terrific traffic jam of city equipment," Flynn said. "Collisions."

"I looked at a district map. In the geographic dead center of the district, at the corner of Breed and Acorn streets, is a gas station."

"And you're going to tell me. . .?"

"The map doesn't say which company runs the station, so I asked a reporter to drive over and look."

"Did he collide with anything?"

"It's an Astro station, Frank."

"So whom are we looking for?"

"A young gas station attendant, who works at the Astro station at the corner of Breed and Acorn streets, and who got off duty at six o'clock."

"Why young?"

"He's moving awfully fast, Frank. Over fences. In second-story windows."

"So he must be agile, and therefore he is probably young. Quick in the knee, as it were."

"And he has access to a lot of Astro gasoline containers."

"All right, Fletch." Flynn's voice lowered. "I'll pull on my pants and wander over to Charlestown. See if I can help out. I have a natural dislike of seeing a city on fire, you know?"

"I know."

"Tell me, Fletcher. After we catch this arsonist boyo, will we also discover he's the murderer of Ruth Fryer?"

"Good night, Frank. If you get the guy, will you call the *Star*?"

"I'll see Captain Holman does."

"Ask him to talk to Jack Saunders."

"I'll do that. I'm always very cooperative with the press, you know."

TWENTY-SEVEN

Driving through the light, Sunday mid-morning traffic in the Ghia, very considerate of the two policemen following him, Fletch easily found 58 Fenton Street in Brookline.

He had had four hours' sleep in one of his own guest rooms.

He had not renewed contact with the guest asleep in his own bed.

Lucy Connors opened the door of Apartment 42 to him.

Purposely, he supposed, she was dressed in a full peasant skirt and a light blouse with low neck and puffy sleeves. She wore no makeup, nor jewelry.

"Martin Head?"

"Yeah," Fletch said. *"Très Magazine."*

Lucy's eyes went from one of his empty hands to the other, possibly checking for a camera or a tape recorder.

"Good of you to see me," he said. "Especially on a Sunday morning."

"I wouldn't dare have you come any other time. It might improve my reputation."

The apartment was the usual one or two bedroom arrangement. A small dining table was in a corner of the living room. Along the wall next to it was a hi-fi rig, with album-filled shelves.

There was a cheap, old divan along the opposite wall, an undersized braided rug in front of it, a saggy upholstered chair to one side.

A drapeless window ran along the fourth wall, letting in a harsh light.

The only wall decoration in the room was a Renoir print over the divan.

"Marsha?" Lucy said.

That was the introduction.

Marsha Hauptmann was stretched out like a board, her slim haunches in the far corner of the divan, the heels of her moccasin topsiders on the floor in front of her, hands in the pockets of her blue jeans. She wore a heavy, blue naval shirt, opened at the throat, sleeves rolled above the elbows.

Her hair was a perfect black, shining pageboy, her skin as translucent as a well-scrubbed child's.

She did not move her head, nor her body, as Fletch entered.

Her dark eyes moved into his, seeing nothing else, expressing more curiosity and challenge than hostility.

Fletch said, "Marsha."

"Would you like some coffee, Martin?"

Clearly, Lucy was nervous. Her new way of life was about to be questioned by a detached professional.

"Not unless you're having some."

"We aren't," said Lucy.

She sat on the divan, a full seat away from Marsha.

Fletch sat in the chair.

"I'm glad you're doing this, Lucy," he said. "People need to understand what you've been through."

"No one has understood," she said. "Not my family, friends. Not Bart. I rather thought Bart might understand, or I wouldn't have been so frank with him. He took it as some kind of a personal insult."

She gave Marsha's forearm a tug, pulling her hand out of her pocket. She held Marsha's hand. "Really, Martin, it's a matter of complete indifference to me as to who understands and who doesn't."

"Of course." He coughed quickly. "You've resolved your problems. Others haven't."

Marsha's eyes warmed towards him.

"I'm afraid most people think this is the problem," Lucy said. "I mean, Marsha and I living together. Like it's acne or the flu or something that will go away." She gave Marsha's hand a self-conscious squeeze. "I guess I went through that phase, too. But why are you more interested in me than in Marsha?"

"I'm interested in Marsha, too," said Fletch. "But you're a little older. You were married. I would guess you gave up quite a lot, in the way of material things, to live with Marsha. I would think you have had to make the bigger adjustments."

"I guess so. Marsha's lucky. She's always been a little dyke." She smiled fondly at Marsha. "Straight through school. All those shower rooms after field hockey, eh, Marsha?" To Fletch, she said, "Marsha went to boarding school, a much better education than I had. Self-discovery. She started sleeping with girls when she was about twelve."

Marsha remained silent, a lanky love object at the end of the divan.

"I had to go through the whole thing," Lucy said. "Boy, was I thick."

"Tell me about it." Fletch took notebook and pen from his pocket. "Tell me about 'the whole thing.'"

"As 'Ms. C?'"

"Absolutely."

"And I get to see the manuscript before you hand it in?"

"Absolutely."

"Okay." She exhaled. "Shit." Still holding onto her hand, she glanced at Marsha. "You know. A nice girl. Brought up. Goals set for me. A role set for me. We lived in Westwood, a lawn in front, a lawn in back, a two-car garage. Dad owned an automobile agency. My mother was neurotic, a pill freak. Still is. I hated Jack, my older brother. He was plain, simply cruel. Big hockey player. I mean, when Mother was freaked out, he'd stick pins in the hamster. He'd stick pins in anything. I barely survived him. Bastard."

Marsha's eyes rolled to study Lucy's face worriedly.

"I was considered good-looking," Lucy said hesitantly. "You know what that means in an American public high school. First one in a training bra, first one to wear falsies, first one to bleach my hair — at thirteen. First one to beat the baby fat off my ass. Goal-oriented. Cheerleader. Little skirts and pompoms. First one to get laid. Very goal-oriented. I didn't enjoy it. Getting laid, I mean. But it was a goal. The first guy to lay me, the fullback, must have weighed two hundred and twenty pounds. A fat, gray belly. It was not fun. Damned near broke me in two.

"I went to junior college. Went with a guy from Babson who played the violin and was full of the secret international commodity cartel he was going to run. A real drip.

"At a party I met Bart. I was getting near graduation. Bart was a goal. He looked normal, acted normal. Dartmouth College, Harvard Law. Going a little bald. Older than I was by twelve years. In a law firm. Very rich. I played innocent and let him thrill me. I was very dishonest, but people are, sometimes, in attaining their goals."

Fletch asked, "Did you have any sexual feeling for him at all?"

"How did I know? I didn't know what sexual feeling was. Look, I had been told boys turn girls on and girls turn boys on and that was it. There was nothing else. Whatever happened between me and a boy I figured I was turned on."

"But you weren't."

"No way."

"Never?"

Firmly, she said, "Never. I hear some are, but not me — ever. It was pure role-playing. I played the game with myself, 'someday my crisis will come.' I wasn't even excited. Only I didn't even know it."

"Come on, Lucy," Fletch said. "You knew such a thing as lesbianism existed."

"No, I didn't. It never entered my head. I mean, I knew such a thing existed. Creatures like Marsha. Way over there, somewhere. Far out. They were different. Really weird. I mean, I didn't relate to them at all. I was very successful at suppressing my own, real sexual nature. Totally successful."

"Okay," Fletch said.

"Soon after we were married, Bart started asking me about frigidity. Conversationally, you know? What did I know about it? He began having these long talks with the woman in the next apartment, and then coming to bed stinko. When he was on trips out of town, I picked up a guy or two. For Bart's sake. Nothing ever happened. I mean, I never got turned on by anybody. So when he suggested a psychiatrist, I went along with it. He was beginning to make me think something was wrong.

"The psychiatrist was a great guy. He got me toward the truth very quickly. I turned him off, ran away from him. Ran away from the truth. It was just too shocking. You know, I was one of those creatures 'over there.' I like girls. I tried to bullshit the psychiatrist. He was a slob, but by then I was too close to the truth. I couldn't bullshit myself. I was listening to myself. This went on a long, long time. A terribly long time.

"I was bitchy, irascible, tough, mean, violent. Bart and I had slugging matches. I hit him. I threw things at him. I mean, I hit him with things, objects, anything at hand.

"You did?"

"Yes."

"I see."

"He had so many goddamned welts on his face, so often, he had to tell the people at the office he was doing boxing as a sport. He might as well have been living with a bad-tempered, second-string welterweight. I was really violent."

"Are you still?"

"No."

Marsha looked at her from beneath half-drawn lids.

"Well, I mean," Lucy said. "Sometimes we play. You know?"

"Yeah," said Fletch.

"I felt I was in some kind of a box, and had to fight my way out. Can you understand that, Martin?"

"Sure."

"It's a wonder I didn't belt a few shrinks along the way. I took everything out on poor old Bart."

"So how did you meet Marsha?" Fletch asked.

"One day I went into a boutique, and saw something I liked — Marsha. She waited on me. I bought a skirt. Next day I went back and bought a pair of pants. The third day I went in and started to buy a bikini. I called her into the dressing room to ask her how she thought it fitted me. I was feeling something. The tingle. I guess I was opened up enough then to the idea of girls. I had been forced to become conscious of my real desires. In the dressing room, Marsha put the palm of her hand against my hip, looked me in the eyes, and said, 'Who are you bullshitting?' " Lucy picked up Marsha's hand, and looked at it, wonderingly. "Her first touching me was the most satisfactory feeling I'd ever had."

They looked at each other, apparently recalling the moment.

Fletch looked at his notebook.

Finally, Lucy said, "Are you straight, Martin?"

"You mean, do I like girls?"

"Yes."

"Yes."

"I guess that's how you can understand."

Fletch chuckled. "I guess so."

"I mean, you don't seem offended."

"I'm not. Why should I be?"

"Would you be if I were your sister?"

"I don't think so."

"Some are."

"Everybody should be what he or she is."

Lucy said, "Bart even suggested religion for me. Jesus."

"How did you handle the marital situation?" Fletch asked.

"First, I went through a long period thinking I could have it both ways. Marsha and I were making it together. Sometimes here. Sometimes at my place. It was beautiful. Too good. It was the real thing. It wasn't a passing phase on my part. It was me. We were getting careless. I mean, we were even doing it at my apartment while a servant was there. Oh, my god. I realized unconsciously I wanted Bart to find out. He was too thick. I finally had to tell him."

Fletch asked, "How did he take it?"

"I said, like a personal insult. He thought he had enough masculinity for both of us. He thought he could snap me out of it, if I just gave myself to him fully. He suggested more psychiatrists. He suggested religion. He even suggested we go into a marriage-of-convenience thing, both of us making love to girls on the side. That was about the last straw. By then Marsha had come to mean just too much to me. As a person, you know?"

Again they exchanged looks. Marsha's hand was squeezed.

"Bart set up the boutique for us. Financially. I mean, the one we now run. You can forget the name of it. We don't need the publicity."

"Does he still own it?"

"He's still financing it. We're not completely divorced yet."

"You say he was hurt?"

"I guess so. I guess this revelation about me caused him to question his own masculinity. I mean, he loved me, he married me, and I wasn't there at all."

"But at the same time, apparently he hadn't found your sexual relations satisfactory."

"He had put up with them. He hadn't thrown me out. It might have been better if he had. Instead, he had tried to help."

"Do you ever see each other?"

"We bump into each other. Boston's a small city. Everybody's always embarrassed. These days, you know, everybody knows everybody else's sexual business."

"Hey, Marsha?" Fletch said. "What do you think?"

Lucy looked at her expectantly.

Bright, dark eyes in Fletch's, Marsha shook her head slightly, and said nothing.

Fletch closed his notebook and put it in his pocket.

"Again, sorry about coming on a Sunday morning," he said. "I tried several times to phone you Tuesday night. Weren't you here?"

"Tuesday?" Lucy looked puzzled at Marsha. "Oh, Tuesday. I was in Chicago, buying for the boutique. I was supposed to fly back Tuesday afternoon, but the plane was late. I was here by nine o'clock. You were here, weren't you, Marsha?"

She said, "Yeah."

"I have to fly out to Chicago sometime soon," Fletch said. "What did you fly, Pan American?"

"TWA," Lucy said.

"That's better, uh?"

"We were supposed to arrive at five, but it was seven-thirty before we got to Boston. Fog."

"Well, Lucy, I thank you very much. Will you keep the name of Connors?"

"I don't think so. I guess I'll use my maiden name. Hyslop. Get out of Bart's hair. What's left of it."

Looking straight at Fletch, Marsha said, "You didn't call here Tuesday night."

"I tried." Fletch stood up and put his pen in his inside jacket pocket. "Phone must have been out of order."

Marsha's eyes followed him as he went toward the door.

Lucy followed him.

Fletch said, "What's this about a murder in your husband's apartment?"

"That's irrelevant," said Lucy.

"I know. I'm just curious. I mean, murders are interesting."

"Not for the story?"

"Of course not. What's it got to do with you?"

"Some girl was murdered in our old apartment. After Bart left for Italy. He rented the apartment to some schnook who says he found the body."

463

"You mean, your husband killed her?"

"Bart? You're kidding. There's not an ounce of violence in him. Believe me, I should know. If he were going to kill anybody, he would have killed me."

"Have the police questioned you?"

"Why should they?"

From across the room, the harsh light from the window streaking between them, Marsha's eyes were locked on Fletch's face.

"You must still have a key to the apartment," he said.

"I suppose I do," she said. "Somewhere."

"Interesting," said Fletch.

"The police probably don't know where to find me," Lucy said. "Everything here is under Marsha's name. You wouldn't have known where to find me, if Bart hadn't given you the number."

"That's right."

"I'm still surprised he did. Bart must be coming to the idea that this situation happens to other people, too."

Fletch said, "Your husband's a surprising fellow."

"How did you happen to meet him?"

"He's doing some trust work for my editor. We all happened to be together in Montreal," Fletch said, "Tuesday night."

Marsha still had not moved. Her eyes, clear and unwavering, remained on Fletch's face. A small amount of fear had entered those eyes.

"When will we see your story?" Lucy asked.

"Oh, a few weeks." Fletch opened the door. "I'll send it to you. If it works out."

TWENTY-EIGHT

The Countess was not at the apartment when Fletch returned.

She had left a note for him saying she had gone to mass.

When the downstairs door's buzzer rang, Fletch shouted into the mouthpiece, "Who is it?"

"Robinson."

It was certainly not the Countess's voice.

"Who?"

"Clay Robinson. Let me in."

Fletch had never heard of Clay Robinson.

He let him in.

Fletch stood in the opened front door, listening to the elevator.

A curly-haired man in his mid-twenties got off the elevator. His face was puffy, his eyes red-rimmed and bloodshot, the pupils glazed. His lips were cracked.

As soon as he let himself through the elevator doors, he returned his hands to the pockets of his raincoat.

"Fletcher?"

"Yeah?"

The man's words slurred.

"I was engaged to marry Ruth Fryer."

Fletch took a step forward with his left foot and swung with his right hand. His fist landed hard against Robinson's jaw.

Going down, Robinson couldn't get his hands out of his pockets.

He crashed against the small table under the mirror across from the elevator, rolled off it, and fell onto the floor, a flurry of raincoat.

Fletch put his right knee at the base of Robinson's rib cage and knelt hard on it.

In the right-hand pocket of the raincoat, inside Robinson's hand, Fletch felt the pistol. Robinson's eyes rolled toward his brows.

Fletch grabbed the gun from the pocket and stood up. It was a .22 caliber target pistol.

Robinson sat on the rug, one arm straight to the floor, a knee up, his other hand gently touching his jaw.

"Come in," Fletch said.

He went into his apartment and put the gun in a drawer of the desk in the den.

When he returned to the apartment's foyer, Robinson was standing in the door, dazed, right hand in coat pocket, left hand rubbing his jaw.

"Come in," Fletch said.

He closed the door behind Robinson.

"I'll put some coffee on. You take a shower."

He walked Robinson down the corridor to the master bedroom's bathroom. Sylvia's things were everywhere.

"Hot, then cold."

Fletch left him in the bathroom.

He heard the shower running while he crossed the hall to the den with a coffee tray.

After a while Robinson appeared in the door of the den, hair wet, tie hanging from his opened collar, raincoat over his arm.

His eyes were less glazed.

"Have some coffee," Fletch said.

Robinson dropped his coat on a side chair, and sat in a red leather chair.

"You've had a rough time." Fletch handed him a cup of steaming, black coffee. "I'm sorry."

Robinson, saucer held at chest level, sipped his coffee, blinking slowly.

Fletch said, "I didn't kill Ruth Fryer. Nothing says you have to believe me, or even can believe me. I found her body. She was a beautiful girl. And she looked like a hell of a nice person. I didn't kill her."

Robinson said, "Shit."

"Shooting me would have been a real mistake," Fletch said. "But I did the impulse."

In his chair, Robinson choked. Then, breath out of control, he put his coffee on the side table, his face forward in his hands, and sobbed.

Fletch went into the living room and studied the Paul Klee.

The noise from the den was a full-chested, strangulated, broken-hearted sobbing. It stopped. Then it started again.

When the pauses became more frequent, and longer, Fletch went back to the bathroom and soaked a hand towel in cold water. He wrung it out.

Going back into the den, he tossed the wet towel at Robinson.

"Anything I can do for you?"

Robinson rubbed his face in the towel, then pushed it back over his hair.

He sat, head over his knees, towel pressed against his forehead.

"Were you at the funeral?" Fletch asked.

"Yes. Yesterday. In Florida."

"How are her parents?"

"There's only her father."

Fletch said, "I'm sorry for him. I'm sorry for you."

Clay Robinson sat back in a slouch.

"I hadn't broken down before this. I guess I've been holding myself pretty tight." He grinned. "The thought of killing you got me through it."

"Do you want some food?"

"No."

"And you don't want anything to drink."

"No."

"Where are you from?"

"Washington. I work for the Justice Department."

"Oh?"

"A clerk. A clerk with a college education."

"How did you meet Ruth Fryer?"

"On an airplane. I was flying some papers in from Los Angeles. We spent the night together."

"You picked her up."

"We met," said Clay Robinson. "Fell in love. We were getting married New Year's."

"I don't remember her wearing an engagement ring."

"I hadn't bought one yet. Have you ever lived on clerk's pay?"

"Yes."

"I came up Tuesday," Clay said.

"To Boston?"

"Yes. I was going to surprise her. I knew she had ground duty all this week. I took some time off. By the time I got to the hotel, she had gone."

"Do you know with whom?"

"No. Her roommate just said Ruth's uniform was there, so she must have changed and gone out. I didn't know about it, about the murder, until next morning when I went to the airport to find her."

"What did you do?"

"I don't know. I don't remember. It was the next morning I called her father and began to make arrangements to fly the body down. The police had already done an autopsy. Arrogant bastards."

"Where did you get the gun?"

"Pawn shop in the South End. Paid a hundred dollars for it."

"This morning?"

"Last night."

"Where did you stay last night?"

"Mostly in a bar. I got pretty drunk. I fell into some hotel at two, three this morning."

"Want some more coffee?"

"I don't know what I want."

"There's an unused guest room in there," Fletch said. "If you want to hit the bed, it's all right with me."

"No." A little more clear-eyed, Robinson looked at Fletch wonderingly. "I was going to kill you."

"Yeah."

"You moved mighty fast."

Fletch said, "What are you going to do now?"

"I'm going to find Ruthie's murderer."

"Good for you."

"What do you know about it?" Robinson asked. "I mean, about the murder."

"It's being handled by Inspector Francis Xavier Flynn of the Boston Police Department."

"Who does he think killed Ruthie?"

"Me."

"Who do you think killed Ruthie?"

"I have a couple of ideas."

"Are you going to tell me?"

"No."

Robinson said, "You have the gun."

"Yeah," Fletch said, "but you might have another hundred dollars."

Robinson's white face moved as slowly as changes in the moon.

"Why don't you go home?" Fletch said. "Go downstairs, get into a taxi, go to the airport, take the next plane to Washington, taxi to your apartment, have something warm to eat, go to bed, and tomorrow morning go to work."

Robinson said, "Sounds nice."

"Thought it would if someone laid it out for you."

Robinson said, "All right."

He stood up stiffly and reached for his raincoat.

"What am I supposed to say to you?"

Fletch said, "Good-bye?"

"I guess if I ever find out you are the murderer, I will kill you."

"Okay."

"Even if they put you in jail for twenty, thirty years, however long, when they release you, I will kill you."

"It's a deal."

At the door, Robinson said, "Good-bye."

Fletch said, "Come again. When you're feeling better."

Before leaving the apartment himself, an hour or two later, Fletch wrote a note to the Countess saying he had gone to the airport to pick up Andy.

TWENTY-NINE

It was a dark brown, wooden Victorian house, three storeys under a slate roof, on the harborside, in Winthrop. It had a small front yard and cement steps leading up to a deep porch.

Looking between the houses, as he walked from where he had parked his car, Fletch saw their shallow backyards ended at a concrete seawall. Beyond was the cold, slate-gray, dirty water of Boston Harbor. The airport was a mile or two across the water.

On the porch, Fletch looked through the front window, into the living room.

At the back of the room, four music stands were set up in a row. Behind them, to their right, was a baby grand piano, its lid piled with stacks of sheet music. A cello stood against the piano. The divan and chairs, coffee table, and carpet seemed incidental in the large, wainscoted room.

Two teenage boys who looked just alike, not only in their blue jeans and cotton shirts, but in their slim builds and light coloring, were setting sheet music on the stands.

A jet, taking off from the airport across the harbor, screamed overhead.

The storm door to Fletch's right opened.

"Mister Fletcher?"

He had not rung the bell.

Flynn's small face, at his great height, peered around the corner at him.

"Hi," Fletch said, backing away from the window he had been peering through. "How are you?"

"I'm fine," Flynn said. "Your police escort phoned me to report you were approaching my house. They fear you threaten our well-being."

"I do," said Fletch, holding out a five-pound box. "I brought your family some chocolate."

"How grand of you." Flynn held the spring door open with his huge left arm and took the candy with his right hand. "Bribery, is it?"

"It occurred to me it was the City of Boston which owed me a bottle of whiskey — not the Flynn family."

Flynn said, "Come in, Fletch."

The vestibule was dark and scattered with a half-dozen pairs of rubbers. A baby carriage was parked at an odd angle.

Flynn led him into the living room.

Besides the boys in the room, one of whom now had a violin in his hands, there was a girl of about twelve, with full, curly blond hair and huge, blue saucer eyes. The color of her short, fluffy dress matched her eyes. The boys were about fifteen.

"Munchkin," Flynn said. "This is Mister Fletcher, the murderer." Flynn pointed off his children, "Randy, Todd, Jenny."

Randy, bow and violin in one hand, extended his right. "How do you do, sir?"

As did his twin, Todd.

"Ach," said Flynn. "My family gets to meet all sorts."

A boy about nine years old entered. His hair was straight brown. Mostly he was glasses and freckles.

"This is Winny," said Flynn.

Fletch shook hands with him.

"No Francis Xavier Flynn?"

"One's enough," said Flynn. "No bloody Irwin Maurice, either."

Elizabeth Flynn entered through a door behind the piano.

Her light brown, straight hair fell to her shoulders. Her body, under her skirt and cardigan, was full and firm. Her unquestioning light blue eyes were deep-set over magnificent cheekbones. They were warm and humorous and loving.

"This is Fletch, Elsbeth. The murderer. I mentioned him."

"How do you do?" She held his hand over the music stand. "You'd like some tea, I think."

"I would."

"He brought me some candy." Flynn handed her the box. "Better give him some tea."

"How nice." She looked at the box in her hands. "Perhaps for after supper?"

"We were about to have our musicale," Flynn said. To the children, he said, "What is it today?"

"Eighteen — One." Todd's Adam's apple seemed too large for his sinewy neck, especially when he spoke. "F major."

"Beethoven? We're up to that, are we?"

Jenny said, "I am."

"Sorry to wake you all up last night," Fletch said.

Elizabeth had come in the other door with tea things.

"Come over and have a cuppa," Flynn said.

While Flynn and Fletch sat over their tea, Elizabeth at the piano helped the children tune their instruments. Todd had picked up a viola. Jenny had a less than full-sized violin.

Fletch spoke over the scrapings and plunks.

"Did you catch him?"

"Who?" Flynn poured a cup for Elizabeth as well.

"The arsonist."

"Oh, yes," said Flynn.

"Was it the gas station attendant?"

"It was a forty-three-year-old baker."

"Not the gas station attendant?"

"No."

"Oh."

"Are you crushed?"

"Why was he burning down Charlestown?"

Flynn shrugged. "Jesus told him to. Or so he said."

"But where did he get all the Astro gasoline containers?"

"He'd been saving up."

Elizabeth was tuning his cello.

"Now, let's see what this is all about."

Leaving his cup drained behind him, Flynn sat behind his music stand.

"Elsbeth usually joins us at the piano," he explained to Fletch, "but Beethoven didn't consider her today."

She came over to the divan and took her tea.

The children were behind their music stands.

The youngest, Winny, was the page-turner.

"Remember to turn me first," his father said. "I've got a memory like a bear's mouth."

They all straightened their backs, like flowers rising on their stems in the morning sun.

"*Con brio!*" their father shouted, in a voice of pleasant threat.

They were off, bows indicating two dimensions in their coming and going, eyes intent upon the sheet music, Randy's violin gracefully indicating, belatedly, a few notes Jenny skipped, her blue eyes getting more huge as they traveled down the page, a few times losing her place altogether (when she had nothing to play, she sighed, then her tongue would sneak out and touch the tip of her nose), Winny back and forth behind them like a waiter, following his father's score, turning his page first, then Jenny's on perfect time (frequently a help to her finding her place and a cause of renewed, more confident playing), then Todd's, then Randy's, every five or six minutes a jet screeching by just five hundred meters above the house, deafening the players (drowned out, they sawed away apparently soundlessly), making them adjust their paces to each other once they could hear each other again, ever and always Flynn's cello playing along, leading from behind (*"Molto! Molto!"* he shouted over the shrieking of a jet during the third section, he was enormous, delicate over his instrument), keeping the pace, somewhat, the tone, as well as it could be kept, Elizabeth sitting in the divan beside Fletch, ankles crossed, hands in her lap, loving them all with her eyes.

Upstairs, a baby mewed.

They sat rigid in their slight curve, shoulders straight, chins tucked, the boys' blue denim stretched over their slim thighs, sneakers angled on the floor like frogs' feet, the sky through the windows behind them going down the scale of gray through dusk to dark, more lights coming on at the airport across the reflecting surface of the harbor. During the fourth section, Jenny was tired and not as practiced. Sighs became more frequent. The tongue crept out to the tip of her nose even when she should have been playing. Even Randy's and Todd's faces shone with perspiration.

Their hair matted on their foreheads identically. For a moment, Fletch looked at the chessmen set up on a board to his right. A game was in progress.

Jenny was vigorous in the last bars, practiced, *allegro*, and finished a little before the others. She looked momentarily confused.

It was a wonderful forty minutes.

"Bravo!" Elizabeth said while she and Fletch applauded.

"Pretty good, Jenny," Randy said, standing up.

Without comment Flynn closed his sheet music and stood to lean his cello in the curve of the piano again.

"Da'?" Todd said. "That should never have been in anything other than F major."

"We all make mistakes," said Flynn. "Even Beethoven. We all have our temporary madnesses."

Elizabeth was hugging Jenny and complimenting Winny on his page-turning.

It was five-twenty.

"I expect we could find a drink for you, before supper," Flynn said. "Elsbeth drinks sherry, and I suppose there's some other stuff in the house."

"I have to get to the airport," Fletch said.

"Oh?" said Flynn. "Skipping town, finally?"

Conversation was suspended while a jet thundered overhead.

The room reeked with accomplishment as the kids moved about with their instruments. They bounced on the balls of their sneakered feet as only happy, accomplished children do.

"Andy's arriving," Fletch said finally. "Six-thirty."

"Is she now? That's nice."

"You'll stay for supper?" Elizabeth said, coming back to where Fletch was now standing.

"He's picking up his girlfriend," rolled Flynn. "At the airport. That will alarm your police escort, I'm sure. I'd better warn them you don't mean to take flight, or they will tackle you at the information counter. They'll watch you, all the same."

"Bring her back with you," Elizabeth said.

Fletch shook hands respectfully with the children.

"I like you," Elizabeth said. "Frannie, this is no murderer."

"That's what all the women say," Flynn said. "I haven't convinced him yet, either."

"His face was good while he listened."

"As long as he didn't hum along," Flynn said. "Tap his toes."

They all laughed at Flynn as a jet whined in a holding pattern over their heads.

"Bring your girl back with you," shouted Elizabeth. "We'll wait supper for you!"

"Thanks anyway," said Fletch. "Really, this has been a wonderful time for me."

Flynn said, "We'd be glad to have you, Fletch."

Fletch said, "I'd be glad to stay. May I come back sometime?"

"What's your instrument?" Winny asked.

"The typewriter."

"Percussion," said Flynn.

"Well," said Elizabeth, "Leroy Anderson wrote for the typewriter."

"You come back any time," said Flynn. "Any time you're free, that is."

In the cold vestibule, Flynn said, "I guess you didn't have the conversation with me this afternoon you wanted to."

"No," said Fletch. "This was much better."

"I thought you'd think so."

"May I see you in your office tomorrow?"

"Sure."

"What's a good time?"

"Five o'clock. Any policeman with good sense is in his office at that time. The traffic is terrible."

"Okay. Where are you?"

"Ninety-nine Craigie Lane. If you get lost, ask the plainclothesmen following you."

They said good night.

Outside, the air was damp and cold.

Fletch stood on the top step of the porch for a moment, adjusting his eyes to the dark, feeling the house's warmth at his back, hearing a bit of early Beethoven scraping in his memory's ears, thinking of the two blue doll's eyes under a doll's mop of tossed, curly blond hair.

Across the street, under a streetlight, he clearly saw the faces of the two plainclothesmen waiting for him. It seemed to him their eyes were filled with hatred.

One of them picked up the car phone, as Fletch started down the steps. Flynn would be telling them Fletcher was going to the airport, and they shouldn't panic . . . but to make sure he didn't get on a plane.

"Jesus Christ," Fletch said.

The scrape of his chin on his shirt collar made him realize he should have shaved.

THIRTY

"Fletch!"

He had never seen Andy in an overcoat before.

After they had embraced and he had taken her hand luggage, her first question was quick and to the point.

"Is Sylvia here?"

"Yes."

"Bitch. What is she doing?"

"I don't know. I haven't seen much of her. I mean, I haven't seen her often."

"Where is she staying?"

"At my apartment."

"Where am I staying?"

"At my apartment."

"Oh, my god."

"How are you?"

Andy's big suitcase was in the way of people coming through the customs' gate. The few porters were being grabbed by artful older people.

"Any luck with the paintings?" she asked.

"Can we wait until we get in the car? How are you?"

He handed her back her purse and vanity case.

"Why did you want to know about Bart Connors?"

"How are you?"

He carried the huge suitcase through the airport, across a street, up a flight of stairs, across a bridge and halfway through the garage, to where his car was parked.

The plainclothesmen, hands in their pockets, followed at twenty paces.

She began her questions again as he drove down the dark ramp of the airport garage.

"Where are the paintings? Do you know?"

"Not really. It's possible they're in Texas."

"Texas?"

"You and I may fly down later this week."

"How can they be in Texas?"

"Horan seems to have gotten all three de Grassi paintings from a man in Dallas named James Cooney. He's a rancher, with eight kids."

"Do you think so?"

"How do I know? I've handled Horan very carefully. His reputation is impeccable. Pompous bastard, but everything he's said so far has been straight. I'm putting a lot of pressure on him to try to crack Cooney's source."

"You mean, find out where Cooney got the paintings?"

"Yes. If putting pressure on Horan doesn't work, then we go to Texas and put pressure on Cooney ourselves."

"What did you do? You asked Horan to locate one of the paintings?"

"Yes. The bigger Picasso."

"Where is that painting now?"

"In Boston. Horan has it. I asked him for it Wednesday. He located it Thursday night or Friday morning and had it flown up Friday night. I saw it Saturday. He doubted the whole thing when I first spoke to him about it."

"What do you mean?"

"Well, he doubted whether the painting existed; whether it could be located; if it was authentic; if it was for sale."

"Is the painting authentic?"

"Yes. I'm as certain as I can be. So's Horan. And, apparently, Cooney is willing to sell it."

After paying a toll, they went down a ramp into a tunnel.

Fletch spoke loudly at Andy's puzzled expression.

"So far, Horan has acted in a thoroughly professional, efficient, routine manner. I don't like him, but that's immaterial."

Driving up out of the tunnel, they faced strata of crossroads, and a vast confusion of signs and arrows.

"Oops," he said. "I don't know which way to go."

"To the right," Andy said. "Go on Storrow Drive."

"How do you know?"

He turned right from the left lane.

"We're going to Beacon Street, aren't we? Near the Gardens?"

"Yeah, but how do you know?"

They went up a ramp onto a highway.

"I lived here nearly a year," she said. "The year I was at Radcliffe."

"Where's that?"

"Cambridge. Go down there, to the right, to Storrow Drive. You knew that."

Her directions were perfect.

"Why did you want to know about Bart Connors?" she asked.

"Because the night I arrived, a girl was found murdered in his apartment."

Her profile was backed by lights reflected on the Charles River.

"He didn't do it," she said.

"You seem pretty certain."

"Yes. I am."

"That's why I yelled at you that night on the phone to get out of the villa. When I asked you to go see him, I did not expect you to take up residence with him."

"You'll want to go left here." At the red light, she craned her head left. "We'll have to go all the way around the Gardens, won't we? Dear old Boston. Or is your apartment down to the right?"

Fletch said, "The police think I did it."

"Murdered the girl? You didn't do it, either. If you did, you wouldn't be trying to blame Bart."

"Thanks."

"Bart's a very gentle man. Wouldn't hurt a fly."

"Boy, when I ask you to do a job for me. . . . Did you check his teeth, too?"

"His teeth," she said, "are perfectly adequate."

"My god."

"So who killed her?"

"Damn it, Andy, there's a very good chance Bart Connors did!"

"No chance whatsoever."

"He was in Boston that night when he wasn't supposed to be! He was seen two blocks away from the apartment in a pub with a girl tentatively identified as the murdered girl just before she was murdered! He had a key to his own apartment! He left on an airplane for Montreal just after the murder! And within the last six months he has received a sexual-psychological trauma, delivered by a woman, which he considered, wrongly, a blow to his masculinity!"

"I know," Andy said. "He told me all about that."

"Great."

"And he told me the night you called you were trying to lay the crime off on him. He asked more questions about you than you've asked about him."

"Andy. . . ."

"Watch out for that taxi. Furthermore, Fletch," she continued, "I can testify that the 'sexual-psychological trauma delivered by a woman,' as you phrase it, has done him no harm whatsoever."

"I bet you can."

"You and I have our understandings," she said. "Stop being stuffy."

"Stuffy? You're wearing my engagement ring."

"I know. And it's a very nice ring. Whom did you make it with this week?"

"Whom? What?"

"I didn't hear your answer. You're not acting like Fletch."

"We need a place to park."

"Over there. To the left."

"I need two places to park."

Headlights grew large in his rearview mirror.

"Absolutely," she said, "I will not help you blame Bart Connors for a crime neither of you committed."

He said, "Such loyalty."

Going up in the creaky elevator, she said, "Try Horan again."

THIRTY-ONE

On the sixth floor landing, Fletch put the huge suitcase down to take his keys out again, to unlock the door.

Sylvia, arms wide, in an apron, opened the door.

Andy and Sylvia clutched and jabbered simultaneously in Italian.

He had to insinuate himself, with the luggage, through the crowded front door.

They sounded like a girls' school reunion.

He understood Sylvia had prepared a magnificent supper for them. A dinner.

He left the luggage in the hall and walked empty-handed down the corridor to the telephone in the master bedroom.

Even through the closed door he could hear their delighted shrieks and exclamations while he dialed.

"Mister Horan? This is Peter Fletcher."

"Ah, yes, Mister Fletcher."

"Sorry to phone on a Sunday night. . . ."

"Quite all right. I'm used to calls from anywhere, at any time. Have you decided to change your offer for the Picasso?"

"Have you spoken with Mister Cooney?"

"Yes, I did. He said he won't respond to your offer at all."

"He wouldn't consider it?"

"No."

"Was he any more open regarding the painting's provenance?"

"No. I said you rightfully had questions. I outlined to him quite carefully what you had said regarding your responsibility to question the provenance. I went as far as I could, short of physically shaking him, which would be difficult over the phone, anyway."

"And you got nowhere?"

"He didn't even deign to offer the usual evasions. He said the authenticity of the painting can't really be questioned. . . ."

"Of course it can be."

"Not really. I have thoroughly satisfied myself. No, he's prepared to stand on the painting's authenticity."

"I see."

"And, by the way, Mister Fletcher, our Texas cowboy friend rather surprised me by repeating something you said."

"Oh?"

"He referred to 'Vino, Viola, Mademoiselle' as a 'most significant Picasso.' He referred to it as the 'key work of the cubist period.' "

"Oh."

"So our cowboy with eight kiddies has no sheep wool over his eyes, if I may coin a phrase."

"If you insist. Mister Horan? Offer Mister Cooney five hundred and twenty-seven thousand dollars for the painting."

"Ah! Mister Fletcher. Now you're in the arena. I most certainly will."

"And you may remember originally I said I might ask you to help me on another problem or two?"

"Yes."

"I wonder if you would ask Mister Cooney if he has another particular painting in his possession?"

"You mean, another specific painting? I don't understand."

"Yes, another specific painting. An Umberto Boccioni entitled 'Red Space.' "

" 'Red Space'? Again you've got me stumped. Mister Fletcher, you go from a key cubist work by Picasso to the work of an only relatively important Italian Futurist."

"I know."

"Fire and water."

"Or water and fire, depending upon your point of view."

"Well, again, professionally, I have to advise you that I don't know if such a painting exists. . . ."

"I do."

"What makes you think Mister Cooney might have such a painting, Mister Fletcher?"

"We all have our little secrets."

"You mean, you want me to ask him straight out if he has this 'Red Space' by Boccioni?"

"Not necessarily 'straight out.' After all, I'm offering him over half a million dollars for the Picasso. . . ."

"It's worth much more."

"I think it's a good enough offer to justify a little conversation. You might say that someone has mentioned the existence of such a painting, and you'd give anything to be able to locate it."

"You want me to exercise craft, is that it?"

"Even deviousness," suggested Fletch. "I'll be interested in what he says."

"It's nearly eight o'clock now," Horan said. "Of course, that's not Dallas time. I guess I can try to call him tonight."

"Will you call me in the morning?"

"If I reach him."

"Thank you. Good night."

THIRTY-TWO

The dining room table had been set with crystal and silver. The light was subdued.

"Oh, it's nothing," said Sylvia, removing her apron. "I'll serve."

Fletch sat at the far end of the table. Before leaving the room, Sylvia indicated Andy should sit to his right.

Sylvia would sit at the other end of the table.

Fletch said to Andy, "Trust you don't feel seven years old."

"What's going on here?"

"Oh!" said Fletch. "Soup!"

"The first course," said Sylvia. "A nice soup!"

In the flat bowls was about a cupful of consommé.

The bouillon cube, worn away only at its edges, sat in an island of its own grease, surrounded by cool water.

"I can tell," said Fletch. "You gave us big spoons."

Applying the tip of the spoon to the bouillon cube accomplished nothing. A minute Michelangelo with hammer and chisel might make something of it.

Stirring the water around the cube only caused it to sway like a tango dancer. The grease reached out in disgusting, finger-like patterns.

Sylvia said, "I thought we all needed a good, hot dinner! Filling and tasty! American cooking, yes?"

Fletch said, "Yes."

"After such a long airplane ride for poor, dear Angela!"

"Yes."

"This beastly, cold New England weather!"

"Yes."

"Good, hot American cooked soup!"

"Most substantial," said Fletch. "Full body, vigorous aroma, the ambience of a bus. . . ."

"You no like your soup?" Sylvia had come to collect his bowl. "You no finish your soup."

"It's taking too long to cool down."

He waved it away.

While Sylvia was in the kitchen, Andy said, "She can't cook. Everyone knows that."

"I'm finding it out."

"Now the fish!" Sylvia announced from the door. "Good American fish!"

A piece of cold, canned tuna fish and a quarter of a lemon lay on his plate.

What happened to the fourth slice of lemon?

"Oh, yeah," said Fletch. "Fish. I recognize it. Glad you removed the head, Sylvia. Never could stand a fish head on a plate. Aren't you glad she removed the head, Andy?"

"I'm glad she removed the lid."

"That, too," said Fletch. "Funny no one's ever made a solid silver can opener to go with a place setting. I'd think there'd be a market for it."

At her end of the table, Sylvia was beaming.

Her neckline disappeared into her lap. Her bilateral, upper structural support systems were more sophisticated than anything used on the Swiss railway system.

It was not the same gagging décolletage she had worn to stun the Ritz.

"Yeah." Fletch chewed the fish. "This is nice."

"Just like a family," said Sylvia.

"Precisely," said Fletch.

"Just like a family, we are together."

"Precisely like a family. Precisely."

"If only Menti were here."

"Now there was a man who knew a piece of fish when he saw one."

"Poor Menti."

"Nice touch, the slice of lemon," Fletch said. "Did you cut it yourself?"

"They've located his body," Andy said.

"Whose?"

Sylvia said, "What?"

"In a pasture. Outside Turin. The police called, just before I left."

Sylvia said, "They found Menti?"

"Really?"

"Sorry," Andy said. "I didn't mean to bring it up at dinner."

"You can't ruin dinner," Fletch said.

Sylvia began in galloping Italian exclamations (at one point, she blessed herself with her fork), ultimately giving way to long questions, which Andy answered tersely. As Sylvia's questions became shorter, she switched to French — the language of reason. Andy, who had attended school in Switzerland, answered even more tersely in the language of reason.

Muttering in Portuguese, Sylvia took the fish plates into the kitchen.

"Now it's my turn," said Fletch.

"The police called just before I left. They found the body in a shallow grave in a pasture outside Turin."

"Do they know it's your father?"

"His age, his height, his weight. They're pretty sure. Dead about three weeks."

"I see."

Sylvia entered with salad plates. The salad consisted of a clump of cold, canned peas huddled together against the rim. On none of the plates had any of the peas broken free of the clump.

"Oh," said Fletch, "a pea."

"Salad!" Sylvia screwed herself into her chair. "Good American salad!" She had added salt. Too much salt.

"I would think," Fletch spoke quietly, "if that were the case, one of you, if not both, should be in Italy to receive the remains."

" 'Remains?' " asked Sylvia. "What's 'remains'?"

Fletch said, "Sort of like supper."

Andy answered her properly in Italian.

Quickly, Sylvia said, "This is not to be spoken of at dinner."

"I thought not," said Fletch.

"Angela," the Countess demanded archly, "why you no stay to accept your father's remains?"

"The police want them."

"Why the police want the remains of Menti?"

Sylvia was getting a remarkable amount of chewing out of her pea.

"They said they had much to do."

"What to do? What to do with the remains of Menti?"

"They have to test his teeth."

"What's wrong with Menti's teeth? He's dead! No good testing
them now!"

Fletch said, "That's how they confirm the identification of a corpse,
Sylvia. The body's been in the ground three weeks."

"Oh. If the body is wearing Menti's teeth, then they know it is
Menti?"

"Yes."

"Ha!" said Sylvia, for some reason victoriously, fork in air. "Menti
had no teeth!"

"What?"

"All Menti's teeth false! His gums were entirely — how you say?
— bareass."

"That's right," said Andy. "I had forgotten that."

"They can identify a corpse by its false teeth," Fletch said.

"How come you know so much?" Sylvia asked.

Andy said, "The police said they would give us a closed coffin
when they are through doing what they can to identify father. We
can have a burial. It doesn't matter when. We've already had the
funeral."

"This is terrible," said Sylvia. "Poor Menti."

Something was sizzling in the kitchen, suggesting the threat of a
fourth course.

"Did you have a chance to speak to the lawyers?" Fletch asked
Andy.

"Yes. I called Mister Rosselli. He said it was good news."

"That your father was murdered?"

"We knew he was murdered. The police said so."

"Sorry."

"He said the will could be read after he gets the papers from the
police."

"What papers?" exploded Sylvia. "Already we have had papers up
the asses!"

"They have to have positive identification, Sylvia," Fletch said. "They can't settle an estate without a corpse."

"Pash!" She shook her fork in the air. "All they want is Menti's teeth! You look in that closed coffin. There will be no teeth! Some police inspector in Turin will wear them!"

Fletch said, "Sylvia. Something is burning."

"Ooo," she said, grabbing up her gown for the run to the kitchen. In their momentary privacy, Fletch said to Andy: "I guess I'm tired."

She said, "That's why we're having such a nice dinner."

"I should have planned something."

"Yes. You should have."

"I never guessed Sylvia would make such an effort."

Andy said, "I don't guess she has."

The entrée was a burned frankfurter each, sliced lengthwise.

At the edge of each plate was a tomato, obviously hand-squeezed. The indentations of four fingers and a thumb were clear. In fact, Sylvia's thumb print was clear.

"Oh, my god," Fletch said.

"What's the matter?" Sylvia was screwing herself into her chair again. "Good American meal! Hot dog! Ketchup!"

Andy said, "Sylvia, really!"

"You live in America, you get used to American food," Sylvia said. "I been here nearly one week already. See?"

"We see," said Fletch.

"Bastard Rosselli say what Menti's will say about my paintings?"

Fletch said, "What paintings? There are no paintings."

"There are paintings." In her insistence, Sylvia leaned so far forward she almost dipped one in the 'ketchup.' "My paintings you two find. If you no look for, why you here? If you no find, why Angela come? Eh? Answer me that, Mister Flesh Ass-pants."

Fletch said, "We just came for dinner."

"Rosselli said nothing about the will, Sylvia."

Fletch said, "I'm in love with Jennifer Flynn."

He made no approach to his frankfurter and tomato. They sat there, burned and thumbprinted, like a victim and a perpetrator.

Andy, using her knife and fork on the frankfurter, was looking at him.

He said, "I would think you'd both want to be in Rome now."

"No!" said Sylvia. "I stay here. Where my paintings are."

Looking at Sylvia, Fletch counted the number of hours of sleep he had had. Then he counted the number of hours of sleep he hadn't had.

"Sylvia," he said. "The paintings are in Texas."

"Texas?"

"Andy and I are planning to fly to Dallas the end of this week."

"Good! Then I go, too."

"Good!" said Fletch. "We'll all go. Just like a family."

Andy's look could have burned through telephone books.

To Andy he said, "I doubt you've ever had Texan chili. Good American cooking."

"Chili sauce," said Sylvia. "You want chili sauce?"

Fletch placed his unused napkin next to his untouched plate.

"Sorry I can't stay to help out with the dishes. I'm going to sleep now."

"Sleep?" Sylvia was prepared to be hurt. "You no want dessert?"

"Don't even tell me what it is," Fletch said. "I'll dream on it."

He went into a guest room, locked the door, stripped, and crawled between the sheets.

The rhythms of exclamations in Italian, French, Portuguese, and English through the thick walls lulled him to hungry sleep.

THIRTY-THREE

"Hi, babe."

In the single bed, he had rolled onto his side.

Light was pouring through the open drapes.

Eyes open, staring at him, her head faced him on the pillow.

The white sheet over her upper arm perfected her smooth, tanned shoulder, neck, throat.

His right hand went along her left breast, under her arm, down her side. She pulled her right leg up, to touch his.

"Nice to feel you again," he said.

She must have entered through the bathroom from the other guest room.

He flicked her lips with his tongue.

Then his left arm went under her and found the small of her back and brought her closer to him.

"Where were you last night?" she asked.

"When?"

"Two o'clock. Three o'clock. You weren't in bed."

"I went out for a walk," he said. "After that heavy dinner."

In fact, between two and three in the morning, he had switched the license plates of the rented car and the black truck.

" 'After that heavy dinner,' " she said.

She giggled.

"Did you use my bed in Cagna?" he asked.

"Of course. Our bed."

He said, "I'm hungry."

She put on a slightly perplexed face.

She said, "This is your apartment."

"Yes."

"How come Sylvia's in the master bedroom and you and I are in a single bed in a guest room?"

"I don't know."

"You don't know?"

"I guess it's like the Latin-American expression, 'I lost the battle of the street.' "

"Was there a revolution?"

"There must have been. I guess I was an absentee government."

"What does that mean?"

"I wasn't here a couple of nights."

"Where were you?"

"I was working."

"Working?"

"At a newspaper. An old boy I worked with in Chicago works for a paper here now. He was shorthanded and asked me to come in. Charlestown was burning down again."

"Why would you do that?"

"Why not?"

"Why should you?"

"I liked it. Anyhow, Jack had let me spend some time at the newspaper looking up Horan."

"Jack?"

"Jack Saunders."

"I doubt it would take two nights for Charlestown to burn down."

"What do you mean?"

"I mean, I would expect your friend to solve his staff problems by the second night."

"I don't get you."

"You said you were gone two nights."

"Did I say that?"

"Where were you the other night?"

"What other night?"

"You were only gone one night?"

"Ah. . . ."

"If you were only gone one night, how come Sylvia has the master bedroom?"

"Um. . . ."

"How come she has it, anyway."

"Who? Sylvia?"

"Were you sleeping with Sylvia?"

"Who, me?"

"You see, Fletch?"

"See what?"

"Don't give me a hard time."

"Did I give you a hard time?"

"About Bart."

"Oh, yeah, Bart the Woman Slayer."

"He needed help, Fletch."

"I'll bet."

"You know why his wife left him?"

"I heard rumors."

"Then this girl he wanted to take to Cagna finally refused to go."

"I know. I found her body. She should have gone."

"Bart never killed anybody."

"Andy, one of three people killed Ruth Fryer. I know I didn't, and Bart tops the list of the other two candidates."

"Tell me about Sylvia."

"Sylvia who?"

"Come on."

"You must have misunderstood something."

"I did not. You've never lost a battle of the street in your life."

"I haven't known many Sylvias."

"What happened?"

"I was raped."

"That's nice."

"Not bad."

"I don't believe you."

"Believe me. I think you've figured out she wants the paintings as much as you do."

"She's not going to get them, is she?"

"I know what she has to offer. What do you have to offer?"

"You know what I have to offer."

"You're skinnier than she is."

"You like that. Skinny."

"Did I say that?"

"Once or twice."

"Was I telling the truth?"

"One never knows."

"We're doing an awful lot of talking. For two friends who haven't seen each other in almost a week."

"I'm not used to making deals in bed."

"Oh. Then feel sorry for me."

"Why should I feel sorry for you?"

"I was raped. I need to get my sexual confidence back."

"You have it back. I can feel it."

"See how much good you've done already?"

THIRTY-FOUR

Fletch went into the den to answer the telephone after a second helping of scrambled eggs and sausage.

It was past ten, and Sylvia apparently had gone out earlier to follow her own investigation, which, Fletch guessed, meant walking through Boston's private galleries with the list of de Grassi paintings in her hand.

It was, finally, a cloudless October day.

At breakfast, Fletch and Andy had decided to spend the day walking the old streets. She said she would show him his American history.

He worried about the moon.

It was Horan.

"Mister Fletcher, I was able to get Mister Cooney on the phone last night, too late to call you back."

"That was very considerate of you. I did go to bed early."

"There was little point in rushing to you with the news anyway."

"Oh?"

"He says he won't respond to your new offer for the Picasso, either. Contrary to my advice to you, he says you're not even in the ball-park."

"Did you remind him he has eight kids to feed?"

"He said he is looking for upwards of a million dollars for the painting."

"Hungry kids. I thought beef was cheaper in Texas."

"That's the lay of the land. I don't know if you want to go further with this negotiation, but I expect you'll want to think about it."

"Would you? I mean, would you go further?"

"I think I would. I think I'd make another offer for it. Of course, I have no idea how much of your resources you want to tie up in a single property."

"Will you make another offer, if I don't?"

"Mister Fletcher, I think I made a mistake there — one for which I apologize — in indicating to you I might be interested in purchasing this painting if you don't. I'm your broker, in this case, and a client should never feel he would be in a position where he must bid against his own broker."

"I was wondering about that."

"I was greatly mistaken. What I meant was, if this negotiation between you and Cooney doesn't work out, after a decent interval of time — and it would be a long, decent interval — I might reopen negotiations with Mister Cooney on my own, or even, conceivably, in behalf of another client."

"I see."

"As long as you leave your negotiation with Mister Cooney open, you will not be bidding against me, or any other client of mine, even potentially. I will continue to give you my best advice, to make your negotiation successful."

"And what's your advice now?"

"First, I think you should think about it. No reason for being too swift in these matters. After you consider your own resources, and the very real question of how much of those resources you want committed to a single property, I'd make a new offer, if I were so inclined."

"How much?"

"The new offer? I think eight hundred thousand dollars."

"I'll think about it."

"All right, Mister Fletcher. Call me any time."

"What about the other painting?"

"What other painting?"

"The Boccioni. 'Red Space.' "

"Oh. A complete blank."

"Really?"

"I guess I was too subtle at first. He had no idea what I was talking about. I finally asked him, more directly. Mister Cooney clearly had never heard of Umberto Boccioni."

"That's puzzling."

"I guess your source of information was dead wrong."

"That's hard to believe."

"Nothing's hard to believe in this business, Mister Fletcher. Whoever told you Mister Cooney owns a Boccioni was incorrect. Call me when you decide about the Picasso."

"I will."

Andy was clearing the dishes from the dining room table.

"That was Horan," Fletch said. "Our man in Texas never heard of Umberto Boccioni."

THIRTY-FIVE

Trusting the two plainclothesmen would not be too puzzled by his not using the Ford Ghia, Fletch took a taxi to Flynn's office on Craigie Lane.

It was a graystone pile at the edge of Boston Harbor. Inside, everything was painted regulation green, except the sagging wood floors, which were soft underfoot.

The policeman behind the counter sent him up a curved staircase with a heavy, carved wooden railing.

Grover was making tea in a corridor alcove on the second floor.

He led Fletch into Flynn's office.

Flynn was behind an old, wooden desk, and behind him three arched, almost cathedral-like windows overlooked the harbor. A few straight-backed, wooden chairs stood about the room in no particular order. Along the inside walls was a long, wooden refectory table.

"Did you bring Mister Fletcher a cup of tea as well, Grover?" Flynn stood up to shake hands. "Pull up a pew, Mister Fletcher. Make yourself at home."

Grover placed the two tea cups at the edge of the desk and went out to get a third.

"We'll have a nice little tea party."

Fletch moved one of the wooden chairs to be at an angle to the desk so he would have solid wall behind Flynn, not the late afternoon light from the windows.

"Homey," said Fletch.

"I know." Behind his desk, Flynn's elfin face looked like that of a schoolboy playing teacher. "I came to look at you in an off-moment, Saturday, and you came to look at me in an off-moment, Sunday. That was our weekend. I learned you're a peeping tom, besides being a reporter and a murderer, either one of which is bad enough, but did we accomplish anything else?"

After handing Fletch a cup of tea, without questions regarding cream and sugar (there was neither in the cup), Grover took his own cup, and dragged a chair over to the long table against the wall.

"You do want me to take notes, Inspector?"

"For what they're worth. I think Mister Fletcher has something important to say, and I want a witness."

Fletch asked, "How's the other murder going? The chubby City Councilperson's murder?"

"Slowly," said Reluctant Flynn. "Very time-consuming, to be sure."

"Was the axe murder solved?"

"Oh, of course. Such things are usually family matters. I don't know why we bother with them at all."

"Look, regarding the Ruth Fryer business. . . ."

"It's called murder."

"Yes. I want off the hook."

"You want to go to Texas."

"Probably."

"We'll be pleased to let you off the hook as soon as we find a more attractive candidate for charging than yourself."

Fletch said, "I would guess not too much has been accomplished in recent days."

"Will you listen to that, Grover? The candidate for hanging is getting impatient. And he had such a great lot of faith in the institution of the Boston Police to begin with."

At the side of the room, Grover sat hunched over his table, writing slowly.

"I quite understand you've got other things to do," Fletch said.

"One or two. One or two."

"And undoubtedly there's a lot of political and press pressure on you regarding the City Councilperson's murder."

"I thank you for making my excuses."

"But I'm being sort of a victim here. I didn't kill Ruth Fryer."

"You say you didn't."

"And the investigation has been dragging on almost a week now."

"Mister Fletcher, the Complaint Department is downstairs. It's a small room, with see-through walls."

"Another person in my position might have hired private detectives this last week. . . ."

"However, being a great ex-investigative reporter yourself, you've done a little investigating on your own. Is that it?"

"Yes."

"And you have come to a conclusion?"

"I think I have."

"Do you want time to sharpen your pencil, Grover? Oh, it's a pen. I don't want you to miss a word."

"Okay," said Fletch. "First of all, it is most likely the murderer must have had a key to the apartment. Not absolutely necessary. Thinking Bart Connors was in Italy and the apartment was empty, Ruth Fryer could have gone to the apartment alone or with some other person to use the apartment for sexual purposes. Or, not knowing Connors was in Italy, to surprise him. She could have had a key, which the murderer then took. Or Joan Winslow, in a state of advanced intoxication, could have let her in."

"All highly unlikely," said Flynn. "The Winslow woman supposedly was at the Bullfinch Pub. Ruth Fryer would have seen your suitcases in the hall, noted the airline's tags in the name of Peter Fletcher and been scared off from whichever course of action she intended. For the last time, Mister Fletcher, I reject the idea that Ruth Fryer killed herself."

"Narrow of you," said Fletch, "but I accept it. So," he continued, "the basic question is, who had a key to that apartment? Me," he counted himself off on his little finger, "Mrs. Sawyer, whom you've investigated. . . ."

"As pure as Little Eva."

". . . Joan Winslow. . . ."

"Ach, she's incapable of anything."

". . . Bart Connors. . . ."

"Now he's a real possibility. How come we haven't thought of him, Grover?"

". . . and Lucy Connors."

"Lucy Connors?"

"Let's consider Bart Connors first."

"You've been considering Bart Connors from the very beginning. You've been after him so, the man has my sympathy."

"Apparently." Fletch was hanging onto his index finger. "Six months ago, Bart Connors had a sexual-psychological shock. His wife left him, for a woman. Mrs. Sawyer said he then became sexually very active. He is known to have brought girls to his apartment. We thought he had gone to Italy on Sunday. He did not leave Boston until nine-thirty Tuesday night, and then he flew through Montreal, a sort of unusual thing to do. Just prior to the murder, Joan Winslow said she saw him in a pub two blocks away with a girl she has identified as Ruth Fryer."

"She's an unreliable witness. Any defense attorney would make hash of her in minutes."

"Flynn, why isn't Bart Connors the murderer?"

"I don't know."

"We know he delayed his departure from Boston because he was trying to talk a girl into going to Italy with him — a girl who ultimately refused."

"Well, I have a prejudice against him. He's a Boston lawyer, you know, an important firm. . . ."

"All of which just means he's smart enough to lay the crime off on someone else."

"I don't know why he'd need to. I don't know why he wouldn't have taken the body and dumped it in some alley."

"He had a plane to catch. He was well-known in the neighborhood. It was still early evening. He knew I'd be arriving."

"All good reasons. But Ruth Fryer had not had sexual intercourse."

"That's it, Flynn. Her rejecting him, after his experience with his wife, may have sent him up the wall."

"May have."

"Frankly, Flynn, I don't think you've paid enough attention to Bart Connors as a suspect."

"Grover, pay more attention to Bart Connors as a suspect."

"Incidentally, something else you don't know is that Ruth Fryer's boyfriend, whose name is Clay Robinson, flew up from Washington Tuesday afternoon to spend a few days with her."

"Did he? Grover, our incompetence is becoming marked."

"Presuming Ruth Fryer knew Bart Connors, and thought he was in Italy, why wouldn't she have taken Clay Robinson to use Bart's apartment?"

"Why would she, when there are hotels?"

"It's a nice place."

"Wouldn't she have had to explain to her boyfriend how it was she had access to such an apartment?"

"I suppose so."

"She had no key we know of, Mister Fletcher. Your tagged luggage was in the hall. . . ."

"Okay. Now we come to Joan Winslow."

"My god, Grover, it's like listening to one of those Harvard-Radcliffe professors — such a pompous lecture we're getting."

"Flynn, I'm tired of being a murder suspect."

"I'd say you've got pretty good evidence those paintings are in Texas." Flynn's voice was barely audible across the desk. "You want to get out of here."

"Inspector, I didn't catch that," Grover said.

"You weren't meant to. Go on, Mister Fletcher."

"Joan Winslow has a key to the apartment. She was in love with Bart Connors. Passionately. He had rejected her quite thoroughly. She hated, absolutely hated, the young girls he had been bringing to his apartment."

"So how would that work in time and space?"

"I don't know. Joan Winslow heard someone in Bart's apartment, knew he was in Italy, went over to investigate, found Ruth Fryer naked, thinking she was waiting for Bart; Joan went into a drunken rage and slugged her with the bottle."

"Who put the other whiskey bottles away? I mean, cleaned off the whole liquor bar?"

"Joan Winslow did. She knew the apartment. I guess she knew I was coming in. Or, she saw the suitcases and knew I was going to return. Or, she simply wanted to frame Bart Connors."

"That's a possibility."

"Joan Winslow has made an even greater effort than I have to blame Bart Connors. She identified Ruth Fryer as being the girl she saw in the pub with him."

"When do we get to consider all the evidence against you? Grover's getting anxious over there."

"I think you've done enough of that. You've considered me such a prime suspect, you've done little else."

"Now, what haven't we done?"

"I'll tell you what you haven't done. You didn't find Ruth Fryer's motel key."

"By the way, you never gave it to me."

"You didn't need it. You didn't know Joan Winslow has a key to Bart Connors' apartment."

"That was thick of us. Sheer inexperience on my part."

"You didn't know Ruth Fryer's boyfriend, Clay Robinson, was in Boston Tuesday afternoon."

"How were we to know that?"

"You haven't talked with Bart Connors."

"Oh. Him again. You sound like a Christmas phonograph — reindeer and snowflakes and bright shining stars over and over again."

"And the most significant thing of all I don't even think you've thought of doing."

"We've had the City Councilperson's murder. . . . ."

"You're not going to send me to prison, Flynn, because you're distracted."

"Such a scolding I'm getting. You sound like Grover. A more experienced policeman might resent it."

"Sorry, Flynn, but I want to get moving."

"You've mentioned it."

"Lucy Connors," said Fletch.

"Ah, yes. Lucy Connors."

"She has a key to the apartment."

"Has she? Have you talked with her?"

"Yes."

"Very enterprising of you. When could that have been? Does she live in Brookline?"

"Yes."

"Ah. You went there Sunday morning, before paying your visit to me."

"Flynn, Lucy Connors flew into Boston from Chicago Tuesday afternoon on Trans World Airlines."

"My god."

"Furthermore, she made an excuse to her roommate for being late. She was late by two or three hours."

"Very enterprising of you, Mister Fletcher. Very enterprising, indeed."

"She has a history of violence, which she admits. She used to beat up her husband — send him to the office with welts. She and her girlfriend still play with sexual violence."

"You must have been a very good investigative reporter, Mister Fletcher, to know what two people do in bed."

"Lucy Connors flies into Boston. Her eye is taken by Ground Hostess Ruth Fryer. She picks her up, maybe with some story about her boutique. Ruth is young and innocent, and never dreams this older woman has sexual designs on her. They go to Ruth's hotel, where she changes into a pretty dress, because, after all, this older woman, her new friend, has been in Chicago buying for her boutique. She doesn't wait for Clay Robinson, because she doesn't know he's coming. Ruth is an airline stewardess, bored in a city she doesn't know, about to get married in a month or two; another girl asks her to join her for drinks, a dinner, the evening. Why shouldn't she go? She feels perfectly safe."

"We have to think in these terms, don't we?" said Flynn.

"A man and a woman can check into a hotel together, but eyebrows still rise at two women doing so."

"I expect so."

"Lucy can't take Ruth Fryer home with her, because Marsha is at the apartment, waiting."

"So," said Flynn, "knowing Bart's in Italy — either not knowing about your arrival, or not caring as she has a perfect right to use the Connors apartment, they not being divorced yet — she brings Ruth Fryer to what is technically your apartment at that point."

"Yeah. And at the apartment, Ruth discovers she, in fact, is being seduced. She's a young girl, she's about to be married, she's not that way. She's straight. She resists. Her dress gets torn from her. She runs down the hall. Lucy, who enjoys violent play, chases her down the hall. Also, Lucy is not very experienced at seducing girls. She loses her head. Maybe she's hurt at being rejected. Maybe she goes into a blind rage."

"And she cracks little Ms. Fryer over the head with a whiskey bottle."

"Dusts the bottle and puts it back. She puts all the other bottles in the salt-and-pepper cabinet, knowing Mrs. Sawyer will have to move them around. Her own fingerprints wouldn't make any difference, anyway."

"And she puts out a carafe of water, knowing that when you return to the apartment and find the body after dinner, it would be any man's normal instinct to pour himself a stiff one at the sideboard. Thus she got your fingerprints on the murder weapon."

"Right."

"Damned clever. How did you get to interview Lucy Connors?"

"I said I was from a magazine."

"I see. It seems you've done better than we have, Fletcher."

"The thing that has been puzzling since the beginning," said Fletch, "is that this murder appeared to be a crime of sexual passion. The victim was naked. She was beautiful. And yet the autopsy turned up no evidence of sexual intercourse."

"That was surprising," said Flynn.

"There would be no such evidence, if the sexual affair was lesbian."

"My God, it's been in front of our eyes all the time."

"Lucy has a key. She and Ruth were at the airport at the same time. She would be attracted to Ruth. Anyone would be. She and Ruth could not go to a hotel, easily or safely. Lucy is known to be violence-prone. Ruth would have resisted her."

"An arrest," said Flynn, standing up from his desk, "is imminent."

"58 Fenton Street, Brookline," said Fletch, also standing. "Apartment 42. Under the name of Marsha Hauptmann."

"Have you got that, Grover?"

"Yes, Inspector."

"Now, Frank," said Fletch. "Would you do me a favor?"

"It seems I owe you one."

"Get your goons off my back."

"I will, indeed. Grover, order Mister Fletcher's tail removed immediately."

"Yes, sir."

"And will you be at home later tonight, Mister Fletcher?"

"I expect to be. Later."

"Perhaps I'll give you a call to tell you how things turn out."

"I'd appreciate that."

"I'm sure you will, Mister Fletcher. I'm sure you will."

THIRTY-SIX

Both Andy and Sylvia marveled when Fletch donned blue jeans, boots, a dark blue turtle neck sweater, Navy windbreaker, and a Greek fisherman's cap, and said he was going out for a while.

He said he would be back for dinner.

He wouldn't.

Although free of his police tail, out of habit he went through the kitchen and down the service stairs of the apartment house. Going through the alley to his garage on River Street was a short cut, anyway.

In the black truck, Fletch put himself on Newbury Street and headed west. (The two top storeys of 60 Newbury Street were lit.) He crossed Massachusetts Avenue, down the ramp, and continued west on the Massachusetts Turnpike Extension.

Lolling along, singing to himself while munching pretzels, he took the Weston exit, went left at a light, and curved right up a grade after a second light. The moon was out. Climbing, after he passed the golf course, he had a better view of the antique farmhouses, close to the road, and the well-separated estate houses, set back.

Passing the Horan house, he noted it showed no light.

He continued on into Weston Center.

Next to a drugstore on the main road was a lit telephone booth. Fletch parked at an angle, next to it, and checked his watch.

It was five minutes past nine Monday night. He had been in Massachusetts about six days and six hours.

Despite the dim light emanating from the drugstore, he knew it was closed.

In the phone booth, he dialed the Boston number of Ronald Risom Horan.

The man answered immediately.

Chewing gum in mouth, thumb pressed against his left nostril, Fletch said, "Mister Horan? Yeah. This is the Weston police. Your burglar alarm just went off. Yeah. The light just lit on the console here."

"Is someone at the house now?"

"Yeah! A burglar is, I guess."

"Are the police there?"

"Oh, yeah. We're sending the car over. As soon as we can locate it."

"What do you mean, as soon as you locate it?"

"Yeah, they're not answering the radio just now."

"Jesus! Listen, you jerk! Get someone to the house right away!"

"Yeah. I'll do what I can."

"I'll be out right away."

"Yeah. Okay. You know where the police station is?"

"I'm not going to the police station, you jerk! I'm going to the house!"

The phone slammed down.

Taking his time, Fletch drove back to Horan's house, down the driveway.

He drove behind the house to the garage. His headlights picked up the dirt track around the right of the garage. He drove around the garage. His headlights swept the area as he turned.

He backed the black truck into the tractor shed and turned out the headlights.

Walking back around the garage, he saw that the back and side of the house were bathed in moonlight. It was easy to find a big enough stone.

On the back porch, being careful to lay his bare fingers nowhere but on the stone, he reexamined the alarm system carefully. There were six small panes of glass in the back door. Each pane had two wires of the alarm system zigzagging through it, from left to right, top and bottom.

Very carefully, with the stone, he smashed the pane of glass nearest the door handle, knocking out both wires.

The alarm went off— a high, excited, shrill, piercing, truly frightening ringing.

His mind's eye saw a light beginning to flash at a console at the Weston police station.

As he went down the porch stairs, he pitched the stone into the woods.

He crossed the driveway to the bushes. In the bright moonlight, he stood, silently, further back in the bushes than he wanted to, but he still had clear views of the driveway, the side and back of the house.

Soon he saw the huge lights of the Rolls-Royce traveling north on the road. It braked as it approached the driveway.

The lights streamed down the gravel.

Horan turned the car so the headlights flooded the back porch of the house. He dashed across the gravel and up the steps. His feet crunched on the broken glass. He stooped to examine the window. Using his key, he let himself into the house.

The kitchen light went on.

In a moment, the burglar alarm was turned off.

No lights went on in the front of the house.

Dim lights, as from a stairwell, mixed with the moonlight on the window surfaces at the back of the house, both downstairs and up-stairs.

Then lights went on in an upstairs room at the back of the house. Light poured through its two windows.

Other than the kitchen, the room in the center of the second storey was the only room fully lit.

There was a noise from the road to Fletch's left.

Blue lights rotating on the top of a police car came down the driveway. There was no sound of a siren.

The light in the room on the second floor went off.

The policemen parked behind the Rolls. Going around it, one of the policemen brushed his fingers along a fender.

Horan appeared at the back door.

"You Mister Horan?"

"What took you guys so goddamned long?"

"We came as soon as we got the call."

"Like hell you did. I got out from Boston sooner."

"Is this your car?"

"Never mind about that. What the hell am I paying taxes for, if this is the kind of protection I get?"

The policemen were climbing the steps, their wide belts and hol-sters making them look heavy-hipped.

"You pay your taxes, Mister Horan, because you have to."

"What's your name?"

"Officer Cabot, sir. Badge number 92."

The other policeman said, "The glass is smashed, Chuck."

"Christ," said Horan.

"Anything missing?" asked Cabot.

"No."

"The alarm must have scared them off."

"The alarm had to scare them off," said Horan. "Nothing else would."

"We can patch that up with a piece of plywood and some tacks."

Cabot said, "Let's look around, anyway."

Lights went on and off throughout the whole house as Horan showed them around.

The ground was cold. Fletch began to feel it in his boots.

The three men were fiddling about the back door. The policemen were helping Horan tack a piece of plywood on the inside of the door, over the window frames.

"You live here, or in Boston?"

"Both places."

"You should get this window fixed first thing in the morning."

"You're no one to tell me my business," said Horan.

The policemen came down the steps and ambled toward their car.

From the porch, Horan said, "Get here a little faster next time, will you?"

Turning, the car reversed and headed up the driveway. Its rotating blue lights went out.

Horan returned to the house and turned out all the lights.

He closed and locked the back door.

Moving slowly, he came down the porch steps, got into the car, reversed it a few meters, and drove up the driveway.

As soon as the Rolls taillights disappeared around the curve, Fletch hurried across the driveway and up the porch steps.

Using his handkerchief over his hand, he pressed in on the plywood through the broken window. The tacks pushed free easily. The wood clattered onto the kitchen floor.

Stooping a little, at an angle, he reached his arm through the window as far as his elbow. He released the locks and opened the door from inside.

Quickly, he snapped on the kitchen light.

Anyone roused by the alarm and still watching the house would think they were seeing a continuation of the previous action, Fletch hoped. The house had been completely dark for only a minute or two.

Turning on lights as he went, he ran up the back stairs, along a short corridor, and into the center back room. The light revealed what was obviously an antiseptic, unlived-in guest bedroom with a huge closet.

The closet door was unlocked.

Light from the bedroom caused shadows from what appeared to be three white, bulky objects — each leaning against a wall of the closet.

He pulled a chain hanging from a bare light bulb in the center of the closet.

In the center of the closet, on the floor, was a Degas horse.

He lifted it into the bedroom.

Gently, he tugged the dust sheets away from the paintings stacked neatly, resting against each other's frames, against the closet walls.

He lifted two paintings out of the closet.

One was the smaller Picasso.

The other was a Modigliani.

These were the de Grassi collection. Sixteen objects, including the horse.

He took the Picasso and the Modigliani downstairs with him and left them in the kitchen.

Then he ran to the tractor shed for the truck.

He backed it against the back porch and opened its back doors.

He put the two paintings from the kitchen into it, bracing them carefully, face down, on the tarpaulin.

It took him a half-hour to load the truck.

Before he left the house, he closed the closet door and wiped his fingerprints off its handle. As he went through the house, he turned off all the lights, giving the switches a wipe with his handkerchief as he did so.

In the kitchen, he replaced the plywood against the broken window, fitting the tacks into their original holes and pressing them firm.

Driving along the highway, back into Boston, he maintained the speed limit precisely.

Fletch continued to have a professionally jaundiced view of the police, but, under the circumstances, there was no sense in taking chances.

THIRTY-SEVEN

"**M**ister Fletcher? This is Francis Flynn."

"Yes, Inspector."

"Did I wake you up?"

It was quarter to twelve, midnight.

"Just taking a shower, Inspector."

"I am in the process of exercising two warrants. Is that how a real policeman would say it?"

"I don't know."

"In any case, I am."

"Good."

"The first is for the arrest of Ronald Risom Horan for the murder of Ruth Fryer."

Fletch kept listening, but Flynn said no more.

"What?"

"Horan killed Ruth Fryer. Would you believe that, now?"

"No."

"It's as true as the devil inhabits fleas."

"It's not possible. Horan?"

"Himself. He's in the back of a car now on his way to be booked at headquarters. Sure, and there's no knowing what's in a man's heart. A respectable man like that." Fletch listened, breathing through his mouth. "We had to wait for the man to get home. He says he took a ride in the country by himself, on this beautiful moonlit night. And, of course, we had to use a pretext to get to see him at all, such an exclusive dealer in art he is, sitting here by himself in this castle. I borrowed a page from your book, if you don't mind — the book you haven't written yet — and made an appointment with him by saying I had a small Ford Madox Brown I had to sell. Do I have that name right?"

"Yes."

"And I said it was a nineteenth-century English work, to show him I knew my potatoes. Was that right?"

"Yes, Inspector."

"Anyway, it must have worked, because he made the appointment with me. Serving the warrant was the easy matter. I let Grover do it. The lad gets such satisfaction from telling people they're under arrest, especially for murder."

"Inspector, something's. . . ."

"The second warrant is to search both this house and the house in Weston for the de Grassi paintings."

"Weston? What house in Weston?"

"Horan has a house in Weston. That's a little town about twelve miles to the west of us. So Grover says."

"There's no Weston address listed for him in *Who's Who*."

"I think your Mister Horan keeps his cards pretty close to his neck-tie, if you know what I mean. He's not in the telephone book out there, either."

"Then why do you think he has a house in Weston?"

"We have our resources, Mister Fletcher."

"Inspector, something's. . . ."

"Now what I'm asking is this: Seeing you're such a distinguished writer-on-the-arts, and all, and therefore can be counted on to rec-ognize the de Grassi paintings, I wonder if you'd be good enough to join me in my treasure hunt? I'm at the Horan Gallery now."

"You are?"

"I am. We'll have a look around here, and if we find nothing, we'll go out to Weston together and have a look around that house."

"We will?"

"You don't mind, do you?"

"Inspector, what makes you think Horan has the paintings? He's a dealer. He works on assignments for other people."

"I've sent Grover to your address. He'll be sitting outside your door in a matter of minutes, if he's not there already. If you'd pull up your braces, however late in the night it is, and let him drive you over here, I'd be deeply in your debt."

"Inspector, something's. . . ."

"I know, Mister Fletcher. Something's wrong. Will you come and correct the error in my ways?"

"Of course, Inspector."

"There's a good lad."

Fletch left his hand on the receiver a moment after hanging up. It was sweating.

In the guest bedroom, he threw his jeans and sweater in the back of a bureau drawer and began to dress quickly in a tweed suit.

From the bed, Andy said, "Who was that?"

"The police. Flynn."

"Where are you going?"

"He's arrested Horan for the murder of Ruth Fryer."

She sat up in bed.

"The girl?"

"He's flipped his lid."

Sylvia, in a flowing nightdress, was in the corridor.

Fletch got just a flash of her fenders as he dashed by.

"What happens? Where you go now? Angela! What happens?"

Fletch ran down the five flights to the lobby.

A black four-door Ford was double-parked in front of the apartment building.

Fletch glanced down the street, at where the black truck was parked in front of the Ford Ghia.

He got into the front passenger seat.

Grover turned the ignition key.

Fletch said, "Hi, Grover."

Grover put the car in gear and started down Beacon Street.

"My name's not Grover," he said.

"No?"

"No. It's Whelan. Richard T. Whelan."

"Oh."

He said, "Sergeant Richard T. Whelan."

Going around the corner into Newbury Street, Fletch said, "Quite a man, your boss."

Sergeant Richard T. Whelan said, "He's a bird's turd."

THIRTY-EIGHT

The street door of the Horan Gallery was open.

Fletch closed it, aware what an open door would do to the building's climate control, and ran up the stairs to Horan's office.

Flynn was sitting behind Horan's Louis Seize desk, going through the drawers.

The Picasso, "Vino, Viola, Mademoiselle," was still on the easel.

"Ah, there he is now," said Flynn. "Peter Fletcher."

"This is one of the paintings," said Fletch.

"I thought it might be. Lovely desk this, too. Pity I haven't a touch of larceny in me."

Fletch stood between the painting and the desk, hands in his jacket pockets.

"Inspector, just because Horan has this painting does not mean that he has the other de Grassi paintings."

"I think it does." Reluctantly, Flynn stood up from behind the desk. "Come. We'll take a quick tour around the house. You'll recognize anything else that belongs to the de Grassis?"

"Yes."

"Good. Then all we need do is walk around."

"Inspector, this painting, this Picasso, is here because I asked Horan to locate it and negotiate my purchase of it. A man named Cooney sent it up from Texas."

"I see."

On the landing, Flynn was stepping into a small elevator.

"In talking with Horan, he mentioned that he had had 'one or two other paintings from Cooney the last year or two.' "

"Hard quote?"

Flynn was holding the elevator door for him.

"Reasonably." Fletch stepped in.

Flynn pushed the button for the third floor.

"And you think those two other paintings he had from Cooney were the two de Grassi paintings that showed up in his catalogue?"

"What else is there to think?"

"Many things. One might think many other things."

On the third floor, they stepped out into a spacious, tasteful living room.

"Isn't this lovely?" said Flynn. "I can hardly blame the man for wanting to hold onto his possessions."

Flynn turned to Fletch.

"Now what, precisely, are we looking for?"

Fletch shrugged. "At this point, fifteen paintings and a Degas horse."

"The horse is a sculpture, I take it?"

"Yes."

"There's a sculpture of a ballerina on the first floor. . . ."

"Yes. That's a Degas," said Fletch.

"But it's not a horse. Saturday in your apartment, you said there were nineteen works in the de Grassi collection."

"Yes. Two have been sold through this gallery. A third, the Picasso, is downstairs. So there are fifteen paintings and the one sculpture."

"And do the works have anything in common?"

Flynn had walked them into a small, dark dining room.

"Not really. They belong to all sorts of different schools and eras. Many of them, but not all, are by Italian masters."

"This would be the kitchen, I think."

They looked in at white, gleaming cabinets and dark blue counters.

"Nothing in there, I think," said Flynn, "except some Warhols on the shelves."

Back in the living room, Flynn said, "Are you looking?"

"Yes."

There were some unimportant drawings behind the piano, and a large Mondrian over the divan.

Flynn snapped the light on in a small den off the living room.

"Anything in here?"

A Sisley over the desk — the usual winding road and winding stream. The room was too dark for it.

"No."

"I rather like that one," said Flynn, looking at it closely. He turned away from it. "Ah, going around with you is an education."

They climbed the stairs to the fourth floor.

The houseman stood on the landing. Thin in his long, dark bathrobe, thin face long in genuine grief, he stood aside, obviously full of questions regarding the future of his master, his own future — questions his dignity prohibited he ask.

"Ah, yes," said Flynn.

In the bedroom was a shocking, life-sized nude — almost an illustration — of no quality whatsoever, except that it was arousing.

"The man had a private taste," said Flynn. "I suspect he entertained very few of his fellow faculty members in his bedroom."

One guest room had a collection of cartoons; the other a photography wall.

Fletch said, "You see, Inspector, Horan didn't really own paintings. Dealers don't. More than the average person, of course, a good deal more, in value, but a dealer is a dealer first, and a collector second."

"I see."

The houseman remained in the shadows of the corridor.

"Where is your room?" asked Flynn.

"Upstairs, sir."

"May we see it?"

The houseman opened a corridor door to a flight of stairs.

His bedroom was spartan: a bed, a bureau, a chair, a closet, a small television. His bath was spotless.

An attic room across the fifth floor landing contained nothing but the usual empty suitcases, trunks, a great many empty picture frames, a rolled rug, defunct lighting fixtures.

Flynn said, "Are the picture frames significant?"

"No."

Again on the third floor landing, Flynn said to the houseman, "Is there a safe in the house?"

"Yes, sir. In Mister Horan's office."

"You mean the wee one?"

"Yes, sir."

"I've already seen that. I guess I mean a vault. Is there a vault in the house, something of good, big size?"

"No, sir."

"You'd know if there were?"

"Yes, sir."

Flynn put his hand on the old man's forearm.

"I'm sorry for you. Have you been with him long?"

"Fourteen years."

The old man took a step back into the shadow.

"This must be quite a shock to you."

"It is, sir."

They took the elevator to the second floor and went through the four galleries there. One was completely empty. The others had only a few works in each, lit and displayed magnificently.

Flynn said, "Nothing, eh?"

He might have been taking a Sunday stroll through a sculpture garden.

"I wouldn't say exactly nothing," said Fletch. "But none of the de Grassi paintings."

Despite the house's perfect climate control, Fletch's forehead was hot. His hands were sticky.

Flynn was in no hurry.

"Well, we'll go out to Weston now." Flynn buttoned his raincoat. "The Weston police will meet us at their border."

Double-parked, Grover waited outside in the black Ford.

"We'll both get in back," said Flynn. "That way we can talk more easily."

Grover drove west on Newbury Street.

Fletch was sitting as far back in his dark corner as he could.

Coat opened again, knees wide, Flynn took up a great lot of room, anyway.

"Well," he said, "I guess I'll miss two o'clock feeding this morning. At least I know Elsbeth can't wait. Have you ever been to Weston?"

"No," said Fletch.

"Of course you haven't. You're a stranger in town. And we've been watching you as if you were a boy with a slingshot since you arrived. I hear it's a pretty place."

Flynn chuckled, in the dark.

"All this time poor Grover up there thought you were the guilty one. Eh, Grover?"

Sergeant Richard T. Whelan did not answer the bird's turd.

"Well," said Flynn, "so did I. More or less. When was it? Wednesday night, I think. I thought we were going to get a confession out of you. Instead, you invited us for dinner. Then that day on the phone, when I couldn't get around to see you, I felt sure I could convince you of your guilt. I decided I had to get to know this man. So on Saturday I invaded your privacy for the purpose of getting to know you — an old technique of mine — and damnall, you still turned up as innocent as a spring lamb."

They went down the ramp onto the Turnpike Extension and proceeded at a sedate pace, well below the speed limit.

"When I heard your voice on the phone early Sunday morning, I thought sure you were calling from a bar ready to confess." Flynn laughed. "Unburden your soul."

"I might yet," said Fletch.

Grover sat up to look at him through the rearview mirror.

Still chuckling, Flynn said, "Now what do you mean by that?"

"I hate to spoil your time," said Fletch, "but Horan couldn't have killed Ruth Fryer."

"Ah, but he did."

"How?"

"He hit her over the head with a whiskey bottle. A full whiskey bottle."

"It doesn't make sense, Flynn."

"It does. It was his purpose to frame you."

"He didn't know me."

"He didn't have to. And, to a greater extent than you realize, he did know you. Although you're a great investigative reporter . . ." — Flynn took coins for the toll out of his pocket and handed them to Grover — ". . . you made a mistake, lad."

"You have to pay tolls?"

"This road is in the state system, and I work for the city. We've got enough governments in this country now to spread thinly around the world."

"What mistake?"

"Matter of days after Count de Grassi is reported kidnapped, then murdered, Horan gets this innocent wee letter, from Rome of all places, asking him to locate one of the de Grassi paintings."

"He knew nothing about the de Grassi murder," Fletch said. "The local papers didn't carry it. I checked."

"I did, too. Earlier today. So I asked the man tonight what paper he reads, and he said the *New York Times*. The *Times* did carry the story."

"Christ. I knew he read the *Times*."

"You had even been mentioned by name, as Peter Fletcher, that is, as the de Grassi family spokesman the day you had the ladies reveal their most intimate finances to convince the kidnappers they couldn't come up with the exorbitant ransom. The *Times* printed it."

"Why would they have? From Italy?"

"You're the journalist. There's no end of interest in crime, my lad."

"Ow."

"You were undone by the press, my lad. You're not the first."

"Horan would have noticed even a small item concerning the de Grassis."

"Precisely."

Fletch said, "He must be in cahoots with Cooney."

"I doubt any man would go to the extent Horan did to protect another man. It's possible, of course," Flynn said. "Anything's possible."

"It's still not possible."

"So you write him this innocent letter of enquiry from Rome, telling him which painting in all the world has caught your fancy, what day you'll arrive in Boston, and where you'll be staying.

"On the day you're due to arrive, the handsome, suave, sophisticated Horan, probably with an empty suitcase, went to the airport, probably pretended he had just arrived from someplace, picks up the Trans World Airline Ground Hostess. . . ."

"I didn't tell him what airline I was flying."

"If he knows what day you're arriving, he can find out what airline, what flight number, and what arrival time with a single phone call. Surely you know that."

"Yes."

"As handsome a man as he is, looking as safe as your favorite uncle, he suggests Ruth Fryer join him for dinner, at some fancy place obviously he can afford. Probably he mentions he's a widower, an art dealer, on the Harvard faculty. Why wouldn't she go with him? Her boyfriend's not in town. She's in a city she doesn't know. Dinner with Horan sounds better than sitting in her motel room manicuring her fist."

"You haven't gotten to the impossibilities yet."

"There aren't any. Ach, another toll." He rummaged in his pocket again. "Don't they ever stop their infernal taxing?"

He handed more coins to Grover.

"He taxies Ms. Fryer to her motel. Allows her time to change. Waits for her in the bar. When she reappears, he has a drink all poured and waiting for her. He buys her more than one. It's his point to give you time to get into your apartment and out again. He's perfectly sure that you, a man alone in a strange city, an unfamiliar apartment, of course will take himself out to dinner. And you did."

Grover steered into the side road which curved up through the woods into Weston.

"Mister Horan was a pretty good predictor," Flynn said.

Ahead, a car was pulled off the road, showing only its parking lights.

"Is that a police car, Grover?"

"Yes, sir."

"They'd be waiting for us. Not only do they have to effect the warrant, but surely we'd never find the house by ourselves in this woodsy place."

Grover stopped behind the parked car.

"Using the excuse of dropping off his suitcase, I'm sure, Horan takes Ruth Fryer to what he says is his apartment, but which is really your apartment. An innocent enough excuse to get a girl home with you." A uniformed policeman from the other car was striding toward them. "You might remember it yourself."

"Flynn," Fletch said. "Horan didn't have a key to that apartment."

"Ah, but he did. A few years ago he arranged some restoration work on Bart Connors' paintings while the Connorses were vacationing in the Rockies. And who'd ever demand a key back from a man like Ronald Risom Horan, or even remember he had it?" Flynn rolled down the window. "You should see the number of keys in his desk. Hello!" he said through the window.

"He told me he had done restoration work for Connors."

"Inspector Flynn?"

"I am that."

"Weston Police, sir. You're here to enter the Horan house with a warrant?"

"We are."

Flynn was hunched forward, blocking the window.

"If you'll just follow us, sir."

"We will. And what is your name?"

"Officer Cabot, sir."

The policeman returned to his car, Flynn rolled up his window, and they started off in tandem at a slow pace.

Fletch said, "Well."

"You see, all the time you thought you were leading him down the garden path, he was leading you down the garden path."

"Because he reads the *Times*."

"You were a great threat to him. He had to get rid of you. If he murdered you outright, he'd be a natural suspect. You were coming to Boston to see him, and only him. So he contrived this magnificent circumstance to stop your investigation before it ever started. It's a good thing I didn't arrest you right away. Isn't it, Grover? The man must have been mighty surprised to have you show up the next day at his office as free as a birdie in an orchard."

"I'm grateful to you."

"Well, we got our man, although I had to withstand more than one tongue-lashing from that boyo up there in the front seat. Terrible tongue-lashings, they were."

They were going down the driveway.

"So Horan bopped the young lady over the head with a full bottle of whiskey, before or after he tore the dress off her, put all the other liquor bottles away, put water in the carafe to make things as easy as possible for you to implicate yourself, knowing as sure as God made cats' eyes any man coming into a strange apartment at night finding a naked murdered girl would go to the nearest bottle and pour himself a big one."

"Except you."

"I might be tempted myself."

The uniformed policemen were waiting for them on the gravel.

"Here's the warrant," said Flynn.

Cabot said, "There was an attempted burglary here tonight."

"Was there, indeed?"

"Yes, sir."

" 'Attempted,' you say?"

"Yes, sir. The burglar or burglars didn't actually gain entry to the house. The alarm scared them away."

"And how do you know that already?"

"Mister Horan came out earlier. We went through the house with him. He said nothing was missing."

"Is that where he was? Now isn't that interesting? He said he was taking a ride in the moonlight. Now why didn't he tell me?"

Cabot said, "In fact, he was here when we arrived."

"Do you suppose he robbed himself?" Flynn squinted at Fletch. "Could he have known we were breathing down his neck?"

Fletch said, "How would I know?"

Flynn looked at Grover, helpless, and shrugged.

"Well, let's see what's inside."

On the porch, Officer Cabot put his hand through the frame of the broken window and pushed the plywood free. It clattered to the kitchen floor. He reached around, released the locks, and opened the door.

In the kitchen, they crunched on glass.

Turning on and off lights as they went, the five men went through the house, the dining room, the living room, the library.

The house was furnished in the worst country house style — ill-fitting, ersatz Colonial pine furniture, threadbare rugs which should have been retired long since.

At the top of the stairs on the second storey, Flynn turned to Fletch.

"Am I wrong, or is there nothing at all of value in this house?"

The uniformed policemen were turning on lights in the bedrooms.

Fletch said, "So far I've seen nothing of value."

Flynn said, "Then why the extensive, expensive burglar alarms?"

They went through the bedrooms. Again like the worst New England country houses, they were all furnished like boarding school dormitories. Everything was solid, cheap, simple, and unattractive.

"From outside," said Flynn, "you'd think this an imposing country mansion, stuffed with the wealths of Persia. Any burglar attracted to this house would be a swimmer diving into a dry pool."

As they had proceeded, Flynn had opened and closed the doors to empty closets absently.

In the middle bedroom, in the rear of the second storey, he opened the closet door.

"Now, that's something. Look at the dust sheets, folded so neatly." He pulled the chain to the overhead light. "Not much dust on the floor spaces near the walls. There's a dust-free space in the center of the floor, too. Do you see?"

Fletch looked over his shoulder.

"Do you think the paintings were here?"

"We'll never know."

He pulled the chain and closed the door.

Climbing the stairs to the attic, Flynn said to Officer Cabot, "Mister Horan was sure nothing was missing?"

"Yes, sir."

"You went through the house with him yourself, did you?"

"Yes, sir."

"Did you go through the closets in the bedrooms with him?"

"Yes, sir. Every one."

After they looked around the attic rooms, Flynn asked Officer Cabot, "And are burglaries common around here?"

"Yes."

The other policeman said, "Three on this road this month."

"Ah, things are getting to a terrible state."

Again standing on the back porch, waiting for the Weston policemen to close up the house, Flynn said, "I don't think the man Horan ever lived here at all. What was the house for?"

"Maybe he inherited it."

Slamming the door behind him, Officer Cabot gave Flynn a friendly nod.

"What shall we say if Mister Horan asks us why we searched his house?"

"Mister Horan won't be asking," said Flynn. "We arrested him earlier this evening for first degree murder."

They were driving east on the Turnpike Extension.

"It's a puzzle," said Flynn. "It is. How could he have known enough to rob himself? And what did he do with the paintings?"

Fletch said, "Perhaps you weren't very convincing as a man who wanted to sell a Ford Madox Brown."

"I spoke to him in German," said Flynn.

"Inspector, I still don't see that your evidence against Horan is any better than your evidence against me."

"It is. His fingerprints were all over your apartment."

"His? I asked you about fingerprints."

"And I told you that we had yours, Mrs. Sawyer's, Ruth Fryer's, and a man's we presumed to be Bart Connors'. We were never sure of the man's prints. Mister Connors, you see, has never been in the service and he's never been charged with any crime. His fingertips are as virginal as the day he was born. There is no record of his fingerprints. And all this time he's been enjoying your house in Italy."

"He certainly has."

"We had Mister Horan's fingerprints because he had been a Navy Commander, you know."

"I know."

"It wasn't until we were chatting over tea on Saturday and you allowed me to know why you were really in Boston — to see Mister Horan — that I considered we might try to match up the fingerprints we found in your apartment with those Mister Horan had on record. A perfect fit. He was a bit careless there. He thought he was so far removed from being a suspect for this particular crime, he never wiped up after himself. Even so, I suspect a more experienced police-man never would have suspected Mister Horan. Such a respectable man."

"Does he know you have his fingerprints?"

"Oh, yes. He's confessed."

"You finally have a confession. From someone."

"It's much easier when there's a confession. It cuts down on the department's court time."

The moon had disappeared.

Fletch said, "Lucy Connors didn't kill Ruth Fryer."

"Indeed not. She's as innocent as a guppy. You must get over your prejudices, lad."

"Did you know Horan was guilty this afternoon when I was talking to you? I mean, yesterday afternoon? In your office."

"Yes, lad. I'm sorry to say I deceived you something terrible. There I was, a wee lad again in Germany, asking you for your autograph while I took your picture to send on to London. By five o'clock yes-terday we had matched up Horan's prints with those in your apartment, and I had made an appointment to see him. The warrants were in process."

"Flynn. Have you ever felt stupid?"

"Oh, yes. A cup of tea is a great help."

Flynn gave Grover money for another toll.

"Good luck on the City Councilperson's murder," Fletch said.

"Ach, that's over, all this long time."

"Is it?"

"Sure, I'm just letting the politicians exercise their bumps so they'll accept the solution when I give it to them. They so want to think the crime is political. They've all demanded police protection, you know. It makes them look so much grander when they go through the streets with a cop at their heels."

"Who did it?"

"Did you say, 'Who did it'?"

"Yes."

"Well, you have your humor yourself, don't you? Her husband did it. A poor, meek little man who's been in the back seat of that marriage since they pulled away from the church."

"How do you know he did it?"

"I found the man who sold him the ice pick. A conscientious Republican, to boot. An unimpeachable witness, with the evidence he has, in a case involving Democrats."

Outside 152 Beacon Street, before getting out of the car, Fletch put his hand out to Flynn.

"I've met a great cop," he said.

They shook hands.

"I'm coming along slowly," said Flynn. "I'm learning. Bit by bit."

THIRTY-NINE

Ten-thirty Tuesday morning the buzzer to the downstairs door sounded.

Fletch gave his button a prolonged answering push to give his guest ample time to enter.

He opened the front door to his apartment and went into the kitchen.

Coming back across the hall with the coffee tray he heard the elevator creaking slowly to the sixth floor.

He put the tray on the coffee table between the two divans.

When he returned to the foyer, his guest, nearly seventy, in a dark overcoat, brown suit a little too big for him, gray bags under his eyes making him no less distinguished, was standing hesitantly in the hall.

Fletch said, "Hi, Menti."

As he shook hands, the man's smile was dazzling, despite the lines of concern in his face.

"I never knew you wear false teeth," Fletch said.

Taking his guest's coat and putting it in a closet, Fletch said, "They found your body a few days ago in a pasture outside Turin."

Clasping his hands together, the guest entered the living room and allowed himself to be escorted to a divan. Count Clementi Arbogastes de Grassi was not accustomed to a cold climate.

He sipped a cup of coffee and crossed his legs. "My friend," he said.

Fletch was comfortable with his coffee in the other divan.

"Now I ask you the saddest question I have ever had to ask any man in my life." The Count paused. "Who stole my paintings? My wife? Or my daughter?"

Fletch sipped from his cup.

"Your daughter. Andy. Angela."

Menti sat, cup and saucer in one hand in his lap, staring at the floor for several moments.

"I'm sorry, Menti."

Fletch finished his coffee and put the cup and saucer on the table.

"I knew it had to be one of them who arranged it," Menti said. "For the paintings to have been stolen on our honeymoon. The theft at that time was too significant. The paintings had been there for decades. The house was usually empty, except for Ria and Pep. Few knew the paintings were there. But Sylvia was with me in Austria and Angela was here in school."

"I know."

Menti sat up and put his unfinished coffee on the table.

"Thank you for being my friend, Fletch. Thank you for helping me to find out."

"Were you comfortable enough in captivity?"

"You arranged everything splendidly. I rather enjoyed being a retired Italo-American on the Canary Islands. I made friends."

"Of course."

"Where are the ladies now? Sylvia and Angela?"

"They flew the coop this morning. No note. No anything."

"What does 'flew the coop' mean?"

"They left. Quickly."

"They were here?"

"Yes."

"Both of them?"

"Under the very same roof."

"Why did they leave, 'flew the coop'?"

"Either they both left together, or Andy left when she heard Horan was arrested, and Sylvia took off after her. It must have been quite a scene. Sorry I missed it."

The Count said, "Are they both well?"

"Grieving, of course, but otherwise fine." He poured warm coffee into the Count's half-empty cup. "I have fifteen of the paintings. Two have been sold, you know. The police are keeping one, the big Picasso, 'Vino, Viola, Mademoiselle,' as evidence. You'll probably never get it back without spending three times the painting's financial worth in legal fees, taxes, international wrangling, and what have you. And we have the Degas horse."

Menti absently turned the cup in its saucer.

"Everything is in a truck downstairs," Fletch said. "You and I can leave for New York as soon as you get warmed up."

Menti sat back, sad and tired.

"Why did she do it?"

"Love. Love for you. I don't think Andy cared that much about the paintings. She doesn't care about the money.

"When her mother died," Fletch continued, "Andy as a little girl, thought she would take her mother's place in your affection. You remarried. She has told me how heartbroken she was, and furious. She was fourteen. When your second wife left you, she was pleased. She thought you had learned your lesson. Because you had been married in France, you could divorce. Then, while Andy was in school here, you married Sylvia. Andy was no longer a little girl. She was old enough to express her rage. In her eyes, you had kept something from her all these years. She took something from you. The de Grassi Collection."

"She wasn't afraid Sylvia might have inherited them?"

"I'm not sure, but I have the impression Andy knew that under

Italian law children of the deceased have to inherit at least a third of the estate. Have I got that right? I'm sure Sylvia had no idea of that. Knowledge of the law could have motivated either one of them to steal the painting — from the other."

"Angela wanted the whole collection."

"I guess so. She doesn't expect much sense of family from Sylvia. People like Ria and Pep are very important to Andy."

"But how did she do it? A little girl, like that?"

"It took me a while to make the connection. I knew Andy had been to school in this country. I hadn't realized her school was here in Boston, or Cambridge, which is just across the river. I knew her school was Radcliffe. I didn't realize that Radcliffe is joined with Harvard. Radcliffe women now receive Harvard degrees. Horan, the Boston art dealer, was Andy's professor at Harvard."

"I see. But I think it would be difficult to get your professor to commit a grand, international robbery for you because you didn't like your father marrying again, no?"

"One would think so. However, Horan, who had gotten used to a very expensive way of life, was going broke."

"You know he was broke?"

"Yes. Five years ago he sold his wife's famous jewel, the Star of Hunan jade, to an Iranian. I knew that before I came here."

"Still . . . such a distinguished man."

"He's also a handsome, sophisticated man, Menti. An older man. For years, Andy had been wanting a certain kind of attention from you. . . ."

Menti's eyes were dull as they gazed at Fletch. "You believe their relationship was more intimate than is usual between a student and teacher?"

"I suspect so. For one purpose or another."

"I see." Menti sipped his coffee. "It happens. So, Fletcher, it was Horan who actually arranged for the paintings to be stolen."

"Yes. You showed me the catalogues from the Horan Gallery. Two of the de Grassi paintings were being sold, or, in fact, had been sold. We made our plan. We left copies of the catalogues for each of the ladies to find.

"Andy was enraged," Fletch said. "She knew Horan had the paintings, of course. She was enraged that he was selling them without her. Did Sylvia react at all?"

Menti said, "She never looked in the catalogues. I couldn't get her to." Menti chuckled lightly and shook his head. "When you called from Cagna saying you were driving down with an upset Angela, it was too late. I could wait no longer for Sylvia to notice. I had to go forward with our plan and get kidnapped."

"I don't know what Andy was really thinking on that drive to Livorno. She was certainly going to you, maybe to confess. More likely, she didn't know what she was doing."

"My disappearance helped clarify things," Menti said.

"Yes. Essentially, Andy sent me here to find the paintings so she could steal them back from Horan. She probably wouldn't have played her own hand out unless she thought you were dead." Fletch swallowed coffee. "This morning Horan was arrested. Exit Andy. Exit Sylvia."

"Enter Menti."

The buzzer to the downstairs door sounded.

"We're taking the paintings to a dealer in New York. A man I trust implicitly." Fletch stood up to answer the door. "His name is Kasner. On East 66th Street."

In the foyer, he shouted into the mouthpiece, "Who is it?"

The answering voice was so soft it took Fletch a moment to assimilate what it said.

"Francis Flynn, Mister Fletcher."

"Oh! Inspector?"

"The same."

Fletch pressed the button that would release the lock on the door downstairs.

Quickly, he grabbed Menti's coat from the closet.

Then he went into the den and took the truck keys from a drawer of the desk.

In the living room, he handed the coat and keys to Menti.

"Hurry up," he said. "Put on your coat. The man who is coming up is a policeman."

Moving gracefully, with speed, Menti stood up and put on the coat Fletch held for him.

"I won't be able to drive to New York with you, Menti. Can you make the trip alone?"

"Of course."

"Here are the keys. It's a black caravan truck, a Chevrolet, parked at the curb outside the apartment house, I think, to the right as you leave the building. The license plate on it is R99420. Have you got it?"

"In general, yes."

"Kasner's address is 20 East 66th Street, New York."

"I can remember."

"He's expecting you this afternoon. Come into the foyer with me, as if you were leaving, anyway."

The doorbell rang.

"Good morning, Inspector."

"Good morning, Mister Fletcher."

The little face on top of the huge body was bright and shining from a recent close shave. The green eyes were beaming like a cat's.

Fletch brought Menti forward by the elbow.

"I'd like you to meet a friend, from Italy, who just stopped by. Inspector Flynn, this is Giuseppe Grochola."

Flynn's eyes went to Menti. He put out his hand.

"Count Clementi Arbogastes de Grassi, is it?"

Menti hesitated not at all before shaking hands.

"Pleased to meet you, Inspector."

Flynn said to Fletch, "I never forget a thing I've heard. Isn't it marvelous?"

"It's marvelous, Flynn."

"And such a great cop I am, too. Didn't I hear someone say that?"

"You did, Inspector."

"Now why do you suppose this man who's supposed to be dead, this Count Clementi Arbogastes de Grassi, is standing here in your front hall?"

"I'm on my way to the airport, Inspector."

Fletch said, "He's been found, Flynn. Isn't that great?"

"It's a wonder he was lost at all."

"A narrow escape," said Fletch.

"It's a confusion," said Menti. "I came here to see my wife and daughter. They, hearing I was found alive, rushed off to Rome, not knowing I was coming here."

"I see," said Flynn. "And how was it, to be dead?"

Menti said, "I'm trying to catch them at the airport, Inspector."

Flynn stood away from the door.

"I'd never come between a man and his family," he said. "Have a joyful reunion."

Fletch opened the door.

"There's some coffee in the living room, Inspector."

He opened the elevator door for Menti.

Flynn had wandered into the living room.

Fletch whispered, "Send me back the license plates. By mail."

From inside the elevator, Menti whispered, "What do I do with the truck?"

"Leave it anywhere. It will get stolen."

Still in his overcoat, Flynn stood over the coffee table.

"There's not an unused cup," he said, "on this brisk morning."

"I'll get one."

"Never mind. I had my tea."

"I wasn't expecting you," Fletch said.

"I suspected as much. I'm only here for the moment. I thought I'd ask you this morning if you've had any ideas at all as to where the de Grassi paintings might be?"

"I've just been through that, Inspector."

"Have you?"

"I told Menti everything."

"You must have been mighty surprised to see him."

"Mighty."

"The ladies have gone already, have they?"

"They were gone when I got back. They must have gotten the news during the night, while I was with you."

"And they didn't wait for you? Your girlfriend and the Countess."

"Menti's discovery was big news, Inspector."

"I daresay it was. And how was he found?"

"Wandering near the steps of Saint Sebastian."

"In a daze, was he?"

"No. He'd been let out of a car."

"Remarkable they'd feed a captive that long. Italian kidnappers must have hearts of honey. A month or more, wasn't it?"

"About that."

"Well, anything is possible under the sun." Flynn turned on his heel at the end of the room. "Now, where do you suppose the paintings are this morning?"

"Well, Inspector, you might believe Horan hid them last night."

"I might believe that, yes. The man doesn't say so himself."

"You asked him?"

"I did, yes."

"But, Inspector, who can believe a murderer?"

"Ach, now there's a point worthy of my own Jesuit training."

"What did Horan say, precisely?"

"The man says he never heard of the paintings."

"Didn't he say a man named Cooney in Texas has them?"

"He says he never heard of a man named Cooney."

"It's a great puzzle, Inspector."

"It is that. The man must have had the paintings, or he never would have gone to the extent of murder to frame and thus dispose of you."

"Perhaps he just doesn't like people named Peter."

"I'll ask him that." Flynn, hands behind back, walked back down the room. "I'd almost think you took them yourself, Fletch. There was a burglary at the man's house last night. If the man hadn't gone out there immediately afterwards and told the police nothing was missing."

"I suppose I could make some tea," Fletch said. "The water's still hot."

"No, I must be going." Flynn headed toward the front door. "Of course, a man may be reluctant to admit something he isn't supposed to have is stolen from him. I mean, how would a man say something I stole was stolen from me?"

Fletch said, "I understand reluctance, Inspector."

"Ach," said Flynn. "A man has no privacy at all."

Before he opened the front door, Flynn turned to Fletch, and said, "Which reminds me, Mister Fletcher. Finally we discovered what else you did on that Wednesday you went in one door of the Ritz and out the other."

"Oh?"

"You bought a truck. The marvelous bureaucracy dropped the registration into my hands just this morning."

Flynn began to rummage in all his pockets at once.

"Now, why would you buy a truck and rent a car the same day?"

"I was going to use it for skiing, Inspector."

"Ach! That's a perfectly good answer. What do you mean, you *were* going to use it for skiing?"

"It was stolen. I've been meaning to report it."

"Ah, Mister Fletcher. You should report such things. And when was it stolen?"

"Almost immediately."

"What a pity. That very afternoon? Is that why you rented the car?"

"I didn't want to have to drive a truck around town."

"Gracious, yes, indeed. I was forgetting about the man's style."

"It was stolen a day or two later. I had parked it on the street."

"Terrible lot of crime around these days, isn't there? The police should do something." Flynn pulled a slip of paper from one of his pockets. "Ah, here's the little darling. A light blue Chevrolet van truck, last year's model, license number 671-773. Is that it?"

"That's it."

"Just the right size truck, I'd say, for transportin' paintings and a sculptured horse."

Fletch said, "Skis, too."

Flynn said, "Do you suppose Horan stole it himself, for the purpose of stealing the de Grassi paintings away from himself?"

"Anything's possible, Inspector. He may have committed that crime, too, and blocked it out."

"Highly unlikely, I'd say."

Flynn opened the door.

"Well, I'll put out an all-points bulletin on this truck immediately. Light blue Chevrolet caravan truck, last year's model, license number 671-773. Seeing you're a friend, been such a help on the terribly difficult case, I'll put the screws to the boyos statewide. There's no chance this truck won't be picked up in a matter of hours."

"Very good of you, Inspector."

"Tut. Think nothing of it. Anything for a friend."

Fletch closed the front door, diminishing the sound of the descending elevator.

His watch said fifteen minutes to twelve. Tuesday.

He was almost perfectly a week late.

In the den, he picked up the phone and dialed a number he had looked up and memorized in the airport the previous Tuesday.

While he was waiting for the number to answer, he pushed the drape aside with his hand and looked down into the street.

Menti was just climbing down from the back of the truck.

He had been looking at the paintings!

"Hurry up, Menti," Fletch said to the windowpane. "For Pete's sake!"

"Hello? 555-2301."

Menti was unlocking the driver's side door of the truck.

"Hello?" the voice said.

"Hello," said Fletch.

He craned his neck. He could see the top of Flynn's head as he walked out of the apartment building.

Menti was in the truck.

"Yes, hello?" the voice said.

"I'm sorry," said Fletch. "Is this the Tharp Family Foundation?"

Flynn was getting into the front passenger seat of a black Ford.

"Yes, sir."

Exhaust was coming from the tailpipes of both the police car and the truck.

"May I speak with your director, please?"

"Who shall I say is calling, please?"

The double-parked police car began to move forward.

Without looking, Menti darted out of his parking space with the bounce and jerk people make when unaccustomed to driving a vehicle.

The police car braked hard, making the front end of its chassis bob toward the road surface.

"Sir? Who shall I say is calling?"

Apparently, the driver of the police car waved ahead the black Chevrolet caravan truck, last year's model, license plate number R99420.

The two vehicles proceeded up the street, the black police car behind the black, jerking truck.

Fletch released the window drape.

"I'm sorry. This is Peter Fletcher. . . ."